More Kinky Friedman

MORE KINKY FRIEDMAN

Kinky Friedman

*

Frequent Flyer

Musical Chairs

Elvis, Jesus and Coca-Cola

faber and faber

LONDON · BOSTON

This edition first published in 1993
by Faber and Faber Limited
3 Queen Square London WC1N 3AU

Frequent Flyer (1989) and *Musical Chairs* (1991)
first published in the USA
by William Morrow and Company, Inc., New York

Elvis, Jesus and Coca-Cola first published in 1993
by Faber and Faber Limited
3 Queen Square London WC1N 3AU

Phototypeset by Intype, London
Printed in England by Clays Ltd St Ives Plc.

A CIP record for this book is
available from the British Library

ISBN 0-571-16714-4

2 4 6 8 10 9 7 5 3 1

Contents

Frequent Flyer

The tattooed lady left the circus train,
Lost all of her pictures in the rain,
I wonder if you're happy, I wonder if you're free,
I wonder if you'll ever know the mark you left on me.

I'm the Wild Man from Borneo
The Wild Man from Borneo
You come to see what you want to see
You come to see but you never come to know.

ACKNOWLEDGMENTS

The author would like to thank the following Americans for their help: Dr Tom Friedman, Dylan Ferrero, John Woodford Rapp, Jr, Alden Shuman, Hilda Pierce, Larry 'Ratso' Sloman, Marcie Friedman, Tony Kisch, and Max Swafford; Esther 'Lobster' Newberg at ICM; James Landis, Jane Meara, and Lori Ames at William Morrow; and Steve Rambam, technical adviser.

The author would also like to thank his five-year-old niece, Amanda, for the phrase 'the grasshopper game'.

It was flyover country.

Flyover country, of course, is what New Yorkers call any place between New York and Los Angeles.

I was standing in a snow-covered cemetery somewhere outside Cleveland, Ohio, and the bagpipe player they'd hired for the funeral was wearing long johns under his kilt. It was so cold the teardrops were turning to sleet before they hit the ground.

I'd gotten the phone call the afternoon before. I'd been dozing at the desk in my loft in the Village. It was a stranger's voice saying, 'You were a friend of John Morgan's, weren't you?' One of those rather awkward, unsettling moments in life just before the past tense hits you like the *Sunset Limited*.

'Yeah,' I said, struggling to regain my spiritual balance.

'John died yesterday in Columbus.'

The voice paused, and I lighted a cigar just for something to do.

'He often talked about when the two of you were together in the Peace Corps. In the jungles of Borneo, wasn't it?'

'Yeah.' I could see the shimmering laughter in John Morgan's eyes. They were the color of banana trees on the other side of a dream.

'The funeral's tomorrow in Cleveland,' the voice said. 'Do you think you can make it?'

'Yeah,' I said.

The guy gave me the time and place of the funeral, and I wrote it down. He told me his name, but by the time I'd cradled the blower I'd already forgotten. If he'd said his name was Zippy the Pinhead, I doubt if it would've blown my skirt up too much. You half listen to those kinds of phone calls. Part of you hears the voice on the other end of the line and part of you strains to hear that faraway sort of music Van Gogh might've composed if he'd poked out his eyes instead of cutting off his ear.

I listened to the music for a while. Then I lost it to the growling of the garbage trucks out on Vandam Street.

I called Kelly, my friendly travel agent, and told her I was going on a trip.

'Is it business or pleasure?' she asked.

'I'm going to Cleveland,' I said.

So here I was in the bone orchard. My thoughts skittered crazily like the snowflakes, and like the snowflakes, crashed in silent finality against cold marble stone.

The priest had said a few *cosa nostras*, and the bagpipe player was bravely squeaking and farting his way through a lilting Irish tune in 15-degree weather at a funeral for somebody he probably didn't know. Bagpipe players don't get a lot of work these days. When a gig comes along, they take it.

If it'd been a wedding I'd probably have tried to stop it. But it wasn't a wedding. It was a funeral. The only funeral you've got a right to try to stop is your own, and that's a full-time job.

I hadn't seen John in maybe five years and had only gotten together with him on four or five occasions in the almost twenty years since I'd been back in the States. I didn't feel too bad about it though. The only way to keep a good friendship going these days is to stay the hell away from people.

Yet when you've lived two years in the jungle with someone, you get to know him pretty well, and when the unctuous undertaker had taken me to the open casket that morning, I knew something was wrong.

I glanced across at John's parents. Subtract twenty years and they looked just like the people in the photograph that John had shown me in Borneo. I gazed around at the rest of the family and friends standing by the casket near the gaping hole in the ground. The grief on their faces seemed deep and genuine.

I was confused, but I didn't think it was the time or place to raise my hand and ask for a point of clarification. I kept my thoughts to myself as I grimly watched them lower the casket into the frozen ground. Five years can change somebody, I thought. But never that much. No, I wasn't imagining things.

I couldn't stop the funeral. And there was something else I couldn't stop. I couldn't stop wondering.

Why was the body they were burying *not* John Morgan?

2

They didn't show a movie on the flight from Cleveland back to New York. They didn't have to. In my head a double feature was going on, and by the time we got to LaGuardia it had pretty well twisted itself into a sick, synaptic pretzel of *Lord Jim* and *Invasion of the Body Snatchers*. They didn't show a cartoon, either. That was coming later, but I didn't know it.

At LaGuardia I grabbed a hack driven by a non-English-speaking Third World gentleman named Hassan. He only spoke enough English, it emerged, to tell me to put out my cigar. I, of course, not wishing to bring additional grief to the Third World, grudgingly obliged.

'The last good Arab,' I muttered as I killed the cigar, 'was probably Muhammad.' I don't know whether Hassan understood, but he made several glottal noises, and off we roared onto the Parkway.

I sat back to enjoy the ride. After visiting America for a while, it's always nice to get back to New York.

Hassan had not heard of things like Greenwich Village or the George Washington Bridge, and he did not take kindly to the news that I was a big admirer of the great Islamic poet Danny Thomas. By the time we got to 199B Vandam, a hard frost had settled both outside and inside the cab. I gave Hassan a tip commensurate with the service. He gave me an unpleasant Middle Eastern sign with his hand as he drove away.

The freight elevator with the one exposed light bulb was in use, so I legged it with the suitcase up four dank flights of stairs. On three, I had to kick a tricycle out of the way and an empty bottle of Early Times. Kid was sloppy, but he had good taste in whiskey.

I unlocked the door to my loft. It smelled like a big cigar had died there. Maybe a small side order of cat shit. It was a lot like love. Sometimes you had to go away before you noticed it. It was about 27 degrees Fahrenheit. Colder than an eccentric old lady's bosom. I went over to the radiator to turn it on, but it was already on. It put out about as well as some broads I've known. At least it didn't want to sit down and have a good talk.

As I walked over to the desk, I noticed a fairly recent cat turd lying equidistant between my two red telephones. Both phones were connected to the same line, sort of to enhance the importance of my incoming wounded. Of course, it wasn't going to be too pleasant answering either one of them with a feline souvenir lying there right in the middle.

Cats often present you with things. Sometimes it's a bird; sometimes it's a turd. This one didn't have any wings.

I was staring at the cat turd, which was shaped vaguely like Nicaragua, when the phones rang. Gingerly, I picked up the blower on the left.

'Start talkin',' I said.

'Are you Kinky?' It was the husky, foreign-flavored voice of a young woman.

'Who wants to know?'

'My name is Carmen,' she said. 'I am John Morgan's fiancée.'

Don't be too sure, I thought.

'Something has happened,' she said. 'I must come to see you.' I felt myself shiver suddenly from the chill in the room.

'Fine,' I said. 'Where are you calling from?'

'A place where people disappear,' she said.

3

I removed the cat turd, but it didn't seem to clear the air very much. Here I was back from Cleveland, and I still hadn't buried John Morgan. Was it possible that out of three hundred or more people at the funeral, I was the only one who recognized that there'd been one minor problem?

I walked over to the kitchen and opened the window. I looked at New York. A cold storage warehouse. A couple of rusty fire escapes. A billboard with an aircraft flying away to somewhere else. Nice view.

But you can't really see New York the way you can see San Francisco or San Diego or Dallas. New York is like a lady standing in the fog. From one angle she looks like a beautiful young girl. From another, she's a weatherbeaten old whore.

In New York you've got to know all the angles.

There are more people, pigeons, and potholes in New York than cross-ties on the railroad or stars in the skies, and there's no elbow room for Daniel Boone. But people in this city have something else. They all feel that it means something just to be here. For example, a mugger in New York knows that he's at the top of his profession. Child molesters, hit men, killer fags, all smile a secret little smile to themselves in New York. They know they are the best that they can be.

From my kitchen window I could see a bench on the corner with a black man and an old white woman sitting on opposite ends. They each appeared to be talking to themselves. Nothing wrong with that. I've talked to myself for years. They say it's when you start answering yourself that you've got problems. I didn't have to worry about that. Tonight I didn't have any answers. I closed the window.

It was a Friday night in the dreary middle of a frigid February. The time was moving inexorably toward eight o'clock, the peak time for millions of people to start actively seeking fun. I was not one of these people. I let fun come to me.

I had promised my friend McGovern earlier in the week that I'd drop by his place this evening. McGovern was a large half-Indian, half-Irish reporter for the *Daily News* who had been grudgingly invaluable to me on several occasions in the past. I didn't see how he could help me now, but you never knew.

If nothing else, tonight McGovern was cooking my favorite: Chicken McGovern.

I put on my hat and coat, grabbed a few cigars for the road, and headed for the door. The cat was still hiding someplace, but that didn't bother me. One less person to say good-bye to.

4

'That couch,' said McGovern, nodding toward the couch I was sitting on, 'has been across the Atlantic twice.' It was a pink velvet affair, and it took up about half of his quaint, newspaper-strewn apartment. McGovern paused to take a long drink from a tall glass.

'Fascinating,' I said. 'When's the Chicken McGovern going to be ready?' The aroma reminded me of curries in the Far East. And of other things. There had to be a mistake somewhere. . . .

'It once belonged to Dermot Purgavie,' McGovern was saying, 'the noted columnist for the *London Daily Mail*, who took it aboard the *Queen Elizabeth II* along with his first wife . . .'

I'd never known John to wear a beard, and yet the corpse had had a beard. But still, I thought, I would've recognized my old friend. . . .

'. . . from New York to a Victorian sitting room in Hampstead, London. After a while, the first wife decided she didn't much like the couch – or Dermot, for that matter. . . .'

. . . Either I was letting my imagination run away with me, or something very peculiar indeed was going on. . . .

'. . . So Dermot took the couch and himself from the Victorian sitting room, traveled across with it again on the *QE2* . . .'

. . . If I wasn't careful, I thought, I was going to need a couch and a shrink to go with it. . . .

'. . . and stored it in a warehouse in New Jersey. Are you with me so far?'

'I'm afraid so,' I said.

'Then fire struck the warehouse in New Jersey.'

'What an interesting story.'

'But it doesn't end there.'

'No, of course not.'

'The couch was declared legally dead. Dermot collected five grand in insurance. The second wife didn't like it any better than the first. And Dermot gave me the couch.'

'Generous,' I said. If John Morgan was legally dead, I thought, and he wasn't the same guy I'd known in Borneo, then where –

'I seem to remember a certain down-and-out country singer who didn't mind crashing on it from time to time. Not to mention Tom Baker, Frederick Exley, Vaughn Meader, and the great Australian journalist Piers Akerman.'

Piers had told me that one night while he was sleeping on McGovern's couch, the gracious host had sat on him, thereby causing grievous injury to his scrotum. But there was no point in bringing that up now; the Chicken McGovern was almost ready. I never discussed religion, or politics, or McGovern anecdotes while eating Chicken McGovern. It gave one gas.

So, as we knocked off the Chicken McGovern, which was killer bee, I told McGovern all about my trip to Cleveland.

'When I get to the paper in the morning,' said McGovern, 'I'll see if I can find him in the morgue.' He laughed his hearty Irish laugh. 'No pun intended.'

5

Walking home in the cold that night, I began to feel like Kafka's character in *The Trial*, raked by situations and circumstances that seemed unreal, far away, and beyond my control or comprehension. It was an uncomfortable, almost frightening feeling.

As I rode up to my loft in the freight elevator, I began to wonder if I wasn't really losing my mind. Like the security guard on the Texas Tower said about the mild-mannered Charles Whitman after he'd suddenly climbed the tower and shot twenty-six people, 'It'll happen to you.'

When I walked into the loft, the cat was sitting on the kitchen table waiting for me. Her eyes narrowed slightly and went from green to yellow like a sentient traffic light. It was enough to make the hairs on the back of your neck come to full attention. The cat always translated my innermost fears with uncanny accuracy. This time there was no mistaking it. Something was as wrong as acid rain.

I fed the cat some tuna. I thought about emptying the litter box.

I walked into the bathroom and peered into the rain-room, where I kept the litter box. With only one unfortunate exception – a morning some time ago when I'd been on the third ring of Saturn – I always took it out before taking a shower. Just a homemaker's tip.

The litter box didn't look too good. Neither did the rest of the world. I decided to let them both be. I was always a little hesitant to empty the litter box these days after my friend Ratso, the editor of *National Lampoon*, in his clever, Watson-like way, had hidden over a quarter of a million dollars of top-quality cocaine in it almost a year ago.

I was the one he was hiding it from, of course.

The results had been very unpleasant.

But I had to admit, however, that, with the exception of the litter-box incident, Ratso had been very helpful with my forays into crime-solving.

I looked in the litter box again. It was good for another few weeks at least. That was more than I could say with any certainty about myself.

I walked back into the living room and thought about John Morgan. It's funny how even a short period of time can create doubts in your mind. Can fade an impression that once you were so sure about. I didn't know what to think.

I poured out a double shot of snake piss into my old bull's horn shot glass and carried it over to the desk. There were a few things I could do, I thought. I could set a fire under McGovern's large Irish buttocks and at least obtain in short order Morgan's obit in the Cleveland papers. Christ, computers were wonderful. I could sit on my own buttocks and wait for the mysterious Carmen broad to reestablish commo. I could call a few old Peace Corps buddies of mine who'd also known John in Borneo and see if they'd heard anything about either his recent demise or to the contrary.

I made a few calls. One to Dylan Ferrero in Texas and one to Joe Hollis in North Carolina. Nobody home twice.

I got up and knocked a few cobwebs off the old stereo. I put on a cassette Ratso had given me. Chinese children singing Christmas carols. Because of my years on the road as a country singer, I had come to hate the sound of the human voice singing. At least with this cassette, I didn't have to understand the words.

I went back to the desk, killed about half the shot, took a cigar out of my porcelain Sherlock Holmes head and set fire to it, always keeping the tip of the cigar well above the flame. I sat back in the chair, put my feet up on the desk, killed the rest of the shot, and listened to the Chinese version of 'Silver Bells.'

Friday night in the Big Apple.

6

It was a coffee-colored river. I could see it clearly as I sat at my desk that night, many shots and many Chinese Christmas carols later. It seemed to flow out of a childhood storybook, peaceful and familiar, continue its sluggish way beneath the tropical sun, and then, at some point that you could never quite see, pick up force and become that opaque uncontrollable thing roaring in your ears, blinding your eyes, rushing relentlessly round the bends of understanding, beyond the banks of imagination.

One of the comforting things about the Borneo jungle, or the *ulu*, as it's called, is that it is fairly immutable. Although evangelical missionaries with third-grade educations portray Jesus as a bogeyman and teach the natives to throw away their beads, cut their hair, and sing 'Oh Susanna,' progress, as we like to call it, is slow. As the Kayan tribesmen tell you when they say good-bye: *'Pleheigh, pleheigh, tuan,'* which roughly translated means, 'Slowly, slowly, lord.'

The Kayans, former headhunters, are a beautiful, gentle people. They wear their hair in sort of an early Beatles' style, as they have for hundreds of years. Tattoos are popular with the men, and the women wear heavy earrings that eventually stretch their earlobes down almost to their breasts.

Kayan men often drill holes in the heads of their penises and insert a length of bone with feathers on each end. This is called a *palang*, and was probably the grandfather of the French tickler. Unfortunately, hemorrhaging often resulted in the female, and the *palang*'s popularity has declined somewhat. My friend Joe

Hollis always wanted a *palang*, but in the end, quite to everyone's disappointment, he settled for a tattoo.

In the West, you never know what's going to happen from day to day. When you wake up in the morning, you've got to wait for Bryant Gumbel to tell you if it's safe to go outside and then you've got to wait for Willard Scott to tell you what to wear. But somehow I was pretty sure Borneo was still as I remembered. Of course, there was no way to really know. Maybe now I was looking at things with different eyes. Twenty years can change a dreamer far more than they can a river.

I closed my eyes and could see John Morgan and me in a small boat in the gathering darkness. We must have been four or five days, as near as I could recall, upriver from Long Lama, the little village we were both based out of. John had told me he'd been working on some kind of community health project in this area. I'd never been this far into the *ulu* before. The trees along the banks of the river looked tall, strange, and vaguely ominous.

'Durian trees,' John said. 'The fruits are encased in a hard, spiked shell, and every so often they fall on somebody's head and kill 'em.'

'That's good to know.'

Morgan smiled mischievously. 'Also,' he said, 'if you eat durian at the same time as you drink *tuak*, the native wine, you'll die.'

'Yeah,' I said, 'but I bet it's a hell of a way to go.'

'Better than having your head lopped off with a *parang* and put in a basket to decorate the *ruai* in somebody's longhouse.'

'C'mon,' I said. 'They don't do that anymore.' John smiled devilishly, and I could see what he'd looked like as a little kid.

'Did Hitler shave his moustache?' he asked.

The trees became invisible, and the sky and water joined together. John had maintained that we were near a longhouse, and I hoped to hell he was right. You don't know what dark is until you've been in the *ulu* at night. There were legends about ghosts, or *hantus*, as the Kayans called them. There was black magic that had been practiced diligently for generations. There were stories of witches who flew, using their ears for wings. The dark night of the *ulu* was closing in palpably around us. It was almost enough to make you want to throw away your beads and sing 'Oh, Susanna.'

After we'd drifted with nothing but a flashlight and a kerosene lamp for a lot longer than I would've liked, we saw lights ahead of us flickering on the river. Soon we could make out men rowing small carved wooden *prahus* and carrying torches.

'What the hell is it?' I asked. 'A war party?'

John laughed. 'More like a fishing party.' His eyes twinkled and, as usual, told more than his words.

We watched the silent torches for a moment gliding slowly toward us on the river in the night. 'Because of the current,' John said, 'and because they get *mahbok* on the *tuak*, they never do catch many fish. In fact, their word for fishing translates into English to mean "visiting the fish." '

I could see John's face in the lamplight – young, unlined, gentle as the spirit of the Kayan people. On that coffee-colored river, at that time, I felt very close to him.

'Visiting the fish,' I said. 'I like that.'

'It's yours,' he said.

7

Saturday morning I nursed a very unpleasant, almost cloying hangover, and listened to McGovern recite John Morgan's obituary from the *Cleveland Plain Dealer*. Hell of a way to start the weekend.

'Not a bad obit, as they go,' McGovern said brightly. 'Maybe a little bit stiff.' McGovern laughed loudly, and my hangover hung over all the way to my left eyeball.

'That's cute, McGovern. Very sensitive to take advantage of a friend in his time of grief.'

'Grief?' shouted McGovern. 'You already said you're not even sure who it was that you buried! The way I see it, you only have two courses of action.'

There was a third course of action, and that was to hang up the phone, but the obit had been so sketchy and unforthcoming that I found myself hopelessly holding on to the blower as if it were a lifeline from the *Lusitania*. About the only thing the obit had confirmed was that Morgan had been in the Peace Corps in South America. Either that was a factual error, or John had really been in the Peace Corps in South America before he'd been assigned to Borneo. An unusual reassignment, but not unheard of. I'd have to check it out.

'The two courses of action being . . . ?' I asked rather testily. I was starting to feel kind of dizzy.

'They should be obvious,' said McGovern.

'If they were obvious, I wouldn't be talking to a large, cheerful mick at nine o'clock in the morning. What the hell are they?'

'Get an exhumation order,' McGovern said, 'or, as you always say, get a checkup from the neck up.'

I followed the third course of action and cradled the blower.

Still irritated with McGovern and half in a throbbing fog, I stoked up the espresso machine, fed the cat, and banged around the kitchen looking for my IMUS IN THE MORNING coffee mug. Apparently, someone had stolen it.

'The theft must've occurred while I was in Cleveland,' I muttered bitterly to the cat. The cat was eating and didn't like to be interrupted. She didn't respond.

I found a chipped but suitable replacement mug, loaded it with thick, steaming espresso, and took it over to my desk. I took a few tentative slurps, fired up a half-smoked cigar I found in the wastebasket, and pondered the mysterious occurrences that had intruded upon my life within the past forty-eight hours.

First there was the bewildering situation in Cleveland, beginning with the phone call about Morgan's death and ending with a large number of normal-looking Americans burying a body that I was almost certain did not belong to John Morgan.

Then had come the phone call from someone who had said that her name was Carmen, that she'd been a friend of John Morgan's and that she was calling from a place where people disappear. I remembered, at the time of the call, feeling a sudden chill. Now, in the pale light of Saturday morning, I felt myself shudder again. I took a healthy slug of the espresso and puffed a couple of times on the cigar to clear my head.

Normally, this would've been enough to fill anybody's plate for a while, but then I'd had to hear McGovern's tedious dissertation about the history of his couch, walk twenty blocks through a dismal, specter-ridden night wondering openly about my sanity, and get home just in time to see the cat's eyes change colors.

I wondered if there was a support group for this kind of situation. If there was, I didn't think I wanted to belong.

Add to all this the disappearance of my favorite coffee mug, and you could see what a fragile state my mind was in. Any shrink will tell you that people who are already under great mental stress and then happen to lose their IMUS IN THE MORNING coffee mugs are only a Texas two-step away from becoming Jesus or Napoleon impersonators.

I was too tall for Napoleon and too o-l-d for Jesus.

Maybe they had somebody else.

8

The only person I could think of who had known John Morgan as well as I had was Dylan Ferrero. I'd met Dylan in Borneo, and when we'd got back to the States, he'd become the road manager for my band, the Texas Jewboys. After the Jewboys had gone on sabbatical, he'd traded in his sunglasses and python jacket for a coat and tie, gotten married, settled down, and become a schoolteacher. Nothing wrong with that. Might've done it myself, but I never could find the right tie.

'Dylan,' I said, 'I think I have some bad news.'

' "Bad news travels like wildfire; good news travels slow." ' Dylan was fond of quoting lyrics from rock 'n' roll songs, a trait that sometimes irritated me, but he had so many good traits and I had so many repellent ones that I usually let it slide.

I told Dylan what had happened in Cleveland. Unlike myself, he was a good listener, and absorbed it all in shocked silence.

Then he said, 'Well, Jesus Christ, hoss, why don't you call his parents and find out?'

'Dylan, it was an open-casket funeral.'

'Shit,' he said. 'I haven't seen Morgan in some years, but the last

17

I'd heard he was back in the Far East. He seemed to hop back and forth pretty often. I just don't believe he's dead. It's kind of like "something's happenin' and you don't know what it is, do you, Mr Jones?" '

'Dylan,' I said irritably, 'were there any strange incidents in Borneo involving John that you can remember?'

'Well, there was the time Morgan brought a tribal medicine man over to Hollis's house one morning to give him a *palang* operation. That was pretty unusual. Hollis had gone fairly native at the time, but he woosied out at the last minute.'

'That's understandable,' I said.

'I guess he figured a bone in the nose was one thing, but a bone in the hose was quite another.'

'Quite,' I said. 'Look, if you think of anything besides the *palang* incident, call me.'

' "If my memory serves me well," ' he said, 'but it was "long ago and far away." '

When I hung up with Dylan, I found myself thinking about John Morgan and smiling wistfully.

9

'That Carmen person sounds interesting,' said Ratso as he put a piece of pork approximately the size and shape of a golf ball into his mouth with a pair of chopsticks. I'd told him the whole story. It was pushing eleven o'clock and we were having dim sum at the Golden Palace on Mott Street. Ratso pronounced the name 'Carmen' like 'common.'

'What kind of accent did you say she had?' he asked. He picked up a piece of shrimp that appeared to be covered with a clear layer of mucous membrane.

'Foreign,' I said.

'That doesn't help much. By your standards, anybody who doesn't say "Thank ye. Y'all have a nice day now" has a foreign accent.'

'I'm not quite that parochial, Ratso. In fact, her accent sounded a lot more pleasant than yours. She sounded kind of like an upscale Mexican.' I helped myself to some tripe in black bean sauce.

All around us four generations of Chinese were chatting mysteriously to each other. Their words seemed to cascade off the ceiling of the big room and flit together like little Oriental birds. Ratso caught me listening and paused to listen himself.

'Sounds nice – almost like music – doesn't it?' he said. 'I wonder what they're all saying.'

'They're probably all saying, "Thank ye. Y'all have a nice day now," ' I said. I took out a cigar and began a little preinflammatory foreplay. I poured us both another cup of hot Chinese tea.

'You know,' said Ratso, 'that "place where people disappear" business seems to ring a bell. Have you given it any thought?'

'Oh, a nightmare or two. I figure she's either calling from the Bermuda Triangle or from the transporter room of the starship *Enterprise*.'

'Let me think about it for a while,' said Ratso in his most Watson-like manner. 'A place where people disappear . . .'

'Take all the time you want,' I said. 'We're not going to bring back the dead.'

'*If* he's dead,' said Ratso.

Later, while walking west on Canal Street, we passed a large flock of flea markets, which put Ratso on cloud eight and a half and bored me right through the pavement. I started to drag Ratso away, but I saw a little flame in his eyes that burned with the spirit of a woman window-shopping at Tiffany, so I went along with him relatively good-naturedly. After all, practically his whole wardrobe came from this kind of place. This was Ratso's Fifth Avenue. Ratso's Savile Row.

By the time we got to Soho, the weather was thawing out a bit. It was almost warm enough to dodge tourists. We were passing a very trendy new store that sold only used dashikis when Ratso grabbed my arm.

'This Carmen person, if she exists – '

'Of course she exists,' I said. 'She called me.'

'Of course,' Ratso said, looking at me peculiarly.

There was an uncomfortable silence during which time Ratso let go of my arm and said, 'Ever heard of the *desaparecidos*?'

'Sure,' I said. 'It's the new Mexican restaurant on the Upper East Side.'

Ratso laughed rather indulgently. 'No, Kinkster, I'm afraid not,' he said. 'The *desaparecidos* are a group of people – many thousands of them – whose views ran counter to certain governments in Latin America. Beginning in the late sixties, this whole group of people seems to have, quite literally, disappeared. Even their own families have no earthly idea where they are.'

I stared at Ratso for a moment. 'Watson,' I said, 'you always cease to amaze me. But how does all this tie in with John Morgan?'

Ratso had a very troubled look in his eye. It was one part sadness, one part doubt, and if I didn't know better, I would've said it was one part pity.

'He was – or is – your friend,' said Ratso gently. 'You tell me.'

10

Carmen didn't call. Blower traffic in general was pretty light. That left a hell of a lot of quality time that weekend for me and the cat.

In the loft above us Winnie Katz's lesbian dance class thudded away at unexpected intervals throughout the weekend. Whenever the thudding ceased, it seemed to be picked up in a growling refrain from the Greek chorus of garbage trucks out on Vandam Street. All in all, it was a peaceful time, quite conducive to self-reflection. Self-reflection, of course, is when you put a slice of your life under the microscope, focus it in, and observe it carefully. Then you stand back and try to avoid projectile vomit.

It was sometime over the weekend that I decided I might like to have an affair with Winnie. She was demurely attractive and quite character-laden, and she reminded me of a kleptomaniac I'd once seen briefly in the police station in Nashville. I was there for urinating off a balcony or whatever songwriters did in those days, and she was there for *goniffing* seven packets of eyeliner or something from one of Nashville's finer department stores. She was well dressed, beautiful, and fragile in tears. Her makeup was running, so it was probably a pretty good thing that she'd lifted the eyeliner. Eventually, her slightly embarrassed corporate husband came down to get her just before she shoplifted my heart. But there was something about the way she looked at me as she left that now made me think of Winnie Katz. In those days it was sicker to be a lesbian than a kleptomaniac, but values are changing.

Obviously, attempting an affair with a lesbian is not particularly best foot forward. Of course, we did like some of the same things.

I lit another cigar and gently stroked the cat.

I must've done a few other things too, because before I knew it, Sunday night had rolled around, and I found myself listening to Ratso's rodentlike voice on the blower.

'Kinkster,' he said, 'I'm coming by to get you in the morning.'

'Why?' I asked. 'Where're we going?'

Ratso's voice had sounded vaguely ill at ease, and it was making me feel uncomfortable too.

There was a rather awkward pause. Then Ratso said, 'It's a surprise.'

I poured a healthy jolt from a nearby bottle of Jameson into the bull's horn. I don't like surprises worth a damn, but I liked the strange tone in Ratso's voice even less. It sounded like an uncharacteristic effort to be patronizing.

I killed the shot.

'Goody,' I said.

11

Monday morning I was warming up a rather elderly bagel when I heard what appeared to be screeching noises coming from the sidewalk below. I walked over to the kitchen window and looked down into the gray February drizzle. At first I didn't see anything. Then three dark forms began to emerge from the bleak background like blurry figures on a photographic plate.

I rubbed my eyes, opened the window, and looked again. Ratso, McGovern, and Rambam, a private investigator I'd sometimes worked with, were all standing on the sidewalk shouting up at me. They looked like three sullen leftover Christmas carolers.

'Throw down the fuckin' puppet head!' yelled Rambam.

I looked on top of the refrigerator, and there it was – the little black puppet head smiling stoically, with the key to the building lodged firmly in its mouth. A little homemade parachute was attached to the puppet head, and when I looked carefully, I noticed that so were a few cobwebs. That was all right. Puppets, like people, sometimes need to rest their weary heads.

I stood in front of the window and gazed fondly at the puppet head in my hand. To some, it was merely a puppet head. Others might think of it as an extremely short concierge. To me, it was a friend.

I threw my friend's head out the window at a slight angle, taking into consideration the way the freezing drizzle was pounding into the building from the south. It took a nice trajectory over the fire escape, drifted gently back toward Hudson Street, caught a little downdraft around the second-floor level, and Ratso came up with it like a desperate bridesmaid.

I got a brief glimpse of the dark expression on Ratso's face as he gripped the puppet head and looked back up at the window, and I realized the quiet weekend was o-v-e-r.

The psychiatrist's office was over on Charles Street, a short but, under the circumstances, extremely unpleasant taxi ride from the loft.

I did not need a shrink. What had occurred in Cleveland was enough to unhinge even a normal person, but every time I tried to bring it up in the cab, Ratso would say, 'Tell it to Dr Bock.'

'But be sure not to tell him that we once burgled his office,' said Rambam. His eyes were the color of steel, and they were looking at me as if I were a lab specimen. Apparently, I was being forcibly taken to the same shrink on whom we'd done a little B & E operation a few years back. That time, I needed the psychic goods on a croaked bisexual. This time, I didn't need a goddamn thing. Well, I'd tell that to Dr Bock.

'It can't hurt to talk to him,' McGovern said, as the four of us crowded into the little waiting room.

'Yes, it can,' I said in a loud, hostile, petulant voice that brought the head of the grossly overweight receptionist slowly swiveling toward me like a large bird of prey. Ratso walked over to the desk and spoke to her, and I sat down and tried to make sense of what was rapidly becoming a rather tedious, not to say undignified, situation.

There were three of them, not counting the big receptionist and the little shrink, who was hiding in his hole somewhere, and there was only one of me, unless, of course, I had a multiple personality and there were several of me. I flatly doubted that. If I was that crazy, the cat would've left me long ago.

Suddenly, forged of necessity, I came up with a great idea. I'd humor my three so-called friends and tell Bock about John Morgan. Then I'd get Bock to hypnotize me. In my conscious mind the memories of Borneo and Morgan were about as faded as my old sarong, but in my subconscious there might just lie the key to the whole baffling situation. It couldn't hurt to try.

When the receptionist called my name, we all trooped into the shrink's office like the Von Trapp family climbing a hill, Ratso and McGovern both, apparently, wanting a prior word with the guy. Bock got up and came over to us, and we all went through the usual unpleasantries. Finally, Bock said curtly, 'I wasn't aware this was a group-therapy session. I'll have to ask all of you, except Kinky, to please wait outside.'

Ratso and McGovern nodded and left, as did Rambam, who, I noticed, had been futzing around in the vicinity of Bock's desk while all the team captains had been introducing themselves. He winked at me as he stepped into the waiting room.

A little over an hour later, I stepped into the waiting room myself, preshrunk, posthypnotized, and extremely pissed. I didn't remember a thing about the hypnosis, and Bock, citing professional ethics, had stubbornly refused to let me have the tape he'd made of the session.

'No tapes are to go out of the office at any time,' he said dismissively. 'Come back next week, and I can discuss it with you.'

'Fat chance,' I said rather thoughtlessly as I passed the receptionist. We all walked outside, except Ratso, who stayed behind, I later learned, to stick me with the bill. In troubled times, there are some constants.

'Jesus, I wanted to hear that tape,' I said, shaking what was left of my head in disgust.

'Go back next week,' said McGovern.

'No need,' said Rambam, pointing to his attaché case. 'I bugged the office.'

I stopped and looked at Rambam with renewed admiration.

'Somewhere,' I said, 'H. R. Haldeman is smiling.'

12

'. . . I feel the nails going into my body . . . I see the blood flowing out . . . I see a multitude of people standing around me . . .'

'Christ,' Ratso said, as back in the loft we all listened to my voice on the tape, 'maybe he's sicker than I thought.' He looked across at me as I sat at my desk. I shrugged.

'Make it a little louder, will you?' McGovern shouted from the couch. Rambam walked over to the attaché case on the kitchen table and adjusted a knob on the little tape recorder.

'. . . Oh, God, stop them . . . they don't know what they're doing . . .'

There was a silence on the tape. Ratso, Rambam, and McGovern were all staring at me. I moved uneasily in my chair. I tried to look relatively sane. This certainly wasn't what I'd expected to hear.

We all waited.

The next voice on the tape was Dr Bock's. He sounded a bit surprised himself, possibly excited in a rather clinical way. Shrinks like a little variety too. He was asking me what I saw now.

'I can hardly wait,' said Rambam.

'. . . they are giving me more tuak to drink . . . more betelnut to chew . . . Morgan is there . . . he is smiling as he hands me a stick of ganja . . . they are dipping the nails in pig fat . . . the people are crowding around me . . . I'm lying on the floor of the ruai . . . I see two small Kayan boys who are identical, maybe eight years old . . . haircuts like

24

little tadpoles . . . one is holding a bottle of tuak *. . . the other is carrying banana leaves almost as big as he is . . . they are native boys, but they both have remarkable, frightening blue eyes . . . blue as the sky . . . I want to ask a question, but I can't . . . the pain is coming back now . . . I am seeing explosions of light . . . Morgan is here again . . . Now they are wrapping my arm in banana leaves . . . Morgan is talking to me . . . "Got some great shots," he says . . . I am looking at my arm, but all I see is blood and banana leaves . . . I close my eyes . . . I hear Morgan saying, "Great-looking tattoo, man. Now your arm's got to be buried in a gentile cemetery." . . .*

'Maybe now,' I said as I got up and poured drinks for the house, 'you three doubting Thomases will finally come to believe that I do not think I'm Jesus Christ.'

'Rather an inversion of the biblical theme,' said McGovern, downing the shot, 'but it does come as a relief.'

'Yeah,' I said, 'and I want to say that your faith in me has been very heartening.' I killed the shot and poured another one for McGovern and myself.

Ratso was still staring at his drink. 'Well,' he said, 'at least we now know beyond a doubt that the John Morgan you claim to have known did exist. Let's see this tattoo of yours.'

I pulled up my sleeve, and the three of them gathered around to look at the bluish markings on my left arm. 'It's a Kayan stylized version of a dog,' I said. 'Here's the jaw, and these are the teeth. This is the eye of the dog,' I continued, pointing to a marking at the center of the rather elaborate design. 'When you die, it's supposed to become a torch and light your way to heaven. It protects my soul.'

McGovern knocked back his second shot. 'It's got its work cut out for it,' he said.

We'd had a few more drinks, and McGovern and I were carrying on a rather acrimonious debate about the Piers Akerman scrotum incident, when suddenly I thought I heard a woman's voice coming from the general area of the attaché case.

'What was that?' asked McGovern.

'I told you,' said Rambam. 'I didn't just record Kinky's session, I bugged the goddamn office. This is his next patient.' Rambam smiled.

'Maybe we should turn it off,' said McGovern.

'Let it run,' said Ratso. 'I've got a graduate degree in deviant psychology. I'm interested.'

'Too bad you didn't take a course in ethics,' I said.

'C'mon,' said Ratso, pouring himself another shot of Jack Daniel's. I'd had to bring in reinforcements for the bottle of Jameson we'd already killed. 'This can't hurt anybody. This'll be fun. Let it roll.'

'So, Winnie,' Dr Bock was saying, 'the last time we talked, you were dealing with guilt feelings about your fascination with a menage à trois involving Edith Piaf and Mama Cass.'

McGovern choked on his drink. Ratso and Rambam laughed so hard we missed a little of the dialogue. I looked up at the ceiling. At least it was quiet up there now.

The next thing we heard was a voice saying, ' – no longer bothers me. I've resolved that. I came to see you today for another reason. But it's kind of embarrassing.'

'Anything you say,' said Dr Bock firmly, 'stays in this room.'

'I'll drink to that,' said McGovern.

'Well, I've been breaking out in a rash all over my – all over my body. It makes it quite uncomfortable to continue giving my dance classes. When you wear tights and leotards and things and you're as physical as I am – well, you can imagine what it's like. Or can you?'

'Of course,' said Dr Bock.

'I've been to three doctors. I've tried everything. It goes away for a while, but it keeps coming back worse than ever.'

'Sounds psychosomatic,' said Dr Bock. 'Possibly related to childhood neglect, adolescent anxieties, adult guilt.'

'But none of that bothers me, Dr Bock. In fact, nothing seems to bother me except – '

'Except what, Winnie? Tell me.'

'Except cigar smoke and cats,' she said.

13

That night I wandered down to the Monkey's Paw alone, looked for trouble, didn't find any, and wandered back to 199B Vandam. They say if you're looking for trouble you'll find it, but the truth is, if you look too hard for anything you probably won't find it. The way you find stuff is not to look for it. You might even try praying for things you don't want. Run in a little reverse psychology on God. You could get lucky.

Of course, sometimes you want what you want.

On this particular evening I wanted some tuna for the cat and some fish ice cream for myself, but both of our cupboards were about as empty as Little Orphan Annie's irises. The cat peered under the counter with me, saw there was no cat food, and turned away in disgust. I offered her the bagel that I never got around to that morning, but she drew a bye. She had very little appreciation for ethnic things.

I had just taken off my boots and was thinking of making it an early night when the phones rang. No big deal. Happens to firemen all the time.

I walked across the cold wooden floor in my tie-dyed socks, which I'd bought from a guy at an arts fair who had a booth that sold nothing but tie-dyed socks. You can imagine what kind of drugs he'd taken in his life.

I made it to the desk and opted for the blower on the left. I almost always opt for the blower on the left. Partly because I'm left-handed, and partly because I'm a creature of narrow habit. Also, I've done pretty well in my life, all things considered, and I don't see any point in changing blowers in the middle of the stream.

It was Carmen. She was at the Pierre Hotel.

'Kinky,' she said, 'can you come over now? I'm scared.'

'Soon's I get my boots on. What room are you in?'

'Eleven-oh-seven . . . I think there's someone following me. I saw him at the airport, and when I was checking in, I saw him in the hotel lobby.'

'Could be coincidence. What's he look like?'

'He's an old man . . . Maybe I'm wrong . . . but something about him gives me the goose bumps. He's wearing a dark suit with white socks and a blue flower in his lapel.'

'Snappy dresser,' I said.

I told her I'd be right over, and to stay in her room until I got there. I hung up, put on my boots, grabbed my hunting vest, coat, cowboy hat, and a few cigars for the road. I left the cat in charge, and headed out into the New York night.

It was after eleven when I hailed a hack on Hudson. A light snow was starting to fall, and under the streetlights it looked almost timeless, like leftover Lindbergh confetti.

'Pierre Hotel,' I told the driver, as offhandedly as I could.

There were shabbier destinations.

14

Whatever the Pierre may have lacked in soul, it made up for in opulence. It wasn't your down-home kind of place, but the people who stayed there weren't down and they weren't home, so why should they give a damn? The place welcomed a Claus von Bulow or a Zsa Zsa Gabor like the Statue of Liberty, but a guy coming in late at night with a cowboy hat, a hunting vest, and a cigar might have to search for the golden door farther downtown.

My friend Bill Osco from L.A. always stayed at the Pierre when he was in New York. Bill used to dress like most rich people in California: crummy jeans, crummy jacket, and a baseball cap. He told me once he'd stayed at the Pierre for two weeks, and every night when he'd come back to the hotel, a security guy in the lobby would come up to him and say, 'Can I help you?' Bill would always answer, 'Yeah. You can get out of my way so I can get to my room.'

As I paid the cabbie and tipped the doorman, who was dressed like that archduke whose assassination started World War I, I visualized myself breezing through security, and damned if it didn't work. Two security guys were harassing some guy in a baseball cap, and I blew right by in a trail of cigar smoke. The lobby wasn't crowded. Nobody was wearing white socks and blue flowers. I found an open elavator, bootlegged the cigar inside, and pushed eleven.

A woman, probably in her late fifties, was already in the elevator. She was dressed like a dead teenager. It didn't take her long to flare her manicured nostrils, fix me with a haughty little moue of distaste, and march off the Otis box at four. You meet all kinds of people on elevators.

I got off at eleven, followed the gilded maze around for a while, and finally arrived at 1107. I started to knock, and realized that the door was not quite shut all the way. Rather careless of Carmen, I thought.

I knocked anyway. Nothing.

I walked in and saw that the room was part of a larger suite. Maybe Carmen was on the other side.

I walked through a kind of sitting room and went into the far end of the suite. A woman's belongings were strewn around, including a purse and a scarf on the floor. Rather sloppy of Carmen, I thought.

I picked up the purse and started to go through it. I felt vaguely like Art Linkletter rifling a strange woman's purse on his old TV show. There was something wrong with going through a woman's purse, even if you found it on the floor of a hotel room. But there are a hell of a lot of things in the world that are a hell of a lot wronger. I could see the reaction to one of them in my eyes in the wall mirror.

Her name was Carmen Cohen, I learned. Melodic name.

From a land where people disappear. Argentina, in this case.

Now Carmen Cohen had disappeared. I felt a sense of confusion mingling with the stronger sense of danger. I was in some kind of unfocused tableau, standing alone in a suite in the Pierre Hotel holding the purse of a strange woman who had disappeared before she could tell me anything about John Morgan, whom I couldn't seem to find either.

I didn't like puzzles that much. Especially those that appear increasingly to be cut from a large, raw, karmic chunk of evil.

15

'Maybe ten thousand young broads a week turn up missing in New York City,' said Detective Sergeant Mort Cooperman as he poked rather desultorily through Carmen Cohen's suitcase. 'Most of them, of course, aren't missing at all,' he added as he gazed somewhat skeptically around the hotel suite.

'Most of them just stood up guys like you,' said Detective Sergeant Buddy Fox from the doorway to the living room. The hotel dick standing next to him nodded his head like a mildly bored robot.

'Most of them,' I said, 'don't leave their purses behind when they go.'

'See, I told you, Fox,' said Cooperman with his back to us, 'it ain't Kinky's purse.' These guys had some sharp banter going.

Cooperman and Fox and I seemed to be fated foils. Circumstances had often thrown us together, and never had it been what you would call pleasant. Shucking all modesty, Ratso and I had arrived at solutions to a number of cases that had baffled the NYPD. To make matters worse, McGovern had flaunted our amateur crime-solving expertise in the *Daily News* to such an extent that Cooperman had probably thought twice before he'd saved my life in a rather terrifying caper the year before at Madison Square Garden. It became quite obvious at times that Cooperman wondered if he'd made the right decision.

This, it appeared, was to be one of those times.

Cooperman now turned to face the rest of us just as Ratso came running into the room, slightly out of breath, wearing lavender slacks, a sweater with little hockey players all over it, and a coonskin cap with the racoon's face, eyes sewn shut, mounted on the front.

Cooperman shut his own eyes for a moment, possibly hoping the vision would go away. When it didn't, he spoke in a voice that sounded remarkably like the hiss of a subway train.

He said, 'Terrific. Just terrific. The goddamn fucking Bobbsey Twins.'

'What did I miss?' Ratso asked.

About five minutes later Cooperman motioned to Fox and they headed for the door. 'We'll file a report,' he said shortly.

'Wait a minute,' I said. 'We're dealing with a missing person here.' I'd already told them about Carmen's call to me and about her fear that she was being followed by an old man with white socks and a blue flower. The story hadn't dented their demeanors noticeably.

'As far as we're concerned,' said Cooperman, 'she's not missing yet.' Ratso and I stared in mild disbelief.

'And if she's any friend of yours,' Fox said with a harsh little chuckle, 'we're not sure she's a person yet.'

'I'll sleep better knowing you guys're on the job,' I said.

Cooperman turned in the doorway so he was facing me. His massive torso practically blotted out the hall. 'If she doesn't turn up, call us back in twenty-four hours. Then she can be declared officially missing, and we'll open a file. There's nothing else we can do now unless she's a minor, a senior citizen, or mentally incompetent.' Cooperman turned and left.

'Like you,' Fox added with a little leer. Then he followed Cooperman out to the elevators.

Ratso and I watched the hotel dick double-lock the room. Then we took an elevator down to the lobby.

'What do we do now?' Ratso asked.

'Make a phone call,' I said.

16

'No problem,' said Rambam, nodding confidently toward the C-note in his right hand. 'I've got the master key to every room in the hotel right here.'

The three of us were sitting in the downstairs bar of the Pierre knocking back whiskey at about six bucks a shot, and I wasn't counting on Ratso to pick up the tab. I'd told Rambam about the cops, the room, the phone call from Carmen, and, of course, the old man, the white socks, and the blue flower. The whole story seemed somehow to have a faint aura of unreality clinging to it.

'You guys sit tight,' said Rambam, getting up from the table. 'I'll just have a word with the bell captain.'

'Make it a quick word,' Ratso said. 'They're closing this bar pretty soon, and loitering in that lobby's harder than it looks.'

Rambam left, Ratso ordered another round, and I thought things over. With security the way it was, it would've been tough to get anyone out of the hotel against her will in the time frame in which we were working. I was betting that Carmen was still in the hotel. And if anybody knew the ins and outs of locked hotel rooms, it was Rambam.

I thought of the time, several years before, when Rambam had provided the final piece in the puzzle that would hang the infamous Hank Williams Killer at the Lone Star Cafe. To do that, he'd had to go unbeknownst into the murderer's locked hotel room. Of course, that had taken place at the Gramercy Park, and this was the formidable and mildly intimidating Pierre Hotel. This would be harder. Much harder. But sometimes in life, what one learns in St Mary Mead does hold true in London. I had confidence in the boy.

Rambam returned just as the impeccably dressed waiter was shoehorning Ratso and me out of the bar. Over his shoulder he was carrying what looked like some dry cleaning with the hotel's fancy paper wrapper covering it. Under the dark gaze of the waiter he walked back into the bar, lifted his glass in a toast to the irritated man, killed the shot, and walked back out to where we were standing.

'One for the elevator,' he said.

We walked over to an alcove near the elevators and sat in a plush forest of expensive-looking, uncomfortable furniture.

'Just like your loft,' said Ratso.

'Just like room seventeen-oh-two,' said Rambam.

'You think she's in there?' I asked.

'I don't know,' said Rambam, 'but that's the room of the old geezer with the white socks and blue flower. Bell captain thinks he's an old queen. Has the look, he says. Also, he saw him with two big blond hunks earlier this evening, so he may not be alone.'

'Maybe they're all havin' an orgy up there,' said Ratso.

'Maybe you can flash your *National Lampoon* press card and they'll let you in,' I said. Ratso tilted his coonskin cap to a rather rakish angle.

'Getting in is no problem,' said Rambam. 'The hard part, in this kind of situation, may be getting out.'

17

'Room service,' said the voice.

The man in the red-and-gold bellman's jacket balanced a tray of food with his right hand. With his left he knocked on room 1702.

'Room service,' he said again, with just a very slight hint of an un-Pierrelike intonation. This time he knocked louder. Ratso and I were waiting about ten feet farther up the hall, but we clearly heard the irritated voice on the inside of the door.

'We didn't order any room service,' it said, logically enough. I would've preferred that he'd said 'I' instead of 'we,' but there wasn't much to be done about it now. Sometimes when you look for trouble you find it.

'Terribly sorry, sir,' said Rambam with a dangerous-looking wink to me and Ratso. 'If you'll please just sign the receipt and state that you didn't place the order. I have to account for the tray to the room-service captain.'

The door opened a crack, and Ratso and I flattened ourselves against the wall. An unseen presence was checking Rambam out. I felt a small wave of pity for the guy behind the door. He had no way of knowing at that moment he was staring into the eyes of probably the most dangerous room-service waiter in America. Of course, at the time, I didn't know whom or what we were dealing with. Had I known that then the little wave of pity would've been buried in a tidal bore of stronger, deeper emotion.

Then the door closed and I heard a muffled metallic noise that sounded like a chain being removed from a door, a weapon being cocked, or, barely possibly, the Tin Man getting a new heart.

The door opened.

A large blond head peered out like an Aryan turtle, radiating evil. The head had a vague familial resemblance to Gorgeous George, the wrestler. It swiveled in an almost mechanical fashion, and suddenly its furtive eyes, like smuggled emeralds, locked with my own. For a fraction of a second I saw a gleam that seemed to emanate from a great and chilling darkness. Then Rambam dropped the loaded tray on Gorgeous's head and rolled across the threshold like a vicious, conscienceless, somewhat larger model of the Little Engine that Could.

Ratso and I heard dull thuddings and muffled shouts as we headed for the open door. Gorgeous came squirting out of the room on two wheels, collided solidly with Ratso, and ricocheted off the wall. He fixed us with a shivery liquid gaze, and then ran down the hallway in the direction of the stairs.

'Forget him,' I said, as Ratso slowly got back on his feet. 'Let's find the girl.'

The two of us were converging on the room again when Rambam yelled, 'Watch out for Goldilocks!' A second man, blond and somewhat bloodied, came crashing through the doorway, hooking Ratso in the gut with his left shoulder. Ratso went down again. The guy bugged out for the dugout.

When Ratso and I finally got into the room, Rambam closed the door behind us. The right side of his face was beginning to resemble the color of his bellman's uniform, but otherwise he looked pretty cheerful. Ratso had taken off his coonskin cap and was trying to decide whether to hold his head or his stomach. The room was empty.

'If she's not in the dumper or the closet, maybe we did break up a poofter's convention,' I said.

'One way to find out,' said Rambam. 'But I'm warning you, it could be ugly.'

I pushed open the bathroom door and walked in. On the floor were a woman's shoes, stockings, skirt, and blouse. I walked back into the room just as Rambam was opening the closet.

'Door number three,' he said as he pulled on the knob.

Inside the closet a woman was tied by the wrists to the clothes rod and gagged with a pillowcase. She was wearing nothing but a pair of lace panties. She was the most beautiful woman I'd seen since Jean Seberg had gone to Jesus.

Ratso dropped his coonskin cap and made no effort whatsoever to pick it up.

Whatever they'd doped Carmen with before they'd tied her up, I wouldn't have minded a few hits of myself. She was definitely out where the buses don't run. Ratso had done a fairly convincing job of getting her into a Pierre Hotel robe and laying her down on one of the beds. Now Rambam and I were studying the jacket that one of our blond friends had left behind in the room. We were studying it on Ratso's body, and he was studying it in the full-length mirror.

'It was probably Gorgeous's,' I said. 'He's about your size, and he left in a hurry.'

'So did Goldilocks,' said Rambam.

'Whatever did you say to him?' Ratso asked. He was going through the pockets of the coat and finding absolutely nothing.

After some time Ratso came up with a small scrap of paper. It was a receipt for a roll of film someone had dropped off at one of those quickie developing places.

'Couldn't have been Carmen,' I said. 'If she stayed in the room like I told her, she wouldn't have had time.'

'I'll ask her when she comes to,' said Ratso.

'You do that,' said Rambam. He was looking for labels in the jacket and finding none. 'That's interesting,' he said at last. 'It's been sanitized.'

'Yeah,' said Ratso, looking at the fabric of the sleeve, 'it's nice and clean, all right.'

'That's not what I meant,' said Rambam. ' "Sanitized" means somebody has taken the trouble to cut all the manufacturer's labels out of a garment. This guarantees anonymity, hides the country of origin and . . .' Rambam looked thoughtfully at the sleeping woman on the bed.

'And what?' Ratso asked.

35

'And means,' said Rambam grimly, 'that we could be in some deep, very unpleasant, international shit.'

I took a few steps back and levelled a measured gaze at Ratso in the jacket.

'It's you,' I said.

18

Tuesday morning broke dark and threatening over New York City. Actually, it was around eleven o'clock when I woke up. Morning, like anything else in this world, is relative. Some people had probably been up since six a.m. doing squat thrusts in the parking lot, eating fibered cereal, and disturbing other Americans with early morning phone calls. If you want to get up at six a.m. and pretend you're Tevye the Milkman, that's your problem. For me, morning begins when I realize that the soft warm body curled up next to me is a cat.

I looked out the bedroom window of the loft and couldn't decide whether it was the window that was grimy or the city. Then the events of the previous night came back to me, and I plunked down for the city. It's pretty hard to find good help willing to do cities these days.

As the espresso machine began to hum happily to itself, I lit a cigar and sat at the desk thinking thoughts as dark as the weather. Carmen was safely stashed away, for the moment at least, at Ratso's apartment in nearby Soho. Whoever was after her would know nothing of Ratso. It was a good place for her to stay for now, if she could stand living in a small apartment with a stuffed polar bear's head, a five-foot-tall statue of the Virgin Mary, three hundred hockey sticks, and roughly ten thousand books, the vast majority of them dealing with Bob Dylan, Jesus, or Hitler. The reason Ratso needed so many books was that none of them, quite understandably, attempted to deal with any more than one of the subjects. You rarely ever found a book about Jesus' influence on Hitler or about Bob Dylan's influence on Jesus. You couldn't very easily find an anthology that included more than one of them between its covers. In fact, there was only one thing I could think of that Jesus, Bob Dylan, and Hitler had in common, and that was that Ratso was an unrecognized world authority on all three.

Thunder rattled the warehouse doors of Vandam Street. I poured myself an espresso and proceeded to ponder particularly paranoid thoughts. Nothing really added up yet, but I was beginning to suspect that the phone call I'd received last week informing me of John Morgan's death might very possibly not have come from Cleveland. I didn't know why exactly I felt this, but the more I thought about it, the more likely it began to seem.

Maybe Carmen would provide us with the answers about John Morgan. It was 11:32 a.m. I called Ratso's number. The phone rang about five times, and I hung up before I had to listen to his gratingly familiar recorded voice. Maybe they were both still dead to the world. Maybe they'd gotten up at six and were still doing squat thrusts in the parking lot. If I didn't hear from them in a while I'd try again. At least Carmen was in safe, if slightly horny, hands.

I'd given the receipt for the roll of film to Rambam to pick up as soon as possible. If one of our blond friends wanted that film bad enough, I was sure he could pick it up without the receipt. I expected to hear from Rambam soon. I expected to hear from Ratso soon.

All I heard was the dull thudding of the lesbian dance class starting up over my head. It sounded vaguely like primitive drums answering the thunder. Man's answer to God. No, woman's answer to Mother Nature. Woman's answer to Father Nature? Whatever it was, it was tedious. But it was somebody's answer to something, which was a hell of a lot more than I had going for myself so far.

I got another cup of espresso and walked over to the kitchen window to watch the rain start to fall. At first it fell with a blue, glinty color, like the eyes of distant women. Then it came down harder and turned to a warm, and somehow comforting, New York gray. Tuesday's child smokes a cigar and watches the rain. There were worse ways to spend a Tuesday morning, I reflected, and in my life I'd tried more of them than I cared to remember.

The cat jumped up on the sill and watched the rain with me. I daydreamed that the cat and I were adrift on a ship in a dark and deep and dangerous ocean. What the cat daydreamed I do not know.

Dreams, they say, can never hurt you; only the dreamer can.

19

I was taking a little power nap on the couch – quite dreamless – when a voice from below, apparently gaining power as it spiraled upward through several concentric circles of urban hell, awakened me. I walked over to the window and looked down to see Rambam standing on the sidewalk. The rain had let up just a bit, but nonetheless he seemed to want the puppet head pretty badly. Pushy New Yorker if I ever saw one.

The puppet head and parachute were still a little damp from the day before, but I opened the window and floated them out with a flourish, like a Madison Avenue ad guy with a great new idea. It was a fairly nice shot, if I say so myself.

Running a puppet-head operation in the rain is not a casual proposition. It requires skills they don't teach you at vacation Bible college. It calls for a time-consuming and extremely high-maintenance relationship between man and puppet head. Of course, if it were easy, everyone would do it.

Rambam came in wearing a trench coat, like a spy in an old London Fog commercial. 'I didn't know you guys really wore coats like that,' I said.

'Oh yeah,' he said. 'It started many years ago in Europe and Latin America, when they had to wait around for a long time for puppets to fall.' He flipped the slightly soggy puppet head over to me, and I replaced it carefully on top of the refrigerator.

Rambam tossed a packet onto my desk. 'Photos,' he said. He walked over to the espresso machine and drew himself a cup. 'Mulberry Street's got nothin' on you,' he said.

'Keep the customer satisfied, I always say.'

'I also got,' he said, taking a healthy slurp, 'some information on who rented the room last night at the Pierre. Between the bell captain, the room clerk, and several other less savory sources, this case is starting to get a little expensive.'

'Put it on my tab,' I said.

'That's what I was afraid you'd say,' said Rambam. He studied his espresso leaves. Then he said, 'The room was rented to the 88 Leasing Corp. out of Bayonne, New Jersey. That mean anything to you?'

'Place to start,' I said. I walked over to the desk, took a cigar out of Sherlock's head, lopped the end off with my cigar guillotine, and set fire to it with a kitchen match, always careful to keep the tip of the cigar well above the flame. Then I opened the packet of photos. Rambam wandered in behind me and glanced down at them over my shoulder.

The first shot was of a tree with what looked like some kind of chalk-marked symbol on it. Maybe an upside-down version of the peace sign the hippies used to use back when peace was happening. I'd almost forgotten what it looked like. Most of the pictures were jungle shots – banana trees, rubber trees, trees big enough for Tarzan's condo, overgrown trails, muddy rivers. There were several shots of what appeared to be an Indian cave painting. The painting looked vaguely Mayan at a glance – sunbursts, primitive animals, the Indian peace sign that was later inverted to make the swastika, a group of stick figures that might've been the ancient ancestors of Sherlock Holmes's dancing men.

In the middle of the roll somewhere there was one terrific shot of John Morgan that nearly brought a tear to my eye. He was smiling from the front seat of a Land Rover pulled off to the left side of a small highway with the jungle rising all around it. On the right side of the road, going in the opposite direction, was a bus with about ninety-seven passengers, not counting chickens and goats. The bus looked like it had once belonged to Ken Kesey. I stared again at John's face. His hair was falling over his eyes, like always, but you could still see that they were sparkling, also like always, with mischief. Sun was dappling his features. He looked happy. That was how I remembered him.

I glanced at the remaining photographs. There was one of two old men standing around wearing panama hats. One of them had a rather prominent gap between his two front teeth. There were no more shots of John. The last picture was the same as the first, a similar chalk marking on the side of a tree. That was the lot.

'Standard South American jungle shots,' I said. 'Twenty-four pictures to the roll. No way to accurately date when they were taken.'

Something was bothering me about the photographs. Like a troublesome insect that somehow had slipped under your mosquito net and wouldn't go away. I'd go over the pictures more thoroughly, I thought, after I'd had a chance to talk with Carmen, but something seemed wrong to me. I just didn't know what the hell it was.

At last I put the photos back in the packet. 'You've seen one jungle,' I sighed, 'you've seen 'em all.' I leaned back in my chair and puffed thoughtfully on the cigar.

'What's even stranger than these photographs,' said Rambam, 'was what the guy at the photo place said to me after I picked them up.'

'What'd the guy say?'

'He said, "Thank you, Mr Morgan." '

20

'Hello,' I said. 'This is Dr Hiram Dickstein. I'm a corporate psychologist.'

The woman's voice on the other end of the blower did not sound overly impressed.

'Yes,' she said.

'This *is* the Secretary of State's Office?'

'Yes.'

'In Trenton, New Jersey?'

'Yes.' Large vocabulary.

'I need some information,' I said, 'on a new corporation. The 88 Leasing Corp.'

'I can give you what we have on file. Just a moment, please.'

I waited. It was almost four o'clock and I still hadn't heard from Ratso. Thoughtful of him to keep in touch. I picked up a half-smoked cigar out of my Texas-shaped ashtray and fired it up. Quite often they were better that way. Quite often a lot of things were better that way. The lady came back on the line.

'Yes, Dr . . . uh . . .'

'Dickstein.'

'Yes, well, I can give you the service address at the time of incorporation.' She read out a lawyer's name and a street address in Bayonne, New Jersey, which I jotted down in my Big Chief tablet. 'It's an active corporation, but it's not a new one. In fact, it's quite old.'

'How old?'

'According to the card file, it was incorporated in 1946.'

I thanked her and hung up. Interesting, I thought. For a company started in 1946, the 88 Leasing Corp. was a strange name.

So, of course, was Dr Hiram Dickstein.

Around five o'clock I went out for a while to get some cat food and some Kinky food. I bought the cat food at a little corner grocery store on Tenth Street near Sheridan Square that was run by friendly foreigners who specialized in cat food and beer. I had dinner – party of one – at a little coffee shop on the square. They gave me a nice table by the window.

The rain-wept sidewalks of the Village shined like mirrors with lines. You could almost see yourself. I wondered if I'd always be a party of one. I wondered if I'd be an old man with a bow tie sitting alone on New Year's Eve looking out the window of some little restaurant at two dogs hosing on the sidewalk. That was certainly something to look forward to.

I walked across the square – past two panhandlers, an albino Negro, and an identically dressed matched pair of homosexuals, all loitering in the park. I thought about loitering myself for a while, but I was afraid I might fit in, so I walked over to the Monkey's Paw. It was a good place to drink and, on a slow night, it was a good place to think. It was a slow night.

Where was John Morgan? I wondered. In South America? In Borneo? In a Cleveland bone orchard? Lurking somewhere in New York? The boy reportedly got around pretty good, but this was ridiculous. Maybe the question should be: Who is John Morgan?

I sipped a Bass ale and turned an empty shot glass of Jameson thoughtfully in a clockwise direction on the mahogany. Carmen Cohen was the key to the puzzle. By now, with any luck, Ratso might have gotten all the answers out of her. The only other active lead, besides the photographs, was the service address of the 88 Leasing Corp. in Bayonne, New Jersey. That was the lawyer's office. So my two best leads were a lawyer and a woman, both, of course, inherently capable of treachery and deceit. Well, you work with what you've got.

When I arrived back at the loft, it was pretty late. I'd done more thinking than I thought. There was a message from Ratso on the machine. His experience with Carmen had been 'very revealing' so far. He wanted to 'explore further' some things with her. At the moment, according to the message, Ratso and Carmen were attending a party at the Egyptian embassy. He could get me in, too, he said, if I desired.

I desired to go to bed. The Egyptians had managed without me for thousands of years, and it was my guess they'd make it one more night. Egyptian culture had been pretty much downhill anyway ever since the Hebrews left for the suburbs.

I was in bed dreaming of pharoahs and kings when the phone rang like a sacred cat shrieking inside a tomb. It was Dylan calling me from Texas.

He'd remembered something.

21

'The four of us,' Dylan was saying, 'had left from Sibu on a trip to try to find the legendary headwaters of the Ulu Ayer. There were six of us in the longboat: Shanahan, Jones, Morgan, myself, and two Iban guides. We had a three-pronged giant hook with us that Shanahan intended to impale a chicken on and troll for crocodiles along the way. We had an RAF silk parachute that made into a great tent in the *ulu* if we needed it. We had supplies for two weeks. The only thing I'd forgotten was my little yellow pills for malaria.

'About six days into the journey we stopped at one of the last civilized outposts on the river, an Iban longhouse. We quickly became friends with the *tuai rumah*, the chief. They were having a festival for the eclipse of the moon, and *tuak* was offered to all of us. As you know, to refuse anything offered to you in the *ulu* is seen as an insult. Not drinking *tuak* is the sign of a woosie. Drinking until you vomit and then coming back and drinking some more is the sign of a real man.'

'I wonder what they think of quiche,' I said. I was propped up on the pillows and beginning to get into Dylan's story. I remembered that Dylan's *ulu* stories were always pretty good, but seldom if ever short-winded.

'So we're all sitting on the *ruai*, everybody – even the little children – are drinking and smoking bark-wrapped jungle tobacco, and the moon is slowly being gobbled up by a *hantuh* – a local ghost of some kind – and all around us people are beating gongs. A few of them are playing the *sapei* – you know, the three-stringed native guitar – and dancing the *najhat*.

'So, suddenly, Jones, who's sitting right in the middle of the whole group, throws his legs over his head and shouts to nobody in particular, "Light me." Nobody makes a move. Jones shouts at the top of his lungs, "Light me!" Shanahan reaches over with a cigarette lighter to Jones's ass and lights it. Jones promptly blasts about a six-inch-long blue darter. One of the best I've ever seen. The Ibans, of course, were completely blown away by it, in more ways than one. It was a form of magic from the red-haired devil that they'd never seen before. It was a little like when the American Indians first saw a demonstration of gunpowder. A very sharing and caring experience culturally speaking.'

'Fine,' I said. I knew better than to tell Dylan to get to the meat of it. He was so into his story that he'd forgotten to speak in song lyrics.

'Anyway, later that night Shanahan decides he's going to try to *niap* one of the native girls. We've all been drinking pretty heavily. A lot of people have already passed out. So a mischievous Iban friend of Shanahan's points to a certain door of a *rumah*, Shanahan tries it and it's locked. So the Iban tells him how to climb over the inside wall of the longhouse and jump down into the *rumah* where the young *prempaun* is sleeping.

43

'About five minutes later we hear a loud cracking noise – you know, the floors are made of bamboo slats – and we all rush over to the door, the *prempaun* opens it, and there's a big hole in the floor. We look into the hole and there's nothing. Silence and blackness. Those longhouses, you know, are built on stilts, some of them are twenty to thirty feet off the ground, or more. So we all go racing down the *ruai*, down the log plank – which is actually easier to do when you're *mahbok* than when you're sober – and we start looking desperately for Shanahan under the longhouse. We're sure he's broken his neck. Finally, we find him facedown in about two feet of pig shit. We get him up and he's all right. All he says is, "Terrific hose."

'About an hour later only the *tuai rumah* and I are still drinking. Everybody else is passed out. The chief is really taking a shine to me because I'm staying with him on the *tuak*. So when we finally crash, he brings me into his own *rumah* and lets me sleep in his own bed. He goes somewhere else. The bed is a beautiful four-poster job like you might find in an elegant old hotel in the States. I don't know where he got it. Anyway, in the middle of the night I start feeling really sick. I get up and I stagger as far as I can and I vomit. Then I find my way back to the bed and I'm out for the night.

'In the morning, when I went out on the *ruai*, everybody in the longhouse was laughing. "What is it?" I asked. "You vomited on the chief," they said.'

I told Dylan to hang fire, got up and found a cigar and the ashtray in the shape of the state of Texas, and scampered back into bed. I usually didn't like to smoke in bed but this was a special occasion. Not that Dylan's story wasn't humorous. It was just that it was longer than the Punic Wars. I lit the cigar.

'Start talkin',' I said.

'It was true. He'd given me his bed, and he'd slept on the floor near the bed. But he was a good sport – he didn't try to take my head or anything. Of course, they had about thirty of forty heads already, hanging in woven baskets from the rafters of the *ruai*.'

'It all sounds like good public-relations work,' I said. 'What happened next?'

'Okay,' said Dylan. 'We go upriver the next day, and we start hearing stories about this great white tiger with blue eyes. It's a *bantu*, you know. There are no tigers in Borneo. There are panthers, orangutans, cobras – '

'An old British ex-pat once told me,' I said, 'that the most dangerous animal in the jungle is the bee.'

'The bee?'

'The bee. A swarm of bees in the *ulu*, if it comes after you, means almost certain death, my lad.'

'Well, *be* that as it may,' said Dylan, 'as we continued upriver, we kept hearing stories from the natives about the great white tiger with the blue eyes. I was starting to have dizzy spells, which, at the time, I mistakenly attributed to *tuak* consumption rather than malaria. I began suggesting that, as long as we were so close to the headwaters, we take a hard left when we got there, and go in search of the white tiger. This would take us, of course, through primary jungle, into an area quite unfamiliar to the Iban guides, just out of reach of Kayan country, and inhabited, supposedly, solely by nomadic Punans, who, as you know, are the only true pygmies of Borneo.

'They all said I was crazy.'

'Pretty judgmental of them, wasn't it?' I said. 'Pray continue.'

'Well, two mornings later, I showed them. Just before dawn one of the guides and I packed up our *barang* and took our share of the supplies – enough, we thought, to get across the Kayan country – and set out through thick primary *ulu* searching for the lair of the white tiger. We left a note in the longboat for the others. I don't know if it was stubbornness or malaria that goaded me to make the trip, but all I can tell you is that I'm very lucky to be alive.

'The *ulu* was so thick that you could go for hours without even seeing the sun. It was like nothing I'd ever seen. By evening of the first day, I was getting cold chills and dizzy spells, and I knew I was running a fever. The whole first day we'd seen no sign of man except for a sacred-hornbill sculpture in a small clearing.

'Toward the evening of the second day we saw something very strange. A fog seemed to be rolling in through the jungle – cold, dense, and – it was the damnedest thing – it seemed to have a kind

45

of life to it. It set the Iban's eyes to rolling, and it gave me a rather severe case of the goose bumps, I can tell you. Of course, it could've been the malaria. Even today, I'm not quite sure.

'Anyway, suddenly, in the middle of a nearby clearing, the fog parts and I see the biggest tiger I have ever seen – in or out of a zoo. It is white as driven snow, and its eyes, about the size of durians, are like pools of blue amber. Trapped in the amber, I can see something horrible beyond imagination screaming to get out . . .'

'Of course,' I said, clearing my throat, 'it could've been the malaria.'

'Don't bet on it, hoss. But I'll grant you, it is possible. Anyway, that's not the end of the story. When I came to, the sun was shining brightly. I was on my back in some kind of clearing. I sat up and looked around for the Iban guide, but he was gone like a gray goose in winter. Couldn't blame him.

'Suddenly, I was surrounded by the strangest-looking men I'd ever seen. Not Punans. Too tall. Not Ibans. Not Kayans.'

'Kenyahs, maybe,' I said.

'Maybe. But whatever the hell they were, I could have sworn that several of them – if I hadn't known better – had looked at me and then given me a Nazi salute.'

'Could've been the malaria,' I said, but a chill tumbled its way like a miniature Austrian avalanche down the slopes of my spine. Neither of us spoke for a moment.

'You still with me, hoss?' Dylan asked.

'I'm afraid so,' I said.

'Well, I got out of there alive, I'm not sure I even remember how exactly, and six months later I'm telling the story to a group of people in a bar in Kuching. Shanahan, Jones, and Morgan are there, and a few others – Dick Myers, John Schwartz, Jim Murchison, Chris Cooke. By the time I get to the end of the story, everybody's blown away. Everybody except Morgan, who sits there quietly nodding his head. "Could be some kind of anthropological land bridge," he says.'

'Sure,' I said. 'An anthropological land bridge. Kind of like throwing away your beads and singing "Oh, Susanna." '

'Yeah,' said Dylan. 'I didn't think much of the idea either. But get this. Two months later I'm leaving the country for good, going back to the States. I'm trying to check up on a few friends before I leave. I couldn't find anybody who'd seen Morgan. So I call your old friend Effendi bin Addis – you were on leave in Thailand at the time, remember, so I didn't see you when I left. I ask Effendi where Morgan is, and guess what he says?'

'Morgan's lighting farts in a mosque in Brunei?'

'Not quite, hoss. Effendi says he's afraid our boy's gone completely *gilah*. He says Morgan's up at the headwaters of the Ulu Ayer. Effendi says Morgan's gone hunting for a white tiger with blue eyes.'

22

Wednesday morning I got up on the wrong side of the bed. That was how I found my IMUS IN THE MORNING coffee mug. I stepped on the bastard, slipped, and damn near broke my neck. Household accident #467. Obviously, a broad had left it there on some recent memorable evening that had slipped my mind. I wound up on the floor, and the mug wound up under the bed.

As I looked for it, I also found myself surreptitiously checking for Nazis, communists, Jehovah's Witnesses, and a few other things that I didn't need lurking on the dark side of my life. Of course, ever since I was thirty-seven years old, I haven't been the kind of person who looks under his bed. I believe so much weird stuff that can mess up your life happens *in* the bed that anything happening underneath is going to need all the help it can get.

I found the mug, kicked the espresso machine into low gear, and frisbeed the fairly fossilized bagel out the window onto Vandam Street, narrowly missing a small group of tourists. I don't know what they were doing on Vandam Street. Maybe they were lost. Unless they came from a country that greatly admired garbage trucks, there was no reason for them to be there.

The reason I knew they were tourists is because they were dressed a little better than your average New Yorkers and they were walking slow and looking at things. Nobody from New York walks slow and looks at things.

Of course, if the bagel had carried a little more to the left, I could imagine the front page story in the *Athol, South Dakota, Gazette*: LOCAL MAN KILLED BY FLYING BAGEL. Well, that was another thing to watch out for in the big city.

When the espresso was ready, I poured a cup, lit up a cigar, and sat down at the kitchen table to read yesterday's fish wrappers. It didn't take long for my attention to wander.

I didn't think there were Nazis under my bed, and I didn't really believe there were Nazis currently weaving their dark and bloody threads into the Made in the U.S.A. fabric of my life. Maybe their shadows were still hiding somewhere in the inside pockets of my youth, but as for them being my modern-day adversaries, I just didn't see it. There's a little bit of Nazi, I thought, and a little bit of Jew in all of us. How we deal with these diverse parts of our being will have a lot to do with what kind of lives we will eventually lead and what kind of world we'll be able to make for our children and our kittens.

I walked over to the desk and called Ratso. It was a deeply gratifying experience to finally be able to speak to him in person. We made plans to meet at La Bonbonniere, or La Lobotomy, as we sometimes called it, on Eighth Avenue at eleven a.m. It was agreed that he would come to breakfast alone. I knew almost nothing about Carmen Cohen, and it wasn't unthinkable that she was not who she represented herself to be. Few people are, when you think about it.

As I fed the cat and got ready to leave, it was dawning on me that, possibly for the first time, I might actually be needing Ratso's help. Of course, he'd helped me before, but that had usually been in a rather Watsonlike manner, showing me quite clearly how not to think, what not to do. As far as Carmen went, I would see what Ratso had learned, and then make arrangements to talk to her myself.

But it was in a deeper way that I now found myself needing Ratso's rather eclectic help. And a grim understanding was coming to me that this help would not be in regard to Bob Dylan or Jesus.

Sometimes, when darkness is moving in all around you, you don't see it because you've been looking for something else. In reality, the darkness has been there all the time, but you don't notice it until it is too late for daylight savings time to reach the western states of your soul.

The light goes down to low interrogation. Then it disappears almost completely, leaving only a candle, shaped maybe like a mushroom, made by the last hippie in the world. Then, quickly, the darkness rises up, snuffing out the candle, suffocating the spirit, and drowning you, inexorably, in an India inkwell of ancient evil.

That's what happens, sometimes, when you look under the bed.

23

'Nice jacket,' I said to Ratso as we sat at one of the little tables near the window. At La Lobotomy, all the tables were near the window. Ratso's jacket was the color of phlegm.

'Thirty-seven dollars on Canal Street,' he said, not without some pride. 'Let's order.'

Charles, the cook and proprietor of the place, took our orders for breakfast. Charles was one of the few Frenchmen I liked, and that was because he was probably a Greek. Charles is a French name and La Bonbonniere is a French name, but the cuisine and ambience of the place were more like a Greek coffee shop than a French restaurant. I like Greek coffee shops more than French restaurants. They're more American.

Charles brought us our coffee. 'I don't think,' said Ratso, 'that Carmen knows much more than we do about all this.'

'That's great,' I said. 'Of course, she knows something. She knew to come here looking for me, didn't she? Maybe you're just a weak Watson.'

'Maybe,' said Ratso. 'Maybe you're just an unpleasant Sherlock.' He sipped his coffee.

'Look, Ratso, you've had plenty of time to get close to her.'

'I *have* gotten close to her.'

'That's what I was afraid of. I expected better of you, Watson.'

We drank our coffee in silence until Charles brought our breakfast.

I chewed a piece of very crisp bacon rather thoughtfully and watched as Ratso cut his eggs into ridiculously small segments with a knife and fork. It was not a particularly pleasant thing to see. I waited.

Ratso put a very large piece of ham into his mouth and gestured with his hand that the Heimlich maneuver would not be necessary. I waited.

Ratso took his time. He chewed, swallowed, belched, and said, 'Morgan told her that at times his job could be dangerous. Not only dangerous to himself, he said, but quite possibly even dangerous for her. He didn't say what the job *was* and apparently she didn't push him on it.'

'Unlikely.'

'Anyway, if something went terribly wrong, he was to leave her a prearranged signal, and she was to leave Argentina as soon as possible. She was not to contact the embassy, the Peace Corps, or anyone else. She was to locate John's old friend from Borneo, a guy named Kinky, who could usually be found in Texas or New York. He'd know what to do.'

I didn't know what to do. I stared mutely at Ratso and ate another piece of very crisp bacon.

'The prearranged signal,' said Ratso, 'was some sort of symbol to be written on a certain tree in Carmen's front yard.'

On an impulse I took the package of photographs out of the pocket of my hunting vest and dealt the top photo across the table to Ratso. The one with the chalk marks on the tree in the jungle.

'Something like this?' I asked.

Ratso looked at the photo, then looked at me. 'Yeah,' he said thoughtfully. 'I'll show this to Carmen.'

'Not yet,' I said, taking back the photograph. 'These are deep waters, my dear Ratso. There's something I have to do first, and

50

then I'll be wanting to speak to Miss Cohen myself. How's she holding up, by the way?'

'As well as could be expected. She's really a fine person, Kinkster.' Ratso's face lit up like a harvest moon over Reno.

'No doubt. Now, Ratso, there's something I need your help with. I know you've been eager to tackle a case that deals with Bob Dylan, Jesus, or Hitler, and I just might have something that falls rather neatly into one of your arcane pockets of knowledge.'

'Great! Which one?'

I took a sip of coffee and looked at Ratso for a moment. 'I could be off on the wrong track, but if I'm correct, you can forget about Mr Tambourine Man and the Baby Jesus.'

Ratso stared at me like I was trying to take away his breakfast. 'Jesus,' he said.

'Forget about Him, I told you.' Charles came over, refilled our coffee, and went back behind the counter. 'Something about that 88 Leasing Corp. rings a distant bell. It may be nothing, but check out that name 88 in relation to your third area of expertise.'

'Okay.' Ratso looked unconvinced but willing. His attitude, in truth, wasn't far off the mark from my own. When it came to wild notions of conspiracy and intrigue, I was usually from Missouri myself. Unless the conspiracy or intrigue took place in Missouri. Then I didn't believe it at all.

'Finally, Ratso, as we conclude the minutes of this Kiwanis breakfast, what else did you find out from Carmen about John Morgan?'

'Nothing. He was her fiancé. They had this prearranged signal – '

'Ratso, I went to Cleveland last week to bury an old and dear friend of mine. I can't tell you what it was like to look down into his coffin and see the body of a total stranger. Then, out of the blue, I hear from this broad in Argentina, who is the one human link that I have to what became of John Morgan. She comes to New York. She's immediately kidnapped, and God knows what else would've happened to her if we hadn't come along just when we did. Then I entrust her to my friend Ratso, who takes her to a party at the Egyptian embassy. Why not take her to lunch at the Carnegie Delicatessen with Henry Youngman?'

'That's this afternoon,' said Ratso.

'Well, goddamnit, I wanted you to pump her.' I must have raised my voice a little more than I thought, because an elderly lady at a nearby table wagged her finger at me. I could live with it.

Ratso was laughing. 'I thought you said *hump* her,' he said.

I smiled and got out a cigar. But I could see that I was going to have to talk to Carmen myself very soon. Any information we'd get from her was not likely to come through Ratso. Something in his eyes told me it was too late to tell him not to get too attached.

As Charles brought the check, an interesting thing occurred. It was sort of like a prearranged signal. Ratso went for the door at almost precisely the same moment that I went for my wallet.

24

Frank Sinatra never sang about Bayonne, New Jersey. The only music I heard as Rambam's black Jag rolled through the gray early dawn streets was a symphony of quiet desperation. It was five a.m. and the graveyard shift was on at the Dunkin' Donuts. In the near distance factories labored inexorably through the night to reverse photosynthesis. It looked like the kind of place Richard Corey might've grown up in.

'Not a garden spot, is it?' I asked, as we passed two cops sleeping in a patrol car on a side street.

'No,' said Rambam, 'and it doesn't smell like a garden, either.'

'Wouldn't know. I haven't smelled anything in seven years.'

'Roll down your window and you'll be born again.'

We drove in silence for a while along a grimy corridor of unhappy-looking warehouses that obscured a city of dreaming Americans. If you had to dream, Bayonne was as good a place as any.

Earlier in the day I'd given Rambam the name of the lawyer and the service address for the 88 Leasing Corp. as faithfully transcribed in my Big Chief tablet. That afternoon Rambam had checked out the building and the attorney who represented 88.

The building, he said, was a two-story converted warehouse that, in Rambam's words, would represent 'no problem.' The matter of the lawyer was even more interesting. He'd been dead for twenty years, but he was still paying the rent.

Rambam wheeled the Jag into a small alley down the street from a two-story office building that had been a warehouse when the world was young. No lights were on in the building as far as I could tell.

'I'm going to the pay phone on the corner to make a call to the law firm and the plumbing-supply company on the first floor. Make sure nobody's home. If a cop comes by, duck. If anybody else comes by and seems suspicious to you, honk.'

'What if a panzer tank comes by and seems suspicious to me?'

'Call General Patton on the car phone,' Rambam said, and disappeared into the gloom. I waited. I noticed there wasn't a car phone.

In a few moments Rambam was back. He opened the trunk, took out a green knapsack and a long, ugly-looking pair of wire cutters, and vanished again. Scarcely three minutes later he reappeared and motioned for me to come with him. I got out of the Jag and crept along behind him toward the back of the building. The Hardy Boys in New Jersey.

Phone wires to the building were dragging on the ground. The door stood open about six inches. 'That's the alarm system,' said Rambam, gesturing to the wires, 'and this is the door.'

'What took you so long?' I asked as I followed him down a short hallway.

Rambam turned on a small flashlight. We climbed the stairs to the second floor and came to another hallway that appeared to have three or four offices opening into it. The 88 Leasing Corp. was not listed on any of the doors, but one door had a familiar name on it. The lawyer had been dead for twenty years, but his name was still on the door. It wasn't immortality, but it wasn't bad.

Rambam took a tool from his knapsack, which looked like it had been made for gutting catfish in a previous life. He did not get to use it, however. As he put his hand up to test the door, it swung open before our eyes like a vampire's vault.

'Strange,' muttered Rambam. But strange, as we would soon find, was relative.

Rambam shone the small penlight around the dead lawyer's office. There was an old desk, a number of metal filing cabinets, and a lot of dust. The light cut the gloom just enough to reveal an open doorway into an adjoining room. We walked over to the doorway, and Rambam poked the light inside the room.

There was an object in the middle of the floor. I blinked my eyes a couple times, but it didn't go away.

'Jesus Christ,' I said in a voice I almost didn't recognize.

The object on the floor was a man with two heads. Both of them looked very dead.

I felt a ghost train shuddering silently along my nerve tracks.

'Two heads are better than one,' said Rambam.

25

As a kid in the dusty summertime, I vividly remember my visits to the Frontier Times Museum in Bandera, Texas. Years later, Piers Akerman, as a large adult Australian, visited the museum and called it 'the attic of the town.' That it certainly was, and more.

I remember kind old Mr Hunter showing us the shrunken head of a South American Indian. It was about the size of a matzo ball, and the hair on the thing had continued to grow at approximately the rate of an inch a year. By now it must have some pretty amazing moss.

Mr Hunter also had a wonderful collection of bells from around the world. He used to ring each one for us. Tibetan temple chimes, Chinese gongs, sleigh bells, cowbells, etc. That was many years ago, and Mr Hunter has long since gone to Jesus, but sometimes, in a reflective moment in New York City, I can still hear the bells ring.

But the exhibit in the museum that truly hypnotized me and caused me to stare for long minutes at a time in transfixed horror was a freak two-headed goat in a glass case. Somehow the eyes of the animal – all four of them – looked almost evil in their innocence. For some inexplicable reason that little goat symbolized to me what could happen to man or beast if, as Sherlock Holmes says, 'he leaves the straight road of destiny.'

Now, decades later, in another time and almost another world, I stared with the same mixture of wonder and horror at the ghastly sight on the floor of the dingy office building in Bayonne, New Jersey. The four dead eyes leered back into the little tunnel of light pouring from Rambam's flashlight. I'd seen dead eyes before, and they're about as pleasant as watching Ratso eat eggs. But these were in a class by themselves. They seemed to struggle out of their sockets in a stalklike, insectine terror.

Rambam and I stepped a little closer. From this angle the creature looked like a radioactive crab on LSD. Both its faces were a healthy purple – healthy if you were an eggplant. Both faces were grinning, quite literally, from ear to ear. *Sardonicus* smiles. Probably nothing to a big-city coroner, but to your average American it was the kind of thing that, as Dorothy Sayers once observed, 'could set one off one's nice beef steak.'

As we walked a bit nearer to the creature, something about it, oddly enough, seemed to strike me as familiar. I knew the faces. I'd seen them before. As my eyes adjusted to the gloomy little room, it became readily apparent, much to my relief, that we were not dealing with a man with two heads. We were dealing with two men – our blond friends from the Pierre Hotel – who'd been tightly bound back to back and dispatched from this earth in a fashion most hideous. One blond head lolled over at an impossible angle to create the eerie illusion of a two-headed man.

But both of them were certainly dead. And death, however you looked at it, was no illusion.

'Poison?' Rambam asked.

'Maybe it was salmonella,' I said.

We looked at the bodies up close. I decided beyond any possible doubt that I was never going to be a big-city coroner when I grew up.

'What now?' I asked, as I followed Rambam back into the main office.

'We do a Jim Rockford. We get out of here. I'll dial nine-one-one on the phone and just put it down on the desk. The cops'll trace

55

it and maybe they'll show up. I'm not going to get my voice recorded.'

'I know what you mean,' I said. 'I'm between labels myself.'

Rambam made the call, put the phone down on the desk, and headed for the door. I was on my way out with him when I noticed something lying in the dust beside an old hat rack that would've been at home in Elliot Ness's office. It was a feather.

I picked it up and was startled to see its very distinctive alternating brown and white bands of color.

'Hold the weddin',' I said, turning the feather incredulously in the palm of my hand. Rambam came back and took a look.

'Probably fell out of somebody's skypiece,' I said.

'Or Big Bird from Sesame Street was here. Let's go.'

'Okay,' I said, 'but there's only one kind of feather in the world that looks like this. And there's only one place you can find it. It comes from the sacred hornbill – the bird that's worshipped by the natives of Borneo.'

'We don't get out of here now,' said Rambam, 'you'll see how that story plays down at the cop shop.'

We left New Jersey on the wings of dawn. The hornbill feather was safely tucked away in the pocket of my hunting vest. But all the way home I thought I could hear the faintest of flutterings in the back of my consciousness. I recognized them for what they were. The wings of the Angel of Death.

26

It felt very reassuring to wake up late Thursday morning and know I was back in the good old wholesome Big Apple. It didn't feel good enough to click my heels together and say, 'There's no place like home,' but it was all right. The only people who might've been inclined to click their heels together were Dorothy in *The Wizard of Oz* or a Nazi. Maybe Dorothy was a Nazi. I resisted the urge to see if she was under my bed. Instead, I made some espresso and called McGovern.

'National desk,' said the familiar voice from the blower on the left.

'I don't know if you remember me,' I said. 'Name is Kinky. Curly-headed fellow from Texas . . . played the guitar . . .'

'Of course,' said McGovern. 'You used to sleep on my couch.' He laughed louder than people normally laugh in the morning.

'Nothing slips by you, does it, McGovern?'

'Nothin' but the scenery on the A-train, baby. What do you need?'

'Two guys got themselves croaked in Bayonne last night. Maybe you could talk to one of your colleagues on the *Bayonne Bugle* or whatever it's called and get me a little inside information. I know there's a kinship between members of the Fifth Estate, and – '

'It's the *Fourth* Estate,' said McGovern a bit testily. 'Think of it this way. There's the First Amendment, the Second Coming, the Third Reich, and the Fourth Estate.'

'That's a handy mnemonic. Look, McGovern, just give me some of the stuff they always hold back from the story. And check with the Coroner's Office too, will you?'

'I'm sort of your leg man, right?'

'Of course not, McGovern. You're not just a leg man. You play a vital role in determining what kind of poison would make two stiffs smile like Dr Sardonicus.'

'Jesus Christ. You saw them yourself?'

''Fraid so. And they weren't just saying "Have a nice day." '

'Well, I'm only your leg man. It's not really my business what you were doing in Bayonne in the middle of the night or whether it involves that friend from Cleveland you've been looking for who might or might not be dead. But you better pace yourself, pal. That's three stiffs in under a week.'

McGovern said he'd call as soon as he had something. I hung up, sipped a little espresso, and waited. I didn't really know what I was waiting for, but it better be good.

It was about twenty minutes later, and I was into my second espresso and my first cigar of the new day, when the phones rang. It was a little too soon to be McGovern and a little too late to be the call that was going to change my life.

On about the fifth ring I picked up the blower on the left and listened to Ratso's rodentlike voice loudly repeating the word 'Kinkstah!'

I took a patient puff on the cigar and waited. In time, I was rewarded.

'I've got something for you, Kinkstah.'

'Lay it on me, Ratman.'

He did.

According to Ratso, 88 stood for the eighth letter of the alphabet, H, repeated once. As in, he said, *Heil* Hitler. Certain organizations and corporations took the code name after the fall of the Third Reich. The Nazi version of 'Save your Confederate money, boys, the South will rise again.' Only these guys *believed* it.

While this revelation didn't really surprise me, it didn't do my nerves much good. Apparently, we were dealing with whom I thought we were dealing with.

Unpleasant.

'Oh, Sherlock,' Ratso said, 'I uncovered something else pretty interesting that you might want to know. It involves the Austrians prior to the time of the *Anschluss*, the German invasion that really wasn't an invasion because the Austrians welcomed the Nazis with open arms.

'Apparently, each Austrian political party had its own flower symbol. The atheists wore pansies. The socialists wore red carnations. And – get this – the Austrian Nazis wore a blue cornflower in their lapels.'

'Interesting,' I said. 'I wonder if that helps explain why so many Austrians today suffer from Waldheimer's Disease?'

'What's Waldheimer's Disease?'

'It's when you can't remember that you used to be a Nazi.'

27

I sipped a luke espresso and gazed at New York from the kitchen window. A wall, a billboard, a fire escape. What else did you need? They ought to put it on the back of a postcard, so I could send one to my Aunt Rhoda in Pocatello. But Aunt Rhoda wants the Empire State Building. Aunt Rhoda wants the Statue of

Liberty. Aunt Rhoda wants the Staten Island Ferry. That's why she lives in Pocatello.

The more I looked out the window, the more I was convinced that this was a classic view of the city. It was undeniably New York; it just wasn't postcard material.

I thought of the postcards that the government of Borneo had issued. Borneo is the only place in the world where tribes of people live communally in longhouses. These majestic, rustic structures, built high on stilts and stretching across a city block of jungle, have never been deemed worthy of postcard status. Nor would the Borneo government ever approve a postcard of a four-foot-tall Punan tribesman holding a seven-foot blowpipe. The postcards of Borneo I'd seen had mostly been of things like a new two-story office building in Kuching, the capital city. No doubt the government was very proud of the office building, but what would Aunt Rhoda think?

I stared out the window into a certain middle distance of the heart, and I felt a numbing loneliness invade my spirit. There were a lot of things they didn't put on postcards. Like a blond girl in a peach-colored dress driving a little white T-bird convertible down a dusty country road. A large white standard poodle named Leo is sitting in the seat beside her. They're listening to country music on the car radio. The sun is shining on the girl's hair, and she's smiling a lovely crooked smile that makes her look a little like Hank Williams. Wish you were here.

I walked away from the window, wandered over to the desk, sat down, and watched the phones for a while. Waiting for McGovern to call was about as tedious as waiting for Godot, though not, very possibly, as existential an experience.

I fed the cat. That was existential enough for a Thursday morning.

I thought about what Ratso had told me earlier concerning the meaning of the name 88 and the blue cornflower business. Ratso and I had also agreed that my having a little chat with Carmen was in order for that evening. I preferred to have the little chat without the presence of a large rat, but I realized that Ratso now too had a special interest in the case. Ratso and I were not the most objective, scientific practitioners of crime-solving under the best of circumstances. I wondered openly about our abilities to solve crimes against humanity.

At around six-thirty, with a rather fitful power nap under my belt, I left the cat in charge, grabbed a few cigars for the road, and started to leave for the Spanish Inquisition.

I had just turned the doorknob to the right when the phones rang. I returned to the desk, picked up the blower on the left, and listened grimly.

Godot had arrived.

28

Vandam Street looked dark and spectral as I made my way to Ratso's place that evening, and my own troubled thoughts mirrored the foreboding ambience of the street. After hearing what McGovern had to say about last night's twin killing in Bayonne, I was convinced beyond a shadow of a doubt that Bob Dylan and Jesus Christ were out of it. And I didn't particularly want to invite home to dinner what was left.

According to McGovern, the two component parts of the radioactive crab, heretofore known as Goldilocks and Gorgeous George, had other names and other games. They were widely known in the New York – New Jersey area as neo-Nazis.

They did not look like neo-Nazis, black yachtsmen, or anything else I'd known in the past. Rambam had once introduced me to a group of neo-Nazis several weeks before he'd visited upon them an event that has since become known as 'the Invasion of the Killer Jews.' But Rambam's neo-Nazis had looked more like what you'd expect neo-Nazis to look like. Prison tans, tattoos everywhere, axle grease from the local body shop under their fingernails. They hadn't looked like the kind of guys who'd need to cut the labels out of their fine Italian jackets.

Of course, I reflected as I crossed Seventh Avenue against the light, you can't judge a book by its cover. Especially once they've burned the book.

But by far the most interesting piece of information that McGovern was able to unearth was the means by which our charming blond friends had been delivered into the hands of Charon, the ferryboatman of Hell. They had been injected with a little-known pesticide called phenoxylcholine.

Now that I thought about it, the Nazis always had been great ones when it came to injections. I remembered the account I'd once read of the German office worker who had recalled that groups of Gypsy children from local orphanages had been taken up the stairway to a room one floor above him in the same building. In that room, good German doctors would inject water, air, gasoline, or toxic chemicals into the veins of the children. The substances would circulate briefly in the veins until they reached the heart, at which point the child would drop dead on the floor. At regular intervals of about sixty seconds the German office worker and his innocuous, bespectacled colleagues would hear the sound of the body of a small child hitting the floor directly above them. They had, so they later contended, no way of knowing what was going on up there. Of course, over periods of some months, groups of children had been led up the stairs, and none of them ever were seen to come down again. But who could tell?

It must also be reported, to the credit of the peculiar, meticulous nature of the German people, that there was no work stoppage among the office workers. Their work, it is gratifying to note, did not suffer like the children.

The more I thought about the sounds of small children dropping dead, the less I was starting to mind Winnie Katz's lesbian dance class.

As I walked up Prince Street towards Ratso's apartment, I leaned into a chill wind and remembered the last morsel that McGovern had come up with. The coroner's lab had run an analysis of the substance that had eighty-sixed Goldilocks and Gorgeous George and subsequently seeped into their Aryan entrails. Phenoxylcholine, according to McGovern, was a fairly archaic derivative of Zyklon-B, the chemical the Nazis had used in the gas chambers.

I had to admit one thing. McGovern was a hell of a leg man.

29

Impressions can often be misleading. My friend Sammy Allred from Austin, Texas, once told me about the time he met a lady who was walking a duck on a leash. 'Where you goin' with that pig?' Sammy asked. 'That's no pig, stupid,' she said. 'It's a duck.' 'I was talking to the duck,' Sammy said.

I didn't know who the hell or what the hell Carmen Cohen was but I was sure the hell going to find out.

Even though she was no longer wearing lace panties or hanging by her wrists from a clothes rod in a closet of the Pierre Hotel, she still managed to look good. You didn't need a sniperscope to see that the broad had a lot of class. Too much class for Ratso, I thought. I'd known outcall masseuses with more class than Ratso.

But I wasn't here to compile information for the Social Register. I was here to try to unravel what had become a rather unpleasant ball of yarn, and I was beginning to wonder what kind of yarn I was going to get from Carmen Cohen.

It didn't take long to find out. Ratso offered me a seat beside him on the sofa with the skid marks on it.

'No thanks,' I said. 'I'll pace.'

Carmen was sitting in a straight-backed chair looking beautiful, sulky, magical, and secretive, like a Gypsy child that the Germans had missed. With only a little goading from me, she launched into her story. It was pretty straightforward as far as it went. There were, however, a few distractions. One was Carmen crossing her legs about eleven times during the narrative. She was wearing a short black leather skirt and long, lovely Latin wheels.

Two was Carmen's pronunciation of the letter *J* like *Y*, so the word 'jungle' sounded like 'yungle.' But this could be overlooked and probably usually was, since it had to contend with distraction number one. I sat down on the couch a little to the north of the skid marks, to listen and to observe.

Carmen's parents had died in a plane crash when she was an infant. She was adopted by a wealthy plantation owner who'd come to Argentina from Europe, where he'd been an engineer of some sort. Sometime in her early teens, Carmen's adoptive parents were divorced, an event that apparently was quite traumatic for her, because she went on about it for some little time.

'Let's just operate on the assumption,' I said, perhaps a bit unkindly, 'that everybody comes from a broken home.'

Ratso gave me a stern look. Carmen, however, appeared unfazed, and continued with her narrative.

She'd met John Morgan about three years ago, when she was only eighteen years old. They saw each other only sporadically for a while, and then, about a year ago, they started to dance pretty close and Carmen brought John home to meet her father.

At first the two men seemed to get along very well. Then something, which Carmen appeared to be rather vague about, happened to poison the waters between Morgan and her father. I pressed Carmen on the point. She maintained she'd never understood what had caused the breach between them. Ratso watched her intently. I lit a cigar and studied her black eyes through a wreath of blue smoke. She was something, all right.

'It's just as if they've disappeared into the yungle,' she said, crossing her legs for the twelfth time. Who was counting?

'Hold the weddin',' I said. 'We know John's missing in action, but who *else* has disappeared recently?'

'My father,' she said.

'She may be dreideling us, Ratso,' I said, as he accompanied me down in an elevator that was at least big enough for several anorectic midgets.

Ratso stared at me in disbelief. 'C'mon, Kinkster,' he said. 'She's been under a great strain lately. You heard what she said. She comes home six days ago. Her father's gone. The place is completely trashed. The only thing missing in the house is a picture of her and John Morgan that she kept on the bureau in her bedroom.'

'And now Morgan himself seems to have disappeared. Maybe they both just vanished into the yungle.'

'That's cute. Leave her alone for a while. She's had a bad shock.'

The hallway to the street in Ratso's building always smelled faintly like urine because Ratso had a pet bum who slept there on cold nights. I lit a cigar as we walked briskly through to the street.

'Oh, she seems to be holding up all right,' I said. 'I'm more worried about the two of us.'

'That's very self-directed, Kinkstah,' Ratso said as he *goniffed* a papaya from the Moonie fruit stand on the corner.

'As Hillel said, "If I am not for myself, who will be for me?"'

'Yeah,' said Ratso, taking an unnecessarily large bite of papaya, 'but can you say that while you're standing on one foot?'

'Of course, but it'd be hard getting home that way.'

It wasn't that I didn't want to believe Carmen's story. I was ready to believe 'The Princess and the Pea,' if it would help me find out what had happened to John Morgan. It was just that all the loose ends in this affair were beginning to flay me to death. Had Morgan been in New York recently? The guy who'd developed the film thought so. And what was it about those photographs that kept nagging me like a mosquito that had slipped under the net?

Why would someone employ infamous Nazi methodology to whack a couple of neo-Nazis? Could this increasingly grotesque puzzle reach back almost fifty years in time and across the length and breadth of three continents? As my friend and personal guru Earl Buckelew always says back in Texas, 'It'll all come out in the wash if you use enough Tide.' All too often, however, there is not enough tide in the affairs of men.

'One point that was interesting,' I said to Ratso, 'was Carmen's comment about John always flying off to Hong Kong. Hong Kong was the hub city en route to Borneo when I went there twenty years ago. I'll bet Borneo was his destination. Now why was he flying back and forth so often, and who was paying for all his travel and accommodations?'

Ratso shrugged and pitched the papaya over his shoulder onto a shiny Porsche parked in front of a wine bar. I didn't like wine bars, and I didn't like Porsches much, either. Papayas were all right.

'It looks,' I said, 'like an extremely unpleasant version of the ol' grasshopper game.'

'Yeah,' said Ratso. 'The ol' grasshopper game.' He turned and started back toward his apartment. A moment later he stopped, turned around again, and shouted, 'What's the ol' grasshopper game?'

I took a last puff on the cigar and killed it in the gutter of Mulberry Street not terribly far from where Joey Gallo got his.

'In due course, Watson,' I said.

30

It's always a mistake to be walking along minding your own business in New York. It's the kind of irrational, bizarre behavioral error that seems to make trouble jump out at you from the hand shadow of a duck. Yet, though it might've appeared that way, minding my own business wasn't exactly what I was doing that night.

I was looking into Carmen's eyes. I could see them almost as an after-image against the hepatitis yellow of the occasional street lamp. They stared seductively at me from behind the bars of first-floor windows. And what was particularly worrisome about them was that they seemed to be telling me something that Carmen had not.

I had shown Carmen the photographs. There had been a noticeable reaction only to two of them. One was the picture of John Morgan in the Land Rover with his hair gently disheveled by the wind and his green eyes shining like a rain forest at dawn. She'd lingered lovingly over that one.

The second photograph that seemed to stop her momentarily was the one of the two old men in the jungle. They were pretty ancient geezers, both wearing panama hats and smiling, and one of them, as I remembered, had a space between his two front teeth, which was better, I supposed, than having a space between your ears. Other than that, there was nothing remarkable about the photo aside from Carmen's reaction to it – a sudden intake of breath before she caught herself.

'Who are those men?' I'd asked her.

'I don't know,' she said, but she'd looked confused. She said she'd seen a picture of one of them before – the one with the little

65

space between his teeth – at John's apartment in Buenos Aires. When she'd asked him who the man was, he'd said, 'Dr Breitenbach, I presume.'

'Dr Breitenbach, I presume,' I muttered to myself as I headed down Vandam Street in the darkness. That told me exactly nothing. But it did sound like Morgan. Enigmatic, playful right to the end. But *was* this the end? Was Morgan really dead, or, as we say in New York, was he just currently not working on a project?

I wondered. But I didn't wonder long.

Five bald-headed geeks had surrounded me. Like malevolent walking cue balls, they slouched languidly, expressionlessly forward in the queasy manner of enemy Martian plants. The light from a distant street lamp gleamed wickedly off their hairless cue-ball craniums. Nobody smiled.

In their small eyes I recognized that their fervent dream was to rack my soul.

31

Skinheads are neo-Nazi groups springing up in America almost as fast as BMW dealerships in southern California. Skinheads hate blacks and Jews, and they don't bother to take into consideration the fact that most Jews and blacks don't even like each other very much.

Cops'll tell you that it's easier to stop a pit-bull attack or a runaway locomotive than to deal with a gathering of skinheads. The reason is because skinheads have no neurons. The casual stick in the eye does not usually faze them. Cutting off their legs just below the knees rarely impedes their forward progress. This is because, from almost any human standpoint, they are dead before they shave their heads.

Things weren't looking too good for me, either. I was standing on a dark, deserted sidewalk in New York City, a block and a half from my loft, like a human wagon train encircled by pale engines of hate. They looked like five aging heavy-metal sidemen with no words and no music. Negative stage charisma.

I remember I was staring at a picture of an eagle on the T-shirt of one guy. It was not an American-looking eagle. Something in its eye told me that it had been an engineering major, and that it wished very much to land upon the bridge of my nose. It was some kind of kraut eagle, I remember thinking.

I was staring transfixedly at the eagle like a large urban field mouse when a searing pain shot suddenly through both of my eyes. I wheeled blindly to the left, leveled a savage kick with my cowboy boot about *huevos*-high, and connected with nothing but the hatred in the air. My eyes cleared enough to notice the metal-stud bracelets the skinheads were wearing. Somebody had slipped around behind me and rasped me across the eyes.

What little I knew about defending yourself single-handedly against a gang I'd picked up from Boris Shapiro's Berlitz combat karate class, from a few tough local micks I knew, and from several friendly individuals in the Jewish Defense League. The situations, however, had always been hypothetical. This one, unfortunately, wasn't. Like so many other aspects of life, the wheels tend to come off when things get nonhypothetical. Only if you're lucky do you live to hypothesize another day. Hypothetically speaking, of course.

I backed up against a brick wall, thereby preventing them from completely surrounding me. The next thing to do, I knew, was to find the leader and do something unpleasant to him if possible, like pulling one of his eyeballs out of its socket. You can usually tell the gang leader, because he's the one doing the most yapping. But it was impossible to make this determination, because all five were ominously silent. Furthermore, they had the same shaved domes and the same dreadful glazed, hate-riddled, halibut eyes. They advanced slowly, then stopped, almost as though they were operating under a hive or swarm instinct. It was as if five dead people were playing games with you.

I decided to go for the guy with the eagle on his chest, but just as this thought struck me, something else did, too. It was a heavy chain that slammed down across the top of my head and flattened my left ear like a silver-dollar pancake. Another chain zinged me heavily on the back of the neck and knocked me to the sidewalk.

I felt hot pain mingling with cold fear. The two sensations

seemed to alternate rapidly, kind of like taking a hotel shower in Mexico. Before I could get back on my feet, I took a black leather boot to the head and one to the solar plexus. Fear went quietly to the back burner. Pain was all I felt. Rough hands, boots, chains, and studded bracelets rained down on me. I tried futilely several times to blink the blood out of my eyes, and then gave it up for Lent.

The pain was now gone. A peculiar and almost peaceful numbness had set in, and I recognized that it was almost time for me to say *adiós* to mañanaland. I could see nothing but blurred images, but I was hearing a new sound – a sickening thudding sound that I assumed was my skull giving way. I could feel very little by now, but the noise was very clear. It sounded like *klaang, klaang, klaang*. Somewhere in the deep recesses of what was left of my brain I remembered that a *klaang* was a canal in Thailand. They don't always come in handy, but it's nice to know these things.

I listened now – which was about all I could do – and I heard it again distinctly. *Klaang, klaang*. Then a hand was on my shoulder and a voice was saying, 'Hey, man, that was a close one. I was waitin' for you on your fire escape, and I saw this going down and rushed over. Just in time, it looks like.'

The hand was now mopping the blood from my eyes with a handkerchief. I blinked a few times and saw Zev standing over me with a blood-soaked handkerchief in one hand and a lead pipe in the other. Four skinheads were gone, and one was sprawled appropriately in the gutter.

Zev was a mysterious friend of mine who'd been rumored to have fought with the Israeli Army in Lebanon and with the Mujahedeen against the Russians in Afghanistan. For many enemies of democracy, Zev had been the last vision they'd seen on earth, and, fortunately for me, he also went in for *klaanging* skinheads.

'Jesus Christ, Zev,' I said in a slurred and subdued voice, 'you saved my life.'

Zev laughed. '*Azoy!*' he shouted.

'What the hell does that mean?'

'Freely translated?'

'Whatever gets you through the night,' I said as he slowly helped me to my feet.

'It's Jewish. Not Hebrew. Jewish.'

'Jewish,' I repeated.

'Freely translated, it means: "We beat the shit out of them." '

Unfortunately, I was busy counting my kneecaps and was not fully able to savor our victory. I felt like the other guy you should've seen. I was weaker than prime-time programming.

'Zev,' I said, 'check that guy in the gutter for papers or identification, will you?' Zev went over to the guy and I started to stumble slowly in the direction of the loft.

'He's clean,' Zev said.

I'd taken about three more steps when I heard Zev speak again.

'He's also dead,' he said.

32

We did a Jim Rockford.

Within minutes I was back in the loft lying on the sofa, chewing a green substance called *gat* that Zev had given me. *Gat* is a clover-like plant that, according to Zev, kills pain, makes you high, and is only chewed by Yemenite Jews. I wasn't a Yemenite Jew, but I was beginning to feel like one.

The cat was watching me anxiously from the rocking chair. Zev was looking down on me with concern in his eyes. I was a lot farther away from New York than Westchester.

'That *gat*'s good stuff,' said Zev. 'You know, in Israel it's actually illegal for anyone except Yemenite Jews to chew it.'

'That's why I love America,' I said.

By midnight my body had settled down to a dull throb. Zev, apparently, had been taking Ratso lessons. He announced his intention, as Ratso had done several times in the past, to stay with me in the loft until I recovered from my little accident. I was fond of Zev and rather grudgingly grateful to him for saving my life, but I didn't want the guy to put down roots. The cat and I had a fairly high-maintenance relationship as it was.

'You're going to be all right,' said Zev. 'Just don't look in the mirror for a couple of days.'

'I look that bad?'

'Worse.'

'It's a good thing,' I said, 'that I'm not an escort in the Miss Mean-minded Vacuous Bitch Pageant.'

I got Zev to rev up the espresso machine, and, miraculously, I found an only slightly crushed cigar in one of the little pockets of my hunting vest where some Americans keep their shotgun shells. I sat up slowly and painfully and began the prenuptial arrangements on the cigar. Sometimes it's good to have something to do with your hands. I lit a cigar, always keeping it slightly above the flame.

Zev brought over two cups of espresso, handed me one, and sat down on the couch. 'I'll stay tonight,' he said. 'In case those guys try to come back.'

'One of them won't,' I said grimly. I took a puff on the cigar. Zev laughed. It was a high-pitched, peculiar, dangerous sound. I took a sip of the espresso, swished it around with the *gat*, and swallowed hard. 'Not bad,' I said. Of course, anything with *gat* wasn't bad.

Zev chuckled. The chuckle was worse than the laugh.

'Zev,' I said, 'let me play psychologist for a moment.' You don't want to be a psychologist for much longer than that. You might find out something you don't want to know.

'Let me ask you a question. A guy got spliced tonight, right?'

'Right.'

'I know he probably tied his shoes with little Nazis, but how does it make you feel?' I took an insightful, other-directed puff on the cigar. The smoke, as usual, was also other-directed.

'How does it make me feel? I'll tell you how it makes me feel.' He got up and walked over to the window. He looked out into the darkness and raised a clenched fist in the air. 'Nazis – six million,' he shouted, 'Jews – one!'

'Yeah,' I said to the cat, 'but who's keeping score?'

It was a few moments after that that I reached into the inside pocket of my hunting vest and realized that John Morgan's photographs were missing.

33

Sometimes you can see things more clearly when they're not there. Most of the great books about human freedom, for instance, were written in prison. From my own personal experience, I have put a black pill of opium into a cup of coffee, drunk it down, stood at the edge of the Borneo jungle staring out across the South China Sea, and seen America more lucidly than at any time in my life. This was made possible partly by the drug, but mostly, I believe, by the physical absence of America.

Following this somewhat distorted but more often than not accurate line of thinking, one might conclude that a man who professes to be searching for a white tiger in the jungle might well be searching for something else.

It was Friday afternoon. Zev had gone back to Brooklyn. I was sitting at my desk with a fresh cigar and a twelve-year-old bottle of Jameson, not looking at photographs and not looking in the mirror. Life, I always say, is what happens when you're not looking.

I poured and killed a shot. Then I took a few puffs on the cigar, closed my eyes, leaned back in the chair, and tried to visualize the photographs that were no longer in my possession. The images ran by like a slide carousel slowly spinning in my brain. A tributary, I supposed, of the Amazon River cutting through the jungle, here and there vaguely reflecting the sky . . . prehistoric trees bearing strange fruit you never see in shopping carts . . . branches brown and gnarled hanging timelessly in the clouds . . . a little highway heading nowhere, sparsely traveled, lighted by the sun . . . a Land Rover pulled off to the left side of the road . . . a bus going by on the right, full of people and chickens and bananas . . . John Morgan's face smiling recklessly into forever . . .

I found it hard to accept that this man could be dead. I held the picture of John in my head and attempted to adjust the focus.

When I did, I realized that something was very wrong with the picture. I'd assumed the little blurs of people on the bus to be South American Indians, peasants, farmers, but now I wasn't so sure. When you're not looking at pictures, you cannot look again and again and sometimes memory will triumph over imagination. Many tribes of people across the globe bear distinct physical resemblances to each other. That was one of the reasons I gave the shrink for not wanting to go fight in Vietnam when my Peace Corps service was completed. After working two-and-a-half years in the Far East, I didn't want to go back and kill the same people wearing the same funny pointed hats. I conjured up the passengers on the bus again and realized they could've been anybody.

Then I noted the direction the bus was heading. Then I backed up one frame and noticed the direction John was going in the Land Rover. Then I opened my eyes and saw that I'd been a world away from the truth.

34

'You see,' I said to the cat, 'unless I'm very much mistaken, there was almost no British influence in Latin America.' The cat scratched her left ear rather irritably with her left rear paw.

'All right, there's the Falkland Islands, I'll grant you that. But what else have you got? British Honduras is now only a stamp.' The cat looked at me and blinked her eyes rather sleepily. The cat had never been much of a philatelist.

'You can see what the problem is, can't you?' The cat shook her head violently. Either there was a flea in her ear, or she couldn't see what the problem was.

I almost hadn't seen it myself.

I had met John Morgan in Borneo, so it was to Borneo that I'd originally looked for possible clues to his mysterious background. But from Carmen's statements and from the increasingly unpleasant Nazi undercurrents in the case, I'd assumed that whatever he'd been up to recently had been based in South America.

Now I saw that the photographs – even in their absence – proved this thesis to be wrong.

Normal people, I thought, drive on the right-hand side of the road. Only where there's been early and pervasive British influence do they drive on the left. But John, to my knowledge, had never been to India or Africa. And couldn't have been driving on the left anywhere in South America. The only jungle terrain in the world with British driving patterns that could logically match the photograph was Borneo.

So the photographs were from Borneo.

The hornbill feather I'd found in the long-dead lawyer's office was from Borneo.

Therefore, whatever nefarious schemes Morgan had recently been involved in had transpired in Borneo. I poured a hefty jolt into the bull's horn and downed it with a shudder.

'So Morgan *had* been searching for a white tiger,' I said to the cat. I puffed a bit on the cigar and ran down the peculiar convoluted affair in my mind for a few moments.

'And I'll bet you a case of Jameson against a case of tuna that that tiger has blue eyes.'

35

Weekends and holidays, I've always thought, are strictly for amateurs. Time for some middle-level German civil servants of all nationalities to adjust their wire-rimmed spectacles and go out and be party animals. I didn't have any wire-rimmed glasses, so I stayed home Friday night. Also, my face was turning a nice purple hue, and I was beginning to feel like the hunchback of New York, so I figured I'd hang around with the cat. The cat didn't seem to mind, though I did catch her looking rather furtively at me a few times. Probably my imagination.

One thing that I definitely knew wasn't in my imagination was the fact that somebody'd set those skinheads on me. Either someone had been watching the loft and tailed me that evening, or somebody'd set me up. And there weren't very many somebodies who knew I was going over to Ratso's that night. I didn't much like where things seemed to be pointing.

Of course, I didn't much like a lot of things, and I would very probably continue not liking a lot of things until the big iron crab grabbed me and they put me in the ground. There was nothing I could do about it. It was part of being an adult. Part of being an American. Part of being. It was life on the Mississippi.

Saturday morning I did not go to the Fun Club to see Tom Mix. I stayed in the loft, chewed a little *gat*, and chewed a little fat with the cat. If you were stationed in the *ulu* and you ever told that many rhymes to anyone in the Peace Corps brass, or you didn't come out of your house for a few days, they'd send in a helicopter factory-equipped with a shrink to pluck you out of there and take you to wig city for observation. I'd seen it happen any number of times. It wasn't *Apocalypse Now*; it was simply that in the *ulu* you became adept at hearing a twig snap, and the Peace Corps brass became adept at hearing a wig snap. That was one reason I rarely spoke to Peace Corps officials the whole time I was in Borneo. Now, rather unfortunately, it crossed my desk that it was mandatory for me to break that silence.

That afternoon I called John Mapes, an old Peace Corps buddy of mine who was currently residing in Hawaii. There were a lot of good reasons to currently reside in Hawaii, and one of them was that characters with blue cornflowers in their lapels didn't follow you around hotel lobbies.

Mapes, who was rather widely known as the barefoot economist for the state of Hawaii, sounded a bit grumpy. The reason, I quickly divined, was the five-hour time difference between New York and Hawaii. It was 7:15 Saturday morning in Hawaii. But in New York, unfortunately, it was past time for me to get my ass in gear. After Mapes had had time to become a little more coherent and civil, I filled him in on the John Morgan situation and, in return, got nothing but perplexing questions. Mapes knew less than I did about Morgan's activities in recent years. He did, however, still have some connection with official Peace Corpsdom in Washington, he said.

'You could call Norman Potts,' he said. 'Remember, he used

74

to be country director. Now he's got some cushy desk job in Washington. Of course, he hates your guts.'

'Yeah, Mapes, but as Gandhi said, "Forgiveness is the ornament of the brave." Surely he's forgotten by now.'

Mapes laughed. 'In your case, pal, not a chance.'

There were many fine people, I was sure, who worked for the Peace Corps in Washington. It was just my luck that the only one I knew was Norman Potts. He never had adored me, but it came as something of a shock that, after twenty years, the guy still wanted to see me in hell. Potts, I remembered, had had me forcibly 'returned to my own culture' after two-and-a-half years in the jungle. That, in military terms, was not as ignominious as a dishonourable discharge, but it wasn't exactly the Distinguished Flying Cross. I'd never forgiven him for it, and apparently he'd never forgiven me for whatever it was that he'd never forgiven me for. By this time I'd forgotten. In twenty years you meet a lot of new people that you can piss off, and you forget just what it was that fired some pompous stuffed shirt's rocket somewhere in the distant mists of the past. At least I hadn't lost my touch.

I talked a little longer to Mapes, then I wheedled Potts's office phone number out of him, said good-bye and rang off. I hadn't seen Mapes in twenty years, but there's always some kind of bond forged between two people who are caught in a monsoon together for several months. I remembered when I'd left Borneo, Mapes had put me aboard a freighter for Singapore. I was shivering with a malarial fever, pale as a spinning ghost, weighed about twenty-seven pounds, and didn't know where the hell I was going or why. Otherwise, I was fine.

The tropics will do that to you. I remember Mapes kissing me good-bye as he put me on the boat. Like he knew he'd never see me again. There was deep generosity and kindness in the man, and there was something very close to pity in his eyes. Now that I think about it.

Sunday passed in a blur about as vague as Jesus' face on the Shroud of Turin. I didn't go to church, I didn't have a Sunday dinner with the whole family, and I didn't give a damn. I was a pagan like Breaker Morant.

75

By Sunday night I'd spoken to Ratso and explained to him the significance of a Land Rover's driving on the left-hand side of the road through the jungle. He was dutifully impressed.

'What now, Kinkster?' he'd wanted to know.

'Well, we can't very well hop a plane for Borneo, can we?'

'Not till we find out if the Rangers get into the play-offs.'

Like I said, he was dutifully impressed.

Sunday night I also got a call from Rambam. He'd done some work on the John Morgan case, he said. It was imperative that the two of us return to New Jersey Monday morning. After some little protestations on my part, it was agreed that he'd pick me up at eleven and tell me the details at that time. He didn't want to talk over the phone. I told him I didn't know why. If the telephone was good enough for J. Edgar Hoover, it was good enough for me. He hung up.

As I lay in bed that night with the cat and a terminal case of insomnia, I plotted the approach I'd use on Norman Potts in the morning. If I could get hold of an actual Peace Corps file, it would go a long way toward at least clearing up the question of who was John Morgan. Once I got that taken care of, I could worry about the Nazis under the bed.

Several of those spectral creatures, unfortunately, seemed to have slithered out of late, and were more than a little determined, apparently, to link their foggy-nighted, kerosene-blooded, ring-less-fingered karma with that of my own.

36

'This is Mike McGovern,' I said, 'with the *New York Daily News*.' I took a sip of espresso and winked at the cat. It was Monday morning and I was on the blower to the Peace Corps Administrative Offices in our nation's capital.

'Norman Potts here,' said the voice on the blower. 'What can I do for you?' There were a few things Norman could do for me, but if I told him what they were, I'd never find out about John Morgan.

'We're doing a follow-up feature for our Sunday magazine on

Peace Corps volunteers who've returned to the States. Jay Maeder, the editor, says he wants a "Twenty Years Later – Where Are They Now?" sort of thing, and I'd – '

'RPCVs,' said Norman Potts.

'I beg your pardon?'

'Returned Peace Corps Volunteers,' he said with just a hint of irritation. 'We call them RPCVs.'

'That's good. We'll use that.' I took another sip of espresso and rolled my eyes in the direction of the lesbian dance class. 'I'd just like to ask you a few questions.'

'Shoot,' said Norman Potts. He was just one of the guys.

'As I told your secretary, we're highlighting one particular, uh, RPCV. He's now a Wall Street success story, but we'd like some bio information and a photo of him from the sixties when he still had dreams in his eyes. His name is John Morgan, and he was stationed in Sarawak, which I located on my map and found to be in Borneo. What we need – '

'That's very curious.'

'Not really. We chose Morgan at random. We just – '

'Not what I'm talking about. Someone called us last week wanting information on John Morgan. Now, when you get two calls concerning one individual in twenty years and they both come within a week of each other, it's rather curious, if you see what I mean.'

I saw what he meant.

'Who was the other caller?'

'Fellow from some European publishing consortium. A West German magazine was doing a retrospective article. "Peaceful alternatives to the Vietnam War." Something like that. Wanted to see the Peace Corps file on John Morgan, a volunteer in Borneo, they said. We don't release files to the press or the public, Mr McGovern. This has always been our policy. You can understand this, I'm sure.'

I understood and lit a cigar at the same time. 'Quite sensible,' I said. 'What did you do? Did you give the caller the information?' If it was the same Norman Potts, all you had to do was wind him up and let him go.

'No. He was very insistent, and I didn't like his attitude. A lot of the volunteers I remember, but this one I didn't. So when he hung up, I checked all the Borneo groups and found no John Morgan. It was rather perplexing, as you can imagine.'

I could imagine. I took a puff on the cigar and imagined quite a lot of things, none of them very pleasant.

'We call this a "news leak," Mr Potts. No doubt emanating from our tabloid competition here in the city. They'll stoop to anything to beat us to a story, and I'm afraid it's created somewhat of a nuisance for you. It's one of the things the Fourth Estate is not particularly proud of.'

'Actually, it made me curious, so I popped John Morgan into the big computer and found he *was indeed* a volunteer at one time. But it was earlier than they'd thought, and it wasn't in Borneo. It was Argentina. 1963.'

'Interesting,' I said. 'Did the caller say who he was or where he was calling from?'

'Said his name was Harvey Pickelner. He was based out of some town in New Jersey.'

'Bayonne ring any bells?'

'That's it. Bayonne. How'd you know that?'

'We've had trouble there before.'

Something ugly was happening, and it was happening on a lot of levels. People who were knocked off, like Goldilocks, Gorgeous George, and the anonymous skinhead, seemed to be being quickly replaced, like worn-out parts of a much larger machine, for a much larger purpose. Good German engineering.

I got some bio information on Morgan from Potts that didn't tell me much. But, much more significantly, he agreed to release a photo of Morgan to my 'stringer' in Washington. The photo, I figured, ought to tell me something.

Twenty years, I noticed, had done little to leaven the cool, cautious, slightly bored, bureaucratic inflections in Potts's voice. Even so, this was the longest, and certainly the pleasantest, conversation I'd ever had with him. Of course, he thought I was Mike McGovern, but you couldn't hold that against him.

'Are you interested in the other volunteer they wanted to know about?' asked Potts. '*Him* I remember very well, unfortunately. *Very* unpleasant fellow. Couldn't deal with authority at all.'

'We've got a few of those right here at the National Desk.' I made an attempt at a hearty, McGovernlike laugh.

'Not like this one,' said Potts. 'He thought he was Lord Jim out there in the jungle. Practically destroyed our working relationship with the host country. No, I'm not likely to forget him.'

I took a slightly paranoid pull on the cigar.

I waited.

'Guy named Friedman,' said Norman Potts.

I exhaled.

37

My 'stringer' in Washington was a Lebanese Druse rock-'n'-roll guitarist named Jimmie Silman, who preferred to be known, cosmically enough, as Ratso. I spoke of him sometimes as Washington Ratso to differentiate him from the New York Ratso, but when I spoke to him I just called him Ratso. I was a two-Ratso man.

Why two adult white male Americans would wish to be known as Ratso in the first place was a mystery to me, but I went along with it. Ratso, I always figured, was a pretty funny name for someone to have, much less two people. Of course, if you stopped to think about it, Kinky was a funny name too.

While waiting for Rambam to show up, I moved smoothly into my second and third espressos, thought about – but decided against – breaking out cigar number two of the morning, and lined up things with Washington Ratso. Washington Ratso had never been a stringer for the *New York Daily News* before, and he was rather excited about it. How is a journalist supposed to act? he wanted to know. I told him that a journalist acts just about like a rock-'n'-roll guitarist except that he should dress a little tackier. Ratso didn't think that would present any problem, said he was between gigs right now anyway, and pledged to personally messenger the alleged photo of John Morgan to me within the next forty-seven hours. I gave him my standard line about time being the money of love and told him to get crackin'. Big-time journalism was tough work, and it was starting to wear me out.

I stood at the kitchen window juggling the puppet head nervously and waiting for Rambam. It was really too much, I thought, to ask somebody to go to New Jersey twice in the same lifetime. Well, we'd work things out when Rambam arrived.

It was a cloudy morning, cold and bleak, with the wind whipping through the rusty slats in the fire escapes. The scenery looked pretty much the color of the lining of your lungs. The only green that met the eye was inside the loft: the houseplants left by the Greek woman I subletted from, who looked like a spider. Every once in a while I'd water the plants or spit a little Jameson on them. At the moment they were thriving better than I was. In fact, they seemed kind of smug. Where in the hell was Rambam?

I put the puppet head back on top of the refrigerator, walked over to the desk, took cigar number two out of Sherlock Holmes's head, set it in the guillotine, lopped off its butt, leaned back in the chair, set fire to the end of it, and took a relaxed puff just as Rambam's voice carried its coarse Brooklyn obscenities through my Manhattan windowpane.

I did not move from the chair.

I haven't seen any studies on the subject from any pointy-headed university professors, but it's my contention that cigar smokers live longer than the average nonsmoker. This is because of our attitude toward life. We don't let people screaming for puppet heads ruffle our feathers too much. Especially when they're not very punctual and they want to go to New Jersey. This is why most cigar smokers live longer than they want to. They also live longer than anyone else wants them to.

Eventually, Rambam entered the door of the loft with the puppet head in one hand and a brown envelope in the other. 'Jesus Christ,' he said. 'What happened to your face?'

'Nothing,' I said. 'It was just a little hunting accident in Peru.'

'Better tell Mother Rambam all about it,' he said, flipping me the puppet head. I walked over and put it on top of the refrigerator and came back and sat at the desk, where Rambam had already pulled up a chair.

I told him the whole saga of the skinheads. I started with the interview with Carmen, my leaving Ratso's place, and my strong suspicions that someone had set the skinheads on me. Rambam listened in silence. When I came to the part about Zev, he laughed and shook his head.

'What's the matter?' I asked.

'Nothing. I'm just glad the little bastard's on our side.'

By the time I finished with the account of the dead skinhead, Rambam was baring his teeth at me in a rather frightening smile.

'What the hell are you smiling about?' I asked.

'I'm just thinking of how much fun we're gonna have,' he said, 'when we finally catch up with these baddies.'

'Yeah,' I said rather doubtfully, as I felt the large, painful, purple swelling under my left eye, 'that *will* be fun.'

38

Rambam and possibly even Zev, I reflected as Rambam nosed the Jag out of the Holland Tunnel and onto the New Jersey Turnpike, were probably not clinically ill. They were, however, a little out of line with the other ducks. I'd seen Rambam with my own eyes waste half a dozen hired gunmen from two warring Colombian cocaine cartels, and the stories about Zev were legend. Zev walking home at two in the morning on the tops of parked cars. Zev allowing himself to be dragged up the stairs of the Lone Star Cafe by the hair. (Thereby demonstrating the strength of his hair. Of course, he was monstered on slivovitz at the time.) Zev delivering things like diamonds and silencers to places even Negroes feared to tread. And then there was Boris . . .

But the main problem I had with all these guys was that they lived in Brooklyn and I lived in Manhattan. These places were geographically and culturally far enough apart even under the best of circumstances, but when some mysterious person in Manhattan was trying to kill you, Brooklyn might just as well be Oz.

This was one of my problems.

Another problem was where we were driving and why. Rambam had shown me the contents of the brown envelope

81

earlier, in the loft. It had contained a federal-government product chart, and the portion Rambam had copied listed all the poisonous chemicals and insecticides imported into America within the past year. He was rather vague about how he'd happened to come by the chart. A guy he knew in customs, he said. But the significant thing about the chart was that the chemical we were looking for, phenoxylcholine, the one that iced our Aryan acquaintances in Bayonne, was handled by only one company in the States. The company was called Interchem, and it was located in Newark, New Jersey.

'Newark is Bayonne's uglier older sister,' said Rambam, as we passed through the same depressing scenery by day that, a week before, we'd only glimpsed in the darkness.

'I'm looking forward to meeting her,' I said. All around us was a landscape of industrial blight. Funnels coughing forth smoke that was a lot more dangerous than the smoke people were always bitching about that flowed cumulusly from my cigar. I didn't see anybody bitching at the funnels. Everywhere there were flat, ugly oil and gas depots and storage tanks. Occasionally, a stunted, distorted little tree that you could be pretty damn sure Joyce Kilmer had never seen.

'Actually,' said Rambam, 'the sunrises and sunsets in this area are supposed to be quite beautiful because of the chemicals.'

'Yeah,' I said, 'but it looks pretty goddamn weak at high noon.'

'Don't worry. We find what we're looking for, we won't be coming back.'

'Alcoa can't wait.'

As we neared the outskirts of Newark, where Interchem was apparently located, Rambam gestured toward the back of the Jag. 'Put on that trench coat back there. With that hat over your face and the sunglasses, you ought to be fine.'

'Maybe you've been watching *The Ipcress File* too much.'

'Look, your face looks like a week-old Chicago-style pizza. You got to go with the hat and sunglasses, and the only thing that'll go with them is the trench coat.'

'There's a logic to that.'

'I'll go with the suit and tie I've got on, and let me do the talking.'

'That's fine,' I said, as I struggled into the trench coat. 'Now that we've got our outfits worked out, who're we supposed to be?'

'We're from the EPA,' said Rambam with a wicked little smile. 'We're Compliance Verification agents.'

'Nice touch,' I said.

39

The two Compliance Verification agents from the EPA walked confidently through the massive warehouse piled to the ceiling with fifty-gallon drums with strange markings on them.

'Haven't seen so many drums and symbols since high-school band practice,' I said.

'Beat on one of these babies, you may get a surprise,' said Rambam.

Interchem, if you believed the signs, was dangerous, caustic, and corrosive. Interchem, I reflected, was, in many ways, a lot like life. Of course, if you wanted to be a philosophical nerd, everything was a lot like life. This beautiful sunset brought to you by Interchem.

We rounded a corner and headed down a drum-lined corridor toward a large, glassed-in office. I took out the walkie-talkie Rambam had given me and said a few imaginary words into it. A walkie-talkie, according to Rambam, beat a phony ID any day.

'Don't overdo it,' he whispered. 'Just look at some drums, write some shit in a notebook, that kind of thing. You wander around. I'll go into the office.'

He went into the office.

There was a guy standing inside with a white shirt and a tie and his sleeves rolled up. I doubted if he was Mr Interchem, but he looked like some kind of executive. Maybe a son or son-in-law. Maybe someday all this would be his.

I could see Rambam showing him some sort of ID and the two of them walking over past a desk and out of my line of vision. I started to wander around. I hoped this wouldn't take too long.

I looked at some drums. I took out a notebook and jotted down some numbers in it. Put the notebook away. Looked at some more drums. The act was getting old fast.

A few workmen in orange overalls were giving me the fish eye, so I took out the walkie-talkie, murmured a few incantations into it, looked up, and they were smoke. Amazing.

I wondered if the technique might possibly have applications in everyday life. Maybe I'd try it on an unwanted housepest some time.

A guy in a forklift was coming toward me, eyeing me suspiciously. I took out the walkie-talkie, and he hooked a left down a side corridor.

I stared at a drum and wondered if life was but a dream. Probably not, I figured. It was probably a drum.

Finally, the door to the office opened again, and Rambam came out. I put the walkie-talkie away, and we both walked briskly and importantly down the corridor, through the large warehouse, and out of the building.

He didn't talk until we were back on the turnpike.

'Wilhelm Stengal,' he said. 'That's our man. The only guy to order any of this stuff on Interchem's records. Only a small sample, but enough to do the job. Lives on East Eighty-sixth Street. Yorkville. Used to be called German Town. My dad told me during the thirties the German-American *Bund* used to march there. Thousands of them filled the streets marching in full Nazi uniform.'

Neither of us said anything until the desolate scenery fell away behind us and we'd reentered the Holland Tunnel. The dim, claustrophobic, unworldly eternal twilight seemed to be closing in on us.

'Apparently,' I said, 'a few of them are still goose-stepping around.'

40

'I'm not *saying* she set me up, Ratso,' I said. 'I'm just saying that *somebody* did.' Ratso was sitting on my couch wearing a labial-pink sport jacket and eating a pork pie from Myers of Keswick on Hudson Street that he'd found in my refrigerator. It was late Tuesday afternoon, and the left side of my face was beginning to clash with Ratso's sport jacket.

'You can take one look at you and see that,' said Ratso with some intensity. 'Somebody probably tailed your ass over to my apartment from here, then arranged to nail you on the way back.'

'The streets were pretty deserted.'

'So's the space between your ears,' he said rather petulantly. Ratso dipped the pork pie into some residual Chinese sweet-and-sour sauce he'd also located in the refrigerator. It'd been there for weeks, but they say it keeps.

'Pete Myers wouldn't like to see you doing that to his pork pies,' I said.

'Let it be our little secret.'

I walked somewhat desultorily over to the kitchen counter, poured a medicinal shot of Jameson into the old bull horn, walked over to the window, toasted another Tuesday in my tragic little life, and killed the shot. I wasn't really feeling sorry for myself; I was just confused. And I felt, down deep somewhere in my bruised bones, that something extremely ugly was about to occur.

I was all for calling in Sergeant Cooperman and picking up Wilhelm Stengal. Old traffic tickets or something. I had come to firmly believe that he was a major piece in the John Morgan puzzle. My theory was that he'd employed the two Aryans, then spliced them in Bayonne for botching the hotel job. A hard man to work for, I thought.

I also believed he was the man who'd lost the hornbill feather among the cobwebs on the floor of the croaked lawyer's office. So he'd been to Borneo. I wondered if he also wore a blue cornflower in his lapel.

Rambam had gotten Boris and a group of Brooklyn myrmidons

to stake out Stengal's house on East Eighty-sixth Street. He didn't think we had enough on Stengal yet to bring Cooperman in. He felt that the Aryans had been amateurs, and that Stengal was an old-time pro. He'd also pointed out, rather gauchely I thought, that I was an amateur.

I'd seen Rambam play this cat-and-mouse game before, and I had to admit that he usually got the cat or the mouse or whoever the hell it was he was after. But in the back of my mind there was the nagging notion that he was never going to bring Cooperman into it. Rambam wanted Stengal for himself.

Rambam, I felt, wanted to hunt Nazis in New York, and I wanted to find John Morgan. What the hell, I thought, maybe we'd both get our chance.

I walked back across the loft to where Ratso was sitting and to where the pork pie was no longer in evidence. Ratso looked up at me almost belligerently. He fairly shouted:

'Maybe Carmen tied and gagged herself and hung herself by the wrists from the clothes rod at the Pierre. Maybe she killed John Morgan, switched the bodies, went back to Argentina, then came up to New York and got you involved in such a baffling, unsolvable case because she heard you were a misogynist.'

'Pull your lips together for a minute, Ratso. All I'm saying is that Carmen tells a strange story, is a beautiful woman, and could be dangerous.' I walked back over to the bottle of Jameson and poured a fair-sized jolt into the bull's horn.

'You *are* a misogynist!' Ratso shouted tauntingly.

I walked rather stoically over to the Sherlock Holmes head, withdrew a cigar, bit off the end, and spat it on the floor. I walked back to the kitchen window, struck a wooden match against a fashionable exposed-brick wall, and lit the cigar. A little theater never hurts when someone is attacking you for being a misogynist.

I puffed on the cigar and watched the gray clouds rolling into the Village for a few moments as if I were struggling to get control of myself. For some reason I thought of Winnie Katz. If I was a misogynist, I wondered, what the hell was she? Finally, I turned to face my accuser.

'I don't hate anyone,' I said. 'Maybe Wilhelm Stengal. Or what I think he represents. But I don't hate lawyers, or Negroes, or vegetarians, or homosexuals, or lesbians, or nonsmokers, or guys who go around wearing dead men's clothing and spouting newly discovered sensibilities . . .'

Here, I killed the shot and looked Ratso in the eyes.

'. . . I don't hate myself – did I mention myself? – and I don't hate cats and I don't hate dogs and I don't hate rats and I don't hate Wade Boggs and I don't hate insane people in mental hospitals who go around rhyming things to some pinhead psychiatrist so he can afford a new BMW . . .

'I have loved certain women in my life . . . I don't profess to love them as an ethnic group. The kind of guy that loves all women and is always pointing out tits and ass to everybody is usually a latent homosexual . . . too bad they don't have a dance class for that kind of guy . . .'

I was standing in the living room and gesturing dramatically toward the ceiling with my cigar, and Ratso was sitting on the couch with his mouth open. In the labial-pink sport jacket and with his mouth agape, he looked like a large, disbelieving codfish.

'I don't *hate* all broads, Ratso. I just think women are wired differently. If you *love* all broads, then I feel sorry for you, because one day, my dear Ratso, fate will pluck you up by your wrinkled little scrotum and you will realize much to your chagrin that you are a latent homosexual, which, of course, is a lot less exciting than being a killer fag, but you take what you can get.

'Our heroic friendship, of course, will continue unchanged. If I should appear to be a little guarded or uneasy around you at times, I'll only be protecting my person from what others might say. We're very into images these days – in fact, we always have been. As Geronimo said, in turning down the offer of a Cadillac from the U.S. Government, "Man ride in car – nobody looks. Man ride horse – *everybody* looks." '

Ratso looked at me like he was ready to run me down to Dr Bock's office again. I was ready to gut an infuriating, oversized, rather smug codfish.

87

Both of us were saved by a bloodcurdling scream from the street.

41

It was one of those moments many people wait a lifetime for. Some, possibly longer. I'd thrown the puppet head out the window to the dark, strange-looking figure standing next to the garbage truck in the gathering twilight. A minute or two passed before we heard the heavy footsteps in the hallway. Then three knocks resounded sharply against the door of the loft.

The housepest in the labial-pink sport jacket with whom I'd been arguing the innocence of women in general and of Carmen in particular now stood by my desk watching the door, his curiosity piqued. In a way, mine was, too.

'Come in!' I shouted.

The door opened slowly, and a figure wearing a blue backpack and carrying a smiling puppet head in one hand slithered over the threshold. He looked, for all the world, like Yessir You're-a-fart's hipper younger brother in Western drag. He walked over to me, gave me a hug, handed me the puppet head, and dumped the blue backpack squarely in the middle of the desk, where the cat sniffed at it curiously for a moment, then went back to sleep.

In silence, I walked with the puppet head over to the refrigerator, placed it securely back on its perch, returned to the desk, extracted a fresh cigar from Sherlock Holmes's head, went through the prenuptial arrangements, and fired it up.

I sat down in the chair, took a few puffs, and watched the hazy blue smoke drift lazily up to the lesbian level.

'Ratso,' I said, 'I'd like you to meet Ratso.'

We could hear Winnie and her girls working out somewhere in the near-distant homosexual heavens, but the loft itself was unusually quiet. A lot had gone down, as it were, on several different levels. On one level, for some strange reason, I hoped there was only dancing going on. But this level, for me, was one of imagination, and imagination, though worshiped by Einstein, was never trusted by Sherlock, and hadn't done me a hell of a lot of good either.

On a more basic level, the one on which the three of us were standing, the Ratso who bore the closest resemblance to Ralph Nader now had the floor.

In 1969, according to Washington Ratso, né Jimmie Silman, a paraplegic in North Carolina named Sid White gave him the name 'Ratso' after a car accident and a long convalescence had reduced him to 119 pounds and caused him to walk with a slight limp. The detailed nature of Washington Ratso's account pretty effectively defrayed any major challenges from New York Ratso. The cat and I, trusting spirits to the bitter end, took him at his word.

In 1978, again according to Washington Ratso, he was introduced to me at the Cellar Door in Georgetown by our mutual friend Tex Rubinowitz. (I don't remember the circumstances of my meeting either Ratso, but as Ingrid Bergman once said, 'The recipe for happiness is good health and a bad memory.' At least I think it was Ingrid Bergman.)

Apparently, I'd just fired a guitar player for 'playing too good,' and had hired Ratso, thereby kicking him upstairs from bass player to guitar player. 'Who's gonna play bass?' he'd wanted to know. 'We don't need a bass,' I'd reportedly told him.

This little exchange will not be very meaningful or, I daresay, humorous to nonmusical types, but it was fun for me to hear it again since I didn't remember any of it the first time. New York Ratso was not amused.

He sat quietly as Washington Ratso went through a hilarious recounting of our exploits later that night at Mr Henry's, a gay bar in Georgetown. When he got to the part about me making eyes at the piano player, a look of confirmed suspicion came into New York Ratso's eyes, and a slight moue of distaste crossed his face like a hint of a shadow falling on a sunny salami sandwich. He walked to the refrigerator in disgust, opened the door, found he'd eaten everything already, and slammed the door so hard it rattled the puppet head.

I poured a round for the two Ratsos and myself, and when

things settled down a bit, New York Ratso began grudgingly to give us his story.

He'd met me in 1973 at Max's Kansas City, where he'd heckled me from the audience with such virtuosity that my brother, Roger, who was then managing my band, invited him backstage. I, of course, had forgotten the incident, but Ratso remembered everything with great clarity. It was, for Ratso, like the day Kennedy died is to everybody else. For me, it was another show in my hip pocket.

In 1974 Ratso met Bob Dylan. Jesus and Hitler he'd met much earlier, he contended, while experimenting with psychedelic drugs in Madison, Wisconsin. But it wasn't until 1975, in a parking lot in Vermont during Bob Dylan's Rolling Thunder Revue that Joan Baez gave Larry Sloman the sobriquet 'Ratso.' She named him that, so she said at the time, because of his unkempt and unpleasant appearance.

'Hard to believe,' I said.

New York Ratso went on to point out that, though Washington Ratso may have been a Ratso longer, he himself had known the Kinkster much longer. Washington Ratso absorbed this rather stoically, poured himself a long one and avowed he had to get on the road pretty soon. He suggested I look inside the blue backpack on my desk. This was fine with me, because the dueling Ratsos were starting to get up my sleeve.

With one Ratso looking over each shoulder, I zipped open the backpack and extracted a large envelope from which I withdrew a black-and-white photograph. I looked at the photo, nodded my head, and congratulated Washington Ratso on being a fine stringer. He hugged me again, exchanged a chilly handshake with his New York counterpart, patted the cat, and headed back to our nation's capital.

When he'd gone, I studied the photograph again. I'd only seen the man once in my life, and that wasn't under the best of circumstances. It was in a pine box in a funeral home in Cleveland, Ohio.

Ratso, I noticed, was gazing at the photo too. 'I thought I was the only Ratso in your life,' he said, a trifle wistfully.

'Part of growing up,' I said.

Soon Ratso too was smoke, and the cat and I were recuperating from our two housepests. I'd just taken my brontosaurus-foreskin cowboy boots off and was settling down to a quiet evening when the phones rang.

It was Rambam. His tone was urgent, and his voice was full of grim determination.

'Get ready,' he said. 'We're hitting Wilhelm Stengal tonight.'

42

I had kind of had it in mind to stay in for the evening. Maybe pop some popcorn. Play Scrabble with the cat. Possibly even give Winnie Katz a call. Class didn't sound like it was in session.

I briefly ran a few of these ideas by Rambam, but they didn't fly. I told him Tuesday night was my bowling night. He was not amused.

'Look, Rambam, I'm not being a woosie here. I just don't think the idea of popping into the home of a big international Nazi who plays with poisons and kills people for kicks is exactly best foot forward.' The cat nodded her head in agreement.

'Listen, Mr Stay-at-home-baby,' said Rambam almost insultingly, 'we can't just sit around and solve this one by deductive reasoning. Boris and the boys have been watching this guy. Boris says the place looks like the American Embassy right before the fall of Saigon. There's barbed wire everywhere, and right now, while we're on the phone discussing this, he's out back burning papers in a barrel. We gotta move on this guy soon, or he's gonna fly south like those fucking hummingbirds you're always talking about.'

There was a crude logic to what Rambam was saying. If Stengal flew the coop, a major piece of the John Morgan puzzle might be irretrievably lost. On the other hand, I had a feeling in my lower bowel that Stengal, though a mystery man himself, was not in a vastly different position than I was. Both of us, I felt, were searching for John Morgan. For John's sake, I dearly hoped I got there first.

If Stengal was indeed the blue-cornflower man, the Zyklon-B-derivative specialist, the slow-leak son-of-a-bitch who sicced the skinheads on me, he could well be an old-time Nazi. The McCoy. The real thing. As such, my attitudes toward his life or death on this planet were probably a little to the left of Zev's. The problem was, I needed Stengal. The problem also was, he thought he needed me.

In this case, it was not nice to feel needed.

'Look, Rambam,' I said, 'we're not going tonight. I've got a strange feeling – '

'Call it a hunch,' Rambam interrupted.

'Call it whatever the hell you want, but Stengal's after more than those photographs the skinheads took from me. Think of a way to get the two of us into his house. I want to see the place. I also want him alive.'

'Ah. Ve have vays to make him talk.'

'That's the spirit.'

'How's tomorrow sound?' Rambam asked, like he was inquiring about a racquetball game.

I told Rambam I'd think about tomorrow, and again reminded him to come up with a way to get us inside without resorting to catapulting the castle. I hung up.

The cat was asleep, but I was starting to feel kind of restless. I'd just thought about putting on my boots and drifting over to the Monkey's Paw, or the Ear, or the Lone Star when the phones rang again.

This time it was Carmen. I asked her where Ratso was, and she said she didn't know and she didn't care. She wanted to come over to my place. She thought it was time the two of us got to know each other. She sounded like she meant it in the Old Testament sense. With only a slight pang of guilt I gave her the directions to the loft. She asked if there was anything I needed. I said I'd let her know when she got here. She said she'd be over soon. I said fine. She hung up. I hung up.

I put on my brontosaurus foreskins.

If you think you may be going for a ride, it's a good thing to put on your boots.

43

An old friend of mine from Texas, Dr Jim Bone, once told me an Indian legend about the content of the Milky Way. The Indians believe that the Milky Way is the lingering smoke from the distant campfires of their ancestors and friends who have gone before them and are waiting for them to arrive. Scientists, of course, know that the Milky Way is comprised of stars, subatomic particles, asteroids, inert gases, and galactic dust. That's a problem we have today: too many scientists, not enough Indians.

Be that as it may, there are some people whom you may have met in other circumstances and whom you suddenly see sitting across the kitchen table from you and realize they could fill an emptiness in your life. Everyone has this emptiness, but some of us have it more than others. It's called being spiritually horny.

As I looked into Carmen's eyes that evening, I saw a timelessness, a warm, primitive presence capable of filling a vast emptiness, like smoke from a comforting campfire that almost lingers long enough to mend a broken heart.

I poured a couple get-acquainted shots from a bottle of Wild Turkey I found in the back of a cabinet. She was, I knew, Ratso's girlfriend, not to mention Morgan's fiancée. Over the years I'd developed a hard-hewn code of ethics; not only did I live by it, but I felt that without it, life itself would have very little meaning for me. On the other hand, I wasn't running for the school board.

We made a silent toast, killed the shots, and looked at each other with a sudden intimacy that suggested no kitchen table would ever be likely to keep us apart.

With a slightly trembling hand I poured another round, deliberately not looking into Carmen's black, unfocused, prehistoric eyes. She seemed too young to be so old. Too shy to be so bold. She grabbed my wrist and held on with her blood-red nails. I felt briefly like I was in danger of being carried off by one of those large, extinct birds with the long names. Maybe it wouldn't be so bad. With my free hand I killed the shot.

'You've got to find him,' she hissed. Her voice sounded a little

93

like air escaping from the tire of a lox-colored '58 Cadillac tearing ass south down the Pan-American Highway in the middle of August. I was at the wheel, and I knew I was in some danger of losing control of my motor vehicle.

'Him?' I said. It was an interesting pronoun, I thought. But then, we lived in a world of interesting pronouns. Fairly tedious people sometimes, but interesting pronouns.

'John,' she said.

'I see.'

I didn't, of course. All I saw for sure was Carmen letting go of my wrist, downing her shot of Wild Turkey, squirming seductively in her chair, and unbuttoning two buttons on the top of her blouse. She was definitely headlighting with her brights on.

The Turkey was opening her up in more ways than one, apparently. She began talking rather freely. As they say in the argot of the West, I let her have her head.

'. . . never had a strong, masculine figure to look up to . . . I can still recall my parents arguing when I was a child. My dad would come home late. I was already in bed, but I could hear my mother saying, "Stay away from me, Bill. Don't come near me when you smell that way . . ."'

I murmured something about alcoholism not being unknown in Latin cultures. Then I poured us both another round, sat back, and waited for more from Carmen.

'. . . so I grew up always wanting a strong, take-charge kind of man. A man who cracks a subtle whip . . . who'll tell me what to do . . . who'll never let me fall . . .'

I sat up a little straighter in my chair. I was thinking of what Charles Manson had said to Squeaky Fromme when they'd first met. They were walking down the street somewhere – I think it was San Francisco – and Squeaky slipped, but Charlie caught her before she hit the ground. He held her tightly by the arm and said, 'I'll never let you fall.'

That macho, take-charge, ride-'em-hard-and-put-'em-away-wet routine works with more broads in this liberated age than the *Ms.* magazine editorial board would care to admit. Or maybe it's just that the Squeaky Fromme gets the grease. Whatever it was, I found myself standing so close to Carmen I could feel her nipples boring into my chest. They were harder than Japanese arithmetic.

I felt a sexy, half-human, half-reptilian kind of claw encircle and slowly close around my *pisang*. It was, in all honesty, a not-unpleasant sensation. *Pisang* is the Malay word for 'banana.'

I closed my eyes.

The next thing I saw was the unwelcome visage of Ratso's large and loyal face looming up suddenly before me like an image shot from a magic lantern. Then I saw Morgan smiling cheerfully at me across time and geography. I pushed Carmen away.

I walked to the table on fairly unsteady wheels, killed my shot of Turkey, and turned to Carmen. Her arms were groping blindly toward me. Her upper lip was perspiring. She looked like a cranked-up, slightly over-the-hill Menudo groupie. A kinder, more classically oriented eye might've regarded her as a Thisbe, in a randy moment, reaching impossibly through the garden wall for her Pyramus.

'Maybe,' I said weakly, 'maybe if Ratso'd never met you, if John Morgan hadn't loved you, if you and I had met somewhere else, maybe in the Peace Corps . . . I could've found it possible for us to have made love. Even now, with – '

Carmen had stormed to the door of the loft. She flung it open wide enough for any eavesdropping lesbian to hear. 'I don't *make love*,' she shouted, 'I *fuck!*'

Then the door slammed. Then the cat and I stared in silence at the closed door. Then we listened to the not-quite-mechanical whine of the freight elevator descending downward into the worldly world.

Then I killed Carmen's shot.

44

To take my mind off of Carmen, I called an old friend of mine, John Rapp. John was the *shabbos goy* of the Blue Nun Wine Company and somewhat of an expert in your Teutonic area. At least I once saw one of those old World War I kraut skypieces with the pointy-looking spike on top at his apartment. Rapp was also the proud possessor of a Luftwaffe toilet-paper holder stamped with the date 1944, an eagle, and a swastika. Rapp had been a country-music lover, and a fan of mine in particular, dating back to about the time the Kaiser first waxed his cookie-duster. I had a certain loyalty to my fans. Even if they eventually turned out to be hatchet-murderers, I somehow tended to trust their judgment. Besides, I thought it might be a good idea to know a little about Wilhelm Stengal's fortress in the event that Rambam and I ever got on the same wavelength long enough to assault it.

'I'm a *Judenfreund* from way back,' said Rapp when I got him on the line.

'Good,' I said. 'Maybe you'll be more help this time around.' I briefly sketched the situation for John and gave him the address of Stengal's brownstone. He knew the place.

Apparently, it had had a long and sinister history, going back to its first owner, who was the *Bund* leader at the time. Though most of the old places in Yorkville had now been transformed into condos and trendy Japanese restaurants, this address had curiously – or possibly not so curiously – remained in the same fascist hands. Rapp suspected there were quite a lot of relics inside the place but, as a *Judenfreund*, recommended I stay the hell away from it. I asked him for an assessment of what the mentality of the current owner might be.

Rapp said, 'Like the guy who kept pigeons in *The Producers*. Remember, Kinkster?'

I told him I remembered, thanked him, and hung up. And I did remember. More than I wanted to about the Germans. I was too young to have been there at the time, but I was a Jew. There would always be a little piece of yesterday in my eye.

It was around nine o'clock when I lay down for a little power nap on the couch. Every time I closed my eyes, I saw Carmen. I recognized the folly of following my *pisang* around the world, but I had wanted Carmen and, apparently, I wanted her now. Though I had been loyal to Ratso, I knew that, like Jimmy Carter, I had lusted in my heart. Of course, I reflected, if you go around worrying about lusting in your heart all the time, you'll probably never get near the front of the line for having big fun on the bayou. Even with the excess baggage that Judaism sometimes brings, I was suddenly very glad that I wasn't a Christian fundamentalist.

I closed my eyes and thought of Carmen again.

The phones rang. Could it be? I wondered, as I got up from the couch and moved quickly for the desk.

It was not Carmen.

It was a heavy Germanic voice that said, 'Herr Friedman?'

'Yeah?'

'Your friend Ratso . . . I'm sorry to say that he is dead.'

The caller hung up, and for a moment I sat there stunned, listening to the dial tone. Then I hung up and, with a sense of dread, picked up the blower again and dialed Ratso's number in New York. I got his answering machine. I hung up.

Frantically, I dialed Washington Ratso's number. It rang five times, and then I got *his* answering machine. I was trying to sort things out, but as I hung up the blower I noticed my hand was shaking. I felt in my guts that it had been no crank call that I had received.

They say home is where the answering machine is. I could wait awhile and call both numbers again, I thought. I could leave urgent messages at each place. But one idea kept coming into my head, and it was having a rather numbing visceral effect.

I was suddenly very much afraid that I was no longer a two-Ratso man.

45

They say you never marry the person you first see *Casablanca* with. They say a lot of things, I thought, as Rambam sliced a vicious right turn off Eighth Avenue onto Fourteenth Street, and they're usually right.

It was ten o'clock, and I didn't know where my children were. I wasn't even sure I had any. All I knew was we were on our way to Wilhelm Stengal's house and Rambam had a plan. I liked a man with a plan.

Before I'd left the loft, I recruited Rambam to help with the Ratso situation. By the time he'd arrived, I'd already called the numbers in New York and Washington several times, leaving urgent messages to get in touch with me at the loft. I gave Rambam the two addresses, watched him make a terse phone call, and did not feel particularly reassured when he promised me he'd be putting a few 'Hebraic irregulars' on it.

To begin with, Rambam had never especially liked New York Ratso, nor did he particularly put much credence in the veracity of the kraut caller's statement. In fact, with another human being in the loft, taking nothing away from the cat, I was beginning to wonder if the call mightn't have been an effort at Bavarian humor myself. Knowing Rambam's distaste for one Ratso, I did not feel it necessary to inform him that the other Ratso was a Lebanese Druse.

Finally, in a mood that had begun to vaseline back and forth between doubt and dark desperation, I'd called Cooperman. After I'd related the situation to him, he'd made what sounded like a sort of choking noise on the phone. Before things became too unpleasant, I was able to give him the actual names and addresses of the two Ratsos, and he was able to tell me that he would do nothing for twenty-four hours, at which time I could file a missing-persons report if I so wished. Then we were both able to hang up.

Now Rambam was taking the FDR like a hack honing in on LaGuardia. The FDR Drive ran along the East River like a narrow, pock-marked ramp to hell, and hell was as good a name as any for where we were going. Every time the Jag hit a pothole, Rambam cursed and I screwed my cowboy hat on a little tighter. It was a nightmarish ride, but it beat the subway.

'In just a minute you're gonna have to lose that cowboy hat,' said Rambam, as he wrenched off the FDR onto Ninety-sixth Street. 'I've got another one for you to wear though.'

'Good,' I said. 'That's the one thing cowboys and Jewboys have in common. We both like to wear our hats indoors, and we attach a certain amount of importance to it.'

'Well, unless we fuck up real bad, you should get a chance to wear a hat indoors tonight.'

'Great,' I said, as I flung the cowboy hat into the back of the Jag. 'Where's the new hat?'

'It's in the trunk,' Rambam said almost to himself as we cruised silently up Eighty-sixth Street.

'That's too bad.'

'It sure is,' said Rambam as he looked at my hair. I lowered the visor and looked in the mirror. My head looked like a rocket ship. My hair had congealed like a gelatin mould into the shape of the inside of the cowboy hat. I'd seen this before. It was an occupational hazard afflicting cowboys with kinky hair and Jewboys who, for inexplicable reasons of their own, insisted upon wearing cowboy hats. Which of the two categories I belonged to depended on how you looked at it. Most people, for reasons of esthetics, preferred not to.

'Dis looks like de place, boss,' said Rambam, pointing out a stately brownstone on the left-hand side of the street. The lights were on inside, giving the building a distinguished, romantic, almost merry appearance. It looked like Nick and Nora Charles might live there. Unfortunately, they didn't.

Rambam made another pass around the block, checked the street carefully, and finally parked the Jag about a block and a half away from the place. We got out of the car, and Rambam walked over to a nearby pay phone and dialed a number. I readjusted my moss as best I could, nodded to a passing young couple, and edged closer to hear Rambam's conversation.

'. . . Yes, sir . . . this is Mr Wallenberg with Con Ed . . . we've received a field report about a potential emergency situation in your area. Our Main Number Thirty-seven on the East Side appears to have ruptured, and we're concerned about the possibility of emissions into residential dwellings . . . Yeah, within the hour . . . an Emissions Detection Team . . . they're in the area right now . . . no problem . . .'

Rambam walked back to the Jag with a satisfied smirk on his face. 'Jesus Christ,' I said. 'Wallenberg?'

'You can call me Raoul, or you can call me Ray,' he said as he opened the trunk.

Five minutes later the Emissions Detection Team was heading

up the sidewalk at a leisurely pace toward Wilhelm Stengal's house. We were wearing yellow regulation hard-hats, bright orange safety vests, and thick leather equipment belts loaded with enough gear to hot-wire the Hindenburg.

Out of the corner of my eye I saw Rambam transfer a small black handgun from his vest pocket to the small of his back. 'That's the one piece of equipment,' I said, 'that I damn well don't want to see you use.'

Rambam smiled.

'Think about it,' he said. 'Here we are going into the home of a World War II Nazi to warn him that he may be in danger of being gassed.' Rambam laughed a faraway laugh.

'The irony,' I said, 'is not lost on me.'

46

'Germany,' said Wilhelm Stengal, 'is the only country in the world that could rise like a phoenix from the ashes of destruction.' It's pretty hard to argue with an elderly fanatic. Especially one who's pointing a Luger at your nose.

I cast a nervous look at Rambam, who was standing about ten feet over to my right and looking like he was ready to wring Stengal's scrawny neck. Stengal was beginning to resemble some kind of horrific chicken, with his slightly stooped shoulders, thin, cordy neck, and large, civilized-appearing head. His hand on the Luger was steady as they come.

'The West Germans, in particular, have done well,' I said, humoring the old man. 'I understand they've come up with a new microwave oven. Seats forty.'

This drew no response from Rambam. With Stengal, however, it was a different matter. His hand tightened almost imperceptibly on the Luger, and for a moment, in the gothic, art-museum lighting of the place, I thought I could see millions of men and military machinery moving behind his gray eyes. Then he did something that chilled me. He let forth with a laugh that sounded more like a cackle. An intelligent, arrogant, almost nostalgic cackle that bubbled with evil.

They say when you laugh, the whole world laughs with you, and they're usually right. Usually.

Just how Inspector Clouseau and I permitted ourselves to get into a situation where an old geezer was pointing a dangerous-looking war relic at my beezer is something neither of us, I'm sure, is particularly proud of. Essentially, he outfoxed us.

I'd told Rambam before we went into the place that we should work on our story, and he said we'd be out of there before we needed a story. I reflected bitterly upon this as Stengal deftly shifted the Luger from his right hand to his left one, and checked the time like the old pro that he was. There was a swastika inside a circle on the handgrip of the Luger. It really was an old war relic, and so was Stengal, and God only knew what might be going on in the ancient, dusty, twisted gray matter department of a World War II Nazi. Maybe he is still following orders.

The other mistake Rambam and I had made was to allow ourselves to be separated. If you're ever visiting an old Nazi's house under the guise of a gas company Emissions Detection Team, always stick together and let one guy do all the talking.

What had actually occurred was that Rambam had wandered off through the living room with an emissions detection device that appeared to fascinate Stengal. It was a scam, Rambam later maintained, that was extremely effective, especially with elderly people. He'd enclosed a light meter in a portentous-looking leather case with only the dial exposed, and as he walked toward the light fixture in the far corner of the room, the thing went crazy. Stengal definitely appeared to be hooked, walking nervously alongside Rambam, wringing his hands. It was at that point that I drifted into a huge adjoining room whose contents would've made the lions in front of the Metropolitan Museum of Art turn green with envy.

If you're one of these pointy-headed intellectual sticklers for the facts, you might point out, probably with your head, that the lions are in front of the library, not the museum of art. To this, however, I would answer, Under the circumstances, what possible difference could it make? Read between the lions.

Unfortunately, I know so little about art that I don't even know what I like, but, unless I missed my bet, this room represented a treasure trove of works that must've been pillaged by the SS from museums and private collections all over Europe. I confess to being mesmerized.

I was staring into the faintly familiar Flemish face of a woman who seemed to be saying, 'I don't belong here. Please take me home with you, mister,' when another voice sounded very close to my left ear. It was also faintly familiar.

'On which side of town is your office located?' asked Wilhelm Stengal very slowly and distinctly. I realized my answer would be a coin toss. I did not turn around.

'East Side,' I said finally. When I felt the gun in my back, I knew that Rambam must've told him 'West Side.'

Such a simple trap, I thought, and there was nothing I could do. East is East and West is West. Especially to a kraut.

I looked up into the friendly face of the Flemish woman. 'I don't belong here either,' I said.

47

Stengal motioned with the Luger for me to get over closer to where Rambam was standing. I did. We were back in the main room of the house. I never went in for art museums much anyway.

'You have your friend John Morgan to thank for this,' Stengal said. 'I cannot let you go now.'

'Where is John Morgan?' I asked.

'When I find him,' said Stengal rather ominously, 'I'll extend to him your regrets. You're the first to try this here, but others, like John Morgan, have tried many times before in South America and other places. Their bodies are occasionally found floating in the Amazon with their testicles in their mouths.'

It was not a pleasant image. I'd heard of pulling a groin, but this sounded, at the very least, unsportsmanlike.

When I looked at Stengal's face again, he was wearing a hideous, forced kind of smile, vaguely reminiscent of an air-scoop vent on a '65 Pontiac.

'I had to do what I had to do,' said Stengal, more serious and strident now. 'I was, after all, protecting the greatest genius the world has ever known!' I looked over to Rambam. He appeared to be biding his time. Unfortunately, it didn't seem as if there was going to be a lot of that left to bide.

'And you still are, aren't you, Stengal?' I asked.

Stengal turned his distinguished eyes toward me and looked directly at me, giving nothing away. He would've made a good poker player, for a Nazi.

Imperceptibly, he nodded. 'I cannot let you go,' he repeated almost sadly, like a rather stilted jilted lover. 'Franz and Erik will be here shortly, and then – '

There was the sound of crashing glass in the front of the house. The three of us turned toward the noise, and less than an instant later the room seemed to be enveloped in smoke and flames. My throat suddenly constricted and became very dry. I was struggling for breath in a rolling blanket of searing heat. Flames leaped up all around us, effectively trapping the three of us in what appeared to be an almost certain dance of death. Just before I heard a motor-cycle roar off into the night, I was vaguely aware of a voice that shouted 'Never Again!'

It was an irony that was not lost upon me.

The next thing I remember was Rambam knocking me down with his shoulder and hollering, 'Hit the floor!,' which, under the circumstances, were easy directions. At the same time, Stengal, coughing, choking, and dodging flames, squeezed off two rounds with the Luger into the air space I'd very recently vacated. The second shot grazed Rambam's left side and made him angrier than an Italian-Jewish bull. He went straight for Stengal like a hate-seeking missile. I stayed on the floor beneath the heavy smoke level and crawled toward the action. It wasn't hard to follow just from the audio portion – coughing and choking sounds, two more shots, a series of retreating Germanic curses, and, several times, a loud and decidedly Brooklyn refrain: 'I'll tear your fucking heart out! I'll tear your fucking heart out!'

I got to sort of a hallway where the smoke wasn't quite as bad, and caught sight of two scurrying figures racing down a spiral staircase. Stengal might've been o-l-d, but he could still m-o-v-e when the notion took him. Walking like a homo erectus again, I followed Rambam's broad back through a doorway into some kind of basement. The fire was beginning to crackle pretty good upstairs. I could hear sirens in the distance. Smoke was already starting to drift down into the basement.

'I don't believe it,' said Rambam, as he leveled a few furious, futile kicks at an iron door. 'The fucker's got a *bunker* down here.'

At that moment steel bars on rollers began rolling down from the ceiling to the floor, effectively shutting Wilhelm Stengal away to a lonely death. 'The way this building's going up,' said Rambam, 'he doesn't have a chance in there. He'll die just like "the greatest genius the world has ever known." '

'I don't think he was referring to *that* "greatest genius," ' I said, watching the smoke start to billow into the basement. 'I think he was talking about another "greatest genius." '

'Yeah? Well, let's hope the two of us are smart enough to get our asses out of here alive.'

For a while, which seemed like a torturous eternity, it didn't seem like we would be. Running back up the basement stairs to the first floor, we were met by a virtual wall of fire. We returned to the basement and began, like two large, white, increasingly frantic rats in a maze, to look about for doors or windows that just weren't there. Things did not look too promising. One corner of the basement was set up as sort of a chemical laboratory with trays and test tubes and beakers, but of course there wasn't a hell of a lot of time to check it out.

I wasn't afraid to die. I'd died onstage a number of times in my life. But I hadn't died yet in Wilhelm Stengal's basement.

I raced up the stairs again until I met with a wave of heat and could go no farther. On my way down again I looked up in despair and spotted something I hadn't seen before. It was about ten feet off the ground, but it looked like a small painted-over window high above the basement steps on the street side of the house. I yelled for Rambam and grabbed what looked like a ceremonial dagger off a nearby table.

Moments later, I was standing on Rambam's shoulders, smashing the window with the pommel of the dagger and shouting for help. I heard voices outside, knocked shards of glass away with the dagger, and, just as the heat and acrid smoke were becoming unbearable, two arms reached through the window and helped pull me out. The arms were attached to Detective-Sergeant Mort Cooperman.

A short while later, Rambam and I were on the sidewalk watching Wilhelm Stengal's empire burn. I showed Rambam the blade of the dagger. It read: '*Blut und Ehre.*'

'That's "Blood and Honor," ' said Rambam. 'That was the motto of the SS. Stengal was an SS man.'

'Nice guy like Wilhelm? Who'd have thought it?'

Fox and Cooperman walked up to us. 'That's a nice outfit, Tex,' said Cooperman. 'Meter reading might be a swell midlife career change for you.'

'That's what I thought.'

'We're takin' you two in as material witnesses,' said Fox. 'Probably more than that before we're through with you.'

They frisked us both and took Rambam's gun. Cooperman took the ceremonial dagger and studied it appreciatively.

'Looks almost like it might be stolen property, doesn't it, Fox?'

'Damned if it don't.'

'It may *look* like stolen property, but it's not,' I said, as they hustled the two of us into the back of a plain-wrapped car.

'It's an heirloom,' I said to the back of Mort Cooperman's head as he gunned the engine and tore out of there. 'It's been in the family almost twenty minutes.'

48

It was one o'clock the next afternoon, Wednesday, by the time Wolf Nachman, the greatest lawyer in the world, was able to get Rambam back to Brooklyn and me back to my cat. I won't bore you with the shunting around from place to place, the holding cells, the bologna sandwiches, or the constant onslaught of tedium from Cooperman and Fox.

Needless to say, I did not get my ceremonial dagger back. Wolf said he'd work on it.

The cat appeared relatively happy to see me, and the blinking red light on the answering machine indicated that four Americans had tried to reach me during the night. I petted the cat and walked over to the machine. I put it on 'rewind,' took a cigar out of Sherlock's head, fired it up, leaned back in the chair, and set the machine on 'play.'

The first voice, to my great relief, was New York Ratso's. He sounded guarded, almost unfriendly. He'd been out to a hockey game and then hit a few bars. He wanted to meet me for lunch today at Big Wong's. There were a few things he thought we ought to talk over.

Now that I knew he was alive, I didn't especially want to go to Big Wong's and talk with Ratso. I didn't know what Carmen had told him but I could imagine, and I almost didn't care. And I was starting to feel tired as hell.

The second message was a rather heavy-handed hang-up. Nothing wrong with that. Some people just don't like to talk to answering machines. Some people really enjoy talking to answering machines. It's a diverse and fascinating world we live in. I took a puff on the cigar and pondered the world for about a microsecond.

The third message was from my old friend Cleve, once the manager of the Lone Star Cafe, now residing at the Pilgrim State Psychiatric Hospital. It's never a really good idea to establish too close a relationship with people in mental hospitals, because one day, usually sooner than you expect, they get out and try to cut your head off. But Cleve claimed he was now in a rehabilitation work-therapy program, and he had a great idea he couldn't wait to tell me about. I could wait.

I figured Cleve wasn't going anywhere, so I'd get back to him when I found out what the situation was with Washington Ratso, fed the cat, and got some sleep.

The last message on the tape took care of whatever lingering doubts I'd had about my little Lebanese brother. The voice was gruff and all too familiar. It was Sergeant Cooperman.

'More bad news for you, Tex . . . I don't know what you've got yourself into, but I'm sure as hell going to find out. Just after we released you to Nachman we got a call from a precinct outside of Washington, D.C. Guy they think is named Jimmie Silman was found burned beyond recognition in his car. The dental records are going to the lab, but the car was his and it was parked in the garage of Silman's house. The garage was destroyed, but they saved the house. And whose name and phone number do you think they found on a pad by his telephone?'

Almost unconsciously, I reached into a desk drawer and took out a kaffiyah, the traditional headgear worn by Arab peoples, and held it in my lap. It'd been sent to me by a Palestinian girl I'd once known.

I heard Cooperman's voice in the blower: '. . . Tex? You still with me, Tex?'

No, I thought, I wasn't.

I gazed at the Peace Corps photograph that had, almost certainly, cost Jimmie Silman his life. The eyes stared back at me like a stranger in a dream. I looked over into the near distance of the kitchen window. Somewhere in the dancing motes of dust threading their way through the gray afternoon light, I saw the other John Morgan whom I knew so well. I saw the glint of green in his impish, mischievous eyes. For a moment, I saw his face smiling playfully back at me.

'. . . John . . . you ol' devil . . . what in Christ's name have you gotten me into?'

49

I slept pretty well that night but I woke up with the kind of headache you'd get if you'd been drinking cheap champagne from a size–14 Cinderella slipper. There was cat vomit on the bed. The phones were ringing, so I stumbled over to the desk to answer them. It was, I noticed between waves of cranial pain, only nine o'clock.

'Kink,' said a voice, 'this is Kent Perkins in L.A. I've got something kind of interesting for you.'

'I hope so,' I said. Kent was an old friend of mine, also from Texas, but I'd met him some years ago out on the Left Coast. He was a big, friendly guy, a producer for NBC television, and, unlike my amateur self, a real private detective. Kent was married to Ruth Buzzi, the actress and comedienne who'd first made her mark on *Laugh-In* hitting people over the head with her purse. At the moment, in fact, it seemed like Ruth was hitting me over the head with her purse.

'A guy died a few days ago,' Kent said, 'in an old folks' home out in the Valley. When they started trying to contact the relatives on file about the disposition of his few effects, they all turned out to be nonexistent. He was a Canadian citizen, apparently, but of European ancestry. Anyway, I start going through this guy's stuff, and I get the definite feeling he's deliberately concealing his past. In fact, I begin to think . . .'

Kent droned on along with my head for a few moments. The cat made a rather clumsy jump onto the desk, wobbled silently, and sat down looking kind of embarrassed. My head was really pounding.

'. . . so I figured the guy must be some high-ranking Nazi.'

My ears perked up at the word.

'Nazi?' I said weakly.

'Not only that, but I checked over his phone bills, and two weeks ago he made a call to a number I recognized. It was rather unusual, I thought, for him to be calling this particular phone number. The number, my friend, is *yours*.'

After I'd rung off with Kent I had a lot to think about, but I didn't really feel like thinking. I started to make some espresso, but then I decided not to. I fed the cat some tuna, but she didn't want any. She was definitely off her feed.

The cat looked at me with slightly crossed eyes like Siamese cats do. Only she wasn't Siamese. She was a New York alley cat that I'd found in Chinatown, so she must be Chinese. And I liked to think she had enough Jewish upbringing that, if a cat Hitler ever came along, she could be in real trouble. But I knew there wasn't much danger of that ever happening. Cats are a very independent and freedom-loving race of people.

I was feeling a bit dizzy, so I went to the couch to lie down for a little power nap. I knew the cat was ill, but just at the moment I didn't much feel like putting her in a pillowcase, lugging her down to the vet in the Village, and standing around in the waiting room with a large number of adult men and their little toy chihuahuas.

The pounding in my brain seemed to be easing up just a hair, and vague, blurry images began appearing in a light red backdrop on the inside of my eyelids. I saw a twisted old Left Coast Nazi sitting, in full uniform, under a large umbrella on a redwood verandah gazing out over Malibu and then dialing my number. I saw Wilhelm Stengal walking elegantly through the lobby of the Pierre Hotel with a blue cornflower in his lapel and with eyes that could change so suddenly from cultured mother-of-pearl to those of an angry skink whose rock's just been turned over and who can't decide whether to run for his life or to swallow the sun. Does a skink have eyes? I'd have to look it up when I got home. Then I saw Jimmie Silman's sad dark eyes. I wanted to help him, but I couldn't. I wanted to warn him, but it was too late.

The last thing I remember before I passed out was turning my head and watching the cat gamely trying to jump onto her rocking chair. Once, twice, three times she tried. Each time she fell unceremoniously back to the floor. It was painful for me to see. But if you're a cat and someone is watching you, it's worse than death.

Of course, neither the cat nor I realized at the time how close to death it actually was.

50

'Open the windows! Jesus Christ! Don't light a match! Call the Con Ed emergency number!'

Very fuzzily, I heard one strident female voice giving orders, and another, softer one, murmuring assent. Suddenly, it had become very cold, and I found myself shivering. I opened my eyes and saw a woman's face bending over me.

'Ruth Buzzi?' I asked.

'No,' said Winnie Katz, 'but I'd like to meet her.'

She put a warm hand on my forehead. 'Why did you do it?' she asked.

When you've done a lot of things in your life, this is always a confusing question. What was she talking about? Could she have found out about Rambam bugging the shrink's office?

'You've got so much to live for! If we hadn't come around and gotten in through the window by the fire escape, you'd be dead. The room's filled with gas!'

It was news to me. Of course, it accounted for everything rather neatly. I hadn't smelled anything in seven years, but this was the first time my beezer'd almost let me down for the count. How could it have happened? My mind was whirring with questions, theories, paranoid notions. My teeth were chattering. Winnie was looking down at me with deep platonic sympathy.

'Where's the cat?' I shouted.

Winnie and the other girl began looking around the place and calling for the cat the way people do who don't know much about cats. I sat up on the couch and shivered.

'Find him a coat,' Winnie ordered the other girl.

'Find the cat!' I shouted. I was still too weak to stand. 'Check under that rocking chair.'

Winnie checked under the rocking chair and extracted a very foggy cat. One would think, after a near-death situation such as this, that a man and a cat would be experiencing a joyous reunion. One can picture the man and the cat running toward each other across the bridge of life. This, however, was not to be. The cat sat up very erect, with her back to me and her eyes on the far wall, doing a slow burn. Under other circumstances, I might've thought this behavior somewhat humorous. Things being as they were, I found it totally uncalled for.

Winnie sent the other broad upstairs, led me to the kitchen table, got the espresso machine humming a familiar aria, and got me into a heavy black lamb's wool coat that made me look like a slightly anemic pimp. Uptown Judy had given me the coat, and it was a hell of an item. A boyfriend of hers who'd been running from the law left it in her apartment and never came back. She had a very private garage sale one night, and I got the coat. If I could stay alive long enough, I thought, I ought to give her a call. Let her know how the coat was doing. Then there was Downtown Judy. But my mind was wandering. I looked up and saw Winnie expertly pouring the espresso.

'You're going to make somebody a very fine something someday,' I said.

'You silver-tongued shithead,' she said as she handed me the cup.

I took a sip and looked at Winnie. She was a very pretty girl. She had freckles. She had intelligent, sexy, hazel eyes. She had a very comforting presence about her.

'You saved my life,' I said.

'That's what they all say,' she said.

By the time the two Con Ed guys got there, I was striding back and forth in my Uptown Judy pimp coat with an unlit cigar in my mouth lecturing Winnie about how sometimes a cigar is just a cigar. She'd made a comment I hadn't liked, and I felt called upon to defend my oral dissertation. The Con Ed guys pretty much ignored the two of us and went to work in the vicinity of the oven. I did notice they did not have an emissions detection device.

The effect of the gas had fairly well worn off by now, except that I had a bit of a buzz going for myself. Winnie was listening to me with rather a smart-ass schoolgirl smile that was kind of fetching in an offbeat way.

'. . . Freud said that every human being has the potential to be homosexual. It's an accident that we become heterosexual, determined by developmental vicissitudes. So you see, cigar smoking is really no big deal. Dr Charles Ansell, the head shrink of the San Fernando Valley and a personal friend of our family, maintains that it "suggests an unresolved infantilism reminiscent of suckling of the breast." Dr Ansell maintains that it can also, of course, suggest fellatio, but you can't have everything. Care for a cigar?'

'Hey, buddy,' one of the Con Ed guys said, motioning me over to the stove, 'you want to see what the trouble was?'

'Yeah,' I said. I walked over next to him. He pointed to an area close to the floor and behind the oven.

'Flex hose worked its way loose,' he said.

'How often does this kind of thing happen?' I asked.

'Depends,' said the Con Ed guy, 'on whether there's an inch-and-a-quarter wrench available.'

51

In Austin, when you die, they say you go to Willie Nelson's house. As I sat at my desk that evening listening to an old Billy Joe Shaver record on the Victrola, I reflected upon a time some years back when I'd gone to Willie Nelson's house without having to make the ultimate sacrifice. Willie'd told me something that night that made quite an impression on my pillow for many years to come. He'd said, 'If you ain't crazy, there's something wrong with you.'

As I listened to the garbage trucks growling along with Billy Joe, I poured a second shot of Wild Turkey into the old bull's horn, flicked a Clarence Darrow-length cigar ash into my Texas-shaped ashtray, and realized that there was nothing wrong with me.

So I had to be crazy.

That would explain a lot of things.

It would explain why, two weeks after returning from Cleveland, I was still on a wild-goose chase looking for John Morgan. It would explain why a lot of people – namely Zev, Rambam, and Winnie Katz – seemed to be saving my life lately. It would explain why I was ready to believe that a World War II Nazi, now residing, thankfully, in whatever the kraut version of Willie Nelson's house is, had called me from southern California as Kent Perkins maintained, and invited me, as I was now beginning to realize, to John Morgan's funeral. They wanted to be certain I didn't get on the trail of the *other* John Morgan. They probably hadn't known it would be an open casket funeral!

Maybe I'd call Cleve and have him reserve a bed for me at Pilgrim State, I thought as I killed the shot of Turkey. It was heavier than Jameson. It was sweeter than Jack Daniel's. It was still pretty damn good if you didn't have the other two. I poured another shot.

So I was crazy. I was a little out of line with the other ducks. Out where the buses don't run. The date on my carton, apparently, had expired. There was nothing wrong with me. I was crazy.

How else could I justify my conviction that some Nazi conspiracy of international proportions was after my ass? Was there a functioning, death-dealing 88 organization? Was this a brotherhood of evil feasting at some satanic banquet, or was I nodding out at a local Lion's Club luncheon?

But with Wilhelm Stengal now a crispy critter, how else could I explain the vengeful irony of method in the morning's attack upon my life and the life of my cat? And with Wilhelm Stengal now a member of the grateful dead – not the rock group – could anyone have known about the gas-leak business Rambam and I had visited upon him?

I thought briefly of going down for another check-up-from-the-neck-up with Dr Bock, but I didn't want to give Ratso, Rambam, and McGovern the satisfaction. Beyond a doubt, the whole world was crazy and I was a part of that world, and when I thought about it, I wouldn't have wanted it any other way. I killed the last shot and went to bed.

52

Friday morning Jimmie Silman, aka Washington Ratso, called. I didn't know if I was in Willie Nelson's house or still dreaming. Fortunately, neither was the case.

'Ratso,' I said. 'Jesus Christ, man, where are you? Goddamn, brother, what happened?'

'Well, let's take the first epithet first. I'm standing in what's left of my house. The place is gutted, my guitars are slightly damp, the car is gone, and the garage is gone. I've been talking to the neighbors and the police, and now I understand that *I* was almost gone. I wander off with a broad for twenty-four hours and *this* shit happens.'

'That's the vengeance of Muhammad being visited upon you for practicing fornication.'

'I was raised as a *Methodist*, for Christ's sake, and I stopped practicing fornication when I was about twelve years old. By now I'm pretty good at it. At least that's what the broad told me. You ever seen a water-logged 1957 Stratocaster guitar built by Tex Rubinowitz?'

'I'm afraid not. Ratso, I don't want to bring up anything unpleasant, but who was in the car?'

'Yeah, that was pretty unpleasant, all right. The cops think it was the guy from AAA. For twenty-four hours after I called them they kept threatening to send someone over to start the car and they never did, so I just left a note on the garage door. Apparently, when I was out with the broad, he finally made it over. He started it up, and the bomb blew him away. Christ.'

Before I hung up, I told Ratso what had happened to me the previous morning, warned him to be extremely careful, and let him know how great it felt for me to be a two-Ratso man again. I was thrilled he was alive and well and I wanted to share the experience, as they say in Hollywood, with someone. I thought about calling New York Ratso, but I couldn't be sure he wouldn't tell Carmen, and I was less sure than ever about Carmen. Also, I didn't want to create feelings of ambivalence in Ratso, letting him know he was the only Ratso in my life for a brief, shining moment but that now the other Ratso had come back into the picture.

I tried to call McGovern, but he was away from his desk. I was away from my desk too. Pouring a shot of Wild Turkey into a cup of espresso and feeding the cat her morning tuna.

Finally, I settled on calling Rambam. I laid out the whole Washington Ratso situation for him, told him my great relief that Jimmie Silman was alive, and told him who the cops now suspected the actual victim was.

'I'm glad it wasn't Ratso,' I said, 'but it's a shame about the AAA guy.'

'That's nothing,' said Rambam. 'I know a Mafia don who lives right here in Brooklyn. Every morning he calls AAA to start his car.'

53

'Gas leaks are more common than you think,' said New York Ratso as we sat at a little table in Big Wong's that afternoon. 'I had one in my apartment last year. Same thing happened. Guys came out and wanted to know if it'd been tampered with. Hell, I told 'em, that stove's never even been used. They don't want you to know how often it happens.' He lifted a rather large portion of roast pork scrambled eggs into his mouth with a Chinese soup spoon.

I was beginning to have my doubts too. Wilhelm Stengal was at Willie Nelson's house, John Morgan might be there too, for all I knew, and I hadn't been beaten up since the last time I'd been with Ratso. Quite possibly, the whole case had died with Stengal. The other theory, that we were dealing with a huge, nefarious, Hitlerian Hydra, lopping one of its skinheads off only to produce ten more, was looking less and less plausible in the pale light of a fading February afternoon in comforting, immutable Chinatown. March was almost here, and I, for one, was ready to goose-step into a new month and a new frame of mind. Get a little mental health on board. Time for visions and revisions.

On the other hand, there was the mysterious phone call Kent Perkins had reported. And there was one less AAA representative in the District of Columbia area. I didn't know what to think. What I need, I thought, is one single shred of hard evidence.

'What I need,' said Ratso, 'is some duck sauce for this roast duck-roast pork over rice.'

'No doubt,' I said. 'Ratso, I want you to do a favor for me.'

'Anything you want, except I won't share the roast pork scrambled eggs.'

'I know things may be a little strained between us right now. I haven't been as open with you as maybe I could about this case.'

'Why is this case different from all other cases? You never tell me shit.'

'Well, I'll tell you something now. I started out looking for my friend John Morgan, and now I feel I'm surrounded by enemies and I'm not even sure who they are or even whether they exist. And I'll tell you something else, in case you may be wondering. I did not hose Carmen.'

'Yeah. She told me. But she said you tried.'

I almost choked on a piece of tripe. I decided to play to Ratso's ego. All friendship aside, I needed his help.

'Okay. So I tried. But I didn't get anywhere. You know me. If I had access to hook-and-ladder truck number four-oh-seven and a heavy-metal *pisang*, I'd probably try to sodomize the Statue of Liberty.'

'What's a *pisang*?'

'Means "banana" in Malay.'

We ate in silence for a while.

Finally, I said to Ratso, 'Okay. Here's what I want. Find this out from Carmen: Was her adoptive father an alcoholic?'

'All right,' said Ratso disgustedly, 'but I'm getting tired of all this cryptic bullshit – the grasshopper game, your doubts and hints and warnings about Carmen, your paranoid behavior about the gas leak. You don't trust me anymore. You keep everything to yourself. You've been working full tilt on this case for quite a while now, and you're still nowhere as far as I can see.'

I took out a cigar, went quickly through the prenuptial arrangements, and lighted it slowly and carefully.

'You know,' said Ratso, with something close to dismay in his voice, 'sometimes I wonder. What fucking detective school did you go to, Sherlock?'

I took a few leisurely puffs on the cigar before I picked up the check.

'Elementary, my dear Ratso,' I said. 'Elementary.'

54

'No, I didn't know that Elvis never played to an empty seat, Cleve, but look where it got him.'

It was later that afternoon, and a squall had blown up across the city. I'd taken time off from watching the rain with the cat to call

Cleve back. Now one end of the blower was at the loft, and the other end was connected to the third ring of Saturn.

'All I'm saying is, it wouldn't hurt you to take a gig every once in a while. You've got a lot of fans out there, big guy. Let 'em know you're still alive.'

I smiled grimly. Maybe my fans knew something I didn't know.

'Yeah,' I said, 'but fans like dead stars better than live ones. Lenny Bruce, Judy Garland, and Elvis all died on the throne, and Jim Morrison in the bathtub, and they have more fans than anyone except Wayne Newton, and he refuses steadfastly to go anywhere near a bathroom because he senses his own mortality.'

'Kinkster,' said Cleve, 'you're running on here a little. You're not being rational.'

'That's because I don't like to be called "big guy." '

'Well, you're being very juvenile, talking crazy. I just want you to listen to this. I've got a great idea.'

I didn't like the fact that Cleve appeared to be patronizing me when I was the one who was supposed to be patronizing him. I had to admit, however, that he sounded pretty lucid.

'I could be a killer agent,' he said.

'That's what I'm afraid of.'

'I could book you on a tour of Texas. They love you down there, Kinkster.'

'To paraphrase Bessie Smith, "It's no disgrace to come from Texas. It's just a disgrace to have to go back there." '

'We'll call it "The Kinky Experience." We'll get Jerry Retzloff and Lone Star beer behind it. We'll make T-shirts that say "I put a Lip-lock on a Longneck and Had a Kinky Experience – Texas Tour '89." What do you think?'

I didn't know which I found more unsavory – the name of the tour, or the slogan on the T-shirt. At least the numerals at the end of the whole megillah weren't ' '88.'

'We can do it, baby!' Cleve shouted in a slightly unnerving fashion. 'You and me against the world!'

'What about Helen Reddy?' I asked.

'She'll open for you,' he said.

'Cleve – '

'I'll get to work on it now. "The Kinky Experience." "The *Kinky* Experience." ' He said the phrase several more times, and each time his intonation became a little more frightening. At least, I thought, he hadn't reached that dangerous, terminally monstro-wigged condition where the patient unconsciously rhymes things all the time.

'Okay, Cleve. Good luck. Stay in touch.'

'You won't regret it, Kinkster,' he said, with a desperate quality in his voice that made me almost certain that I would. I started to cradle the blower, but Cleve, apparently, had more to tell me.

'Mickey says it's time to go. Give a little pat to the cat – hat – rat.'

55

I stayed in all that weekend, but it wasn't quite as monastic an experience as it sounds. Saturday night I went dancing. You don't always have to go out to go dancing. Sometimes you can just go up.

That's what I did.

I walked up one flight of stairs, knocked on a door, and there stood Winnie Katz looking receptive, radiant, and ravishing. If heterosexuality was an accident, I felt like I'd just been T-boned by the *Sunset Limited*. How Winnie felt, of course, I couldn't say. But she did smile when she told me to park my cigar at the door.

It wasn't quite as sperm of the moment as it sounds. That morning Winnie'd been coming into the building with one of her girls and I'd been walking out carrying about four tons of cat shit in a large plastic tray. It was not an especially romantic encounter, I remember thinking at the time, but romance is so often not what we think it is, who can ever tell? The net result was that I dumped a grotesquely large amount of cat litter in the dumpster but did not return to the loft empty-handed. Winnie'd said if I had nothing to do I should drop by later that night. That was how I happened to be parking my cigar at the door of a lovely lesbian's loft, the occupant, now standing to one side, staring at me with an almost scientific curiosity, as if I were a rare specimen of a vanishing breed of colorful tropical fish that only thrived in some distant

lagoon in Borneo. There were other fish in Borneo, I thought –
bigger and more dangerous fish – but why let them ruin a
pleasant, platonic Saturday night?

I crossed the threshold.

None of Winnie's girls were there. Only one girl. And that was
Winnie. She took my hand and showed me around the place. Soft
music was playing from somewhere. We had the whole dance
studio to ourselves, like Adam and Eve in the Garden of Eden
trying to make up their minds whether the fruit was forbidden or
merely tedious. The lights were suggestively low.

'Do you dance?' she asked.

'No,' I said, 'but I know Tommy Tune.'

'He's not gonna help you much tonight, but I will.'

What followed, a dance lesson of sorts, began rather awkwardly
and asexually, yet ended in a moist and dreamy embrace. Many
thoughts ran through my mind. The last time I'd been up to Winnie's loft I'd had to step over a dead Colombian. This time, I
reflected, I might've had to step over something even stranger. I
didn't know what it said about a man to be so attracted to a
lesbian, but there wasn't time for me to call Dr Charles Ansell and
ask.

I kissed her tentatively at first, like a guy somewhere in Alabama making love for the first time with his cousin. I caught a look
at her eyes before she closed them. They were as big as Susan B.
Anthony silver dollars. Then we kissed more passionately.

'You're the first person,' she said, 'who's made my knees trem-
ble since I was twelve years old.' It was very flattering.

We drifted over to a bedroom and sat down on a tofu mattress.
It looked like the same one I'd killed a Colombian on the year
before. That was about the most comfortable thing you could do
on a tofu mattress. He was the only man I'd ever killed in my life,
and I was pleasantly surprised to find how little sleep I was losing
over it. Of course, I didn't *sleep* on a tofu mattress. It had been
self-defense, but that wouldn't have made too much difference
anyway. As I've often pointed out, you have to kill two people in
New York before anybody notices.

On an old black-and-white TV set in the corner Humphrey

Bogart was talking to Ingrid Bergman. Winnie went over to the set and turned the volume up a little. Then she came back and sat down next to me on the tofu mattress, taking my hand and holding it in her lap. She looked at me and smiled a smile that was almost heartbreaking in its innocence. Then her eyes drifted back to the flickering image of Humphrey Bogart smoking a cigarette.

'I've never seen this before,' she said. 'Is it *Casablanca*?'

56

It was two nights after I'd become the first person Winnie Katz had ever seen *Casablanca* with that I got another mysterious phone call from a kraut. I could tell by the way he rolled his *r*'s when he said the words 'Herr Friedman.' It was hard to determine if it was the same guy who'd called to tell me Ratso was dead. All Orientals look the same to you, all krauts sound the same to me.

To make a long and rather painful story short, the guy claimed to have information concerning the whereabouts of John Morgan. This, of course, I doubted. The guy wanted to meet me that night at a certain place and time I won't bother you with, to give me the information. This, of course, I suspected to be a trap.

The 88 organization, or whatever it was called, if it existed at all, had to comprise a small group of rather geriatric bad sports who refused to admit that they'd lost the war. No doubt they had the funds to recruit the occasional young skinhead or neo-Nazi lunatic along the way, but their hopes for taking over the world could probably be postmarked Fat Chance, Arkansas. This did not mean, however, that they would hesitate to kill a few more people in the glorious, mindless pursuit of their lost and hopeless cause.

I did not wish to become one of those people. I wanted to live another day so I could argue with Ratso. But it was a chance I had to take.

I noted the time and place of the assignation, told the kraut voice I'd be there, and cradled the blower. Then I called Rambam, Boris, and Sergeant Cooperman, told them each about the mysterious call (Cooperman was the least happy with this information), gave them the details of time and place, and cradled the blower three more times. I took a few cigars for the road, grabbed my hat and coat, and left the cat in charge.

Then I went to the place and waited for the time.

Time passes rather slowly when you're waiting for a mysterious kraut who you feel almost certain is not going to show up, but who you know, if he does, is going to try to kill you.

I can't say nothing happened. I'm sure, while we waited, many things did. Generations of Italian immigrants arrived on our shores, worked their way through life in the inner city, and moved out to the suburbs. A child playing with a paper boat in a gutter probably had time to grow up to be Lord Jim. Somewhere in New York a guy got a table in a restaurant.

Down the block in the gloom I was barely able to make out the shape of a car parked on the side of the street. This I took to be Cooperman, but I suppose it could've been Rambam or Boris as well. It never moved, and I couldn't tell if anyone was in it. Whoever it was, he was doing a pretty fair impersonation of a parked car.

It was a cold, foggy night, drizzling on and off. A good night to kill someone, as they go. Once I thought I saw a shadow moving along the side of a nearby building. Another time I heard hoarse shouting that sounded like it might've been in Russian. It wasn't guttural enough to be German, and it didn't much sound like the kind of English you'd hear in Texas. I crouched down and listened intently for a while until I realized it was two cab drivers yelling at each other.

A few people walked rather close to where I was standing, but if one of them was a Nazi he kept it pretty much to himself. Besides, the party I was looking for was not a three-hundred-pound woman, a man with a turban, or the young Negro who had just passed by with his shoelaces untied, his hat on sideways, and a handful of gold watches. Racists came in all sizes and colors, I thought, but you could count on Nazis at least to always be white.

After standing in the cold for what seemed like an eternity but was probably only a little under an hour and a half, Rambam stepped out of the darkness, waved, and shouted that he'd see me back at Vandam. Then the lights on the parked car came on, and it rolled up the street in my direction. When it came to a stop, I could see Cooperman and Fox in the car. Cooperman waved me over to the sidewalk. I lit a cigar and walked over to the car just as Cooperman chucked the butt of a dead Gauloise onto the curb. Fox's face was sneering like a cheerful Halloween mask.

'Sorry, fellas,' I said, as I rubbed my hands together in the cold. 'False alarm.'

Cooperman pushed his hat back on his head and rubbed his forehead with his hand in a gesture of frustration. He lit another Gauloise.

'Tex,' he said in a tired and world-weary voice, 'a wise man once said, "When baiting a trap with cheese, always leave enough room for the mouse." '

57

I didn't own a mouse but I had a cat, and the cat was sitting on my lap when Rambam came through the door of the loft later that night with the puppet head in his hand.

'Nice domestic scene,' he said.

'Don't rub it in.'

'You feelin' all right?'

'What are you, a doctor?'

Rambam shot me a strange look, and if I hadn't known better I would've thought there was pity in his eyes. He set his black knapsack down on the couch, mentioned some errands he had to run, and headed for the door.

'I'll be back to check on you later,' he said.

'We'll be here.'

When Rambam had left I checked my travel alarm clock on the desk and noticed that it was pushing midnight. For some reason the loft seemed strangely empty and vulnerable now. Maybe the cat was just a cat. Maybe I was alone.

Suddenly, I felt nuts, paranoid, inordinately out of line with the other ducks. Strange thoughts came into my mind. How well did I really know Washington Ratso? What if someone had blown up his car for an altogether different reason, totally unrelated to me? And what about the gas leak and the two mysterious kraut phone calls? If these weren't the work of some far-flung member of 88, there was only one other possibility. And I didn't think I liked it at all.

Clearly, either the pieces of the John Morgan puzzle would have to come together soon, or I was in great danger of going to pieces myself. I looked at the phones. Whom could I call? Dr Bock? Dr Ansell? Dr Ruth? I would've gotten up to get a shot of whatever snake piss happened to be around, but I didn't want to disturb the cat.

Not that I wasn't already somewhat disturbed myself. But people who love cats learn to think of the cat first and themselves second. Albert Schweitzer, who was left-handed, had a cat who always liked to sleep on his left arm. This forced Schweitzer to write much of his diary and many of his prescriptions with his right hand, which is why they remain almost illegible to this day. There is also a well-known story about Muhammad waking up at dawn to go to mosque and finding his cat sound asleep on the sleeve of his robe. Because of faulty record-keeping in those days, we do not know if it was his left sleeve or his right sleeve. All we know is that he took out his knife, cut the sleeve off his robe, and slipped out of it without awakening the cat. Possibly some of the other Arabs kidded him that morning at mosque about the appearance of his robe, but guys like Muhammad and Jesus were never very big in their sartorial area anyway. Of course, Ratso wasn't much in his sartorial area, and he hated cats. But Jesus loved cats. But then Jesus loved everybody. What did that prove?

This is the way the mind of a detective works, I thought. This is the way he sorts things out.

Then there was Winston Churchill's cat, Jock. During most of his later adult life Churchill refused to eat until Jock was seated at the table, and would not sleep until Jock was in bed with him. Maybe I was only a *little* out of line with the other ducks.

The phones rang.

The cat twitched an ear, and I reached across for the blower on the left.

It was Ratso.

'So aside from carrying on an affair with a lesbian, having an agent who's booking you out of a mental hospital, and refusing to tell me what the grasshopper game is, what else is going on?' he asked.

It's hard to keep a secret in New York.

I smoked a cigar, stroked the cat, and had a long and oddly comforting talk with Ratso. We discussed everything from Hitler to hockey and back to Hitler again. We talked about some of the cases we'd solved together in the past, some of the exciting times we'd had, some of the close calls. For a moment it almost felt like it was all over. Ratso and I were o-l-d, sitting on the porch of some bungalow in the Shalom Retirement Village, resting up between shuffle-board games.

This sensation, fortunately, did not linger long. The conversation hit a jarring note when Ratso told me that Carmen had told him unequivocally that no one in her family had ever been an alcoholic. I said, 'That fits.' Ratso said, 'What fits?' I said, 'I can't tell you yet.' Ratso said something that was quite unprintable.

'I'll let you know soon,' I said.

'Promise?'

'As my friend Fred Katz says, "My word of honor as a furrier." '

We hung up in our normal state of rancor.

I got up, which greatly irritated the cat – who probably didn't realize that I couldn't go on sitting there for the rest of my life – went into the bedroom, got out of my clothes, and put on my sarong and my T-shirt with the picture of Elvis shaking hands with President Nixon on the occasion of Elvis being made a drug-enforcement deputy. I may have played before a lot of empty seats in my life, I reflected, but I was doing better than either of them.

I didn't know when Rambam was coming back, and I wasn't going to wait up for him. Just before he'd left I'd given him an extra key so the puppet head and I could get some sleep. But, as I Indian-wrestled with Morpheus, I wondered what or who it was that John Morgan had stumbled upon that might've placed his life and mine in the danger I now believed us to be.

There was a big fish out there somewhere. It was deadly and it was deep. And it was lurking just beyond the shadowy waterline of my vision.

58

A train roars through the night and the fog. The cowboy stars stare with empty eyes into the lonely attic. Faces crowded together on the train. Eyes like black smudges against the black forest night.

A wall of a laboratory consisting of a solid mass of human eyeballs. A lampshade, upon close inspection, appears to be made of the stretched skin of human beings.

It's the kind of dream that is so close to reality that it doesn't make any sense at all.

Heaven can't hear this train. Railroad ties can't bind the hopeless wound it cuts in the world. This is the train that Frank and Jesse James cannot stop.

It runs like a silent screaming souvenir of evil that no one will save and few will remember. Only the cowboy stars who shudder against the wall as the wind sweeps the little attic.

The train stops at a station on the way to eternity. There is a debonair young man with shiny black boots and a space between his teeth. He is shouting a strange word in a strange tongue. The word sounds like '*Zwillinge! Zwillinge!*'

The children are walking away from the train in twos, like a little, human Noah's Ark.

A terrible page torn clean from the Old Testament and thrown to the wind.

Sometimes a songwriter has a dream in which he hears the words and the music and he knows, even though he's dreaming, that they've come together right. When he wakes up, the first thing he does is rush for a pen and paper to get it all down just like it was in the dream. He acts with great intensity, because he knows from experience that sometimes it's still there and sometimes it's gone.

The sensation I felt was an equal mixture of exhilaration and frustration. I had it and I didn't want to lose it. It had to do with 'the greatest genius the world has ever known.' It had to do with Morgan's pictures of the old man in the jungle and the young man with shiny black boots at the train, both of whom had a space between their teeth. It had to do with the vision of the two little native boys with blue eyes I saw in my delirium when I was receiving the tattoo that I now hoped to God would protect my soul.

Suddenly, it all came together very vividly. The music in the dream was of a heavily Dopplered, distorted, Wagnerian, country-rock flavor. It did not sound like it would cross over. The lyrics were sort of a subliminal rap of all the evil murmurings in the world.

Crazy as dreams can sometimes be, I knew in my heart that this one would still be true when I opened my eyes. I knew where the big fish was. Not only that, I knew his name.

But a new sensation was now rolling over me like waves of terror. I felt or saw or somehow sensed a presence in the room near the bed. A man in a peaked cap. For a moment I thought that a doorman from the Helmsley Palace had wandered into my bedroom.

Another wave of terror crashed into the dream. Now I was looking through the eyes of the brilliant, hard-living journalist Piers Akerman. Piers had been born in New Guinea, and what I was now experiencing seemed to have a very primitive, cannibalistic ambience about it. Ambience is only important in two places: dreams and restaurants. If this was a dream, it was becoming almost as unpleasant as what passes for reality. If it was a restaurant, it was time to tell the waiter to eighty-six the raspberry sorbet and drop the hatchet.

But it was not a restaurant, and it was apparently not entirely a dream. I was Piers Akerman and I was floating somewhere out to sea in a big storm. The vessel that was carrying me looked and felt uncomfortably like McGovern's couch.

An Irish buttocks the size of a Liberian-registered tanker seemed to loom over me like the long-forgotten playground shadow of a childhood bully. I was not Piers Akerman. I was myself. I was in great danger.

I opened my eyes.

Someone was indeed standing there. It took a second or two for my dream-frazzled orbs to adjust to the gloomy room. Then I saw who it was.

It was not McGovern.

It was Wilhelm Stengal.

59

I felt like I'd just gotten a wake-up call in hell. Maybe I *was* in hell, because Stengal, I knew, was dead: he even looked a little dead. Like death lightly microwaved. And if I wasn't in hell, what was Stengal doing in New York?

Of course, normally I did not think of hell as a geographic place. But fear is a funny thing. Sometimes it'll make a Catholic schoolchild out of you. For about sixteen seconds there it had me reaching for my rosary.

Then logic kicked in.

Like Descartes, I deduced something very basic. There is an elderly Nazi standing in my bedroom, therefore I am.

I took a closer look at Stengal's hat. It was better than looking at his face. There was a silver skull-and-crossbones on the front of the hat. I remembered vaguely that I'd seen hats with emblems such as this in old World War II movies on late-night television. They were worn by some kind of SS death-squad guys. But the war was over. Almost fifty years had passed. It seemed incredible that so much had happened in the world since then and that so little had changed inside Willhelm Stengal's head.

Suspended between the dark cap and a black shirt was a face that I now gazed upon with something near to amazement. It was shocking in appearance. It looked like a cold, wrinkled mask of white, withering, genocidal hatred.

Then he smiled.

It was charming in a rather diseased way, but the longer you looked at that smile, the more horrific it became. Many years ago it might've won over a *Fräulein* or two, but now it was only the wax lips of an old man forever smiling when the obvious intent was a rather sinister sneer. That, or the whole world was upside down. One possibility was about as likely as the other.

Against the black of his shirt was a red armband with a black swastika set in a white background. Nice color scheme.

How Stengal had survived the fire storm on East Eighty-sixth Street, I did not know. Maybe the bunker had a secret emergency exit. Maybe Satan watched over child molesters and old Nazis. Possibly the bunker was fire-proofed. As Smokey the Bear always says, 'Never leave the site of a campfire until you're sure the crispy critter is fried just the way you like it.'

Stengal had the Luger out again, and this time I wasn't taking any bets against his chances of squeezing off a successful shot. His eyes were shining like moonlight on the Rhine. He loved his work. He was an old Nazi, and I was becoming rapidly resigned to the fact that I might never get to be an ancient Jewish person and move to the land of my people, Miami.

We watched each other's eyes, if not with trust, at least with understanding. It was almost as if we were savoring the moment. For we, along with John Robert Morgan, shared a monstrous secret.

A chill passed through the room encompassing both of us. It was too much power, too much history, too much responsibility for the mind of man to feel comfortable with. Stengal, like the other Nazis, I'm sure, felt he was 'not responsible.' Not responsible for trains, smoke, or children. Not responsible for man-made lime-laden valleys of death where countless thousands were buried together alive or almost alive. Not responsible for the Jews. Not responsible for the Gypsies. Not responsible for sailing a paper boat down a river of blood or watching the sun set over a hill of human hair.

Who *was* responsible? The Red Baron? Hansel and Gretel?

I could tell, looking into Stengal's eyes in the half-darkness, that he now felt responsible for something. He felt responsible for keeping the secret. I, I'm sure he knew, felt responsible for telling the secret to the world.

Neither of us probably knew exactly where John Morgan was. But we both knew one thing. John, while deep in the jungles of Borneo, had indeed stumbled upon a white tiger with blue eyes.

The secret was that the tiger walked on two legs.

60

I looked from the gun, to the swastika, to the skull-and-cross-bones, to the eyes. The eyes had it.

As I searched for a hint, even a glint, of humanity, I found them empty as an office building in Texas. They shone like a glass skyscraper in the winter sun, with that cold, brittle light that emanates from the Dallas of the soul.

As I watched, Stengal's eyes began to blink rapidly. As Ratso would say, not a good sign. He was blinking rapidly and I was thinking rapidly, and this went on for about seven years.

Then he reached his left hand over to steady his right wrist. Every muscle in my body tensed.

His face was as somber as an old German clock, and as he blinked, the wrinkles at the corners of his eyes seemed to tick away the seconds of my life. Then, suddenly, the nervous blinking stopped, and the old man's eyes opened wide as ovens.

'Heute, Deutschland,' he shouted, 'Morgen, die ganze Welt!'

'Hold the weddin', pal,' I said, in what I hoped was a soothing, rational voice. 'We're both after the same thing.' This, of course, was a fatuous lie. I didn't feel, however, it was the kind of thing that, if Stengal were to blow my brains out, Saint Peter would hold against me.

'Once we find Morgan,' I continued in an even tone, 'then we can settle our differences. As Ted Kennedy said, "We'll cross that bridge when we come to it." '

'Juden raus!' Stengal roared, waving the Luger wildly. 'Juden raus!'

I sensed that he wanted me to leave. I also sensed that he wasn't going to give me the chance. I didn't have my German-English dictionary by my bedside, so I was flying by Jewish radar in more ways than one. He seemed to be growing rather frighteningly irrational and agitated, which rarely bodes well for you when you're sitting third row center to a Luger.

'I'm not here alone,' I said. This was patently false, and we both knew it. I could almost hear my voice echo through the empty loft. I was trying to stall Stengal in the slim hope that Rambam might return in time to save my life for the fourth time this month. Maybe the Baby Jesus was trying to tell me something. But Rambam, I knew, when he went on an 'errand,' might not be back for a week.

'You won't get away with this, Stengal.' I was pulling out all the clichés, or, rather, fear was pulling them out of me. I knew the likelihood was that Stengal *would* get away with it, and Stengal, for his part, didn't seem to really give a damn.

They would find me, I suspected, many months later. The cat and I would probably be in rather advanced stages of decomposition. Maybe a Jehovah's Witness who was overly zealous would come to the door one day and smell us. 'Zealous' and 'smell us,' I thought to myself, made a rather nice rhyme scheme. I also realized that that was exactly the kind of nonsense that probably cluttered the minds of most men seconds before their deaths. It probably also cluttered the minds of the Clutter family. Well, there was nothing to do but think crazy thoughts. Any attempt at vocalization seemed only to rile Stengal, and that was certainly to be avoided.

It was funny, I reflected, but McGovern and I had set up the man-in-trouble hotline for precisely this purpose. So that if anything happened to us, a Jehovah's Witness who was zealous wouldn't come to the door and smell us. McGovern and I called each other on a fairly regular basis, opening the conversation with the acronym 'MIT . . . MIT . . . MIT.'

If you lived alone in a major city in North America, you needed the MIT hotline. In a fraction of a second I worked out what everybody else in my life would think if Stengal were to pull the trigger, then slip quietly out the fire escape. They would all, of course, get my answering machine. Ratso would assume, when I didn't return the call, that I was miffed about something. That would miff Ratso, and it'd be a while before he called again.

Decomposition would begin. Winnie would call, and when she didn't hear back from me, she'd assume I had a fear of intimacy or something. She'd harden her attitude toward men. Maybe after a few weeks she'd tell Dr Bock about it. Decomposition would continue. A sample call might be from my friend Sal Lorello, who ran a limo service out of Chappaqua, New York and who'd once acted as road manager for me when Cleve was busy listening to Hank Williams records. Sal might say, 'Okay, Kinky Man, I guess you're out raising hell tonight. Call me when you get in.' He might or might not say, '*Ciao*.' When I didn't call Sal back, he'd watch a few Giants games, meet a few new beautiful women, then, eventually, get around to checking back on me again. This time he'd say, 'Kinky Man! Where are you? Okay, you must be in Texas. I wish I was with you. Tell your dad and Marcie hello for me.' Decomposition would progress rather alarmingly. The lack of adequate heating in the loft might retard it somewhat, but you couldn't really count on something like that. Cooperman might even call just to rattle my cage. I kept no regular hours, so if he called me late at night he might just assume, as others would, that I was out on a tear. He might say something patronizing like, 'Tex? You keepin' your powder dry?' Decomposition.

Actually, by the time I saw Stengal's index finger tighten, I was almost looking forward to it. Decomposition was probably preferable to a lot of things. One of them was looking at Stengal's eyes.

Then the cat jumped on the bed.

Stengal shot an irritated glance at the cat, then took two steps closer. I reached out and patted the cat on the head. Stengal shifted the Luger to his left hand. It looked like he'd had about enough. He raised his right hand high in the air. I couldn't decide if it was absurd or terrifying, but it was clearly Stengal's final statement. A Nazi salute.

'*Sieg Heil!*' he shouted. '*Heil* Hitler!'

The cat looked at Stengal, then looked at me questioningly. One of the most difficult things we ever have to do in life is explain a Nazi salute to a cat. I figured I'd wait until she got a little older.

I wondered very fleetingly what the girl in the peach-colored dress would say when she called my answering machine. Stengal shifted the Luger back to his right hand, steadied his wrist, and took aim.

Just as Rambam roared through the door and hit him like the Rockaway shuttle, he pulled the trigger.

61

I figured it was about time I got out of bed. The cat was nowhere to be seen. There wasn't a hell of a lot to be seen, in fact, as I stumbled through the gloom and made a determined effort to find the light switch. I could hear Rambam and Stengal struggling somewhere on the floor between the far side of the bed and the wall. The acrid smell of the gun shot in the small room was powerful enough for even my beezer to pick up on. Just as I hit the lights, a second shot rang out.

I looked across the room, but my vision was obscured briefly by the bed. Then Rambam stood up with the Luger in his hand and something approaching a little Charles Whitman smile twitching on his lips.

I walked across the room on tiptoe for some reason, remembering as I did that that was the curious way John Morgan often walked. I stood at the foot of the bed and peered over the far side of it. Stengal's waxen face was just visible. One eye was gone. Well, it wasn't really gone. It was somewhere deep in the base of his skull looking around like a child in the Black Forest at the dark and twisted branches that extended through his gray matter department. I couldn't be sure what, if anything, Stengal himself was seeing, but one look at his body was enough for me. I was as close as I ever wanted to literally finding a Nazi under my bed.

Rambam, however, was excited by something. He motioned me to come closer, then lifted Stengal's left arm to reveal a tear in his shirt that had been incurred during the struggle.

'See that jagged scar under his armpit?'

'Yeah,' I said in a thick voice. It isn't everybody, at four o'clock in the morning, who gets to see a scar under a Nazi's armpit.

'That's where SS men always tattooed their blood-types. After the war, they often had the tattoos removed, sometimes somewhat clumsily, to hide their identity. It was in case they were wounded in battle. Helped the doctors in giving them transfusions. Too bad Stengal removed his tattoo. Maybe we could've helped him.'

Rambam smiled.

I walked into the other room, poured two double shots out of a new bottle of Jack Daniel's, downed one of them, found a cigar, lit it, refilled my bull's horn, and waited for Rambam to come out of the killing fields.

Moments later he came in, pitched the Luger onto the kitchen table, and lifted his glass.

'Here's to the occupants of Muranowska Seven,' he said.

'Here's to the Chicago Seven.'

'Very funny. Muranowska Seven was the address of the command bunker at the Warsaw Ghetto.'

'A fairly obscure toast, but I'll drink to it.'

'*L'chaim*.'

We killed the shots, and I paced back and forth a little in the kitchen, smoking the cigar and figuring out what the hell to do next. It was an unusual American, I thought, who could make a toast 'to life' only moments after splicing a man, even if the stiff was a Nazi. But then, who among us is without his little foibles and inconsistencies?

'Glossing over the fact,' I said, 'that you saved my life, what purpose did it serve to kill the old bastard? He might've been holding back some information on Morgan. Maybe the authorities would've wanted to talk to him. You didn't have to ice the geek.'

'The gun went off in the struggle,' Rambam said with an amiable grin. 'That's my story, and I'm sticking to it.'

'Of course, I have to call Cooperman,' I said. The thought was not a particularly pleasant one, but it was nicer than the notion of hiding a Nazi under your bed during the advanced stages of decomposition.

'You could make German sausage out of him,' said Rambam as he poured himself another shot. 'Keep him in the freezer along with your five-alarm Lone Star Cafe chili.'

'No, I don't think so. There's two occupational groups that I never wish to see in action: politicians and sausage-stuffers.'

Rambam thought about it for a moment and shrugged his shoulders. 'Hell of an idea,' he said.

I walked over to the kitchen window and opened it a couple of inches to let in some air but not far enough for the cat to fall out. People say cats won't fall out of windows, and if they do they always land on their feet. If that's what you think, you ought to talk to Joel Siegel. His cat took a nosedive off the sixteenth floor onto Riverside Drive. The results were not pleasant.

I walked back over to the desk and called Cooperman.

'This better be fucking good, Tex,' he said.

'Not to worry.'

When I cradled the blower, I checked the clock and walked back into the kitchen area of the loft. It was four-thirty of a chilly Tuesday morning in March of the year of our Lord 1989, if you followed the Gregorian Calendar. If you followed the Jewish Calendar, it was the month of Adar in the year 5750. Only a minor discrepancy in the dates. I'm sure they could work it out.

'Cooperman coming?' Rambam asked. I nodded. He was now seated at the kitchen table, upon which rested the cat and the Luger. Rambam picked up the Luger.

'Why don't you try playing Russian roulette with it?' I asked.

Rambam ignored me. He put down the Luger, walked over to the sink, washed his hands thoroughly with soap and hot water, dried them off, went back over to the table, and picked up the Luger again. He took out a handkerchief, walked back into the bedroom. The cat watched him disappear into the bedroom, then looked at me. I shrugged my shoulders.

I stoked up the espresso machine and put it in gear, and soon Rambam, the cat, and I were sitting around the kitchen table, Lugerless, sipping espresso and waiting for Cooperman. All except the cat, of course. The cat didn't like espresso. It's an acquired taste. Rambam was making loud mewing noises to the cat. The cat didn't much like that either.

'Well,' I said, 'isn't this nice?'

'The fucking Bobbsey Twins in the country,' said Rambam, as he sipped his espresso.

'I've got to call Ratso,' I said, a bit uncomfortably. 'I want him to tell Carmen for me.'

'Tell Carmen what?'

I looked over to the window. I could hear the sounds of a tire squealing against the curb and two car doors slamming.

'Tell Carmen that we've found her father,' I said.

62

Cooperman was not pleased. He tried to conceal his irritation, but I could tell.

'You don't fuckin' discriminate, do you, Tex?' he shouted from the bedroom.

I had the right to remain silent, and I did.

Cooperman came out into the living room. By now the loft was a hive of activity. Technicians were measuring the angle of the bullet in the headboard of my bed. Technicians were photographing the body. Technicians were dusting the Luger. I considered asking one of them to take a look at some of the problems I was having with my old black-and-white television set, but it was a little late for levity.

Fox and a burly party I'd never seen before were working over Rambam in a far corner of the loft. The discussion seemed to be throwing off a nice number of sparks. Fox was becoming more and more agitated. Rambam was coming up with a wide enough repertoire of hand gestures to have been directing traffic in Times Square. I couldn't tell if the influence was from the Jewish or the Italian side of the family, but as the conversation became more and more animated, it began to look like it might be the Italian.

A little after five in the morning Cooperman flew out of the bedroom like a large and extremely angry bee and started circling counterclockwise around my head. I was sitting at the kitchen table studying the leaves of my seventh espresso.

'Last year,' he snarled, 'we get a call to come over here and we extricate seven wasted Colombians. This time, we come over to your place and what do we find? A dead kraut!'

'I'm an equal-opportunity employer,' I said.

Cooperman had a few choice words, then left in the direction of the stiff trailing more steam than a train pulling out of Grand Central. Fox drifted by and helped himself to a cup of espresso. When he walked back past me, he was holding his cup like a demitasse in an exaggeratedly effeminate fashion.

'You must tell me where you get your coffee,' he said.

'When my lawyer gets here.'

'You know, Tex, I know how you feel,' Fox said with a razor-thin grin. 'I lost my favorite uncle in a concentration camp.'

'Sorry to hear it,' I said as I set fire to the end of a cigar.

'Yeah, poor ol' Uncle Max.' Fox took a sip of espresso, timing his delivery. 'He was makin' the rounds one afternoon when he dropped his swagger stick. Prisoner jumped up and choked him to death.' Fox chuckled like a rabid chipmunk.

'Sorry to hear it,' I said.

Fox chuckled again and went back over to Rambam. Cooperman came out of the bedroom, went over to the desk, made a phone call, walked over to where I was sitting, pulled out a chair, and sat down across the table from me. He took a Gauloise out of his pack and, with a thoughtful and almost conciliatory expression in his eyes, lit it slowly with his Zippo.

'I don't know, Tex, what you've got yourself into this time. What with the disappearing broad at the Pierre Hotel two weeks ago, the unsolved bombing of your friend's car in Washington, the mysterious fire at the brownstone on East Eighty-sixth Street, and this elderly skell showing up in his Halloween suit – you're gettin' into an area that ain't really my beat. Maybe you need Interpol or Mr Spock or somebody. I saved your ass at the Garden last year, but if this *ain't* a Halloween suit this stiff was wearin', I may not be able to always be around to hold your hand.'

Cooperman stood up, killed the Gauloise, gave a sign to Fox, lit another Gauloise, and looked at me with a kind of tough wistfulness through the smoke.

'I know you admire Nero Wolfe,' he said. 'But just remember,

Wolfe only arranged to have the *suspects* come to him. He didn't always have their goddamn dead *bodies* lying around his house.'

As if on cue, two guys began carrying what used to be Stengal through the living room. He was wrapped up so you couldn't see him, but you could feel an evil aura almost pulsate from the body bag as they passed between the desk and the kitchen table.

'Get him outta here,' Cooperman snarled, waving off the stiff like a guy passing on a hand of cards.

Not too much later, everyone else was gone, too. There were still things Cooperman wanted to talk to me and Rambam about, but that, apparently, was it for the night. It was a good thing too, because the sun was peeking in the window from the east.

I picked up the cat and carried her over to the couch, where both of us lay down to take a little power nap together. I didn't feel like walking all the way to the bedroom.

63

'Believe me, Ratso, Carmen's adoptive father was an SS man named Wilhelm Stengal. Probably since some time shortly after the war, he's been protecting a major Nazi fish who's been in hiding deep in the jungles of Borneo. No one would think to look there, and no one did until John Morgan, who was looking for him in South America, tumbled onto his true whereabouts.'

It was ten o'clock Tuesday morning, A.P.N. (After Power Nap), when I finally got around to the rather unpleasant chore of calling Ratso. The cat, a lit cigar in an ashtray, and a cup of hot chocolate with mini-marshmallows were arrayed before me, perfectly positioned in true Hercule Poirot style between the two red telephones.

I was downshifting from a fairly steady diet of espresso, which will burn your brain cells out at almost the rate of Peruvian marching powder but is, of course, cheaper. The hot chocolate always seemed to go well with a cigar, and it was a welcome change from the ground Colombian fast lane. It was like stopping to smell the flowers, if your beezer could smell the flowers. If it couldn't, you could practice tonguing the mini-marshmallows out of the hot chocolate. Never know when it might come in handy. I tongued a few mini-marshmallows and listened to Ratso's incredulous, rodentlike tones.

'That's abso-fucking-lutely ridiculous,' he said.

'Not when you consider that Stengal came to my loft last night and tried to kill me. Fortunately, Rambam walked in just at the time, and Stengal was killed. Gun went off in the struggle.' I was almost beginning to believe the last part. It was starting to have a nice ring to it.

'You're kidding.'

'I'm not kidding. Where's Carmen now?'

'She's still asleep.'

'Okay, then pull your lips together for a minute and I'll explain. Carmen and her father kind of had a relationship like Patty Hearst and that guy – what was his name? Bocephus?'

'Bocephus?'

'You know. The guy that was head of the SLA.'

'Oh, Cinque.'

'You're welcome. But you see, she lived in fear of him, but for a long time he was all she knew. Stengal – '

'Bocephus? Jesus Christ.'

'Stengal, according to Carmen, was an engineer from Europe, but what he really was, was a *chemical* engineer from Hitler's Germany, an SS man, and the keeper of a terrible secret that I will reveal to you at a later date. He knew about Zyklon-B derivatives, had a chemical lab set up in the basement of his brownstone, and he wasn't an alcoholic, so when Carmen told me she'd once heard her mother saying, "Stay away from me, Bill. Don't come near me when you smell that way," it either means he'd been working in a lab all day with extremely pungent chemicals and his wife was a kind of ball-busting, insensitive twit, or that he had a rather tertiary case of halitosis. Are you with me so far?'

'I read you, Bocephus.'

'Carmen's mother called him Bill, so it was Wilhelm to William, William to Will, Will to Bill, or something along that order. Add to this the fact that when Carmen talked to me at this loft she kept wanting me to find *him* not *them*. She'd forgotten that her father was supposed to be missing too, because actually he wasn't. I now believe the abduction at the Pierre was a setup that didn't quite come off, and I know she was involved in setting up the skinhead attack on me. She was the only one, other than you, who knew when I was coming, when I was going, and had the time to do it. You don't get five skinheads out of Central Casting that fast. The attack was prearranged, and when you and I left your apartment, she called somebody, probably Stengal, to tip him off. That's the only way it could've happened. I don't blame her. She was under Stengal's powerful influence since she was a small girl. Adopting a Jewish child, keeping her original name, and turning her to his own purposes probably appealed to Stengal's perversity. Also it provided good cover for him.

'When you tell her about Stengal's death, break it to her gently, Ratso. I still want to talk to her about Morgan. Let's have dinner tomorrow night at the Derby. Bring Carmen if she wants to come. I'll fill you in on the rest of it.'

'Okay,' said Ratso. 'I'll wake her now.' His voice sounded different, like all at once he was immeasurably older.

I hung up the blower, patted the cat, took a sip of hot chocolate, leaned back in the chair, and puffed the cigar, and suddenly I felt very sorry for Ratso.

64

I had lunch at an all-day dim sum place in Chinatown with Mike Simmons, who was on the wagon again and therefore a rather stultifying luncheon companion. For all I know, he probably thought the same of me. Gone were the golden days of innocence and truth when Mike would vomit on the head of the woman at the next table and I would threaten to stick my fork in the waitress's eye. My excuse was that I only had chopsticks. Simmons's excuse was that it was no fun to go around walking on your knuckles in southern California, where he was now spending most of his time, because everybody did there. He proceeded to give me many reasons why he did not like southern California and why he missed New York. I empathized.

It is a fact of life today that New Yorkers are fast moving out of New York to live in other parts of the country, and, upon arrival in Buttocks, Texas, or Plymouth Rock, or wherever they wind up, they never stop bitching about the absence of things that they never gave a damn about when they lived in New York. While this does not endear them to the locals, it does make people begin to wonder what they might be missing by living in Buttocks, Texas. So they try to accommodate. The result is that today you can get a bagel in Texas, but you can't really get a *bagel* in Texas.

There is very little danger of the rest of the country becoming more like New York or New York becoming more like the rest of the country. That would be terrible. Soon someone would come up to you on a street in Manhattan and say, 'Have a nice day,' before they mugged you.

But the main result of this migration of New Yorkers is that people in small towns and communities throughout mid-America are becoming ever-so-slowly aware of attitudes, values, and a unique cultural upbringing that probably is totally foreign to their own. Their growth and enlightenment is interesting to note. Now we can all sit back and wait for the fifties to catch up with them.

Unfortunately, the eighties had caught up with me, and they were doing a pretty good job of pulling my coattails. Somewhere between the dream I'd had the night before and my waking up staring into the barrel of Stengal's Luger, I'd known there was a call I had to make. It was already a lifetime too late, so I didn't figure a few more hours were going to make a hell of a lot of difference. Nevertheless, as soon as I got back to the loft, I sat down at the desk and picked up the blower.

My brother, Roger, who works in our nation's capital, had once given me the name of a friend who held a high-level position in the Justice Department. His name was Nathan Gabriel, and he was involved with the Office of Special Investigations. I dialed Information and got the number. I extracted a cigar from Sherlock Holmes's head, lopped the end off in the guillotine, set fire to it with a kitchen match, took a healthy puff, and called Gabriel.

'This is not a secure line,' was the first thing he told me after he identified himself.

I told Gabriel, outlandish as it may have seemed, what I believed to be the truth.

'Very unlikely,' he said. 'I've been to Brazil and seen the dental X rays and other evidence two years ago. The root-canal work he had done shortly before he died. His personal diary written in his own hand. Of course, we have had and continue to have some terrific sightings. He's been seen playing in a marimba band in Las Vegas. He's been seen dealing cards in Atlantic City. He's been spotted on the staff of several major hospitals in New York and Philadelphia. But frankly, he's dead.'

It took some time, but I gave Gabriel everything I had. All the personal, firsthand evidence, unusual as it was, to bolster my strong belief that he was wrong. When I finished, there was a long, reflective pause on his end of the line. When he spoke again, there was a different tone in his voice.

'What you say is very interesting. I don't know what we can do about it, but there are those who might wish to take action. I'll see that the information is passed on to the Israelis, the West Germans, and the Simon Wiesenthal Institute in Vienna.

'Of course, you are not alone in your view that he's still alive. There are thousands of people in a group they call "the Candles" who believe him to be such a clever fiend as to be quite capable of fabricating his own death. The group is also known sometimes as the "*Zwillinge* Organization." '

I almost dropped my cigar. It was the word I'd heard in my dream.

'*Zwillinge*,' I said. 'What does that word mean?'

'*Zwillinge*?' said Nathan Gabriel. '*Zwillinge* is the German word for "twins." '

65

At around nine-thirty on Wednesday night, I was sitting at the bar in the Derby Restaurant chatting it up with a very skinny woman with convex breasts who was about nine feet three inches tall. I was drinking a Carta Blanca and smoking a Romeo y Julieta cigar that said 'Habana' on it and had been sent to me from Switzerland by a lady named Rocky. Andrew's son, also very inventively named Andrew, was behind the bar serving the skinny broad a large number of straight shots of a thick yellow fluid that I hoped wasn't Galliano.

'This was Churchill's favorite cigar and Travis McGee's favorite beer,' I said.

'Who's Churchill?' she wanted to know.

I was watching the door for Ratso, but so far I hadn't had any terrific sightings, as Nathan Gabriel would say. I turned back to the woman.

'He's a high school in upstate New York,' I said.

'Who's Travis McGee?' she wanted to know. I was beginning to get a little worried about Ratso.

'Look it up when you get home,' I said. She downed the shot, and Andrew was rather hesitantly pouring her another one when Ratso walked in wearing slacks and a sport coat almost identical to the color of the fluid she was drinking. He looked like a slightly overstuffed canary who'd been eaten by the cat and lived to tell about it. He again had on the coonskin cap with the tail on it and with the little face affixed to the front. He signaled to me and walked directly to a booth in the front of the place. He was noticeably without Carmen. I wasn't greatly surprised.

As I got up to join Ratso at the table, the lady at the bar stood up, knocked back the shot in front of her, turned around, and looked down on me like I was a low-flying snail-darter.

'Who're you?' she wanted to know.

'I own this restaurant,' I said.

I joined Ratso at the little booth, and it didn't take long for me to realize that he was going to be about as much fun as the lady at the bar.

'She's gone,' he said.

'Carmen?'

'Who the fuck do you think?'

I motioned the waiter over and ordered a couple of stiff ones. When they arrived, we killed them in silence and ordered two more. The waiter was an older gentleman whom a former girlfriend had once told me had the nicest face she'd ever seen in her life. She'd never liked mine too much, of course, but that's the way it goes. I was better off without her, anyway. She was pretty neurotic. Whenever I'd offered her a piece of gum, she'd always asked for the second one from the top. She didn't want to take a piece that might have some 'pocket juice' on it. I was blinded by love at the time, so I thought this was cute. I'd told Ratso about it once, however, and he'd said it was the most disgusting thing he'd ever heard in his life. Looking at the waiter's face as he brought the second round, I reflected that love may be grand and love may be blind, but the fear of getting pocket juice on a piece of wrapped gum should never be categorized as attractive behavior.

We ordered the meal, worked more slowly on the second round of drinks, and looked at each other. There was nothing I could really say to Ratso that would help. There are some things you never get over. You just get above.

'Face it, Rats, she was engaged to Morgan, sleeping with you, and coming on to me when it suited her. She wasn't very loyal to you or to John, and when Stengal got liquidated, she just bolted. There was nothing else she wanted here.'

'I know,' said Ratso.

'As my friend Alden Shuman says, "She was one of those women who will stick with you through thick." '

'I know,' said Ratso. I could see that he didn't, but who the hell was I to talk? I'd gone around for five years thinking 'pocket juice' was cute.

When the meal arrived, Ratso brightened somewhat, even to the point of asking me again what the grasshopper game was, and who was the big fish I'd been making veiled references to recently. I told him I'd discuss it with him after the meal.

It was Nero Wolfe's dictum never to discuss business during a meal, and besides, the big fish being who he was, I did not wish to discuss him while eating the Catch of the Day.

'It was the gap between his teeth that first put me on to him. The photographs that Morgan sent Carmen. One of them was of an old man in the jungle with a panama hat and a gap between his two front teeth. The skinheads later stole the photographs, but, like the gap in the Watergate tapes, the absence of something is sometimes more telling than its presence. I've done a little checking up, and it was one of the best-known features of the man.'

The waiter had cleared the dinner plates, and Ratso and I were drinking coffee and sipping sambuca. Ratso also was busy attacking a piece of the Derby's dessert speciality, walnut-apple-pecan cake, which was roughly the size of his hat.

'In connection with that photograph, you'll remember, was a rather cryptic comment from Morgan to Carmen: "Dr Breitenbach, I presume." That checks out as one of the four or five regular aliases he used. I've already told you, I believe, how and why I place the suspect in Borneo – Morgan's Land Rover being driven on the left-hand side of the jungle highway.

'What I think happened was this. Morgan was in South America, probably already on the trail of the suspect – remember the photo Carmen found in his apartment of the gap-toothed man?

'Morgan, like the pro that he was, ran into this Peace Corps volunteer down there, a guy named John Morgan from Cleveland, Ohio. The guy I know as John Morgan got hold of the Peace Corps kid's passport, identification papers, and even old photos of his parents, had them copied and maybe doctored a bit, and picked up what's known as a "floating identity" he could use for himself. When the suspect fled to Borneo – he might've gone back and forth many times – Morgan wasn't far behind. That's where I met Morgan, naturally assuming he was who he said he was.'

'This is all very circumstantial,' Ratso said between large chompings of walnut-apple-pecan cake. 'There are probably lots of old men hanging out in weird places with panama hats and gaps between their two front teeth. Where does it all lead?'

'Well, it didn't lead anywhere for a long time. The big fish was lurking at the very bottom of a very deep pool. All I could see was his shadow in the water. Then I started putting together some things that some people had told me. My friend Dylan's account of his malarial attack in the *ulu* when he was trying to run down the legend of the white tiger with the blue eyes. After seeing the tiger – obviously a malarial hallucination of some kind – he passed out. Upon awakening, he was surrounded by a group of native men, who, if he hadn't known better, he said, had looked at him and given him a Nazi salute. Of course, later Dylan wrote this off as a fevered vision just like the sighting of the tiger. The tiger might've been only in his mind, but the native men giving him the Nazi salute was for real.

'I ask you, Ratso, where did those Kenyah tribesmen learn a Nazi salute?'

'Maybe they watched late-night movies like the rest of us.'

'I'm afraid they don't have Manhattan Cable in Borneo. In fact, no television at all, no VCR, no stereos, no McDonald's.'

'That *is* primitive.'

'I'll tell you where they learned a Nazi salute. Like the Kayans learned "Waltzing Matilda" from Aussie paratroopers. Like the Ibans learned to cut their hair, throw away their beads, and sing "Oh, Susanna" from moronic missionaries from West Memphis, Arkansas. The Kenyahs learned a Nazi salute from a Nazi. The Japanese were in Borneo during the war. Many of their skulls still decorate the *ruai* of longhouses. But there were no Germans there during the war.'

'So this tribe – what are they, the Ubangis -?'

'The Kenyahs.'

'The Kenyahs,' said Ratso thoughtfully. 'They learned a Nazi salute from a real Nazi in the years after the war.'

'That's correct, Watson.'

'Interesting.'

'Add to that that John Morgan would've never used the phrase "anthropological land bridge," as Dylan asserts that he did when Dylan told him the story of the white tiger and the Nazi salute. Morgan didn't know any anthropology. And he wouldn't go to the headwaters of the Ulu Ayer unless there was damn good reason. And he had one. Find the guy who taught a gentle, primitive tribe, isolated for centuries from the outside world, the Nazi salute.'

'So far, so good.'

'In a manner of speaking. Now we know we have a Nazi in Borneo after the war. How do we determine his identity? We have

145

the very telling gap-tooth business and the name Dr Breitenbach. Add to that Stengal's remark to me that he was protecting "the greatest genius the world has ever known." '

'He was protecting Spinoza?'

'Not quite, Watson. Remember when Rambam bugged Dr Bock's office? We were in the loft listening to my voice speaking under hypnosis, recounting the time, deep in the *ulu*, when I was getting a Kayan tattoo. Morgan was there, too, by the way, and probably not by accident. Anyway, remember the two small native boys I saw who appeared to be identical and had those startling blue eyes? They were twins, Ratso. *Twins*. What does that bring to mind?'

Ratso stared at me in mute horror. A large piece of walnut-apple-pecan cake that had been balancing rather precariously upon his fork fell off and made a three-coffee-bean landing in the middle of his glass of sambuca.

'In Auschwitz and in all of miscreation there was only one fiend whose speciality was experimenting upon twins. Though "experimenting" is far too kind a word to use.'

'So is "fiend",' said Ratso.

I watched as his eyes took on an horrific understanding like a cold dawn over a parking lot that used to be the world.

'That's right, pal,' I said. 'The man Morgan was after was Dr Josef Mengele.'

66

'Too bad they don't serve German chocolate cake here,' I said as the waiter brought Ratso a fresh sambuca. Ratso still hadn't said a word. He was just sitting there and slowly shaking his head.

'Abbie Hoffman,' I continued, 'once gave me a great recipe for German chocolate cake. The first step is, you occupy the kitchen.'

Ratso chuckled a small chuckle, took a swallow of sambuca, and looked at me with a genuine fondness in his eyes.

'And it's just crazy enough to be true,' he said. 'You *are* amazing, Sherlock.'

'You say that to all the guys.'

'I guess something's being done about Mengele.'

'Everything that's possible,' I said, 'which, I'm afraid, isn't much.'

The waiter brought the check.

'Now tell me,' said Ratso, 'what the hell's the meaning of the grasshopper game?'

I chewed a coffee bean slowly and considered his question. I chased it down with the last of the sambuca. I looked at Ratso's gentle, intelligent eyes.

'I'd rather leave you, my dear Watson,' I said, 'with at least one mystery in your life.'

Ratso got up abruptly, put on his coat, and walked to the door. At the door he turned to face me.

'I'd rather leave you, Sherlock,' he said, 'with the check.'

67

Two days later, on a windy, rain-streaked Friday afternoon, I got a package in the mail from Wolf Nachman's office. I don't trust packages from lawyer's offices, so I opened it rather gingerly. Inside was Stengal's ceremonial dagger. The one that said *'Blut und Ehre.'* Also inside was a bill from Nachman that was so monstrous it was going to require more blood and honor than I had to pay.

I gave the dagger to John Rapp that evening at a Thai restaurant on Eighth Avenue and Twenty-second Street that he claimed was the best in the city. As well as being an expert on matters of a Teutonic nature, he was also a prominent authority on Thai food. That's what we call eclectic.

John assured me that the SS dagger would be the centerpiece of his collection and he'd place it squarely between the World War I pointed hat, which is always better than a pointed head, and the 1944 Luftwaffe toilet-paper holder.

I did not tell Rapp that if you viewed his little collection from left to right, it would make, in many ways, a fairly accurate representation of the spiritual development of the German people.

There were a few more little problems that nagged at me that weekend, but after what I'd been through, they were nothing I couldn't deal with. The first was an irate phone call from McGovern, which I handled horizontally at 9.02 on Saturday morning.

'Who is this Peace Corps fuckhead who keeps calling me about some story I was supposed to write about John Morgan?'

'McGovern,' I said rather groggily, 'many thousands of young Americans served their country in the Peace Corps. I was only one of these idealistic young people. What makes you think I know anything about this matter?'

'Because I see a fine Jewish hand at work here,' McGovern sputtered. 'Last month you come over to my place to enlist my support in locating your old Peace Corps buddy John Morgan. I pitched in. I got you the obit from the Cleveland paper. I got you that coroner's report from my press contacts in New Jersey.'

'Okay, McGovern, so I used your name in vain so I could get some information from the Peace Corps in Washington.'

'That's the thanks I get for being your fucking leg man. Now the guy's hounding me and my editors every day to find out when the John Morgan story hits.'

'You've got to admit,' I said, 'it'd make an interesting piece.'

McGovern said something that was pretty unpleasant to hear at any hour of the day, and told me, in precise Irish terms, that it'd be to my advantage to call the guy off. I said I would.

Of course, I didn't. That was because I never really liked to talk to Norman Potts twice in the same twenty years. I figured either Potts would eventually wise up and stop harassing McGovern, or that sooner or later McGovern would cave and do a story on Morgan. He'd certainly covered more sordid stories than this. Where was his enterprising journalistic spirit? What would H. L. Mencken say? Probably not much, I thought. He'd been dead for thirty-two years.

I rolled over on my back, the cat curled up beside me, and we both went back to sleep.

It might've been eleven minutes later when Cleve called. If you think McGovern might be difficult to deal with on a Saturday morning, you should try talking to Cleve sometime.

'Kinkster!' Cleve shouted. 'We're happenin', baby! "The Kinky Experience" is happenin'!' It was brutal.

'Great,' I said so unenthusiastically that only a crazy person could've misconstrued my lack of interest.

'And the *T-shirts*, dude, the *T-shirts!*'

'The T-shirts?' The only possible use I could think of for a T-shirt was to crush Cleve's larynx.

' "The Kinky Experience" T-shirts! I've ordered ten thousand of them! My cousin Lissa is already selling them in the Lone Star gift shop. Lissa says they're the hottest-selling item she's ever had. We're committed, baby!'

'*You're* committed,' I said, perhaps a little unkindly.

'Oh, that's no problem. My psychiatrists will let me go on the tour as part of a work-release therapy program. I only stay out for the duration of the tour. You're the one who signs me out.'

'That's nice.'

The conversation rattled along like this for a while on a very dangerous track, and finally, with Cleve and me shouting at the tops of our lungs and the cat bolting in terror for the living room, it jumped the trestle altogether. Cleve was shouting about his reputation being at stake, about contracts being in, and about the fact that if I didn't sign them he'd come over in person and see that I signed them. For my part, I kept repeating in loud, frazzled tones that The Kinky Experience was one experience that I never wanted to share with anyone, least of all Cleve.

Cleve ended the conversation on a mildly threatening note, alleging that if I didn't proceed with the tour he'd kill me, blow up the Lone Star Cafe, and assassinate the governor of Texas. He hung up with the threat still hanging in the air. It didn't sound too bad, actually. If he killed me, all my troubles would be over. If he blew up the Lone Star, we wouldn't get stuck for quite so many T-shirts. And if he assassinated the governor of Texas, who would notice the difference?

Later that afternoon Cleve's shrink at the hospital, a Dr Numbnuts or something, called me to say that Cleve had had a little setback and wouldn't be eligible for the work-release therapy program after all for at least another four months. He reprimanded me rather strongly for encouraging Cleve with the idea in the first place, and wanted to know what he should do with the bill for the ten thousand T-shirts Cleve had ordered.

I told him.

'That,' said Dr Numbnuts, 'is an extremely immature response, Mr Friedman.'

'That's good,' I said. 'I was afraid I was losing my touch.'

68

One night the following week I was walking home from the Monkey's Paw alone in the gloom. Without Stengal around, the thought of skinheads hardly crossed my mind. Carmen was gone. The Left Coast kraut that Kent Perkins had uncovered was dead. Mengele, if he was still alive, had to be around seventy-seven years old, cowering somewhere in the jungles of Borneo. The case appeared to be fairly well wrapped up from this end. The only thing I still didn't know was the thing that had gotten me involved in the whole mess in the first place.

Where was John?

I drifted back to the time when I first thought of joining the Peace Corps. I'd told my friends at school that I was thinking of going, and if I went I'd be earning approximately eleven cents an hour. Most of them had said something like, How can you afford to go away for that long? When you come back, they'd said, we'll be in medical school. We'll be finishing law school. Where will you be? What will you have?

Now, many of them are working in their third careers and wrapping up their second divorces, and I'm a country singer turned amateur detective living in New York City with my cat. Things seemed to have worked out pretty much the way they weren't intended, but as Joseph Heller says, 'Nothing succeeds as planned.'

I'd already felt the angel's wings brushing against my cowboy hat a few more times than I would've liked in the past month or so. Even without a family to look after, or a structured type of job to confine me, what else could I possibly do to find John Morgan?

How much time could you afford to take out of your life in 1989 to search for a friend from the past?

There are still a few trees left in the city, and I happened to glance up into one of them, and suddenly I saw the monkeys. It was in the early days of my time in Borneo when I'd first met Morgan at a little marketplace in Long Lama. We'd gotten along right off the bat, had a few drinks together, wandered down a nearby hill, and watched the little Kayan kids with their haircuts that made them look like tadpoles, playing on the banks of the Baram River. Women were washing clothes in the river. It looked like a good idea, so I jumped in with all my clothes on. John jumped in too, but before he did, he took off the new shirt that he'd just bought and laid it on the branches of a nearby tree.

We were both swimming around in the middle of the river when I first saw the monkeys passing John's shirt back and forth up in the treetops. The kids on the shore were watching soberly, waiting to see what John would do. John yelled at the monkeys, 'Hey! Give me back my shirt!' The monkeys started to get worried. They began passing the shirt around more frantically. Then they started tearing it up in little strips and passing the pieces of colored cloth back and forth in the bright sunlight. It was really something to see.

I don't know who started laughing first, but now that I think about it, it was probably John. Then all the kids started laughing. Then all the monkeys started laughing. Okay, chattering.

As I walked along the cold sidewalk in New York, even I had to smile. We were two young Americans, each weighing in at about 120 pounds, with, as I thought then, nothing heavy in our hearts, not a trouble in the world. It was a moment of pure joy. That was the way I would remember John.

I hadn't known what John was up to at that time, and when I considered it, I didn't really know one hell of a lot more about it now. That's why they invented 'floating identities.' I wasn't sure if John was dead or alive. I only knew he was in the world as long as I followed my heart and did what I wanted with my life.

Like Jesus, John Brown, or Joe Hill, Morgan had dealt largely in the casino of the spirit, and perhaps, like them, he'd bet a little too heavily on people. If I was ever going to find John Morgan, I'd pretty well decided, I was going to have to find him in myself.

I took a right on Vandam Street and walked briskly back in the direction of the loft.

There were a few more trees along the way, but I didn't see any monkeys.

69

I woke up one morning about three weeks later with a strange itch inside my heart. Everybody needs a vacation, they say. Of course, when your whole life's a vacation, it's sometimes hard to tell when's the best time to leave. This time I knew.

I called Winnie to see if she'd take care of feeding the cat and checking the answering machine while I was gone. In the background I could hear her putting her girls through a rather up-tempo version of 'Gonna Wash that Man Right Out of My Hair.' I tried not to take it personally.

Winnie wasn't overenthusiastic about my plan, but after a little bit of good-natured cajoling, she agreed.

'Thata girl,' I told her.

'How would you know?' she asked.

I said I might be gone a little longer than expected, and I asked her if I should drop the key off at her place or if she'd rather just continue using the fire escape.

'Drop the key off, Bogie,' she said.

I did.

Winnie took the key, along with a little kiss from me, and closed the door. I went back down to the loft.

I turned off the espresso machine, picked up my suitcase, and walked out the door.

I left the cat in charge.

70

It was a coffee-colored river. It seemed to flow out of a childhood storybook, peaceful and familiar, continue its sluggish way beneath the tropical sun, and then, at some point that you could never quite see, pick up force and become that opaque uncontrollable thing roaring in your ears, blinding your eyes, rushing relentlessly round the bends of understanding, beyond the banks of imagination.

Musical Chairs

This book is dedicated to the memory of
Floyd E. Potter, Jr.
Friend, teacher, tireless defender
of Texas wildlife

and to the memory of
Joan B. Potter
who had that lost human
talent for finding something
to like in everyone

Homo Erectus
Got to connect this
Bone that I discovered yesterday
Tyrannosaurus
Lived in the forest
Died because its heart got in the way

1

It was Christmas Eve and all the salamis in the window of the Carnegie Deli had been hung with care. It was two o'clock in the morning and I was drifting by the window like a secular ghost in the rain when suddenly, between two salamis, I saw something that made me stop on a dime and pick it up. Standing in the middle of the restaurant, bathed in that incandescent, celestial light you only see coming out of heaven or a jukebox, was Leo Steiner.

In Leo's case, I thought I knew where the light was coming from. Leo was dead.

At least I hoped he was dead – we'd buried him almost a year ago.

Leo had owned and operated the Carnegie from 1976 to 1987, during which time he'd managed, using an equal mixture of pastrami and charm, to turn the place into a cultural institution, a veritable haven for wandering Jews of all creeds and religions.

Leo was the man who first made me believe that New York could be my home.

Now Leo was holding some menus and laughing and talking to Adlai Stevenson, Jean Seberg, and Thurman Munson, one of those rather unwieldy parties of three, apparently, and trying to find them a nonsmoking table not too near the kitchen. For a moment I thought of what my father says whenever a waiter or maître d' gives him a table anywhere near the kitchen. My father says: 'Why don't you just put us right *in* the kitchen.' Neither my father nor the waiter ever seems to find anything funny in this line, but, at the moment, it was about the most humorous thing I had going.

I was beginning to wonder, as I stood out on the frozen sidewalk watching this unworldly scene unfold, if I hadn't been T-boned by a runaway Volvo and just didn't know it yet. But I could see that I wasn't in heaven and, quite fortunately, it didn't look a hell of a lot like Kansas. The celestial, half-blinding light from inside the Carnegie Deli continued to pour rather eerily out onto the street. Could it indeed, I wondered, be reflecting from the cherubic cheeks of some large luminous buttocks?

I rubbed my bloodshot orbs and looked away for a moment to that dead Dixieland of the spirit that, just when you don't really need it, will sometimes rise again. My gaze fell upon a bag lady, her earthy possessions gathered around her in ragged splendor, sitting on the curb with her feet in the gutter, warming her hands over a steam vent. When she smiled at me I saw in her face all the regrets of my life.

I looked between the salamis again and Leo and his cool customers were gone. It was just another store-front now, I thought, and Christmas Eve was just another night to me. Chestnuts might've been roasting on the open fire for some Americans, but, right at the moment, my own nuts were about to freeze off. I hailed a hack and headed for 199B Vandam.

I watched New York slide by beneath streetlights that had seen it all and still wanted more. From the cab it seemed like a forgettable familiar film caught in the projector in an old movie house when you were a kid. A body lying on the sidewalk, people walking over it. A skinhead sullenly aiming south, kicking at pigeons. A new Mercedes with tinted glass windows and a vanity license plate that read 'GREED.' I wondered where the hell the angels were. Maybe they were hanging out in Herald Square.

By the time we got down to the Village, the third McCartney song in a row had come to an end.

'What happened?' I asked the driver. 'Paul McCartney die?'

'It's a tape,' he said.

2

The period between Christmas and New Year's can be a rather lonely time for those of us married to the wind. Old people living alone tend to leap from their top-floor balconies in greatly increased numbers, sometimes taking until Purim to hit the pavement. Young people who feel alone see the holiday season as a pretty good time to end it all before it begins. They hang themselves while listening to albums by Whitesnake, overdose on St

Joseph's baby aspirins, or just wander away, having always dreamed of someday seeing themselves on milk cartons.

It's not a very good time either for the 'in-between people,' as the Koreans call the children of mixed ancestry left over from the war. They stay home alone sifting the ashes of their childhoods, dreading becoming o-l-d, and wondering if this could signal the fearful, muted arrival of middle age.

It could.

I was sitting in my loft the day after Christmas smoking a cigar and killing a medicinal shot of Jameson's Irish whiskey when I found myself vaguely wishing I was a Young Republican. I never liked Young Republicans much but I'd never seen an unhappy Young Republican and I kind of wondered what their secret was. I wasn't really feeling sorry for myself but I wasn't feeling much of anything else, either.

I stroked the cat, poured another shot, and looked at the calendar. I'd sort of penciled in a New Year's date with Winnie Katz, the girl who ran the lesbian dance class in the loft above me. Of course, with a lesbian, you never really know how things stood, or lay, as the case may be. There was some fine, slightly twisted silk machinery in their minds that no man would ever be able to observe intimately. It was hard enough understanding normal broads which, in itself, was about as likely as making eye contact with a unicorn.

Winnie and I'd been kind of on-again-off-again for the past year or so, and anytime I heard the lesbian dance class starting up over my head I knew we were off-again.

'At least,' I said to the cat, 'I'm not playing another New Year's Eve gig at the Lone Star Cafe.' The last time I'd done that had been several years back and the results had been most unpleasant, not to say painful.

The cat didn't say anything, but looked at me with a rather jaundiced expression. She'd been burned out on country music for some time now. The last thing she'd really liked was 'I've Got a Tiger by the Tail' by Buck Owens. I never cared for Buck Owens myself, though I had to admit he didn't much sound like a Young Republican.

The cat and I had rather diverse musical tastes but somehow we managed. We'd gotten along in a cold, drafty loft at 199B Vandam Street, New York City, for almost five years together. That's more than you can say for most urban couples.

When I thought about it, there'd been an absence of music lately in both my life and the cat's. I killed the shot and thought about it, took a reflective puff or two on the cigar, and thought about it some more. Because of my years on the road as a country singer I had come to hate the sound of the human voice singing. That was understandable, I figured. Sonny Bono never lets his young wife play rock-'n'-roll music. Elton John never goes to concerts unless they are his own. Of course, his close friends call him Sharon, but the point is that too much of a good thing can get pretty tedious.

Things for me, however, hadn't always been this way. I took a nostalgic puff on the cigar, blew the smoke upward toward the now silent Isle of Lesbos, leaned back in the chair, and drifted daydreamily off to a girl in a peach-colored dress. Her eyes kept staring at me like they belonged to a Mexican picture of Jesus.

She was out of the picture, so to speak. She'd married a highly successful shoe distributor in Seattle and was now about nine months' pregnant with twins. That was about as out of the picture as you could get. I had, however, suggested to her that if one of the twins turned out to be a girl, they might consider naming her Kinkadora.

Suddenly, there was a ringing in my ears.

They say if there's a ringing in your left ear it usually means someone's saying something bad about you. They say if there's a ringing in your right ear – which is, of course, a far more rare occurrence – someone's saying something good about you.

As it happened, no one was saying anything about me. The two red phones were ringing on my desk. I watched them ring for a long time. Then I picked up the blower on the left.

'Start talkin',' I said.

'Kinky, this is Tequila. I'm here in New York.'

'Tequila,' I said with a fairly undisguised lack of enthusiasm. Tequila'd been a guitar picker with my old band, the Texas Jewboys. In the thirteen years since the band had broken up I hadn't seen or spoken with Tequila and there'd been a damn good reason for it. Trouble followed the guy like a tornado homing in on a mobile-home park.

'Wondered if I could crash at your place for a couple days. I got to talk to you about something. You're some kind of big private dick now, aren't you?'

'That's what she told me last night.'

You never know what kind of paint-by-the-numbers hell you're going to get yourself into when you pick up a blower these days, but having done so, reluctantly, I also, reluctantly, gave Tequila my address. He said he'd be right over.

'By the way, Tequila,' I said, 'what do you need a private dick for?'

'Oh, I forgot to tell you,' he said. 'Somebody's trying to kill my ass.'

3

One of the things I didn't need in my life just at the moment was a ghost from Christmas past. I stoked up the espresso machine and the cat and I walked around the kitchen looking into empty cabinets, seeing what provisions I didn't have for a housepest I didn't want.

'Well,' I said to the cat, 'at least he won't be staying long.' The cat didn't say anything but she raised her eyes to the ceiling in a look of disgust. Cats, as a rule, hate housepests of any kind because they view them, most of the time correctly, as agents of change. To a cat, all change is extremely unwelcome. They are lovers of the status quo who do not embrace strange people with strange habits intruding upon their orderly world. Cats, as a group, are a little to the right of Judge Bork.

I walked into the bathroom to throw some cold water on my face and I happened to glance in the mirror. Maybe it was the lighting but it looked like I was beginning to resemble Judge Bork. I hadn't shaved in a few weeks apparently and I damn sure wasn't going to start now just because I had a housepest coming over. After all, he wasn't Prince Charles; he was a burned-out, paranoid guitar picker with a dark streptocumulus cloud the size of Bangladesh hanging over his head. And he thought somebody was trying to kill him. Should be a nice visit.

I sat back down at the desk to wait for Tequila. I found a half-smoked cigar in the wastebasket that had a kind of nice, earthy look to it and fired it up. Cigars, like love, are often better the second time around. There are other parallels and analogies between cigars and love and I might've drawn quite a few of them if I'd been in a romantic or philosophical mood, but I wasn't. I was waiting for Tequila.

Stupid name, Tequila. All the time I'd picked with the guy on the road I never knew his real name. What, I wondered, would make a guy want to call himself Tequila? Why not pick a name like Kinky?

I was jolted out of my reverie by a muffled shout from the street. I got up rather grudgingly and walked over to the kitchen window. I opened the window just enough to lower the temperature in the loft another forty degrees. If it got much colder I could grow orchids in hell.

I looked down into the frozen, gray, viscous afternoon and saw a large black hat seemingly levitating about five feet four inches above the sidewalk. Tequila was not tall but he did wear a big hat. Possibly because he didn't want the pigeons to shit on his lips.

I reached up to the top of the refrigerator and took down the puppet head with the parachute attached and the key to the building wedged in its mouth. It was a friendly Negro puppet head that I'd picked up at a flea market on Canal Street once while waiting for my meticulously selective friend Ratso to Christian the guy down on a pair of dead man's shoes.

The puppet head was about the only housepest that the cat or I were ever likely to abide on anything like a permanent basis. It always had a smile for everyone and a little twinkle in its eye that seemed to say 'Have a nice day' without, of course, being so drivingly tedious as to actually *say* 'Have a nice day.'

I threw the puppet head out the window using the big black hat as a target. The colorful parachute drifted through the drizzle in slow motion like some exotic jellyfish floating just across Jacques

Cousteau's nose. I figured even Tequila could work out what to do with the key and find his way up to the fourth floor. I closed the window, went back over to the desk, poured a small jolt of Jameson's into the old bull's horn, killed the shot, and waited for my most unwelcome housepest.

'I never should've given the bastard our address,' I said to the cat. The cat said nothing, but it wasn't hard to see that she was irritated. Her eyes had turned from a peaceful green to a rather dangerous-looking yellow.

I heard somebody stumbling on the stairs. I heard voices in the hallway. I looked at the cat and the cat looked at me and I tried, only partially successfully, to dodge the little feline daggers that were clearly coming my way. More voices in the hallway. I took a patient puff on my cigar.

I waited.

There are those who say heaven belongs to those who wait. Obviously, they've never tried to buy theater tickets.

4

It was taking Tequila a hell of a lot longer than your average American to find the loft. Maybe he'd run into a bass player from L.A. lurking somewhere in the hallway and they'd gotten into a jam session. I killed the cigar deep in the heart of a Texas-shaped ashtray, sighed rather deeply, and glanced uneasily at the door. Nothing.

I was just starting to get up and walk over to the door when I heard a loud, persistent rapping like a rather repellent raven on Methedrine. I went to the door, opened it, and there he was. Hat, coat, gloves, knapsack, duffel bag, guitar, face like a road map with more lines than I remembered, topped off with a twitchy little Richard Speck smile.

'Hey, brother,' he said as he threw his arms around me in the kind of hug you get only from a fellow road musician or a favorite Jewish aunt. It all came back to me now. I could see that gritty, dusty, long-ago road zigzagging its way like life itself. From Austin to Nashville. From Nashville to L.A. From L.A. to New

York. Punctuated by every one-night stand along the painful parade route to eternity.

'Good to see you again, Tequila,' I said with a truthfulness that surprised me. 'Long time between dreams.'

The cat was checking out Tequila's guitar case, which was covered with stickers from every band he'd ever picked with, the way some elderly couple might plaster the back of their RV with things like 'We Saw Niagara Falls,' 'We Visited the Grand Canyon,' 'We Don't Believe in Anything That Can't Be Reduced to a Bumper Sticker.' I walked over to the counter to pour us both a shot.

'You look good, Kinkster,' Tequila said, nodding his head like an approving parent.

'Clean living. You don't look too bad yourself,' I said.

He looked like shit.

Tequila not only had the ambience of the road about him, he seemed to have a lot of the road physically on him. And in his eyes I could see the dulling pain of being out of the limelight once you'd gotten used to it.

'Been ridin' the couch circuit for a while,' he said, like he'd been reading my mail. He seemed to shiver for a moment and then sneezed three times in rapid succession. When he'd run through his repertoire I handed him the glass and he raised it in a toast. 'To the Texas Jewboys,' he said.

'May they rest in peace,' I said.

I told Tequila that my loft was his loft, showed him the couch, and gave him a big green beach towel from Hawaii, which he promptly sneezed into several times.

'Gettin' a cold?' I asked.

'No, man. I think I'm just allergic to cats.'

He shook his head and wiped his nose on the beach towel. I was glad it was green.

'Jump in the rain room,' I said. 'Take a hot shower. I've got to go out for a minute and get some groceries.'

'It's a thought,' said Tequila. 'Wash off some of this Tennessee mud and Georgia clay.'

'Make room for some New York pigeon shit.'

Tequila smiled. It always made his eyes look even sadder when he smiled.

When I heard the water running I put on my coat, grabbed a few cigars, and headed out into the darkening afternoon. I left Tequila in the loft, closing the door softly like you would for a pilgrim in a sanctuary.

5

There is a difference between the street and the road. I thought about it as I walked down one and remembered the other. Shadows seemed to shiver around me as I went down Vandam and hooked a left somewhere before Seventh Avenue. I must've wandered for a while because by the time I got to the little corner store that specialized in beer, cat food, and perma-logs, I felt like a shadow myself, only there was nowhere for me to fall. The afternoon, like a well-rehearsed magician's trick, had turned into the night.

The guys who ran the store were of a heavy, rather uncertain ethnicity. They looked Italian, Greek, Lebanese, or Pakistani, depending on how you were feeling at the time.

That evening they looked Pakistani. I wasn't wearing seven gold chains with evil-looking icons around my neck but I was feeling somewhat Pakistani myself. Nobody was from here anyway, I thought. Nobody, spiritually speaking, was ever from anywhere. Every place and every person was merely a station on the way. This was the legacy of the road.

I bought a can of 9 Lives tuna for sixty-seven cents. I bought a weird thing that could have been a Vietnamese salami, some coffee, toilet paper, and a few more cans of 9 Lives tuna for sixty-seven cents apiece. I didn't want Tequila telling anybody I didn't take good care of my housepests.

I paid for the stuff and headed home through the gloom. In my memory, I saw a picture of a dusty station wagon pulling an overloaded U-haul trailer. Like *A Thousand Clowns*, it was crammed full of people and it rolled easily across the Arkansas of the mind. We'd just tennis-shoed the bill at the Little Rock Holiday

Inn and were racing to Dothan, Alabama, to open a show for B. J. Thomas . . .

A doorknob distributor or a circuit rabbi or a traveling nipple-jewelry salesman may think they know the road and perhaps they do. It's their territory, they say. But a country musician's attitude toward the road is that of a jet-set gypsy. The road does not belong to him; he, like Jack Kerouac, belongs to the road.

I stopped off at a liquor store on the way home and picked up a bottle of tequila for Tequila.

By the time I got back onto Vandam, the road had receded to a lukewarm memory and I knew I was back on the street. I trudged the final few blocks of urban tundra, groceries in hand, past garbage trucks, bag ladies, people in a hurry. A bright-red Porsche with is burglar alarm blaring was parked downwind from a garbage truck. Porsche probably belonged to one of Janis Joplin's friends. It did not seem out of place in the frozen, reeling emptiness of New York night. Nothing ever did.

I commandeered the freight elevator with the one exposed lightbulb up to the fourth floor. It was an uneventful trip. There wasn't even an elevator operator to say 'Nice ride' to.

In front of my doorway someone had dropped a guitar pick. Probably Tequila, I thought. But it was funny that I hadn't noticed it on my way out to get the groceries. I turned the pick over and saw that it said 'Kinky Friedman' with a Star of David dotting the *i* in *Kinky*. I thought of what Robert B. Parker, my adult pen pal, had once said about the way I signed my letters to him: 'Anyone who dots their *i*'s with a Star of David can't be all bad.'

In 1974 I'd had the picks made and given them to the band and a few close friends while they'd lasted. The picks, that is.

I turned the pick over in my fingers and smiled wistfully. *Had* to be Tequila, I thought.

When I opened the door to the loft I heard the shower still running. When I went over to the counter to set down the groceries I noticed that the kitchen floor was wet with water flooding out of the bathroom. When I shouted, 'Hey, Tequila, keep the damn curtain inside the tub!' there was no answer. Like a fairly pissed-off modern-day Jesus, I walked on the water all the way to the bathroom, pounded loudly on the door, and shouted, 'Tequila!'

Nothing. Not even a sneeze.

I listened for a moment and thought about my hot-water bill. I opened the bathroom door and the loft suddenly felt like a Navajo sweat lodge. I cut a determined swath through the blanket of steam, trying to focus on anything other than the hot white gauze that kept wrapping itself around my orbs.

I spotted the green beach towel still hanging on the hook. The shower curtain was halfway open and the water flowing out of the tub was a blushing pink slowly going to red like a Hawaiian sunset. What was not very pretty was the jagged hole that was visible waist-high through the curtain.

I took a few steps closer and saw the dark form of a body lying in the tub. One quick glance caused the hair along my forearms to wave like miniature fields of grain. I couldn't say for sure but I made an educated guess about the object that was plugging up the drain.

The thing looked a hell of a lot like what was left of Tequila's head.

6

'No, McGovern, I can't meet you at The Corner Bistro,' I said into the blower on the left. The loft was crawling with cops of all shapes, sizes, and personality profiles, one of the more unpleasant being Detective Sergeant Mort Cooperman, who was standing by my left elbow glinting at me through the cigar smoke.

'Why not?' McGovern wanted to know.

'There's been a little, uh, urban hunting accident over here.' I took a nervous puff on the cigar. Cooperman made a little gesture of irritation and I shrugged helplessly and pointed to the blower.

'Is there a story in it?' I heard McGovern ask.

'Oh, I don't know, McGovern,' I said, casting a sideways look at Cooperman. 'There's about seven hundred cops in the place and there's a stiff in my rain room. Might make a nice little human-interest feature for the Sunday magazine.'

'You knew the guy?' asked McGovern.

'I'm afraid so,' I said.

'Anybody I knew?'

'I'm afraid not.'

'Maybe I ought to get to know him. Every other stiff I've become involved with through you has always led to a good story.'

'This one'll be a little harder to get to know, McGovern. His face's been blown off.'

'I'll be right over.'

'Shall I chill the red wine or the white?' I asked, but McGovern had already hung up. It's safer to get between a pit bull and a throat than it is to stand between a newspaperman and a story. I cradled the blower and turned to find Cooperman still glaring malevolently at me.

'You know something, Tex,' he said, 'you must be a magnet for deep shit. Last time I was here there was a croaked Kraut. Time before that, it was something else. What was it, Fox?'

Detective Sergeant Buddy Fox was standing nearby in the kitchen, apparently studying his gaunt, sinister features in the shiny reflection of the espresso machine. 'Spliced spics,' he stated succinctly.

'Yeah,' continued Cooperman, 'you got a real problem here, Tex. You're livin' in a two-bit loft that seems to want to be a killing field when it grows up.'

'And it ain't doin' bad,' said Fox with a sandpaper chuckle. He stopped admiring himself, turned, and walked across the loft to the living-room couch, where two cops were crouching and tentatively toying with Tequila's pathetic possessions, gypsies poking at camp-fire embers.

'I know it's a little difficult,' said Cooperman, 'to make an identification when the party you're identifying ain't got a face, but let's share the experience, Tex.' He headed for the crime scene at a casual clip and gestured brusquely for me to follow him. I got up stiffly from the chair. I'd never quite realized how far the desk was from the bathroom door. To Cooperman, I knew it was just routine, but there was something inside me that wasn't all that eager to go back into that rain room. Sooner or later, of course, I'd have to.

For one thing, the faster I cooperated with Cooperman, the faster the cops would bug out for the dugout. For another, I had to urinate like a racehorse. Of course, when I thought about my going face-to-bloody-pulp with Tequila again, it seemed mildly preferable to just go outside and take a whiz on an electric fence.

As I took the long walk toward death's steamy threshold, the protective state of shock seemed to wear off and left me to deal coldly in the down-home, nightmarish casino of reality. For the first time since the murder I consciously thought of what Tequila had told me over the phone. 'Somebody's trying to kill my ass.' I entered the bathroom and forced myself to look in the tub.

I didn't know who the somebody was but they'd done a pretty damn good job.

7

Cooperman led me through the crime scene with all the panache of a used-car dealer. There were, according to Cooperman, some interesting dissimilarities between the wound in the victim's body and the wound in the victim's head. The blast that had caught Tequila in the lower chest had been fired, apparently, from a greater distance. There was no evidence of powder burns, which Cooperman explained was called 'tattooing,' in the chest wound. The head wound, on the other hand, was delivered from a much closer distance and did evidence clear tattooing, as Cooperman, with only faintly concealed pleasure, made a point of emphasizing. Much of Tequila's head was beginning to resemble the extra-lean section at the supermarket meat counter. No eyes, no nose, and definitely low in the fat and cholesterol department. I fought back a sudden tendency to gag.

Cooperman picked up on my discomfort and, with this added encouragement, plunged headlong into a closer examination and explanation of the chest wound. He pointed out the plastic particles from the shower curtain that were clearly visible in the bloody mess. I nodded and tried not to throw up my toenails.

'Isn't this a job for Quincy or somebody?' I asked.

'Yeah,' said Cooperman, 'Quince'll be along any minute. While we're waiting, suppose you and I have a little chat. What's this guy's name?'

'Tequila.'

'Tequila?'

'Tequila. Guitar player used to be in my band. Hadn't seen or spoken to him for thirteen years until today.'

'Well, this is what sometimes happens when old friends get back together, isn't it, Tex? It's never quite the same as it used to be.' Cooperman winked at me and nodded toward the body in the tub. 'You kill him, Tex?'

I explained to Cooperman how I left Tequila in the loft, went out for a while, walked around, bought groceries, bought the bottle of tequila, came back, and found the body.

Cooperman made some notes in his little notebook and flipped the page over the top. A few more characters started to drift in and out of the bathroom. They were talking pro football. I made a move to leave but Cooperman stood his ground with his little book.

'What was his real name?' he asked.

I explained that the only name I'd ever known him by was Tequila. Cooperman laughed unpleasantly to himself.

'That's nice,' he said. He shook a Gauloises out of his pack and lit it up with a Zippo. He inhaled and studied me for a moment. Then he said: 'Not that we don't trust you, Tex, but where did you buy those groceries?'

'It's a little corner store somewhere over by Tenth Street. Run by Greeks, or Italians, or Pakistanis, or – '

'Make up your rabbit mind, Tex,' said Cooperman gruffly.

'Lebanese,' I said.

After what seemed like forty days and forty nights Cooperman and I finally left the dumper. We wandered into the kitchen where he sat down at the table and stared at me and I busied myself with the espresso machine so I wouldn't have to stare back at him. He was asking me about how I'd first met Tequila when a rotund little man with an ill-fitting leather coat came rolling into the room like a sentient bowling ball. Without breaking stride he nodded to Cooperman and headed toward the door of the bathroom, which, in terms of activity, was beginning to resemble a recently molested dirt dobber's nest.

When the little man disappeared into the bowels of the rain room Cooperman looked up and smiled the nearest thing to a real smile I'd seen from him in several years. It didn't noticeably warm the loft. It looked more like he was halfheartedly auditioning for 'good cop' and didn't much care whether they gave the part to somebody else.

'That,' said Cooperman, 'was Quincy.'

The smile disappeared quicker than a rain forest. Cooperman was now glaring at the doorway to the loft which was mostly filled with a large uniform and the even larger form of McGovern.

'Mike McGovern, *Daily News*,' said McGovern, holding his press card and introducing himself like a huge, rather shy, adult Mouseketeer.

'This is fucking terrific,' said Cooperman with disgust. Then he rather grudgingly pulled a chair out for McGovern. Like most cops I'd run into, he was ambivalent about the situation. He loved and needed the press. It was reporters he hated. I poured three espressos, collared a nearby bottle of Jameson's, and managed, with some little risk factor, to get them all over to the table in one trip.

'You should have been a waitress in a hash house,' said McGovern. This was followed by his hearty Irish laughter which was always a little too loud. Particularly on this occasion.

'I thought about waitressing for a while,' I said as I sipped my espresso, 'but the opportunities and benefits in the dental hygiene area finally won me over. Sorry we're out of whipped cream, McGovern. I could've served you an Irish coffee.'

McGovern poured an extremely large portion of Jameson's into his espresso. 'That's all right,' he said.

8

The espresso was hot and bitter and the conversation was starting to turn that way. McGovern could see that the rain room was indeed the storm center of quite some little activity, could see the flashes from photographs being taken, could see plain-clothes dicks and uniforms drifting in and out like human flotsam and jetsam in a tide of events he was not being allowed to be a part of. Apparently, McGovern was not to be privy to the privy, and this did not go down well with the polite, but very large, Irishman. Every time McGovern would make a comment like 'So there really *is* a stiff in there,' Cooperman would respond with a grim 'Sit tight' and stare malevolently into his espresso leaves. And I still had to urinate.

This rather unpleasant Hispanic standoff continued through another round of espresso and several direct shots of Jameson's fired point-blank down the necks of McGovern and myself. Cooperman, of course, did not drink on the job, but it was difficult to see what the job was unless you wanted to count restraining a large and increasingly angry Irish journalist, which I guess, in all fairness, you could say was a job. But Cooperman loved his work and must've said 'Sit tight' about five times before Fox finally walked over and interrupted the tension convention with a little tension of his own.

'Sorry to bust up your little tea party here,' he said, 'but we've found something in the luggage. If these two fine gentlemen don't mind, I think you ought to come have a look.' He smiled a vaguely serpentine smile in the direction of myself and McGovern and motioned with his head for Cooperman. Cooperman got up and followed Fox over to the other side of the living room.

Fox's gesture with his head, I reflected, was somewhat reminiscent of the way the natives of Borneo pointed things out from time to time. In Borneo, it's considered quite rude to point with your hands, so the people there point with their heads or stick their lips out and point with their lips. By the time the U.S. Peace Corps forcibly returned me to my own culture, I'd gotten pretty

good at pointing at things with my lips. Unfortunately, this particular talent did not have great application in the Western world.

I wondered for a moment whether all cops and all natives of
Borneo made similar gestures with their heads. Was this significant? Could there be other similarities between the two tribes?

Of course, I decided, there were things the two did not have in
common. The natives of Borneo are a gentle, peace-loving people.
Also, they are almost never rude. In defense of cops, however, it
must be said that during a murder investigation, etiquette, as well
as a number of other things, often quite rightly must go over-
board. One of those other things was my bladder, and I was just
thinking of the possibility of urination in one of my landlord's
potted plants when I saw McGovern get up determinedly from his
chair and start moving like a surly aircraft carrier toward the rain
room.

Very unpleasant, I thought.

Halfway there I caught up with McGovern, but my efforts to
stop his forward progress were somewhat similar to a valiant
young water spider trying to reason with a right-wing hippopota-
mus. In a last-ditch effort I got between McGovern and the bathroom and attempted to establish eye contact with my friend who,
more and more, was taking on the behavioral traits of an escapee
from the gorilla house at the Bronx Zoo.

'McGovern!' I shouted in a hoarse stage whisper. 'Hold the
weddin'! The body's not going anywhere!'

Concerning this last, I was very wrong. What finally stopped
McGovern was the sight of a small parade of men trooping out of
the bathroom carrying a body bag. McGovern and I stood aside
and watched in silence as they carried Tequila across the kitchen
and out the door of the loft.

'Well,' said McGovern, 'that's that.'

'Not quite,' said Sergeant Cooperman, looming surprisingly
close to my left shoulder like an unpleasant parrot. 'Want to tell
me again why you agreed to let . . . uh . . . Tequila stay here?'

'I already told you,' I said. 'Tequila called. He needed a place to
crash, he said. He'd been ridin' the couch circuit for quite a while
apparently. So I told him he could stay here for a few days.'

'Isn't that interesting,' said Cooperman.

'Not especially.'

'Oh, I think it is,' said Cooperman smugly.

'Why is that?' I asked with just the slightest qualm of anxiety.

'I've got to call the boss and I'll want you and McGovern here to witness this, but we've found something a little unusual in . . . uh . . . Tequila's duffel bag.'

'Like what?' I lit a fresh cigar and took a tentative puff or two.

'Like twenty-five thousand dollars in cash.'

McGovern's eyes got a great deal wider. Then a large smile spread across his face. I don't know what my face looked like but an involuntary intake of breath caused me to choke momentarily on my own cigar smoke. Always a bit of a social embarrassment. When I did recover my poise, my mind was whirring with the implications of this latest finding.

'Well,' asked Cooperman, 'what do you have to say for yourself, Tex?'

'He could've stayed here all week on that,' I said.

9

'Music's a gift,' said McGovern, shouting over the jukebox at the Corner Bistro. 'It brings people together! It makes people happy! You're blessed, man, you're blessed!'

'Yeah,' I said. 'Maybe I could play rhythm guitar for the Dalai Lama.'

It was after two in the morning and I was just grateful that I'd finally had the chance to grab my Republican by the neck and then get the hell out of the loft. I thought for a while I'd need a forklift to get Cooperman out but he finally left, promising, like Mac-Arthur, to return, and, like MacArthur, I knew he'd probably be pretty tedious about it when he did.

McGovern motioned to Dave the bartender for another drink. McGovern was drinking a Vodka McGovern. Dave, of course, was more than a little familiar with this drink: a rather large helping of vodka, soda, fresh orange juice, and a squeeze of lime. Not a woosie little piece of lime peel. It had to be a *squeeze* of lime. The

Vodka McGovern was one of the few things in this world that McGovern could be said to be truly meticulous about. He could always tell you and always *would* tell you if it was wrong. Dave, according to McGovern, made just about the finest Vodka McGovern in Manhattan. Dave put another one together with the speed and agility of a neurosurgeon, placed it before McGovern, and looked questioningly at me.

'I'll have a diet hemlock,' I said.

I didn't enjoy having a friend of mine, even one I didn't like all that much, go to Jesus in quite this violent a fashion. And how did I know whether or not I liked Tequila? I hadn't really seen the boy in thirteen years and now it looked like it might be a while before I woke up next to him in hell.

The jukebox had thankfully gone silent and the place was starting to thin out. I was trying rather unsuccessfully to rid my mind of the image of Tequila's bloody body lying in my bathtub, and McGovern and Dave were standing across the bar from each other just to the left of me talking about Portugal.

Strangely enough, I was starting to miss Tequila. I took the guitar pick out of my pocket and gazed at it as if it were a tiny mirror to my memories. McGovern had asked me an excessive number of questions about Tequila and had found it rather irritating that I knew almost nothing about the murder and not a hell of a lot more about the man. Of course, performers often tend to shroud their origins in mystery because it makes for better press. Then they start believing their own press and pretty soon they can't remember who they actually are. Back when I was touring with the Jewboys I used to give a different age and place of birth in every interview. Tequila, now that I thought about it, had probably had something of the same idea and that was why nobody really knew dick about him.

'It was about one hundred eighty miles west of Jib,' I heard Dave saying.

I turned to McGovern. 'Jib?' I asked.

'Gibralter,' said McGovern. 'Dave once owned a bar on the southern coast of Portugal. When was that, Dave?'

'Sixty-eight.'

'What was that place called? The City of Light?'

'It was a little fishing village,' said Dave, 'called Playa de Luz. Means "Beach of Light." '

McGovern was moving smoothly through his fourth Vodka McGovern and I was drinking whatever it was that Dave was putting in front of me. It might've really been diet hemlock because it was taking a while to kick in.

'Of course it's not the City of Light, McGovern,' I said. 'The City of Light is either Paris or heaven or wherever Jerry Lewis isn't.'

McGovern laughed his hearty Irish laugh. The one that was just a little too loud for indoor use. I made the mistake of mentioning it to McGovern.

'Well, isn't there such a thing,' he said not quite innocently, 'as hearty *Jewish* laughter?'

'I'm afraid not, McGovern. The Jews have very little in this world to laugh about. Almost as little as the Irish.'

'That's why we laugh,' said McGovern.

Two rounds later Dave had told us all about Playa de Luz, the bar called Godot's, the little terrace that extended out over the Atlantic, the ex-French Foreign Legionnaire who helped him run the place, and the large old hound dog named Dingus that, much to his regret, he'd had to leave behind in Portugal. The southern coast of Portugal was so beautiful and the people were so great, Dave explained, that eventually he got tired of it and had to come back to New York.

I watched the vague, dreary, late night with David Letterman shadows move by the windows of the Bistro and wondered wistfully whether any people in Portugal were standing at a bar talking about New York. Probably not, I figured.

Suddenly I felt as tired and used up as the year itself. By my latest calculations there were five more days to go till New Year's and I wasn't at all sure that the current year or I was going to make it. And Tequila was seeping back into my mind again or maybe he'd never left. Besides the tragedy of the whole thing, I still felt some lingering shock that somebody would blow a guy away in my bathtub while I was out shopping for groceries. It was an invasion of privacy.

178

I thought of the huge caseloads the NYPD routinely handled and I was not optimistic about Cooperman's chances of ever nailing the killer. I thought of Tequila again. How ragged but righteous his face had looked. How he'd hugged me.

As I listened to Dave and McGovern droning on in the near distance I felt like a child hearing his own secret messages in adult cocktail chatter. A child staying up late. Listening to muffled voices in the hallway.

10

There was something I probably should've been doing besides tying and macraméing my nose hairs, but I couldn't figure out what it was. There is a time after the death of someone you know that leaves you shocked, confused, and as rattled as a tin can tied to a cat's tail by a mischievous little neighborhood boy with a cute cowlick in a painting by Norman Rockwell. Life might've been a magazine but if this state of ennui and troubled inactivity went on much longer we'd both be out of circulation. A friend of mine had been whacked right under my nose and I had to do something. I just didn't have a clue as to what that something was.

When I woke up it was Monday morning. A numbing cold had invaded the loft, a dreary mask of gray urban oblivion had descended upon the city, the garbage trucks were grumbling loudly outside my window, and I realized I was not in Portugal. I also realized that I was freezing my balls off.

The cat was curled up tighter than a fossil snail on top of my stomach and did not seem to be eager to move. I lifted my back off the mattress a few times and made a couple of false starts toward getting out of bed but the cat wasn't buying it. One fast sit-up, I thought, would've probably shot the little booger right off the bed and onto the floor but there was no telling what she might've grabbed on the way down. It wasn't the most serious quandary I'd ever been in in my life but it was a problem.

Even if you hate cats it's usually not a good idea to try to shove one off your stomach. Cats like stomachs, they don't like to be shoved, and, if you try to shove one of your stomach, it won't like you. Not that it liked you a hell of a lot to begin with.

If you love cats, the problem becomes even more difficult because you have to contend not only with the logistics of removing the cat from your stomach but also with the expression in its eyes, which, under the circumstances, could be that of betrayal, anger, or even shocked disbelief. Painful for any cat lover. Distressing for any sensitive American. More than most New Yorkers would care to deal with before breakfast. A foot away, a face full of freeze-dried feline hatred staring down past your irises into the back of your head, coldly observing the weather-beaten remnants of your dreams.

By grabbing the comforter on either side of the cat and gently but firmly stretching it tight, then wriggling slowly to my right, I was able to slip out from under the problem. I put on my purple bathrobe with cat hairs all over it and the cigar hole burned through it, walked purposely over to the espresso machine, fed it with a little of my special Kona-Kilimanjaro mix, and turned on the juice and cut the damn thing loose.

I lit my first cigar of the morning with a kitchen match, took a few puffs, opened the window, looked out at the gray people scurrying here and there across the gray morning. It wasn't a bad feeling not to be one of them.

I glanced into the bedroom. The cat had not moved a muscle. This was good. If I could round up a reasonably well-preserved bagel and a can of tuna, the cat and I could have a late power brunch together. Sort of get the week off on the right footing.

I looked back out the window again, thought gray thoughts. Getting out from under a cat was one thing, I reflected. Getting out from under some of the other problems in life could prove a bit more tedious. Like the ramifications of having an old friend blown from your rain room all the way to kingdom come and then finding twenty-five thousand dollars in his duffel bag. That one could turn out to be a little gnarly. The case was full of loose, untidy threads, I thought. If things didn't go well I could always open up a tailor shop.

I turned and glanced briefly at the solitary, unopened bottle of

180

tequila still standing like a lonely sentry on the kitchen counter. If things didn't work out with Winnie for New Year's Eve, I could always have a date with that bottle, I figured. I walked over to the espresso machine, which was humming and steaming and beginning to make little Jimi Hendrix noises, drew myself a cupful, walked back over to the window, and looked at some more gray.

I was semiconsciously humming 'Oh, What a Beautiful Morning' when I noticed two figures coming toward my building from across the street. I'd just gotten to the line 'The corn is as high as an elephant's eye' when I noticed that one of them was Winnie Katz.

I took a slight step backward so that I could see the parties in the street but they couldn't see me. It was a technique I'd learned from *Rear Window*. The girl walking next to Winnie was one I hadn't seen before. She had a huge, gorgeous mass of reddish-blond moss, only a portion of which was shoved under a cute black cowboy hat, and slightly Oriental-looking orbs that were so green they shined like smuggled emeralds. Both girls looked flushed and radiant as if they were coming back from a break after a workout or something.

I leaned forward over the sill as Winnie was negotiating the lock on the front door of the building and from four floors up I could see that even among dancers' asses, this girl had a dancer's ass. Maybe the nicest one I'd seen since a few years back when a little Palestinian friend of mine had gone to the arms of Allah. Some guys had all the luck.

They were just two broads walking into a building in New York City, but as I watched the big metal door swing open I saw something that caused a little louvered cat door in my heart to swing shut.

They entered the hallway holding hands.

It was the first time I'd ever been jealous of a broad and I wasn't even sure which one I was jealous of. I took a bitter sip of espresso, closed the window, and walked numbly back toward my desk like a journeyman fighter who'd just had his bell rung again.

181

It was about that time when I first noticed that both my phone book and my puppet head were missing.

11

A power brunch with a cat will take you only so far in life. After that you've got to go out and make things happen for yourself.

I went into the bathroom to take a Waylon Jennings Bus Shower in the sink and to think about shaving. During these unsavory ablutions I registered for the first time the fact that Cooperman had taken my shower curtain as evidence. At this moment, Quincy and his personable Japanese assistant, Salmon Skin Roll, might be poring over the curtain in the lab looking for whatever vestigial brain cells Tequila hadn't already fried with the Texas Jewboys on the Left Coast. I couldn't imagine what else they could be doing with the curtain. Fingerprints maybe. I didn't know a hell of a lot about guns and I didn't really want to, but I did know that running a ballistics test on a shotgun blast was about as practical as pissing up a rope.

I left the cat in charge and snaked my way through the bleak afternoon until I reached the din and racket of Canal Street. I'd been on Canal Street many times in the past but this was the first time I'd ever gone there shopping for a shower curtain. Almost makes you feel like a young suburbanite buying decorative things for the home until you stumble on a large Samoan selling used dildos on the sidewalk. You can buy anything on Canal Street if you're crazy enough to want it.

The first store I went into sold pornographic books, hassocks, handcuffs, and World War II incendiary bombs. It was sort of a country store in the city. There was a fat guy in charge wearing a Giants warm-up jacket. A large dog was lying on the floor. Part German shepherd, part mutt, with big brown eyes that looked almost as sad as Tequila's. Jewish shepherd, I decided.

'Do you have any shower curtains?' I asked.

'Louie!' he shouted to the back of the store.

A guy who looked like a human groundhog gradually emerged

from somewhere in the musky, raincoat-wrapped, extended bowels of the shop.

'Shower curtain!' the fat guy in the warm-up jacket shouted.

Louie turned at about a 78-degree angle and made a beeline for the far corner of the place. I edged past the nose of the Jewish shepherd and followed Louie, my Virgil of Canal Street, into an era that had ended before I was born but was constantly being brought back from the dead by trendy Americans, if only sartorially. I felt a little uneasy, like a kid just before he gets lost in a museum.

For a moment I thought of my friend Ratso, the editor of *National Lampoon*. He was loyal, seedy, parsimonious to a fault. This was his kind of place. Practically his whole wardrobe was lying around on open tables and in cardboard boxes. Ratso'd been a lot of help to me in the past on a number of pretty unsavory cases. I would've liked to have talked to him now about Tequila, but Ratso was in California working on some kind of screenplay for a while. This was Ratso's kind of place, but he wasn't here.

In a few minutes I had the curtain and was heading back to pay the fat guy. He was now fairly busy picking his nose with a camouflage handkerchief and examining the contents.

'Find what you were looking for?' he asked.

'Yeah,' I said, holding up the shower curtain. 'These little boogers are hard to come by.'

'So are these,' he said as he shook out the handkerchief.

I paid the guy and walked out into the pale, refracted light of the last decade of the twentieth century and didn't even blink.

I walked up Canal, took a right to Mott Street past the Chinese dwarf-painting pastel pictures, and realized that Big Wong's was closed on Mondays. Big Wong's is always closed on Mondays. In all the excitement of shopping for a shower curtain, I'd forgotten.

I went two more blocks up Mott Street and turned into one of those twenty-four-hour places that Jack Kerouac used to hang out in. I didn't see Jack but my waiter looked a lot like Allen Ginsberg.

When you go into an all-night place in the afternoon there's a certain carryover of spirit sometimes that kind of warms the soul. There were few patrons at this time of day but you could almost hear the leftover conversations and smell the whiff of sweet-and-sour stale perfume wafting in with the wontons.

I used an entrance line that my old pal Dylan Ferrero, road manager of the Texas Jewboys, had often used in the past.

'Sirhan Sirhan,' I told the waiter, 'party of one.'

I put the shower curtain on the table, gave my order, and smoked a cigar while I waited for the food. Another nice thing about twenty-four-hour Chinese restaurants is that they don't give a damn whether you smoke a cigar, put a shower curtain on the table, or hang yourself from the shower rod.

I thought about one bleary night about a year ago in Chinatown when Goat Carson was sucking up a large oily-looking plate of snails at three o'clock in the morning and reminiscing about dancing with Judy Garland at the Salvation Club just two weeks before her death. He said she looked like 'a marshmallow with two little toothpicks for legs.' I thought, strangely, about the last time I'd hugged Tequila.

My mind drifted macabrely to the little particles of plastic shower curtain embedded like highway reflectors in the wound to Tequila's body. The wound that had not evidenced the tattooing effect. I thought of the wound to the head that had evidenced tattooing but had contained no embedded shower-curtain particles. There was meaning in this somewhere but I couldn't figure out what it was. Not for the life of me.

If Cooperman did not come up with something fairly soon I was very much afraid that I was spiritually obligated to get involved in this one myself. And this one looked like it might go a lot deeper than the water running over the tub.

'What you got in package?' the waiter asked.

'Curtains for somebody,' I said.

12

By the time I got out of Chinatown it was pushing five o'clock and there was a long line of honking four-wheeled penises struggling to get the hell out of Manhattan. Many of them were on their way to God's country. New Jersey. The sooner the better, I thought, as

I lugged the shower curtain up Hudson like a weary circuit preacher hugging a ragged Bible.

When I got back to the loft there was one note under my door, one message on the answering machine, and one cat who did not seem particularly pleased to see me.

'Honey, I'm home,' I said to the cat.

The cat did not answer. Cats can be clever, wily, ruthless, and brutally persistent, but the ability to understand facetiousness is not a quality that is often found on their dance cards.

I decided to ignore the cat and open the note at the same time. Kill two birds and get stoned. The note was from Winnie. It said to call her. I did.

'Hello . . .'

'Win, it's Kinky. About New Year's . . .'

'Let's discuss it later.'

I lit a cigar and waited. There wasn't a hell of a lot of later, I thought. When she spoke again it was in a softer voice.

'I'm sorry to hear about what happened to your friend. He seemed very nice.'

'You met Tequila?'

'We met in the hallway when he was looking for your loft. He seemed like such a lost little lamb.'

I took a disbelieving puff on the cigar, thought of Tequila with twenty-five thousand simoleons in his duffel bag, coughed politely a few times, and rolled my eyes at the cat. Never eat at a place called Mom's, I thought, and never underestimate the charm of a road musician.

'Lost little lamb,' I said. 'Go on.'

'He said you were the only one he trusted.'

'Guy was in worse shape than I thought. What else did he say?'

'He said that he'd come all the way from Sixteenth Avenue and now he was lost in the hallway. That's in Brooklyn, isn't it?'

'The hallway?'

'Sixteenth Avenue, shrimp dick.'

Because of the fact that they don't have a shrimp themselves, lesbians may, at times, become a bit acerbic with the opposite sex. There were slightly adolescent things I could've said to Winnie at

185

the time, like 'You'll eat those words,' or 'Someday you'll come to realize, quite literally, probably, that I have a giant prawn.' Fortunately, my roots are firmly enough grounded in my manhood that I can be gracious about these things and need not resort to such petulant, prepubescent rejoinders.

'Mr Shrimp Dick, to you,' I said as I calmly cradled the blower.

I had other fish to fry. I had a phone message to check on that could conceivably represent the call that could change my life, I had a shower curtain to hang, and, if those things weren't enough, my mind was already beginning to worm its wandering way down to Sixteenth Avenue.

If Winnie wasn't willing to walk beside me, she could get the hell out of my way.

So could everybody else.

13

The shower curtain was a piece of cake, the phone message was a piece of work, and Sixteenth Avenue, I soon came to learn, was a piece of real estate you'd better not buy if you ever wanted to play monopoly again. But first things first.

As any good bisexual interior decorator will tell you, having the rain room in order often can set the mood and decor for the rest of the house. It is commonly called the centrepiece on the table of interior decoration. Having the curtain strung nicely across the shower rod gave me such a sense of peace and completion that I took a bottle of Jameson's over to the desk and poured a celebratory shot into the old bull's horn. I broke out a fresh cigar, lopped the butt off in my desk-sized guillotine, fired it up with a kitchen match, took a few relaxed puffs, then killed the shot. Then I played back the message on the answering machine.

It was not music to my ears.

It was Cleve.

Cleve was a former road manager of the Texas Jewboys, a former musician, a former manager of the Lone Star Cafe, and a current occupant of the monstro-wig ward at the Pilgrim State Mental Hospital. He was there for murdering not one, not two, but three country singers as well as seriously injuring my scrotum. For a while I thought I might have to become a traveling falsetto yodeler, but, as they say in Hollywood, time heals everything. Even your scrotum.

It wasn't that Cleve actually caused trouble anymore. It was just that he was sort of a harbinger of trouble. Whenever he called with some new idea for reviving and revitalizing my somewhat dormant musical career, I soon seemed to find myself quite pre-dictably in a world of shit. This time I hadn't even needed Cleve's help to get there but he called anyway. I figured I'd get it over with and call him back. He answered on the first ring and he knew who I was as soon as I spoke. At least his hand-to-ear coordination and the voice-identification centers of his brain were functioning.

'Kinkster!' he shouted in the brittle, barely modulated tone of all seriously ill people. 'Your pet shark here has a whale of an idea this time!'

'I'm sure you do, Cleve,' I said. If they ever let him out of there there'd really be hell to pay, I thought. I puffed a couple of preparatory puffs on the cigar and then said: 'All right. Spit it.'

'We do a reunion tour of the Texas Jewboys!'

I sat in a stony silence. The idea was so far off base, even Luis Aparicio would've gotten picked off for nurturing it.

'Cleve,' I said in what I hoped was a calming, rational tone, 'the guys in the band hated each other's guts, they've been scattered to the winds for thirteen years, and, at our peak popularity, we barely had the commercial success to make a national tour, much less a reunion tour more than a decade later. And on top of that, I'd rather go on a lifelong bean-curd diet than go back out on the road again.'

'I anticipated there would be problems,' said Cleve.

I smoked the cigar and looked at the cat, trying to pretend that no conversation had taken place. It worked for a few seconds, until Cleve started going over the imaginary itinerary in his mind with me. He'd anticipated there would be problems, I said to myself as Cleve recited the names of various American cities as if he were reading them off the moving destination roll on the front

187

of a Greyhound bus stopped at a little station on a rainy afternoon before the world went digital and something was lost.

'Cleve,' I said hopelessly.

'New York, Boston, Philadelphia, Washington – '

'Forget it, Cleve.'

'Chicago . . .'

I knew from experience that when Cleve got a hot new idea it usually required a fired-up Gurkha unit to disabuse him of the notion. I wasn't up to the task and I knew it so I did what everyone does with the criminally insane. I agreed with him.

'Sounds like a winner, Cleve. We'll have to talk about it.'

'Oh, I've already talked it over with most of the guys. They're up for it. A few may require a little arm-twisting but that's what you have your pet shark for. I also talked to a reporter about the idea and he sounded very interested.'

'It wasn't Bob Woodward, was it?'

'I don't remember his name. Said he'd call back to flesh it out. You don't have Tequila's number, do you?'

Tequila's number was up, but there was no point in disturbing Cleve's precarious emotional architecture with the truth. There wasn't going to be any reunion tour anyway. I figured my musical career had pretty well bottomed out and might be in position to rise modestly again if Cleve could pull his lips together for a while. I shuddered at the thought of the possible media fallout of having a career comeback being put together by an agent/publicist operating out of a mental hospital. I'd worked very hard to get my career to bottom out and I wasn't going to have somebody blow it for me now.

'Tequila's going to be on the road for a while,' I said.

'Well, when you see him, tell him to give me a call.'

'Sure thing, Cleve.'

'Detroit, St Louis . . .'

After I'd hung up with Cleve I paced around a bit and noticed it'd gotten very dark in the loft. I turned on a few lights here and there but it didn't seem to make much difference.

14

All that night I remained physically at Vandam Street but mentally my address was somewhere along Sixteenth Avenue. I had Noxema or amnesia or whatever you call it when you can't sleep, so I didn't. I sat up with the cat and drank Jameson's and thought about Tequila.

In the early hours of the morning I took a long shot and called Cooperman. I hadn't heard from him since Tequila had gotten himself capped. Not that I expected all that much from the NYPD. I never had liked or trusted cops, especially New York cops, who were recruited from little towns in Alabama, looked like Hitler Youth, and crucified you for jaywalking. New York cops, at least, never cared much what you did. There hasn't been a moving violation issued to anyone in New York City for at least twenty years. Killing one person in New York is all right, but you can get your wrist slapped if you ice two people. If you smoke more than two people you might find yourself organizing reunion tours.

'Sixth Precinct,' said a bored and grumpy voice. I identified myself, asked for Detective Sergeant Cooperman, and was put on hold.

I held.

At 2:45 in the morning it beat having a nightmare about a large green whale landing like a helicopter on Vandam Street with Texas state troopers pouring out of its mouth to arrest me for retroactive obscenity in a show I did in Dallas in 1973. Cooperman came on the line after I'd just about given up on him, like a verbal bulldozer knocking down Tom Joad's farmhouse.

'You're in luck, Tex. I'm here. What in the fuck do you want?'

'I was just calling, Sergeant, to inquire if there's been any progress on the Tequila situation.'

'Yeah, Tex. We got him ID'd. Name's . . .' Here there was a pause of about half a minute in which I could hear Cooperman riffling through papers and cursing all Americans who'd come to New York from the great state of Texas. People in Texas didn't generally hold New Yorkers who'd moved to Texas in very high regard either, but this didn't seem like the time or place to communicate this information to Cooperman.

'. . . Kirby McMillan,' said Cooperman.

'Kirby McMillan?'

'Kirby McMillan.'

I was going to say 'Kirby McMillan?' again but I thought better of it. Tequila as Kirby McMillan would take some getting used to. Of course, now there was all the time in the world to get used to it.

'Fairly Yuppie name for a country guitar picker,' I said.

'Aw, you know these country entertainers, Tex. They got all kinds of funny names. Used to know a guy named Kinky once. Wasn't much of a guitar picker so he thought he'd turn to crime-solving. Sort of a mid-life career change. Well, he had a little beginner's luck at first. Then one day he got in over his head and – '

At this point I put the blower gently down on the desk, took a cigar out of my porcelain Sherlock Holmes head, lopped off the butt, and lit it with my latest Bic, a hot-pink little number that I'd bought from a Negro with no legs on the Bowery. It worked fine, I'm happy to report.

I'd heard Cooperman's whole, rather tedious megillah on a goodly number of occasions and it always started the same way, rolled along for a seeming eternity, and then ended with something grotesque and horrible happening to Kinky. The only place where Cooperman provided any variety at all was in what particularly sordid and macabre ending befell the perpetrator. In this case, me. It was kind of like watching a fairly familiar soap opera where you know the characters and what they usually would do and you only really watch for the little twist at the end.

I picked up the blower just in time to hear Cooperman saying: '. . . found his left arm – the one with the Ubangi tattoo – floating in the East River still holding on to that little pickaninny puppet head, and his right arm – the one he picked the guitar with – was found crammed into the mouth of that big lizard on top of the Lone Star Cafe . . . had all its fingers cut off . . .'

'And they found the body,' I injected, 'in the trunk of a fifty-seven DeSoto at JFK.'

'Newark,' said Cooperman.

'Look, Sergeant,' I said, 'a woman I know in the building has told me – '

'The dyke upstairs?'

' – has told me that she spoke to Tequila just before he came into my loft. He told her he'd come all the way from Sixteenth Avenue.'

'Now, isn't that interesting.'

'Yeah. It's Brooklyn, isn't it?'

'Yeah. It's Brooklyn. It's also Bensonhurst. It's also the Gambino family's backyard.'

'Maybe they'll invite us over for some barbecued cannolis.'

'This is a red-hot potato, Tex, and it's not my fucking beat. I'm gonna lateral it off to the OCCB.'

'What's the OCCB?'

'The Organized Crime Control Board.'

'Yup. All the initials check out.'

'Twelve million people in this city don't fucking get involved, Tex. You don't want to end up visitin' the fish, you goddamn sure better see you're one of them.'

'I'll do my best,' I said. 'You guys didn't by any chance take my little black book with phone numbers in it, did you?'

Cooperman laughed a hoarse, gravelly, but seemingly genuine, laugh. It sounded like somebody shoveling a light layer of snow off a driveway.

'Don't flatter yourself,' he said.

15

I never got around to asking Cooperman whether or not he'd taken the puppet head but it was probably just as well. There were a lot of ways not to get involved with this thing and all I had to do was find one and run with it. It didn't seem like that tough a job. But life sometimes is like a kitten with a ball of yarn. It starts out going harmlessly along in one direction and before you know it, it rolls under the couch and you reach under there to get it and before you know it, you're staring into the limpid blue eyes of a twelve-year-old member of Future Hatchet Murderers of America who's hiding from imaginary Iroquois and he kills you and before you know it, the kitten is using your scrotum for a bean bag. Next thing you know, you're on Paul Harvey, page four.

Essentially, I'd known all this since I was eight years old playing baseball in my backyard. Still, I figured if I was careful enough, I could explore around the edges of the thing without actually becoming involved. This notion proved to contain a small amount of pilot error on my part, but we all have a different interpretation of what 'not getting involved' means. That's what makes for horse racing. It's also, unfortunately, what makes for waking up next to a horse's head.

It was Tuesday morning. Tequila'd been croaked on Sunday. There were four days left in the old year and something told me each of them would be tie-dyed with his blood.

In the aftermath of the murder I had, perhaps, not been thinking as clearly as I might've. It was now very apparent to me that I had *not* misplaced my little black phone book. Nor did I need my local pointy-headed ACLU representative to tell me that the cops legally couldn't've lifted it. The conclusion was inevitable. Tequila's murderer had goniffed my phone book. I found speculating *why* to be a moderately frightening experience.

On impulse, I walked over to the refrigerator and stared somberly at the empty space on top where the puppet head usually resided. You could probably concoct numerous reasons why a killer might steal a little book with phone numbers and addresses in it, but what rational homicidal maniac on the planet would goniff somebody's puppet head? It was one of those senseless crimes.

In desperation, I looked into the dark, cobwebby space between the back of the refrigerator and the wall. Once my eyes adjusted I saw a little black face smiling up at me. It was like finding an old friend you thought had been lost from your life.

I picked it up, dusted it off, and put it gently back on top of the refrigerator. As a test, I opened the refrigerator door and slammed it shut hard. I repeated this Butt-Holdsworth Home for the

Bewildered-type behavior several more times but the puppet head did not move. Its smile did not even noticeably quiver.

I never like to lift anything heavier than a Freudian slip, but, subconsciously, I sort of knew something was forebodingly wrong. By the time I consciously figured out what it was, of course, it was too late.

16

Friday evening I was coming home from miniature golf or something when I found Ratso's body lying on my doorstep.

Ratso was not even supposed to be in New York. He was definitely not supposed to be sprawled facedown in my hallway. He was supposed to be in L.A. working on screenplays and getting acclimated to the Southern California life-style so he could move out there and eat yogurt happily ever after. At the moment, that didn't look like a real viable possibility.

'Who did it, Ratso?' I shouted. 'What happened?'

Ratso said nothing. He just lay there like a large, ill-proportioned doormat.

I thought fleetingly of the many times Ratso and I had teamed up together to tackle cases that the NYPD had already consigned to its 'open' file. I thought of Ratso, my old pal, in his seedy sartorial splendor sallying forth in a spirit of stumbling ingenuousness. If the soul of Dr Watson could be said to be alive today, it surely dwells in the large and sometimes rather unhygienic temple of Ratso's body. Now I was very much afraid that I was witnessing the final destruction of that temple.

'Get up, Ratso!' I whispered hoarsely. 'You don't know where that floor's been.'

Ratso didn't move.

I thought of what all New Yorkers say to comfort themselves when confronted with the death of someone they know. 'He's not really dead,' I told myself. 'He's just not currently working on a project.' It didn't help.

I crept closer, reached down, and tried to find signs of a pulse in Ratso's wrist. He didn't seem to have any veins. I remembered what William Burroughs had once said to the shoeshine boy in New Orleans: 'If I had veins like that, I'd have myself a party.'

I felt around a little closer to his hand and pressed my thumb down harder. I felt faint flutterings like the kind that might emanate from a beautiful butterfly in some idiot's collection when nobody's looking.

I knew it wasn't wise to move someone like Ratso. You could further injure the victim and, very possibly, you could injure your scrotum. I unlocked the door, ran to the blower, and dialed 911. I gave them everything but my shoe size and they said they'd be right over. I stepped over Ratso, went back down the stairs, left the front door of the building open, climbed back up the stairs, stepped over Ratso again, went to the counter, and poured a rather shaky shot of Jameson's.

As I killed the shot I heard a grinding, growling noise that sounded like it should've been coming from my stomach but wasn't. It was coming from the hallway and it was not a very pleasant thing to hear but, in this instance, it sounded as comforting as the music from the harp in the lobby of the Omni Berkshire where you can have tea and crumpets, talk about Ambrose Bierce or pork-belly futures, and hear otherworldly notes peacefully penetrating your soul whether you like it or not.

The noise from the hallway came again. It sounded quite a bit louder this time, like a dog working Yorick's skull. You couldn't keep a good rat down, I thought, as I poured a celebratory shot of Jameson's into the bull's horn. I killed the shot, walked over to the door, and very carefully slid Ratso into the loft like a large sack of incoming mail. I was rewarded with a series of grunts and grinding noises but no words. It was one of the more pleasant conversations I'd had with Ratso in a long time.

Eventually, the paramedics showed up, checked Ratso over, and determined that he had a concussion and a broken jaw. They put him on a stretcher and carried him down to the meat wagon. I got in back with Ratso and off we drove to St Vincent's.

I won't trouble you with the tedium of the next few hours. Filling out forms, calling Cooperman, greeting Cooperman at the hospital, telling Cooperman I didn't know a damn thing about what had happened.

But in spite of all that, I was glad I'd accompanied Ratso to the hospital. If I hadn't, they probably would've admitted him as Ratso Doe or something. Also, it wouldn't have been too pleasant if I'd stood at the kitchen window and watched them take him away alone in the meat wagon.

Every time you watch a meat wagon drive off, it takes a little piece of you with it.

17

It was after four in the morning when I got back to the loft, and by the next day at this time it would be what is designated by certain Western cultures as the New Year. In certain Eastern cultures it's business as usual. Kill a Jew for Allah. Kill a Sikh for Buddha. Poke the prisoner's eyes out with bicycle spokes. Worship a cow. Shun a pig. Have sexual relations with a chicken. In the West, of course, we had all we could do just to kill an evening for Christ.

Ratso had now been at St Vincent's for several hours. I was sitting at the kitchen table smoking a cigar. The cat was sleeping on my lap. I just wished there was a place I could bring the old year, leave it out on the lot. Don't know who they'd sell it to. Some hapless, death-bound American teenager might like to kick its tires. Maybe an old, friendly Caribbean yardman from somebody's childhood. Might've been the kind of year he'd like to drive around in.

I didn't know if it was hot or if it was me and I didn't really care. I put the cat down on the kitchen table and walked over to the window. I tried to raise it but it was jammed. Always live in a house that's older than you are. You may get a stuck window now and then but the wisdom of the ages will seep into your very being. Of course, many may prefer windows that open.

I walked over to another window and tried to raise it. It was jammed, too. I looked over at the cat to see what she thought about the situation. She was sitting upright on the kitchen table staring directly away from me. Still miffed that I'd gotten up while she was sleeping on my lap. She didn't understand that if you wait for a cat to wake up you'll never be vice-president of Dow Chemical.

I took a closer look at the windowsill and the window jam. Then I walked around quickly and checked the other windows in the loft. Every one in the place had been nailed shut.

They say when the Lord closes the door He opens a little window. But if it took Him all night to pull three little nails out of Jesus, He was going to be working His buns off on this job. I walked into the kitchen puffing on the cigar. I looked at the cat.

'I just hope He does windows,' I said.

18

'If I had a hammer,' I thought, 'I'd hammer in the morning . . .'

I didn't have a hammer.

When you don't have a hammer you can't open windows that've been nailed shut unless you're close friends with Uri Geller. I didn't even know who to call at this hour. I thought about Pinocchio's father, Geppetto the carpenter, but he wouldn't've believed me. The only other carpenter I could think of was Jesus, but all the lines were probably down because of heavy calling from television evangelists.

In a rising panic I thought of places I could go to get away from some seriously unthreaded individual who was nailing my windows shut. For some reason I thought of my old college friend Joe Kboudi, who'd retired from the human race about twenty years ago and now owned a record store called All That Jazz in Steamboat Springs, Colorado. Joe skied every day. Lived in a house he'd built with his own hands, and, though he'd never been married, claimed to have been divorced twice. I thought of the way most people lived in New York and Joe's life-style suddenly seemed pretty damn good. 'You ever tried cross-country?' I asked the cat. Apparently she hadn't.

Flying by Jewish radar, I walked over to the door of the loft, opened it, and took a good long look at the lock. I didn't see anything unusual but the light in the hallway wasn't that great. I got out my hot-pink Bic, fired it up, and took a closer look. Inside the tumbler, the pins were scratched. I could see where the metal gleamed bright against the dull surface of the inside of the lock. Clearly someone had picked the lock, come inside, and nailed the windows shut. But why? I thought about this all the way over to the bottle of Jameson's.

I poured a shot. It was cold as hell outside and, whether the windows were open or closed, the loft was usually cold in winter and hot in summer. Yet here it was the end of December and I was feeling hot in the loft. It didn't take a detective to determine that I must be feverish. I put my hand to my forehead, then put my hand to the cat's forehead, then checked my own again. I was definitely feverish. Maybe I was coming down with the Epizoodic or something.

I wondered very briefly if someone had released some kind of deadly microbes in the loft. I discounted this possibility for three reasons: one, the cat wasn't sick; two, the forced lock and nailed-down windows were a rather crude modus operandi to be associated with the placing of deadly microbes; and three, life rarely imitates James Bond. Life is grainier and not quite as diverting. The popcorn, however, is always better with the movie.

So, if it wasn't microbes, why would someone force their way in and nail down the windows? Even given that the windows were an overdramatic touch, if the party had wished to kill me, why not wait *inside* the loft to accomplish it? Especially after picking the lock? Why wait outside on the staircase where, I surmised, the perpetrator was lurking when Ratso's untimely arrival surprised him?

I was starting to sound like Cooperman, I realized to my slight discomfort. Well, why not? I was obviously becoming more professional with experience. And, I noted, what seemed to be absent from the methods of the intruder was exactly that professional touch. Among professionals, of course, I wasn't a professional, but, compared to this guy, I was smoother than Lord Peter Wimsey. Of course, Lord Peter Wimsey wasn't a professional either, but he was an aristocrat, so you couldn't tell the difference.

Coming as quickly as it did after the murder of Tequila, the

197

break-in could very well be connected. Possibly the killer thought Tequila had certain information which he'd imparted to me. That scenario seemed particularly unfortunate. I'd hate to die for withholding information I didn't have.

I sat around drinking and smoking and stroking the cat for a while, and eventually, the fever seemed to diminish. By just before dawn it was gone. Jameson's will cure anything if you drink enough of it.

Suddenly, I felt a great need to talk to someone about this latest episode. I couldn't call Ratso till the late morning at the earliest. Rambam, my private-investigator friend, would surely have an angle on it, but he was jumping this month with a crack Guatemalan airborne unit called 'Los Cobras.' Maybe that's where I should've been. It sounded safer at the moment.

I settled on calling McGovern. He picked up the phone on the eleventh or twelfth ring and he didn't sound real happy about it.

'Leap sideways, McGovern,' I shouted. 'MIT – MIT – MIT!' 'MIT' was our special coded signal for the Man In Trouble Hotline in case something happened to either of us and nobody came around to check on us until the body had decomposed. McGovern had read on the wire where a guy in Illinois had died in his apartment and wasn't discovered for six months. The purpose of the Man In Trouble Hotline was to avoid such a situation if possible.

Finally, I heard McGovern's groggy reply: 'MIT – MIT – MIT . . .' To an untrained ear, the conversation might've sounded like a mating call between two large, rather ill birds.

'McGovern, I've got a problem. I had to call someone.'

'Why me, lord?'

'Because you're my friend and you have a very large head that contains a great deal of knowledge. Also, you're the only one who'll listen.'

'Makes sense.' If it made sense to McGovern, I thought, I was really in trouble.

'Okay. Tequila gets blown away in my rain room a few days ago.'

'I covered the story,' said McGovern irritably.

'Right. Well, before he went to Jesus he'd mentioned something about coming from Sixteenth Avenue. That information plus the large amount of cash that was found made Cooperman turn the whole case over to the OCCB. You know what that is?'

'Too bad it wasn't the OTB,' said McGovern. He laughed rather loudly for that hour of the morning. Then, just as abruptly, he stopped just short of driving off in a 1947 snit. 'Of course I know what it is.'

'Well, get this. Tonight I get home and find Ratso, who's supposed to be in California, knocked colder than a stuffed flounder at my doorstep with a broken jaw and a concussion. I notice the lock's been picked and when I check the windows, they've all been nailed shut.'

'Holy shit! The last time that happened was in the thirties. You ever hear of Legs Diamond?'

'Yeah. He was a bad Broadway show.'

'That's how they killed Legs Diamond. He kept getting away from them so they nailed his windows shut, came in, and blew him away.'

I was starting not to like the Sixteenth Avenue aspects of the case. I was beginning to feel that not only were the windows nailed shut but the walls seemed to be doing a pretty fair impersonation of closing in on me. Kind of claustrophobic in the loft. It was hell not to get involved when you didn't know what it was you weren't supposed to get involved in.

'Hey, Kink. I've got a good idea for you.'

'What?'

'Have you thought about going to Portugal?'

19

A long time ago my mother told me a story about a friend of hers who once spent the night at a big hotel in St Louis. When I was a child all hotels seemed very big and St Louis seemed very far away – almost as far away as childhood seems to me now. Be that as it may, here is what all of this has to do with the windows. The woman in the story left her window open while she slept that night and somehow a bird got into the room. The bird dived and flew around the dark room, waking the woman up and scaring the hell out of her. For the rest of her life, I was given to understand, the woman could not eat chicken, turkey, or any kind of fowl. If she did, the reaction, apparently, was always the same. Projectile vomit.

The Legs Diamond death scenario being operative that night, I figured no bird, roach, or Stealth Bomber would be getting in under the windows. All I had to do was get up and bar the door. I did.

In the morning, I could call the super about the windows. If I wanted faster action I could go down to Canal Street and buy a hammer at the same place I bought the shower curtain. See if the guy was still picking his nose with the same camouflage snot rag.

Around dawn or so I killed the lights, got into bed, and went to sleep more easily than on any night since Tequila had nodded off forever.

I'd check on Ratso in the morning.

I'd fix the windows in the morning.

I'd explore the Egyptian ruins of my social life in the morning.

But before the morning came something else did. It belonged to the ugly, unwelcome, sifting-the-ashes-of-childhood department, and it told me in no uncertain terms that no matter what happened in the morning I was very soon karma-bound to reap an ill-winded, inexorable harvest of hate.

20

Scientists don't know where dreams come from. Of course they don't; that's why we call them scientists. But, in all fairness, very few other Americans know where dreams come from either. Dreamers, for instance, don't know where dreams come from. Of course they don't; that's why we call them dreamers. But there is one man who does know where dreams come from. He's a guy I went to high school with who I used to call Wally but who now operates under the moniker Dr Wallace P. Mendelson. Wally wrote a book called *Human Sleep and Its Disorders* which he once sent me a copy of. The problem with the book is that it's a very learned, well-researched, scientific study, and by the time you get to the part that tells you where dreams come from you're usually on the nod.

In layman's terms, Wally's main contention is that dreams and nightmares, more often than not, are caused by gas. It is a thesis I am not prepared to argue with, having had in my life many dreams, many nightmares, and, of course, rather large amounts of gas. Wally levels a few fairly fetid blasts at the school of frilly Freudian lingerie thinking and I can't say I disagree with him. I say only that my nightmare came from somewhere pretty unpleasant and it didn't get in through the windows.

My friend Captain Midnite always maintains that the first time he met me I was hanging from a cross outside the Nashville Holiday Inn. That was where the dream started. And, like many dreams these days, it got worse.

To my left from high upon the cross, I saw the Day-Glo skeleton of Ernest Tubb sinuously weaving its way up lower Broadway singing, 'I'd waltz across Texas with you in my arms.' To my right all I could see was a huge sign that read: BAPTIST BOOK STORE. I looked straight ahead and saw the lights of the city of Nashville below me. It reminded me of the old Tom T. Hall song 'I Flew Over Our House Last Night.' As my friend Dave Hickey says: 'I like all of Tom T. Hall's songs and both of his melodies.'

There wasn't a hell of a lot else to see. It might be exciting to Jerry Falwell or somebody like that, but I think most people would find hanging around on a cross all night pretty goddamn boring. I decided to come down and maybe get a big hairy steak in the little restaurant that Midnite always referred to as 'Hillbilly Heaven,' and which, as things evolved, was an extremely appropriate name. But I'm getting ahead of my dream.

It must've been the late sixties or early seventies, judging by the taillights, yet when I went inside Hillbilly Heaven the ragged group sitting around the table stared back at me with eyes that were timeless as the rain. They were too degenerate to be King Arthur's boys, and, though several of them looked rather like Dorothy Parker, they lacked the sophistication to be confused with the Algonquin Hotel crowd. Nonetheless, they were destined for their place in history. This band of brigands was the Texas Jewboys, soon to travel across America, racing to stay one step ahead of angry Jews, Negroes, rednecks, and women in their relentless effort to piss off everybody.

Captain Midnite himself was sitting at the head of the table discoursing to the group about Billie Jean Horton, the woman who had had the misfortune to be married to both Hank Williams and Johnny Horton. 'People say Billie Jean was a witch,' intoned Midnite. 'They say she killed Hank Williams and Johnny Horton and stunted Faron Young's growth.'

Billy Swan took out his glass eye and dipped it in his drink. Willie Fong Young, the 'Singing Chinaman,' made a lurch like a lizard's tongue for the waitress's left breast. Not all the Texas Jewboys were Jewish, but all of them were Jews by inspiration.

Next thing I knew I found myself blithering down a vaguely familiar street in Nashville with a couple of the guys in the band and a bottle of Jack Daniel's approximately the size of Webb Pierce's guitar-shaped swimming pool. I took a slug from the bottle and the water from the pool all sloshed over to one side. Through the pool, which was now inside the bottle, I could see the dark form of the German battleship *The Bismarck* sailing directly toward my uvula at an unpleasantly brisk clip. The background music for this part of the dream was Johnny Horton singing 'Sink the Bismarck.' I passed the bottle to the drummer, Major Boles. He made the observation that his come count was redlining and passed the bottle to the bass player, Brian 'Skycap' Adams. They were talking to a broad who looked a lot like the green-eyed blonde I'd last seen holding hands with Winnie Katz. Probably the same one who was going to shoot me out of the saddle for the New Year's date, I thought, but there wasn't time to dwell on it. The street was running with blood.

Tequila's face floated by in the gutter like a discarded fright mask. Workmen were hammering on a sign that read: WELCOME TO MUSIC ROW. The hammer blows came irregularly, sounding like gunshots. The blood was rising rapidly in the street, slightly discoloring my brontosaurus foreskin boots.

Music Row, I said to myself. Music Row.

It was only after I'd awakened from the dream that I realized what should've been obvious to me some time ago. What was now called Music Row in Nashville had for many years been known to all of us by another name.

'Music Row' had once been Sixteenth Avenue South.

21

New Year's Eve came around relentless as a tedious housepest. You can coddle a tedious housepest, pretend you like him, ignore him, but he'll still be hanging around like a bad smell unless you get a forklift and get him the hell out of there. New Year's Eve was the same way – unforgivable and unforkliftable. Like Exxon or a twenty-four-hour Chinese restaurant, New Year's Eve didn't care if you sang, danced, or hung yourself from a shower rod. The only remedy was to sleep through the bastard like a bad dream, and I'd already had one of those too many the night before.

At least the super had showed up and, for a small honorarium, had unpried the windows, which was a good thing because I was beginning to worry a little that my entire loft might be developing a crucifixion complex. It was a couple of minutes after ten – less than two hours before the arrival of that smarmy, smirking little rug rat in a diaper that symbolizes all our hopes and dreams for the future – when I opened the bottle of tequila.

The fact that Sixteenth Avenue South in Nashville could've quite logically been what Tequila'd been talking about before he died, rather than Sixteenth Avenue in Brooklyn, was still on my mind. The fact that I, with the New Year coming, felt myself being spiritually sucked into the vortex of Kirby McMillan's (a.k.a. Tequila's) murder case was also on my mind. About the only thing, in fact, that was not on my mind was Georgia.

Then I took the first strong shot of tequila, felt my scalp tingle, and felt the brain under that scalp grow as empty and as blank as the blue eyes of a bimbo in love. Tequila'll do that to you. It'll send you to a different planet than a white wine cassis.

After another shot or two, with the lemon neatly quartered and the salt sprinkled sparingly on the back of my wrist to cut the bite the tequila was taking out of my heart, an entirely new scenario was filling my mind, a bold new attitude taking over my being. I was on a planet with Tom Mix, John Wayne, Steve McQueen, and my old friend Tom Baker, and, I was pleased to observe, I felt I belonged there.

Cleve's crazy dream of a giant Texas Jewboy reunion tour didn't seem so bad to me suddenly. I could see us back in '73, '74, '75, at Armadillo World Headquarters in Austin, Liberty Hall in Houston, Max's Kansas City in New York, the Troubadour in L.A., electrifying the crowds with avant garde insanity. In all its old glory, I thought, the band was really something. Of course, it's hard to be avant garde on a reunion tour. But, after all, we were cultural pioneers. Before MTV. Before Watergate. Before Christ. Before –

There was a loud noise in the hallway. It did not sound like applause. It sounded more like the wail of a wildly distraught woman. I killed another shot of tequila, which was going down a lot more smoothly now, and I lit a cigar. The noise did not seem to be going away.

I licked some residual salt from the back of my wrist, took a few irritated puffs on the cigar, and, very reluctantly, headed for the door. That hallway was going to get me into trouble yet.

22

'Of course you couldn't've known she was a lesbian, Kelli,' I said reassuringly. 'They don't have lesbians in Texas.' We were standing by the counter after I'd coaxed the young blond, green-eyed dancer into the loft, coaxed her name and port of origin out of her, and coaxed her into taking several stiff shots of tequila. Now, if I could coax her into bed with me, the New Year might yet come in with a bang.

'It's not that,' said Kelli, wiping two blue teardrops from her green, green eyes. 'I've been a dancer all my life. I've got an ex-boyfriend in Texas who's been harassing me and threatening to come up here. I just got rid of him and now this woman thinks she owns me. I thought she was a friend.'

I handed her my snot rag and she dabbed at her pretty eyes again. 'With friends like that,' I said, taking a patient puff on the cigar, 'who needs lesbians?'

She nodded as if she understood whatever the hell it was I meant. I thought very fleetingly of the first time I'd seen her from my kitchen window. She was crossing Vandam Street, I reflected, on those muscular, perfectly formed dancer's legs. She'd really knocked the helmet off my Nazi love puppet. It was a good thing, too. You never get a second chance to make a first impression.

Kelli smiled a little and seemed to loosen up a bit. She took out a pack of Merits, shook one free, and let me light it for her. I liked dancers who smoked Merits. I liked broads who smoked anything; you could get on a coffee-and-cigarette wavelength with them on rainy days after you'd done a little horizontal hokey-pokey and then in the evening go out to romantic little Spanish restaurants and get drunk with colorful, bohemian friends. Also, broads who smoked tended to bitch less about my cigars.

As Kelli and I developed a rapport of sorts, midnight was slipping up on Vandam Street. There was definitely some kind of organic chemistry between us.

'Actually,' I said, 'I really do know a lot about dancers. Do you know how you can tell when your date is a dancer?'

'How?' she asked in beautiful, breathless innocence.

'When she does splits on your face,' I said.

Black and white images of black and white people were seething, snaking, and shimmering all across the screen of my black and white television set. They were all watching a ball drop. Like a baby's untried, trepid testicle descending into the netherworld of Times Square, it appeared about the same size, shape, and consistency as a fairly healthy boysenberry. Kelli and I watched this rite with varying degrees of fascination.

'We should be there,' said Kelli.

I remembered being there once. Thirty seconds after the ball fell, a group of black youths, as they're called, beat a seventy-nine-year-old Frenchman to death with his own cane right in front of his granddaughter. I got there just as the black youths were vanishing into the crowd and they were beginning to load one stiff Frog into the meat wagon. Though a noninvolved passerby eagerly provided me with a blow-by-blow description of what I'd missed, I did witness a burly white youth picking up a funny-looking little beret from the sidewalk, putting it on his head, and blowing a noisemaker that seemed to stretch out like the tongue of an avaricious anteater and reach all the way to the beaches of Normandy.

'Happy New Year,' I said as I poured out two shots of tequila.

We were clinking our glasses together in a toast and I was staring into the rather promising depths of Kelli's green eyes when there came the sound of someone knocking at my chamber door. A woman's voice could also be heard and the voice was saying my name. The voice sounded a lot like Winnie Katz's.

'Oh, God,' said Kelli. 'Not that – that creature!'

'Who?' I said ineffectually. 'Where?'

It wasn't my idea for Kelli to hide in the linen closet. It just seemed like the appropriate thing to do under the circumstances. Try putting yourself in her place. You're a young dancer from Texas and a large, athletic, cranked-up New York bull dyke is standing at the door ready to huff and puff and do a few other unpleasant things if she discovers you're here.

She'd probably drill you like your friendly neighborhood dentist. Of course, dentists, like bull dykes, like many other Americans, spend most of their lives drilling in the wrong places and that's why they not infrequently commit suicide. I have very little sympathy for people who take a brodie. I agree with my friend Nelda from Medina, Texas, who, whenever she hears of someone taking his own life, always remarks: 'Wish I could of handed 'em the gun, the chickenshit!'

I opened the door to the hallway.

Winnie was wearing a smile I could not read and something that looked like a teddy for cooler weather that I could not take my eyes off of and she was holding a large bottle of some kind of château de cat piss.

'Happy New Year!' I said. I had a rather distinct feeling that it wasn't going to be one for very long.

Winnie brushed past me into the loft at about the same time that Kelli sneezed in the linen closet.

'What was that?' asked Winnie.

'What?' I said. 'Where?'

Kelli sneezed again. It was a cute little sneeze and I wanted to throttle her for it.

What happened next was not all that pleasant but it was better than what happened after that. But let me tell the events in the order they occurred, for there is a place for everything under heaven . . . turn, turn, turn. I turned, all right. Just in time to see Winnie yank open the door to the linen closet and Kelli come flying out like a belligerent blond bat for her throat. Was this my innocent little dancer from Texas?

I didn't have a hell of a lot of time to wonder. Winnie did not shirk from the action and soon they were kicking and flailing, and choking, and scratching, and cursing, and screaming, and carrying on, in general, like a married couple. The cat and I both jumped repeatedly out of the way and finally I stood on the sidelines wondering whether to be jealous, smug, or ambivalent. I won't repeat some of the things that were said, for they certainly belong to the argot of the gutter.

Kelli threw my 'Imus in the Morning' coffee mug at Winnie and it crashed into an expensive-looking picture of a ballet dancer that belonged to the Greek woman I subletted the loft from. That's the way it goes. Winnie picked up my porcelain Sherlock Holmes head in which I kept my cigars and rocketed it at Kelli's skull. It was a large object and, when Kelli ducked, it smashed into the wall above the refrigerator, sending the puppet head and a small covey of expensive cigars flying off in all directions. Great material damage was done to the loft.

The skirmish seemed to go on forever but, in reality, lasted for only a few minutes. It ended when the two combatants, the cat, and myself all suddenly realized that the four of us were not alone in the loft.

A large, fairly deranged-looking man was standing just inside the doorway and watching the action with eyes that glittered dully like pinballs. He had a tavern tan and it appeared as if he'd been sleeping in his hat and coat for a couple of years. He had no facial hair except for a rather evil-looking 'white man-hater' that grew from his lower lip like a black orchid and made him look like a drunk who'd missed the mark on Ash Wednesday. He sprayed evil around the place like a blue-balled tomcat.

'Let me guess,' I said. 'You're Kelli's boyfriend from Texas.'

'Wrong,' he said as he took out the gun. 'I'm Winnie's husband from Sing Sing.'

23

Lately the atmosphere of the loft had seemed to vaseline violently back and forth between long periods of enormous ennui and brief, intense intervals of frenetic activity, both polarities being rather unpleasant. The cycle had appeared to begin the day I went out shopping for a bottle of tequila for Tequila, each of which vessels, of course, were now empty. Whether Winnie's husband from Sing Sing was really Winnie's husband from Sing Sing was something we could discuss later if there was a later. Whether he had decked Ratso, deep-sixed Tequila, and done some unauthorized carpentry work on my windows could also be given consideration at a later date. As far as the Texas Jewboy reunion tour went, we'd have to put that one on Hollywood hold for a while. Take a spiritual raincheck.

I looked at the man with the gun and saw that his dark, furry white man-hater was bobbing up and down and that meant he was flapping his lips. His voice was soft.

'Don't worry, baby,' he said to Winnie. 'I'm not gonna kill you. I'm just gonna give you something to remember me by every time you look in the mirror.'

From a pocket in his overcoat he extracted a clear bottle about three-quarters full of a clear liquid. I noticed for the first time that he was wearing gloves. His orbs were starting to run through a few REM movements I hadn't seen before.

Winnie and Kelli were visibly shaken and I wasn't feeling too good myself. I looked at the two of them and registered that there was something very beautiful and arousing about a woman in a high state of danger and vulnerability, no doubt one of the things that delights the esthetic eye of the rapist. They were both chalky-white, like statues of minor Greek goddesses smiling with fear.

I made myself focus on the bottle in his hand and wished I'd paid a little more attention in high school chemistry. I did remember that almost all acids have a kind of dirty clear color and have to be kept in brown bottles or they lose their potency. I made a judgment call that the bottle was not the McCoy. If this was true, the only little problem was the gun.

The cat hopped up on the desk next to where I was standing. As she walked to the far end, an idea crossed my desk as well. I picked up the cat and held her protectively, stroking her head as if to soothe her. I hoped to hell she'd cooperate. The cat hated to be picked up.

'That ain't the pussy I'm gonna hurt,' said the man with the gun. I looked in the direction the gun was pointed and saw, incredibly, that the two girls were now hugging each other. Women.

I waited till the guy started futzing with the cap of the bottle, then I threw the cat in his face. With the same motion I went for the gun. The cat made a beautiful four-point landing on the guy's mug and promptly put down some rather sharp roots.

Two hours later, it was all over. Just me and the cat. Cooperman had un-hog-tied the guy and taken him away, the girls had left together, and I was still slightly shaken by the revelation that the gun hadn't even been loaded.

'Well,' I said to the cat, 'that was great teamwork. Now I'll just clean up the guy's urine sample or whatever the hell it is from the kitchen floor and we'll go to bed.'

I've only owned one rug. It was a beautiful, very expensive Persian, one given to me some time ago by a little Armenian friend. I speak of it in the past tense because when I finally got over to look, it was still smoking with a hole in the middle roughly the size and shape of the Louisiana Purchase.

24

Sunday morning, the first day of the New Year, I was wandering my weary way over to the St Vincent's Hospital Broken Jaw Ward. Thirty-seven years earlier, to the day, I reflected, Hank Williams had died on a one-way ride to Canton, Ohio. Maybe in a hundred years, I thought, there'd be a St Hank's Hospital in New York.

Maybe not.

As I walked through the Village I noticed that people had already started chucking out their Christmas trees onto the curb. When I was a kid we used to collect them and build Christmas-tree forts to protect ourselves from wild Russian boars, imaginary Iroquois, or the bullet-heads from the next block. Now that we live in an adult world, of course, the currency of old Christmas trees has fallen off a bit. It was kind of ironic, I thought. Now was the time that we really needed Christmas-tree forts.

Ratso looked green for some reason. Maybe it was the lights. Maybe it was the Jello-O.

'You're always visiting me in hospitals,' I said. 'I thought I'd visit you in one.'

'Hrrmghh,' he said. It was painfully obvious they'd wired his jaw.

'What's the matter, Rats?' I asked. 'They give you a charisma bypass?'

'Yechhuuum!' Ratso said, a bit more demonstratively.

'Well, maybe it's a blessing this happened,' I said. 'You've seen what Hollywood did to F. Scott Fitzgerald. They weren't very nice to the Lone Ranger, either. Wouldn't even let him wear his mask at county fairs. Mind if I smoke?'

Ratso made a noise in his throat that I took for an affirmative. I checked the hallway, saw that the coast was clear, lopped the butt off an English Market Selection Rothschild Maduro, and fired the little booger up.

'Well, I don't see Big Nurse out there,' I said. 'All I see is Big Nerd.' I looked at Ratso and smiled a warm, lighthearted, engaging smile. The muscles in his jaw rippled a few times like an overly zealous B-movie star and his lips twitched a bit grotesquely. I decided that must be the way people with wired jaws laughed.

'Screenwriting's like putting together lawn furniture,' I said. 'Not a hell of a lot of creation there. You should stay in New York with me and we'll put those little gray cells to work on this latest case that seems to have fallen into my lap like a bowl of matzo-ball soup. Of course, I guess that makes me a spiritual *shlemazel*, right? The *shlemiel* is the one who spills the soup, I believe. The *shlemazel* is the one who gets the soup spilled on him. Or is it the other way around? I knew I was one of those guys.'

At this point I laughed in good-natured self-deprecation. Ratso made another noise in his throat. Sounded like a slow, and very unpleasant, child learning how to chuckle.

I took it as a positive sign. I sat back in my chair and puffed on the cigar a bit. The Maduro cigar is of a very dark color and brings to mind obvious racial as well as Freudian implications but has a nice, toasted aroma that I felt could only enhance the ambience of the sterile, spiritless room.

I filled Ratso in on what had happened at the loft both before and after his little accident. I started with the circumstances of Tequila's death that Sunday evening exactly one week ago. I mentioned the business about Sixteenth Avenue, the missing phone book, and the temporarily missing puppet head, and then I fast-forwarded to the Friday night I'd found Ratso lying on my doorstep. Ratso reacted to all this in stoic silence, which is about the only way a person with his jaw wired shut can react. If he had any thoughts he kept them to himself.

Finally, I briefed Ratso on the events of the previous night, featuring Winnie's husband from Sing Sing. When I'd gotten to the part about finding the giant hole burned in the Persian rug by the acid, I saw the first smile come to Ratso's lips since I'd entered the room. It was a painful thing to see, but there it was. It looked kind of like a frozen Jackie Kennedy funeral smile.

'Here, Ratso,' I said, handing him a blank page from the little notebook I carried with me. 'Write everything you saw about the person who did this to you.' I handed Ratso a pen and he was scribbling maniacally on the page when the Big Nurse finally did come in and began to gag on the cigar smoke. She gave me the old fish-eye, then wheeled in my direction and came toward me at a surprisingly accelerated pace for such a large woman.

The nurse did not quite actually chase me around the room. She only appeared to do so as I lunged for the bed, grasped the paper Ratso was extending toward me, asked 'Is that everything?,' received a curt nod from Ratso, then ran around the back of the bed about two steps ahead of the huge, increasingly ominous-looking white-clad Fury with a stethoscope around her neck about the size of the Holland Tunnel. I speed-walked to the door as quickly as dignity would allow.

Out on the street, I took in the grim, cold, debris-blown visage of the New Year as a man about half my age plundered a nearby garbage can. I didn't know if he happened to be one of the wonderfully weak-willed generation of Americans we seem to be breeding lately, an outpatient from the Butt-Holdsworth Home for the Bewildered, or a guy kind of like myself who had run out of people to see and places to go. He was a small part of the wretched refuse from that teeming shore that, unfortunately, now seemed to be our own. Shore, that is.

I walked up the block to a French laundry that was now run by a Chinese family. I waved to a little Chinese kid inside and he waved back. I didn't know if they still sautéed pinafores, or whatever French laundries were supposed to do, but at least this one was friendly.

I stopped a little upwind from a guy urinating on a brick wall, flipped my cigar into the gutter, and took the crumpled page out of my coat pocket. The page on which Ratso had written everything he'd observed about his attacker. It was broad daylight but I semiconsciously stepped under a streetlamp to read it.

On the page was a somewhat crude, childlike drawing of a fist, the four knuckles of which had been tattooed with the letters L-O-V-E.

Almost precisely my sentiments for the season.

25

The phone book was still missing when I got back to the loft and so was some of my eagerness to jump into the quirky quagmire of the case without at least testing the water with my big toe. A week had gone by since Tequila's human contents had been punctiliously poured into the River Styx and there was still nothing new unless you wanted to count the New Year which, as far as I could see, didn't look too damn good.

Whether Ratso stayed in New York or went to California it didn't appear as if he'd be able to be much help for some time to come. Working on a murder case without my faithful Dr Watson would be lonely going, but, as my old friend Tom Baker used to say: 'There are worse things in life than being lonely.' Unfortunately, Tom failed to impart to me what these things were prior to his unscheduled exit.

The action seemed to be coming at fairly regular intervals right into my loft. If I leaped into the middle of things, I wouldn't have to jump too far.

I lit a cigar, sat down at my desk, and took the jump.

The first thing I needed to check on, even before I waded through Tequila's murky background, was the matter of the tattooed fist. Winnie's husband from Sing Sing, though he'd been wearing his little glovies the night I'd seen him, looked like a logical candidate for that kind of decorative self-expression. Tattoos of that nature, L-O-V-E on one fist and H-A-T-E on the other, were common in prisons and biker gangs, though they were not very popular yet among Young Republicans.

The point to settle was whether Winnie's husband from Sing Sing was also Ratso's attacker. Once this was established, a nice sliver of light might possibly be shed upon the identity of Tequila's attacker as well. All three violent incidents had occurred at my loft within one week. I didn't know if the crime rate was down in the city, but it seemed to be up in my apartment.

I puffed purposefully on the cigar for a moment, weighing the tedium of talking to Winnie with the unpleasantness of calling Cooperman.

Winnie won.

Not that I have anything against cops; cops are important and lesbians are important. It's just that if you don't really need a cop, sometimes it's better to make do with a lesbian.

I made myself a cup of espresso, got settled back at the desk, took a few tentative puffs on the cigar, and called Winnie. The ceiling seemed pretty quiet at the moment. When I got Winnie on the phone and asked her about her husband from Sing Sing, she seemed subdued and almost apologetic about the events of the previous night.

'I haven't seen my *ex*-husband, Bud, in eight years, fuck-face.'

'Sir Fuck-face,' I said.

'If he had the Gettysburg Address on the tip of his dork I wouldn't have known it.'

'David Allen Coe has a snake tattooed on the tip of his penis,' I said. I glanced briefly at my cigar but didn't take a puff.

'Who's David Allen Coe?' she asked.

I took a somewhat chagrined slurp of espresso. I have found that one of the rather disconcerting things about lesbians is their almost total lack of appreciation for country music.

'Country singer,' I said.

'What do you have tattooed on the tip of your dork?' she asked. 'A liver fluke?'

Out of the blower came a sexy, almost-growling lesbian laugh. I chuckled along to show that I was a good sport and that my masculinity wasn't threatened.

'Jewish people aren't allowed to have tattoos on the tips of their penises,' I said calmly. 'If they do, then their penises have to be buried in Gentile cemeteries. Of course, sometimes we'll just take the tattooed tips of the penises, wrap them up, and send them over to Russia. The Russians plant them over there. Grow little dictators.'

Winnie did not laugh. She said, 'That's precious,' then she hung up the phone.

I was not making a lot of headway, as it were. All I'd learned was that the guy was her *ex*-husband and his name was Bud. I was not surprised that he wound up in Sing Sing. Guys named Bud usually do get into some kind of trouble. Even Robert Young's son on *Father Knows Best* got himself into trouble apparently, according to the *National Enquirer*. And if you're in the *National Enquirer* and you're not an astrologer or a Brazilian midget, you're definitely in trouble.

I took a sip of espresso but it was already tepid. I took a puff on the cigar but it'd gone out. I reached for my phone book but it wasn't there.

Sometimes, even if your name isn't Bud and you're not a Brazilian midget, life can be tedious.

26

Later that Sunday evening, as darkening shadows fell rather gingerly across the garbage trucks parked on Vandam Street, I reached out and touched Sergeant Cooperman. He was not greatly pleased to hear from me. During the course of our brief conversation I managed to pick up several semicogent pieces of information. Sing Sing was now known as the Ossining Correctional Facility. I conveyed to Cooperman my regret that a colorful, poetic name like Sing Sing should be changed to a dull, almost prison-gray, bureaucratic one such as the Ossining Correctional Facility. Cooperman belched lightly into the phone.

I also learned that Cooperman would have Bud's Department of Corrections file checked for tattooing on his knuckles and would get back to me on the matter. Finally, I learned that Bud would not be getting out anytime soon, a fact I heartily disbelieved, knowing the ridiculous release policies of New York area prisons and mental hospitals. I was a *Post* reader and I remembered the story about the guy who cut off his mother's head, was held briefly for observation, then was released and promptly cut off his ex-wife's head. The headline, I believe, had been TWO HEADS ARE BETTER THAN ONE. I thought fleetingly of Cleve for some reason.

The conversation ended rather abruptly when Cooperman got a

ten-four or whatever they call it and hung up on me just as I was saying 'Good-bye, Sergeant. Thank you.'

When you're left stranded with a blower in one hand and a cigar in the other, it's always a good idea to cradle the blower and light the cigar. I performed those acts. The cat did not applaud.

I still missed my phone book. Even if there'd been someone to call, there was no way to call them. Maybe I should've done what my friend Don Imus does every New Year's Eve. Throws his phone book into the fire. I'd had mine for so long it was starting to read like the *Book of the Dead*. It's all very well to sit back and let people call you, but when you're attempting to conduct an investigation into a murder, that particular passive dog usually won't hunt.

I took the guitar pick out of my pocket and studied it on my desk. Yep. They'd spelled my name right.

I thought of the painstaking process that was going to be required to gather the phone numbers of the people who'd been in and around the Texas Jewboys. They were the ones, I thought, who were most likely to still be hanging on to one of these guitar picks after thirteen years.

Some of the people and some of the picks could be accounted for, I reflected, and some of them couldn't. For instance, I'd given one to my Peace Corps buddy John Morgan who'd once used it – successfully, I might add – to get backstage at an Eric Clapton concert. Later, both Morgan and the pick had gone mysteriously missing and I suppose there were times you could've said the same about Eric, but that's rock 'n' roll. I'd finally found out what had become of John in Borneo, but the circumstances had been of such a peculiar nature that the subject of the pick, or Eric Clapton, had, of course, not arisen.

But what bothered me most was the fact that the water'd been running when I left the loft last week and I hadn't noticed the pick in the doorway on my way out. So it was logical to think that whoever'd whacked Tequila had also dropped the pick, and I was rapidly coming to realize that, if Tequila hadn't dropped it on the way in, it might've been placed there on purpose. The person who'd done that, I theorized, had also taken my phone book. The bastard. But why? What numbers could possibly be in that book that a murderer would want to get his bloody hands on?

I thought about it as I fed the cat a late-night snack of tuna. I thought about it as I sat at the kitchen table alone smoking a cigar. I thought about it as I listened to the rhythmic thuddings of the lesbian dance class as it started up somewhere over my head in the night sky of New York.

I was still thinking about it later that night in bed when I got the phone call from Dylan Ferrero, the first road manager for the Texas Jewboys. Dylan told me that Raymond Boatright, the keyboard player for the band, had just been discovered dead from an apparent drug overdose in Dallas. An autopsy was to be conducted.

Boatright had been found, according to Dylan, sitting in his apartment, looking over an old scrapbook of the Texas Jewboys.

27

There was a time in rock 'n' roll, during the late sixties and early seventies, when the death of a band member was considered to be a very fashionable and fortuitous thing. After the demise of said dead individual, the band would succeed to far greater heights than they'd ever dreamed of or, in fact, usually deserved. Now, with the legacy of Nancy Reagan's persuasive 'Just Say No' program and George Bush's equally effective anti drug policies, drugs and, for that matter death, are not as popular as they used to be. They're both still around, however. If you want them, you can find them.

For myself, I stopped snorting cocaine several weeks ago, when Bob Marley fell out of my left nostril. Haven't touched it since. Cocaine, that is. I still touch my left nostril every now and then when I think nobody's looking. I was touching my left nostril that Wednesday morning while standing at my kitchen window and, sure enough, somebody was watching.

It was a figure with a very large head, standing out there on the freezing sidewalk. The head was looking up at me. It was either

McGovern or a very good McGovern impersonator, and it didn't matter which because it didn't look like it was going away.

'Stop pickin' your nose,' it shouted as I opened the window and threw down the puppet head. The puppet head made a graceful little trajectory, temporarily blotting out McGovern.

Trajectory. I thought of something Kelli Tuck, with her perfectly formed, muscular dancer's legs, had mentioned to me on New Year's Eve. Her father, Grady, had a theory he called 'life as trajectory.' Just as NASA, when trying to land a rocket on the moon, for instance, would aim a little above the target. Grady believed you should always aim a little higher than your dreams.

I watched as the puppet head, with its colorful parachute, completed its own little trajectory and fell directly in front of McGovern's face. I watched as he reached for it and missed, and the puppet head bounced painfully several times, puppet head first, onto the heartless, Paleolithic sidewalks of New York. I watched as the little head rolled off the sidewalk and the large form with the large head scuttled after it like a giant sun being drawn suddenly into the gravitational orbit of a small, black tennis ball in the gutter.

So much for life as trajectory.

It might work in theory, but in practice, I always felt you'd meet with less disappointment if you adhered to Tom Lehrer's attitude toward life. 'Life,' said Lehrer, 'is like a sewer. What you get out of it depends upon what you put into it.'

Scant moments later, McGovern and I were sipping carefully at two very hot espressos. It was not theories of life that the two of us were discussing. It was theories of death.

On the table between us McGovern had thoughtfully provided his rather lurid *Daily News* account of Tequila's murder. I scanned it until I came to the phrase 'brains down the drain,' and then, like Hercule Poirot, placed it perfectly symmetrically back on the table between us.

'That's somewhat graphic, isn't it, McGovern?'

'You should've seen the *Post!*' McGovern laughed his loud, hearty Irish laugh. It would always be too early in the morning for that laugh.

'McGovern,' I said with some heat, 'not to take away from the *great* writing you've done in the past . . .'

'Lots of it about you.'

'Of course. Not to take away from *that* – but if I took a Nixon at Grand Central Station and read the men's room walls, I could save thirty-five cents.'

McGovern looked hurt and I instantly regretted the remark. But he took a sip of espresso and brightened immediately.

'You'd only save a dime,' he said.

'Why's that?' I asked. I lit my first cigar of the morning and waited.

'It costs you a quarter to take a dump at Grand Central,' he said. Then he laughed even louder.

Suddenly, McGovern became very serious. 'It's hard to believe a guy was murdered right here in your loft just ten days ago.'

'No harder than believing in never-never land,' I said. I took advantage of the absence of Irish laughter to refill both espresso cups and to mention to McGovern the news Dylan had told me several nights before.

McGovern stared at me thoughtfully. I shrugged amiably and took a puff or two on the cigar. 'Just one of those little coincidences of life,' I said.

'Or death,' said McGovern.

It was a coincidence, all right. How strange after all these years that Raymond Boatright and I should suddenly be on the same wavelength. I'd been up here in New York pondering, resisting, wrestling the notion of going back out on the road with the band. Raymond, so far away in terms of time and geography, digging up strikingly similar bones. A scrapbook of the Texas Jewboys.

We drank our espresso in silence. The cat jumped on the kitchen table and McGovern patted her head like he was very gently dribbling a basketball. McGovern loved everything, but he hadn't had a lot of luck with animals. He'd once sat his large Irish buttocks down on a couch without looking and seriously injured his girlfriend's lap dog.

'You know,' he said, 'the first shot that hit Tequila was a gut shot. It was fired right through the curtain and probably didn't kill him. Then the killer throws the curtain open, sees who his victim is, or, possibly, thinks he's been recognized, and finishes Tequila off almost point-blank to the head.'

I puffed patiently on the cigar and waited. You had to wait a lot when McGovern was theorizing.

'That first shot,' he said, 'the one fired through the curtain – '

'Get to the meat of it,' I said irritably.

'That first shot,' said McGovern, 'was meant for *you*.'

28

I didn't really buy McGovern's theory but I thought about it all the way to the bottle of Jameson's. McGovern was a large, colorful, kind, humorous American, but he was also a very smart American. He was the only person at the *Daily News* who'd been a Nieman Fellow at Harvard, one of journalism's highest accolades. He was also the only Nieman Fellow who'd never finished high school.

And McGovern thought the first shot was meant for me. I poured the kind of shot I liked a hell of a lot better and killed it. Nice way to start the day. Drink a shot of Jameson's and begin to realize that somebody'd been trying to kill you. Not that I hadn't been aware of that possibility. It was just that when McGovern said something he believed deeply, it always carried great spiritual force.

I poured another medicinal shot to settle my nerves. It was very early for me. Almost eleven o'clock. Maybe I'd go out to an Indian restaurant. Were any Indian restaurants open yet? Did Indians eat breakfast? What'd they order – blintzes *vindaloo*?

I was getting set to kill the second shot when the two red phones connected to the same line rang at once on both sides of my desk. They always rang at once, of course. That's what happens when you connect them to the same line. But it creates an urgency and an importance that I kind of like. You feel like you're doing something vital, like manning the crisis hotline for the National Bulimia Society.

I carried the shot of Jameson's over to the desk and, picking up the blower on the left, heard the unmistakable, grating, gravel voice of Sergeant Cooperman.

'No initials, Tex,' he said. 'No L-O-V-E, no H-A-T-E. Not even M-O-M.'

'That's too bad,' I said. The thing had looked too easy anyway.

'What's wrong, Tex? You wanted initials? You got a thing about initials?'

'Not really. I never like to say 'fuck' in front of a C-H-I-L-D, but that's – '

'You know, Tex, I've had to come over there twice this week. Three times could be the charm. What you need is to get out of the city for a while. Talk that little bull dyke upstairs into going on a vacation with you. Take her to Niagara Falls.'

Possibly because of Cooperman's homophobic nuance I thought of Oscar Wilde and what he'd reportedly said upon seeing Niagara Falls: 'Second greatest disappointment for American brides.' They weren't makin' fagolas like Oscar Wilde anymore. They were making a hell of a lot of homosexuals these days, especially for a group that couldn't reproduce itself. But none of them were as clever or as funny as Oscar Wilde. Of course, nobody else was either.

'I hear Portugal's nice,' I said to Cooperman.

'Look, pal, let me tell you something. I don't know what's goin' on, but you're definitely in the middle of a mess that's probably gonna turn out pretty fucking ugly. In fact, it already has. We ran the prints on this Kirby McMillan Tequila character and came up with nothing. Also, the OCCB's come up empty so far.'

'What about Bud from Sing Sing? I mean the Ossining Correctional Facility? Ratso got decked in the hallway last week by a guy with L-O-V-E initialed on his fist. So obviously, it wasn't Bud. But who says Bud couldn't have been hanging around here the week before and knocked off Tequila?'

'I says,' said Cooperman. 'He would've had to have had a fuckin' out-of-body experience. He wasn't released from prison until New Year's Eve.'

After I'd hung up the blower with Cooperman, I fed the cat some tuna, took the two espresso cups off the kitchen table, and walked them over to the sink where they'd feel more comfortable in the company of some friendly cockroaches and all the other unwashed crap. I looked around the loft and it suddenly appeared to my mind's myopic eye that the place seemed dusty, cold, empty, and unlived-in, like an attic that didn't want to think about its memories.

I left the cat in charge, grabbed a few cigars, put on my old cowboy hat and hunting vest, and bugged out for the dugout. I took Vandam to Hudson to Eighth Avenue, and by the time I walked into LaBonbonniere and waved hello to Charles, the proprietor, my nose hairs were hanging down like frozen stalactites.

There was a new waitress there with an interesting mouth and about twenty-seven bracelets and legs that reminded me a little of Kelli's. She asked me what I wanted and I ordered bacon and eggs, honeymoon style.

'What's honeymoon style?' she asked as she adjusted several of her bracelets.

'Straight up and hard,' I said. I don't remember whether she laughed or not, but the fat lady at the nearby table didn't appear to find it all that amusing.

I studied the fat lady as I ate my breakfast. She weighed in at almost three hundred pounds and the guy across from her, whom I took to be her husband, looked just like your normal guy. You see a lot of fat ladies like that who all seem to have average, fairly nice-looking husbands. I asked my friend Dr Jim Bone about it once and he said it was the Jack Sprat Phenomenon.

Something was definitely wrong with the picture at the nearby table and I guess the Jack Sprat Phenomenon explained it as well as anything, but it didn't account for what was wrong with the picture in my mind. Nobody lives forever, but two members of the original band, the Texas Jewboys, had just gone to Jesus inside of one week. When I got back to the loft I planned to call Dylan and get an update on Raymond Boatright's death, but Tequila's croaking was starting to really puzzle me. Something was all wrong about it, that much I knew. Something I'd seen but I hadn't really observed.

I drank my coffee and looked out the window onto Eighth

Avenue and thought of all the things that happen every day that we don't appreciate the significance of as they occur. For instance, it is recorded that on Tuesday, July 14, 1789, the day the mobs stormed the Bastille, King Louis XVI of France wrote in his diary the word 'Nothing.'

I drank more coffee and looked out the window as history slowly ticked by on the already ancient street outside. The past and the present are deeply intertwined, I thought. History is what happens when one of them gets a little ahead of the other. When a couple of kids on skateboards rolled by I closed my eyes for a moment and it almost sounded like a streetcar.

29

'Linguini and yogurt?' I said.

'Don't you like it?' I heard Kelli ask in a tone that was almost maddening in its childlike innocence.

'Of course I like it,' I shouted. 'Everybody in America likes linguini and yogurt.' I blew some cigar smoke up at the lesbians and made a face at the cat. The cat didn't respond but I knew damn well she wouldn't like linguini and yogurt. Linguini and tuna, maybe.

'So save your appetite. This should be really good. The dinner's at the home of some friends of mine, some dancers I'd like you to meet.'

'I've already got a pretty good appetite,' I said, 'for you doing splits on the bridge of my nose.' Kelli chuckled indulgently. So did I.

It was moving in on two-thirty when I hung up with Kelli. The plan was for me to pick her up around eight at her place on West Eleventh Street, and then together we'd venture into the East Village for linguini and yogurt. I'd already had my hip card fairly well punched in the funk department, but this promised to be the kind of experience very few Americans would ever get to have in the course of their lives. I owed it to myself. I owed it to my country.

Going over the day's correspondence, I noticed that I also owed quite a bit to Con Ed, New York Telephone, and the rather unpleasant Greek woman I subletted the loft from. I couldn't go on, I suddenly realized, being an unemployed youth forever. You can't eat a jukebox. My bank account was beginning to resemble that of Dr Martin Luther King at the time of his death. I thought fleetingly of rounding up the Texas Jewboys and going back out on the road. Then I thought of Tequila. And Raymond. There'd been several incarnations of the Jewboys, and there were guys who'd gladly fill in for the two of them, but it wouldn't be quite the same. Of course, if I was the kind of person who wanted everything the same I wouldn't be going to the East Village tonight for linguini and yogurt.

I decided not to worry about money. Like I'd always said: 'Money may buy you a fine dog, but only love can make it wag its tail.' Unless I missed my bet, that tail was damn well going to be wagging the dog later tonight on Vandam Street.

Around five-thirty, when I thought Dylan would be home from teaching his fourth-grade class in San Antonio, Texas, I reached him on the blower.

'How was school today?' I asked.

' "Teach your children well," ' he said. Dylan had the endearingly exasperating habit of frequently speaking in rock lyrics. It wasn't as bad a habit as, say, picking your nose, but sometimes it required the even-mindedness of the Mahatma on the part of the listener.

'Anything new on Boatright's autopsy?'

' "Don't send me no more dead flowers, baby, no." ' How did he teach?

'The autopsy, Dylan. Anything?'

' "Nothing was delivered," ' he said.

After some wheedling and cajoling, I was able not only to understand Dylan but to, at least temporarily, wean him from his lyrical mode.

'So it looks like an intentional drug overdose,' I said. 'That's too bad.' It was too bad. But lately I was fresh out of sympathy for drug overdoses, intentional or unintentional. Too many people who'd wanted to live on this rotting grapefruit of a dying star had already been indiscriminately eighty-sixed. Somebody up there was asleep at the switch.

'It's pretty strange, hoss,' said Dylan. 'Ray wasn't one for suicide. And he knew the dangers of drugs pretty well from all his years on the road.'

'It's always the best swimmers who drown,' I said.

Dylan also revealed that he'd gotten a phone call the day before from Snakebite Jacobs, the horn player for the Jewboys, who was living in New Orleans. Snakebite, apparently, had heard from Boatright in the days just prior to his death, and Raymond had sounded fine.

'In fact,' said Dylan, 'Ray had asked Snakebite for your phone number but Snakebite didn't have it. He also wanted the number of somebody else in the band.'

'And who would that be?' I asked with a slight sense of dread.

'He wanted Tequila's number. You don't know how to reach Tequila, do you?'

'No,' I said.

After I hung up I looked over at the cat. 'I could've given him 1–800-CROAK,' I said.

30

The East Village is like any other village except that it's seedier, funkier, and more violent. It is inhabited largely by witches, homosexuals, and drug addicts, and, of course, the few bad apples that you'd find in most any community.

'There better be one hell of a lot of linguini and yogurt,' I said as we ankled it up seven flights of dark, dank stairs in the middle of nowhere. 'What I'd really like is a big hairy steak.'

'That's disgusting,' said Kelli, turning up her cute, health-oriented nose as we made our way down a hallway almost big enough for a conga line of pygmies. Strange music was emanating from behind a shabby door. Sounded like somebody'd left their Ravi Shankar record out in the sun too long.

Kelli knocked.

I knocked.

We both knocked.

Eventually, the door was opened by a rather peevish pansexual with green hair who said, '*Entrez-vous*.' We did.

The place was lit by candles and redolent with incense. Judging from the appearances of the fourteen men and the one woman who were there, it had the mildly unhealthy ambience of a cheerless, homosexual Haight-Ashbury.

'I'll just help myself to the linguini,' I said as the men and the woman began to gyrate wildly around the small room, all of them with their eyes closed.

Our host ignored my needs. Instead, he spoke patiently to Kelli and me, as if we were students in Dylan Ferrero's fourth-grade class. 'Kundalini yoga,' he said, 'is a very old East Indian form of yoga. It involves shaking your body up and down in order to excite and encourage energy to go up and down your spine.' He closed his eyes and gave us a very sick little demonstration. I gave Kelli a very thin little wintry smile.

'Kundalini yoga,' I said, nodding my head sagely.

'Kundalini yoga?' she said to the thing with green hair, but he was now spinning around with his eyes closed and couldn't be bothered.

'The green moss is about the only normal thing about the guy,' I said. 'So much for linguini and yogurt.'

'I'm sorry,' Kelli said. 'I must've been listening to these New Yorkers with a Texas accent.'

'*These*,' I said, indicating the fourteen men and one woman who were now madly gyrating around the room, 'are *not* New Yorkers. *These* are creatures from a distant doughnut. Their sexual identity is a multiple-choice question.'

'They do have some nice moves,' she said.

'It's a marvelously self-expressive form,' I agreed. My head was aching and I was about ready to pass out from hunger, but you've got to humor a dancer if you ever hope to have her help you do the horizontal hustle.

Eventually, Ravi Shankar expired, the dancers stopped moving and languidly held their positions like anemic, degenerate department-store manikins, and a weird little guy came over to us as cheerful as a second cousin at a bar mitzvah. He hugged Kelli and introduced himself to me as Bongo, a dancer Kelli'd once worked with when she was doing a show in Las Vegas. He, apparently, was the one who'd gotten me into this nightmare and I wanted to beat him like a drum.

'What do you think?' he asked, all smiles as he gestured around the room at the dancers who now looked only slightly more substantial than the melting candles. The whole scene made you feel like you were living inside a depraved, human birthday cake. I'd've gotten the hell out of there but it didn't look like I was going to get to make a wish. I damn sure wasn't going to blow any candles.

'Great,' said Kelli.

'Really something,' I said.

'But that's not all,' said Bongo. He ushered us over to where everyone was eagerly forming a rather unpleasant circle on the floor in the full-lotus position. I hadn't sat in the full-lotus position since I'd been a fetus.

After Kelli and I'd taken our places in the circle, Bongo introduced us to the group. Then, one at a time, each person shared his own intimate feelings, now that the magic of kundalini yoga had put all of them in touch with the energy in their spines.

'I feel utterly consumed by love for everyone,' said one young man.

'I feel great anger at my parents for not letting me be myself,' said another, who obviously held a black belt in Jewish whining.

The woman, for some unknown reason, began to sob. Her sobbing continued for some extended time so, thankfully, she missed her chance to share her experience.

'Next,' I said quietly. Kelli elbowed me in the ribs and, before I knew it, a guy across the circle from me was orbing me rather heavily.

'I feel a great love for Kinky,' he said.

31

Later, out on the street, I grabbed the first hack I saw, aimed it at Little Italy, and took Kelli to Luna's Restaurant on Mulberry Street where we finally ran down some real linguini. Luna's was the place Ratso and I'd had dinner with Mike Bloomfield several weeks before his death. Every time I went in there I thought I heard diminished guitar chords.

Luna's never changed. You had to walk by a loaded scullery sink just to get in the place. The waiter, a cheerful, obese, Italian version of a character from *Deliverance*, came up to the table singing 'She'll Be Comin' Round the Mountain When She Comes' before he chucked the menus at us. Yola was the lady at the counter. She was Ratso's friend and was currently busy handling the Jewish piano and watching reruns of *Barnaby Jones*. The pasta was the best in the world.

The waiter had brought a large carafe of red wine and a loaf of Italian bread, and was onto the last chorus of 'She'll Be Comin' Round the Mountain,' when Kelli excused herself for the ladies' room. For a brief, shining moment there I'd had wine, woman, and song, if you counted 'She'll Be Comin' Round the Mountain.' Now, with Kelli and the waiter gone, I just had the wine. I could make it.

I gazed across Mulberry Street at the little Franciscan monastery. The Church of His Precious Blood. I thought of the wine as Michael Bloomfield's blood. He was a Jew like Jesus. Skinny like Jesus. Died pretty young like Jesus. All Jesuses died young, I reflected, as the waiter brought two heaping orders of linguini with red clam sauce and a large pungent bowl of *zuppa di pesce* with everything but the scullery sink floating in it. It was hard to imagine what an old Jesus would've been like. A ragged, unemployed, homeless old fart in a frayed purple robe hanging out at domino parlors and bocci courts, irritating tourists with his eccentric antics. It was probably a good thing he died young, I thought. Like aging movie queens and aging homosexual queens, for an aging King of all mankind, the market just wasn't there. I poured another glass of wine and started in on the soup.

When Kelli returned to the table she sat down across from me and gave me a forced little smile. 'Don't wait for me,' I said. 'Go right ahead.'

'I found something in my purse,' she said.

'That's fairly remarkable in itself.'

Kelli smiled wearily. 'Remember that ex-boyfriend I told you about? For some weeks he'd been calling me from Texas in the middle of the night. I told him not to call, I hung up on him repeatedly, but nothing worked. On his birthday he called me at four o'clock in the morning and, in a weird voice, sang "Happy Birthday" to himself.'

'My heart breaks for guys like that.'

'Anyway, last week the calls suddenly stopped and I thought I was finally through with him. Now I go into the ladies' room, fumble around in my purse, and find *this*.'

'So he's here in New York?'

'It looks like it,' Kelli said with a hint of fear in her eyes.

'Let's see that note,' I said. Kelli handed it over, and I unfolded and studied it on the table just to the left of my linguini. It was one of those sick things that serial killers and Son of Sam types often put together to maintain that deadly balance of fame and anonymity that they crave. The words were neatly cut from newspaper print and pasted on the page.

A very faint shudder went through me. I wasn't sure if it was the note or the *zuppa di pesce*. But there was something about people who wrote and sent notes like this. The crimes themselves, if and when they were ever committed, might be fairly routine. But the very act of cutting up words of newsprint and pasting them onto a page, unless you were a child or an old lady making a scrapbook, usually meant you were a creep.

I glanced at the note again. It read: 'the EYES of Texas are UPON you. YOU cannot Get AWAY.'

32

'The problem,' I said to the cat, 'with being a country singer-turned-amateur detective is the clients you tend to attract. Even if I'm able to resolve the situation with Kelli's crazy ex-boyfriend from Texas, it'd be inappropriate, not to mention difficult, to collect a fee from a dancer. Of course, it'd be easier than collecting a fee from Tequila. You see the problem?'

It was a cold, dreary Tuesday afternoon and the cat, unfortunately, didn't see a damn thing except the large fly crawling up the side of my mug of hot chocolate. I did not wish the fly to attach itself to one of my melting mini-marshmallows. Nor did I wish for the cat to take a swipe at the fly and spill hot chocolate on my scrotum. My only wish was that I wasn't wading Watson-less into a world of wickedness.

'I know you hate every living thing except yourself,' I said to the cat, perhaps a bit harshly. 'As far as you're concerned I could be a country singer-turned-homosexual, or worse, an accountant. Then I could carefully calibrate your meals and you'd never be without your beloved tuna for the rest of your life. You'd like that, wouldn't you?'

The cat said nothing, but a positively wistful look came into her eyes. I lit a cigar, took a sip of hot chocolate, and took stock of what I had. I wrote it down in rough form on my Big Chief tablet and looked it over for a while, maybe trying to read more into it than was there. The Big Chief tablet read:

Sunday, December 26th, Tequila croaked in rain room.

Friday, December 30th, Ratso zimmed in hallway. Windows of loft nailed shut.

Saturday, December 31st, Winnie's ex-husband, Bud, intrudes himself upon quiet domestic scene, burns a hole in the middle of Persian rug big enough for me to put the whole thing over my head and wear it as a serape.

The first two entries, I figured as I puffed the cigar and studied the Big Chief tablet, could very easily be seen as attempts on my life. Obviously, neither one had been successful. That was why I was smoking a cigar and studying a Big Chief tablet instead of whiling away eternity as worm bait in some suburban bone orchard.

The third entry on the Big Chief tablet, Bud's crashing of my little New Year's Eve party, seemed unrelated to the first two. I would've liked it to be related because Bud seemed a good perpetrator for just about anything, but his alibi was too tight. I still had almost nothing to go on in the riddle of the killer's identity. I was clearly going to need to recruit a new Watson, but there was a problem of a totally different nature that seemed to be nagging at the corners of my mind: Kelli's persistent, slightly deranged noodnik of an ex-boyfriend from Texas. I knew not to take him too lightly. After Charles Whitman, Richard Speck, and Charles 'Tex' Watson, I wasn't going to be taking any chances with good ol' boys from Texas who liked to cut words out of newspapers, paste them into messages, and slip them into dance bags. No, Bubba.

If I had the chance, I certainly planned to find this guy and rearrange his bolo tie for him, but first there were other liver flukes to fry. I had to locate the five remaining former Texas Jewboys and the small handful of people who'd worked the closest with the original band. I had to talk to all of them. Try to flesh out some kind of background on Tequila. It wasn't going to be easy without my address book containing their telephone numbers. Tracking wandering Jews could shape up to be a formidable task under the best of circumstances, I thought. I empathized with the committee that had been given the job of writing the Old Testament.

I made a short list on another page of the Big Chief tablet of all the former Jewboys and road crew who'd been with the band from the start. I puffed on the cigar, took a few sips of hot chocolate, tongued a mini-marshmallow, and looked over the list. It read as follows:

Band Members:
Snakebite Jacobs, Billy Swan, Willie Fong Young, Little Jewford, Major Boles, Wichita, Panama Red, Skycap Adams.

Others:

Cowboy Jack, Dylan, Big Jewford, Bo Byers, and my brother, Roger. Deceased: Tequila, Raymond Boatright.

Of course, Tequila and Boatright hadn't lived or died in anything like the same manner, but dead is dead. Once deceased, always deceased. It didn't matter who you were or what you were. As Bum Phillips once said: 'The thing that's going to decide the size of your funeral is the weather.'

I looked out the window and the late-afternoon January sky seemed to be bleeding a frozen, semiviscous, gray-green ooze. Not a fortuitous day for a large funeral.

I called Dylan first.

'So how was school today?'

' "Don't know much about a science book. Don't know much about the French I took." '

Over the next few hours I spoke with a couple of voices from the past and learned a number of things including more than I ever wanted to know about the effects of time on wandering Jewboys and other assorted Americans. I logged all information I gleaned, trivial or inconsequential as it seemed, into the Big Chief tablet. Many of the numbers I called had been disconnected. Some had taped referrals. Others had happy Puerto Rican families residing at them. Most of the time I had to leave messages on machines or with people I didn't know.

Around seven I closed shop for the day, put on my hat and coat, and grabbed a few cigars out of what was left of Sherlock Holmes's head after a little reconstructive surgery with Elmer's glue. I left the cat in charge and the answering machine to do the work. I had my lines out across the murky bayou of the years and the miles. Now all I had to do was wait for the fish.

Of course, by the time I caught them they'd probably smell worse than Winnie Katz's workout shorts.

33

'I just don't know,' said McGovern, shaking his great head with an exaggerated sarcasm I felt was hardly warranted. 'Moving up from your leg man to your Dr Watson. I'm not sure I can handle the responsibility. The enormous trust you're somehow willing to place in me. I'm thrilled, of course, beyond words, but I can only pray you find me worthy.'

'Put a sock on it, McGovern,' I said irritably.

We both sat in silence for a while and watched a wooden chair burn in the fireplace of McGovern's quaint little newspaper-strewn apartment on Jane Street. We were drinking double shots from a giant bottle of Black Bush that I'd bought at great personal expense in an effort to soften McGovern's reticence toward actively helping me with the Tequila murder case. So far it looked like I was out fifty-eight bucks.

'The thing is,' I said, 'Ratso's out of commission for a while and Rambam's jumping with Los Cobras in Guatemala – '

'And you're here in my apartment jumping through your ass-hole for America.' McGovern laughed loudly in the little room and knocked back a healthy jolt of the Irish whiskey. A sudden dignity came into his demeanor and, as the light from the crackling fire was reflected in his eyes, I thought I caught a glimpse for a moment of the part of him that was Indian.

'Of course I'll help you,' he said. 'Anybody who's in as deep shit as you are and doesn't even know it needs all the help he can get.'

I stood up and grasped his hand firmly. 'Welcome, Watson,' I said.

Watson poured us both another double shot of Black Bush. He lifted his glass. 'Here's to us, Holmes,' he said. 'We're all we've got.'

My drink and I wandered over to McGovern's famous pink velvet couch, sat down, and loitered for a while as McGovern performed the final touches on the Chicken McGovern that had been obscenely bubbling in a pot for several hours now. Hopefully, it'd be ready before Elijah returned and discovered that he didn't have reservations.

Billie Holiday was on McGovern's old Victrola. The apartment had no television set or radio. In the time I'd known McGovern, since Christ was a cowboy, he'd never owned a television or a radio. I wasn't even sure he knew what they were. If giant ants from the third ring of Uranus attacked the world and you were staying at McGovern's apartment, you wouldn't know it until the invasion was pretty far along. You'd be sitting on a couch that'd been across the Atlantic twice, sipping a little Black Bush, listening to Billie Holiday, and reading a rather dog-eared copy of *The Great Gatsby*. Of course, if giant ants from the third ring of Uranus ever attacked the world, that wouldn't be a bad way to go.

'Chicken McGovern's ready,' said McGovern finally.

'This place'd never make it as a fast-food joint,' I said.

We both sat down at the little table against the wall to the left of the fireplace. The ancient Smith-Corona typewriter that had once belonged to McGovern's mother remained on the far side of the table like a short, rather quiet dinner companion.

'Who's going to say the prayer?' asked McGovern.

'How much prayer should a Chicken McGovern get?' I asked, somewhat rhetorically because a large drumstick was already on the way at a very rapid pace to my uvula.

'Prayer,' said McGovern, pausing to take a large swill of the Bushmills, 'is never out of place for a good Christian or a good Jew.'

'I'm a pagan,' I said. 'Like Breaker Morant.'

'Me too,' said McGovern.

'That's obvious from your table manners.'

McGovern laughed. 'Me,' he shouted. 'You're the one eating like a young porker!' The Chicken McGovern was undeniably killer bee.

'Never say "young porker" in front of a Jewish person,' I said. 'It causes us to have gas which leads to diarrhea and, quite often, simultaneous projectile vomiting. In layman's terms, squirtin' outa both ends. And, as you probably know, if you are experiencing diarrhea and projectile vomit and, at the same time, happen to belch, you will die.'

'Yeah,' said McGovern, 'then who's going to say the prayer?'

Toward the end of the meal I reached into one of the inside pockets of my youth and pulled out the newspaper-print note from Kelli's Texas ex. I handed it to McGovern and explained a few of the circumstances of its coming into my possession.

'Of course, the main case we'll be working on is the matter of who lunched Tequila in my rain room,' I said as I got up to pace off a little of the Chicken McGovern. 'But we might be able to clear up this little item quite quickly, and it may prove to be diverting. Good way to get your feet wet, Watson.'

McGovern nodded agreeably as he glanced at the note on the table. 'Yes, boss,' he said in what apparently was a rather weak, Irish-inflected Rochester impersonation. He studied the note more closely.

'Most dancers carry dance bags with them to classes and just about everywhere else they go. The dance bags are like portable attics. They keep their purses in them along with most of their worldly possessions. Everything from tampons to tap shoes. You with me so far?'

'No,' said McGovern. 'It's too hard to follow.'

'Spare me your quaint Irish witticism,' I said. 'The guy who sent this is clearly deranged and certainly very potentially violent.'

'In other words, your typical Texan.' I ignored McGovern's remark.

'The guy could've slipped this note into Kelli's dance bag some time ago when she was back in Texas. She might've not known about it until she fumbled around and found it last night. So the good news is that while the guy's a strange bird, he very probably could be safely nesting somewhere back in Texas.'

McGovern got up from the table, picked up the note, and held it against the light. 'That's the *good* news,' he said.

I walked over to the kitchen and poured a little after-dinner drink. 'Go on,' I said.

'Many newspapers opt for distinctive makeup. Format, column size, typeface, and so on. The New York dailies fall into this category, as do, of course, the *International Herald Tribune, The St Louis Post-Dispatch, The – '*

'So what the hell's the *bad* news?' I asked.

McGovern walked over to the table and took a somewhat theatrical swallow from his tall glass. He set the glass down slowly, folded the note, and handed it back to me rather grimly.

'He's in New York,' he said.

34

I hadn't spoken to Willie Fong Young, the original bass player for the Texas Jewboys, since I'd passed on an invitation to his wedding in order to attend the bas mitzvah of my cousin's daughter. Willie's wedding was in Nashville, and Steve and Loni Samet's daughter Erin was to be bas mitzvahed on the same day in San Antonio. Tough choice for the old social calendar. I figured I'd get sick drunk on Champagne at either affair, but at the bas mitzvah I could wear my Yamaha on my head. With the Jews, you can wear a Yamaha or a tractor seat or a backyard satellite dish on your head and burp all you want as long as your head is covered. I wasn't so sure that the same rules applied for Willie's rather formal country-club affair.

I told Willie at the time that blood was thicker than water, that my whole family would be at the bas mitzvah, and that, as much as I'd like to go to his wedding, 'In the eyes of God, when a young Jew is thirteen years old, the person becomes a man or a woman according to the Torah.'

Willie's response, 'Why don't you go fuck yourself,' showed a certain lack of understanding of Judaism, Christianity, and several other religions, possibly even Islam. Now, as I dialed his number in Nashville, I hoped 'The Singin' Chinaman,' as I lightheartedly referred to him onstage, had softened his attitude toward me.

'Hey, Willie,' I said. 'How's the marriage holding up?'

'Just fine, bagel-nose.' When a Chink from Arkansas calls a Hebe from Texas 'bagel-nose,' sometimes it's almost enough to get your Irish up. Remembering all the times I'd introduced him as 'The Southern Slope,' I let it pass. Besides, I needed Willie's help.

The other Jewboys I'd contacted had mostly reacted positively to the notion of a Jewboy reunion tour, but when I came to information about Tequila it was like a missing chord in a faded melody. Of course, I hadn't heard back from Snakebite or Wichita yet, but it didn't seem as if anybody knew much more about Tequila's life since the band broke up than I did. All of them, however, seemed shocked to hear about his death.

Now, with Willie on the line, it was time to set aside the tension conventions of the past, stir-fry his brains, and maybe come away with a little take-out order of Tequila's movements, other than bowel. I made small talk for a while to steer the topic away from weddings and bas mitzvahs, then I dropped the news of Tequila's murder.

'Jesus Christ!' said Willie.

'I'll see that Jesus and raise you a Peter,' I said. 'Had you been in touch with Tequila at all over the years?' I held my breath. *Somebody* must've been in touch with Tequila since 1976.

'The last time I saw Tequila was in that godforsaken motel someplace in Colorado. The band had just broken up and nobody knew what the hell they were going to do. I walked into his room to say good-bye and he was arguing with Sharon.' Sharon was a belly dancer, a free spirit, and Tequila's wife, roughly in that order. She'd called herself by any number of names, including Fatimah, Sheena, and Madame La Tush. Not only did I not know where she was anymore, I wasn't even sure *who* she was.

'They were always arguing,' I said.

'Yeah, but this one sounded especially vicious. Of course, she never argued with me. She was a pussycat, if you know what I mean.'

'Cast your mind back,' I said. 'Can you remember anything they were saying when you came into the room?'

'Shit. It's been so long. I think – wait a minute – they were yelling about something that happened on a train.'

'You sure it wasn't something that happened on *cocaine*?'

'On that tour, everything happened on cocaine. But it was something heavier than that. Tequila was livid with rage.'

'Cocaine,' I said rather wearily, 'almost ruined my life.'

237

'What do you mean "almost," said Willie.

That was the trouble with having once lived in the fast lane. Every time you sniffled or cleared your throat people thought you were still on drugs. If you'd been known to take a drink in the past and then gotten a divorce, people blamed it on alcohol. Drugs and booze were always blamed for life's failures. My experience has been that drugs and booze tend to make dull people more interesting and interesting people more dull. Of course, if you're on drugs and booze at the time, it's often hard to tell the difference.

'Did Tequila say anything else?' I asked.

'Well, he was pretty bitter as I recall. He said he might just take a trip down to Mexico. And then he said something about you.'

'Spit it,' I said.

'You sure you want to hear it?'

'Look, Willie, Tequila's dead. This happened over thirteen years ago. What could he possibly have said that could hurt me now?'

'He said you were a burned-out star.'

Later that evening I paced the loft, trailing cigar smoke and thinking about my conversation with Willie. What's past was past, I thought. Seine yesterday for clues but don't get caught in it. Life as trajectory, I said to myself. Life as trajectory.

I walked over to the kitchen window and looked up through the rusted fire escape into the narrow New York sky. No stars out tonight. But I knew they were there. Emily Dickinson wrote: 'What are stars but Asterisks to point a human life.'

It was a nice sentiment and one I could relate to, but maybe she should've gotten out of the house a little more.

35

Thursday morning, when Snakebite Jacobs called back, I was able to update my Big Chief tablet a little further. Snakebite had continued to play music in New Orleans since the band broke up. We talked about that a while, commiserated about Ray Boatright a bit, then I laid the news on him concerning Tequila. Snakebite, too, was shocked. I pushed for more on Tequila.

'Haven't seen him since the Jewboys,' said Snakebite, 'but Sharon was through here about three years ago.'

'Through New Orleans?'

'Through my bedroom, actually. She'd cut her hair Egyptian style and called herself Cleopatra.'

'And you were the asp, right, Snakebutt?'

'That's *bite*,' said Snakebite, 'Snake*bite*.' This was an old stage routine that we'd used about eleven times every show. It became progressively more humorous to the audience but I never could tell whether Snakebite liked it or not.

'Cleo said she'd been divorced from Tequila for years. In fact, hadn't even seen him for years. She thought he'd gotten himself into some trouble in Mexico. We didn't talk about him all that much.'

'I can understand that. What happened to – uh – Cleopatra?'

'When she left here she was heading for Vegas. Got a call from her a few weeks later in Miami.'

'Belly dancers move around,' I said.

'You know, one thing was kind of funny about her, though.'

'What was that, Snakebutt?'

'*Bite*,' he said. 'Snake*bite*.'

'What was it, Snakebite?'

'As far as she was away from Tequila and as long as it'd been since she'd seen him, she seemed almost *afraid* of him.'

'If you hear from her again,' I said, 'you can tell her not to worry.'

After I'd hung up with Snakebite, I looked over the notes I'd made on the Big Chief tablet. I'd talked to, or left messages for, everybody except Wichita who now lived in Tulsa. I'd given him more rings than Elizabeth Taylor but still hadn't gotten through to the boy.

Of course, there were other Jewboys I could've called, but they'd come into the band later down the line and had known Tequila only in passing, pardon the expression.

I thought fondly of Van Dyke Parks, Country John Mankiewicz, Roscoe West, and Jimmie Don Smith, the brilliant blues guitarist who'd died of cancer in '86. I remembered our old bus that had broken down somewhere outside of Dolopolous, Mississippi. I smiled in spite of myself. Everything's funny if you wait long enough.

I decided not to contact these latter-day Jewboys just yet. They'd be great to fill out the band for some kind of imaginary childhood reunion tour, but they didn't know much about Tequila. Of course, nobody else seemed to, either. *Somebody* had to, I reflected. Otherwise I wouldn't've had to buy a new shower curtain.

At straight up Gary Cooper time I called Kelli.

'This is the Dancer,' she said as she answered the phone.

'This is the Kinkster,' I said.

'Oh, I was hoping it was you.'

'Your wish has come true.'

'Can I make another?'

'Well, it is my dime, but go ahead.'

'Can we have lunch somewhere?' I could think of a few places I wouldn't've minded eating lunch with the Dancer. One of them was at the Y.

'You know, Dancer, I think you're going to be a piece of cake.'

'You're wrong, darling. All good dancers are very tough. We only appear to be easy.'

'That's what I was afraid of,' I said.

Half an hour later I strolled up to Kelli's building on West Eleventh Street just half a step ahead of the mailman. We rang the buzzer together and I noticed he was carrying a package about the size of a shoe box.

'Too big for the box,' he said.

'That's what she told me last night,' I said. The mailman scowled and said nothing. Reminded me of my cat.

'Hi, Mr Mailman,' said Kelli brightly as she came out onto the front step and kissed me on the cheek.

'Name's Gene,' said the mailman sourly. He handed her the package and turned his attention to the mailboxes on the wall.

'He doesn't like it when I call him Mr Mailman,' said Kelli as she led me down the little hall.

'How can you tell ?' I asked.

She fumbled with the key in the lock for a moment and soon we were inside her first-floor apartment which, more than anything else, resembled a hall of mirrors. The mirrors almost completely covered the bottom third of three of the walls in the large room. On the exposed brick wall, above the little fireplace, was a large framed photograph of a very familiar-looking ass and pair of legs, also exposed.

'Nice decor,' I said.

Kelli set the box down on a small table and eyed it suspiciously. 'That better not be from Travis,' she said.

'Travis, is it?'

'Travis Parnell.'

'What does this Travis Parnell look like?'

'He has blond hair. Very handsome. Comes from an extremely wealthy and prominent family . . .'

'Anything good about the guy?' I asked. I stood in the middle of the mirrored room and lit a cigar with my hot-pink Bic. I took a few reflective puffs.

'He has boots just like yours,' said Kelli.

'Nobody has boots like these,' I said a bit brusquely. 'They're brontosaurus foreskin. They cost two or three hundred. What else about the guy?'

'He usually wears a bolo tie,' said Kelli meekly.

'Every nerd in the world wears a bolo tie *now*,' I said. 'If he'd worn one thirty years ago I might've been impressed with him. Of course, he probably wasn't born then. How old is he, anyway?'

'He was twenty-nine the night he sang me that spooky happy birthday song to himself.'

'Oh,' I said, 'he's a kid.' Kelli smiled indulgently and so did I.

'He's a cowboy,' said Kelli.

'You mean he *thinks* he's a cowboy,' I said. 'There's only one real cowboy left in the world and that's Earl Buckelew who lives just outside of Medina, Texas. Of course, a lot of guys think they're cowboys. That's all right I guess unless they run into somebody who thinks he's an Indian.'

I thought about it for a minute. I was jealous of Travis. I didn't like to admit it, but it was true. I also thought about the other

241

person who'd come to me recently with a story about somebody being after him. I'd have to do a little better job watching Kelli than I'd done with Tequila.

'That's very funny,' Kelli said, staring at the box again, 'but he's scaring the shit out of me.'

'I'm sorry,' I said, and I took her in my arms. She felt very childlike and fragile and vulnerable. My eyes wandered up the photograph above the fireplace. It was amazing, I thought, how many women a woman could be.

'Let's open the package,' I said.

We went to the small table by the doorway and I picked up the box. There was no return address. It was postmarked New York. We opened it together.

Inside was a doll. A ballerina. She didn't look like she'd be doing any dancing soon. Her legs had been severed.

36

That night I decided to put the Tequila file on the back burner and turn my attention to Travis Parnell. Tequila's unfortunate croaking was almost two weeks old but it seemed like a lifetime, so to speak. I was tired of talking to long-distance voices from the past; the trail had grown old and cold.

I still had operatives working in the field. Captain Midnite in Nashville was poking around about the twenty-five thousand dollars and the Music Row-Sixteenth Avenue South connection. Billy Swan was in Los Angeles running down some drug rumors he'd heard about Tequila and his wife. Cleve was calling periodically with highly annoying 'tour updates.' And I'd contacted just about everyone I could think of with the exception of Wichita who, of course, lived in Tulsa.

I wasn't the FBI. I wasn't the NYPD. The only real manpower I had was me and McGovern and sometimes I wasn't so sure about McGovern.

I placed the Tequila file, which looked a lot like a Big Chief tablet, in the desk drawer with the book, lyrics, and music for *God's Other Son*, the Broadway show that Don Imus and I had been working on for about forty-nine years now. By this time, we'd both hoped to have some homosexuals tap dancing, but it just hadn't come to pass. These things take time, the lawyer said. Lawyers, like cats and Moslem fundamentalists, have no notion of time. If you die, they know they'll be dealing with your estate. If your lawyer dies, you still have to get another lawyer, who, of course, looks happily forward to dealing with your estate. Where there's a will, there's a lawyer, I always say.

I closed the drawer, took a fresh cigar out of Sherlock's fractured skull, lit it with my pink Bic, and swung it around rapidly with my left arm in three complete arcs like I'd seen a guy in Austin do once. I figured this maneuver either produced an even burn or the guy was an outpatient trying to land imaginary Nazi aircraft onto the bridge of my nose.

I puffed peacefully for a while and thought about Travis Parnell. He'd grown up in Kerrville, Texas, according to Kelli, and his family still lived there. Kerrville is a beautiful little town, but, like all beautiful little towns, it has spawned a few rather ugly incidents over the years. One was the infamous slave-ranch situation that had occurred several years ago just outside of Kerrville near Mountain Home. Hitchhikers were picked up, forced to work on the ranch, at times at gunpoint, and at least one of them had been tortured, rather slowly, to death. The ranch was owned by people who could best be described as a sadistic, cedar-chopping *Bonanza* family gone bad.

The other unpleasant incident had happened even more recently and involved the horrific nurse Genene Jones, who'd made her rounds in San Antonio and Kerrville for several years, administering deadly injections to babies and then trying to save them. Not always successfully.

I wasn't going to sit around on my introspective Jewish buttocks and wait for Travis Parnell to create incident number three. I don't like waiting. And I know something about the waiting game. If you wait around long enough for your ship to come in, your harbor'll sink.

37

'It's no disgrace,' I've often heard, 'to come from Texas; it's just a disgrace to have to go back there.' Whether or not I went back there now was beside the point, of course, because a little ray of Texas sunshine was apparently already here in New York. Its name was Travis Parnell.

But I was not without friends and connections in the Texas Hill Country. As luck would have it, the only two Jews the people down there knew were me and Jesus Christ, and I was the only one they knew personally.

I called my friend Max Swafford in Kerrville, Texas. Max worked as a counselor who officed in an institution called the Alternative School, which worked with emotionally troubled youngsters who couldn't get along within the educational mainstream. I'd thought about enrolling there several times myself.

Max was a very responsible and character-laden American who'd once served as my press secretary when I ran for justice of the peace in Kerr County. As I recalled, he'd done a fine job until he left in the middle of the campaign to search for a gold mine in southern Mexico.

Unfortunately, my fellow Kerrverts had returned me to the private sector. They hadn't responded too well to my campaign slogan, 'I'll keep us out of war with Fredericksburg.' Fredericksburg was a little town about twenty miles down the road.

As I dialed Texas, I remembered that Max had grown up in West Texas close enough to Mexico to, rather annoyingly, pepper his speech patterns with Spanish. I don't understand Spanish and I don't much like the fact that, at bullfights, Spanish custom dictates they cut the tongues out of the horses so the people won't hear them scream when they get gored. Otherwise, I have nothing against Spanish-speaking peoples.

'¡Hola! ¿Como está?' said Max when he answered the phone.

'Yeah, Max,' I said irritably. 'This is Kinky.'

'¿Qué tal, Señor Friedman?' It was maddening.

'I'm playing with my piñatas here in Nuevo Yorko,' I replied to whatever the hell Max was asking me about. 'Look, Max, I've got a little problem here.'

I explained that I needed a brief thumbnail on Travis Parnell yesterday. I also needed him to try to pinpoint Parnell's present location. I puffed rather plaintively on the cigar and said: 'I need your help, Max.'

'The last time I helped you,' he said, *'perdiste tu culo.'*

I took another patient puff and asked: 'What the hell does that mean?'

'The last time I helped you,' said Max, 'you lost your ass.'

It was creeping up on ten o'clock when I hung up with Max and snow was beginning to fall outside the kitchen window. I was getting that New York trapped-rat feeling that occasionally pervades the soul of all modern cliff dwellers, so I shut down operations, got inside my coat and hat, left the cat in charge, and began to walk up Vandam Street, threading my way through the crazy canopy of God's white geometry.

I was sure that Max would deliver the goods on Travis Parnell. After all, he'd been a great press secretary in the justice of the peace race. Max had a theory that I was only good interpersonally for about five minutes. When people met me as a candidate, they invariably thought I was very charming and entertaining for the first two or three minutes. After that, they usually began to have their doubts about the wisdom of electing me judge. I'd often become rather nervous and defensive then, and start chain-bumming cigarettes and saying things like: 'I'd be a fine judge if I'm any judge at all,' or 'When I get to be governor, I'll reduce the speed limits to 54.95.'

Max would slip in at that point, take my arm, and say something like 'The governor's on the phone for you, Mr Friedman.' Yeah, I thought, Max would deliver the goods on Parnell. When I got to Hudson I took a left and kept walking.

It's funny what you think about when you're walking in the snow alone. Though the case of Tequila was still firmly on the back burner, I could see his face very clearly, along with the others, in some long-ago middle distance between the flakes. The band was getting together to rehearse for our first big national tour. It must've been around '73 because everybody looked young, happy, and full of hope. Time and the road, like two sculptors, were just picking up their chisels.

I could see the place, too. It was an old house on a small isolated ranch out in the Texas Hill Country. My family'd owned it for a while, then sold it to some guy in Houston who'd used it only during hunting season. I didn't know who owned it now.

We called the place Rio Duckworth, after an elementary school teacher my brother Roger had once, Miss Duckworth. We all thought Rio Duckworth was a pretty funny name for a ranch, but, then again, it was 1973 and a lot of things were funny then that now seem almost kind of sad.

Like snowflakes.

I walked into the Cottonwood Cafe, a haven on Bleecker Street for transplanted Texans.

'I'll have a chicken-fried snake,' I said to the girl in the Dallas Cowboys sweatshirt. 'And give me the most esoteric Texas beer you've got.'

'What's esoteric?' she asked.

'This restaurant,' I said. I looked over to the picture of James Dean from the movie *Giant*. It was cool to be cool in the fifties, I thought. In the nineties, it was cool to be hot. Maybe somebody'd been screwing around with the thermostat.

'All we have is Lone Star,' she said.

'That's a wide selection,' I said. 'Tough choice for an indecisive guy like me. Christ. Let me think about it for a minute. Okay, I got it. I'll have a Lone Star.'

Her smile was paper-thin and very brief. Almost a tic. I never did too well with waitresses or stewardesses but I never let it bother me much.

When I'd finished putting my choppers around the chicken-fried snake, for $9.50 plus tax, and knocked off another bottle of Lone Star, I fished out of my pocket the photo of Travis Parnell I'd commandeered from Kelli and showed it to the waitress. Travis looked cute with his shy smile, his hunting rifle, and his military fatigues, but the serene face of the dead Angora goat he was holding up by the horns seemed to exude more humanity. Compared to Parnell, it glowed like the dead face of Christ.

'Know this guy?' I asked.

'No, but I'd like to,' said the waitress.

I looked over at James Dean. He'd died two weeks after filming *Giant* and you could see it coming in his eyes.

'Maybe I can arrange it,' I said.

38

It was still snowing Friday morning when I got up. Out on Vandam Street the garbage trucks seemed to shiver slightly under a thin blanket of off-white. Nothing stays clean very long in New York, not even the garbage trucks. But you get used to it. Like my friend Rambam said in teaching me one of the most important lessons in life: 'Never eat pasta with a white shirt on.'

The cat and I sat by the kitchen window and watched the little people running hither and thither like notes on a zither. Possibly it was the chicken-fried snake, but I felt like someone was taking zither lessons in my colon. For $9.50 plus tax, I hoped they were getting their money's worth.

It was a week into the New Year and it felt old already. Time flies when you're tracking psychos, I thought as I sipped a hot chocolate and wondered what to do next. I stood up to get a better view of the street, and the cat jumped off my lap and onto the windowsill. We watched the snow fall for a while in silence, each of us lost in our own whirling ephemeral dreams.

'Where would you go,' I said to the cat, 'if you were a displaced Texan on your own in New York?' The cat just kept watching the snowflakes. She'd never been to Texas. In fact, like many other folks in the city, she'd never been out of New York. To her, Texas might just as well have been the South Pole. Of course, the Texans might have something to say about that. So might the penguins.

'Put yourself in four of Travis Parnell's boots,' I said to the cat. 'Where would he be hanging out when he's not busy trying to terrorize Kelli?' The cat watched the snow.

'He could go anywhere, of course, but it's good odds that, being

247

a Texas kind of guy, he'd've checked out a Texas kind of place. The girl at the Cottonwood said she's there every night and hadn't seen him. What does that leave us?'

I walked over to Sherlock's head and got a Romeo y Julieta Cedros de Luxe Number Three from Switzerland by way of Havana. A lady named Rocky'd sent me a box and the cigars had that old Cuban flavor that can't quite be described but is a cross between a hint of chocolate and a hint of vanilla. Gives you sort of a protein rush like you get from eating sushi after a bad night. The best Cuban cigars come from Switzerland and that's about all there is to say for Switzerland but it's usually enough. The only way to get cigars this good in America is if your favorite rich uncle gets run over by a book-mobile and leaves you his humidor.

When I got back to the window the cat was pacing back and forth on the sill. 'Relax,' I said. 'I'll make you some breakfast.' I reached under the counter and came up with a can of tuna. Nothing earth-shattering about that. Every can down there was tuna. Cats are creatures of narrow habit and so are most people and that's what keeps amateur detectives in business.

'There's always the Lone Star Roadhouse,' I said. 'Everyone from Texas makes a pilgrimage there.' The cat jumped down from the windowsill and began hungrily attacking the tuna. I continued my relentless monologue. I'd worked harder rooms than this.

'Then there's the Cadillac Bar, Alamo, the Yellow Rose of Texas, and what's that new place on Hudson? It's just up the street from Pete Myers's place, Myers of Keswick, where they have those great pork pies. You ought to try them sometime. You ought to try anything sometime.'

I puffed appreciatively on the Cuban cigar. The cat hadn't even looked up. Like a performer in front of an inattentive dinner-club crowd, I went staunchly on with my routine. Following Travis Parnell's mind around Manhattan.

'Cowgirl Hall of Fame,' I said. 'That's the new Texas place in the Village. I'll check it out, also. See if their chicken-fried snake costs more than nine-fifty plus tax. See if it tastes as good as tuna.'

The cat had stopped wiping the tuna crumbs off her whiskers and was staring at me when the phones rang. I walked over to the desk and picked up the blower on the left. It was 11:47 a.m. by the alarm clock that had once belonged to Captain Midnite. He'd slept through five careers with it before he'd given it to me. I'd moved it recently from the bedroom to the desk. I didn't think I had that many careers left to sleep through.

'Señor Friedman,' said the voice, 'this is Max.'

'Shalom,' I said.

'You're dealing with a real bad *hombre* here, *amigo*. A girlfriend of mine used to date him some time ago until he got mad one night and broke her fingers.'

'Okay, so he's not Alan Alda.'

'There's another story about him pushing a girl over a cliff on a skiing vacation in Utah. Almost killed her.'

'Well, there's not much to do in Utah.'

'Believe me, he's a badass with men, women, and animals. If you're gonna tangle with him, be careful.'

'So where the hell is he, Max?' I was starting to like Travis Parnell even less than I thought I would.

'Nobody seems to know for sure. But I did talk to his family. All they know is that he left home a few weeks ago. He said he was going on a hunting trip. Said he wasn't coming back until he killed something.'

'That's what I live for,' I said.

39

I spent the rest of Friday afternoon cutting my nose hairs and listening to a Caruso tape I'd bought in a bargain bin on Canal Street for a lot less than I'd paid for the chicken-fried snake. It was still snowing outside and colder than Cooperman's eyes, so I figured I'd at least wait till the snow stopped before I continued my odyssey of Texas cultural oases in New York City. Unless I got very lucky indeed, the next move, unfortunately, seemed to be Travis Parnell's. Given his modus operandi – the late-night calls, the note culled from newspaper headlines, the ballerina with the severed legs – I did not think ol' Trav was the type to move in for the quick kill. He was more like a cat who liked to play rather extensively with the mouse before – well – before he killed it. That gave me, if nothing else, a little time.

I'd warned Kelli to be on the alert and to call me immediately upon the next sighting or contact with the out-of-state creature. She hadn't wanted to move out of her place, so the only other thing I could've done was to take a large bottle of Jameson's and a box of cigars and move into the hall of mirrors with her. It did have possibilities.

I called Ratso that afternoon just to check his pulse. His voice still sounded like the brakes on a subway train, but he said he was feeling better. He'd decided not to go to California until the spring. His jaw would be wired for about another month, and, after that, he looked forward to resuming his role as Watson if I hadn't already solved the case. I felt a small twinge of guilt for not telling him I'd hired McGovern as my new Watson, but there was nothing I could do about it. The dogs may bark, but the caravan rolls on.

Around four o'clock it stopped snowing. Up and down Vandam Street it looked like someone had laid a beautiful mantle of white over the pavement, the potholes, the garbage cans, the parked cars, the sidewalks, the rusted fire escapes, the pathetic big-city detritus that seemed like so many little children's toys left out in the snow. I toasted the view with a shot of Jameson's. It wouldn't last long, I thought. Nothing this nice ever did.

On my way out I passed Winnie on the stairs. We each said hello but the frosty look she gave me made it seem positively warm by the time I got outside. Too bad she was a lesbian. You couldn't just buy her a new pair of shoes and everything would be all right. I wasn't sure if that worked with anyone anymore. We live in a fucked-up, complex world where women are men and men are women, where JFK's an airport, RFK's a football stadium, and Martin Luther King's a street running through your town. Life's a magazine, love is pain, and death is waiting at the end of a needle or a prayer. Waiting like a rat in the gutter to snatch away the last crumbs of somebody's crumbling dream. One new pair of shoes, more or less, wasn't going to make a hell of a lot of difference anymore.

As I made my way through the snow, Tequila kept weaving his way into my consciousness. Sometimes in life, I have found, it's hard to keep things on the back burner on the back burner. I took Parnell's picture out of my pocket and studied it deliberately to banish Tequila's face from my mind.

'Sorry, Tequila,' I said. 'I'll get around to you.'

I walked a lot of snowy streets that evening and took four hacks, the drivers of which, incredibly, all were born in places that begin with an *I*. The first one was an Israeli, the second was from India, the third was an Iranian, and the fourth was an attractive dark-haired woman from Shenandoah, Iowa, with whom I was able to exchange phone numbers and hobbies.

I hit the Lone Star Roadhouse first and talked to Bill Dick, the owner, and Big Mike, the bartender. Neither had seen Parnell, but they helped me circulate the photo among the waitresses and bus-boys, an exercise which, unfortunately, came up empty. Bill launched into a massive clinical recall about his new 47-foot boat which had a 973 Slivovitz-Fuckhead engine in it or something like that.

'Sounds hot,' I said.

'Is that a boat or is that a boat, Kinkster?' Bill asked, somewhat rhetorically.

'That's a boat,' I said.

Before I left, Big Mike and I had a double shot of Jack Daniel's for the road. 'Have you seen Cleve?' he asked.

'Never could see Cleve,' I said.

'But you've heard from him,' Mike persisted.

'I'm afraid so,' I said.

I blitzed the Cadillac Bar, the Alamo, and the Yellow Rose of Texas with similarly discouraging results. Travis Parnell was a spinning ghost. No one had seen him. But, then, New York, like Texas, was a big place. I knew he was here. I could hear his chains clanking in the dark, snowy side streets. I could feel strange, chilly gusts of air when everything around me seemed still.

Parnell had committed no crime and there was nothing I could go to Cooperman with, but, for some reason, the whole thing was becoming almost next door to scary. Not really frightening, in the true sense. But slightly spooky in spite of itself. Like staying up late alone and finding yourself suddenly being sucked spiritually into a Japanese monster movie.

40

'The chicken-fried *steak* is $10.95,' said a somewhat effeminate-looking young man in a Roy Rogers suit at the Cowgirl Hall of Fame. It was beyond imagination that anyone could charge these prices for a product that in Texas was more mundane than the hamburger. Of course, in New York, who knew?

'Plus tax?' I asked.

'I'm afraid so,' he said worriedly. '*Everything* today is plus tax except love.'

'They've got a tax on love, too,' I said. 'It's called marriage.'

He twirled a little gold tassel on his shirt. 'What do you want to drink?' he said.

We went through the routine about esoteric Texas beers and he returned with something called Rattlesnake which, after the third bottle, was biting me in the ass so well I had to order a Wild Turkey chaser.

'That chicken-fried snake was killer bee,' I told the waiter when I finished.

'Chicken-fried *steak*,' he teased. If he could play the horn, and anything ever happened to Snakebite Jacobs, we could pop this guy into the reunion tour and put him out on the road. He was already wearing his high rodeo drag.

I showed him the photo and he shrugged his Roy Rogers suit. I paid the check, admired the Cowgirl's rather extensive barbed-wire collection, and, in what was becoming a fairly tedious routine, made the rounds of the waitresses and bartenders. Parnell's photo was becoming rather dog-eared and smudged with fingerprints, but somehow, vaguely suspecting the current state of his brain, I didn't think he'd mind.

I'd about decided that the boy either hated Texas culture or he'd blipped off the screen when my eye caught a cute blond cowgirl who worked sort of as a Joe Louis greeter in the place. I was leaving so there wasn't that much for her to greet, but I showed her the photo anyway.

Pay dirt.

'He came in here early last week,' she said. 'Monday or Tuesday night I think. It was late and it wasn't very crowded. I was working the bar. Are you a cop or something? You don't look like a cop.'

It was important to keep this broad loose and flowing with the information. Keep everything lighthearted and easygoing. If she clammed up, I was going to have to crucify her on the barbed-wire collection. Upside down, like they did to St Peter.

'Of course I'm not a cop,' I said. 'I work for Kodak. How'd you like your photo in the next issue of *Guns and Ammo*?'

She flashed me a country-cute smile.

'Did this guy say anything?' I asked.

'He said he'd just got to town a few days before. Said he was here for a shoe show. Said he was tired of hanging around drinking with Dylan Thomas's ghost. Will that do?'

'Shoe salesmen are getting pretty literary these days.'

'And Kodak representatives are getting kind of pushy.'

Now she was really smiling. I may not do that well with waitresses or stewardesses, but give me a little time with Joe Louis-type greeters and I'm not without charm. I asked a few more questions and got a few more answers, none of which amounted to anything. Parnell hadn't told her where he was staying.

'Who are you, anyway?' she asked.

'My Christian name is Friedman,' I said. Then I ankled it out of there before the saloon doors hit me in the ass.

41

Ten-thirty on a Friday night was not the time most people chose to take a power nap, but I'm not most people. As far as most people are concerned I just continue to follow my lifelong motto: 'Fuck 'em and feed 'em Froot Loops.'

'Most people, be damned,' I said to the cat as we lay down together on the couch. I leafed through the little booklet that had come with the Caruso tape. I read a small portion of it to the cat. ' "Enrico Caruso," ' I began, ' "was the most celebrated and sought-after singer of his time, and possibly the greatest tenor of the century." '

The cat was watching me intently. *'Possibly?'* I said. The cat blinked. I continued.

' "Born in Naples in 1873, he was the fifteenth of twenty-one children." ' The cat was watching me now like a bird in the garden.

'That's quite a litter,' I said.

The cat's eyes were perfect pinwheels, like a heroin addict's. 'Have you been shooting up again?' I asked. The cat did not say a word, but her face took on an expression of haughty disgust. No sense of humor at all.

' "His early musical and general education," ' I continued to real aloud, ' "was given by the church – " ' which also,' I said, departing from the text, 'gave us the Crusades, the Inquisition, and the Holocaust.'

The cat began to make irritating kneading movements with her claws on my chest. I returned to the manuscript proper.

' " – where he sang as a choirboy in his beloved Naples. Finding a voice teacher proved almost impossible, as each teacher told him that he had neither voice nor talent"!'

'So much for most people,' I said. The cat yawned. So did I.

Travis Parnell was stalking me with his hunting rifle. I was moving leaden-footedly, backward in time, through a tropical jungle of rambutan and durian trees that must've been somewhere in Borneo. I was heading desperately toward the long-ago safety of a childhood chinaberry tree that had stood in the front yard of our house in Houston. My mother was sitting beside the tree, and I knew as I saw her that I wasn't going to make it. In dreams, you rarely win these kind of races. In life, you never do.

Parnell was getting closer and periodically taking aim with his rifle, which had a scope about the size of the Palomar telescope and flashed maddeningly in the sun. Suddenly, my friend John

Morgan was there running beside me. ' "After the first death," ' he said, ' "there is no other." ' Then he was gone.

I was running as fast as I could but Parnell was moving relentlessly closer with a sickeningly engaging smile on his face. The leaves became familiar faces. I saw Tequila's and one that might've been Boatright's detach themselves, and, in slow motion, whirl hypnotically to the ground.

I had to run faster. There was kind of a fractured, country-western version of 'Chariots of Fire' going on in the background, and I thought of the Christian runner Eric Liddell's words: 'Where does the power come from? It comes from within.' I ran faster.

I ran through the trees like Bambi's mother with Parnell moving as if on a track behind me. A full moon was rising and it seemed to have cross hairs on it. South American peasants began burning the trees as I moved past. Smoke got in my eyes and I ran blindly into the growing darkness. At one point, I saw a beautiful, delicate, nearly translucent butterfly whose wings seemed to embody the gentleness of my mother's hands. When I got to the chinaberry tree, my mother was gone.

I knew where she was, though. She was within.

I woke, at first, as a child. Then the reality of the years rushed back like a toxic Love Canal torrent of loneliness into the loft and I felt my heart ache for dreams that become true and truths that become dreams.

It was 2:15 a.m. I put my cowboy hat and my hunting vest with the little stitched pockets for great white hunters to keep their bullets and shotgun shells in. What wonderful sport, I thought, to send a tiny metal projectile crushing through the skull of a peaceful, harmless animal. I stuffed three cigars into three little stitched pockets and headed grimly for the door.

I figured I finally knew where I could find Travis Parnell.

42

'After the first death, there is no other,' I said to myself in the back of the hack.

'Say what?' said the driver.

Dylan Thomas had been right, of course, spiritually speaking, but, in a practical sense, he might've been very wrong. Thomas had led an extremely funky, full-tilt, self-destructive life, but I didn't remember ever reading about anybody getting blown away in his rain room.

That quote, the one Morgan had recited to me in the dream, was a line from one of Thomas's poems that I first read because it had such a wiggy title. The title, 'A Refusal to Mourn the Death, by Fire, of a Child in London,' was a poem in itself. It showed that not only was Thomas a very angry man but he also had a pretty good sense of humor. Might've been a few of the reasons why a young songwriter from Minnesota named Bob Dylan had decided to borrow his name.

As I read it, there were only two possible places Parnell could've been referring to when he told the broad at the Cowgirl that he was 'tired of hanging around drinking with Dylan Thomas's ghost.' I should've got it then and there, but sometimes things need to percolate through your dreams a little before you understand them.

The two places where Dylan Thomas's ghost might've been hanging around were the White Horse Tavern, where Thomas had reportedly drunk eighteen straight shots of Old Grand-dad, passed out at the bar, and been dumped out on the sidewalk, and the Chelsea Hotel, where he was taken and, apparently, did his dead-level best to 'rage against the dying of the light' for the last time. His death certificate stated that Thomas had died of 'acute insult to the brain,' a phrase demonstrating that coroners have a sense of humor, too.

There was no reason for Parnell to be hanging around a bar and hamburger joint in the Village, even if Dylan Thomas had, unbeknownst to himself, put it on the map. Parnell more likely had become bored hanging around his hotel. And the Chelsea had a plaque out front commemorating the fact that Thomas had lived and died there.

Of course, Sid Vicious's girlfriend had lived and died there, too, but it doesn't have quite the same ring to it when you tell someone you're tired of hanging around drinking with Nancy Spungeon's ghost.

It was slightly after two-thirty when the driver let me off in front of the Chelsea Hotel. I'd been there before. It was the first hotel the Jewboys had stayed in when we played Max's Kansas City on our first New York gig in 1973. It was also the place where I'd first met Abbie Hoffman.

If you've ever stayed at the Chelsea for a while, a little bit rubs off on you and, though you may check out, you never quite leave. Then there are those, like Dylan Thomas, who checked out when they checked out. I wasn't eager to join that select group tonight if I could help it.

The lobby of the Chelsea looked like a cross between an art museum and a methadone clinic. A young girl was staring off into space. A man and a woman were arguing with each other. The paintings and the sculpture appeared to be done by Dalí, and might've been. The people in the lobby might've been the models he'd used.

It all came rushing back. How proud, seedy, and soulful the place seemed when you walked in the door. How perfectly the old, eccentric hotel seemed to suit the spirit of the band that cold winter night when we checked in there for the first time. Dalí could've painted us, too.

The night clerk at the desk, perpetually bored yet halfheartedly trying to seem busy, looked like an undertaker out of Charles Dickens. As I spoke to him, his eyes flickered with what could almost pass for interest. Was Travis Parnell staying at the Chelsea? The answer, apparently, was yes and no.

I pushed; he hedged. I cajoled; he wavered. The story, when I finally got it, was interesting and somewhat suggestive in terms of time frame. Parnell had checked in about twelve days ago, right about the time I'd been staring at salamis in the window of the

Carnegie Deli. He'd paid for the week in advance. When the week was up, the hotel had tried to contact Parnell about leaving another deposit, but he hadn't responded to the phone messages they'd left or the notes they'd slipped under his door. A day later, the management moved Parnell's luggage down to the storeroom and rented the room to somebody else.

Ten minutes and forty dollars later, I was down in the dank Chelsea Hotel storeroom with the night security man, who had a buttocks about the size of the rear end of the squad car he'd once, no doubt, driven. The only thing more tedious to deal with than a cop is an ex-cop who still thinks he's one. That, however, was not my problem.

My problem was being in a small, dusty, poorly lit room at three o'clock in the morning, trying to navigate around countless trunks, boxes, and suitcases, racks of unclaimed fashionably forties clothing, one beautiful brown Borsalino hat that looked like it'd been there before the war, and one large, ubiquitous ex-cop's buttocks. A treasure map might've helped, or maybe my dad's World War II navigational bombing maps of Germany. These days it'd be easier to find a needle in the Chelsea than Parnell's suitcase.

'Welcome to the Bermuda Triangle of all lost luggage, fella,' said the security guy. I began checking the tags on suitcases while he stood just inside the door of the crowded little room. A look of disgusted impatience was on his face, like he was in a hurry to get back to sleep.

'Whatever happens to ferry-boat captains?' I said as I performed a slight variant of the Virginia reel, moving through all the crap in the storeroom.

It didn't take as long as it might've, but it took long enough. Travis Parnell's suitcase was an expensive-looking hand-tooled leather affair that had been shoved against a wall directly behind a steamer trunk that looked like it'd come over on the *Golden Hind*.

It wasn't locked.

Inside the suitcase were clothes, toilet articles, shaving cream, and a paperback of Robert B. Parker's *Looking for Rachel Wallace*.

Underneath the first archaeological layer I found two cases of forty-five caliber bullets and a photo of Kelli Tuck.

'Judy Garland's luggage doesn't appear to be here,' I said. Toward the end of her life, Judy'd been unable to pay her hotel bills, and several New York hotels had reportedly impounded her possessions. While this information was probably only of great interest to the homosexual community, it was more pleasant to think about than the implications of what I'd found in Travis Parnell's suitcase.

'Got what you wanted, fella?' asked the security guy as he moved to the door.

'Yeah,' I said. 'All that's missing is a man and a gun.'

43

'Rectal realism,' said Goat Carson as he stood in my loft smoking one of my cigars and drinking about five fingers' worth of my Wild Turkey, 'is a school of art my brother Neke created here in New York in the early seventies.'

It was Saturday afternoon and I was half listening to Goat, as I always did, and half watching the garbage trucks pull out of their staging area on Vandam Street. The city looked like a bomb had hit it. With the snow partially melting, you could see unpleasant-looking objects lying around everywhere, and the street itself looked like something that'd come out of Jimmy Buffett's blender.

'How interesting,' I said.

'He wants you to have this,' said Goat.

'Who wants me to have what?' I asked.

Goat unwrapped a large canvas on the kitchen table and leaned it against the counter. 'This once hung in the National Gallery in Washington before it was stolen, but that's another story,' he said. 'Neke wants you to have it for catching that queer a few years back who was strangling the blond women in TriBeCa. Neke had a beautiful blonde then who lived down there and he feels you helped prolong his sex life.'

'Ah, yes,' I said. 'The Bruce the Ripper Case, I believe.' McGovern had called it that in the *Daily News* and somehow it'd stuck.

That particular case had brought me just about as close to death as I'd ever come, but it had given Ratso a chance to explore his sexual identity.

'What do you think of it?' Goat was saying.

'What do I think of what?'

'The fucking painting,' Goat shouted. He adjusted his little black-leather hat to a rather rakish angle and took another hearty shot of Wild Turkey.

I didn't know a hell of a lot about art. I wasn't sure I even knew what I liked. I figured I might as well walk over to the table and find out. I did.

It was a portrait of Andy Warhol.

'Andy videotaped Neke,' said Goat, 'as Neke was painting Andy.'

'That Andy,' I said.

'It's got a very primitive sort of Grandma Moses look to it, doesn't it?' Goat downed another shot of Turkey and cocked his head to one side, admiring the work.

'Very primitive,' I said. I killed a shot myself. We both studied Warhol's bland countenance for a moment or two. The only thing Warhol had ever done that I liked was to put my friend Tom Baker in his movies. But there was something rather appealing about the painting. Warhol looked very colorful in his colorless sort of way.

'This may be a stupid question,' I said, 'but why is this called rectal realism?' If you don't ask, I thought, you'll never know.

Goat waxed professorial, like a deeply degenerate graduate hoping for tenure in the University of Life. He cleared his throat and repeated the phrase *rectal realism* several times. Then he began his little lecture.

'In the early seventies, when Neke was experimenting with rectal realism,' Goat intoned, 'he always favored a very short easel. When he was working, more than anything else, he probably resembled a center in football. Every now and then, he'd look between his legs at his subject. This work in oils of Andy Warhol is, I believe, one of his finest efforts, but he painted many other canvases in this fashion. Once he painted a very fine likeness of the audience from the stage of a Martin Mull show.

'During this period of his creative life, Neke employed specially rubberized tips on the ends of all his brushes. Then, placing the canvas either on the floor or on the very short easel, Neke would take the brush and . . .'

'You don't mean . . .'

'Yes, I do,' said Goat, nodding appreciatively at the student's sudden grasp of the subject matter. He poured us both another shot of Wild Turkey. 'Yes, I do.'

'You're not really saying . . .'

Goat put a hand up to stop me. He made a rather obscene gesture with the other hand.

'I'm telling you,' said Goat, 'that Neke painted this portrait with his ass.'

'My God,' I said. 'It's a masterpiece.'

Later, after Goat had taken his departure, I threw out an empty bottle of Wild Turkey and wondered where to hang my new art acquisition. The dumper was certainly a possibility, but somehow, it just didn't seem right. On the other hand, if you're going to have somebody watching you take a Nixon, Andy Warhol's about as good a choice as any. Out of respect for the artist, however, I finally jetted the idea.

Eventually, I chose an esthetically pleasing, high-profile locus on the wall above my desk where many Americans would see it when they walked in the door and realize I had a little more refinement than they'd suspected. The downside of this particular portrait placement was that people who live alone never seem to be able to hang pictures straight because they've got nobody to stand by the door and say, 'A little to the right.'

Now anybody coming in the loft would immediately suspect I was a highly refined, pathetically lonely bastard, and it wouldn't even be true. I'm not that refined.

As Saturday evening cradled the city in a muffled, moth-eaten blanket of horns and darkness and sirens, I found myself still silently staring into Andy Warhol's Evian water eyes. For the first time in my life, I looked upon Warhol with something almost akin to empathy. I was the one who was supposed to come up with the answers. I was the one who was supposed to seek out the truth. Yet I felt like a befuddled participant-observer of life. With all the many dark and deep and blue currents swirling about my head and eddying into my life within the past two weeks, I still had done little, and knew even less.

I thought, with a grim smile, of the phrase Truman Capote had once used to describe Warhol: 'A sphinx without a secret.'

44

On Sunday morning, with a cup of steaming espresso in one hand and the first cigar of the day in the other, it did not take me long at all to realize that Andy Warhol's eyes were inspiring me even less than they had the night before. Taking nothing away from the unique, dexterous talents of Neke Carson, I was beginning to feel very strongly that either me or Andy had to go.

If the portrait had been of, say, Ernie Kovacs, Hank Williams, or Anne Frank, it would've been a very different matter. They were my three patron saints; I admired these people, and privately believed they were all Jewish and all born in Texas. I believed the same about Gandhi, Emily Dickinson, and Tony Curtis, and admired them greatly, too, though I wasn't sure about Tony Curtis being born in Texas. I admired Ira Hayes, the American Indian who was one of the four men who raised the flag at Iwo Jima. I also admired Isaac Hayes, Gabby Hayes, Helen Hayes, and Woody Hays. And 'Purple Haze.'

I did not particularly admire Andy Warhol, and judging from his rather limpid, Aryan, pastel expression, he did not particularly admire me. It was nothing personal. Tom Baker had introduced us once at the Lone Star Cafe and we'd gotten along fine. It was just that his demeanor always seemed to evoke the essence of a Campbell's soup can. I needed the lost recipe for that Jewish Hungarian goulash that Ehrich Weiss's mother used to make for him before he grew up and changed his name to Harry Houdini.

These were the Sunday morning thoughts that were going through my head as most of my fellow Americans were in church praying to Jesus to help them make the payments on their latest four-wheeled penis. Jesus, of course, was Jewish also, though he, quite obviously, had not come from Texas. He was still batting .500.

I turned the chair away from the desk so that it faced the window. The view was fairly weak but it beat gazing at Andy Warhol's lips. I made another cup of espresso and gave the blower a little workout just to keep my left ear warm.

I called Kelli and got her playing the blues harmonica on her answering machine. I called Cooperman, and got put on hold three different times by three different cop-shop functionaries, and then got cut off before I could leave a message. I called Winnie but she slammed down the phone as soon as she heard my voice. Reaching out and touching someone was not what it used to be.

I decided to take a break from the blower for a while, got my pliers and Phillips screwdriver off the shelf, and located a rerun of *Quincy* on my old knobless black and white television set in the living room. I'd seen this show before, but I liked Quincy and Quincy liked me and I needed to talk to someone. The first adult I ever saw carry on a conversation with a television set was my old friend Slim back in Texas. Slim used to talk to *Bonanza*.

After the vignette that runs at the end of each *Quincy* had reached its final poignant freeze-frame, I turned off the set with the pliers, took a large blob of Lone Star Roadhouse five-alarm chili out of the freezer, served the cat some tuna, and we both had Sunday brunch together. When the brunch was over, the cat curled up in her rocking chair and I put on the Caruso tape and schlafed out on the couch for a little power nap. Now that I knew he had no voice and no talent, I had a new and greater respect for Caruso.

Around four that afternoon I was able to reach McGovern at the National Desk of the *Daily News*. 'McGovern World Head-quarters,' he said.

'Watson,' I said, 'I need you.'

'I didn't know you cared,' said McGovern, sending small tidal waves of chuckles crashing deep into my inner ear. At least Ratso had laughed more infrequently.

'We need to get together,' I said with some urgency. 'We need to have a Watson Transitional Power Caucus as soon as possible.'

I quickly brought McGovern up to speed on the fact that Travis Parnell was lurking around somewhere with a gun and a bad attitude, and gave him my considered opinion that all hell might break loose at any time and possibly from several directions at once. It was imperative that our relationship be functionally operative in case the unforeseen occurs, as it almost invariably does.

McGovern informed me that he was wrapping up a story about the very large and terribly overweight visiting Russian female downhill bobsled team, and would be ready to assist me in my crime-solving efforts a little later that evening.

As fate would have it, things came to a boil a little sooner than that. I was standing on the chair, reaching high above the desk, in the midst of a little spontaneous Andy Warhol relocation project, when the phones rang. Without personal injury, I was able to collar the blower on the left after the fourth ring.

'Start talkin',' I said.

She did.

I didn't recognize the voice, but as she talked, I did recognize that something terrifyingly, timelessly evil was taking place. By the time I hung up, I'd also recognized something else.

The back burner was on fire.

45

'Wichita was killed in Tulsa?' McGovern said incredulously as he eyed the tall Vodka McGovern on the little table. We were sitting in a dark booth at the back of the Corner Bistro, about as far away from Portugal as you could get.

'Hunting accident,' I said. 'That's what his sister told me when she called.' I knocked back about half of a healthy shot of Jameson's.

McGovern's intelligent eyes met my own. Then he shrugged and picked up the Vodka McGovern. 'Hunting accident,' he said.

'Wichita had a little cabin on some land outside of Tulsa. They got a severe cold spell last week and the plumbing froze up. He went out in the woods with a roll of toilet paper and . . .'

'Somebody blew his shit away,' said McGovern.

'That's a rather coarse way of phrasing it, but it's essentially correct.' We drank for a moment in silence.

'In 1980,' said McGovern, 'Tulsa was the number-one city in the country with over two hundred thousand population in terms of accidental fatalities per capita.'

'Watson,' I said, 'you always cease to amaze me. What other enlightening spiritual trivia do you have filed away in your head?'

'I'm on the National Desk,' said McGovern a bit defensively. 'That's what they pay me for. But since we're on the subject of accidents, who was the pilot in the first fatal plane crash?'

'Let me think,' I said as I signaled Dave for another round of drinks. 'Pontius Pilate?'

'That's a good guess, Sherlock, but it's incorrect. The pilot in the first fatal plane crash was Orville Wright. It occurred on September 17, 1908. Orville survived but his passenger died.'

'Oh, the humanity!'

McGovern looked at me. 'You're not really so sure Wichita's death was an accident, are you, Sherlock?'

'Well,' I said, 'Wichita and Boatright appear to have died accidentally, and Tequila's manner of croaking was quite obviously murder.'

'Quite,' said McGovern as Dave brought the drinks to the table.

'But that makes three former Texas Jewboys who've all made the one-way trip to Hillbilly Heaven within the space of two weeks. It *could* be coincidence, but I doubt if even a Brooklyn bookie would give odds on that.'

McGovern was silent for a moment. Possibly he was considering placing a bet.

'And there's something else that's rather suggestive,' I said. 'Wichita's sister told me – these are not her words – but before Wichita went outside to take the last Nixon of his life, he'd been playing the guitar. That's what he did about twenty-four hours a day, which is one reason why so many musicians tend to get up your sleeve after a while.'

'Present company excluded, of course.'

'Of course. But near Wichita's guitar, the state police found the musical charts for 'Ride 'em Jewboy,' a song off my first album. That didn't mean much to them, but it tells something to me.'

'Maybe he was just indulging in a bit of nostalgia,' said McGovern.

'Unlikely, my dear Watson, unlikely. You only use charts when you're unfamiliar with a song. Wichita'd played that tune thousands of times on the road. Why would he need charts?' I killed the shot of Jameson's and went about initial preparations for lighting a cigar.

McGovern seemed to be lost in thought. Still in somewhat of a semitrance, he got up and walked over to the jukebox. I knew he was onto something because he'd left his Vodka McGovern on the table. Soon Billie Holiday was singing in the Corner Bistro. It was the kind of place she would've liked.

When McGovern returned to the table, his eyes were shining with triumph. 'I've got it,' he said.

'Watson, don't tell me you've cracked the case?'

'No, but I've got the headline.' I winced slightly and lit the cigar.

'Christ,' I said rather irritably. 'Lay it on me.'

McGovern took a long drink from the tall glass. He leaned back in his chair and stared intently at me across the little table.

'SOMEBODY'S KILLING THE JEWBOYS OF TEXAS,' he said.

46

One of the most frightening aspects of childhood ghost stories is that some of them tend to haunt us for the rest of our lives. When I was a kid at summer camp, just outside of Kerrville, Texas, our counselor, Vern Rathkamp, told us one particular late-night tale that I've never forgotten. It was called 'The Last of the Thirteen.'

Vern was very big and very tall, and though I was ten years old at the time, I still think of him that way today. I can see the sleeve of his T-shirt rolled up to hold his packet of cigarettes. I can see all of us, staring with the ingenuous eyes of the early fifties over the edges of our bunk beds as Vern told his story, occasionally pacing back and forth like a tiger in the semidarkness. And no matter how nonsensical, disjointed, and downright ludicrous they may appear today, when you're ten years old every story is true.

It was Sunday night and I wasn't sleeping anyway. So I sat at the kitchen table in my purple robe, drank black coffee, smoked Cuban cigars, and let my mind wander back to Echo Hill Ranch, a little green valley full of smoky campfires and dusty dreams. Through the ears of a child, I heard Vern again telling 'The Last of the Thirteen.'

When Vern was very young he'd met a man on a train about half an hour before midnight. The man was not an old man, but the striking feature about him was that his hair was pure white. Every few minutes or so the man would ask Vern, 'What time is it, son?' and Vern would tell him. As it grew closer to midnight, the man became increasingly nervous in the service, and finally unburdened himself of what had been, for many years, his own private hell.

Some time ago, when he'd been a freshman in college, the man with the white hair had joined a fraternity. During that first year, as part of the hazing process, he and his twelve pledge brothers were blindfolded and taken out into the country by the upperclassmen. When the upperclassmen had dropped them off and driven away, the pledges took off their blindfolds and realized that they were lost in the middle of a dark forest.

'What time is it, son?'

'It's a quarter to twelve, sir.'

They wandered through the forest and stumbled eventually upon an old abandoned house. It was very dark and they had no flashlights or camping gear and they were exhausted, so all thirteen of them slept in the living room of the creepy old house. At dawn, they left and found their way back to the city.

In the next four years, they finished college, graduated, and went their separate ways. Several years after graduation, the tragic word arrived that one of the young men in that freshman pledge class had fallen down the stairs in the basement of his home and died. The only unusual thing about the unfortunate accident was that, when they'd found the body, the young man's hair had turned white.

'What time is it now, son?'

'Ten minutes till midnight, sir.'

The following year it was learned that another member of the group had been killed in a one-car accident on a lonely road around midnight. His car had run into a tree, killing him instantly. His hair was white as driven snow.

During the next five years, five more from the freshmen fraternity class died. One fell off the roof of a tall building. Another jumped off a diving board into a pool without any water. Another choked to death in a fancy restaurant where no one felt it was appropriate to give him the Heimlich maneuver. Still another died when his Honda Civic was T-boned by a shuttle bus. Yet another died of mysterious causes, possibly brought on by the ennui engendered by his hearing about the deaths of all the others. In every case, the hair of the victim was white as a suburb.

'What time is it now, son?'

'It's five minutes to midnight, sir.'

The remaining six men decided it was about time they got together for a little power caucus. They met in the same city where they'd attended college. They discussed the deaths of their friends and surmised that some strange kind of curse must have been responsible. They thought back over their years at college. The only thing they could recall that all thirteen of them had done together was spend the night in that old house in the middle of the forest.

So they went back to the house. They went back on a dark, stormy winter night, but this time they brought flashlights, weapons, and overnight gear. The place looked a lot spookier than they'd remembered. Tall spruce trees grew in front and shrieked in the wind. Inside the living room, all the furniture was covered with sheets, and cobwebs and dust were everywhere. The old house creaked and shuddered from the storm outside and the devil knew what inside. They looked around with their flashlights but found nothing of interest until they saw a picture over the fireplace. It was a painting of a very old and wrinkled woman. A witch to the superstitious mind.

'What time is it, son?'

'It's almost midnight, sir.'

The man with the white hair on the train told Vern that nothing had been resolved. They each returned to their separate lives, and every year or so he'd hear of another strange and tragic accident. At this point the man became very highly agitato. Vern, of course, asked him what was the matter. He said he was going to tell Vern something that he'd never told anyone, but Vern must promise never to tell a soul. Vern promised a promise he had broken only now, many, many years after meeting the old man on the train.

Vern's voice was like a hushed whisper as he told us the words the white-haired man had told him. 'Son,' he'd said, '*I am the last of the thirteen.*'

Then Vern screamed so loudly that it scared the shit out of every single one of us.

I poured myself a fresh cup of black coffee and sipped it with a large Jack Daniel's chaser. I paced the loft a little and smiled to myself. But at the same time I was smiling, I felt the hair on my forearms rising involuntarily. It was amazing how much that story had frightened me when I was a kid.

What was even more amazing was how much the story frightened me now.

47

Monday morning I'd fed the cat and had my first cup almost to my lips when Cleve called from the Pilgrim State Mental Hospital. It wasn't the way I would've chosen to start the week, but maybe things would pick up.

'Hey, dude,' said Cleve shrilly. 'The responses are rollin' in!' I've acclimated myself to the younger generation referring to me as 'dude.' In fact, I think I like it a little better than 'mister' because it means they think I'm hip, with it, now, today, or mod, as my father calls it. But when a man in his forties who lives in a mental hospital calls you 'dude,' it's a rather saddening experience for more reasons than I wish to go into here.

'What responses, Cleve?' I asked.

'What responses? To the questionnaire, of course.'

'What questionnaire, Cleve?' It's an unsettling feeling on a Monday morning to realize that every sentence of conversation you conduct is brick and mortar binding you irrevocably closer in a relationship with someone who is criminally insane. But you can't hang up on a monstro-wig. They take it personally.

'The questionnaire I sent to all the Jewboys.'

'And what did you ask in the questionnaire?'

'I asked would they be able to come to New York by the end of the month to rehearse for the tour?'

I paused for my first sip of espresso. I didn't say anything. There wasn't a hell of a lot to say.

'Oh, I asked them other things, too,' said Cleve in a frighteningly toneless voice.

'Like what?' I asked.

'Like any changes in addresses or phone numbers. Any picking they'd been doing in the past few years. I've got to be sure they're keeping their chops up. Whether they've seen *Ghostbusters II*.' Cleve's voice trailed off.

'Had they?'

'Had they *what*?' shouted Cleve.

'Seen *Ghostbusters II*.'

'No.'

Cleve didn't enlarge upon his answer and I didn't deem it wise to inquire further into the matter. I sipped my espresso, lit my first cigar of the morning, and looked reassuringly toward the cat, my companion in relative sanity.

'The responses about doing the tour have been very positive,' said Cleve a bit petulantly. 'I've heard from everyone but Tequila, Wichita, Raymond Boatright, and Willie Fong Young.' Not hearing from three out of the four was pretty understandable, I thought.

'Willie's probably just miffed because I went to the bas mitzvah instead of his wedding.'

'Those bar mitvahs'll get you every time.'

'*Bas* mitzvah,' I said. 'Bar mitzvahs are for boys and bas mitz-vahs are for girls.' I was sure this information would do Cleve a lot of good.

'What's a Botswana for?' he asked. I puffed the cigar patiently and looked at the cat.

I took a deep breath and made a decision. Either Cleve was crazy or the whole world was crazy and Cleve was sane, and either way I couldn't see that it really made a hell of a lot of difference. So I told him about Tequila, Boatright, and Wichita.

Cleve didn't say anything for a moment. Then I heard a strange, flat whistling in my left earlobe. Cleve was whistling a little tune. It sounded kind of familiar. Then he supplied the words.

'This old man, he played three./He played knick-knack on my knee.'

'Yes,' I said, 'you could say that.' Most people wouldn't, of course, but there was a reason Cleve was where he was.

There was a long and uncomfortable silence. I looked up and met the cool gaze of Andy Warhol. That picture had to come down. Suddenly, I had a sperm-of-the-moment idea.

'Cleve,' I said, 'tell me about that interview you mentioned last time we talked. Who was the reporter? What was the newspaper? What'd he ask you?'

'Sir?'

Now Cleve seemed to have a nice little multiple-personality thing going for him. 'Come on, Cleve,' I said. 'Try to remember.'

The voice on the line was a strangled, whiny affair that came out of nowhere and disturbed me greatly. It sang: 'Try to remember the kind of September/And follll . . . oooowwwwww . . .'

In what I hoped was a calm, rational voice, I tried to get Cleve back in the remote vicinity of the target. He maintained he could remember long-ago things like they were yesterday, but he had a hell of a time remembering yesterday. That sounded so normal it scared me.

About all I was able to get out of Cleve finally was that the interview was a lengthy one with the reporter asking a lot of questions about the band. He couldn't remember the reporter's name, but he thought the paper had been the *Daily News*. I thanked him and told him he'd been very helpful.

There was a rather lengthy silence, and then Cleve said: 'So *they* probably didn't see *Ghostbusters II* either.'

'Cleve,' I said wearily, 'that's something we'll never know.'

48

That evening the Dancer and I had a little dinner date in Chinatown. Big Wong's was, of course, closed on Mondays. Even on the days when Big Wong's was open, if you got there after eight o'clock at night, they started running out of things. One of them was charm.

Kelli and I walked leisurely down Mott Street, drinking in the sights and smells and sounds of people living their lives in a manner that is raw and beautiful and close to the ground. Maybe it was my years in Borneo that kept the East always close to my heart. Maybe it was a Chinese girlfriend of mine who went on to marry a Kraut. I don't recall being heartbroken at the time, but they say once your heart's been broken it's not always so easy to tell when it happens again. I wouldn't know. I do know that if I ever get married the first thing I'm going to do is hire a nanny and adopt a couple of little Oriental kids. I have no plans, at the moment, however, to adopt an adult Korean.

We picked a restaurant on Mott Street a few blocks down from Big Wong's and took a booth by the front window fairly close to a large squid hanging on a hook. We sat across from each other in the booth.

'You can always tell rednecks from normal Americans,' I said to Kelli, 'because the man and the woman tend to sit together on the same side of the booth, leaving the other side, possibly, for Elijah.'

'I've noticed that,' said Kelli, looking over the menu.

'You're a bright kid,' I said. 'You don't miss much.'

Kelli continued happily studying the menu's vegetarian section and didn't seem too put off by my yammering on so I continued. Maybe she was in some advanced state of kundalini yoga that normal Americans didn't know about.

'The reason the rednecks like to sit on the same side with each other is because they're more visceral than the rest of us. They're kind of raw and beautiful and close to the ground, very much like the Chinese. Of course, never tell a redneck that.'

'I'll have the Chinese vegetables over pan-fried noodles,' said Kelli.

'Sensible order,' I said.

After I'd chosen a few dishes from the nonvegetarian portion of the menu, the waiter took our orders and buzzed off into the bowels of the kitchen. Kelli and I sipped hot tea and discussed Travis Parnell a bit.

'That rather unpleasant package he sent you was postmarked just before Christmas, you know. Packages take forever to arrive this time of year.'

'Hmm,' said Kelli. 'I'll have to mention that to Mr Mailman.'

'There wasn't much luggage of his at the Chelsea. He might've just got tired and fed up with hanging around New York and buggered off somewhere else. Almost everybody in New York feels that way. They just don't leave. That's why it's such a friendly place.'

'It's been five days since I got that horrible doll. I haven't received any more late-night calls. Maybe he *is* gone.'

'Let's hope. Of course, you do have probably the best country singer-turned-amateur detective in the city on the case. Just be sure to stay on your toes.'

'A dancer,' said Kelli, 'always stays on her toes.'

Turning the subject deftly away from Travis Parnell, I talked for a while about some of the cases I'd worked on in the past. Then, just to keep it light, I launched into my views of the art scene in New York.

I hadn't gotten too far along into explaining rectal realism when I realized it wasn't really going to fly. Dancers are often nonverbal childlike creatures and they don't always like to put into words the things that they feel. They don't like to hear anybody else do it either. I steered the subject delicately away from rectal realism.

'Let's redirect the conversation back to myself,' I said.

Kelli sipped her tea. It's hard to tell with dancers whether they're happy or pissed off or just content to sit there across from you sipping their tea with their lips resembling the beak of a cute, sexy, little bird. And you never know when that bird may turn into a giant, angry cassowary and try to kick your balls off under the table. That's probably another reason why rednecks always have the women sit on the same side with them.

Since Kelli was in a fairly inscrutable, nonverbal mood, possibly quite understandably because of the strain she'd been under lately, I left her alone at the table for a moment and went into the little hallway to call McGovern on the pay blower. It was broken, so I went outside to find another one on the street. Just up the block I found a phone booth with a pagoda on top of it. I put a quarter in and, sure enough, the voice on the other end sounded farther away than usual. It wasn't even McGovern's.

'Kinky! My hero!' said Tony Burton, the feisty Brit who'd worked with McGovern at the *Daily News* from the days of pencils to typewriters to supercomputers. He'd met McGovern working on the Richard Speck case in Chicago and was responsible for McGovern's coming to New York twenty years ago. If it hadn't been for Tony, I'd probably be tackling two very dangerous cases totally Watson-less right now. Tony did have, however, one rather tedious habit. Almost everything he said could be taken as either high praise or low ridicule, and Tony wasn't going to help you figure out which it was. That was your job.

'It's a rare privilege to hear your voice,' said Tony. Possibly it had something to do with his British background.

'Yeah,' I said. 'Is McGovern in?'

'No,' said Burton, 'but I've been graced to have seen a bit of the piece he's working on. The "Somebody's Killing the Jewboys of Texas" piece. I must say McGovern has certainly again risen to the high plain of journalism we've all come to expect of him. And I've every confidence, Kinkster, you'll soon be wrapping this one up and adding it to your growing list of triumphs.'

'Thanks,' I said. 'And Tony, will you ask McGovern to call me as soon as possible?'

'About the case?'

'Affirmative.'

'Roger. You're my hero, Kinkster.'

'I'll try not to let you down.'

'Pip pip, old chap.'

I hung up the phone wanting to believe that Burton was coming from a sincere place. For some reason, I didn't want to let him down. It was as good a rationale as any for toiling on this planet: so I wouldn't let Tony Burton down. What else was there to life? But there was the distinct possibility, I thought, that in a very abstract, twentieth-century sense, I was a hero to Tony Burton. Adults had been known to have some pretty weird heroes.

With a little more pride in my step, I walked back up Mott Street and into the restaurant. By the time I got to the table, Kelli was about halfway through eating the Chinese vegetables over pan-fried noodles.

'Don't wait for me,' I said. 'Go right ahead.'

Kelli gave me a nice smile and continued eating. I could start to like these nonverbal types. Of course, it's hard to be very verbal with a mouth full of Chinese vegetables over pan-fried noodles.

I could be nonverbal, too, I thought. She could be the Dancer and I could be the Strong Silent Type. We could sit forever eating Chinese food and occasionally smiling at each other in a little frenzy of autism. At the moment, with New York City hurriedly clanging by in all directions around us, it didn't sound too bad.

I was starting in on my spare ribs with black bean sauce, and the waiter was just approaching us with a very handsome-looking steamed flounder, when I heard the shot out in the street and saw blood suddenly spurt across the table.

49

Most of the customers in the place were Chinese and they hit the decks probably thinking it was a tong war. Kelli was sitting quite still across the booth from me, still holding a bloody set of chopsticks. I reached low across the table and pushed her down against the seat almost like a rag doll. Then I hit the decks myself. I knew it wasn't a tong war.

We all studied the gum under the tables for a frozen moment or two, and then the place came slowly back to life. Cautiously, I stood up and looked past the ugly little hole in the front window out into the street. No one out there except the usual crowd of onlookers on the near sidewalk staring at us in expectation, waiting to see if there was going to be a second act.

I looked over at Kelli. She seemed to be fairly fossilized but unhurt. I asked her if she was all right and she nodded her head. Then I looked over at the waiter. Blood was spurting at regular intervals from somewhere near the top of his left bicep. I grabbed a linen napkin, stepped over the flounder on the floor, and took a closer look.

There was a small hole going into the man's arm and a much larger one going out. From the way the blood was continuing to spurt, an artery had apparently been hit. I quickly found several more linen napkins and wrapped them tightly around the wound to cut down the loss of blood. Miraculously, it seemed to work for the moment. Kinky Nightingale.

We sat the waiter down in a chair to wait for the paramedics. I was standing by the table talking to Kelli when a customer from one of the other tables came rushing over.

'I saw man with a gun,' he said excitedly, pointing to a spot somewhere on the far sidewalk. 'Wore big hat just like yours. Cowboy! Just like *Dallas*.'

'Remember,' I said, taking Kelli's hand, 'he only *thinks* he's a cowboy.'

50

The following afternoon, a Tuesday, it was raining cats and dogs in New York. My cat was safe and relatively warm in the loft. She was sitting on the windowsill watching McGovern's large form cursing and chasing around a little puppet head on the rain-wept sidewalk.

'See the funny man,' I said to the cat.

The cat said nothing.

The night before, I'd taken Kelli back to her place, watched her throw about half her apartment into a big red suitcase, hustled her down to Grand Central Station, and put her on a fast train for my nation's capital. Not that Washington, D.C., was a particularly safe place to be, but under the circumstances, it beat New York with a tire iron.

My kid sister, Marcie, who lives in Washington and works for the Red Cross, had just moved into a large, new apartment. One dancer more or less wasn't going to make that much difference for a week.

'What kind of person is Kelli?' Marcie had asked when I'd called to let her know about her imminent housepest.

'Well, when she was a child, she used to talk to the old Christmas tree ornaments before her mother hung them on the back of the tree. Kelli'd tell them that the back of the tree was a very important place to be.'

'That's sweet,' said Marcie. 'I hope she doesn't hang herself.'

'No problem. However, she does have a slightly arrested case of social development. Most of her friends today are Christmas tree ornaments.'

'She'll fit right in,' said Marcie.

Presently there came a loud knocking on the door of the loft. The cat and I both looked up. I went over and unbolted the door. There was a time when I didn't usually keep the door bolted but this wasn't it.

A large McGovern head and a little puppet head came in the door together. Both were soaking wet. 'Ah, Watson,' I said, 'good of you to drop by.'

'I've been standing outside in the rain for the past fifteen minutes,' said McGovern, taking off his drenched trenchcoat. His hair was pasted down over his eyes. McGovern didn't own a hat because men didn't make hats as big as God had made McGovern's head. In spite of his travails, he laughed good-naturedly, a very Watsonlike temperament, I noted with approval.

'The whole time I was in the street shouting for you, that fucking cat was sitting on the windowsill watching me with a smile on her face.'

The cat stared at McGovern and blinked several times rather rapidly, a sure sign of displeasure. I turned to the cat.

'Why didn't you tell me McGovern was out there, darling? Why didn't you let me know?'

The cat did not respond.

'Why don't you ask her to pour me a drink?' said McGovern.

Later, with McGovern and myself sitting at the kitchen table, and the cat and a bottle of Jameson's sitting on the kitchen table, we discussed the two current cases that suddenly seemed to have risen up like evil twin trade towers to dominate the landscape of my soul.

After a few shots of Jameson's, I recounted to McGovern the specific details of the previous evening's events in Chinatown. 'Travis Parnell,' I theorized, 'being a hunter and probably a crack shot, could've easily spliced Kelli if he'd wanted to. But he seems to still be playing his twisted little game of making her life a living nightmare. So he shoots the waiter in the arm instead.'

'Charming fellow,' said McGovern.

'Nothing worse than a good old boy turned bad,' I said. I lit a cigar, McGovern poured us both another round, and we sat in silence for a moment or two, watching the rain slant down onto Vandam Street.

'Tony Burton said you wanted to talk to me. What do you want me to do? Round up a posse?' I looked at McGovern.

'You're big enough to be a posse yourself,' I said.

'Yeah,' said McGovern, 'but who'd lead?'

I killed half the shot and thought about it. It wasn't a bad question. Being a perennial unemployed youth, I'd sat at my desk for some time now, opening the occasional bill or bar mitzvah invitation with my Smith & Wesson knife. The cigar smoke at times had grown stale. The medicinal shot had aged for the better perhaps while settling into the old bull's horn. Cobwebs, at times, had extended from my cigar to my nose to my two red telephones, and, no doubt, into the little gray cells of my atrophying brain as well.

Those were the fun times.

Now, suddenly, a vortex of hatred was swirling around me. A

maniac with a gun and a mission was on the loose, bent, apparently, upon the gradual emotional and physical destruction of a young lady who looked to me for wisdom and advice and protection. And if that wasn't enough to keep me busy, a horrific childhood ghost story appeared to be coming true right before what Emily Dickinson had called my 'unfurnished eyes.'

Coming up against these seemingly inexorable twin terrors were myself and the large, friendly, intelligent Irishman sitting across the little table from me. We were the forces of good, I thought, rather wryly. If there were ten good men in the world, which at the moment I wasn't at all certain of, McGovern and I were surely two of them. On the other hand, if there were ten good men in the world, that left a hell of a lot of bad guys running around out there. I suddenly felt colder and more evanescent than the rain outside the window.

'Watson,' I said with a quiet determination, 'from now on we shall handle these two cases simultaneously. We shall take up both the Travis case and the Tequila case, and we shall crack them both or die trying.'

'Here, here!' said McGovern as he poured another round into my already-full shotglass. The Jameson's flowed into a clear little puddle and dripped off the edge of the table like rain falling inside a distant, half-remembered dream. It wasn't going to be pleasant, I thought.

Since it was a rainy, thundery day, I took the opportunity to briefly recount the story of 'The Last of the Thirteen' for McGovern, who at least had the courtesy not to rush to the phone and try to commit me to the Pilgrim State Mental Hospital. Reflecting upon the Pilgrim State Mental Hospital brought me back to Cleve and that brought me back to what I'd needed from McGovern in the first place.

'Sometime in the past couple of months,' I said, 'Cleve gave an interview to a reporter about the Texas Jewboys. Cleve doesn't seem to remember much about it anymore. Cleve goes in and out of lucid periods like some guys change their underwear. Except me, of course. I don't wear any underwear. It's a little hygiene trick I learned in the tropics.'

279

'How clever of you,' said McGovern.

'Anyway, Cleve thinks he gave the story to a guy from the *Daily News*.' McGovern's interest perked up noticeably.

'You want me to find the article? You think it's connected to this "Last of the Thirteen" business?'

'I won't know until I see it, but I'll tell you this,' I said, pausing to puff the cigar rather dramatically. 'It's the only lead we've got.'

'If it can be found, I'll find it.'

'Good man, Watson!'

'Let's take these cattle north,' he said.

As McGovern was rather laboriously putting on his coat to leave, I reflected grimly that it was already too late for Tequila, Boatright, and Wichita. Some diabolical curse was definitively operative here. There had to be a way to push aside this curtain of Transylvanian mist to reveal the mind and hand of a modern-day murderer. And time, I thought, was doing a pretty good job of running out.

At the door, McGovern turned and looked at me. 'It's too bad,' he said, 'that Big Wong's was closed yesterday.'

'Why is that, McGovern?' I asked.

'WAITER WINGED AT WONG's has kind of a nice ring to it,' he said.

51

The next few days passed rather uneventfully. For all the excitement they were fraught with, I might as well have been a witty, young CPA or a born-again proctologist. I knew what brand of cigars I smoked. I knew the cat ate only tuna. About the only difficult decision I had to make was one morning when I couldn't decide whether I wanted to drink hot chocolate, coffee, or espresso. I imagined that the loft was a large, wide-bodied airplane and that there was a lithe, blonde stewardess standing next to me saying 'Hot chocolate, coffee, or espresso?' with a rather stern yet whimsical expression on her intelligent, sulky, languorous lips. It didn't help me decide what I wanted to drink, but it did make me want to ask the stewardess if she had a layover in Dallas.

The weather was as gray, somber, and monotonous as my

mood. If I was going to get in a brighter, more positive mood, I was going to have to do it without the help of January. I took a certain cold comfort in Sherlock Holmes's assertion that all great artists are very highly influenced by environmental conditions. If I was such a great artist, how come I didn't understand the violent abstract of life that was hanging in the corner of my mind's eye and nudging the elbow of my soul like a bottle imp? As a child, I never really understood the nature of the curse of 'The Last of the Thirteen.' As an adult, for something like this to occur in real life was yet further beyond my ken. Hell, I didn't even understand rectal realism.

At night, visions of Kelli would dance intermittently through my dreams. By day, other visions, darker and bloodier and more foreboding, seemed to gnaw their way, like a Blakeian worm in a rosebud, through the pupil of my left eyeball and ejaculate evil onto my brain. If these visions were sugarplums, the date on their carton had expired.

Kelli and Marcie had called to let me know that all was okay in my nation's capital, but just to be sure, I assigned Washington Ratso, a Lebanese rock 'n' roll guitar player with a band called Switchblade, to look after them. His real name was Jimmie Silman but he'd been called Ratso longer than Ratso had been called Ratso, although Ratso had met me before Ratso had, or was it the other way around. At any rate, I called him Washington Ratso to differentiate him from New York Ratso. Life can be complex when you're a two-Ratso man.

Washington Ratso had once helped me locate a rather unpleasant Nazi who was trying to kill me. I figured if he could help find a Nazi, he could entertain and keep an eye on a dancer and my little sister. Don't hose 'em, just show them the town and keep a mild surveillance on them, I'd told Washington Ratso. Not to worry, he'd replied in some kind of unpleasant-sounding, exaggerated Arabic accent.

I'd felt better after talking to Washington Ratso. If you couldn't trust a Lebanese Druse Christian who'd once played with the Texas Jewboys, who could you trust? There were a number of people who'd played with the Texas Jewboys, I reflected. But there weren't that many of what we liked to call original Texas Jewboys. And from that small handful of chosen people, you could now subtract three, I thought grimly.

Friday afternoon looked like it was going to roll uncomfortably along pretty much like Wednesday and Thursday had. No progress. No sunshine. No joy. No phone calls that promised to change my life.

Around three o'clock, the cat vomited. That was always something to be on the planet for. There was a little scurry of action as I rushed to get an old towel to clean it up and the cat rushed into the bedroom, I suppose to hide her Cheshire chagrin. Eventually, she came back into the living room and I poured a tall shot of Jameson's to relax after all the activity.

I killed the shot.

I seemed to be spending an inordinate amount of time glaring up at Andy Warhol, and he seemed to be spending a commensurately inordinate amount of time glaring down his rather fragile nostrils at me. Of course, neither of us had that much going on.

'What the hell am I going to do with that thing?' I shouted to the cat as I gestured disgustedly toward the wall above the desk.

The cat said nothing.

Warhol said nothing.

I poured another shot of Jameson's and walked it around the loft with me. I certainly couldn't move the picture to the far wall. That wall was entirely filled with the huge Patton-like American flag Vaughn Meader had once given me. In the early sixties, Vaughn had created the enormously popular 'First Family Album,' in which he'd done a brilliant impersonation of JFK. Vaughn had traveled around the country doing his JFK act and making a fortune until one day in 1963 when he'd gotten into a cab at the airport in Milwaukee and the driver had said: 'Did you hear about the President getting shot in Dallas?'

'No,' Vaughn had answered. 'How does it go?'

From that moment on, Vaughn's record sales and appearances had declined so drastically that later that week it had prompted Lenny Bruce to mention it in his act. 'There'll be two graves at

Arlington tonight,' Bruce had said. 'One for President Kennedy, and the other for Vaughn Meader.'

Some years after that, Vaughn had gone fishing up in Maine and never bothered to come back. Couldn't blame him really. I'd rather be fishing myself. I looked up at the giant flag and thought of Vaughn and myself and Tequila, and Raymond, and Wichita, and I was suddenly filled with some kind of strong emotion that I couldn't quite identify. It was too deep and close to the heart to be patriotism and too lonely to be love.

Later that day, as the evening shadows fell gently across the gray afternoon like an Indian blanket from your childhood, I found myself standing at the kitchen window talking to the cat about McGovern.

'He's the kindest, most decent person I know,' I said. 'He's smart enough to know how very useless and futile life is, and yet he lives it to the fullest. He's one of my dearest friends and I would trust him with my life. He's smart, he's sincere, he's impeccably slovenly, he's unworldly, he's a mensch – all important Watson-like qualities – yet I sometimes wonder what put it into my head that I could ever be a Sherlock.'

The cat lowered her head, intently studying a cockroach as it slowly moved along the windowsill.

'But that large head of his is filled with pubescent headlines. He cares more about covering the case than he does about solving it. And when Ratso finds out that McGovern's working with me, he'll be so miffed he'll never want to help me again. I need Watson! I must have Watson!'

The cat looked up at me for a moment and then went back to the cockroach. I lit a cigar and stared out at the blue-black densely populated emptiness. My heart was out there somewhere alone. Alone like my old friend Slim used to be back at the ranch, adjusting his little paper Rainbow Bread hat and leaning back on an old wooden Coca-Cola carton against his ancient green trailer that was never going anywhere again.

Slim used to say: 'You's born alone. You dies alone. You might as well get used to it.'

The phones rang.

I walked over to the desk, picked up the blower on the left, and listened for a while. I puffed with satisfaction on the cigar. At one point, I looked over to wink at the cat, but she was already curled up asleep on the rocking chair.

'Excellent work, Watson,' I said to the blower. 'Excellent work.'

52

He looked like a slightly confused Moses. An old man with long gray hair and beard with his palms outstretched. As I got closer I saw the sign around his neck. It read: I'M 69 YEARS OLD, HOMELESS, AND DYING OF CANCER. I took a few bucks out of my pocket and started to hand them to him when he began screaming like a maniac. You can meet some interesting people on the way to McGovern's house.

'Get away!' the old man shouted. 'Don't come near me with that cigar! I'm anemic!'

Feeling somewhat shaken, I put the money back in my pocket and kept walking. Another aristocratic freak, I said to myself. He's not only anemic, he's crazy as a bedbug. It'd take a social worker driving a Zamboni to straighten out this guy's attic.

'Basically, I feel rejected,' I said to McGovern, after I'd told him of the encounter over shots of Black Bush. 'When a sixty-nine-year-old homeless man who's dying of cancer turns you down, you've got problems.'

'You forgot anemic,' said McGovern. He laughed and I did too. I laughed what I imagined to be hearty Jewish laughter, which is kind of nice because you don't hear it all that often. I killed the shot and McGovern poured me another.

'So you found the interview Cleve couldn't remember giving?'

'It wasn't easy,' said McGovern, getting up and pacing around the little room. Looked like he'd been taking Kinky lessons. I lit a cigar and waited.

'Newspaper morgues are filled today with people who have master's degrees in journalism but have been reduced to clipping articles from back issues because of the heartbreak of what journalism has become. These people are understandably difficult to deal with and you've got to work to try to keep them sober,' said McGovern as he walked around the room with his drink in his hand. He crossed over to the mantel and started fishing around in a large mess of papers under a framed photograph of Carole Lombard.

'Don't tell me you've *lost* the son of a bitch?'

'Not hardly,' laughed McGovern as he continued to shuffle stacks of aging newsprint. 'It's here.'

'So's the Magna Carta,' I said.

'It turned out,' said McGovern, 'that it wasn't a *Daily News* piece after all. It was in *Newsday* sometime in late November. And get this. It was written by Dennis Duggan.' Duggan was a star columnist for *Newsday* and a friend of both mine and McGovern's.

'Jesus,' I said. 'Not only is it a rather tedious world, it's a small one, too.'

'Not when you're looking for something that isn't where you left it,' said McGovern as he moved farther down the mantel, past Carole Lombard and over to a large campaign poster from my ill-fated race for justice of the peace. It was slightly unnerving that I didn't remember autographing the poster. I looked at the inscription now as if reading it for the first time. It read:

To McGovern –

> *A good American,*
> *A good Christian?*
> *A good friend.*
> *Fuck yourself,*
> *Kinky*

I chuckled as I read the inscription. Sometimes I really slayed myself. But it wasn't all that humorous watching McGovern, now searching with what I thought was a touch of desperation, around and behind the poster. I knocked back the shot of Black Bush and puffed impatiently on the cigar.

'Look at this,' said McGovern. I glanced up hopefully. McGovern carefully extracted a piece of yellowed journalism from a pile.

'It's from back when I was covering the Charles Manson trial out in Los Angeles.'

'This is exactly what I didn't want to happen,' I said to myself, shaking my head disgustedly.

'Certain court officials took money from spectators,' said McGovern, 'to let them watch on monitors as Manson was being strip-searched. Charles Manson had a rather legendary *schlong*, you know.'

'That's a piece of information you don't learn at vacation Bible school,' I said.

'Not only that,' said McGovern, 'but according to the British tabloids, Roman Polanski, whose pregnant wife was murdered by the Manson Family, made films of his wife being hosed by Yul Brynner, Peter Sellers, and Warren Beatty, among others. Those films, apparently, were what Manson was really looking for that night.'

'What about Bob Hope?' I asked. 'Was he one of the guys Polanski filmed hosing his wife? That'd be a good piece of information to add to the Bob Hope obituary you've been writing for the past ten years.'

'I haven't *been writing* the Bob Hope obit,' said McGovern indignantly. 'I *wrote* it ten years ago. I've been *refining* it.'

I was thinking of going into the bathroom and looking for a shower rod to hang myself on when McGovern suddenly rushed into the bedroom and emerged moments later clutching a fluttering clipping in his large hands. 'Here it is,' he shouted jubilantly. 'The Dennis Duggan story!'

'Have you ever thought,' I asked, waving my hand around casually at the piles of old newspaper, clippings, and magazines squirreled all over the little apartment, 'about computerizing this setup?'

'Why would I want to do that?' McGovern asked, his face shining with an almost childlike candor. 'The system works.'

Dennis Duggan's article was a retrospective on the Texas Jewboys, including a rather lurid account of the crimes Cleve had committed in order to get where he was today. The piece also made note of the fact that, while Cleve seemed somewhat disoriented about the present, he remembered yesterday with an almost uncanny lucidity.

As I continued to read the piece on McGovern's little kitchen table, I felt fingers of ice moving along the base of my spine. At first I attributed it to the ungodly draft that moved through McGovern's apartment like a Texas blue norther. It was a small apartment but it had a big draft. McGovern poured us both another round of Black Bush and that warmed me up a bit.

Cleve had provided Duggan with several colorful anecdotes from the road, involving people and situations I'd long ago forgotten, that now came rushing back in a surge of nostalgia. I said as much to McGovern.

'There's a lot of that going around these days,' he said as he refilled our glasses again.

'Abbie Hoffman said: "Nostalgia is a symptom of illness in an individual or a society." '

'That's too bad,' said McGovern, looming over my shoulder like the Chrysler Building, 'because sometimes I think nostalgia's all I've got to look forward to.'

'It's all anybody's got to look forward to,' I said, 'after five rounds of Black Bush.'

I tried to concentrate on Duggan's article but my eyes were beginning to wander. Then something got a hold of my optic nerves and riveted my vision to the page. It was the last portion of the story. Duggan had written a 'Where are they now?' closer, and it listed the names of all the original Texas Jewboys, what instrument they played, where they were living, and what they were currently doing or not doing.

'McGovern,' I said, 'read this "Where are they now?" section.' McGovern picked the article up from the table and scanned it for a while.

'Well,' said McGovern, 'I don't want to bruise your ego, Holmes, but this is what our modern culture calls trivia. It's almost as popular as nostalgia.'

'You mean it's almost the same as nostalgia.'

'That's what I mean, but I was too sensitive to say it.'

'This is no time for sensitivity, Watson. Listen to what Duggan says about the first three names on the list: "Tequila – guitar. Still true to the gypsy spirit of the road, Tequila has no known address today. Says Cleve: 'We get a postcard from him once every ten years whether we want to or not.' Last heard from in Mexico.

' "Raymond Boatright – keyboards. Lives in Dallas, Texas. Works as piano tuner.

' "Wichita – guitar and fiddle. Lives in cabin with no indoor plumbing twenty miles outside of Tulsa, Oklahoma. Still plays local gigs whenever he can." '

'Jesus, Mary, and Joseph,' said McGovern.

'I'll see your Jesus, Mary, and Joseph,' I said grimly, 'and raise you an Abraham, Isaac, and Jacob.'

'The first three names on this list – '

'That's correct, Watson,' I said. 'This may look like an interview with a guy who needs a checkup from the neck up. It may appear to be a "Where are they now?" trivia piece. But it's also something else.'

Suddenly the icy fingers made themselves felt again on my spine. I killed the final round and puffed almost paranoically on my cigar. The little apartment seemed colder than it had any right to be.

'What I believe we have here, Watson,' I said, 'is a road map for a killer.'

53

'Well, you've got to admit,' I said to the blower on the left, 'that three Jewboys in a row dying in the same sequence they were listed in a *Newsday* story is a bit suggestive.'

It was a little after ten o'clock, Duggan's article was spread out before me on the desk in my loft, and Cooperman's voice was growling into my left ear like a pneumatic bulldog.

'Okay, Tex, Tequila was iced, I'll give you that. But these other two birds you're telling me about sound clearly like accidental deaths. Maybe your band was accident-prone.'

'I've got this "Where are they now?" story right here in front of me. Suppose somebody else is looking at it, too. Suppose some-body's checking his list and killing people.'

'Were they naughty or nice?' Cooperman asked.

Before our intercourse was terminated, I was able to give Coop-erman the details of the two out-of-state deaths, and he was able to tell me that since things were sailing along so smoothly in the city and there was nothing much for cops to do, he'd try to check it out and try to get back to me. I told him I'd try to hold my breath.

I fished an old, half-smoked cigar out of the wastebasket and fired it up. Sometimes when you resurrect one after a few weeks or so it gives you a little buzz. The way things were going I was going to need a little buzz. Also, the Black Bush was beginning to have a rather undulating effect on my medulla oblongata. I had to think clearly. A little alcohol will help you think clearly. A little more will usually have an undulating effect on your medulla oblongata.

I walked over to the espresso machine, performed the necessary ablutions upon it, and kicked it into gear. Soon it sounded like Orville Wright coming in pretty low. I poured a healthy steaming portion into my old 'Save the Males' coffee mug. Not a bad choice of receptacle, I thought, all things considered.

Duggan's list was still waiting for me when I got back to the desk. I puffed the remains of the rather elderly cigar and took a few tentative sips of espresso. Then I focused my orbs on the fourth name on the list. It read: 'Major Boles – drums. Lives in St Louis but still does regular session work in Nashville and per-forms with his own band.'

This brief account, I felt, failed to capture the Major. Like all drummers I'd known over the years, the Major was, of course, clinically ill. You have to be to want to be a drummer. He was also a very colorful American who often could be heard to complain that his 'sperm count was redlining.'

That was another problem with drummers. They were always horny. Drummers were horny, bass players were Austrians who wished they were Germans, horn players all thought they were black unless they were black, in which case they thought they were white, and lead-guitar players thought they were Jesus

Christ. Once you understood this you could lead a band right into the Valley of Death, which, unfortunately, looked to be a fairly close approximation of exactly where the Texas Jewboys were headed.

A little after Cinderella time, I called Dennis Duggan. It wasn't that easy to call Duggan. You had to dial his number, let it ring twice, then hang up and call again. Obviously, there was somebody Duggan didn't want to hear from. All of us have somebody we don't want to hear from and all of us have somebody we do want to hear from. The problem is getting them to realize who they are.

'Kinkster, my lad,' said Duggan after I'd identified myself, 'what can I do for you?' Aside from already providing what I increasingly believed to be a guidebook for a murderer, there wasn't a hell of a lot Dennis could do for me. Still, it never hurts to check your sources.

'Dennis,' I said, 'that story you wrote about the Texas Jewboys was aces.'

'Thanks, Kinkster. That friend of yours, Cleve, is really – uh – '

'He certainly is.'

'Are you really considering getting the old band together for a reunion tour?'

'You never know, Dennis. We may get our aluminum walkers all shined up and head out for the road again any day now. I wanted to ask you about that list of Texas Jewboys you ran in your article.'

'The old "Where are they now?" list. We'll all be on that roll one of these days, Kinkster.'

'Some of us already are,' I said. I paused to take a few puffs on what was left of the old cigar. 'Dennis, I'm interested in the sequencing of that list. Was the sequencing of the names your idea? Was it all done in a random and haphazard order?'

'Neither,' said Duggan. 'The names were listed in precisely the order they came to me out of Cleve's head.'

'And that,' I said, 'is no order at all.'

When I hung up with Dennis Duggan, I scanned the list again. Tequila, Boatright, Wichita, Major Boles, Bryan 'Skycap' Adams,

Billy Swan, Little Jewford, Willie Fong Young, Panama Red, Snakebite Jacobs, and tour manager Dylan Ferrero. They had all been there in the early days of the band. There were others who came to mind, but most of them joined the band a little later down the road. And these were the ones who came out of Cleve's head.

The list by now had taken on a rather foreboding quality. I could see all the names in some frightful roll call of the dead. It seemed certainly appropriate to inform these people of the danger they were in, even if I turned out to be wrong and nothing ever came of it. Yet a still, small voice that wasn't quite my conscience kept nagging at me. It didn't want me to tell them yet.

A few things were beginning to add up but many seemed to make even less sense than ever. I still didn't understand why the puppet had been hiding its head behind the refrigerator or why somebody'd bothered to nail my windows shut and not wait inside to finish me off. Why wait out in the hallway where some innocent lesbian or troublesome Ratso might wander along? Especially once you'd picked the lock.

Given Duggan's piece in *Newsday*, the stolen address book seemed to fit into the picture a little better. But the specter of Travis Parnell loomed as foggy and fearsome as ever. Of course, he didn't really have anything to do with the Jewboy situation, but, for some reason, he kept popping into my thoughts like a smiling, inflatable good-ol'-boy doll.

Eventually, all the Black Bush, the cigars, the stress of doing battle with enemies you couldn't see, and the wretched weight of the world began to lower my lids like a merchant shuttering his shop in Chinatown. I killed the lights in the living room, wandered into the bedroom, got undressed, put on my old batik sarong from Borneo and my Canadian Wildlife sweatshirt with a picture of a cuddly little baby seal, and got into bed. I was just beginning to count Young Republicans when the phones rang. I could've picked up the phone by the bed, but it sounded like the kind of call that ought to be taken on the blower to the left. I got up and stumbled out to the desk. In the tired, refracted New York moonlight, Warhol looked positively evil.

'Start talkin',' I said.

'Tex,' said Cooperman, 'you're on what we at the Sixth Precinct like to refer to as a wild fucking goose chase. I checked with the boys in Dallas and in Tulsa. They've both conducted thorough investigations and they've both resulted in findings of accidental death. Not the slightest sign of foul play. The files have been closed. They're convinced, and so am I, that you're wasting your time. You're also wasting *my* time. Why don't you wait a few weeks before you bother me again.'

Cooperman hung up. I held on to the blower for a moment as if there were more to say, then I hung up, too. There was always more to say, I thought. That was probably why so few people ever did anything.

Regardless of what Cooperman thought, I could feel an almost palpable presence irradiating my existence with a jagged, eternal evil. Somewhere, I believed, there was a mystery man, and in his head and in his hand he kept the bombing maps of his own private Germany. For whatever rhyme or whatever reason, I knew, beyond the shadow of the grave, something horrific was stirring. And it was out to get the Jewboys again.

54

It was Saturday morning and it was time to gather in the Texas Jewboys from their musical Diaspora. I felt it was essential to get as many members of the original band as possible to New York, if for no other reason than to get them the hell away from wherever they were. At least in New York, I could keep an eye on them and not be gradually informed by long-distance phone calls that life, indeed, was imitating some fantastic childhood ghost story.

The band could rehearse in New York and, if things went well, maybe we really *could* go out on a big reunion tour, make it all into a financial pleasure, leave the curse of the Texas Jewboys far behind us, and, of course, retire again. We could all look forward to living in little pink houses by the airport, with white picket fences protecting us from the past. We could spend our weekends washing our lox-colored '59 Cadillacs and watching our kids grow up to be lawyers and fagolas and BMW distributors.

Anything but a road musician.

The object of this protection plan was, of course, to make it harder for someone to know 'Where are they now?' And, as the large tribes of Philistines attacking ragged little bands of long-ago Jewboys always used to remind each other: 'There's safety in numbers.'

That's why they call them Philistines.

Of course, if you're going to go on a big road tour with a band you might as well get the best pickers possible. I thought of some of the hottest musicians I'd played with in recent years. Larry Campbell, an all-around virtuoso and great producer as well, was in New York, but how interested he'd be in a road tour I didn't know. Lee Roy Parnell (no relation to Travis) was a very hot original new songwriter and guitar player. But he'd just recorded an album and was getting his own band together in Nashville. Neil Kulhanek was one of the greatest steel-guitar players in the world but he was currently with a band in Austin and it might be hard to get him away.

There was one thing lacking, however, in all three of these world-class performers. None of them had been an original Texas Jewboy. Under the circumstances, that certainly appeared to be their good fortune.

The first action I took was to ring up Dylan Ferrero in San Antonio. He didn't have to go to school today and I didn't either. He was also the one guy who could pull this little temporary relocation project together and keep it rolling long enough for me to nail the killer before he decided to get busy again.

'Dylan,' I said, 'how'd you like to have your old job back for a little while? Take a few weeks' sick leave. Road-manage the Jewboys on a little reunion tour. What do you say?'

Dylan said: ' "Left a good job in the city/Workin' for the man every night and day – " '

'So you like the idea,' I said.

Dylan did not respond immediately. When he did, it was with a rather marked reticence.

'What's the matter,' I said. 'You're afraid to try something new?'

' "What's new, pussycat?" ' said Dylan. I waited.

'I don't know, hoss,' he said. 'I've got a suit and a tie and a job and a wife and a house and a dog.'

'You mean you traded that swell python jacket you got in Singapore for *that*?'

' "That ol' rockin' chair's got me," ' said Dylan.

'Why do I always feel like a middle-aged Peter Pan trying to get Tinkerbell off of standby?'

Dylan said 'I don't know, hoss' a few more times and I realized I was going to have to show him a couple of cards.

'Look, Dylan,' I said, 'I told you about Tequila and you told me about Raymond Boatright. Now Wichita's dead, too. A story about the band ran in *Newsday* a couple of months ago. It listed the original Jewboys by name and gave information about where they were currently living. I think somebody's using that article to find and kill the members of the band. You may not play an instrument besides the Jewish mouth bow but you were part of us and you still are. That's why your name's on that list.'

I let my last words sink in for a bit of effect. Dylan remained silent. He had the right. After all, this wasn't the best-dressed list or the employees of the month. This could easily be the most unpopular list to be included in since the group called up some years ago before the House Un-American Activities Committee.

'If anything should mysteriously happen to you,' I said, 'then you won't have to worry about your dog and your house and your wife and your job and your suit. Did I forget anything?'

'Tie,' said Dylan. 'I always kind of liked that tie.'

In the end, Dylan took the new job I'd offered, which was really an old job, dealing efficiently and sensitively with people and music and the road. Few had Dylan's smooth, magical, part flim-flam man, part Pattonlike aptitude for this highly unspecialized line of work. The only two Americans I knew who could touch Dylan with a barge pole when he was on the road were Gary Shafner, who'd worked with Bob Dylan, and Sandy Castle, who'd worked with the Band. But they weren't really Americans; they were Californians.

' "Give me weed, whites, and wine," ' said Dylan. ' "Show me a sign, and I'll be willin' to be movin'." '

Before we hung up, Dylan and I agreed to try like hell to get the band to New York in two weeks' time, without alerting them to the reason behind our urgency. We would lure them up instead with the promise of a big, glorious, profitable, fun, nostalgic reunion tour. And we would keep our fingers crossed that nothing unpleasant would happen before they got there. I was also keeping my fingers crossed that the concert promoters wouldn't find out that my booking agent was operating out of wig city.

I felt a certain sense of relief mixed with a sidecar of fatalism after hanging up with Dylan. The reunion tour would help protect the band and might just be fairly lucrative as well. But I had another reason for wanting to bring the Jewboys to New York, one I didn't wish to reveal to Dylan, McGovern, the cat, or anyone. It was looking more and more to me like the killer was one of the original Texas Jewboys.

55

Ten tedious days later on a brisk Tuesday afternoon I walked up Fifty-second Street with a strong case of déjà Jew. Now that the band had arrived in the city and I'd be seeing them again in a matter of moments, the years since we'd been together seemed to telescope down to almost nothing at all. Like a boxer whose adrenaline starts flowing on the way to the ring or a thoroughbred kicking up as he walks to the starting gate, I could feel the road humming in my blood. Already bits and pieces of music, lyrics, and stage patter were running through my head. It would be easier this time. Much easier. I could almost hear the applause of the crowd as we hit the stage.

Fleetingly, another train of thought seemed to move through my mind. It was not a very pleasant train. Its freight was human doubt and uncertainty. Car after car roared across rusty lifelines from the past, over high, rattling trestles of terror that made me wonder at the wisdom of what I was embarking upon. Could I protect the band from an unknown enemy any better in New York than if I'd just let them be? What would happen when we got out on the road? Was it wise to keep them in ignorance of the pattern of danger that I foresaw in the days ahead? This train of thought was still a distance away but it was getting closer. And it looked like it was coming toward me on the same track.

I lit a cigar, put all negative thoughts from my mind, and took a sharp right into Gallagher's Steak House. Dylan had called the night before to inform me that everyone was checked into the Chelsea Hotel – might as well dance with who brung you – and our first band meeting would be over lunch at two o'clock at Gallagher's. I was running fashionably late like Marilyn Monroe. The band had waited thirteen years for this; twenty minutes more or less wasn't going to make any difference now. I wasn't sure that anything was going to make any difference now if I didn't find out pretty fast who was snuffing semiretired rock 'n' rollers.

It wasn't hard to pick out the Jewboy table at Gallagher's. It looked like a group of fallen disciples assembled at a rather licentious, middle-aged Last Supper. James Clare, the charming, dapper Irishman who runs the place, had given me special dispensation from the Pope to wear my cowboy hat in Gallagher's. He understood that Jewboys and cowboys both like to wear their hats indoors and attach a certain amount of importance to it. The fact that he understood this rather stubborn, arcane notion, and created a spiritual loophole in the policy of the restaurant, defines fairly well the difference between the Irish and the British.

Shouts, greetings, and embraces were exchanged and the years all but melted away. When James Clare sent over a couple of bottles of champagne, it seemed almost like old times. I was happy to note that our little group did not bear much similarity to the gross caricatures you usually see at high school reunions. Maybe the road had served us well. It certainly wasn't the result of clean living, I thought, as I sipped a champagne toast Snakebite Jacobs was making. The waiter filled the glasses again and I looked carefully at Snakebite.

A gray hair here and there, but he looked great. In my mind I could see him playing two saxophones at once in front of a wild crowd in San Francisco. I remembered how I used to introduce Snakebite, telling the audience that I'd found him in an alley playing his saxophone with a coat hanger around his neck. Suddenly, I had an image of Snakebite's dead blue face with a coat hanger tightly twisted around his neck. I shook off the macabre picture and thought of my brother Roger's line that I'd often used onstage: 'If you want to wake up in the mornin' smilin' go to bed with a coat hanger in your mouth.' It was a slightly nicer image.

Billy Swan looked almost distinguished now, a far cry from the wild child I'd known in Nashville. He'd played in Kris Kristofferson's band both before and after the Texas Jewboys, so his chops, I knew, were always up. When Billy Swan smiled, in his eyes you could still see a twinkle of the road. Swan could play any instrument known to man and some that weren't. Dylan and I'd moved him to keyboards for this tour because Little Jewford had had to stay in Houston. That made Jewford the only living original member of the band not making the reunion tour. The thought gave me pause. I drank another toast someone was making. Champagne was not my drink of preference but if you drank enough of it, you forgot which one you preferred.

I scanned the rest of the table. Willie Fong Young looked as if marriage had been good for him. Also, I noticed with some relief, he didn't seem to be bearing any further grudge about my boycotting his wedding in favor of the bas mitzvah. Some people could carry grudges for a long time, I reflected, as James Clare sent over another two bottles of champagne.

Panama Red's mouth still resembled Mick Jagger's more than I would've liked, but there was nothing I could do about it except hire a rabid kangaroo to jump up and pluck his lips off. Panama was wearing his Panama in January in New York in Gallagher's Steak House. He wasn't Jewish or a cowboy, but if his sky-piece was good enough for James Clare, it was good enough for me. I could see Panama under the lights, wailing away on his electric, metallic cocaine bebop guitar. Panama liked to think he played rock 'n' roll with a country sensitivity and I liked to think that I played country with a social conscience, but basically, I made their eyes wet and he made their crotches wet. That was the real difference between country and rock 'n' roll.

Bryan 'Skycap' Adams got his name when the band was passing

297

through the airport in Kansas City and we heard them paging Skycap Adams. He dressed in sort of a mod, Negro style with flashy suits and droopy, velour skycaps. I could hear Skycap snartin' and fartin' on the Tennessee walkin' bass. He still looked like a kid.

Major Boles was bitching already about the first rehearsal, which Dylan had announced would be at the midtown studio he'd rented at two o'clock the next afternoon.

'Two o'clock's too early,' said the Major. I used to say that I'd found him in the Congo beatin' on his bongo, and he pretty much looked the part. Sometimes, when the mood hit him, the Major would play the drums with little American flags waving from his sticks.

Dylan looked like Dylan. He'd taken his python jacket out of mothballs and replaced his squares with an old pair of sky-shooters from the seventies. I didn't even remember if Dylan had eyes. But he'd been in contact with Cleve, with McGovern, even with Duggan, with Bill Dick at the Lone Star Roadhouse just down the street, and with about forty other people. If anybody could get this large, awkward, very-endangered bird into the air, it was Dylan.

Somewhere during my revery, eight steaks had been ordered and eaten along with about seventeen different kinds of Gallagher's potatoes. Everything was killer bee, including James Clare's personally guided tour of Gallagher's meat locker – one of the few peaceful places in New York.

A few people ordered dessert and a few ordered coffee. The waiter came over to Willie's end of the table and stood next to him.

'How would you like your coffee, sir?' he asked.

'Black,' said Willie, 'like my men.'

Swan was keeping his eyeball in his head and everybody appeared to be in a pretty good, confident mood. There isn't a murderer in the crowd, I thought. There couldn't be. Musicians were gentle people. They just weren't cut out to be premeditated murderers. Maybe Cooperman was right. Maybe Wichita and Raymond Boatright had gone to Jesus by accidental death.

James Clare had sent over still more château de cat piss and I was half-buzzed and lifting my glass to make a toast, when I remembered something McGovern had told me recently. 'Charles Manson,' he'd said, 'was a musician.'

'Charles Manson was a musician. Charles Manson was a musician,' kept playing over and over in my head – like a bad champagne trip.

I got to my feet, struggling slightly to keep my balance, and lifted the glass higher. Somehow, 'Charles Manson was a musician' didn't seem like it'd make a very good toast. But as I looked around the table, I couldn't honestly say for sure whether these people were murder suspects, innocent victims, or just old friends getting together again.

'The future,' I said.

If I could've seen the future, I never would've made the toast.

56

I don't remember getting home that night or going to bed but I do remember waking up early Wednesday morning with one of the worst hangovers in my life, picking up a jangling telephone, and finding Cleve on the other side of the line.

'I'll see you at the rehearsal this afternoon,' Cleve seemed to be saying. My head was pounding like I'd taken up residence inside Major Boles's bass drum.

'You will?' I said, in disbelief I didn't even try to hide.

'It's cool,' said Cleve. 'It's cool.'

It was cool, all right, I thought. With Travis Parnell biding his time somewhere in the underbrush, and an unidentified madman out there who was express-mailing Texas Jewboys to Hillbilly Heaven at fairly regular intervals, all I needed was a criminally insane idiot savant booking agent loitering around the band rehearsals. Of course, it was extremely doubtful that Cleve was going anywhere, I figured, as I managed to coax him off the phone. He only thought he was going to the band rehearsal. A lot of people in this world thought things that weren't true. Possibly, even myself.

I drank about a gallon of espresso that morning, and, when the hangover finally went away, the weight of my responsibility for the lives of the band members began to reassert itself. It'd been about three weeks since Wichita'd gotten himself croaked ostensibly by a stray shot from a hunter. Travis Parnell was a hunter, I thought, as I lit my first cigar of the morning. But I just didn't see where he fit into this picture. Tormenting Kelli was one thing, but what could he possibly have against the Texas Jewboys? A lot of people hadn't liked our music, of course, but why wait thirteen years to start doing us in?

The killer, I figured, was someone other than Travis Parnell. Someone who hadn't made a move since whacking Wichita more than three weeks ago. If I was right about Wichita and Boatright not dying of accidental causes, it was about time for the other cowboy boot to drop. Not for a New York minute did I believe that bringing the band up here would make them all invulnerable. I just felt I would be able to keep a closer eye on things. Show business, like politics, is a very open, public casino of endeavor. The biggest, most powerful people in the business, with all their bodyguards and security fences and disguises and bulletproof limousines, can't stop some lightly salted assorted nut from abruptly terminating their careers if his parakeet continues to send him coded messages. Sometimes this manifests itself in nasty letters to Michael J. Fox. Sometimes it results in the death of John Lennon. It depends on the parakeet.

I puffed the cigar, sipped a little espresso, and thought about it for a while. Even with someone who was out where the buses don't run, there had to be a motive. The motive, usually, was out where the buses don't run as well. So, in order to understand the motive, you had to get out there yourself. You had to walk a long, tortuous journey far into your own mind and your own memories. Once you get there, of course, and you understand the motive, the truly frightening thing is that it doesn't really seem so crazy after all. You've probably had the same thoughts yourself at one time or another. Something very deep and essential within the mind of man has always wanted to impress Jody Foster and kill Ronald Reagan.

I sipped some more espresso. Voltaire, I remembered reading somewhere, had drunk more than seventy cups of coffee a day, and, though the doctors said it would kill him, he figured it must be a pretty slow poison because he lived to be one of the oldest and smartest frogs in the pond. I sipped some more espresso.

If some kind of 'Last of the Thirteen' – type curse was in effect upon the Texas Jewboys, something was going to happen pretty soon and it wasn't going to be something very nice. Though Vern's ancient ghost story, like so many aspects of life on this planet, never resolved itself, the bunch of white-haired guys did rack their brains to discover what it was that they all had in common that could've engendered such a curse. In the story, the only shared experience they could remember was the night they'd all stayed in the old haunted house in the middle of the forest.

I sipped some more espresso.

What would be the modern, nonfictional equivalent to the guys with the white hair spending the night together in the old haunted house? What act or experience did all the band have in common that could now be causing someone to wreak some kind of crazy vengeance upon us? I thought about it for a long while, but, in the end, nothing was delivered. We'd done a hell of a lot of things together on the road and off. None of them seemed serious enough to have invoked this kind of hatred upon the band.

I would have to warn Major Boles, of course. He was the fourth name on Duggan's list, and, if things ran true to form, the killer being a methodical, compulsive type, the fourth place on the list was not a healthy place to be. I, as fate would have it, was not on the list, but I'd been dealt with by Duggan earlier in the article. I wondered now about the time shortly after Tequila's death when someone had nailed my windows shut for obviously more nefarious purposes than keeping out the draft. Maybe I'd been the first intended victim. But why hadn't the bastard, once he'd already picked the lock, waited inside to finish me off? Instead, he'd waited out in the hallway, bopped Ratso when he'd come along, got spooked and fled, and then continued his way, apparently, down Duggan's list, giving me a temporary reprieve.

He'd iced Tequila, then gone to Dallas to croak Boatright, then traveled to Tulsa to splice Wichita. Armed with Duggan's information, my telephone book, and the insight and focus that only a murderous mind possesses, he seemed to move pretty much at will. He seemed to enjoy traveling. I wondered if he flew business class.

I looked up and observed that Andy Warhol seemed to be gazing down upon me with a rather thin, slightly condescending smile. He had white hair, too, I noticed. I glanced over at my old guitar leaning against the wall. It was about two hours until the rehearsal. Why not rehearse? I thought. If we were all going to die soon, we might as well give the folks their money's worth.

I sipped some more espresso.

'The monkey ain't dead and the show ain't over,' I said to the cat.

57

Divorces and IRS audits are the only things in the world, I'm told, that are more tedious than rehearsing a band. I've never been divorced mainly because I've never been married, and I've never been audited because I've got a black accountant and the feds always leave him alone. But I have been to a lot of band rehearsals and they were roughly up there, in terms of tedium, with four hours of root-canal work by a glib, heavy-handed, possibly suicidal dentist.

I won't bore you with a detailed description of a band rehearsal, but you should know that the first hour and a half is usually eaten alive by the drummer hitting his drums repeatedly as loud as he possibly can and the bass player striving valiantly to match him in both volume and monotony. The rest of the band often takes this opportunity to urinate, go out for a drink, do drugs, or hang themselves from a shower rod. Finally, the whole band takes the stage and then the bickering starts.

There are also beautiful, private moments, without press, onlookers, or audience, when a handful of musicians who've known each other for years become something bigger than themselves, and fly on the majestic wings of music played well together. It was into one of these moments that a startling and disconcerting thought came into my head. I thought about it for a good while as I sang and played the guitar with the band. Sometimes when you're performing, your thoughts can travel elsewhere with an almost brilliant clarity. In fact, if the audience ever found out what most entertainers are thinking while emoting from the stage, they'd demand their money back.

What I was thinking about was that the original Texas Jewboys had existed as a viable entity only for about three years, from 1973 to 1975. After that, I'd toured with Bob Dylan, played the Lone Star on a regular basis, and, later, made the rounds again with resurrected versions of the band. At one time I had a group of Texas Jewboys in New York, one in L.A., and one in Texas. After all, I wasn't Chuck Berry. I couldn't just pick up a house band anywhere I played and expect them to know 'They Ain't Makin' Jews Like Jesus Anymore.'

From 1973 to 1975, I thought. That had to be it. If there'd been a 'Last of the Thirteen' incident, it had to've happened during that time. And it must've happened on the road because that was the only time we were all together during those three years. That did narrow things down.

As the band plowed painlessly through the set, I did some more reflecting upon things past, but nothing earth-shattering came to mind. That had always been a problem with me. I never remembered things until somebody reminded me about them. Then I never forgot. It was either burned synapses or the Baby Jesus was protecting me from my past. It was kind of like the chorus from a song of mine, 'Silver Eagle Express': 'And I'll ride the Silver Eagle to the last town on the line. There's nothing to remember if there's nothing to remind.'

But Dylan remembered yesterday. And, God help us all, Cleve remembered yesterday. I'd have to have a serious power caucus with those two. Of course, other guys in the band no doubt remembered yesterday, too. The problem was that one of them, I was very much afraid, remembered something about it too damn well.

When the band took a break for dinner, I noticed that the rehearsal studio was beginning to develop a little traffic of well-wishers and kibitzers, most of whom I knew. It was nice to see

303

that Ratso had come down, though he seemed a bit quiet, tight-lipped, and almost thin, very un-Ratsolike qualities. McGovern had come around, too, and was listening to Major Boles and Panama Red swap tales of conquest on the road.

'. . . the redhead with the giant zubers in Denver,' the Major was saying.

'I hosed her, too,' said Panama. 'The next night in Boulder.'

'They *were* boulders,' said the Major.

'You hold her, I'll milk her,' said Willie Fong Young as he walked by.

'She was a newcomer to my cucumber,' said Snakebite.

'I should've been a musician,' said McGovern.

'You're not kiddin,' said the Major. 'In Chicago on that first tour there was a knock on my door about four o'clock in the morning. Tequila's wife. I porked her till her nose bled.'

Panama smiled knowingly. Then he said: 'Too bad about Tequila.'

'Life's a bitch and then you die,' said the Major.

'Let me write that down,' I said.

'I hosed these two sisters in San Antonio once,' Panama said. McGovern was listening in rapt attention. The Major gave me a broad wink. 'One was named Trixie and one was named Dixie.'

I felt a tap on my shoulder and turned to see an attractive, well-dressed, dark-haired woman wearing those large, black glasses that women sometimes wear to show that they're not there to have fun.

'I'm Dr Allison Klitsberg,' she said.

Next to her stood Cleve, humming some song in his head, a sick, little smile on his face, and looking, generally, like he belonged on the third ring of Saturn.

'Cleve is here with me,' said Dr Klitsberg, 'as part of our resocialization program.'

I took another look at Cleve. He didn't even recognize me. I turned back to Dr Klitsberg, who was now drawing approving nods from Panama and Major Boles.

'Good luck,' I said.

On the way to the men's room I was accosted by Dylan and a

tall, thin Charles Manson look-alike who hugged me and picked me up off my feet. When he set me down I realized it was Bo Byers, who'd done the sound for the band and was with the road crew on the first tour. Bo and I exchanged a few somewhat more subdued greetings, then he drifted over to say hello to the other guys.

'Might as well make the reunion tour as authentic as possible, hoss,' said Dylan. 'Bo's been knocking around for a while and he said he needed the work, so I took him aboard. He came in last week from Tulsa.'

'Why does that ring a bell?' I said.

58

'I know it sounds a little far-fetched,' I said.

'No, it doesn't sound far-fetched,' said Major Boles. 'It sounds abso-motherfuckin'-lutely crazy. Of course, people are gonna die in thirteen years. They'll also get married, get divorced, go to bar mitzvahs – '

'Don't say "bar mitzvah" in front of Willie.'

The two of us were sitting in a little Irish bar on Forty-third Street a few blocks over from the rehearsal studio. The rehearsal had been brutal but the band sounded a lot tighter than I'd ever have believed after all that time off the road. It was almost eleven o'clock. On the jukebox the Irish Rovers were singing 'The Unicorn' in a thick Irish brogue. The song was written by Shel Silverstein, who no one ever mistook for being Irish.

'I'll admit,' said Major Boles, 'that the three of them checked out in a pretty short period of time, but sometimes things happen in threes. Like airplane crashes.'

'They weren't on airplanes,' I said as I signaled the bartender for another round of Jameson's. 'They were murdered.'

'You say that. What do the police say?'

I killed the shot and chased it with a little Guinness. I looked out the window into the street. 'They say people go to bar mitzvahs,' I said.

'Ah ha!' said the Major. I looked at him for a moment. His face still seemed to have the disbelief and recklessness of youth about it. You had to look closely to see the fine lines of time and worry that had etched themselves around his eyes like side roads and minor tributaries on an old map of Kansas before Dorothy left. The Major was not that much younger than myself, but he was young enough to make it still rather hard to convince him that his life might be in danger.

I took the clipping of Dennis Duggan's article out of the pocket of my hunting vest and spread it on the mahogany in front of the Major. 'You'll notice,' I said, 'that the three names directly above your own are all recently deceased. They were croaked in the order they appear.'

I let the Major study the crumpled little hit list while I studied my empty glass and motioned the bartender for another round of drinks. 'What do you think?' I asked, finally.

'Where are they now?' said the Major facetiously. 'I'll tell you where they are. They're right exactly just in the same goddamn place they've always been. Nobody really changes much, you know.'

I looked at the minor tributaries again. 'That's what I'm counting on,' I said.

The bartender poured another round. 'Humor me,' I said to the Major. 'Just assume someone's behind these deaths, methodically trying to kill off the band.'

The Major belched.

'Can you remember anything the whole band did that could've provoked someone into seeking this kind of vengeance? Can you remember anything at all?'

'I can't even remember the Alamo,' said Major Boles.

If he hadn't been a drummer I probably could've made him see the light. But you can't warn anybody about anything today. Half the world's a bunch of paranoid nerds who are afraid of life, and the other half just don't give a damn. The latter group is usually more fun to drink with.

Nothing ever happens when you expect it, even if you're ready for it. But there is an uncanny timing to certain events on this planet that leads one, if not to believe in the Baby Jesus, at least to realize that somebody's building a lot of time-share condos in hell.

It was almost midnight, the time the white-haired man on the train was waiting for, when we finished the last round. Major Boles had folded Duggan's article into a paper airplane and headed for the door. I refolded the clipping, put it back in my pocket, and paid the bill. I took out a cigar and started to light it in the doorway.

The Major was standing in the street yelling something when a pair of headlights swam by me like a laser shark. A speeding taxi cab with its radio blaring hit him with that deep, sickening 'WHUMP' sound that, once you've heard it, resonates forever in your fondest nightmares, like a horrible human bell.

59

'Well,' said Sergeant Cooperman, 'I asked you not to bother me for a couple weeks and that's about how long it's been.'

It seemed like Cooperman and I'd been out on Forty-third Street long enough to start asking people for spare change for a sex change. The guys from the stiff casino, with the demeanor and emotional range of workers fixing a pothole, had finally taken Major Boles's body away. My heart felt like it'd lost its rhythm section.

'You didn't get the license number or the number on the cab?'

'It happened too fast,' I said. 'I don't think there was a license plate. Just the headlights. The loud music. It seemed like it all occurred in the time it took to strike a match and set fire to a cigar.'

'Maybe you shouldn't smoke,' said Sergeant Cooperman as he took a Gauloises out of a crumpled pack and, narrowing his eyes like a street cat, lit it with a Zippo. We both stood under a street-light looking at the place where Boles's broken body had lain. There'd been a shoe and a smashed pair of shades there too for a while, but they'd taken them downtown, too. He'd been killed instantly, the medical examiner had said, but I'd known that already.

Traffic was rolling on the street again. The excitement was over.

I looked away for a moment and then back to the place where he'd died. I wasn't exactly sure where the place was anymore. Places change, they say. I put my hands into the pockets of my coat to keep warm.

My fingers fumbled onto something in my left pocket and my hand came out with Dennis Duggan's story. I gave it to Cooperman. He unfolded it and I pointed out the top four names on the list.

'Christ,' he said. 'Too bad we're not at the racetrack.' He'd read the story he said. He knew the list. 'Describe the driver again.'

'I told you. All I saw was a brief impression of a blur going by with a hat pulled down over its face.'

'Maybe it was James Cagney.'

Cooperman was hot tonight, I thought. Death seemed to sharpen his wit. He asked a few more questions. I gave him Dylan's room number at the Chelsea and the names of the guys in the band that were staying there. Finally, he put his little notebook away. He lit up another Gauloises and I began the spiritual foreplay that is occasionally required of lighting a cigar at certain measured moments of your life.

Cinderella's coach had retro-metamorphosed rather unpleasantly to a leering jack-o'-lantern several hours ago. Cooperman and I still stood there, almost friends, watching cars go by and vagrants peer into garbage cans, looking for the world. The brash loneliness was achingly vibrant; it seemed to belong to another place and another time. Casablanca. The Paris of the twenties. New York did not feel like my home anymore. Maybe it never had. Maybe I belonged in Texas. The Texas of the nineties, I knew, was not the Paris of the twenties, but how many kinds of sauces can you put on a chicken-fried steak?

At last, Cooperman shook his head and began walking toward his generic squad car. I turned and started to head for Seventh Avenue.

'Hey, Tex,' he said. I stopped and turned again.

'You said the driver of the vehicle was playing loud music as he drove past?'

'Yeah,' I said.

'What kind of music was he playing, Tex?'

Something made me stop for a moment. Auditory and visual images seemed to be slowly sorting themselves out in some jumbled federal office building of my mind.

'Country music,' I said.

'Figures,' said Cooperman as he got into the car.

60

When I got back to the loft it was two-forty in the morning and I hit the blower running. Most people, for reasons I've never understood, don't like to receive phone calls at two-forty in the morning. As my friend Marvin Brener always tells me: 'People have their lives.' They do, indeed. They have their tragic little lives and a horrible thing like a late-night phone call from New York is just too much for them to handle gracefully. It's foreign to their suburban souls to have a voice from the past intrude itself across a wire into the shipwreck they've made of their lives. Oh, there were people I used to be able to call late at night but they are almost all dead. Now I can still call them anytime I want, only they never answer. All the circuits in hell are busy. Of course, many so-called living people are dead and in hell, too, they just don't know it yet.

I think late-night phone calls can be spiritually important and the absence of them is a significant index of the advance of middle age. When you've truly reached middle age, the only late-night phone calls you get are wrong numbers or news that somebody died. Well, somebody had died. Four somebodys had died.

'Why did you call me?' asked Little Jewford.

'To see if you were there,' I said.

'Where the hell else would I be?' he wanted to know. 'It's two o'clock in the morning.'

'It's an hour later here,' I said. 'Should we circumcise our watches?'

The conversation was fairly brief and it wasn't too pleasant, but it did prove that Little Jewford was in Houston, and it's hard to commandeer a hack in New York if you're in bed in Houston.

I called Max in Kerrville. He wasn't ecstatic either. He had to work in the morning.

'I don't know what you're bitching about, Max,' I said. 'It's an hour later here.'

Max said something in Spanish that didn't sound nice.

'Listen, Max,' I said, 'we've got to pull out all the stops on Parnell. There's a guy in a cowboy hat killing people up here and every time I mentally round up the suspects, he's always up there at the top of the list. He doesn't seem to have a motive, but he does have a cowboy hat.'

'So does Gabby Hayes,' said Max.

I got Max to promise to call Parnell's family again in the morning and to press them on his whereabouts. He would call me as soon as he talked with them.

'*Buenas noches*,' said Max sleepily.

'*Salamat mimpi*,' I said. It was about all the residual Malay I remembered from Borneo, unless, of course, I was drunk. Then I remembered a lot of Malay and a lot of phone numbers that were no longer working in Los Angeles. *Salamat mimpi* meant 'safe dreams.' That was about the nicest thing you could wish anybody, I figured.

When I hung up with Max I called Dylan at the Chelsea Hotel but his line was busy. I left a message with the night-clerk, and, in honor of Dylan Thomas's last residence on this particular planet, I located a bottle of Old Grand-dad hiding behind a bag of cat litter. It was covered with cobwebs and dust and looked like it'd come with the loft. I poured a shot into the bull's horn to settle my nerves. I raised the bull's horn in a toast to Major Boles. The cat sat on the counter looking bored.

' "After the first death there is no other," ' I quoted. I was beginning to wonder if Dylan Thomas knew what the hell he was talking about. I downed the shot.

The Old Grand-dad was funkier than Jack Daniel's and gave the certain impression of being capable of inducing degeneracy faster than Jameson's. But it cut the phlegm.

'You know,' I said to the cat, 'that time at the Chinese restaurant when Parnell winged the waiter?'

The cat looked at me. She blinked several times.

'Suppose it wasn't Travis Parnell.'

I had a few more Old Grand-dads just to unwind a little bit and think things over. I was sitting at the kitchen table with the cat when the phones rang. It was almost four o'clock in the morning. I might be a lot of things but at least I wasn't middle-aged. I walked over to the desk and lifted the blower on the left. It was Washington Ratso telling me that the girls were safe and having a great time and why didn't I tell him that Kelli had very well-shaped buttocks and my sister had terrific breasts. He didn't say it all in precisely those words, but that was the gist.

'It's nice to know you're looking after them,' I said.

'They're pretty hard to miss,' said Ratso. 'I've really enjoyed working with you on this one.'

I lighted a cigar and listened as Ratso went into a little more anatomical detail than I would have liked. Finally, he said: 'Hey, I read in the paper that you're getting the Jewboys together again for a big reunion tour.'

'We've run into a few problems,' I said. 'Or rather, they've run into us.'

'Well, if you need a Lebanese Jewboy who plays a mean butane guitar, I'd love to come.'

'Sexually?' I asked.

'No,' said Ratso. 'I mean join the tour. Sure you don't need a guitar player?'

'Too bad you don't play the drums,' I said.

It was a quarter after four by the time I killed the lights, said good night to the cat, and got into bed, with images of Major Boles still very vivid in my mind. I'd almost gotten into the fitful-tossing-and-turning stage when the phones rang again. Maybe I was younger than I thought.

I collared the pink princess phone by the bedside that the Greek woman I was subletting from had left along with her green plants and ballet poster. It was Dylan.

He said: ' "I Fought the Law and the Law Won." '

'Ah, so Sergeant Cooperman's been to see you.'

'They came through here like the "City of New Orleans." '

I talked to Dylan for some time, and as we talked, the sense of personal loss we both felt became evident. My friend Dr Jim Bone says that everyone has two families: the one you're born into and the one you make for yourself. The Texas Jewboys, with all our strife and separation, were a family, and this latest loss diminished us all.

Cooperman and his boys had interviewed everyone in the band about Major Boles's death, getting background, establishing alibis. The only two people whom they still hadn't located were Snakebite Jacobs and Panama Red.

'Not unusual for musicians not to be in a hotel at four in the morning,' I said. 'Or anywhere else.'

' "Four o'clock rock," ' said Dylan.

After I cradled the princess I lay back in bed and stared for a long time at the paint peeling off the ceiling. A few more lesbian dance classes, I figured, and there'd be nothing left to stare at. A numbing hard-edged guilt was beginning to settle somewhere deep in my soul. I'd brought the band to New York. It was my brilliant theory that they'd be safer here. I was the leader of the band. I was responsible in a large way for what had happened to the Major.

I did my dead-level best to push the guilt out of my mind. Catholic and Jewish people, as well as practically everybody else, seem to enjoy engendering guilt in others, but it serves no one well to experience an undue amount of guilt yourself. Even if you deserve it.

I thought about Snakebite and Panama Red. I didn't lamp Snakebite as a killer. I couldn't really see Panama murdering anyone either. Maybe he could flog somebody to death with his lips. And he did wear a hat all the time. But it just didn't make sense. It was impossible. Or was it? Charles Manson was a musician, I said to myself. It was almost becoming a mantra.

I finally got to sleep and, sure enough, I had a hideous, slow-motion, Technicolor dream about Major Boles.

But first there were a few short trailers. I got a Mr Pibb and some Milk Duds and hurried to my seat just as the lights went down.

61

Dale Haufrect, the kid who lived across the street, reached his hand into the goldfish bowl. I must've been very young because I regarded my three goldfish as my secret friends. An adult, of course, can look upon goldfish as secret friends, too, but it's usually not considered all that healthy a relationship. Dale Haufrect took the goldfish out of the bowl one by one and slit their sides with his thumbnail before dropping them on the floor. I watched in that state of suspended animation that only a four-year-old or an adult New Yorker who doesn't want to get involved can obtain.

But the goldfish never came back to life like Dale Haufrect said they would. Instead, little drops of cotton-candy-colored blood fell from the fish to the floor and my own eyes of ancient childhood filled with tears.

All my youth, I suppose, I've waited for those three goldfish to come back to life, but they never have. Maybe they moved up to the next incarnation. Maybe God sent them back as Goodman, Schwerner, and Chaney. Sounds like a law firm, but it isn't.

I did a few bed turns and vaguely, sadly, semiconsciously realized that one of the things that God probably couldn't do was bring dead goldfish back to life. Not even Dale Haufrect could do that.

I spun a few more times in the shallow grave of Morpheus and the dream fast-forwarded about twenty-four years or so to a large, dank basement of some club in the Village. Several hundred people were crowded around staring at a screen upon which appeared to be a home movie of a fairly large goldfish. The goldfish seemed to have a wound in its side out of which periodically would seep cotton-candy-colored blood. In the dream, I couldn't understand why several hundred people would be standing in a room at rapt attention staring at the rather gory spectacle of a dying goldfish. I was older now and it wasn't quite that traumatic an experience. You could see a dying goldfish on your way to work.

I scanned the room for a familiar face and finally orbed Ratso waving to me with one hand and holding a large, heaping plate of food in the other. The hand he was waving had what looked like a corned beef sandwich in it. I walked over. Next to Ratso stood Allen Ginsberg wearing little Tibetan finger cymbals.

I heard Ginsberg say to Ratso in a soothing, almost hypnotic voice: 'Why don't you try on these finger cymbals?'

Ratso replied: 'I can't. I'm eating a sandwich. They could give me lead poisoning.'

Ginsberg then offered the cymbals to me but I, too, declined. Then Ginsberg smiled beatifically and began playing the little cymbals himself, dancing around, and chanting, as near as I can remember, the following poem:

> Live when you live
> Die when you die
> Laugh when you laugh
> Cry when you cry
> Fuck when you fuck
> Shit when you shit
> Pee when you pee

'Excuse me,' I said, 'but why is everybody watching that goldfish die?'

Ginsberg and Ratso both started laughing, and Ratso laughed so hard I was glad I hadn't accepted Ginsberg's offer. It's hard to give the Heimlich maneuver when you're wearing Tibetan finger cymbals.

Ginsberg started to play the finger cymbals and jump around again. This time he chanted gleefully: 'It's Abbie's dick, it's Abbie's prick, it's Abbie's dong, it's Abbie's *schlang*, it's Abbie's thing, it's his *I Ching*, it's Abbie's dork, it's in New York.'

'Come again?' I said.

'It's a movie,' Ratso said, 'that Abbie Hoffman had made of his recent vasectomy.'

'Hell of a cinematographer,' I said.

'It's Abbie's penis, gonna send it to Venus,' said Ginsberg.

I walked over to the doorway and was trying to light a blue

bubble-gum cigar when a hack high-beamed me from the left wing and slowly moved past like a yellow fog of death. In horripilating slow motion I watched the hellish hack reduce Major Boles to eleven different herbs and spices. I heard the loud, familiar country music again as it ricocheted off the buildings and Dopplered down to me in the dream. It was the same snatch of music I'd heard earlier in the evening when Major Boles had been killed on Forty-third Street. But this time, in the dream, I clearly heard the words *Ronnie Reagan*.

When I woke up it was still dark, but I'd seen the light. At least I'd seen enough of it to know I was on the right track. I still didn't know where the hell I was going, of course, but, I could decide that when I got there. For starters I'd have to talk to Captain Midnite, Willie Fong Young, Skycap Adams because he was next on the list, and Dylan, because he remembered yesterday. So did Cleve, of course, but it was chancy because he might forget it by tomorrow.

I programmed the espresso machine, chased some cockroaches out of the frying pan, and made some scrambled eggs with a heavy dollop of frozen Lone Star five-alarm chili, throwing in some red Vietnamese peppers a little friend had sent me recently from Arkansas. As dawn broke over the warehouses I had breakfast and thought about my dreams.

All of them stemmed from real incidents, of course. Dale Haufrect had killed my goldfish when I was a little kid. I'd performed some songs at a party for Abbie Hoffman where he'd shown a movie of his recent vasectomy. I'd opened for the vasectomy. Two weeks later, Abbie'd jumped bail and gone underground. Now he was underground for good, I thought sadly. Well, at least he'd feel at home there.

As far as 'Ronnie Reagan' went, I was now sure I'd heard the same music at the actual time of the hit-and-run accident. 'Ronnie Reagan' was part of a line of a song, the whole verse of which went like this:

> It's retro-rocket time inside my attic
> I'm all wrapped up in the flag to keep me warm

I've got my brain locked in to cruise-o-matic
Rollin' Ronnie Reagan in suppository form.

The song was called 'Flyin' Down the Freeway' and it was writ-ten by a young songwriter in 1973 in Nashville. I remembered it well. I ought to.

I was that songwriter.

62

Later that Thursday morning I called Captain Midnite in Nash-ville. He had that certain renaissance in his voice that you hear only from soulful former disc jockeys.

'Little Jimmie Dickens International Fan Club,' he said. I identi-fied myself.

'I was going to make a big donation this month to the United Jewish Appeal,' said Midnite, 'but I'm a little short.'

'Yeah. Midnite, have you got anything for me?'

'I gave you that alarm clock seventeen years ago.'

'You'll be gratified to know it still works,' I said. 'Otherwise I might've slept through this conversation.'

'I do have some news for you. Tompall Glaser injured himself trying to sing as high as his brothers. Now he walks with a lisp.'

'I was looking for something unusual or unpleasant that might've happened to Willie Fong Young.'

'Well, he went up to New York to do that reunion tour with you. That's unusual and unpleasant.'

'Midnite, you know how Willie is. It'd take me days to get anything out of him and I don't have the time. Has he been in any accidents or near misses that you know about?'

'Come to think of it, his car was totaled about three weeks ago. Brakes went out.'

'Willie didn't mention it.'

'That's because he wasn't in it. He'd loaned it to his smother-in-law.'

'How is she?'

'Sexually?'

'Walked into my own trap, didn't I? You've been taking Kinky lessons. What's her condition?'

'Willie's smother-in-law? Broke her leg is all. Cast was a bit unwieldy. It was made of chopsticks.'

'I picked right up on that.'

'Since the accident she's been a shell of herself. When Willie visited her in the hospital he lifted her up and held her to his ear to see if he could hear the ocean.'

It was getting interesting. After terminating social intercourse with Midnite, I paced the loft a bit, puffing on a Punch Rothschild Maduro. If I was right there were four victims. There were certainly four stiffs, and I didn't have to extrapolate things too far to see that they were all victims of the same maniacal, methodical mind. You could add to that the failed attempt to eighty-six Willie Fong Young, resulting in the injury to his smother-in-law. You could also add two attempts on my own life, for I now thought it more likely that a poor marksman had been gunning for me rather than Travis Parnell deliberately winging the waiter to send a message of terror to Kelli. Hadn't heard much about Travis Parnell lately. I wondered who his agent was.

Images of the Major kept intruding themselves into my mind's bloodshot eye. Try as I might, I just couldn't quite see the whole picture. The style was obvious. The method. The pattern. But the work remained unsigned, unfinished, insidious, foreboding. You couldn't really tell what it was going to be when the artist was through. It seemed as if an insane Impressionist were carefully creating an abstract painting, splashing fresh bright blood onto the beckoning canvas, cocking a grinning, almost apologetic face to one side, not quite entirely happy with his macabre, death-wreaking work. Rectal realism was never like this, I thought.

Through the blue haze of cigar smoke I saw the Major standing in the street calling me. I just couldn't hear his words. It tore at my heart and at my conscience. I paced a little more rapidly and the cat followed my movements back and forth across the loft from her perch on the counter. She looked like a slightly bored spectator watching a rather slow tennis-match, except that she flicked her tail occasionally in irritation, to be sure that I knew she didn't give a damn who won or lost.

Gradually, it became clear to me what I had to do. This was no time for grief. It was no time for guilt. The reunion tour must proceed as scheduled, fraught as it was with danger and death. I was convinced it was the only way to catch the killer in the act. The only other option would be for the band to scatter itself to the winds, and then to learn at fairly regular intervals, like the white-haired man on the train, of the demise of every single member of the original Texas Jewboys.

Around noon I called Dylan. He told me that Snakebite and Panama had gotten in early that morning and Cooperman planned to talk to them. I did, too, I said. I told Dylan to go ahead with all rehearsal and tour plans as scheduled. He wasn't surprised and allowed that he'd come to the same conclusion himself. For some reason, I felt better when I heard that. If we were both wrong, we'd soon find out.

'I'll get a new drummer for the tour,' I said. 'Corky Laing may have enough of a death wish to want to do it.'

' "Drums keep poundin' rhythm to the brain," ' said Dylan.

'I'll also be checking with Cleve today about the itinerary. I'm going to get him to try to add a date sometime next week at the Lone Star to sort of kick things off. Maybe we'll be able to resolve this madness before the actual road tour starts. I hope Cleve's mental hygiene's in a little better shape than it was at the rehearsal.'

' "Here comes your nineteenth nervous breakdown," ' Dylan said.

'Anybody in the band who wants to bug out for the dugout has my blessing. I know a lot of guys who would love to be in this band.'

There was a brief silence on the line. Then I heard the high, Brenda Lee-like, unmistakable sound of the expulsion of gas occurring fairly close to the receiver of the phone.

'I'm telling you, Dylan, this reunion idea is going to prove triumphant yet.'

' "The magical mystery tour," ' said Dylan, ' "is coming to take you away." '

63

'Of course I'm staying,' said Skycap Adams, 'but it's going to be kind of hard to rehearse the band without a drummer, don't you think?'

'We could go on the road with one of those drum machines they use in lounges at Holiday Inns.'

I'd just returned from the Monkey's Paw where I'd had a liquid lunch with McGovern and brought him up to date on the situation. In tune with the new freedoms in Eastern Europe and the easement of apartheid in South Africa, the management of the Monkey's Paw had decided to lift the ban on McGovern for peeing on the leg of a lady standing at the bar in 1974. 'Free at last,' McGovern had said to me as he'd sipped a tall Vodka McGovern.

'We could give Wayne Newton a Hebrew natural and a cowboy hat,' Skycap Adams was saying, 'and maybe he could take *your* place.'

'He'd probably want an entourage of forty-nine buttboys.'

'You got to get a drummer, Kinkster.'

'I was thinking,' I said. 'You remember Cubby? Used to play drums for the Mouseketeers? I wonder what he's doing?'

'Probably wishing he was still staring at Annette Funicello's tits.'

I told Skycap to be on the alert. I warned him again that his life was in grave danger whether he stayed with the band or not. I told him I was sorry about Major Boles, very sorry. I knew Skycap had been close to him.

'When you play with somebody that long,' said Skycap, but he didn't finish the sentence.

'All I can tell you,' I said, 'is what the great producer Huey P. Meaux once told me: "All musicians are brothers in music." '

When I hung up the phone with Skycap I walked over to the window and stared silently at the unfocused street.

'All but one,' I said to the cat. 'All but one.'

Snakebite Jacobs, Billy Swan, Panama Red, Willie Fong Young (possible), Skycap Adams (possible), and Bo Byers (looks like Charles Manson and just came in from Tulsa).

That was the list of suspects I was perusing in my Big Chief tablet late Thursday afternoon as frightening February shadows reached their tendrils across Vandam Street and into the little loft. The only other possibilities I could think of – Dylan, my brother Roger, Little Jewford, and his brother Big Jewford – were so thoroughly alibied by virtue of their teaching, professional, and family structuring that I now ruled them totally out. As a rule of thumb, I always permitted the accusatory finger to point at every conceivable individual connected with a case, regardless of my subjective feelings for them. Of course, if things continued at the current killing pace, all my potential suspects would soon become victims and there'd be no one to blame at all. It's always been my personal policy to leave the blame for God and small children but, unfortunately, in a murder investigation, somebody's got to be 'it.'

Another distant possibility crossed my desk. Could the killer be someone outside the band who was nonetheless close enough to the band to have motive, method, and means? If there was such a person, I wished he would please step forward. Country bands on the road are like small nuclear families, and outsiders can usually get only as close to them as the one-night-stand permits. A lot could occur on a one-night-stand, but nothing I could think of that might carry such a long-smoldering vengeance across so many years. Hatred, very much like love, is a thing that must be nurtured.

My mind went back to the idea of some kind of curse upon the band. It was far-fetched, fantastic, next door to ridiculous. Yet four methodical murders of people with nothing in common except their membership in the Texas Jewboys was enough to give even a non-superstitious person a measure of pause. And even something as melodramatic and medieval as a curse, if it occurs in what we like to think of as real life, must have a motive.

I wished fervently that my old camp counselor Vern would suddenly spring up in the loft and scream, and the story would be over. But I knew that he wouldn't and it wouldn't. It was remarkable, I thought. Here I was, an adult, looking out the window for something between the faltering light and the insidious shadows of the February of the soul. And yet I felt like a small child in a summer cabin, peering frightfully over the edge of my bunk into the inexplicable, ever-darkening darkness.

64

I was having shredded wheat and rambutans for breakfast Friday morning when Cleve called from wig city. He sounded very lucid, almost businesslike.

'You're going to the wake for the Major?' he asked.

'Yeah,' I said. 'They called me about it last night. It's at the Lone Star at ten o'clock.'

'I'm not sure I can go. Dr Klitsberg's concerned about the ambience there reawakening certain anxieties of mine.'

'Well, the doctor knows best.'

'She's got some nice nay-nays on her, too, doesn't she?'

I ate some shredded wheat. Cleve hummed to himself a little.

'Cleve,' I said, 'can you get us a warm-up gig at the Lone Star? Say, sometime next week? It'd be good to have one show under our belt before we hit the road.'

'Done, dude,' said Cleve.

'Also, can you make a little list for me of any incidents or unusual experiences you remember that everyone in the band was involved in?'

'Done, dude.'

This was really reaching, I thought. Asking a criminally insane mental patient if he could remember anything that might help me find the origin of a supernatural curse. It wasn't standard detection procedure, I was sure. Neither was pissing up a rope.

'Thanks, Cleve. Give Dr Klitsberg my best.'

'Done, dude.'

Rambutans are hard to find in the States. So are durians. They're both native fruits of Borneo. If you eat a durian and drink alcohol, they say it'll kill you. There haven't been too many studies done on rambutans and shredded wheat, but sometimes you've got to take chances. If you want to try rambutans or durians, you can find them, occasionally, in Chinatown. They'll usually be tucked away somewhere between the octopus beaks and the Michael Jackson posters.

When I finished breakfast I fed the cat some tuna, took a cup of coffee over to the desk, sat down, lit a cigar, took a few puffs, and tried to make sense of a situation that made no sense at all. We couldn't afford to lose any more Jewboys. There weren't that many of us to begin with.

I was not looking forward to attending Major Boles's wake. Going to a wake was like going to a bar mitzvah without the bar mitzvah boy. Going to a wedding without the bride and groom. People wandered around saying how much he would've appreciated that, and the stiff was already worm bait spinning in limbo. Wakes were for the living, not, as advertised, for the dead. Like my friend Tim Mayer once told me: 'We mourn for ourselves, Kinkster.'

The Timster himself, a great American, went to Jesus a few years back. I didn't go to his wake. I know he wouldn't have minded.

I used up what was left of the afternoon calling Westport, Connecticut; Montreal; and several less glamorous places in an effort to locate Corky Laing and offer him a gig with the Jewboys. I left a spate of messages scattered around for him and then tried Max in Kerrville and Kelli in Washington, neither of whom were home.

By the time the Corkster got back to me I was in the dead middle of a power nap and I had a minor problem identifying who he was and why he was calling me. Then I had the little problem of making the offer sound attractive.

'We've had a few, uh, accidents occur to band members recently.'

'So I've heard,' said Corky. 'Just between us girls, you guys are being talked about kind of like the Average White Band.'

The Average White Band was the average white band until one of its members brodied on drugs. Then they suddenly became media darlings and their price went through the roof.

'We could do worse,' I said.

'And you have,' said Corky, somewhat insensitively.

The Corkster was now a big-time record executive in Montreal and he was a long way from throwing his drumsticks up in the air at the Lone Star and catching them without missing a beat.

'So you don't want the gig,' I said.

'I didn't say that.'

'Corkster, I knew you'd come through. You're still running on rock 'n' roll time, baby. All musicians are brothers in music.'

'How much are you paying?' said Corky.

We haggled like Turks in an alley for a while. The Corkster insisted upon ridiculously exorbitant 'hazard pay.' I did my best to Christian him down. Eventually, a compromise was hammered out.

'We need you for rehearsals this weekend, Corkster.'

'I'll get down there if it kills me,' he said.

When I got off with Corky I thought about the 'accidents' that had befallen the Jewboys. Only three of them had been made to appear as accidents. Of course, it's pretty hard to blow a guy away with a riot gun in a rain room and make it look like death by misadventure.

I was struck fully for the first time by this radical departure of MO. That's *modus operandi*, if you never took Latin. Most cops never took Latin either, but they know that it's strange for the same killer to alter his work methods drastically. Why would the same person cap Tequila and then take such great pains to make the other three murders look accidental? That was the question. I had the answer right on the tip of my Smith & Wesson knife but I just couldn't see it. If I could've, more tragedy might've been averted.

I had a few shots of Jameson's, thought about the problem from a few rather oblique angles, then threw in the towel. But something was nagging me about this convoluted case. There was a very simple explanation, I figured. All things that appear complex are actually very simple. And all things that appear very simple are actually quite complex. It was a variation on a theme my father had developed about relating well to people. He said:

323

'Always treat children like adults and adults like children and you'll never go wrong.' He didn't say anything about lesbians, bass players, or murderers, but some things you've got to find out for yourself.

I had to get ready for a wake. Whether you like them or not, I suppose it's always a good idea to attend wakes when you get the chance. One thing's for sure: You'll never get to go to your own.

65

The Major would have liked the wake. Almost nobody else did, but what did he care? He didn't have to listen to a pretentious, posturing, heavy-metal band called No MSG for three and a half hours. The Major didn't have to do anything but look down (or up, as I suspected) upon us, shake his head, and say: 'I'm glad I didn't have to sit through *that* shit.'

There was a quantity of alcohol consumed, possibly because, by this time, the band had put two and two together and come up with something approximating 'The Last of the Thirteen.' They did not, for the most part, seem to suspect murder in the three deaths that appeared to be accidental. They felt the deaths were strange, unlucky, an omen, but they spoke with the same sense of fatalism as the Major had when he told me about plane crashes coming in threes. Nonetheless, I found myself attempting to answer as many questions as I felt myself wanting to ask. At a wake, after you've gone through the drill of what a wonderful guy the honoree of the function was, the topic swiftly moves to other areas. To spend the whole time talking about the dear departed stiff would be morbid.

So it was that what conversation was possible with No MSG cacophonating all around us drifted to the past eventually, to memorable events and incidents on the road. That topic suited me fine.

We sat in a big corner booth by the bar: Dylan, Billy Swan, Willie Fong Young, Snakebite Jacobs, Skycap Adams, Panama Red, and Bo Byers, the latest addition to the reunion-tour road crew. It was a small wake, but it was a small world. I noticed, with some relief, that Dr Allison Klitsberg had not seen fit to allow Cleve to attend the wake. The doctor knows best, I thought.

It was a strange feeling to sit at a wake, even a hip, little informal job like this, and realize that somewhere among us very probably was a murderer moonlighting as a mourner. I figured I'd leave the alibi department to Cooperman. A killer as clever as the one I was looking for was clever enough to be somewhere else when he was supposed to be. As I saw it, my job was to encourage everybody to take a little walk down memory lane, an easy task at any wake, and see what joint experiences emerged. Not that I believed for a moment in the notion of a curse upon the House of Jewboy. I just had a feeling that somebody might slip, that something germane to the recurring nightmare we were all experiencing might be said.

Billy Swan remembered the time in 1974 when the entire band got stuck in an elevator between floors at the Sunset Marquis hotel in LA. 'It was the show at the Troubadour,' said Swan, 'our big debut on the West Coast. We were supposed to open for Tony Joe White. We were in the elevator, about ten of us, but it felt like a cast of thousands. Four and a half hours in that elevator and Kinky had to smoke his fucking cigar. Some of the guys really wanted to kill you, Kinkster.'

Maybe somebody hadn't gotten over it, I thought. I downed a shot of Jameson's and asked Swan quietly about his researches into Tequila and his wife's drug-dealing habits.

'Oh, I was going to tell you,' said Swan, 'it was mostly Sheila. She was pretty big time in L.A. back then apparently. I don't think Tequila knew how big.'

'Sheila?'

'Sharon,' said Billy. 'Her West Coast drug alias was Sheila.'

A drug dealer by any other name, I thought. But it was interesting. Maybe there was a drug angle in this that the OCCB hadn't uncovered. One matter I decided was long overdue. Finding Sharon.

Skycap Adams recalled the infamous gig on the campus at Buffalo. It was just when women's lib was becoming a hot issue. 'We'd just launched into "Get Your Biscuits in the Oven and Your

Buns in the Bed," ' he said, 'when these cranked-up diesel-dykes started attacking the stage in waves. Looked like a Kraut's-eye view of Normandy. Then they started smashing the amps and pulling the cords out of the walls. The cops carried them out as the broads wept hysterically. We needed a goddamn police escort to get off the campus. Remember that?'

We all remembered. I killed another shot of Jameson's. Could a woman be behind these killings, I wondered? Driving a speeding hack with a hat pulled low over her face?

'Remember that slit,' said Panama Red, 'that terrorized the band up in Denver? Crazy Helen, I think they called her. She followed us everywhere we went for a while. One night she went into Kinky's room, stayed there for a time, then went into Dylan's. After she left, I asked them both if they'd hosed her. They each said, "No. We just gave her money. We felt sorry for her." '

'And I remember what you called both of us,' said Dylan.

'Homos?' said Panama.

'Worse,' said Dylan. 'You said Kinky and I were "a couple of Peace Corps nerds." '

Everybody laughed. I killed another shot of Jameson's. Crazy Helen had been too crazy to pull something like this off, I thought. But women were better than men at carrying grudges for long periods of time. At least that's been my experience.

'That San Francisco gig at the Old Warehouse was the scariest,' said Willie Fong Young. 'We were co-billed with Buffy Sainte-Marie and the audience was about half Kinky cowboy types and half American Indian Movement braves on the warpath.'

'That was the show,' said Panama, 'where Kinky had that ugly gold costume bracelet in the shape of a snake. He showed it to the audience there in San Francisco and told them: "Janis gave me this." The crowd all went "Ahhhhhh." Then Kinky says: "Janis Bormaster. From Houston, Texas." And the crowd started booing." '

'There were a lot of gays in the crowd, too,' said Bo Byers. 'Half the audience looked like it was trollin' for colon.'

Everybody laughed. Billy Swan said: 'Back to your story, Willie.'

'Anyway,' said Willie, 'we had that song "Kind of Like an

Indian,'' and Kinky had a big Indian headdress. Whatever happened to that headdress?'

'It's down at Duckworth,' said Dylan, 'with everything else.'

'Too bad,' said Willie. 'We could've used it on the tour. We're not doing any shows with Buffy Sainte-Marie, are we?'

'Get on with the story,' somebody said.

'Well, Kinky's headdress had feathers hanging all over it and everything and the song featured a repeating chorus of "Hi-a-wath-a Ooo-guh-chuk-aas." After Kinky'd worn his headdress for a while, Snakebite and Jewford both donned these little dime-store Indian headdresses that kids wear. They looked very unhealthy on the heads of adults and really funny contrasted with Kinky's big headdress. We were about halfway through the song when I saw somebody coming onto the stage through the back-stage curtain. It was Buffy Sainte-Marie and she stalked right between me and the Major toward Kinky. If looks could've killed, we'd all have been dead.'

We may still get our chance, I thought. I killed another Jameson's. Willie continued the interminable tale.

'Then Buffy, who was such an authentic Indian that she had her hair in braids and had on a leather miniskirt, comes right at Kinky, who wisely tries to stay out of her way. She's grabbing viciously for the headdress, trying to pull it off of Kinky's head. The crowd now, of course, has taken sides and fistfights are breaking out in the front row. Half are cheering for Buffy and half are cheering for Kinky and diehard A.I.M. followers are moving menacingly towards the stage.'

'How'd we get out of that one?' asked Snakebite. 'I forgot.'

'Buffy got the headdress,' said Bo, 'and ran off-stage with it. Kinky launched into "I'm Proud to Be an Asshole from El Paso" and then, during Buffy's set, I liberated the headdress from her dressing room and put it back in the U-haul.'

'That was a pretty ugly show, all right,' said Snakebite, 'but it wasn't as bad as the one at the Bluebonnet Club in Temple, Texas. Now, that one was almost mortal combat.'

'I think I missed that show,' said Swan.

'You were already back with Kris by that time,' said Dylan, 'but, believe me, you didn't miss a thing. Except maybe Van Dyke Parks. He was on keyboards then. He was brilliant. Wore a white aviator jumpsuit with little American flags sticking out all over it. He was afraid of Texans, he said.'

'Turned out he was right,' said Skycap.

'Anyway,' said Snakebite, 'back to the Bluebonnet. Van Dyke was with us and Roscoe West and Jimmie Don Smith. Van Dyke had this great intro, a combination of "Exodus" and "I've got Spurs That Jingle Jangle Jingle." The show was one of the best. We were rockin' along and then we noticed a real surly looking Texas highway patrolman standing by the door. You couldn't tell if he hated the show, or the song "They Ain't Makin' Jews Like Jesus Anymore,' or if he just had hemorrhoids.'

' "You never know what the monkey eat until the monkey shit," ' said Dylan, quoting our old friend Slim. 'I get twenty years to the gallon on that one.'

'Well,' said Snakebite, 'it didn't take long for the monkey to shit. Before we knew it there were two deputies there. Then four. Then pretty soon there were ten of them. And they all looked like their guppies just died.'

'Sounds like a nice house to work,' said Swan.

'The crowd wasn't that big to begin with,' Snakebite continued, 'and soon there were almost as many Texas state troopers and sheriff's department deputies in the place as there were patrons. Van Dyke, among others, was not pleased.

'The next thing we know, the troopers and sheriff's deputies are grabbing guys out of the crowd and dragging them out of the place, kicking and struggling. Some of the guys' wives and girl-friends were crying. And Dylan kept shouting: "Keep playing. Keep playing." '

I thought back to the grim scene which now seemed quite funny. When violence broke out in a place, the best thing to do was to keep playing. This usually, though not always, tended to place you above the fray and discourage all hell from breaking loose.

'We kept playing,' said Snakebite. 'And the fuzz kept dragging people off in handcuffs. Finally, there were about twenty people left in the crowd, if you wanted to call it that, and the sheriff's deputies were right at the lip of the stage, showing no sign of slowing their forward progress. Dylan yells: "Everybody back-stage!"

'We didn't have to be told twice. With Van Dyke in the lead – I think this was his first trip to Texas – we got out of there quick. It turned out the owner hadn't paid his liquor license or something, but we didn't know that until much later. That was the first time I've ever seen an audience get arrested.'

'I went in later,' said Bo, 'to take a farewell dump in the men's room and there was the Major who'd just finished dumping and wanted to show me something he'd written on the men's room wall. I didn't want to go in the stall, but he was so insistent that I put on my hydrogen mask and went in and took a look. This is what he'd written on the wall.'

Bo cleared his throat a few times and downed a shot of Wild Turkey. Then he recited the following verse:

'Here I sit, stainin' my pooper
Tryin' to give birth to a Texas state trooper.'

Everybody cheered. Panama stood up. 'Here's to the Major,' he said, lifting his glass. I looked around the table as everyone stood up and raised his glass in a toast. If there is a killer in the group, he could've fooled me.

We all toasted the Major for a last time. There wasn't a hell of a lot else we could do for him. Except find his killer.

66

As Blane Borgelt, a white lawyer who wants to be a black preacher when he grows up, often says: 'Life knows you better than you knows yourself.' Life knew me well enough to know that this case was bringing me alarmingly close to squirtin' out of both ends. It was Sunday morning, the day after the wake, and there seemed nothing to look forward to but a week of rehearsals for what was almost certain to be a disaster.

It was exceedingly frustrating to be dealing with a killer who left only tracks, it appeared, that were intended to be seen. Not only did I not seem to be making much progress on the Jewboy case, but Travis Parnell apparently had pulled off the best disappearing act since Ehrich Weiss. These could be the first two cases, I thought with chagrin, that might have to be lamped into the Kinky Open file. So much for my vaunted reputation, such as it was.

There were things to do, of course, other than just staying home and playing hide the helmet. I could try to find Sharon, which wouldn't be easy because her name frequently wasn't Sharon. Quite frankly, she seemed to be just about the last lead I had in the case. Everybody in the band knew her, most of them, it appeared, in the Old Testament sense of the word.

It was also just faintly within the realm of conceivability that Sharon was keeping such a low profile currently for a very good reason. Suppose Sharon was the killer. Suppose she'd had some reason to splice Tequila, brooded over it for thirteen years while she hosed various members of the band, then tracked her ex-husband down and blew his gray-matter department all over my soap dish. The spouse or the ex-spouse is usually the one behind most unsolved violent murders. Somehow, though, this case seemed too complex, too intricately interwoven, to be resolved by finding a woman whacking her long-ago ex. The scenario didn't take into account, either, what this rather far-fetched virago might have to gain by continuing to knock off Jewboys after eighty-sixing Tequila. Was she trying to cover her tracks in the first killing? Was she overcome by a fiendish lust for blood? Was she still rankling over the band's performance of 'Get Your Biscuits in the Oven and Your Buns in the Bed'? Somehow, as a murder suspect, Sharon left a great deal to be desired.

Not wanting, however, to appear a male chauvinist pig in my now almost desperate search for the killer, I decided to try to get an update on any Sharon sightings from the boys in the band. Swan's last news of her drug deals in L.A. using the name Sheila was almost ancient history. Snakebite's account of his fling with 'Cleopatra' was over three years old. Willie hadn't seen her since the original band had broken up thirteen years ago and she and Tequila had been arguing in their hotel room about a train, or a boat, or a plane, none of which would quite explain Tequila's brain going down my drain. The Major, of course, had said he'd hosed her in Chicago, but, unfortunately, he was no longer around to provide me with the color commentary.

I called the remaining personnel: Skycap, Panama, Dylan, and Bo. Bo said he was too busy screwing with all the equipment and sound to have time for somebody's wife. Dylan allowed as the opportunity had presented itself once a long time ago, but he had not permitted himself to succumb to the flesh.

'You *are* a Peace Corps nerd,' I said.

' "Lay, lady, lay," ' said Dylan.

Panama and Skycap, however, came forth, so to speak, with tales of a slightly more sordid nature. Panama had hosed her 'and everything else that moved' in 1974.

'When you're on the road,' he said, 'you let the little head think for the big head.'

'Maybe that's what I need to do to solve this case,' I told him.

Skycap, it emerged, had had the most recent encounter with Sharon. It'd been two and a half years ago in Knoxville, Tennessee, and she'd called herself Regina.

'Nice name,' I said.

'I remember leaving her at some little motel by the highway,' said Skycap. 'She was standing there in the parking lot and she picked up this stray cat and held it in her arms and said: "How do you like my nice little pussy?" '

'Thank you for sharing that poignant, rather personal moment with me, Skycap. I think I've heard enough.'

In truth, I'd heard more than enough. I felt vaguely ashamed for looking into the pathetic details of a dead friend's unhappy love life. But this was just one of the seedier avenues I needed to explore in thoroughly looking into the case. It was a commentary on husbands and wives, men and women, the loneliness of the road. It made me sad and lonely. And looking back over an achingly empty expanse of time and geography, mournful music seemed to carry across the years, making the endless highway seem like the ribbon in the hair of the girl I used to know.

331

67

Sunday was the Lord's day of rest, but, for the Jewboys, it was another day of relentless rehearsal. The first gig at the Lone Star, according to Cleve, was now set for Thursday night. Corky Laing, hopefully, would be arriving in time for the rehearsal in the afternoon. If not, I thought, we might *have to* get one of the automatic drumming machines from the Holiday Inn lounge.

It was 11 a.m. and I was already up and about. I'd fed the cat and had my own breakfast, which consisted of a cup of semiviscous espresso and a rather sad-looking banana with liver spots that probably wished it was back in Guatemala and I was a tarantula.

I called Max again in Kerrville and got some not entirely unexpected, but, nonetheless, unsettling news. Travis Parnell's parents were now very worried about him. They'd notified the local authorities and were wondering openly if their boy had gone off the deep end. 'Hunting season is over and he's still not back,' his mother had told Max. She probably didn't know, I thought grimly, that hunting season in Manhattan is year-round.

I wondered about Travis Parnell, Texas's version of the elusive butterfly of love, all the way over to the espresso machine. It was not always easy to keep the two current cases separate and distinct in my mind. Sometimes it seemed like I was schlepping around a rather unpleasant pair of Siamese albatrosses. The only thing the two cases appeared to have in common was that they were both going nowhere at a fairly tedious clip. Yet somehow, for no reason I could name, I felt there was an overlappage between the two. Maybe it was because the time frames of the cases were fairly similar; both had managed to cut severely into my cocktail hour over the past month or two. Maybe it was only in my mind that the two cases seemed to embrace each other like the Pacific Ocean and the nighttime California shoreline. Maybe I needed a checkup from the neck up.

It was pushing Gary Cooper time when I raised Kelli on the blower in our nation's capital. She wasn't as restless to come back to New York as I'd hoped. As well as being a dancer, Kelli was an interpreter for the deaf, and she'd become involved in a new project in Washington. She'd been commissioned to choreograph a number for the dance troupe at Gallaudet University. The subject matter was to deal with saving the rain forests, and the troupe was slated to perform the number at the Kennedy Center and the White House. Kelli and Marcie had become good friends and Kelli hadn't been thinking about Travis Parnell at all. It didn't sound, from the conversation, as if she'd been thinking too much about the Kinkster either. Hell, I was endangered, too. I didn't even have a support group.

When I was through talking to Kelli I'd learned more about Gallaudet University than I needed to know, though some of it was quite interesting. Gallaudet is an old school. Abraham Lincoln, Marilyn Monroe's favorite president, was the one who signed the proclamation making Gallaudet into a university. Daniel French, the sculptor, created a statue for the campus, a young girl learning to sign. During the time he was building the statue, French became interested in sign language and learned it himself. I asked Kelli if French had also looked into rectal realism at the time, but she didn't find it all that amusing.

When Lincoln was assassinated, French was the man they tapped to design the Lincoln Memorial. And that is why, if you look closely at Lincoln's hands as they rest on the arms of the chair, you'll notice that Lincoln is signing 'AL,' the initials to his name.

This bit of spiritual trivia I found fascinating as I lighted a cigar and sipped my third cup of espresso. Daniel French had made a timeless, poignant statement that was so subtle, even the tour guides probably didn't know about it. It was a little thing representative of a big thing.

I thought about who might be killing the Jewboys of Texas. The fact that most of them weren't Jewish and many of them weren't even from Texas was beside the point. They were Jews by inspiration. They were Texans by inspiration. That was all I needed, I thought. A little bit of inspiration.

Later that afternoon, as I was getting ready for the rehearsal, I felt more than ever convinced that the whole case would turn on some little thing. Some little thing that millions of tourists to Washington every year would never notice. I felt like one of those tourists myself. The little thing, I knew somehow, was already there. I just couldn't see it.

68

The next three or four days, filled as they were with rounds of rehearsals and press interviews, flew by like an angry Texas turkey buzzard, on occasion pausing very briefly to take a little peck out of my heart. By Thursday afternoon, the day of the gig at the Lone Star, the Average White Band Syndrome had kicked into high gear. Dylan and Cleve were sharing the responsibility of fielding the press and, between the two of them, had their hands full. Cleve had heard from almost all of the New York press establishment, other than McGovern and Duggan, who were both keeping close tabs on me and seemed to be enjoying my life a lot more at the moment than I was. Andrea Stevens from *The New York Times* planned to cover the Lone Star gig. Jann Wenner of *Rolling Stone* was sending somebody to stay with the tour as long as it lasted.

'He may have to get his story in pretty quick,' I said.

'We've also got a call from *Feeble* magazine,' said Cleve.

'You're sure that's not *People* magazine?'

'It sounded like *Feeble*.'

'Maybe it was,' I said.

'We've also heard from Dave Dawson and Jim Oram in Australia. Maybe we could do a tour there sometime. Call it the "Come Home in My Pouch Tour." '

'I'll jump right on it,' I said.

Dylan, similarly, was swamped with morbid fascination on the part of the press. People who had never cared whether I lived or died now wanted to know if I had any pet peeves. I did. I wanted to know why the press and Hollywood had ignored Ava Gardner and her career for almost forty years, then, when she died, alone and broken-spirited, slapped her on the cover of *Feeble* magazine next to the words 'The Last Goddess.' I had a few other pet peeves, too, but I figured they'd keep.

According to Dylan, almost every newspaper in Texas was chomping at the bit for an exclusive interview with anyone in the band down to and including the auxiliary buttboy. Ratso was off his sickbed, covering the tour for *National Lampoon*. Boyd Matson had a camera crew ready to drive the band around for the syndicated show he did from his 1958 fire-engine-red Cadillac.

'The Jewboys in the Jew canoe,' said Dylan. 'That's the angle Boyd's looking for.'

'The old Jewish Cadillac,' I said. 'Stops on a dime and it picks it up.'

'There's twenty years to the gallon in that one,' said Dylan. 'Did I mention that Jay Maeder wants us for his next cover of the *Daily News Magazine*?'

'It may have taken Major Boles to put us over the top,' I said grimly, 'but obviously we're hot. Piers Akerman called from Adelaide. He's the editor now and he's planning to come here to cover the tour himself.'

' "Tie me kangaroo down, mate," ' said Dylan.

'Look, Dylan,' I said, 'we can't let all this attention, pleasant as it is, go to our heads. Nor can we allow the possibility of tragedy interfere with doing a fine performance on every gig. We need to keep our eyes open, yet still follow our lifelong watchword: "Another show in our hip pocket." '

' "Money doesn't talk; it swears," ' said Dylan.

'Assume,' I said, 'that the threat of death does not hang over us like the sword of Damocles. Assume that this is just another tour, full of all the innocence and exuberance of the old days.'

'Assume this,' said Dylan. There was a slight pause. Then there was the unmistakable sound of a large amount of gas escaping through a rather small orifice.

69

From the stage of the Lone Star Roadhouse that Thursday night, the crowd looked pretty much like any other crowd I'd ever played to. There was a familiar face here and there and, every once in a while, a friendly, encouraging smile from someone you don't know who really seems to be enjoying himself. As my friend Will Hoover once wrote in a great country song: 'Sometimes that's all that keeps you goin'.'

Looking out over a crowd of people from a stage, along with evoking many other emotions, never fails to remind you that you're alone. A Judy Garland-like rapport with an audience can carry you so far, but it never quite carries you all the way to the shelter of the warm applause and the easy laughter on the other side of the microphone.

One reason I felt alone, of course, was because I was. I was closing the first set with a solo version of Woody Guthrie's classic, 'Pretty Boy Floyd.' The band had already performed one encore with 'Waitret, Please Waitret, Come Sit on My Face,' a barroom ballad written by Major Boles, Roscoe West, and myself. Because of being passed along in the oral tradition, it was well on its way to becoming a minor American classic. As we'd sung the rather raunchy song, the crowd had all joined in, and for some reason I'd found myself thinking about the Major and realizing that, eventually, the song becomes the singer. But that moment of performance insight was brief.

With 'Pretty Boy Floyd' I was flying pretty much on Jewish radar, just thankful that, musically and physically, we'd all survived the first set. Shucking all modesty, the crowd really seemed to love everything we did. Of course, people don't come to a reunion show prepared to sit on their hands. They're there because they want to sift the ashes of their misspent youth, recreate the ambience of a happier, simpler time. For the band's part, we were all veteran applause junkies by this stage of our lives; when the crowd cheered, we'd pick up our little umbrellas and go right back up on the high wire.

In a semidream state, like a fairly ethereal Texas politician working the house, weaving my way through the crowd, I accepted the praise and adoration gracefully. I used to have trouble accepting praise. When somebody'd say it was the greatest show they'd ever seen, I'd say 'Well, the monitors weren't working very well,' or 'The drummer was getting a little carried away.' I always liked to scapegoat the drummer. But the older you get, the easier it is to accept praise. Just remember you probably deserve it as much as anybody. Don't make excuses where you don't need any; just nod your head a few times, and smile. Remember, they came to see you. You're merely there to re-create the ambience of your billfold.

About halfway to the dressing room, I realized that I was following Dylan and Dylan was following Cleve. Cleve, I noticed, was following Dr Allison Klitsberg who, apparently, had decided that a little ambience wouldn't do him any harm either. What the hell, I thought, as I wormed my way through the final fringes of the crowd. It was a resocialization experience for all of us.

To get up to the dressing rooms at the Lone Star Roadhouse, Bill Dick has thoughtfully provided about half a dozen very long, very steep staircases, an aerobic experience not particularly appreciated by middle-aged musicians. Most of the band was already at the top of the building in the dressing room, probably the shabbiest penthouse in New York, as our little entourage started the steep climb. We were halfway up the second set of stairs, Dr Allison Klitsberg still in the lead, when we observed a cop and a small knot of people on the second-floor landing. Two bodies lay sprawled out on the small, cold, concrete landing, as if they'd been hurled down the steep stairs to their deaths.

'Oh, my God,' said Dr Klitsberg. 'Isn't that your bass player, what's-his-name?'

'Skycap,' I said. Skycap lay very still, his head turned at an impossible angle.

'This is horrible,' said Dr Klitsberg. 'Who's the big one?'

The other body, lying equally still, was indeed a large one. The

337

face had a startlingly serene appearance, not dissimilar to what the big man might've looked like when he'd been a small boy.

'That's Mike McGovern,' I said. 'My favorite Irish poet.'

70

We stared at the two still bodies from the limbo of the second staircase for what seemed like an eternity, then a uniform took us down to a small office on the first floor. Panama Red was sitting at a desk smoking a Kent cigarette.

'I was just coming down from the top of the stairs,' said Panama. 'I heard a shout and then it sounded like Samson was bringing the temple down.'

I lit a cigar and noticed that my hands were shaking. The only one in the room who looked completely at ease was Cleve, who'd picked up a menu off the desk and was studying it with a little Tweety Bird smile on his face.

'Can I have a cheeseburger?' he asked Dr Klitsberg.

'Cleve,' she said as one might reproach a five-year-old.

'Can I? Can I? Can I?' said Cleve.

This was not the most conducive environment, but I knew I had to do some serious thinking. The way the steep stairways were constructed, anyone could lurk just below a landing and hurl someone down below with a very good chance of doing them grievous bodily harm. There was virtually no security along the stairwells until you got to the fifth floor and the dressing room. Very few people ever went up that far anyway unless they were working on their Royal Canadian Air Force exercises.

I was sick at heart about McGovern. I'd asked him earlier in the day to shadow Skycap, and obviously he had. The killer had flung them both down the stairs, apparently, one after the other, like a crazed jai alai player. The killer still could've been anyone in the band, or anyone in the house for that matter. Skycap had known the risks and had elected to stay with the band. He was a helpless victim of this monster and he would be sorely missed. The tour was going to be over almost before it had begun. Jumbled

338

thoughts were running through my head, but the one thing I didn't think I could accept was a McGovernless world.

'You didn't see anybody going up or down the stairs?' I asked Panama.

'Not a soul,' said Panama as he chained another Kent. 'Everybody else was in the dressing room.'

'Where were you going?' asked Dylan.

'Just out to get some air.'

'And you didn't catch a glimpse of *anyone* on the stairs?' I asked.

Panama stood up. 'What the hell's the matter with you guys?' he shouted. 'You think I killed them?'

'Double cheese,' said Cleve, still looking at the menu and smiling. 'Drag it through the garden.'

I turned to Dr Klitsberg. 'Can't you get him to pull his lips together?' I asked.

'He needs the release,' said Dr Klitsberg.

'Maybe it's time to release this,' said Dylan. I walked to the other side of the small room just as he farted. Dr Klitsberg's body stiffened as if she'd been hit with a load of buckshot.

It was into this tense and rather fetid ambience that Sergeant Cooperman's large, scowling visage intruded itself. His eyes glinted a peculiar mix of disbelief and raw malice. He closed the door behind him, shook out a Gauloises from his pack, and lit it with his Zippo. He looked haggard from chasing death, and mean as hell.

'I'll take a cheeseburger,' said Cleve to Sergeant Cooperman.

When all the excitement died down, Cleve, along with Dr Klitsberg, was on the other side of the door and Cooperman was stomping out his Frog fag on the floor as if it was a rattlesnake.

'Fuckin' skell,' he said. He shook out another Gauloises and lit it with an almost poetic economy of motion. Cop ballet.

Dylan, Panama, and I waited and watched. For some superstitious reason I didn't vocalize my thoughts about McGovern, but Cooperman must've read my mail.

'Your pal McGovern may make it,' he said. 'They've taken him to the hospital but he hasn't come to yet. We'll be guarding him.

339

He may have something interesting to say. The other one – what's his name?'

'Skycap,' I said.

'That's a good name for him,' said Cooperman, 'because that's where he is.'

Panama chained another Kent. Dylan took off his sunglasses. I sat down in a chair and felt like crying but no tears came. We mourn for ourselves, I thought.

Cooperman left the room for a moment and when he returned he was carrying two plastic bags. He put them on the desk. I got up from the chair and walked over to look. Inside one bag was a note, handwritten in big block capital letters. It read: 'WAS IT WORTH IT?' In the other plastic bag was a little yellow rubber duck like a kid might play with in a bathtub.

Cooperman said: 'The note was found in the left pocket of the sport coat Skycap was wearing. The duck was found in the right. Mean anything to you guys?'

We looked at the strange and pathetic objects in the little plastic bags. Then we looked at each other.

'It means,' said Dylan, 'that it's time for dis band to disband.'

71

The stewardess on Continental Airlines was young, attractive, honey-blond, and sounded as if she had a hint of an Australian accent. Her name tag said, 'Terri.'

'How do you take your coffee?' she asked.

'Black,' I said. 'Like my men.' She handed me the cup and gave me the Jackie Kennedy frozen funeral smile number forty-seven. She asked the guy in the next row how he took his coffee. Definitely an Australian accent, I thought. It was early Sunday morning, a 'Bloody Mary morning,' but on this occasion I was sticking with black coffee whether Terri liked it or not.

The plane was headed for San Antonio, Texas, with a stopover, of course, in Dallas, home of the majestic memorial plaque to President Kennedy which had about the size and spiritual impact of a commemorative stamp. Out my nonsmoking window, New

York was beginning to look pretty much like a commemorative stamp as well, and what it had commemorated recently wasn't especially nice. But as I sat back in my seat and sipped the tepid coffee, I felt more at peace than I had in months. After all, I knew who the killer was, and unless I missed my bet, I'd be seeing him soon.

72

The solution to the puzzle of who was killing the Texas Jewboys had not come easy. It'd taken almost three days of wandering the streets, hitting every gin mill in the Village, until the Swiss cheese effect was totally in control of my mind, and little particles were suddenly able to get through the intellectual Seine all of us have been constructing since kindergarten. Like the song, I was convinced that little things mean a lot. When strung together, they shone like highway reflectors on a rainy night and led me down the mental road to the identity of the killer. Now all I had to do was prove that I was right.

McGovern was still in a coma. The doctors at St Vincent's had told me that only the family could see him. I told them that there wasn't any family. They said then that nobody would be able to see him. I didn't trust the doctors at St Vincent's. Dylan Thomas had died there, and though he might make McGovern's idea of perfect company, I didn't want McGovern to get any ideas about joining him yet. The world needs its McGoverns. There's damn few of them as it is. Guys who don't own a television, a car, or an answering machine are hard to find in New York unless you look in the men's shelter. The world always needs people who won't let their apartment go co-op even when everyone else in the building is for it; who trust a guy who owns a little pizza joint to work out their taxes for them; who take on a dangerous assignment from a friend so diligently that now they lie in a coma at St Vincent's. There's lots of guys in this world with MBAs or BMWs, and many, probably, with both, but none of them ever thought to brush their hair before meeting a racehorse.

There was nothing I could do for McGovern, I realized, that I

341

hadn't already done. I'd been a friend, hadn't I? Maybe I could've been a little better one, a little kinder one, but if I'd been very much different McGovern probably wouldn't've been my friend in the first place. By the time somebody's in a coma or in a box it's a bit late to worry about what you can do for them. 'Seeing' them or sending them flowers is a poor excuse for living. As Allen Ginsberg says: 'Love when you love.'

I pushed the vision of McGovern's bright Irish mind lying brain-dead in his large, sad, comatose body out of my thoughts. Clap your hands if you believe a guy like McGovern can make it in this world. I didn't hear anything but the engines and the guy behind me droning on about real estate values someplace he was never going to live. On to more practical things, I thought.

I'd spoken to Kelli late Saturday night and I replayed part of the conversation so I could hear her voice.

'You're saying it's okay to come back now?'

'Yeah.'

'And Travis?'

'He's not in New York, Dancer.'

Marcie had spent a lot of time in Mexico, was fluent in Spanish, and had connections with the Mexican Red Cross. When I talked to her I asked her to check a little matter out for me, though I thought I pretty well had the answer. Might as well cross the *i*'s and dot the *t*'s.

On Saturday I'd also called Rambam's lawyer and told him I'd be leaving for Texas sometime this weekend and if anything should happen to me Rambam could have my Smith & Wesson knife and my Caruso tape. I'd talked to Dylan, too, and asked him if he wouldn't mind sticking around a couple of days to take care of what was left of the band. Some guys had already split apparently, and some were still hanging around the city. Dylan said he'd stay.

'I'm leaving the cat in charge of the loft,' I said to him, 'and you in charge of everything outside the loft.'

' "Nobody feels any pain," ' said Dylan, ' "tonight as I stand inside the rain." '

The only thing I did all weekend for my own personal therapeutic amusement was to call my old friend Nick 'Chinga' Chavin, the country music porn star turned highly successful ad exec. I had him mail a copy of his essay 'Prison Rape As a Positive Experience' to Dr Allison Klitsberg.

I chuckled dryly to myself and the next thing I knew I was in one of those semiconscious eight-mile-high dream states rolling across the Arizona desert in an old red pickup truck. My pal Jerry Rudes was at the wheel and we had in our possessions what Chet Flippo in *Rolling Stone* magazine had called 'the quasi-legendary living-room tapes' of the Texas Jewboys. It was the swerving tail end of the sixties and we were on our way to California, on a path more crazy and circuitous than either of us had dreamed. Jerry'd been living in the south of France for almost twenty years now – Christ; could it've been that long? – and I'd been living the life of a jet-set gypsy. I could see that red pickup truck flyin' down the freeway into L.A. and I smiled. At least, I hoped it was a smile. When you're in a semiconscious eight-mile-high dream state it's sometimes hard to tell if you're smiling or mourning for yourself.

They say Texas is a state of mind and maybe it is. It provides the physical and spiritual 'elbow room' that Daniel Boone was always looking for. The Texas tradition of music is so deep and multilayered it would require seven archaeologists with seven brooms seven years just to clear away the dust. When they got to the bottom, after digging through village upon village, they'd probably find Bob Wills's cigar lying next to Mance Lipscomb's guitar.

The influence of music upon Texas and of Texas upon music is enormous and farther-reaching than you might think. Not only did Buddy Holly influence the Beatles and T-Bone Walker influence the Rolling Stones, but Texas's early singing cowboys reached higher into the firmament than they might've known. A girl named Anne Frank, with just a fountain pen, reached the conscience of more people than the entire propaganda machinery of Hitler's Third Reich. After the war, local authorities checked the secret annex in which she and her family had lived. In Anne's little corner of the annex, pictures of American cowboy stars were still fluttering from the walls where she'd left them.

In small, unconscious ways all of our lives were as insulated as

Anne Frank's. I'd made an educated guess as to the killer's identity and his current location. If I was wrong, Kelli was in danger, the remaining Texas Jewboys were in danger, and I was in for a long ride back to New York. If I was right, it could even be worse.

As Slim had said: 'You never know what the monkey eat until the monkey shit.'

73

The usual flotsam and jetsam of well-wishers and teenaged geeks in overgrown cowboy hats was surging around the gate as we deplaned in San Antonio. I scanned the crowd partly out of recent and long-term New York paranoia, and partly out of wishful thinking. I'd had a lot of airport rendezvous in my time. Some of the broads were good at missing planes and all of them were good at messing up my life. There was something about airports. Especially airports the way they used to be. The last memorable thing I could think of that happened at a Greyhound station was when Holly Golightly said good-bye to Buddy Ebsen in *Breakfast at Tiffany's*. And I wasn't doing a lot of steamship travel these days. So if something unexpected was going to happen it was probably going to be at an airport and this one didn't let me down.

I didn't say romantic. I said unexpected.

Right between an obscenely obese Mexican lady in a 'Fat Is Beautiful' T-shirt and a fervent young man holding some flowers was a dark, familiar face that had once had a pretty fair tavern tan. The face was supporting a Yankee baseball cap that was precariously tilted over one eye. The rest of the guy was decked out in full camouflage battle fatigues complete with combat boots. A green military duffel bag was hanging from his left shoulder with a pair of red Israeli paratrooper's wings on it.

It was Rambam.

'Got tired of swatting mosquitoes down in Guatemala,' he said. 'Thought a little backup might be in order.'

'So you just dropped in?'

'Didn't like the sound of what you told Wolf Nachman.' Wolf

Nachman, I thought, was either the world's best or the world's worst lawyer, if there was any difference. The jury was still out.

'So how the hell'd you know I'd be coming in this morning and what flight I'd be on?' It was a logical question.

'No problem,' said Rambam. 'You told Wolf you'd be coming to Texas sometime over the weekend. I just had a friend of mine hack into the airline's computer system.'

'Can you do that?'

'Easier than jaywalking in Beverly Hills.'

As we went through the terminal and out into the parking garage, it felt better and better having Rambam along for the ride. I wasn't exactly sure what I would find on this trip, but if I found it I was very sure it wasn't going to be an egg cream soda. I'd asked Max to drop off the old ranch pickup truck for me at a designated place and to leave the keys on top of the right rear tire. That's what Todd Miller, the owner of the 'Happy Hooker 23-Hour Wrecker Service' in Kerrville, always did. Hadn't got my *Playboy* calendar from Todd yet this year, I thought. When he gives you a calendar he always says: 'Twenty-four tits.' We found the truck and we found the keys.

'Is this truck dusty or is it gray?' Rambam asked.

'A lot of both,' I said as I started her up. There was no accelerator pedal in the truck. You just put your foot down and it usually went. I was gratified to see that it hadn't forgotten how.

'I like that "Eat More Pussy" bumper sticker,' said Rambam admiringly. 'Where'd you get it?'

'My friend Bob McLane sent it from Shreveport. Bob used to be chairman of the Gay Texans for Connolly Committee. Now he sells bumper stickers at Grateful Dead concerts and bikers' conventions in South Dakota. It's pretty lucrative, he says, but bikers who're getting tattooed sometimes come up and ask him, "How do you spell Aryan?" '

'I can think of a number of ways to spell Aryan,' said Rambam.

'That's because you're not an Aryan,' I said. But I wasn't thinking about Aryans. I was thinking about tattoos.

We got onto I–10 West, set our ears back, and made it to Kerrville in a little under an hour. On the way I filled Rambam in on where we were going and what I thought we might find when we got there.

'Sounds like good ol' Texas fun,' he said.

By the time we were rolling through the streets of Kerrville, people were already coming out of church. I pointed out a few of the local tourist attractions to Rambam as we drove past.

'That building over there's the oldest Methodist Church in Kerrville. Recently, they lopped the cross off of the steeple and put in an aluminum drive-up window. Now it's a savings and loan.'

'Now, *that's* progress,' said Rambam.

'Some things change,' I said, 'and some remain the same. You'll be pleased to know that on the posted regulations of the Kerrville Bus Company over there it's still prohibited to transport bull semen by bus.'

'What they need,' said Rambam, 'is a law prohibiting Texans from transporting bullshit by mouth.'

'We'll get there some day,' I said. 'You New Yorkers are just more progressive.'

I took Rambam to the Del Norte Restaurant for lunch, and, like all Yankees, he ordered a chicken-fried steak. I went through the buffet with about forty good little church workers, almost all of whom were senior citizens.

'Great demographics in this place,' I said as I rejoined Rambam at the table. 'Always makes me feel young.'

'The Prime of Miss Kinky Friedman,' said Rambam.

'Last time I was here they had these hunting brochures that advertised Christian hunting guides. I guess they ran out of brochures. Hunting season's over.'

'Not for us,' said Rambam.

Later, in the Del Norte parking lot, I was deeply dismayed to find that, while Rambam and I were having lunch, someone had ripped off my 'Eat More Pussy' bumper sticker. The culprit had left a note under the windshield wiper which I read aloud to Rambam in the cab of the truck. I read as follows: ' "Your bumper sticker is, or was, most disgusting and I assure you that the wrath of the God of Israel is going to be on you either now or forever more." '

'Why doesn't the guy make up his mind,' I said. It continued: ' "I do not wish to explain your bumper sticker to my five-year-old kids." '

'They'll probably think you want to eat their cat,' said Rambam.

'He ends it on a nice note,' I said. ' "Repent and be baptized for the remissions of sins." '

'I didn't know Jimmy Swaggart lived in Kerrville.'

'Jimmy wouldn't mind an "Eat More Pussy" bumper sticker. He might get a little upset about a "Look at More Pussy" bumper sticker.'

'Maybe it's an out-of-work Christian hunting guide,' said Rambam.

As we drove out of the parking lot and headed for Highway 16, we tried to decide what to do with the note. Rambam wanted to burn it. I wanted to frame it and put it on my hero wall. Rambam then suggested rolling it into suppository form and seeing if I could fly. Finally, we put the note in the glove compartment, forgot about it, and watched the Texas countryside gently roll away.

But the wrath of the God of Israel, unfortunately, wasn't the kind of thing we were going to shake that easily.

74

Like a biblical curse, the mid-afternoon skies had grown dark and threatening, and, when we turned off the highway, thunder rolled across the heavens as the dusty pickup rolled across the old cattle guard. Rambam, by this time, was smiling and drumming his fingers on the window frame, ready for action. I was smoking a cigar and thinking about serial killers.

Sergeant Cooperman once, in a rare moment of sharing and caring, had given me a cop's-eye view of the anatomy of a serial killer. Leaving out some of the police jargon, here's the gist. When a man smokes his first victim, according to Cooperman, he may find he likes it more than he expected. He may feel the same exhilaration a kid feels the first time he rides a bicycle or learns to swim. Only more so. Maybe the killer never intended to go any further than whacking one person. Probably you don't start out thinking you'll be a serial killer. But when you discover how easy it is sometimes to take a fragile human life, how powerful and Godlike it makes you feel, something like blood lust comes over you. By the time you cap the second victim and the third victim, you find you're really starting to enjoy your work and you become more brazen. Big-time serial killers often record or even videotape their performances these days. They begin to feel a veil of invulnerability falling over them. They may start to challenge or to bait the police or the newspapers, or to leave behind deliberate clues. It's almost as if the serial killer is saying: 'Look, Ma. No hands!' Judging from the condition in which certain of the victims were found, that statement is sometimes literally true.

As we rolled along the dusty county road past several ranches, over three or four cattle guards, I grimly contemplated what I might find three miles or so ahead. I'd finally been able to assemble the chain of clues, some of them deliberate, some of them not, and it seemed to hold together close enough for color television. I was correct about the identity of the killer, I thought. The only question was whether he'd be here in person or just leave another clue, like a grotesque adult scavenger hunt.

Just as the storm broke and rain and hail began pelting the windshield, we pulled up to the place. There were steep cliffs on one side of the little valley, and a river on the other with two beautiful waterfalls that I remembered from long ago. The old house and the forlorn-looking garage that used to be a barn seemed pretty much the same as they had before. Maybe it was the storm and the dark, rolling clouds that made them appear so desolate and foreboding. There was no sign of an automobile and no sign of any people. A gate on a rusty hinge swung closed somewhere in the vicinity of the old barn. It sounded like part of a soundtrack for a mystery program on the old-time radio. I stopped the truck on the gravel drive in front of the weed-infested yard.

'Place looks deserted,' I said.

'They always do,' said Rambam.

'I'll check the house,' I said. 'You check the barn.'

'Fine,' said Rambam. 'If I run into Norman Bates I'll give him your regards.'

We both got out of the truck into the driving rain. Rambam took off in the direction of the barn and I ran for the safety of the overhang of the house. I didn't quite get there in time to prevent my cigar from getting soggy. The door was unlocked. I walked into the front room. The place looked like it'd been uninhabited for a long time. I shook the rain from my hat and walked into the old living room. It really took me back.

The walls were covered with cobwebbed memorabilia from the seventies. A mirrored poster from Bob Dylan's Rolling Thunder Revue. A handbill from Willie Nelson's Homecoming at Abbot, Texas. I'd been so wired and inspired on that performance I'd almost strangled myself putting on my guitar. I remembered Sammy Allred of the Geezinslaw Brothers telling the crowd: 'All right. We'll get Kinky to do a few numbers. Then he'll sing some songs for you.'

There was another poster from a show we'd done with David Allen Coe. It's funny what you think about when your mind is on other matters. I recalled asking Willie Nelson if there was any truth to the rumor that David Allen Coe had a snake tattooed on the tip of his penis. 'I don't know,' said Willie. 'It's never come up.'

A lightning flash and a loud clap of thunder shook me out of my little reverie. There was a smell in the air that did not seem to be all that pleasant. My beezer hasn't been working too well for about seven years, but when I do detect an odor filtered through all the cat hair, cigar smoke, and Bob Marley residue, you can usually bet that it ain't nothin' nice. I followed my nose into the bedroom.

There, on a little cot, was the body of a woman. She was wearing a white Mexican wedding dress. Her hands were folded beneath her breast, holding something that might've once been a flower. Her face was bloated like a moon pie and several species of insects seemed to be having a convention in her wide-open, sightless eyes. The only name she'd ever answer to now was dead.

'I believe you two know each other,' said a familiar voice. It wasn't Rambam.

I turned around and saw a figure wearing an Indian headdress, a sickening smile, and red war paint that appeared very much like it might've once had a cholesterol rating. The figure was holding a double-barreled shotgun.

'I hold all of you accountable,' said the voice, 'but you, Kinky, I hold personally responsible.'

On the backs of his ever-whitening knuckles I noticed the tattooed words L-O-V-E and H-A-T-E. L-O-V-E was the one that pulled the trigger.

75

'Then I heard two deafening blasts,' I said as I paced McGovern's little hospital room. With McGovern's large form schlafed out in the bed with tubes and things still in him, there wasn't a hell of a lot of room left to pace. I did my best.

'As I hit the floor I saw these colorful feathers flying everywhere. It looked like the Jolly Roger had scored a direct hit on Long John Silver's parrot. Then I heard a voice echoing across the world and I didn't know if it belonged to God or Satan. It said: "This property's protected by Smith & Wesson." It was Rambam, of course.'

A little smile came to McGovern's lips and he almost laughed. His eyes followed me as I paced.

'When I found the puppet head behind the refrigerator I should've known I'd been looking at things all wrong. That was the first major tip-off, so to speak.'

'So it *was* Tequila,' said McGovern in a weak, barely recognizable voice. It'd been a week since his little fall from grace and the doctors now assured me the prognosis was excellent for full recovery.

'Yes,' I said. 'You correctly ID'd him for the cops a few days ago when they showed you the old Jewboy photos. Tequila *was* talking about a train when he was overheard arguing with his wife in a hotel room years ago. He was accusing her of "pulling the train." In other words, hosing everybody in the band. That was the one experience all of us had in common.'

McGovern nodded his head and kept following me with his eyes. I was heartened to see that McGovern's eyes looked clear and alert and filled with intelligence, just like my cat's.

'Marcie checked her Red Cross sources in Mexico and found that Tequila had been in prison there for ten years. That's when he got the tattoos and also, apparently, went around the bend rather irrevocably. The thought that he'd been cuckolded by the entire band sautéed what was left of his brain. When he got out he took a small fortune he'd stashed away from black-market schemes and began his crusade. He didn't care how much it cost him to exact his revenge. The twenty thousand samoleans he left behind in my loft was only a portion of what he had, but it was enough to put us all on the wrong track. The Sixteenth Avenue business only indicated that he'd come to New York from Nashville where he'd tried unsuccessfully to knock off Willie Fong Young. Unfortunately, he honed his act as he went along.

'The reason Travis Parnell blipped off the screen so completely was that he must've followed a tip from a loose-lipped lesbian and stumbled into my loft right after Tequila'd arrived and I'd left to get groceries. Tequila saw it as a perfect means to take himself out of the picture and proceed, quite unsuspected, with his ruthless campaign of revenge and death. There was a struggle between the two during which someone was thrown against the refrigerator, causing the puppet head to roll off. It was a little thing and it took me a long time to realize how significant it was. Tequila'd already had the water running and had stepped into the shower before I'd left. For him to have gotten out of the shower, struggled extensively with an intruder in the kitchen, then wound up dead in the rain room again with a hole shot through the curtain just didn't wash. Obviously, he'd finished showering and was back in the loft when Parnell wandered in and offered a perfect opportunity for Tequila to stage his own death by planting him in the bathtub.

'Which brings us, of course, to the little rubber duck and the note found in Skycap's pockets. The note said "Was It Worth It?" meaning was it worth hosing Sharon, and the answer, after what we've seen, clearly was no. But put *duck* and the word *worth* together and you have *Duckworth*, the name of the ranch we once owned in Texas where the band first went to live, rehearse, and become inextricably intertwined in questionable karma.'

McGovern seemed to be making little chirping noises with his mouth and pointing to the window. Watching each other was wearing both of us out.

'Oh,' I said, 'you want to know why Tequila hid in the hallway once he'd nailed my windows shut? Well, I eventually narrowed it down to either Tequila or Sharon, because she was the other one that might've had motive and means to be behind the whole thing. Even the puppet head clue didn't rule her out. She could've capped Tequila in the rain room. But, according to Skycap, she once held a stray cat in her arms and said: "How do you like my pussy?" That lets her off the hook. Because the reason Tequila refused to wait inside the loft where he'd surely have killed me, and chose instead to lurk out in the hallway where, fortunately for me, he encountered Ratso, is quite simple. Tequila, you see, was allergic to cats.'

McGovern stared at me for a long moment. 'Let's take these cattle north,' he said.

I thanked McGovern for his courage and invaluable help and, after I'd left, I felt very confident about his chances for full recovery. It wasn't because the doctors had said the prognosis was excellent. I never believed in doctors. And McGovern didn't look all that good. He still was weak, lethargic, and shockingly pale. But when I'd turned to say good-bye at the door I'd noticed something that lifted my spirits tremendously. Irish eyes were smiling.

76

Later that evening down at Gallagher's, I was having a drink at the bar with Dylan and James Clare when Billy Swan, Snakebite, Willie Fong Young, and Panama Red came into the place.

'I thought you guys had bugged out for the dugout,' I said.

'Hell, no,' said Snakebite. 'We came here to play on a reunion tour of the Texas Jewboys and that's what we're going to do.'

'The whole world is waiting for us,' said Willie. 'This is no time to woosie out.'

'We'd need more guys,' I said. 'Roscoe West is doing very well as an artist these days. Washington Ratso is getting to be a big shot on television news in our nation's capital. Van Dyke Parks, as well as scoring motion pictures, is now a distinguished lecturer at Harvard. Country John Mankiewicz has become a big Hollywood producer. It may be hard to convince these guys that what they're doing isn't more important than pickin' in a country band.'

Panama lit up a Kent. 'Nothing in the world,' he said, 'is more important than pickin' in a country band.'

With that sentiment in the air, James Clare bought all of us a round of drinks on the house. I thought of some of the great musicians I'd known and loved who'd gone to Jesus and would never play their music live again. Lowell George, Phil Ochs, Jimmie Don Smith, Mike Bloomfield, Ron Slater, Buffalo, Paul Butterfield, David Blue, Jesse Ed Davis. And I thought of Tom Baker, who wasn't a musician but who had beautiful music in his soul. And I thought of John Belushi who loved the blues.

I looked at Billy Swan. He shrugged. Then he smiled. Then I saw a million miles of road shining brightly back at me in his eyes.

'Well,' I said, 'what are we waiting for?'

' "On the road again," ' said Dylan.

Around midnight Kelli came over to the loft. I was just pouring us a few drinks when Winnie called to thank me again for giving her the lovely portrait of Andy Warhol.

'All my girls adore it,' said Winnie. 'It's so compelling and sensitive. I don't know how the artist captured Andy so completely! It *was* done in oils, wasn't it?'

'Something like that,' I said.

When I rang off with Winnie, I told Kelli the whole story about Tequila and Sharon and the Texas Jewboys and Travis Parnell. When I finished the story, I poured us both another stiff shot and made a toast.

'Here's to Anna Pavlova,' I said, 'the great ballerina whose last words were: "Get my swan costume ready." '

We both killed the shots.

Then Kelli asked: 'How did you know about Anna Pavlova?'

'It's my business to know things,' I said.

'Then there's something *I'd* like to know,' said the Dancer. 'You said all the guys in the band slept with Sharon. Did *you* sleep with Sharon?'

I walked over to the window and looked out as the Pacific Ocean embraced the nighttime California shoreline. Summertime. A little motel near Malibu. Another dancer's legs, lithe and steamy. A whiff of jasmine. A taste of the sea.

'*Did* you sleep with her?' said Kelli's half-pleading voice from over my shoulder.

My gaze strayed farther down the coast to a lone chinaberry tree. I turned around and looked in Kelli's eyes. Hope burned green in them. They wanted to believe. For an instant I saw the face of the child who'd once talked to the old Christmas tree ornaments. Maybe the back of the tree *was* an important place to be.

Life is moments, I thought. Disappointments, pleasures, tragedies, dreams, failures, and triumphs, all strung together like a bad puka necklace.

'No,' I said.

Kelli smiled. Then she took my hand. Then she led me into the bedroom. Then we danced together for the very first time.

Elvis, Jesus and Coca-Cola

At Tom Baker's wake, quite well attended, as the wakes and funerals of misunderstood people usually are, I sang 'Ride 'em Jewboy.' The song is a western translation of what is essentially an eastern experience, the holocaust. It is not surprising that this song had been a favorite of Baker's. As Brendan Behan said: 'The Irish and the Jews do not share a nation; they share a psychosis.'

Goat Carson recited a poem he'd written for the Bakerman, the last two lines of which I remember: 'Between the gutter and the stars/People are what people are . . .'

Tom Baker was.

I first met the Bakerman on the gang plank of Noah's Ark. The last time I saw him, the lifespan of a sea tortoise later, was from the frosty window of a hack at four o'clock in the morning out in front of the old Lone Star Cafe in New York. It's not there anymore, the Lone Star. The neighborhood needed another Bennigan's. New York's still there, of course, in a manner of speaking. At least it still exists in the recently colorized imagination of terminally ill children. And who of us isn't one of them?

The Lone Star was heavily shuttered, the Bakerman was heavily monstered, standing on the curbside wearing old trousers, a long gray woolen coat from some forgotten war, a blue knit cap, and an intransigently Irish expression halfway down a country road between happiness and despair. I remember snowflakes dreideling down all around him like slow motion tears from a burnedout guardian angel.

Baker had been one big, tough, talented charming crazy, greeneyed Irishman who men respected and women invariably loved. He was an actor but, because Hollywood was Hollywood and the Bakerman was the Bakerman, most of his more memorable performances were offstage and off-screen. He was a star who only really had the chance to shine into the lives of those who knew him.

Life and death are not without their little ironies and one of them was that Tom Baker died on stage. It was a small stage. It was in the loft of his close friend Bob Brady, an acting coach. Officially, it was called an overdose, but this doesn't tell us much because sooner or later everybody suffers from an overdose. Too many over-the-counter dreams. Too much Early Times. Too many Sunday nights in Los Angeles.

I met Tom Baker's dad for the first time at the wake and noticed in him many of the gestures, mannerisms and voice inflections that you take for granted until you have a dead friend. Tom's father mentioned a film that his son had been working on at the time of his death. I knew about it. Tom had spent a great deal of time and effort on the project. Tom Baker, Movie-maker, he'd called himself. Tom Baker, Trouble-maker, others called him.

The film was a documentary on Elvis impersonators. And, according to Tom's father the film, along with Tom, of course, was missing.

'Do you think you could help us find it?' he asked. 'Our Tom was very proud of it.'

'No prob,' I said confidently. 'Most likely it's just been mis-placed. I'll run it down for you in the next day or so.'

I shook his big, sad hand and felt the Bakerman slipping away.

I'd find the film, all right. It couldn't be that difficult, I thought. It had to be somewhere between the gutter and the stars.

2

There is a period of time after the death of someone very close to you when everyone you meet appears to be a nerd. You can't understand why elderly women would take the time to knit them sweaters. Quite possibly it is that there have always been a high proportion of nerds in the world and that it requires the cauteriz-ation of someone with sparkle to highlight the tedium of almost everyone else.

'At least all cats are pretty hip,' I said to the cat. 'My beautiful little pet.'

'It's not your pet,' said Ratso from the couch. 'It's your animal companion.' Ratso was my sometime Dr Watson and oft-time housepest. When he wasn't busy getting up my sleeve, he was the editor of *National Lampoon*.

I thought about it for a moment as I lit a cigar with a kitchen match, always keeping the end of the cigar just above the level of the flame. I didn't answer Ratso or really take notice of him. Neither did the cat.

'Pet is a demeaning word. Animal companion,' he repeated. 'That's the correct way of stating it.'

'*You're* my animal companion,' I said.

It had been several days since Tom Baker's wake and Ratso had been logging considerable time at my humble loft on Vandam Street. His claim was that the plumbing in his apartment building was being worked on but ever so often I thought I caught him glancing at me with pity in his eyes. Maybe I was just getting paranoid like everyone else in New York, but it crossed my desk several times that he knew how close I'd been to the Bakerman and maybe he was here on some skewered kind of suicide watch like you read about in the *National Enquirer*. On the other hand, the plumbing in Ratso's apartment left a lot to be desired.

At last, I could no longer take Ratso's eyes following my movements around the living room. The more he watched me like a giant hood-eyed tropical bird, the more nervous I became and the more intense became my pacing back and forth across the loft. The cat, as a kitten, had been fascinated by this pacing and used to follow back and forth in my footsteps. As she grew older she tired of this ridiculous activity but still seemed to enjoy watching me pace much in the manner of a slightly bored British matron watching a badminton match. Now that the cat was reaching *The Prime of Miss Jean Brodie*, she could care less whether or not I got a pogo stick and jumped through my asshole for America.

The cat, of course, had never particularly liked Ratso. I didn't know if this was instinct, anti-Semitism, or merely feline malice. I wasn't sure I wanted to know.

'Ratso,' I said, after several more hours had ticked by, 'are you here because I have a broken heart or because you have a broken dumper?'

'Either would seem a compelling reason,' said Ratso. 'Why do you wish to know?'

'Because if you're worried about me hanging myself from a shower rod, I'm going to get a forklift in here and get you the hell out of here. *Then* I'll hang myself from a shower rod.'

'Sounds sensible,' Ratso said.

We bantered on in this fashion for an interminable length of time, whereupon Ratso finally took his leave. He said he had to check his plumbing but I could tell he was going out in a snit. I also observed that he left a large valise containing the viaticum of his life behind the sofa. Like a clockwork MacArthur, I knew someday he'd return.

I appreciated Ratso's concern but I needed to be alone. For one thing, I'd already checked with Bob Brady, Baker's close friend, who'd scoured the loft where Tom had lived and not found a trace of his final cinematic effort. One of Tom's assistants on the film, a guy named Legs, had already reported to Baker's father that the film was missing from the lab. If the film wasn't in the loft and wasn't in the lab that meant I only had to look everywhere else.

Later, in the week following the Bakerman's wake, I reoccupied my old base camp in the foothills of Mt Depression. I stayed in the loft like Emily Dickinson, smoking cigars, drinking coffee, periodically feeding the cat, and occasionally feeding myself some warmed-over detritus from the back of the refrigerator, the dates on both of our cartons seemingly having expired.

I did observe a minor behavioral change on my part during that time. I'd taken to farting loudly, ostentatiously and, I felt, rather humorously, on the increasingly rare occasions when friends of mine, including Ratso, came by the loft. I don't know why I did this.

Maybe it was a cry for help.

3

It was at this time that I began seeing some rather uncanny parallels between my life and the life of Jesus. Both of us, of course, were of the Jewish persuasion. Neither of us ever really had a home to speak of. Neither of us ever married during the course of our lives. Neither of us ever actually held a job during the course of our lives. We both just basically traveled around the countryside irritating people.

'Maybe Jesus can help us,' I said to the cat. 'Maybe He can find the missing film about Elvis impersonators.'

The cat looked at me as if I were clinically ill, but she stood her ground beside me on the desk. Thus encouraged, I continued.

'Maybe Jesus can help me run down this Legs character. I've left three messages on his answering machine but he's not responding to therapy.'

The cat looked at me as one stares at a place where a rainbow has recently been.

'Stop looking at me with pity in your eyes,' I said, as I attempted to brush her off the desk. She moved down a bit just out of my reach and continued to stare at me.

'Let us pray,' I said to the cat. We both bowed our heads.

'Dear God, Jesus, Buddha, or L. Ron Hubbard, please help us find this documentary about Elvis impersonators. We trust the Bakerman and Elvis are with you now and should vouch for the sincerity of our efforts. We know you will enjoy the company of the Bakerman. Elvis, of course, during his entire career never played to an empty seat. Towards the end, unfortunately, he became somewhat of a chemical puppet and had to have his rather protuberant stomach wound extensively with saran wrap prior to going on stage, but Christ, you know how it is with idols.

'As I look at what's going on in the world I can see that you guys have been very busy watching every sparrow – '

Here I winked at the cat.

' – nonetheless, we'd appreciate hearing from you soon.'

The cat blinked both eyes rather doubtfully and looked at the ceiling.

I didn't really expect to hear from L. Ron Hubbard. And Buddha hadn't spoken to anybody in years. But I did hope that God or Jesus might be more forthcoming. They'd been almost garrulous in recent times, speaking to psychics, football coaches, political candidates, and Oral Roberts to name only a few. I was quite hopeful.

I made an espresso, puffed on a cigar and encouraged the cat to be patient. I took the espresso over to the kitchen window sill where the cat joined me. We waited. I did not bring an ashtray. The world was my ashtray.

Two espressos and half a cigar later there had been no sign from the heavens. The view from the kitchen window was pretty ho-hum. A riot of gray. God and Jesus, apparently, were not saying dick. Either they didn't exist, they didn't care, or they were both autistic.

'The power of prayer,' I said to the cat.

I picked up a *Daily News* and, somewhat desultorily, turned a few pages looking for my pal McGovern's by-line. It would've been heartening to see something like: 'Kinky, your little friends are wrong.' But there was nothing.

Well, almost nothing. *The Daily News* had occasionally taken to giving McGovern the 'People Page,' thereby making him the only super-intelligent, six foot five inch, two hundred and forty pound Irish society editor in the world. In today's column McGovern pointed out that for the past decade, developers and pollution had threatened Henry David Thoreau's Walden Pond, and that over the years various groups had been fighting to keep the pond pristine and primitive as it had been in Thoreau's time. Of course, there were others inexorably moving toward making the pond look like New Jersey. Both groups were distasteful in their own way and, I reflected, as I lit a fresh cigar, so was McGovern. I didn't think too highly of vapid pop stars who pirouetted up from their sound stages and multi-track studios to embrace global causes. But global causes needed all the help they could get. Just because Michael Jackson was the proud owner of the skeletal remains of the Elephant Man, was no reason for me to cast asparagus on these nerds trying to save Walden Pond.

The developers, of course, were the bad guys, but at least in a somewhat perverted way, they were honest. All they wanted was a lot of money so they could buy a big hairy steak, a trophy wife, a boat, and time to kill a few bambis on the way to Belize. Developers, in fact, sounded rather dangerously like normal Americans. Rock stars saving the world could be equally tedious. McGovern appeared to agree with me for at the bottom of the page he ran a large glitzy photo of a group of celebrities dressed to the hilt in chic, Hollywood drag at a cocktail party to save Walden Pond. Under the photo McGovern ran a quote from Thoreau: 'Beware any enterprise that requires new clothes.'

I looked out the window again and at last I saw a vision. It was not clear if the vision was biblical or not, but I certainly hoped she was. Time would tell. A gorgeous blonde about nine foot tall in some kind of endangered species coat was crossing Vandam toward my loft. She appeared to be walking two little pet squirrels on leashes. Or maybe they were her animal companions. One thing was for sure, they were the luckiest squirrels in New York.

She looked up for a moment and I saw her face. That was a vision, too. She did not have that humorless, cold, brittle, Teutonic look. She appeared vibrant, full of fun, adorable – and it's hard for tall women to appear adorable. She looked very sophisticated and, at the same time, like someone you might've left at the county fair of your dreams. Someone that should've always been with you.

I watched her till she walked out of sight. Then I watched the fire escape, the exposed brick walls of the warehouse down the street, a dollop of gray sky, a limo, a slow-motion man going through a garbage can in the world of the dimly lit. My fellow Americans, I thought, rolling around in the ancient streets like dung-beetles grimly pursuing happiness as they're being run down by life.

I smoked the cigar. I stroked the cat. Then I closed my eyes and looked out over Walden Pond.

4

Sometimes life jumps up and bites you in the ass. Like the joke: 'What has four legs and an arm?' The answer: 'Pit bull.' Very few people find that joke humorous. Even fewer find life humorous, but maybe that's part of the problem.

For me, at the moment, life was about as funny as Clint Eastwood's monkey. Not only was I suffering the loss of a man whom I was belatedly realizing to have been my best friend, but I was rapidly coming to the conclusion that when I did finally locate his assistant, Legs, I was going to have his broken. My lonely, hermetic, disenfranchised Emily Dickinson mood was turning positively Kafkaesque. I needed some fun in my life whether I wanted it or not.

I was sitting at my desk in the loft one cold stormy afternoon trying to decide whether to kill myself or go bowling when the phones rang. I let 'em have their head for a while. Didn't want anybody to think I was lonely or hungry or looking for work. Hell, I might be busy as a bee for the rest of my life looking for this Elvis impersonator documentary. I didn't mind hearing the phones ring a bit. It meant somebody somewhere wanted me. You take your comfort where you can.

My phone set up was about as interesting as collecting chinch bugs in Uganda, but it was all I had going at the moment. Two red phones on my desk, one for each half of my brain, were both connected to the same line. There was little practical value to this but when they rang together, which they always did, it made you feel like somebody. I had a slightly effeminate pink pastel princess phone in the bedroom which lately had interrupted me only during the rare occasions of sleep or sexual intercourse. Some day when I'd made a million bucks I planned on getting a phone in the dumper.

I picked up the blower on the left.

'Start talkin',' I said.

'Hi, baby. Do you know who this is?'

I hated it when this happened because most friendly familiar women out of the distant past seemed to sound rather similar to me. I was always caught between being rather surly or going on an extremely unpleasant fishing expedition.

'Can you give me a multiple choice?' I said.

'No,' said the voice.

'Well, let me see,' I said. 'A. Eleanor Roosevelt. B. Squeaky Fromme. C. Mama Cass – '

'Kinkster, you *know* who this is.'

I did.

It was Downtown Judy. She just didn't know she was Downtown Judy because she didn't know there was an Uptown Judy. Both of them thought they were just Judy and that was the way I wanted to keep it. They'd both come into my life, along with a number of others who weren't named Judy, some years ago at about the same time. It was also a time when I was usually so high I'd needed a stepladder to scratch my ass. Neither Judy had been quite the answer, so an elaborate juggling system had evolved, providing for rather exciting near-misses that, on several occasions, brought me fairly close to becoming a castrato in the Vienna Boys Christmas Choir. Keeping the two Judys in ignorance of each other kept me busy and, as an added benefit, kept me in ignorance of joint checking accounts, vacuum cleaners, and booster chairs in family-oriented restaurants. Now was the time, I thought, for the two Judys to make a reentry into my life. I hadn't really spent time with either of them for a while.

By the time I'd hung up the blower it'd been arranged for Downtown Judy to come over to the loft that evening for a little slumber party. Downtown Judy had been a pretty fair actress at one time. Now she was a pretty fair social worker. Her goal, as I understood it, was to use her second career to try to uplift all the people she'd had to step on in her first one. Tonight I was hoping she'd uplift Mister Pinky.

Blower traffic was light that afternoon; I was receiving almost no incoming wounded. As the day grew darker and stormier I seemed to become increasingly disenfranchised from both the rat race and the human race, and began experiencing an inability to differentiate between the two. A possible index of my extreme loneliness was that, after no small degree of personal turmoil, I picked up the blower on the left and called Ratso at his office.

'*National Lampoon*,' said a female voice.

'May I speak to Ratso, please?'

'May I tell him who's calling, please?'

'Gerald McBoing-Boing.'

'May I tell him who you're *with*, sir?' said the secretary, with just the slight flutterings of irritation.

'The Butthead Group.'

'May I tell him what this is in regard to?' she said curtly.

'You can tell him that it's in regard to the little-known fact that many centuries ago Tahitian sailors were believed to have made their way to the Hawaiian Islands in rudimentary canoes, and these noble, primitive men, as they crossed thousands of miles of uncharted, often starless seas, in order to detect ever-so-subtle ocean currents, were said to have, on occasion, placed their scrotums on the wooden floors of their canoes for navigational purposes.'

'Did you call last week?'

She put me on hold.

It wasn't the first time this had happened in the brief, torturous pilgrimage of my life and I doubted if it'd be my last. But holding for Ratso invariably tended to give me pause. Which, if you stop to think about it, is a good thing to have if you're on hold.

'Kinkstah!' Ratso finally said. 'Kinkstah! The Rangers are playin' the Bruins tonight! Got two tickets from J.D.'

J.D. was John Davidson, great former Ranger goalie and friend of mine and Ratso's who'd done a very rare thing – beautifully transitioned from star player to star television commentator. In hockey that doesn't happen often. Of course, not all of the players speak English.

I told Ratso that I had some scoring of my own to do that evening and he took the news good-naturedly, warning me against high-sticking and circus accidents.

'It's gonna be a great game,' Ratso tried one more time. 'You're gonna be sorry you missed it.'

'I'm sure I will,' I said. I had no idea at the time how true were those words. I was just grateful Ratso'd gotten his plumbing fixed.

Sometime later, during the empty walk-in closet of eternity that often passes for dusk in New York, the phones rang in the loft. This time it was the call I'd been waiting for. It was Legs.

'Look, man, I've got something important to talk to you about, but I've got to run.' No pun intended apparently.

'Fine,' I said. 'When can I meet you?'

'Tomorrow afternoon at three. The Monkey's Paw.'

'I know the place.' I'd fried half of my brain cells out in the men's room there, I ought to know the place.

'Ciao,' he said, and was gone.

I cradled the blower.

'Ciao,' I said to the cat.

The cat looked at me questioningly. I blew a nice trail of cigar smoke up at the ceiling.

'Rhymes with meow,' I said.

5

From the kitchen window I could see Downtown Judy coming up Vandam Street like a red tide at sunset. Somewhere in the world there was a sunset. In New York, where there was often no sun or sky to speak of, garish shadows fell like elderly people onto the sidewalks and the dull gray blanket turned darker and bone-chillingly colder, and underneath it the rats and people scurried around faster and faster.

Judy waved up at me from the sidewalk. I opened the window just enough to toss down the little Negro puppet head with the key to the building wedged in its mouth. Ratso had once stumbled across a basket of little Negro puppet heads at a flea market on Canal Street and managed to christian down some guy in a turban for the whole lot. In his enormous generosity he'd given me one and I'd developed a rather close rapport with it. What Ratso had done with all the others only Allah or Uncle Remus knew and neither seemed to be talking.

The puppet head, more durable than most human heads, had already burned through any number of brightly-coloured para-chutes and was currently sporting a product I sold at my shows, the 'Honor America Bandanna', otherwise known as 'the Kinky snot rag'. It was an American flag with fifty stars of David, a picture of the Kinkster, and the slogan: 'Sold American.' As a song, 'Sold American' had been in the top ten on the country charts in 1973. That same year it had been number one in Cadillac, Michigan. As a slogan for a parachute, 'Sold American' shot by the junkies on the sidewalk of normal society a little too rapidly to mean a hell of a lot. Unfortunately, it was the story of many of our lives. But at the moment that didn't mean dick to a tree or to me. My main concern was closing the window before my nose hairs turned to stalactites.

With parachute and puppet head in hand, Downtown Judy opened the large metal door to the building and began the laborious climb to my fourth floor loft. I began the rather laborious task of deciding where to take her for dinner. I wished I could say I loved her. I wished I could say I loved anyone. The way I loved the cat and the Bakerman. Historically, I thought, cats and dead people had always been cheap dates. Easy to love. Easy to keep in your heart.

I took Downtown Judy to the Monkey's Paw. I ate five Jack Daniels and several Dr Peckers on the side as well as about half of a shepherd's pie. Everybody in the place looked vaguely familiar, especially after the third shot. Downtown Judy ate the other half of the pie, along with some kind of Chateau de Cat Piss and we both celebrated the occasion with a small aluminum foil package of new improved Tide that she'd purchased from a nervous pale little man called the Weasel who didn't know he was called the Weasel, just like Downtown Judy didn't know she was Downtown Judy. I reflected, as I killed the fourth shot, how few of us in this crazy world actually know who or what we are. Maybe I was an impeccably dressed, uptight, corporate kind of guy trapped in the shell of a country singer turned amateur detective. Maybe I was an escargot.

I was in relatively high spirits and pretty well walking on my knuckles by the time we got back to the loft. I'd down-shifted to Jameson's Irish Whiskey which I was drinking from my old bull's horn. Between the unpredictable jabbing pain of the Bakerman's death and the quite predictable teeth-grinding effect of the Weasel's product, there were moments when I felt almost human.

Winnie Katz's lesbian dance class in the loft above seemed to have suddenly kicked into high gear. Downtown Judy had kicked off her shoes and stockings and various other extraneous paraphernalia, and the cat, who very much preferred Downtown Judy to Ratso, was purring quietly on the kitchen counter. What more could a man want?

'You know,' I said, as Judy unbuttoned her blouse, 'that I've been impotent now for about twenty-five years.'

'Well, that'll work out fine because I'm afraid this just happens to be that time of the month.'

'You're fuckin' kiddin',' I said.

'I'm not fuckin' kiddin',' said Judy. 'I'm not fuckin' at all.'

The cat and I both looked at Judy. Winnie's dance class continued unabated somewhere in the sky. I killed a subdued shot of Jameson's.

'We could cuddle,' she said.

It was later that night when the phones began to ring rather ominously. I uncuddled myself from Downtown Judy and got out of bed noticing that my Borneo sarong had ridden up to my armpits and quite possibly would've choked me to death if not for the sudden fortuitous circumstances of cuddlaribus interruptus. Some mildly foreboding, unkenable instinct warned me that this was a call that ought to be taken at the desk. Walking on tiptoes (a spiritually transferred trait from my friend John Morgan who'd always walked that way), I made it to the desk by Jewish radar and collared the blower on the right.

It was Sergeant Mort Cooperman, a homicide dick that I'd had some rather extensive and often fairly repellent social intercourse with. Unpleasantries were exchanged. Eventually, he got to the point.

'You know a skirt named Judy?' he asked. The tone and texture of his voice would've jump-started Lauren Bacall.

'Yeah,' I said cautiously, as I made an effort to peer through the gloom into the bedroom. Everything was still.

'Known her long?'

'I've known her for a while,' I said with a hint of irritation. Something was suspish.

'You been in contact with her lately?'

'Yeah,' I said. 'I was in contact with her when you called. Now I think she's adjusting her French Maid costume.'

There was a long, somehow menacing silence on the other end

of the line. I glanced nervously into the bedroom again. Judy was still asleep.

When Cooperman spoke again he was giving me an address. It sounded familiar. It was an uptown address.

'Better get over here now,' said Cooperman. 'Otherwise, I may have to book you for necrophilia.'

6

The ride uptown in the hack was uneventful except for a minor altercation between myself and the driver whose appearance and brusque behavior clearly indicated that he came from a country that began with an 'I'. He felt that smoking regulations should be strictly enforced. I felt that, under the circumstances, a little slack might be acceptable. Unfortunately, I wasn't quite sure myself what the circumstances were.

Several potholes and a few near misses served to awaken me a bit from my fairly brain-dead state. Obviously, Cooperman's call had been in regard to Uptown Judy. Remembering how she used to carry a hand gun in her purse, and how occasionally she seemed to be cookin' on another planet, either she'd offed somebody or somebody'd offed her, and neither would've really surprised me. Of course, very little that occurred in New York surprised anybody these days except maybe finding a parking place.

I didn't have a car.

I sincerely hoped nothing had happened to Judy. The last I'd really spoken to her had been months ago. I'd seen her at the Bakerman's wake but she hadn't talked to me. That was strange now that I thought of it. Maybe she'd thought she was giving me my space but I didn't really want my space. I'd been parked in a spiritual towaway zone for years and I wasn't going to start feeding the meter now.

The other thing that was peculiar about all this was why Cooperman was calling me. I'd had fairly peripheral involvement with Uptown Judy, and I didn't really know much about her life. I wasn't exactly her significant other or her next of kin. I hoped to hell she was okay and I'd help her if I could but I was on my way now to meet a homicide dick. I caught a glimpse of the driver's flat, curry-colored eyes glaring at me, shifting with evil intent like the sands of distant dunes.

'Why me, Allah?' I said.

The driver growled something in a language that sounded like a pit bull arguing with Dr Doolittle. He swerved the hack rather violently across Third Avenue narrowly missing a little Korean on a bicycle.

'Allah be praised,' I said. I saw six thousand years of bad karma staring back at me through the rearview mirror.

When the pilgrimage finally ended at the near corner of 83rd Street I realized I didn't want to stay in the cab but I sure as hell wasn't eager to get out and see whatever Cooperman wanted to show me in Uptown Judy's apartment.

'Where're you from?' I asked as I gave him a twenty dollar bill.

'Tel Aviv, man,' he said.

Country *did* start with an 'I'.

'Shalom, brother,' I said as I got out of the cab. 'Keep the change.'

I walked up 83rd until I came to a familiar building. I wondered, do we ever really know the people we know? I pushed a buzzer, got buzzed in, and, taking the familiar elevator up to the third floor, began to lose my buzz. I walked down a familiar hallway. Do we ever know shit?

A slightly bored uniform was standing in front of Judy's door.

'Can I help you?' he asked. It was always a funny thing to say. A cop could say it in death's doorway. A salesperson could say it at Bergdorf-Goodman's. Not so long ago I could've said it to Tom Baker or Uptown Judy.

The uniform stuck his head into the apartment, exchanged a few muffled words with someone inside, then opened the door for me and melted out of the way.

The sweet and sour smell of death still hung in the heavy air as palpably as a christ on a cross. The whole apartment looked trashed – closets ransacked, drawers hanging out like tongues trying to tell you something. Even the door to the refrigerator was open.

371

Standing in the middle of the disarray was Detective Sergeant Mort Cooperman. The serpentine figure of Detective Sergeant Buddy Fox was studying the contents of the open refrigerator. Two techs were busy photographing the floor, dusting the furniture, and performing various other arcane procedures which only a mad scientist in a Walt Disney movie would understand.

Uptown Judy was nowhere to be seen.

Cooperman motioned me to follow him into the bedroom. I swallowed hard and walked in. The bedroom had also been tossed. No Judy.

'That look like her handwriting?' said Cooperman, nodding toward a bedside table. On the little table was a notepad. The top page had only one name and one phone number scrawled on it. Unfortunately, both were mine. I nodded to Cooperman. It did look like her handwriting.

I followed Cooperman back into the living room where the two techs were hunkered down near the middle of the floor. They were studying two faint but visible red lines across the wood that led to the door. Something about those lines caused the little hairs on the back of my neck to snap out of parade rest.

'Those're drag marks,' said Cooperman, matter-of-factly. 'Caused by a body being dragged along the floor. She must've been wearing a pair of red pumps or something. Can't find any in the apartment.'

'Cowboy boots,' I said. 'Red cowboy boots.'

Like a man in a dream I watched the two techs in their workmanlike fashion removing a small chip from the dark, dry stain on the floor, placing it in a glass tube of light blue liquid, holding it up to the light as it fizzed and bubbled and turned a darker color like a high school chemistry experiment, except it wasn't. The techs nodded at each other like two strangers on a commuter train. Then the guy holding the glass tube nodded at Cooperman and Cooperman nodded at him and I almost nodded out trying to decipher what was going on. Cooperman looked at me with a grim little smile ticcing lightly on his lips.

'It ain't Heinz 57,' he said.

7

Sergeant Cooperman had never been my idea of a father confessor figure. Sitting in Uptown Judy's apartment that night with the refrigerator door still standing wide open and with Cooperman across the little kitchen table instead of Uptown Judy was an extremely tedious experience at best.

The idea that Uptown Judy was dead, or at the very least, abducted and grievously wounded by God knows whom, was forcing me to sort out some thoughts of my own. Many of these I did not particularly wish to share with Sergeant Cooperman.

After all, the notion of having a relationship secretly and simultaneously with Uptown Judy and Downtown Judy that spanned several years was not especially wise or clever. It was more an admission of my own inability to love just one person. It was also a bit like sticking your kielbasa in a light socket while playing Russian roulette with the breaker switch.

For too long I'd condemned the two Judys to be more or less a station on the way. This did not make me proud to be an American.

'So you're fuckin' both these young ladies for two or three years on a fairly regular basis and they don't know about each other?'

'That's correct.'

'They both cared about you? Trusted you?'

'You'd have to ask them.'

'That may be a little difficult. How did you feel about them?'

'Who are you? Barbara Walters?'

Cooperman laughed a grating, malicious laugh. 'Just answer the questions. How did you feel about them?'

I wasn't in love with either of them, but I cared about both of them. Between the two of them they filled up an otherwise empty life. Sort of. And, of course, they cared about me in the normal perverse way women care about men who they think don't really give a damn.

'Nobody got hurt,' I said.

'Until now,' said Cooperman, lighting a cigarette with his zippo.

'What're the chances of finding Judy alive?'

'About the same as Hitler shavin' his mustache. Several hours ago a neighbor reported hearing a gunshot and a scream. You see what's left.'

Here Cooperman paused dramatically and gestured across the empty apartment. Fortunately, I reflected, I'd been right in the middle of someone at the time – well, actually not quite – but I'd been with someone earlier in the evening, so at least I wouldn't be one of the usual suspects – this time. But I still wanted to know more about what had happened. It was Cooperman, however, who was asking most of the questions.

'Where'd she work?'

'Madison Square Garden.'

'What'd she do?'

'I don't know.'

'Know anything about her family?'

'No.'

'Her background?'

'No.'

'Sounds like a deep relationship.'

'It had its moments.' Most of which, I reflected, were fairly horizontal.

'There is something you oughta know,' said Cooperman ominously. 'This broad's been in danger for some time. We always knew something like this could happen. I know you've got a tendency to snoop around in the area of crime now and then. You've had a little beginner's luck a few times out. You also almost got yourself polished a couple of times.'

'Why was Judy in danger?' I asked.

'Believe me, Tex, you don't want to know. This one you stay the fuck out of.'

Cooperman nodded and got up and it looked like our little chat was over. I had a lot of questions but, judging from his demeanor, I figured I'd save them for another time. I walked over to the door of the apartment and glanced back at the techs packing up their gear.

'You will let me know,' I said, 'when you find Judy?'

'You'll be the first on your block,' said Cooperman. 'Don't leave the city,' he shouted after me as I walked down the hall.

I'd had no great rapport with Cooperman in the past and it didn't look like things had gotten any better. He was a dedicated cop and he knew his job. I just didn't have any great confidence that he was going to find Uptown Judy very soon. And something in the back of my mind was telling me that very soon was not going to be fast enough.

I caught a hack and headed back down to the village. My thoughts were a troubled, jumbled embroidery of love, loneliness, distance, life and death. New York flashed by like the blurry, pastel view from a childhood carousel. Maybe, I thought, that's all it really was.

When I got back to the loft, Downtown Judy was still asleep. I didn't bother to wake her.

8

By the time I woke up Downtown Judy was gone and so were the dreamy shards of any youthful notion that life would go on forever. Like every other graffiti-strewn, ennui-driven subway train to nowhere, life would come to a screeching halt and all the passengers would have to get off. Anything left unsaid or undone would have to be forwarded to Fat Chance, Arkansas.

'Looks like a nice day,' I said to the cat. The cat could see that it looked like a perfectly hideous day, with a stultifying layer of gray over the city, out of which simultaneously emanated rain, sleet, snow, and every other inclement condition a postman prides himself in getting through.

The cat, of course, said nothing.

It was half past Gary Cooper time when Downtown Judy jumped through the blower on the right to ask me where the hell I'd run off to the night before. I asked her to give me a spiritual raincheck and I'd explain it to her over dinner at the Corner Bistro.

'Why can't you just tell me now?' she wanted to know.

'Because there is a large, old-fashioned wooden clothespin holding my lips together,' I said.

Judy went into a minor snit at that point and my mind was whirring with adequate lies to cover the situation. Our current level of understanding and communications was about the same as most married couples, I figured. At least, I had a reason for the subterfuge. Not only did I not want Downtown Judy to know about Uptown Judy's existence, now somewhat ironically, I had to also protect her from the knowledge of Uptown Judy's disappearance. The former knowledge would be merely unpleasant; the latter could be hazardous to her health.

'I'll tell you the whole story tonight,' I said, 'at the Corner Bistro.'

'You'd better,' she said.

Cooperman did not call. No one else did either which was fine with me. I suddenly had no desire to converse with the living. If Tom Baker or Uptown Judy had wanted to reach me on heaven's radio I'd have given them a big ten-four. But you can't very well loiter around your loft waiting to hear from dead people. Even Houdini's wife Beatrice had gotten tired of waiting for him to contact her as promised from the other side. 'Ten years is long enough to wait for any man,' she'd said.

At two o'clock I told the cat she was in charge and left the loft for my meeting with Legs at the Monkey's Paw. Walking up Vandam I couldn't believe the Bakerman was dead – that I wasn't going to meet Tom, just some friend of his I didn't know. It was going to take more getting used to than I was used to.

Moving briskly through cold, damp Village streets toward Sheridan Square, I began seeing two long red drag marks somewhere along some dim and distant horizon of my brain. I realized that wherever Tom Baker was, it was more than likely that Uptown Judy was now keeping him company. The afternoon was so chilly and brittle it seemed like New York might break like a heart. I hoped the two of them had dressed warm.

By the time I descended from Christopher Street into the

smokey bowels of the Monkey's Paw, the cold had brought tears to my eyes. It was for that reason, possibly, that I hadn't seen Mick Brennan, internationally acclaimed photographer and trouble-maker, sitting at the bar. I was soon made aware of his presence.

'Sit down here, mate,' he said. 'Let us pour a few pints down your neck.' It looked like Mick had poured quite a few down his own neck already.

I took a stool next to him and let him order the drinks. The Monkey's Paw had seen better days, I thought, as I glanced around at the seedy interior. So had I.

'Sorry to hear about your mate goin' South,' said Brennan.

'Yeah,' I said, and I drank about seven gulps of Guinness.

'You seem to be holding up. You can still fly a barstool.'

'I'm handling it well,' I said. 'Right now I'm happier than about 90 per cent of all the dentists in America.'

Brennan laughed and ordered another round. 'If you do top yourself,' he said, 'I could use that loft of yours for a photographic studio. Always wanted a place in the Village.'

'Well,' I said, 'It's a bit of a premature ejaculation just yet.'

Brennan laughed again but his eyes were sad. He was a good man to be with when death was in the air. He didn't pander to it. During the Falklands War he'd covered the Argentine mainland as a Brit photographer and he didn't mind telling you about it several times an evening. His repellent behavior could clear a room with the best of them. But he was not without charm. And he had an uncanny ability to know the news before it hit the papers.

I watched the door for Legs. I didn't know what the hell he looked like, only that he had a funny name. Of course, he might be saying the same about me.

'I hear your old girlfriend Uptown Judy's disappeared,' said Brennan a bit too casually.

'How the hell do you already know that?' I said. 'It happened late last night and Cooperman was taking great pains to keep it away from the press and to keep me from snooping.'

'I'm afraid we never divulge our sources,' said Brennan. 'However, you might talk to a large Irishman with a large head.'

377

I walked over to the payphone by the doorway. I'd forgotten all about waiting for Legs. I called McGovern at the *Daily News*.

'Mike McGovern World Headquarters,' he said.

'MIT – MIT – MIT!' I said. That was our code for the Man in Trouble Hotline we'd established since McGovern had found a story about a guy in Chicago who'd been dead in his apartment for six months before anyone had found him. We weren't going to let that happen to us. Of course, in a manner of speaking, it already had.

'MIT is right,' said McGovern in a low serious whisper. 'You never told me Uptown Judy's last name.'

'It's Sepulveda,' I said. 'So what?'

'So her father was Don Sepulveda.'

'I don't care if her father was Sunset Boulevard.'

'It's not a name,' said McGovern. 'Her father was *Don* Sepulveda. He was rubbed out by the Columbo Family five years ago.'

9

I was one clean shirt away from hanging myself from a shower rod. It'd been a ball-dragger of a weekend. Still no word from Cooperman on Uptown Judy which I took to be a bad sign. Still no word from Legs which I took to be a tedious sign. I wasn't an Indian or a psychic; I didn't read signs. But I knew something very repellent was in the air and it probably wouldn't be long before it wafted into my loft.

That evening I called Cooperman but he was out. Probably walking his pet stomach or playing miniature golf or possibly staring stoically at Uptown Judy's puffy face looking up at him from an over-sized ice tray. With the background McGovern had given me, there was no way I could see a happy ending to Uptown Judy's story. Maybe Hollywood and the fairy tales had used so many happy endings there weren't any more in stock.

I left a message for Cooperman to call me but I wasn't going to hold my breath. There was damn little I could do about the situation. At the moment it seemed even risky talking about it more than absolutely necessary. If the same guys who'd polished Judy's father had also spliced her, they'd either had a hell of a long-time grudge or they were looking for something. They also had my name and phone number now from the pad in Judy's apartment. If they wanted any Sepulveda Family secrets from me, however, they were barking up the wrong disappearing rain forest. I'd known nothing about Judy's background. And the only secrets I'd ever kept were the ones I'd forgotten.

'Judy,' I said, as she stared expectantly at me through the candlelight and din of a back table at the Corner Bistro, 'I really wish I could tell you more about what happened last night.'

'How can you tell me *more*?' she asked reasonably. 'You haven't told me a thing yet.'

Downtown Judy's hazel eyes and red hair seemed to be burning with righteous anger. I knew 'I went to see a man about a dog' wasn't going to cut it. I looked her in the eyes and had to avert my gaze to the obscenely large Bistroburger on the plate before me.

'I didn't want bacon,' I said.

'What!'

'I told 'em to drag it through the garden but I didn't want bacon.'

'Listen! You tell me where the hell you went last night. Now!'

'I'll tell you. Just don't make a scene in here.' It would've been hard to make a scene in the Corner Bistro. Two hermaphrodites could hose each other right on the counter and not too many people would notice.

I couldn't tread water in the Rubicon much longer. I looked at Downtown Judy's face, now angry, but basically honest and trusting, and I tried to imagine Uptown Judy's features. I was amazed to find that I couldn't clearly remember what she'd looked like. Is that what happened when you died? You just blipped off the screen and people forgot you? It was also possible, I thought, that just as McGovern and I taken together pretty much represented an adequate human being, the two Judys taken together pretty much represented an adequate relationship for me. Not that I was all that demanding.

'Okay,' I said. I took a large bite of my Bistroburger and chewed it 97 times for good digestion. I nodded my head encouragingly at

Judy so that she might do the same but she continued to stare at me. No one likes social workers to watch them while they eat.

'Okay,' I said. 'I got a call from Sergeant Cooperman, a homicide dick. You were sleeping so peacefully I didn't want to wake you.'

'Now we're getting somewhere,' Judy said, rubbing her hands together like an insect. I recalled how interested Judy'd been in some of the cases I'd been involved with in the past. Possibly she saw herself as Nancy Drew and me as Thomas Hardy or whatever the hell his name was. Frank and Joe.

'Cooperman told me to come to a certain address – I don't remember exactly – it was uptown – and he asked me if I knew this person – '

'Who was the person?'

I took another bite of Bistroburger. It wasn't bad, even with the bacon. I gave Judy a little gesture that indicated I would swallow quickly and tell her what she wanted to know or possibly I would need a Heimlich maneuver. Unfortunately, I'd never been a very good liar. My only chance, I figured, was to tell the story exactly as it happened but substitute another party for Uptown Judy. I swallowed, took a nicely paced gulp of Prior's Dark, and went on with it.

'There was a guy,' I said. 'Friend of Tom Baker's. Name was Legs. He'd worked on a film with Tom which, by the way, has turned up missing. Along with Tom, of course – '

'So you left the loft – '

'Went up to the address Cooperman had given me. To the guy's apartment. The neighbors, apparently, had reported that a shot had been fired. There was dried blood on the floor. There were drag marks where someone'd dragged the body out the door.'

'Wow,' said Judy enthusiastically. Heartened by her response, I continued.

'So Cooperman asked me how I knew the guy – '

'Wait a minute,' said Judy. 'Wait a minute.'

I waited.

'How did Cooperman know you knew Legs? Why would he call you?'

'Well,' I said, 'that part's kind of interesting, or maybe it's not, depending on how you look at it.'

'Just tell me, goddammit!' Judy was buying it but she wanted her money's worth.

'There was a pad of paper on a bedside table. The only thing on it was my name and phone number.'

'Jesus,' said Judy. In her mind she was probably getting her flashlight and parka out so the two of us could go about solving 'The Secret of the Old Mill'. Unpleasant. It was now my turn to toss down a little sidecar of Wild Turkey and watch Judy thoughtfully munching a Bistroburger that was about the size of her head. The road to hell, I figured, was paved with social workers eating Bistroburgers.

After dinner, Judy and I went our separate ways, she vowing to help me solve the mysterious disappearance of Legs, and me promising to keep her posted on developments as I heard them from Cooperman. We probably would've spent the night together but it was still that time of the month and I was emotionally and spiritually wasted. Also, Judy had some kind of support group seminar she had to chair at some ungodly hour in the morning. As I walked up Vandam to the loft I reflected that one of the more attractive features dead people had going for them was that they didn't need support groups.

The phones were ringing as I opened the door to the loft. I walked over to the desk, patted the cat, and gingerly picked up the blower on the left.

'Start talkin',' I said. It was Sergeant Cooperman and he did. He gave me an address and told me, not quite in these words, to get over there right away.

'Sergeant,' I said, 'you're starting to repeat yourself. You called me around this time last night and you wanted – '

'Get over here now,' he shouted. 'We got a notepad on the table with your name and number on it and this time we got a fuckin' stiff to go along with it.'

'Is it Uptown Judy?' I asked, not sure I really wanted to know. Still holding the blower, I hurriedly put my coat back on and grabbed three cigars for the road.

'Hell no it ain't Uptown Judy,' said Cooperman. 'It's a guy named Legs.'

10

Legs' apartment wasn't quite as nice as Uptown Judy's. What was inside it wasn't quite as nice either. I hadn't known what Legs had looked like before but, whatever that had been, he didn't look that good now. Where one of his eyes had been there now resided a crusty crater large enough to house a small grapefruit. Just glancing at the wound was enough to make you not wish to think of grapefruit. It rather put one off one's nice fried kippers. The eye that was still in Legs' head was brown and sensitive and looking right at me.

'Don't you normally close the eyes or something?' I asked Cooperman.

'If we can find 'em,' said Cooperman. 'Your name seems to be poppin' up a lot lately.'

'That's the price of fame,' I said.

Cooperman looked at me malevolently. He was not pleased. One of the techs from the night before seemed to recognize me and looked up briefly. When he saw Cooperman's demeanor he went back to work. Cooperman went back to glaring at me with dead cop eyes that were only slightly less unnerving than Legs' Cyclopean gaze.

'Take a good look, Tex,' said Cooperman, indicating the rather obvious stiff on the floor of the little apartment. 'What does this look like to you?'

I tiptoed a little closer to the body. I don't know why people always walk quietly around stiffs. Stiffs could give a damn. Maybe supposedly live people are afraid some of the supposed death will rub off. I didn't answer Cooperman.

'See the entry wound there behind the left ear?' Cooperman pointed it out to me like a guy explaining a dishwasher. 'See the exit wound where the right eye used to be?'

'Yeah.' Legs' good eye seemed like it was trying to say something. Whatever it was would keep, I guess.

'What's it look like to you?' asked Cooperman. 'I mean with your vast experience in the criminal field, I'm sure you can shed some light on this.'

From the other side of the room Fox laughed a nasty laugh. The sick little smile lit Cooperman's face briefly then was gone like a twitch. When two dicks want to get hard with you they quite often start out with what they think is funny. It's best to play along with them, I've found. Be a good sport. They can always take the ball and go home and, very possibly, it might be one of yours.

'Looks like a garden variety execution-style wing de-icing,' I said.

'Very good,' said Cooperman with sarcastic icing of his own you could've cut with a plastic birthday cake knife. 'Execution-style,' he nodded at Fox. Fox nodded back and beamed at me.

I took the compliment graciously and glanced around the place. It had been tossed and trashed much in the manner of Uptown Judy's.

'Whatever these guys are looking for,' I said, 'I wish they'd hurry up and find it.'

I also wished Cooperman and Fox would hurry up and let me get out of there. I hadn't brought my toilet kit and I didn't want to have to ask Cooperman if I could borrow his toothbrush. It was at least two hours before I was allowed to bug out for the dugout and drink myself into oblivion on a bar stool at the Monkey's Paw.

The story of my searching for the missing documentary on Elvis impersonators sounded phony even as I told it to Cooperman and Fox. God knows how it played with them. The fact that my name and phone number had been prominent at both murder scenes seemed to be about the only obvious lead they had and they were damned if they were going to let go of it. It seemed fairly logical to me. Uptown Judy hadn't seen me in a while and she was planning to call me. Legs was just returning my calls regarding getting together to discuss the Elvis film's disappearance. Cooperman and Fox didn't quite see it this way.

They felt that two in a row wasn't good. That I must, in some impalpable way, be inextricably bound to both incidents. They thought there must be something I wasn't telling them. If I knew what the hell it was I would've hired the Goodyear Blimp.

Later, at the Monkey's Paw, with Tommy pouring me a succession of shots of Jameson's, I wondered about a few things myself. They say drinking hinders thinking but that's only partially true. Practically all of the first rank Pulitzer Prize-winning novelists in our country have also been horrific piss artists. This has to count for something. It might mean that life itself is so hideously twisted and convoluted that only a drunk can effectively attach or convey any real meaning to it. There's more dead doctors than there are dead drunks and I hoped things remained that way. It wasn't much fun drinking with dead doctors. Unless they were Dr Seuss.

I couldn't for the life of me see any connection between the two incidents, other than my name and phone number and the fact that both times someone had been looking for something. A lot of people are looking for something. Most of the time, of course, they never find it. But at least it keeps them on their toes until they grow up and get to be a dead doctor. The Jameson's was really starting to kick in.

By the time I left the Monkey's Paw I was confused, depressed, thoroughly demoralized, and practically walking on my knuckles. I was a man without a zip code. It was a good way to start the week.

11

Legs' eyeball was still staring at me the next morning from my espresso cup. In a macabre sort of way I was starting to feel I knew the guy. It was not a particularly healthy sensation. Of course, interpersonal relations had never been my long suit.

Later in the morning Ratso called and managed to insinuate himself into what I liked to think of as my life. When he walked into the loft with the puppet head in one hand and half a pastrami sandwich in the other, he seemed to have a very determined Watson-like gait.

'So tell me,' he said, as he took a chair near the desk, 'about these skid marks on Uptown Judy's floor.'

'Drag marks, Ratso,' I said. 'Not skid marks. Skid marks are what you have on that old sofa in your apartment.'

'Mike Bloomfield and Phil Ochs never complained about it.' He started in on his sandwich.

Michael Bloomfield was a great rock guitarist and Phil Ochs had been a seminal folk singer of the sixties. Both had gone to the pearly gates, no doubt eased along, at least in part, by the skid marks on Ratso's couch.

'No,' I said, lighting a cigar, 'I'm sure they didn't. Mind if I smoke?'

'Go right ahead,' he said, as half his head disappeared in a cloud of blue-gray smog.

I asked Ratso how he knew about the drag marks and he told me he'd heard it from Brennan. Brennan had probably heard it from McGovern. It looked like the Village Irregulars were at it again. No point in trying to keep things quiet if the whole damn town already knew about it. And to be perfectly fair, Ratso, McGovern and Brennan had all contributed significantly to cases I'd worked on in the past. Rambam and Boris had saved my ass a couple times, too, though I hoped this time things wouldn't go that far.

'What else do you know?' I asked Ratso casually.

'I know Judy was shot and dragged from her apartment and is now most likely dead.' He masticated rather unpleasantly for a long moment. 'Sorry, man,' he said.

'Well, you know, it's been a long time since Judy and I were close – if we ever were. I knew her mostly during my blue period – '

'You mean when you were fucked up.'

'I prefer to say slightly amphibious.'

'I'm surprised you remember anything,' said Ratso, shaking his head in disgust.

'Oh, I remember, all right.' I took a somewhat pontifical puff on the cigar and looked quizzically at Ratso. 'What was your name again?' I said.

I was not particularly upset that Ratso, McGovern and Brennan knew about Uptown Judy. About the only person who didn't know was Downtown Judy. When the body was found and the news finally hit the papers big-time I might have to do some rather intricate explaining. In the meantime, I had enough trouble figuring the damn thing out for myself.

What the hell. If Ratso knew about Uptown Judy he might as well know about Legs. Sherlock would've told Dr Watson. Nero Wolfe would've told Archie Goodwin. Besides, Ratso was an expert on Bob Dylan, Jesus and Hitler. In his apartment were over ten thousand books that in some arcane way dealt with the lives of these three timeless troublemakers. Ratso was precisely the kind of guy that might be able to shed some light on Elvis and his legion of impersonators.

So I told Ratso that both Tom Baker's film and Legs' eyeball were now missing. Both items were, apparently, news to him, though he had discussed the film with Baker some time ago.

'Baker was telling me something about it but I can't remember exactly what. Anyway, Elvis doesn't quite belong in a league with Jesus, Hitler and Bob Dylan.'

'And he certainly doesn't belong in a league with you. That'd be 20,000 *Leagues Under The Sea*.'

I poured us each a cup of espresso and found an old half-smoked cigar in the waste basket. I fired it up with a mucus-colored Bic that had been in the family for about forty-eight hours.

'Resurrecting a dead cigar always gives me a little buzz,' I confided to Ratso.

'That's probably how Lazarus felt when he saw Jesus on the fifth day.'

I puffed a few times and looked admiringly at the cigar stub. 'Very possibly,' I said.

About two hours after Ratso had departed the phones rang. I went for the blower on the left.

'Start talkin',' I said.

'It's Ratso.'

'Long time between dreams.'

'Yeah, well I thought you'd want to know. I remembered what

Baker told me about the film. He was saying that he was going through some kind of real weirdness with these impersonators. He seemed really shook up about it.'

'Pardon the expression.'

'He said the way things were going, before he finished the film he might be meeting Elvis.'

12

Early that evening I was trudging up Vandam Street returning from a shopping spree. I was carrying two bags full of cat food, cigars, and toilet paper – all the essentials. The sky looked like it might snow but didn't really give a damn. I was wearing a heavy coat, cowboy hat, and hunting vest with cigars stuffed in the little stitched loops instead of shot gun shells. That didn't mean I wasn't going hunting. Actually, it might have to be more like poaching. Especially if Cooperman was never going to declare the season open.

As I climbed onto the freight elevator in what passed for the lobby of the building, I thought again of the comment Tom Baker had made to Ratso. I watched the one exposed light bulb sway slightly back and forth and remembered something Captain Midnite had once told me about Elvis. Midnite had known Elvis since Christ was a cowboy. He contended that Elvis had been turned into a chemical puppet very early on through drugs given him by bluegrass and gospel groups who were, for all practical purposes, out where the buses don't run. By the time Elvis hit it big, he had enough stock to open his own Walgreens.

Stepping out of the elevator onto the fourth floor I heard a strange high-pitched yapping noise coming from the stairwell. Two small dogs, one white and one brown, headed straight toward me and began running madly around in tiny concentric circles of hell at my feet.

'So they're not squirrels,' I said to the footsteps coming up the stairs.

The footsteps were auditorially attached to the longest legs I'd ever seen in my relatively short life. It was the beautiful blonde from the county fair.

'They're not squirrels,' she said, 'but evidently you are.'

There's very little that any faintly heterosexual male can say to a woman that breath-taking. And I didn't. Fortunately, she carried on the conversation.

'This is Pyramus,' she said, pointing to the brown one who was tugging at my jeans. 'And this is Thisbe.' Thisbe was trying to flatten herself like a tortilla and slide under my doorsill. The cat, who I could hear on the other side, was not amused.

'What kind of dogs are they?' I said when I got my voice back. This girl was really killer bee.

'I'm so glad you asked,' she said with a sort of sexy sarcasm as she smiled down at me. She was wearing heels and she looked to be about nine foot three.

'I should've worn my brontosaurus foreskin cowboy boots,' I said.

She looked at me again. 'It wouldn't have helped,' she said. She smiled and I knew she was right.

'Well, they're very cute little boogers, whatever kind of dogs they are.' I'd had some experience with tall people who owned little pets – or rather animal companions – and the little ones were absolutely the way to the big one's hearts. Still, there was something almost poignant about this statuesque beauty's obvious attachment to her two little animal companions. I wouldn't't've minded trading places with either one of them as long as I could still smoke cigars.

'You're a cute little booger, too,' I said.

'C'mon girls,' she said as she started up the stairs for the fifth floor. Her two animal companions followed faithfully. This was one of those rare situations where the view from the rear was at least as good as the view from the front.

About halfway up the flight she turned and fixed me with an almost biblical blue-eyed gaze. Nobody turned into a pillar or anything but it sure made me want to lick her salt block.

'Pyramus is a yorkie,' she said, 'Thisbe is a maltese, and *you* are a fuckball.'

I summoned up all the talent I had in initiating relationships with truly beautiful women which, rather unfortunately, was little.

'That's Mr Fuckball to you,' I said.

She came very close to laughing, I thought, but apparently, decided against it and walked on up to the fifth floor. I heard a door being unlocked, opened, closed, and locked again, kind of like my heart.

Emily once wrote: 'Hope is the thing with feathers that perches in the soul.' Well, hope was flappin' like a November turkey at the moment.

And I damn well didn't want it to come to roost in Winnie Katz's loft.

13

Later that night as I was relaxing in my loft, having a little liquor drink to cut the phlegm, I found myself listening now and then for little yapping noises in the hallway. The yapping noises which had once seemed like somebody was piercing me with white hot needles, I now thought of as music from the baby Jesus's own little Jew's harp. Of course, I don't know what I'd have done had they come to pass my doorway. I thought of several possible opening lines. 'Now which one's the yorkie again?' 'Would you like to come in and meet my puppet head?' 'Did you know you got a bull dyke living across the hall?' At least I hoped she was across the hall.

I poured another shot to celebrate my good luck concerning the girl's geographic desirability. Quite cosmic, I thought, that she lived in the same building. I killed the shot and poured another and things seemed even more cosmic. I got up and put an old recording of *South Pacific* on the victrola. It was the original stage version featuring Mary Martin and Ezio Pinhead. Both of them, of course, had gone to Jesus, but their voices, perfectly mated spiritually, sang to me that night in such a celestial fashion as to make me almost wonder if I'd been along on the trip.

There is a story about Mary Martin that I often tell after four or five drinks. Usually after Mick Brennan's through telling his Falkland War stories. To the common man both of our ramblings would probably seem to be drunken, irrelevant, and frankly, rather tedious. But, as Thomas Jefferson used to say: 'Beware the common man.'

Mary Martin was arriving at LAX some years ago and her son, Larry Hagman, the J.R. of *Dallas* fame, was down to pick her up. Because of the bubble popularity of *Dallas*, swarms of fans were frantically beating their wings around J.R. and almost nobody noticed his frail mother descending from the corridor. As J.R. went forward to meet Mary, some of the crush of his rather boorish fans almost knocked her off her feet. To J.R.'s credit he caught Mary by the arm before she fell, just as Charles Manson reportedly once caught Squeaky Fromme by the arm before she fell. Manson's line at the time had been: 'I'll never let you fall.' J.R.'s line to Mary Martin was: 'Don't worry, mom. It's just showbusiness.'

That night, Mary Martin was to be honored at a gala dinner at the Century Plaza Hotel. Sir Laurence Olivier, Elizabeth Taylor, Cary Grant, Kirk Douglas, and anybody who was anybody on stage and screen were there resplendent in gowns and tuxedos. When Mary Martin was introduced, the crowd of over a thousand stood up as one and gave her an ovation that is said to have lasted for twenty minutes. During this ovation, Mary leaned over to J.R., who was also on the dais, and said: 'No, son, *this* is showbusiness.'

I killed a shot and poured another. If the squirrels were barking in the hallway I never would've known. Ezio Pinhead was transporting me and the cat with 'Some Enchanted Evening.' Of course, Hollywood did not deem Ezio Pinhead or Mary Martin worthy to star in the movie version. That's one reason the original stage version, if you can get it, is so much better than the movie soundtrack. Also, in the movie soundtrack, someone decided, in the song 'Bloody Mary', to take the phrase 'Her skin is tender as DiMaggio's glove' and transform it to 'Her skin is tender as a baseball glove'.

This change may seem minor but it is representative of Hollywood's take on a lot of things. The attitude is un-Italian, and un-

American not to mention unmetrical. Paul Simon says: 'Where have you gone, Joe DiMaggio?' I wasn't sure where the hell he'd gone either. I just wanted to tell him: Don't forget to take your glove.

Around one in the morning I got a call from Downtown Judy. She sounded highly agitato. She'd read a story in the *Daily News*, McGovern no doubt, that Legs had been murdered the night before, and she'd been clever enough to realize that the killing had occurred *after* I'd told her about it at the Corner Bistro. She was coming over now and she wanted answers. I could've used a few myself.

I walked to the espresso machine, stoked it up, and kicked it into high gear. I fed the cat a midnight snack of tuna. The place had gotten a little chilly so I threw on an old purple bathrobe, lit another cigar, and paced a while. I didn't want to have to tell Downtown Judy about Uptown Judy but I didn't really see any easy way to avoid it. If Judy was going to be working with me and the other Village Irregulars she would find out sooner or later but I had a strong suspicion that later would be a lot more unpleasant.

I poured a cup of steaming espresso, noting with some relief that Legs' eyeball didn't appear to be an ingredient in the new batch, and I sat down at the desk with the cat waiting for the inevitable. The seeds we sow. Of course, nothing in life ever looks as good as it does on the seed packet.

'Time to face the music,' I said to the cat. The cat said nothing. It looked upward in the direction of a loud thudding that had begun to emanate from the ceiling of the loft. Winnie Katz's lesbian dance class was apparently conducting, possibly literally, some kind of nocturnal drill. The cat appeared to be rather irritated with the noise. It flicked its tail violently from side to side. If I'd had a tail I'd have been doing that too, trying to decide whether to investigate the Uptown Judy case, search for the Elvis impersonator film, or kill Winnie Katz.

'Don't let it bother you,' I said to the cat finally. 'It's just show-business.'

391

14

By the time Downtown Judy walked into the loft, the only one smiling was the puppet head. Though anger indeed did serve to make Judy very attractive and sensual, it nonetheless wasn't something social workers like to hear. I kept the observation to myself. It was about all I'd be able to keep to myself, I figured. From the look on Judy's face it was past due for me to spit it.

Judy settled herself into the main chair behind the desk and gestured for me to sit in the guest's chair.

'No thanks,' I said, 'I'll pace. Care for an espresso?'

'No thanks,' she said sweetly. 'I'll just rip your heart out with my bare hands if you ever lie to me again like the other night.' Strong words for a social worker, but of course, I had better manners than to mention it. Also, I needed my heart for another decade or two, I thought. Otherwise, what would people have to break?

'There was a very good reason why I told you what I told you,' I said. Now, I thought, if I could just think what the reason was. I took a long time lighting a cigar. Then I walked determinedly over to the espresso machine and began drawing two cups.

'I don't want any espresso – '

'Hold the weddin' now, girl. We've got to have espresso like all good little Turks before we discuss any really important matters of business.'

I made a great pretense of futzing around with the espresso machine and the two cups. Actually, I didn't know if the Turks drank espresso, Turkish coffee or Mr Pibb before discussing important matters of business. If they did, it was about the only thing I admired about them.

When Hitler's aides suggested to him that the world would never let him get away with murdering so many millions of Jews, he'd asked a simple question: 'Who remembers the Armenians?' he'd said.

I did. But the Turks had massacred over a million and a half

Armenian men, women and children, and, like that pesky dental appointment, most of the world had forgotten it.

I handed her the cup of espresso which she received gracelessly. It made me wish for a moment that the Turks would massacre Downtown Judy.

'Look,' she said, 'I know you don't love me like you loved your girlfriend who died in Vancouver – What was her name?'

She'd kissed a windshield at about ninety miles an hour in her Ferrari and now it almost seemed like it'd happened in another lifetime. But those cracks in that windshield that I only saw in my nightmares had reverberated outward in ever-increasing timeless rainy night spider webs until one lazy afternoon they shattered my soul. These days it didn't seem to matter too much what I actually felt or who I really loved.

'Kacey,' I said.

I took a sip of hot bitter espresso. It tasted like tears. There was a distant yapping in the hallway.

'What was that?' asked Judy.

'New neighbor. Has a little dog.' Kacey'd told me about the dog they'd had when she was a child. It's name had been Pepper. Kacey and Pepper'd been together for a long time now.

'I'm your friend,' Judy said. 'Be straight with me. Tell me whatever's going on. Maybe I can help you.'

Maybe New Jersey would melt tomorrow. But her eyes seemed innocent of guile. What the hell.

'Okay,' I said.

I told her about Uptown Judy. About her existence, my relationship with her, her disappearance. Downtown Judy took it well.

'You're a pathetic, slow-leak, sniveling asshole,' she said, setting her espresso down with cold fury on the desk and staring at me as if I were a cockroach.

'Tell me what you really think,' I said. 'Don't hold it back.'

Judy leaned back in the chair and sighed a deep, troubled social worker's sigh. 'How was she?' she asked.

'How was who?'

'Goddammit, how was she?' she screamed, pounding the desk

393

for emphasis. The cat enjoyed this prepubescent display almost as little as I did and jumped off the desk and onto the counter.

'Now you've done it,' I said. 'You've upset the cat.'

'The cat's going to be more upset when she sees your dick flying out the window.'

I puffed on the cigar and tried not to think Freudianly perverse auto-erotic thoughts. I needed to give Judy time to allow her temper to cool down at least to three-digit Celsius. Unconsciously, I walked over to the window, looked out at the street, and tried to collect my thoughts. What *was* she like?

I stood at the window for a long time until, almost in a post-hypnotic trance, I began imagining I'd seen a pale, meteoric after-image of a dick sailing slowly down onto Vandam Street. At that point I turned and walked back to the desk. I told Judy the truth, if there was such an animal. No doubt on the extremely endangered list.

'She was nothing special,' I said, in what I hoped were sooth-ingly sincere tones. 'I didn't love her. It was purely a physical thing. If I hadn't been fucked up as Grogan's goat I probably never would've touched her with a barge pole. Is that good enough?'

A strange expression briefly crossed her features. It could've been something almost akin to disappointment, or possibly simply anger in a quick fade to relief. Whatever it was, it was soon gone and she was in my arms and I was thinking of her in that very sexual, earthy, naturally nasty way that only certain red-heads have the ability to engender in their prey. Like the insect on my bolo tie, I wondered if she'd eat the male after mating.

I went to sleep quite a while later with her taste on my lips and her scent in my nostrils and our bodies melded together. But when I dreamed, I dreamed of Kacey. Then I slept like a spent shell on the beach. If you'd held me to your ear you'd have heard the sound of the Pacific Ocean embracing the night-time California shoreline.

Sometime before dawn a noise awakened me. It sounded like it might've been the cat but instinctively, I didn't think so. Judy was still sleeping soundly beside me. I put on my sarong from Peace Corps days and wandered fuzzily into the living room. The cat was sleeping in her rocker. For the same reason a child looks under his bed, I went to the door of the loft, unlocked it, and opened it slowly.

Standing in the hallway was a pair of red cowboy boots.

15

Business was light at the cop shop that morning. I only had to wait about forty minutes on the wrong side of the pebbled glass to get an audience with Cooperman. I waited in the little foyer with my tall green plastic garbage bag that contained Uptown Judy's tall red cowboy boots. I felt like a rookie bag lady. I didn't know if fingerprints were possible on leather or drag marks could be matched up with the boot heels. I just had the feeling that the point of the whole exercise was to let me know in some mildly Sicilian way that everything was o-v-e-r as far as Uptown Judy was concerned. Someone seemed to be trying to tell me that I was wasting my time hoping to find her alive. At least I didn't have to wait around for the other shoe to drop.

When I did finally get in to see Cooperman he was not excited to see me and even less excited to see the cowboy boots. Fox wandered over from a nearby office and saw the red boots on Cooperman's desk.

'We'll have 'em ready for you on Friday,' he said.

'Look,' I said, 'they're definitely Judy's boots.'

'That's what you say now,' said Fox, 'but could you pick 'em out in a line-up?' Cooperman either laughed or coughed. Whichever it was was equally mirthless. The whole situation was fresh out of mirth.

'Can't you run a lab test on 'em? Match 'em with the drag marks?'

'Fuckin' A – Tweety,' said Cooperman. 'We'll jump right on it. We won't let the little fact that the boss has taken us off the case and given us another one as top priority influence us at all. There ain't even a fuckin' stiff in this case.'

'Gotta have a stiff,' said Fox, smiling.

'Legs didn't look too shabby in the stiff department,' I said. I started to light a cigar.

'Don't smoke that in here,' said Fox. 'We got new regulations. No Jewish cowboys can smoke cigars in homicide. The passive smoke could cloud our thought processes in solvin' all these murders.'

'Anything else you'd like?' said Cooperman. 'Maybe some nice sliced apples and cheese?'

'I'd like to know if Legs had possession of Tom Baker's film on Elvis impersonators. I don't know why but I think these two murders are related. I don't know whether Judy knew Legs but she was friends with Tom Baker, the guy who made the film.'

Cooperman leaned back in his chair. He shook a Gauloises out of a crumpled pack, lit it with his Zippo, and coolly blew the smoke at me. 'I've got a theory on this,' he said, in a tone of deep confidentiality. 'We may be dealing with an Elvis impersonator who killed a Judy impersonator and you're an amateur detective impersonator who may end up worm bait.'

Fox clapped his hands. His eyes lit up with a reptilian glee. 'Then we'll have a stiff!' he said.

Walking home from the Sixth Precinct in a cold, light rain, I pondered the next step in the labyrinth. Bringing the boots to the cops had gone over like a turd in a bottle of Evian water. I should've given them to Ratso. He had a penchant for dead men's shoes. Maybe he'd like dead men's boots. Dead *person's* boots. The politics of it all didn't matter quite as much, of course, when you were dead. When you were a stiff it didn't matter if they called you Ms or His Holiness the Pope, or 'Hey, you!' It wasn't exactly a death wish but I found myself mildly looking forward to going to Jesus, albeit, in a rather offbeat, cerebral way.

My cowboy hat liked the rain and so did I. It was almost beginning to clear my mind and give my soul a Waylon Jennings Bus Shower which is where you splash water from a sink under your armpits and other appropriately funky areas and hope for the best.

The linkage in the two murders was now quite obvious to me. Both victims had known Tom Baker. Both had been shot, though no bullet was recovered at Judy's place to match with the one Legs had caught. Still, it was the same modus operandi – shot with a gun, apartment trashed because someone was looking for something. Also, both victims had been meaning to or attempting to contact yours truly.

Patterns were emerging in my mind that the NYPD was not taking the time to see. How I wished that instead of Cooperman and Fox, I could have dealt with Inspector Maigret of the Paris police. With Inspector Maigret beside me, walking in the rain, hands thrust into the pockets of his ancient frog overcoat that was now coming into fashion in the States, smoking his old pipe, quite possibly upside-down, in the rain – with Maigret beside me, the two of us could seine the frantic human kaleidoscope of the city – any city, no matter how big or cold or busy; we could find the time to make things rhyme – little things that one day would hang the murderer from a gibbet.

Now I felt Maigret walking with me. I could not see his face – no one ever has – but I could feel his mind. Gravely, with deep humanity, it was processing permutations and possibilities that computers could only dream of. Maigret was an expert in human nature. Human nature was the skeleton key to open the gates of the white castle, to reveal the secrets in the blackest mind.

Maigret left me at the freight elevator. He wandered out onto Vandam Street and vanished into smoke and rain. I knew what I had to do. It was time to forget about technicians, ballistics labs, beakers of blood. It was time to put on my lobster bib and call a formal meeting of the Village Irregulars.

16

At two o'clock the following afternoon I addressed the multitudes who stood assembled in my loft. I intoned the words of Wavy Gravy: 'Mistakes are good. We like mistakes. They mean we're human.'

'Cut the shit, mate,' said Mick Brennan. 'Tell us what we're here for.'

'If you'll be quiet and give him a chance,' said Downtown Judy rather stridently, 'he'll try to tell you.'

From the forest of Guinness bottles near the neighborhood of where McGovern and Brennan were sitting, the word 'cunt' was heard to be muttered rather distinctly. Judy visibly tensed; nonetheless it did seem to have the rather gratifying effect of having her pull her lips together.

'Pardon the Shakespeare,' I said, pouring myself a medicinal shot of Jameson's.

Rambam looked on in bored amusement from near the doorway. As a private investigator, he was the only one in the room with even the nuance of any professional training in the field, and it was not clear how he would suss out the little scenario. I wanted to draw him in because, unorthodox and both-sides-of-the-law as he was, if things got ugly we'd certainly need him.

Pete Myers had catered the affair from his gourmet British food shop, if there is such a thing, Myers of Keswick on Hudson Street. He'd laid out a fine spread of pork pies, pasties, mashers, bashers, other things with weird names, and sausages that tasted killer bee but you didn't want to ask too many questions about them. Ratso, of course, had established squatter's rights in a chair adjacent to the Myers of Keswick table. Myers himself was deftly slicing a beautiful chunk of red roast beef almost as large as McGovern's head.

'Let's take it from the top,' said Ratso. 'Tell it from the beginning. We all need to be on the same wavelength.'

'Good luck,' I heard Rambam mutter from the doorway, and I began my recounting of the facts as I knew them. Not surprisingly, it didn't take very long.

'In summing up,' I said, 'we want to find the killer of Judy and Legs and find the Bakerman's missing film about Elvis impersonators. I'm pretty well convinced that when we find one we'll find the other.'

'Got another pork pie over there, mate?' Brennan called out.

'Ratso ate all of them,' said Myers.

'Rotten luck,' Brennan said.

'Look,' said McGovern, 'I've got a deadline here. Let's go ahead and get a division of labor going that's a little more effectual than the way we divided up the pork pies.'

Ratso, looking sated and rather sullen, nonetheless retorted gamely. 'These fuckin' pork pies have been sitting here for over two and a half hours. Irish people like to drink, Jewish people like to eat. I don't know what British people like to do.' At this last, Ratso stared pointedly in Brennan's direction.

'We like to complain about Irish people and Jewish people,' said Brennan. 'Like what's a Jew doing eating pork?'

'Anti-semitism rears its ugly head,' said Ratso with an almost Gandhi-like dignity.

'Boys!' said Judy sharply. 'You all have various talents and skills. We'll need your cooperation to get to the bottom of this. McGovern's a fine, experienced reporter, Mick is an internationally recognized photographer – '

'Yeah,' said Ratso. 'He can keep the scrapbook.'

'You can keep your mouth shut, mate,' said Brennan. For every pork pie Ratso had scarfed, Brennan had poured a bottle of Guinness down his neck. If there'd been an entry in the Guinness Book of Records for drinking Guinness, Brennan was in the hunt.

'Rambam is a registered private investigator,' Judy continued. 'I'm sure he'll be helpful.' Rambam lifted a glass of whatever he was drinking in a mock toast to the assembled group.

'Your immediate death,' he said. Then he took a drink, swallowed, and belched rather loudly. He didn't say anything else but his eyes roved menacingly around the circle of faces. It did not appear from his demeanor that he would be as helpful as Judy had hoped.

'And Ratso,' said Judy. There was an uncomfortable pause as she struggled to pinpoint what it was that Ratso would do to help the group. Ratso looked crestfallen and I felt it was time to take the baton from Judy if possible.

'Ratso's already been very helpful to me,' I said. 'He knew Tom Baker well, as all of you did, and he's provided me with some interesting insights. If any of you remember anything else Baker did or something he said to you that might shed some light on

399

these mysterious matters, please don't fail to call it to my attention in the arduous days ahead.'

'What's she gonna do?' Brennan inquired loudly of the Guinness bottle sitting in front of his nose.

'Judy's a trained social worker who'll be working to keep the rest of us from de-balling each other. She'll be working closely with me.'

'Very closely,' said McGovern. He laughed his loud, almost obscene Irish laugh, which always seemed a little too loud for indoor use.

'Okay,' I said. The group was starting to get a little restless, not to say stultifyingly bored. 'McGovern, you research the relationship between Judy and her dad, Don Sepulveda. Anything you find on him will be helpful. Mick, you stay tuned. We're going to need your services before this is over.'

'I won't leave the city,' slurred Brennan.

'Ratso,' I continued. 'You keep digging on the little Elvis research project we discussed earlier. Give Hitler, Jesus, and Bob Dylan a rest. Concentrate on Elvis.'

'I'll try to find some information on Elvis's last British tour,' said Ratso.

'Elvis never played the UK, mate,' said Brennan.

'I know that,' said Ratso. 'He was probably afraid he'd run into your ass.'

'And Judy,' I said, 'I'd like to thank you for taking copious notes on this meeting. If you'll stick around afterwards I have something in mind for you.' McGovern laughed again, louder, if possible, than before. Judy looked down at the big chief tablet I'd given her which had a few notations on it that looked like they'd been written by a spider. She smiled bravely.

'And finally,' I said, 'Rambam. Do you have any last words for us?' Everyone looked at Rambam who walked slowly around the counter and approached the group. He was dressed in suit and tie, possibly over-dressed for the occasion, especially when compared to Ratso who seemed to be wearing Sonny Bono rejects. Rambam assumed the demeanor of one who was about to address a group of killer Kiwanians.

'I'm going to take our esteemed leader on a building sweep tomorrow – '

'He doesn't do windows,' said Ratso.

Rambam continued smoothly. ' – Of the two murder sites. For the rest of you. There is a killer out there. We don't know who it is. But very soon he'll start to know who we are. The cops won't help us on this and they sure aren't going to save our ass. So be forewarned.'

Rambam fixed the little group with a cold eye. 'You may be the Village Irregulars, but this is some dangerous shit.' He paused and straightened his tie for dramatic effect. Everyone waited.

'Don't think you can just reach for the Metamucil,' he said.

17

If Cinderella thought sweeping a building was tedious she should've tried working with Rambam. He worried the occupants of Uptown Judy's apartment house like the Hound of the Baskervilles gnawing on Yorick's skull and then some. Many of them no doubt were wishing they'd seen or heard something just to get Rambam's foot out of their doorway.

'They didn't waste any time renting out Judy's apartment,' I said to Rambam as we reached the third floor.

'Landlords love to cut through those scene-of-the-crime banners like politicians enjoy snipping ceremonial ribbons. Head 'em up. Move 'em out. In the language of your people.'

'Jesus Christ, Rambam, we're not even sure Uptown Judy's dead.'

Rambam gave me a look that would've withered a flower pressed in a book containing the poetry of John Keats. '*Some* of us aren't sure,' he said.

He handed me a walkie-talkie and knocked on Judy's door. Judy didn't answer. Nobody else did either.

'New tenant's probably out buying a throw rug to cover the drag marks,' said Rambam with a little smile. We walked over to the apartment to the left of Judy's and Rambam knocked again.

'Who is it?' came a voice that sounded like an inebriated macaw.

'Investigators,' said Rambam.

'What do you want?' cried the voice.

'To investigate,' said Rambam.

I held my walkie-talkie and waited. A lock clicked on the other side of the door. Then another lock.

Rambam leaned toward me and said softly: 'White, early sixties, two hundred pounder, wearing floral houserobe that hasn't been washed in twenty years.'

A chain was unlatched from inside the door and then it opened. Even through a thin veil of cigar smoke I could smell the fetid creature. She bore an uncanny resemblance to Rambam's description except that there were no flowers on the bathrobe. Phlegm-colored goldfish appeared to be swimming in its massive and murky folds, fighting like hell not to go belly-up.

'Wait one minnow,' I said. 'Something's fishy.'

'It's him what done it,' she shouted, pointing across the hallway to the apartment directly opposite hers.

'Him what done what?' Rambam inquired. The woman's whole apartment smelled like dying goldfish. I thought very briefly of Dale Haufrect, the childhood neighbor who'd once killed my gold-fish and taught me my first lesson in mortality. Dead creatures stay dead. I thought of Judy's red cowboy boots standing at the front door of my loft. Could they not conceivably indicate that Judy was alive just as well as dead? On the other hand, or foot in this case, if she were alive, wouldn't it be more likely that she would be in them? Instead of rotting like a dead goldfish some-where in the East River?

'It's him and his goddamn microwave what's puttin' these water blisters on my nose,' said the woman.

Even Rambam didn't have an immediate answer for that one. He did, however, lean slightly closer to her nose to observe that it did, indeed, contain a rather unsavory network of water blisters.

'Have you thought about taking some tinfoil and making a little shield and wearing it on your nose?' Rambam said. Now we were getting somewhere, I thought.

'That might be a good idea,' the woman told Rambam. I told him it might be a good idea if we tried another apartment.

Before we departed, Rambam asked the woman at last about the night in question. She maintained adamantly that she had seen nothing unusual that night and had heard nothing from the apartment next door.

'Curious,' said Rambam, as we walked past Judy's former home and approached the apartment to its immediate right.

'Not to say unpleasant,' I added. I'd long known New Yorkers had a reputation for being somewhat eccentric, but the water-blister woman was definitely out where the buses don't run.

Rambam knocked on the door of the other bookend to Judy's place. As he waited for an answer he said: 'You did say Cooperman told you there'd been a call to 911 about a shot having been fired?'

'Ten-four,' I said into the non-functional walkie-talkie, just as the door opened and a slight white male in a pastel-colored floral kimono squinted out at the two of us.

'Hi,' he said, with a smile that was far too friendly for a New York heterosexual.

'There's my floral houserobe,' said Rambam, with a slight hint of triumph in his voice.

'You can have it if you want it,' said its owner invitingly. 'Why don't you guys come inside for some banana bread and brie? But leave that smelly cigar in the hall.' He wrinkled his nose in an exaggerated fashion that might've been sexy if he'd been a pretty young girl from Texas. Hell, maybe he was a pretty young girl from Texas.

'Can't leave the cigar in the hall,' I said. 'I might have an anxiety attack.'

He scrunched-up his nose again. 'Well, why don't *you* come in and let your friend go smoke his big ol' smelly cigar somewhere else?'

'We're investigators,' said Rambam. 'We've got to do the whole building.'

The guy's face lit up. 'If you're gonna do the whole building, why not start right here!'

'That's not what I meant,' said Rambam. 'We want to know if you noticed anything – loud noises, a gunshot, sounds of a struggle, any strange men – having to do with the apartment next door earlier in the week.' Rambam gestured with his head toward Judy's flat in an effort to help the guy remember.

' – Any strange men?' the guy asked himself out loud. The guy obviously was stymied. He was shaking his head rather wistfully either indicating he'd seen and heard nothing or that he wished he had so Rambam would come inside his apartment.

He kept shaking his head, pursing his lips, and occasionally, glancing over at me and wrinkling his nose. He was starting to get up my sleeve.

'Just the facts, ma'am,' I said.

Rambam looked at me with a gaze of cool amusement, then ran it all down with the guy again, coming up empty just as before.

'I hope you'll come back when you're through investigating. Maybe I'll remember something,' he teased.

'Nice housecoat,' said Rambam, as we moved on to the next apartment and knocked on the door.

Hours later, in a trendy little bar along Third Avenue, Rambam and I were dusting off some of the cinders from the building sweep. I was having a Vodka McGovern and Rambam was sipping the most arcane and expensive cognac in the house. Rambam was in a slightly more positive and optimistic frame of mind than I was. So were Kafka and Edgar Allan Poe.

'Jesus Christ,' I said. 'Now I can truly empathize with Jehovah's Witnesses.'

'Don't get too fucked-up. We still got to sweep Legs' building.'

'But what the hell are we accomplishing? Nobody claims to have seen or heard a thing. Maybe everybody in the building's autistic.'

'This is what most detective work is all about. But it's very interesting to me that none of the people we interviewed seems to remember anything pertinent about the night in question.'

'None of the people we interviewed would've remembered the Hindenburg if it fell on their head.'

'That's true,' said Rambam, offering me a sip of his drink. It was the kind of cognac that was so expensive it smelled like somebody's feet. It didn't taste too bad but after two Vodka McGoverns bile doesn't taste too bad.

'The people in that building remind me of that dog in the Sher-lock Holmes story,' said Rambam.

'Oh yeah, I know the one. You mean that rottweiler that Sher-lock's brother Mycroft tried to command to have sexual relations with Dr Watson?'

Rambam laughed. 'No,' he said. 'I was thinking of the time Sherlock solved the mystery because of the clue of the dog that didn't bark.'

'You know what I think?'

'Of course I do but tell me anyway.'

'Give me another sip of that Louis the whatever-the-fuck-it-is and I'll tell you.'

'It's Louis the Thirteenth and it's only about sixty dollars a glass but help yourself.'

I took a healthy swallow this time. It did taste better than bile. I took another swallow and Rambam grabbed his appropriately stemmed glass back from my hand.

'So what the fuck do you think?' he said.

'I think that same dog might've called 911.'

18

The occupants of Legs' building in the Village were equally tedious but slightly more forthcoming than the ones in Judy's building. Not that Legs or Judy gave a damn. Of course, in Legs' case many had seen the body being carried out by the coroner's men and most had read accounts of the murder in the papers. In Judy's case, they were still wearing little tinfoil shields on their noses. In both loci it hadn't been a banner day for building sweeps.

'Maybe we should've been chimney sweeps,' I said to Rambam, as we hauled ass out of the building with the super threatening to call the cops.

'Wait a minute,' said Rambam in the little foyer. 'What's this?'

'Whatever it is I'm sure it'll still be here when we come back in the year 2007.'

Rambam was looking at the row of rusty mailboxes built into the wall like homes for Lilliputian cliff-dwellers. He took something out of his pocket that looked like a putty knife.

'Why don't you just loiter in the lobby for a while?' said Rambam.

'This *is* the lobby,' I said. I looked around nervously for the super but he seemed to have blipped off the screen. Probably had to get back to *Barnaby Jones*.

'Why don't you loiter in that lesbian bar across the street. This shouldn't take long. Looks like the dear departed received some recent correspondence that the NYPD hasn't monitored too carefully.'

'Hard to believe.' I watched Rambam begin to jimmy with the mailbox. 'I can't loiter in that lesbian bar across the street. I tried one night and they wouldn't let me in.'

'Seems like you've got a good discrimination suit you could bring against them. "Kinky Friedman vs The Cubby Hole". You should talk to Wolf Nachman. He's the greatest lawyer in the world.'

'I'd like to talk to you about hurrying up with that fucking putty knife.'

At that moment a middle-aged guy, kind of non-descript for New York, came in the front door and started futzing with his own mailbox about four feet away from Rambam. Rambam turned his body slightly in an effort to hide the putty knife, but the guy hardly noticed. He looked like an accountant or serial killer-type. Definitely one of the service industries.

'One of these days they'll fix these mailboxes,' Rambam said to the guy. I laughed in a good-natured way and wished the lesbians would've let me loiter in the bar across the street.

The guy paid no attention to me or Rambam. Just got his mail and went upstairs.

'That's one advantage New York's got over everywhere else,' said Rambam. 'Nobody cares enough to be nosy.'

'Yeah,' I said. 'It's kind of refreshing, isn't it?'

Rambam opened the box, removed a small stack of letters and bills, and placed them in my hand.

'Just remember,' he said, 'you didn't see me do this.' He folded the putty knife and put it back in his pocket.

'Do what?' I said.

A short while later, loitering in the lobby of my own building, waiting for the doors of the freight elevator to open, I heard familiar yapping noises echoing inside the elevator shaft. When the door finally opened, my tall blonde vision was standing eye-to-eye with my cowboy hat.

'Hi, Pyramus, hi, Thisbe,' I said to the yorkie and the maltese. I paused and lit a cigar for dramatic effect. Then I said: 'By the way, I forgot to ask what your name was.'

'Stephanie DuPont. And now I say, "And what's your name?" '

'And now I say "It's Richard Kinky 'Big Dick' Friedman".' I moved into the elevator and took a few puffs on the cigar. 'My close friends call me Fuckball,' I said.

When she was standing safely in the lobby away from the cigar smoke she said: 'I'll just call you Dick.'

'Look,' I said, 'I'm very busy right now, but seeing as we're neighbors and all, why don't you come down sometime. Have a little liquor drink to cut the phlegm.'

She stared at me as if I were an out-patient.

'Banana bread and brie?' I suggested.

'You don't smoke that cigar in your loft, do you . . . Dick?' I liked the little emphasis she placed on the dick.

'No, of course not,' I said. 'I only smoke in elevators. I'm a thoughtful American.'

'Maybe I'll come down sometime,' she said. 'But *I'll* come down to see *you*. I don't want to walk out of my apartment some day and find you licking my door frame.'

'Don't go giving me ideas,' I said, as the elevator doors closed inexorably between us.

Moments later, still basking in reflected beauty, the cat and I were at my desk like two employees routinely working the dead letter department. Legs had six letters which wasn't bad for a dead man. Of course, most of them were bills.

'Con Ed's gonna have a hell of a time collecting on this one,' I said to the cat.

The cat was not amused. While cats sometimes seem capable of great coldness, not to say cruelty, they have a rather rigid morality when it comes to appreciating attempts at humor about the recently deceased. In fact, cats, to the best of my knowledge, appear to have no sense of humor at all. Unless, of course, you want to count the time the cat took a Nixon in one of Ratso's red antique shoes that had once belonged to a dead man. Ratso was not in the shoe at the time. Neither was the dead man.

'Ah,' I said, as I puffed the cigar and continued the morbid task, 'an invitation to an opening of what looks like a new and very coochi-poochi-boomalini restaurant.'

The cat looked mildly impressed. Either that, or I'd forgotten to feed her today.

'It says "Coat and tie required". Well, Legs certainly ought to meet that prerequisite. What else have we got here. Ah, a personal letter in a feminine hand.'

I showed the letter to the cat. The cat half closed her eyes, a sure sign of agreement, communication, or, possibly, ennui. It crossed my desk that at this moment there were, very probably, men masturbating in mental hospitals who, in their quite ample spare time, showed letters to cats. This dark thought did not unduly distress me. Many fine and talented people have hung their hats and, occasionally, themselves, in mental hospitals. Van Gogh died in one. Countless Zhivago-like Russians have wasted away in wig city over the years, ending their lives showing letters to cats. Nothing wrong with that. If they'd had mental hospitals in biblical times they'd probably have put Jesus in one and told him he had a Christ complex. Like the Lady of Shalott, I was 'half in love with madness.'

The cat nodded out, but I was still flicking my tail.

I opened the letter.

Reading a personal letter to a dead man is not something you want to do every day. Most of the time it's depressing enough just reading personal letters addressed to yourself.

'Dear Legs,' the letter began.

'It is difficult for me to tell you this but I don't think we should see each other again.'

Great. I took a puff on the cigar and poured a tall shot of Jameson's into the bullhorn. I killed the shot, scanned the letter for any clue to Legs' murder, then placed it under the cigar humidor in the shape of Sherlock Holmes's head. Sherlock himself had said: 'I have never loved.' Maybe that was the way to go. It was certainly healthier to abstain from love altogether than to try to encourage a rottweiler to hose Dr Watson. There are many who feel that both of the Holmes brothers probably should've been in a mental hospital, along with Jesus, Van Gogh, and the woman who keeps trying to break into David Letterman's house.

I opened the last envelope. Bingo.

It was a receipt signed by somebody at the Joe Franklin Show. It said they'd received the film Legs had sent them and were taking it under review. It said of course he understood the film would not be returned.

'We'll see,' I said.

The cat sat up. Then she opened one conspiratorial green eye. Then she vomited on my desk.

19

'Yes,' said Ratso, with some little pride, 'I have been on the Joe Franklin Show a great many times.' He took a large bite of the big hairy steak on the platter before him.

'In fact,' I said, 'isn't it true that you've appeared on the show more times than anyone else?'

Wooing Ratso by taking him to the Derby Steak House was one of the things you sometimes had to do if you wanted to be a successful little detective. He was close with Joe Franklin and he seemed like he might make a perfect vehicle for goniffing the film. But I had to play my cards carefully.

'That is not technically true,' said Ratso between mouthfuls. 'There are two other people, according to Joe himself, who've been on the show more times than I have.'

'You're kidding! Who are they?' I said, exhibiting a good deal more interest in the subject than I felt.

'Guess.'

'Foghorn Leghorn and Ezio Pinhead,' I said, somewhat irritably.

'You're close. It's Georgie Jessel and Otto Preminger.'

'Ah, well.' I tried some of the sliced steak with Colman's hot British mustard. Killer bee.

'Do you think Joe would have you on the show again anytime soon?'

'Well, that's hard to say,' said Ratso, cutting his steak importantly. 'He certainly won't be having Georgie or Otto on anytime soon.'

'Look,' I said, 'I'll put it on a bumper-sticker for you. I think Joe Franklin has a copy of Tom Baker's documentary on Elvis impersonators. I think there must be something in that film that brought about the murder of Legs and Uptown Judy.'

'Jesus,' said Ratso.

'I'll see your Jesus,' I said, 'and raise you a Peter.'

'Well, once they've formally accepted it, a television show will only return something to the party that submitted it.'

'That may be a little difficult in this case,' I said. 'Legs sent the film to Franklin.'

'I'm sure the show's got some kind of policy protecting it that would make it tough for anyone to obtain the film from Joe. Now that Legs and Baker are dead it may soon become very valuable or sought after.'

'It's very sought after right now, numb-nuts. I want that film.' I made a theatrical gesture with my fork toward Ratso. He parried neatly with his knife.

'Look, I can talk to Joe but I doubt if he'll let it go. I wouldn't, in his shoes.'

'Joe's pretty o-l-d. You'll probably be wearing his shoes fairly soon.'

We both took a little sambuca break at this point to calm down and think things over. Ratso adjusted his coonskin cap with the little eyes of the animal pathetically sewn shut. It was not dissimilar to the way many Americans went through their lives, I thought. I'd remember to keep my own orbs wide' open just in case anything besides Ratso's steak started to get hairy.

'There is a way you can help,' I said, finally. 'And it'll go a long way toward getting you into the Village Irregulars' Hall of Fame.'

'Whoopee,' said Ratso, with very little discernible enthusiasm.

'You go on the show as a guest and the rest of us will come along as part of that small, informal studio audience he always has. While you're on the show with Joe, his producers and crew – '

' – You'll take the film.'

'Correctimundo.'

Ratso hesitated. Then he said: 'I'll do it. But if Joe finds out I was part of this, I'll never be on the show again.'

'He won't find out,' I said. 'But in the unlikely possibility that he does, at least some good luck will come out of it.'

'What's that?'

'Georgie Jessel and Otto Preminger will finally be able to rest in peace.'

Later that night, Downtown Judy and I strolled the cold, beautiful, half-deserted streets of Little Italy where I could always hear tinny Italian music playing whether it actually was or not. Judy wanted a cappucino, a cannoli, and any new developments that the Village Irregulars had uncovered and, in their petty male chauvinist fashion, hadn't thought to share with her. I wanted about six more sambucas.

'You know, Judy,' I said, as we passed a display of Mussolini T-shirts, 'you should think of it as an honor to be the first woman accepted into an organization that has always been exclusively male.'

'Big fucking deal,' she said.

'That's hardly the spirit.'

'But how can I help if I don't know what's going on?'

'You know everything the rest of us know which, unfortunately, isn't a hell of a lot.'

As we walked, I filled her in on the events of the day, even down to the water blisters on the woman's nose at Uptown Judy's apartment building. As I talked, a clearer picture was emerging in my own mind as well. The Uptown Judy case and the Legs case were hanging together by the merest piece of spit. All they had in common was the eerie way both their places had been torn apart, the fact that they'd both wanted to get in touch with me, and the certainty that they'd both known Tom Baker. It wasn't much but, as I told Judy about the Joe Franklin Show scenario, I knew beyond a doubt that I had to get hold of that missing Elvis film.

'It's not only our best lead,' I said. 'It's our only lead.'

We went to a little coffee shop with outdoor tables even though the night was cold. The building next to it was painted red, white, and green like the Italian flag.

'Did you ever take *her* here?' Judy asked. Even in death, Uptown Judy was making her presence known.

'No,' I said. 'But I imagine her father might've walked with her in these streets when she was a child.'

Downtown Judy shuddered involuntarily.

'Cold?' I asked.

'No,' she said, sipping her cappucino, 'I was just thinking what it must've been like having a father like that. Repairing your bicycle in the backyard with all that blood on his hands and you don't even know it.'

'Fixing your hopscotch games,' I said.

Judy did not laugh. She merely stared down into her cappucino. I tossed down my sambuca and ordered another as I chewed thoughtfully on the coffee beans.

'You know,' I said, 'they're both outside of the mortal equation now. Uptown Judy's gone and her father, Don Sepulveda, was hit by one of the other families in what they tried to pass off as a "boating accident" in the Caribbean five years ago. Supposedly, there was enough power behind the explosion to destroy a small city.'

'No one can escape his or her destiny,' said Judy quietly to the capuccino cup.

'You lives by the watermelon, you dies by the watermelon,' I said.

I drank some more sambuca. If everybody drank enough sambuca we could probably solve all the major problems of the world. Religious conflicts and ethnic violence would no doubt disappear. National boundaries would disintegrate and the world would at last realize John Lennon's dream in the song 'Imagine'. Such is the power of sambuca. Of course, before all this happened, it might be a good idea, just in case, to buy up a large quantity of coffee bean futures.

'So you seem to think,' said Judy, 'that Judy was caught in the same web of the past that finally did in her father.'

'Without a doubt,' I said. 'Regardless of her innocence. It's very difficult to truly escape the bonds of who you are. God knows, I've tried by taking Peruvian marching powder – '

' – Until you had to stop because Bob Marley fell out of your left nostril,' Judy said, repeating a line of mine in a rather tiresome impersonation of a Texas drawl.

'I knew drugs weren't the answer. I just had to find out for myself. As old Slim used to say back on the ranch: "You gotta find what you like and let it kill you." '

I asked Judy if she'd like to try a sambuca but she passed. So I ordered myself another sambuca and another cappucino for 'my lady' as Wayne Newton would've said.

'You don't try sambuca,' I said, 'you stand in the way of global harmony.' Judy looked at me as if my cowboy hat had exploded. I was feeling very peaceful and wise but I could already envision some problems. Sambuca hangovers causing border skirmishes, civil wars in small nations, things like that. Maybe the world needed a little hair of the dog that bit it.

'Well,' said Judy, 'at least I prefer the kind of asshole you are on sambuca to the kind of asshole you used to be on the other stuff. Sometimes, even when we were in bed together, you acted like you didn't even know who you were with.'

'After cave trip, everybody happy – Burma Shave.'

Downtown Judy made a little moue of distaste. She took a rather desultory sip of cappucino. I lit a cigar and let the sambuca do the talking.

'Once, many years ago, when I was in the Peace Corps in

413

Borneo, I spent several months in a place where so-called civilized life couldn't touch me. I lived among the Punan tribesmen, a nomadic group of pygmies who roamed the dark heart of the jungle eating monkey brains and killing wild boar with blow pipes. I felt at peace within the power of their primitivity.

'Once every twenty years or so a western concept deflected upon this tribe like an errant moonbeam looking for a lover. Their only contact with western ideas of any sort had come through the rare interlude with the lost missionary or the rogue mercenary. The only English words that created even a glint of recognition in their brown eyes of innocence were Elvis, Jesus, and Coca-Cola.'

'Elvis, Jesus, and Coca-Cola,' said Downtown Judy.

'Yeah. Sort of a timeless trinity. Like the Old Man, the Boy, and the Spook. I mean, Michael Jackson, Mickey Mouse, and Madonna might be nipping at their heels, but Elvis, Jesus, and Coca-Cola will always be the big three.'

I took another healthy slug of sambuca. Judy stared thoughtfully into the endless Italian night.

'There are, no doubt,' I said, 'other primitive enclaves on this planet, possibly in the outback of Australia, in New Guinea, in the secret hearts of Africa and South America. But these peoples and places are as fragile and ephemeral as a smile in childhood. Yet they do exist. Cultural and spiritual oases where you may truly escape what we have come to think of as the world. Like taking a walk down Yesterday Street. Dancing to music that was written and recorded before you were born. In these places you are safe from harm and sheltered from sorrow.

'If you ever find one of these places, and then leave it, as I have done, you may spend the rest of your life with the better part of your soul living in the shadow of regret.'

Downtown Judy looked across the little table at me with a new-found sparkle in her eyes.

'I'm going with you to the Joe Franklin Show,' she said.

20

The next day was a busy one around 199B Vandam. Ten thousand garbage trucks came grinding through the most hideous hangover I'd ever had in my life.

'To hell with global harmony,' I said to the cat. 'I'll never drink that shit again.' The cat began chasing a cockroach around the loft, leaping from place to place, and doing the whirling dervish routine which was not pleasing to me or my hangover.

I put on my old purple bathrobe and my mental hospital slippers, swallowed about seven St Joseph's baby aspirins from what looked like one of those antique, purple-colored bottles you find at old dump sites, kicked the espresso machine into high gear, and waited for something to happen. At least I ought to get a little buzz, I figured.

The bottle was purple, the robe was purple, the sky was purple, and I was purple. I was also having some pretty unpleasant problems in my gray matter department. I now thought I knew what went on in the mind of an Elvis impersonator.

I poured an espresso and my hands trembled like an alcoholic surgeon's in a B movie. The first sip burned my upper lip rather severely. I put the cup down on the desk and did my best to light a cigar. The lesbian dance class in the loft above me chose this moment to begin a marathon number somewhat reminiscent in length to the choreography in 'They Shoot Horses, Don't They?' I had six million things to do and all I could remember was to feed the cat.

I fed the cat.

The business day began at about 11:45 Jewish Standard Time, when the two red phones on either side of my desk began ringing urgently. I took a few preparatory puffs on my cigar and dumped the ash into the cup which had recently held my third espresso. Cup number four I'd just pour in over the top and drink it ashes and all. I've heard it makes you leap sideways.

I picked up the blower on the left. It was the unmistakable New York-inflected voice of Ratso, which never really sounded right unless it had subway trains and sirens in the background studio mix. This time he had the works going for him including what sounded like a guy breaking up the street with the steam drill that tried to beat John Henry. All the sounds seemed to be emanating from a locus about four inches from Ratso's nose.

'Kinkstah!' shouted Ratso. 'Kinkstah!'

'What hath God wrought?' I said.

'God's wrought me a slot on the Joe Franklin Show! One of the guests suddenly cancelled for tomorrow night!'

'Could you please modulate your voice?' I felt like I'd been recently crucified. Ratso, not quite hearing me correctly, began speaking in a louder, more piercing voice.

'One of the guests suddenly cancelled for tomorrow night!' I briefly held the blower away from my left lobe.

'Did you hear what I said?' shouted Ratso.

'Where the hell are you?' I said, in the barely controlled monotone of a seriously ill person.

'I'm right down the street. I can see your cat in the window.'

I looked to the window and, indeed, the cat did appear to be staring with some distaste at what I could only assume to be either Ratso or a Sonny Bono impersonator.

'Come on over,' I said, 'and bring a large iceberg for my forehead.'

By the time I hung up the blower I was about ready to swoon. I poured a fourth espresso over the cigar ashes and took a healthy slurp. Suddenly, the lesbian dance class went silent. A little man somewhere in my cranium hit a mute button and my headache went away. I took another sip. The sun came out over the city. I felt like the guy who'd discovered penicillin. The absence of pain is a truly wonderful feeling, unless, of course, you happen to be a masochist.

By the time Ratso walked in the door I was wearing a smile almost as big as the one on the puppet head.

'Ratso, my lad,' I said, 'the cat and I welcome you to our airy, spacious loft.' Spacious it may have been, but a thick layer of cigar smoke hung over the place like Mexico City on a bad day and geological formations of unchanged cat litter didn't help the ol' beezer much either. The place smelled as if it couldn't decide whether it wanted to be a hospital or a whorehouse.

'That fucking cat never liked me and never will,' said Ratso. This was undoubtedly true, but the moment called for a diplomatic reply.

'Give her time, Ratso. She'll warm up to you.'

Ratso looked dubiously at the cat. The cat gave him a little mew of distaste.

I poured Ratso an espresso, without cigar ash, and placed him in the chair near the desk.

'I just thought of something,' he said. 'What am I going to do on the Joe Franklin Show?'

'You could pull out your penis like Jim Morrison,' I said.

'Seriously,' said Ratso, as he got up and walked over to the refrigerator, 'the last five times I've been on the show I've talked about my book, *On The Road With Bob Dylan*. Now the producer tells me he wants me to talk about some new project.' Ratso reached into the refrigerator and came out with a to-go order of spare ribs and black bean sauce that had been left over from the Ming Dynasty.

'Well,' I said, 'you can't blame the producer for not wanting a talk show guest who's trapped like an insect in amber.'

'I'll think of something,' said Ratso, as he dug into the culinary artifact with a nearby fork.

'How about "How to Dress for Success?" ' I said.

21

After I'd gotten Ratso saddled up and headed north, a rather laborious task, I finally found myself with some time alone to think. I lit a fresh cigar and paced purposefully around the loft a bit. Some fairly cohesive vines were beginning to grow together in my mind. It was time to swing on one of them. I was looking at the Shroud of Turin and I wasn't sure if there was a face on it or not. When I did see the face, it wasn't Jesus. It was Elvis.

I thought about a story McGovern had covered several years before, about a fourteen-year-old girl, a leukemia victim, who'd

417

died somewhere in Kentucky. Her family and the hospital staff were at her side when she died. They were dumbfounded by her last words: 'Here comes Elvis.'

Tom Baker died as he was in the process of finishing a film on Elvis impersonators. Had he wrapped the film before his death? I couldn't ask him. Legs had worked on the film with him as his assistant. Couldn't ask Legs either.

It was well known that the Bakerman had been casual friends with Uptown Judy. His female admirers were legion. Could Tom and Judy have been dancing a good bit closer than anyone suspected? Couldn't ask Tom. Couldn't ask Judy.

Did Judy ever meet Legs? Couldn't ask Judy. Couldn't ask Legs.

There was no evidence of foul play in Baker's death, but then no one was looking for foul play. He was making an Elvis film and had mentioned to Ratso that he was afraid he'd end up meeting Elvis and he did. Legs was helping Baker with the documentary. He ended up meeting Elvis, too. Could either of them have shown the film or talked about the film with Uptown Judy? Even assuming they had, what then? What was it about Elvis or a flock of pathetic impersonators that could set in motion the deaths of three people? Maybe it was far-fetched. Maybe it strained logic. But it was all I had.

I sat down at the desk and laid the cigar gently in the ashtray. I poured a strong portion of Jameson's into the bull horn and poured the bull horn down my neck. I looked at the cat across the darkening, desperate afternoon.

'Here comes Elvis,' I said.

On an impulse, I called the cop shop and, after a fairly interminable wait, got Fox on the blower.

'Tex,' said Fox, 'I'm glad you called.'

'You are?' I said warily.

'Yeah. As you probably know we got a light workload around here and all, and we had a little extra time to go over some of the details of the case of your girlfriend that disappeared. We think we've got a good theory as to what occurred.'

'What's your theory, sergeant?' I said. I lit an old half-smoked cigar and waited.

'Our theory,' said Fox, 'is that she clicked her red boots together three times and went back to Kansas.'

Fox laughed until it sounded like he would choke to death. He recovered, however, and, in a voice that was void of all mirth said: 'Boots are in the property locker. You can pick 'em up.'

'Look, sergeant,' I said, hiding my irritation, 'I don't have a photo of Judy. Did you happen to come up with one I could have?'

'We could get one if we were on the case, but we ain't on the case. And there were no photos of her in the apartment.'

'You don't find that strange?' I said.

'In this town?' said Fox, and he hung up.

I poured out another shot of Jameson's and with some little pain cast my mind back to the foggy, sordid, almost sepia nights in Uptown Judy's apartment. At least I thought they were sordid. It was hard to tell. It was like dreaming about a dream. But I knew I remembered photographs. Photographs on the table. Shots of Judy in some tropical place. Photos on the dresser. On the book shelves, too, I thought. Framed photographs of Judy and her friends and lovers and family. Of course, I hadn't known that her family was family. But that notwithstanding, it was passingly strange. Could I have been so totally ripped that I was unconsciously transferring the images from one blurry scene to another? The two Judys weren't the only women I'd known in my life and my life at that time was pretty damned out of focus.

No, I thought, the photographs were at Judy's. So? What happened to the pics? The question hung in my mind like a loose thread on an old Elvis scarf. I was still thinking about it when I called McGovern's office at the *Daily News*.

'McGovern World Headquarters,' said McGovern.

'Mit,' I said.

'Mit! Mit! Mit!' said McGovern.

'I need help,' I said. 'I need you to help me find a photo of Uptown Judy. They all seem to have disappeared along with the girl herself. Maybe Brennan can talk to some labs and studios and turn up something. Maybe you can run a piece on her in the paper. Might jar somebody's memory, shake something loose. God knows we need a break.'

'I'll do what I can,' said McGovern, 'but I'm running the "People Page" these days. Can't put her in unless she was somebody.'

'Christ, McGovern, she *was* somebody.'

'I mean a *socialite* or something,' said McGovern. 'Then I could say "Socialite Disappears Mysteriously". Maybe nothing would come of it but at least my editor'd be happy.'

'Well,' I said, 'she *was* a kind of socialite. She did have sexual intercourse with *me* on several occasions.'

McGovern laughed his loud Irish laugh. I puffed rather self-righteously on my cigar and waited.

'A woman who has sexual intercourse with you can be called many things,' he said. 'But one of them is not a socialite.'

22

I had a little time on my hands so early that evening I walked over to the cop shop and picked up Judy's red cowboy boots. On the way home it started to rain and I carried them under my coat. Now, as they stood up on the counter in my kitchen, I could almost imagine Judy dancing in them. It was hard to believe they'd spooked me so bad the morning I'd found them on my doorstep. Of course, they hadn't walked there themselves. Someone was sending me a message. Judy's dead. Lay off looking for her. It was like some strange force had taken Judy away, removed all traces of her image from the planet, left nothing but a pair of red cowboy boots to say that she was ever here. They seemed small and almost poignant now up there on the counter. Bookends for a life unlived.

These were the somber and mortal thoughts that came to my mind like the heavy gray raindrops to the windows of the loft. It was past time for me to call Tom Baker's dad with some kind of progress report. Somehow the call was difficult to make. Hearing Baker's voice in the voice of his father. Why was this a problem for me? I could already hear Baker's voice in the raindrops.

I figured I'd wait a day or two until after Ratso's appearance on, and hopefully, the film's disappearance from, the Joe Franklin Show. Then, at least, I might have something to report. On the other hand, the unpleasant possibility existed that the receipt Rambam had goniffed from Legs' mailbox was for something else that had nothing to do with Elvis or the Bakerman. In that case there'd be nothing to tell Baker's dad and it'd be time for me to call in the dogs and piss on the fire as we say in Texas.

I poured myself a shot and killed it. The cat slept. The rain fell.

For no reason at all I heard the Bakerman's voice telling me some ridiculous story about a Chinese cab driver he'd had once who, during the course of the ride, found himself strongly desiring to take a Nixon. Baker'd suggested he just stop the cab and go into a restaurant or bar or someplace and he, Baker, would wait for him in the cab. The hack didn't like the idea much and instead took Baker on a route through Chinatown where he finally stopped the cab.

'Must go familiar place,' he'd said.

For some reason Baker had loved that line and repeated it to me many times during the subsequent months rather like an unpleasant mynah bird. 'Must go familiar place, must go familiar place.' Baker, of course, did a pretty good impersonation of the oriental cab driver and seemed to derive an enormous amount of pleasure in irritating me with the repetition of this particular phrase. Back then I sort of swatted it off. Never thought it was very funny. Back then.

I poured another shot and watched the sleeping cat and the falling rain and thought how really humorous the whole notion of Baker harrassing me with this anecdote was. Now that Baker was dead it not only seemed very funny, it almost seemed kind of mystical. I tried it out a few times.

'Must go familiar place,' I said softly so I wouldn't disturb anybody. 'Must go familiar place.' There was something to it all right. It could almost be a mantra for the modern world. Almost. I laughed to myself and repeated the phrase. In my own voice I could hear Baker's voice in whose voice I could hear the Chinese cab driver's voice when suddenly, from the hallway, I heard another voice.

It said: 'Pyramus. Thisbe.'

Then I heard the barking of dogs so small that the sound pierced like the sting of tiny baby scorpions into my gray matter department. This intrusion was followed by several sharp knocks on my door.

I got up and walked over to the door and opened it and Pyramus and Thisbe roared in like two miniature freight trains. The cat woke up from her slumber on the desk and couldn't believe her eyes. I couldn't either when I saw Stephanie DuPont, who'd obviously had a few drinks herself, bringing up a beautiful, languid caboose to the whole situation.

'Come in,' I said to the empty hallway. Then I turned around and saw the cat perched on the edge of the desk like a buzzard on angel dust. Certain death emoted from her eyes as the two little dogs yapped obliviously and traversed rapidly up and down like furry yo-yos in front of the desk. It was a catastrophe waiting to happen. And, sure enough, it did.

The cat, arching her back like a small, land-dwelling dinosaur and making noises that should've frightened any sentient being, had finally had enough. With a particularly well-timed and vicious forehand, she clipped Thisbe just as the little maltese reached the top of one of her piston cycles and sent her crashing into the kitchen counter like a bloody tennis ball.

The barking of the dogs, which, to this point, had been merely unpleasant, now reached a certain crescendo of tedium that taxed both human and feline sensibilities to the limit. Stephanie rushed over to Thisbe and found, apparently, that she was all right. The little dog, indeed, was soon back in her piston rotation in front of the desk.

Stephanie was not pleased by the situation. In a manner not terribly dissimilar to the cat's, she hissed: 'Do something!'

'Can you call the dogs off?' I asked.

'No,' she said, 'but I can call you an asshole. Call your sick cat off.'

This, of course, was not really an option. In as long as mankind has inhabited this weary, star-crossed planet, no one has ever truly called a cat, once committed, off. In fact, no one's ever actually called a cat. Like experienced lovers, they come when they wish.

During the height of all this activity, of course, the phones rang on either side of the three combatants, driving all of them into an almost unimaginable state of frenzy. Picking up either blower would've constituted a hazard to my health so I let them ring. Probably Ratso wanting to brainstorm for subject matter on the Joe Franklin Show. Ah well, there are times in life when all of us have to go it on our own.

After what seemed like the month of Ramadan, things finally began to ease a bit. Stephanie was able to reclaim her two little darlings and cater to their injuries which, thank the Lord, were minor. A dead Thisbe would've made Kinky sexual futures with Stephanie almost unthinkable. It would be fairly long odds as it was.

Stephanie sat down in my desk chair mopping up Thisbe with a warm washcloth. The cat had departed for the bedroom in a rather graceless snit. I knew better than to try to talk to her for at least several hours so I busied myself with being a good little hostesticle.

'Would you care for some banana bread and brie?' I asked Stephanie.

'That sounds nice,' she said.

'Well, I don't have any,' I said. 'How about some Irish Whiskey to cut the phlegm?'

Stephanie nodded sulkily and I poured the drinks into the two most appropriately stemmed vessels I had, a coffee mug and the bull horn. I let Stephanie have the bull horn and told her a little about its history and how I'd acquired such an unusual object. She seemed interested.

'You're the first person I've ever let drink from the bull horn,' I told her truthfully.

'It's grotesque,' she said, holding the bull horn at arm's length. 'If anything happens to Thisbe because of your sick cat I'll sue your ass for everything you own.'

'Well,' I said, 'you'd have to talk to my attorneys about that.

They're an old, well-respected firm. Schlemiel, Schlmozzel, and Dealkiller.'

Stephanie smiled fleetingly then began gathering up the dogs, her purse, and one black pump she'd thrown at the cat during the peak of the earlier unpleasantness. The pump had gone wide but I was sure the cat had filed Stephanie's face away in her feline hall of hate which now included almost all living things. I'd filed Stephanie's face away, too. It was so beautiful it was hard to look at directly. As ol' Rapid Robert once said, you had to just 'shovel a glimpse' every once in a while.

As I was walking her to the door, Stephanie noticed Judy's red cowboy boots on the counter.

'I like those boots,' she said. 'Whose are they?'

'Oh, a friend left them some time ago. She's not coming back. Want to try 'em on?'

Stephanie walked back to my desk chair, sat down, took off her shoes, and waited. I went over to the counter, got the boots, and brought them over to her. She did not make a move to put them on.

'You do it,' she said.

'Okay, Cinderella.'

Though I suspected that most career shoe salesmen were probably sick chickens, I had to admit that it was exciting helping Stephanie DuPont put on those boots. I would've gladly let her keep them if they fit. I was beginning to regard the boots as some kind of albatross or bottle imp anyway, and I'd just as soon they walked out of the loft before they brought more tragedy into my life. I was enough of a shoe salesman, however, to want them to fit.

They didn't. They were too big.

'Jesus,' said Stephanie, 'this whore had big feet.'

As I took the boots off her I noticed they were custom made with the name of the maker inside the boot. That was a lead that needed to be followed and one I should've lamped to long before now.

Stephanie put her own shoes back on and I walked her to the

door. I gave her a little kiss on the cheek as she went out carrying Pyramus and Thisbe.

'Stay a while longer,' I said. 'Let's at least exchange phone numbers and hobbies.'

'No, my prince,' she said, 'I have to be home by midnight.'

'Why?' I asked. 'Does your tampax turn into a pumpkin?'

I looked at her and wished, not for the first time, that she'd never leave. She must've seen it in my eyes, for she turned around in the hallway.

'Goodnight, parakeet dick,' she said.

23

Around three o'clock the following afternoon I walked into the green room at the Joe Franklin Show and found a middle-aged psychic studying her tarot cards, a buxom transvestite straightening his pantyhose, and, at a little corner refreshment table, Ratso eating a pizza.

'Nervous?' I asked.

'Hungry,' he said.

In keeping with general green room demeanor, neither of us said much and we kept our voices down to an unnatural level that might've been suitable to a library in wig city. In fact, upon closer scrutiny, the other two occupants of the room looked like they'd just come from hanging out with Van Gogh and Jesus.

'Who goes on first?' I asked Ratso.

'Dame Margot Margot-Howard,' said Ratso, adjusting his dark skyshooters and coonskin cap. I looked at the two other occupants of the room.

'Which one is she?' I said.

Ratso nodded discreetly as he ever did anything toward the guy straightening his pantyhose. Maybe they were long sheer stockings of some kind. I didn't want to look too hard. In my own out-dated quixotic way, I believed there were some things you just weren't supposed to know too much about. I didn't believe in witnessing babies coming out of wombs or seeing the face of the bride before the wedding ceremony. This, very possibly, was the reason I didn't have any brides or babies. Of course, I didn't have any transvestites, either.

'How do I look?' Ratso asked, as he took another slice of pizza out of the box.

He was wearing a pair of red knit pants of some kind and a lox-colored tie, the end of which was very cleverly shaped like a human penis. He had on a cowboy shirt that looked like it might've once belonged to Spade Cooley before he stomped his wife to death in front of the kids.

'Perfect,' I said. 'I especially like the silver collar tips with the little gold square dancing couples on them.'

'Five bucks on Canal Street,' said Ratso with some little pride.

'You're kidding,' I said.

Franklin's studio was in a large television complex situated somewhere deep in the bowels of New Jersey. The three guests on the show appeared well-dressed for the venue. The psychic looked almost like a bag-lady. The transvestite looked almost like an attractive woman. And Ratso, God bless him, looked like Ratso. I was glad there weren't any mirrors in the room or I might've realized that I belonged.

'Know what you're gonna talk about?' I asked Ratso in the lowered voice. Didn't want to disturb anybody who was trying to get a wiggle on.

'Sure,' he said. 'Got it covered.' He reached for another slice of pizza and I took a cigar out of my hunting vest and began my pre-ignition rituals.

I was holding the cigar about a hundred-eighths of an inch above the flame of a kitchen match when my peripheral vision picked up a slight movement over on my left wing. It was the tv, who'd evidently straightened out his pantyhose and was now trying to straighten out me by a prissy little warning gesture with a highly-lacquered finger. I ignored it and him.

'Yoo-hoo,' he said, in an androgynously repellent lilt. 'Smokey The Bear.'

I lit the cigar.

'You get out of here right now with that thing,' shrieked the transvestite, 'or I'll call security.'

'I know you,' I said. 'You were the executive producer of the Howdy Doody Show.'

I left the green room to its rightful occupants. They went back to their slightly nervous little pre-game putterings and I went out into the rather less rarified air of the mundane hallway. I saw a janitor, a secretary, a security guard, a few studio audience types. The folks who'd probably live their whole lives without ever seeing the inside of the green room. I didn't feel too much at home with them either.

I puffed langorously on the cigar for a few moments and then the security guy, always looking for something to justify his existence on the planet, came over and told me to put it out. I did. Didn't want to make a scene. Not quite yet.

I wandered out into the parking lot and, by prearranged plan, waited for various members of our entourage to appear. I lit up a fresh cigar in the fresh New Jersey air and leaned against some kind of nondescript New Jersey motor vehicle. Like everything else in New Jersey it looked weary and rusty and fairly frazzled. It looked like I felt.

I puffed on the cigar and looked around. The view was pretty weak. I'd loitered in finer places than this. But there wasn't any other option. I wanted to go over plans once more with the Village Irregulars before we went into action. At this rate, I was going to miss Dame Margot Margot-Howard.

At about the time I was fresh out of charm everybody showed up. Almost everybody. Mick Brennan, according to McGovern, was hot on a lead. He'd run into a photographer who knew a photographer who'd worked for a time in a lab that had once processed some photos of Uptown Judy.

'How can I put this delicately?' asked McGovern rhetorically. Rambam, Downtown Judy, and I waited.

'Why don't you get to the point?' said Downtown Judy.

'The point,' said McGovern, looking at Downtown Judy, 'is right on top of your head.'

'Look, you two,' I said, 'the altercation is not to occur until Ratso's taping his portion of the show. Hopefully, it'll provide

427

additional cover and distraction so Rambam and I can find what we're looking for. So don't peak too soon.'

'What I'm telling you,' said McGovern, 'is that these photos, that you've set Brennan after, aren't the kind you'd want anybody to know about.'

'Especially your family,' said Rambam. 'With emphasis on the word "family".'

'It's an interesting wrinkle,' I said, 'but it's one we'll have to iron out later. Right now, the Joe Franklin Show must go on.'

We entered the building like typical studio audience types, dulled by life, no sharp edges, ready to let other people get our kicks for us. The security guy in the foyer didn't even look twice at us. It almost hurt my feelings.

Inside the studio, cameras were rolling and Joe Franklin was already talking with Dame Margot Margot-Howard. Ratso was still most likely in the green room. I hoped he wasn't getting pizza on his penis-shaped tie.

McGovern and Judy took seats near the front and Rambam and I sat down close to the hallway exit. Seating selection was easy since there were only about eighteen people in the studio audience and half of them looked like they were on methadone.

'Robert Frost was right,' I whispered to Rambam.

'He sure was,' said Rambam. 'What'd he say?'

'Hell is a half-filled auditorium.'

It was not precisely clear whether or not Joe Franklin knew that Dame Margot Margot-Howard was a man, but, in a cosmic sense, it didn't really matter. He treated her like a lady. She warmed to the role. She was such a faithful caricature of a society woman that millions of viewers out there in Buttocks, Texas or wherever the hell they were, quite possibly were fooled. The studio audience appeared to care less. As for Joe Franklin, he had his hand on Dame Margot Margot-Howard's shapely knee as she explained that she was head of the Mary Queen of Scots Preservation Society and proceeded to correct many popular misconceptions about Mary Queen of Scots that the viewers in Buttocks, Texas had probably never dreamed of entertaining if, indeed, they'd ever heard of Mary Queen of Scots in the first place.

Dame Margot was explaining how her work as head of the Mary Queen of Scots Preservation Society had led to her writing a book entitled: *I Was a White Slave in Harlem* when I noticed Ratso and the assistant producer entering the studio. This was our cue.

I nodded to Rambam and we slipped out the side door just as Dame Margot was sliding sinuously down the couch closer to the Ed McMahon position and Ratso was depositing himself between her and Joe Franklin. He was on his own now. Flying by Jewish radar.

Rambam and I had our troubles, too. The security guard in the hallway was giving us the old fish-eye.

Rambam walked right up to him. 'Which way's the men's room?' he said.

'I gotta urinate like a racehorse,' I added for good measure. The guard seemed impressed. He pointed down the hall.

I'd covered this territory before earlier in the day. The men's room was around the corner out of sight of the guard unless he came down there looking for trouble. Across from the men's room was the producer's office and next door to it was Joe Franklin's office. We walked down the hall in the general direction of the aforementioned men's room. When we'd rounded the corner I pointed out the two offices to Rambam.

'If I were Baker's film,' I said, 'I'd be in one of those two offices.'

'Let's try door number three,' said Rambam and we went into the men's room. Once inside, Rambam said: 'You take Franklin's office, I'll check the production office. How much time you think we'll have?'

'Depends on how much of a diversion McGovern and Judy can make.' Rambam opened the door very slightly and listened. I could hear the sounds of an altercation coming from down the hallway. Judy's shrill, argumentative tones. McGovern using the 'c' word repeatedly. The guard trying unsuccessfully to keep a lid on things.

'Music to my ears,' I said.

'Cavalry, charge!' said Rambam.

In a nano-second we'd crossed the hall and were in our respective offices. I saw immediately that finding anything in Franklin's office was hopeless. The detritus of a lifetime was piled toward the ceiling like the skyline of a small city suffering from urban blight. More than anything else, it resembled McGovern's apartment. If Baker's film was somewhere in Franklin's office, I was going to have to get the psychic to tell me where it was.

I was starting to admit defeat when Rambam came scurrying into the office holding a large film canister in his hands.

'Elvis Lives!' he said, 'Tom Baker. Right on top of the guy's fucking desk. Now we got to find a way to slip it out of here past the tension convention in the hallway.'

It was true that things in the hallway did not sound as if an accord had been reached. The thing seemed to have grown into a major hubbub. I suddenly had an idea.

'Take the film into the dumper, lock yourself into a stall, and wait for me,' I told Rambam.

'Okay,' he said, 'but if you don't come back pretty quick I may start writing graffiti.'

I strode purposefully down the hallway as if I were a busy little television producer myself, but I could've been on a motorized skate board just as well. All the attention in the hall was focused on the security staff and production crew trying with great valor and diplomacy to force McGovern's large Irish body out of the building. I ducked into the green room, smiled at the psychic, grabbed the empty pizza box, and headed back to the dumper.

Moments later, the Bakerman's documentary safely ensconced in the pizza box, and the pizza box firmly in both of Rambam's hands, the two of us headed for the foyer. Rambam had a little Navajo chant going for him even before he got there. He said repeatedly to himself in a loud voice with great concentration: 'They *ordered* pepperoni. I *brought* them pepperoni. They don't *want* pepperoni.'

The security guy smiled at Rambam.

'I'll be back,' said Rambam to the guy.

'That's what my ex-wife told me,' he said.

As we left the building, I noticed a television monitor set into

430

the wall near the front entrance. On the monitor, the Joe Franklin Show was in progress. I stayed long enough to hear Ratso say to Dame Margot Margot-Howard: 'You did say Mary *Queen* of Scots?'

Then I got in a motor vehicle with Rambam and a pizza box containing a friend's final artistic statement. Then I lit a cigar and asked myself once again if a documentary on Elvis impersonators could conceivably create such a trail of doom and destruction.

Life, I reflected, was nevertheless more exciting with a game of chess in it. What you had to watch out for was that sometimes the size of the pieces tended to get rather large.

24

That night, with Uptown Judy's red boots still standing on the kitchen counter and Tom Baker's final cinematic effort still safely ensconced in the pizza box on my desk, the loft seemed to be taking on all the warmth and humanity of a wax museum. Somewhere between the boots of a dead lover and the last crazy creation of a dead best friend, on some metaphysical surveyor's fragile, unworldly plumbline, as yet invisible and unintelligible to mortal man, lay the point called the truth.

I was sitting roughly between the boots and the pizza box, smoking a resurrected cigar, hoping that by mere physical positioning some cosmic awareness might accrue to my weatherbeaten spirit. There had to be a connection somewhere. When I did find it, I had the clear and disturbing feeling it was not going to be the kind of thing you'd want to plug a blow-dryer into.

I turned my attention away from the boots toward the Bakerman's film. I was glad I'd decided to keep it in the pizza box. Stays warm that way.

I had lots of things I needed to do, but now that I had the Elvis impersonator documentary in my possession, I felt a subtle sense of focus and control asserting itself. I needed to keep calm now and think and act rationally.

In the manner of Agatha Christie's great detective, Hercule Poirot, I began straightening objects on the desk, beginning with the pizza box. I worked on that box like Jesse James fastidiously hanging a picture on a wall. It was the last thing Jesse ever did. That dirty little coward Robert Ford shot him in the back just as Jesse's wife was saying 'A little to the right.'

It was as I was straightening other objects on the desk to precise horizontal and vertical positions, that I made a rather disconcerting discovery. The cat had vomited in my pipe.

It was an unpleasant thing to deal with but it was an easy thing to forgive. No doubt, with all the mordant vibes in the loft lately, the cat had become a little nervous, too. I carried the pipe carefully over to the sink, knocked out the vomitus, and ran a little hot water into the little meerschaum bowl that was in all respects an exact replica of the head of President John Fitzgerald Kennedy. Unfortunately, the hole in the pipe where you placed the tobacco was almost precisely in the location of the hole in the President's head created in Dallas, Texas. I finished cleaning the pipe and brought it back to the desk. I didn't agonize over it. I wasn't a conspiracy theorist.

The pipe episode notwithstanding, it was time for one man to act alone. Namely myself. I had to call Tom Baker's dad. I had to find out any information I could from the place where Uptown Judy had bought the boots. I had to set a bonfire under Brennan's arse to find a photo of Uptown Judy. And lastly, and no doubt most important, I had to arrange for a private screening of Baker's Elvis documentary. Hopefully, it'd provide a clue to whatever the hell was going on. As they say in Hollywood, always eat a pizza when it's hot.

I picked up the blower on the left and called Nick 'Chinga' Chavin who, though he was now a successful ad exec, still had some peripheral ties to nefarious individuals from his days as lead singer with the band Country Porn. As I waited for Chinga to answer I hummed a few bars of the band's hit song, 'Cum Stains on the Pillow (Where Your Sweet Head Used to Be)'.

When Chinga picked up, I explained to him what I needed and, being an ad exec, he quickly grasped the concept.

'When do you need it by?' he asked.

'Yesterday.'

'That's a ball-buster of a deadline but let me see what I can do.

432

You need a place to screen a film in private and it's got to be quick.'

'Correctimundo,' I said.

'I'll do it if it harelips the pope. Call you right back.'

Like most high-ranking executives, Chinga rarely called back when he said he would. I lit a fresh cigar, stoked up the espresso machine and settled in for a wait. About a fortnight later, it seemed, the phones rang.

'Start talkin',' I said.

'I spoke to Charlie Chopbuster. He can get a semi-private screening for you late tomorrow night.'

When Chinga told me the new venue for the screening, I was somewhat credulous.

'Fort Dix?' I said. 'The military base?'

'No,' said Chinga. 'Fort *Dicks*. It's a gay club, but not one of those really seedy ones. You could say it's the cream of the crop.'

'What do you mean by semi-private?' I didn't know exactly what the documentary contained but I did know I didn't want to share it with half of the sentient universe.

'Well, at two o'clock in the morning there won't be hardly anyone in the place. But Charlie can't throw out the few who've paid admission. Anyway, they'll probably be glued to their seats, so to speak.'

'Charming,' I said. I took a few Freudian puffs on the cigar. 'That's the best venue you could get, right?'

'Well, the Helen Hayes Theater was already booked. What're you screening?'

'*The African Queen*.'

'They'll like that at Fort Dicks.'

After I hung up with Chinga I paced the loft a bit and went through a brief round of regret about the choice of Fort Dicks to hold the semi-private screening on the following night. There must be other places in New York where we could screen the film. If I wanted total secrecy I could transfer it to microfilm and hold the screening on the bridge of my nose. At one point in my pacing I began carrying on an animated dialogue with the cat.

'Forget about the pipe,' I said. 'Don't be nervous.'

The cat swished her tail furiously from side to side and her eyes flashed a satanic green.

'Just because the ornaments of death are all around us is not sufficient reason to set us off our nice tuna. Let's work with death if we can. Imagine that we're both unctuous funeral home directors. We come from a well-respected family of feline morticians. Been in the croaking business for generations, passed on from cat to kitten, so to speak.'

Here the cat appeared to display a modicum of interest in the subject. She sat stock still on the counter next to Uptown Judy's boots and stared at me with the intent gaze usually reserved for a cockroach. Possibly, she was watching the pattern of smoke billowing forth from my cigar. Possibly, she was genuinely interested.

'We live and work in a great plantation house with huge white columns in front. Maybe it's in Mobile, Alabama – '

Here, quite abruptly, the cat jumped from the counter to the rocking chair, from there to the sofa, and from there, she scurried rather rudely into the bedroom without a backward glance. Like a great many New Yorkers, the cat had an innate bias against southerners and all things southern. This was most clearly expressed in her absolute refusal to even taste Southern Gourmet Dinner.

I located another dead soldier in the waste basket, poured another espresso and continued pacing the lonely loft into the night. If the path I transversed had been in a straight progression I probably could've walked to Mobile, Alabama. Then where would I be?

I decided it was too late to call Baker's father. Too late in more ways than one. I'd call him after I'd had a chance to see Tom's film. I thought again of calling Chinga back and changing the venue from Fort Dicks to someplace more private and appropriate. But that would only take more time and besides, I didn't want Charlie Chopbuster or his patrons to get the word out in New York circles that I was alarmingly homophobic. Best leave things as they stood. Tomorrow I'd call the Irregulars and invite them down to see the film. I needed every unjaundiced eye I could get. Somewhere in the documentary, I was convinced, might be some clue to the deaths of Uptown Judy, Legs, and possibly, something to cast the shadow of foul play even upon the death of Baker himself.

Death was in the air, all right. The cat knew it and I knew it and the boots and the pizza carton weren't letting us forget. I wondered what Baker's documentary would be like. Well done, I was sure. All of the Bakerman's work had been clearly chiseled and finely polished. Such a shame he couldn't be here to enjoy it and the subsequent pleasure it might bring to others.

I killed the espresso machine and the lights and put on my old faded sarong. I moved the cat over slightly and got under the covers still pondering the curious relationship between death and art, art and death. I didn't want to end up like Van Gogh, masturbating in a mental hospital, my paintings all stacked neatly somewhere in the attic, unsold and unseen. Sometimes it takes longer than a life. I prayed to St Dymphna that this would not happen.

St Dymphna, as very few psychiatrists but a great many out-patients know, is the patron saint of the insane.

25

The Village Irregulars trooped up to Fort Dicks like parochial children on a field trip to the other side of a dream. And a wet dream, at that. Chinga, curiosity having gotten the best of him, met us at the front of the place.

'Hope you like ammonia,' he said.

'What's an "All-Live Daisy Chain"?' asked Downtown Judy, reading from the marquee.

'That usually happens earlier in the evening,' said Chinga, 'when they have a crowd in here. It's an audience-participation kind of thing. Maybe ten or twelve people'll come up on the stage and join the performers. They take all their clothes off, lie down on the stage, and get in a position with each one's head near the next one's pee-pee. Are you with me?'

Judy nodded her head as if Chinga were explaining photosynthesis.

'No, I'm not, mate,' said Brennan to the empty street. I held the pizza box a little tighter. The film reel had seemed small and vulnerable without the pizza box there to protect it, so I'd brought it along.

'Then they lie there on the stage in a big circle,' said Chinga, 'and simultaneously suck each other's dicks.'

'All the projection rooms in all the cities in the world,' said McGovern, 'and we gotta walk into this one.'

'Let's get it over with,' said Rambam, with a surprising tenseness in his voice.

I was gratified to see the Irregulars turn out en masse for this event. All of them had known Baker to varying degrees and felt, I thought, a sense of personal involvement in seeing this through. Also, they may have correctly assessed the situation: the Elvis film we were about to see had the potential to break the whole case wide open. Even at two o'clock in the morning in front of a seamy, all-male burlesque house the green light at the end of Daisy Buchanan's pier beckoned us onward. Not, of course, to be confused with daisy chain.

Chinga introduced us to the night manager, a sixtyish guy with black leather yachting cap, black leather vest, and black engineer's boots.

'This is Master John,' said Chinga.

'I didn't order a pizza,' said Master John, looking at the package under my arm.

'Let's get it over with,' said Rambam.

The first real wave of ammonia hit us as we walked into the dingy little lobby, faithfully following Master John.

'They wash this place down about every two hours,' said Chinga in a loud whisper.

'Maybe they should go for every hour on the hour,' I said. Ammonia was an interesting thing, I thought. It could erase the smell of sex or death. Yet its very presence, though momentarily fooling the senses, soon came to represent those very things and almost make their impact stronger.

436

I was surprised to see a popcorn and candy counter with licorice sticks, milk duds, and snicker bars. The popcorn looked like it'd been popped by Orville Redenbacker's grandfather. It seemed somehow unwholesome in a place like this. I was not surprised to see Ratso walk up to the counter and start negotiations with the guy behind it. The guy seemed pretty stale, too.

'Ask him if he's got butterfingers,' Chinga said, in a voice a little louder than necessary.

Moments later we entered the darkened theater.

'The popcorn sucks,' said Ratso.

'So do the customers, mate,' said Brennan.

A second and stronger wave of ammonia hit us as we walked past rows of deserted seats. Here and there, as my eyes adjusted to the tundra-like darkness, were sprinkled occasional patrons – life's little failures – nondescript, gray, excited forms with glasses glinting. On the stage, wearing nothing but a contemptuous smile, was a blond burlesque dancer named Jo-Jo. He was tossing his curls and making his grand exit as our little party took our seats along the third row.

'Best seats I've had on Broadway in years,' said McGovern.

'I went through hell to get 'em,' I said.

'Milk dud?' Ratso asked, offering me the package.

'No thanks,' I said. 'I had an apple on the train.'

Chinga signalled me to come with him to give the film reel to Master John to give to the projectionist. Rambam went along with us. On the way up the aisle a young man passed the three of us, then stopped, turned, and made rather serious eye contact with me.

'Everyone loves a cowboy,' said Rambam.

'Except Crazy Horse,' I said.

'He's dead,' said Chinga. 'Unless they try to dig him up and use him as a hand puppet. So what's this big premiere we're gonna be seeing?'

'Tom Baker's documentary on Elvis impersonators,' I said.

'Tom Baker, Movie-maker,' said Chinga. He'd known Baker distantly. Baker'd known a lot of people distantly.

437

'That's the one,' I said. 'What do you know about Elvis impersonators?'

'I heard they all have little dicks,' said Chinga.

In the lobby a middle-aged guy in a trench coat started staring at my ass. He was close to drooling.

'*Every*one loves a cowboy,' said Rambam.

I took off my hat nervously but soon realized that, because of my kinky moss, my head looked like a rocket ship, and so I put it back on again. All the while, the guy continued to stare at my ass, occasionally licking his lips.

'Unpleasant,' I said.

Rambam shooed the guy away and I gave the reel to Master John who said he'd get it on right away. Charlie Chopbuster was one of Chinga's advertising clients apparently and he'd told Master John to take good care of the straight party that was coming in tonight. Thus, as I turned to walk back into the theater I heard Master John call out to me.

'Look, man,' he said, 'I'm not trying to tell you your business, but if you keep that brown bandanna in your left hip pocket it means you like to shit on people.'

I thought about it for a moment. While there were some aspects of truth to the sentiment, I felt, in practice, it was giving out a false message. I switched the bandanna to my right hip pocket.

'Look, man,' said Master John. 'That might not be a really good placement idea. Brown bandanna in your right hip pocket means you want someone to shit on you.'

'Well, shit,' I said.

'I'm not into it,' said Master John. He chuckled somewhat in the manner of an old-time children's radio host. I stuffed the brown bandanna deep and out of sight into my coat pocket.

'Now, if it'd been a yellow bandanna – ' said Master John.

'Let's get on with it,' said Rambam.

Master John nodded and headed up to the projection room. The three of us headed back to our seats.

'Christ,' said Chinga, 'how does a 'mo even get to pick his nose?'

'Carefully,' said Rambam.

We took our seats just as the house lights went down.

26

Some years ago, on the left coast of North America, according to a friend of mine who was there, another private screening occurred. It did not take place inside a gay men's burlesque theater, nor did it involve a recently deceased friend's film on Elvis impersonators. Nonetheless, in its own way, it was an equally ill occasion. It was the first private screening of a video to promote the new Michael Jackson doll.

An obscene amount of money had been spent creating this video, apparently, and all the architects and producers of the piece, the best that money could buy, were present in the room.

According to my friend, as the video was being shown, all the top producers and directors who'd put it together were giving a running commentary as the footage rolled. Their comments went something like this:

'Brilliant! Beautiful!'

'Perfectly on target.'

'So accessible.'

'Genius.'

As the video ended there was a brief, almost religious moment of silence. Then a voice from the back of the room could be heard. It was a soft, high-pitched, slightly petulant, bird-like voice. It said: 'I don't *like* it.'

It was Michael Jackson.

Then the Hollywood hot-shots began falling all over each other, tearing their hair, and covering their Armani suits with ashes. Their comments went something like this:

'Christ, what a terrible piece of shit!'

'It's the worst crap I've ever seen in my life!'

'Oh, God, I must've had a nail in my head!'

This little story, which I've since come to refer to as 'The Michael Jackson Anecdote', contains many wonderful lessons in life for all of us. One is: Never underestimate by what a fragile and ridiculous tissue of cat vomit people are attached to their beliefs and convictions in the face of a sickly stage whisper from an androgynous space alien worth twelve billion dollars. The second lesson is more to the point. Whether you're selling Michael Jackson dolls to Third World countries or clearing away the fog on the moors of several unsolved murders, you must be very careful to let those helping you form their own opinions. A chance comment, a reduced cue of some kind, could lead them off on a wild goose chase. I had fourteen eyes and fourteen ears and I was determined to use them.

Thus, I made a point of sitting quietly in my seat as the film began and the voice-over commentary of Tom Baker rolled across the fetid darkness of the little room like balm to my soul. In spite of my determination toward total objectivity and my clinical approach to the project, I found myself overcome by the voice of my friend.

'Hey, Tom,' I said softly.

McGovern looked over, nodded his head once, and smiled.

Then, in a darkened porno theater, as millions slept all around us and dreamed of some day arriving at their own private Camelots, we seven watched a succession of shadow men luxuriating each in his own tiny splinter of light from a distant dead star that would forever be a hard act to follow.

There were Elvises beyond the imagination. Negro Elvises, dwarf Elvises, female Elvises, Norwegian Elvises. There were young fat Elvises, skinny old Elvises, in between Elvises. There were Elvises that in no physical way remotely resembled Elvis, yet, in some uncanny after-image, looked like Elvis. There were Elvises with no voice, no rhythm, and no talent except the ability to make you think, if you put your hand over your face and slowly looked between your fingers, you were seeing Elvis.

There was an Elvis impersonators' convention in Las Vegas at which the legions of participants were interviewed by the Bakerman. One of the common denominators was that virtually all of them appeared to be men of quiet desperation. The Bakerman was non-judgmental.

There was also the mandatory pilgrimage to Graceland, Elvis's home in Memphis. The impersonators, descending upon the place like eager locusts, tended to lose whatever star appeal they may have had the closer they got to the King's home. At Graceland, possibly not surprisingly, they went through empty postures and rote mannerisms but clearly emerged as what they truly were – fans. Fans with a curious admixture of love, passion, envy, anger, and beneath that, some arcane form of self-doubt, and what almost seemed to be clinically ill self-loathing. In other words, they were just like the rest of us.

Through all of this, like the muddy, winding river of life, travelled Tom Baker's resonant Irish voice – seeking, encouraging, comforting. In the dark burlesque house, I momentarily stripped away the Elvis impersonators and communed with that disembodied voice I knew so well. I'd taken for granted that it would always be with me. Now, I felt a great inner peace, as if I'd died and gone to the Baby Jesus or Buddha or L. Ron Hubbard and then suddenly realized they were all in attendance at the same AA meeting in the sky. It was almost a mystical experience for me – almost as if I'd been working out for an hour and a half on my Thigh-Master – but it wasn't helping me find out who killed Uptown Judy or who croaked Legs.

Suddenly, a large, dark, muscular figure leapt to the stage. Because of the pose he struck, at first, I had him lamped for an over-zealous Elvis impersonator. All he was wearing was a codpiece about the size of Moshe Dayan's eye-patch. It looked like it had a Volkswagen double-parked behind it. Nonetheless, the man was strikingly handsome, and not without a certain effortless Latin charm as he began giving *lambada* lessons to the sparsely populated room.

'And step, step, step. And step, step, step,' said the man. The Elvis impersonators gyrated obliviously behind him on the screen, their hips undulating in a fashion not dissimilar to his own.

I looked at our small group of theater-goers. Ratso, Rambam, Brennan, and McGovern were all convulsing with laughter. Judy looked like she'd been hit with a pile-driver. And Chinga, turned fully toward the projectionist, was shouting: 'Stop the film! Stop the film!'

441

'And step, step, step,' said the man. 'And hip, grind, THRUST!' He was becoming increasingly animated even as the film froze behind him.

Chinga grabbed me now and spoke very fiercely and intensely close to my ear. He said: 'Look, I've been in advertising long enough to know what doesn't belong in a picture. I don't look at what the magician wants me to see.'

'Pivot, lunge, and dip!' shouted the *lambada* instructor, performing the insane motions alone on the stage.

'I notice the car that somehow sneaks into the frame in the commercial of the Old West,' Chinga hissed.

At this point, the male dancer leapt off the stage and grabbed the person seated closest to him. It was Ratso. Ratso's drink spilled all over him and the popcorn and milk duds went flying.

'There was something very familiar in that last segment,' Chinga continued. 'Where the Elvis impersonator was singing in that Italian restaurant.'

The next thing I knew, the guy had Ratso in an iron grip, pulling him tightly against his practically naked, heavily sweating body. We all stood up to get a closer look at the couple doing the *lambada* on the dance floor.

'Loosen your hips!' the guy shouted to Ratso. 'Follow my lead!'

' "I saw a man dance with his wife," ' sang McGovern.

'Don't look at your feet,' the guy told Ratso. 'Look in my eyes.'

Eventually calm was restored, and everything in the little theater went back to merely sordid. A much-relieved, out-of-breath Ratso returned to his seat as Master John very apologetically hustled the guy out of there. I gave Ratso my brown bandanna to wipe his sweater. Chinga signaled the projectionist. The film rolled again.

What we saw now was some footage of an Elvis impersonator performing before some tables of old men in what looked like an old Italian restaurant. Baker's voice-over was saying: 'We traveled all the way to Sheepshead Bay, Brooklyn to catch this next pretender to the throne.'

Chinga stood up and shouted: 'Stop! Stop the film!'

We all saw it at the same time. It *was* a familiar face.

Sitting at a corner table in the background, sipping an espresso and smiling blandly, was Don Sepulveda.

27

It was four-thirty in the morning and only paranoia was keeping us awake. Rambam had driven me, Ratso, and Mick Brennan back to the loft for coffee and cordials and the four of us along with the prodigal pizza carton were now squeezed into the freight elevator too tightly to even look at our shoes.

'You think anybody there besides our little party saw Sepulveda in the film?' Ratso asked.

'Doubt it,' said Brennan. 'Everyone'd left by then and Master John was out in the lobby probably inspecting handkerchiefs or something.'

'What about the guy showing the film?' Ratso said.

'He didn't see a thing,' said Rambam. 'That little skell was running on eleven different kinds of herbs and spices.'

'My dear Ratso,' I said, 'you're projecting your paranoia on the projectionist.'

Though I didn't say it, I shared Ratso's concern. Judy had left Fort Dicks in a semi-snit and McGovern and Chinga both had pleaded heavy workloads in the morning and had gone home, too. But the seven of us – the Village Irregulars – now shared a dark and potentially quite dangerous secret. Don Sepulveda was alive and well – not rubbed out five years ago as the world had thought. Every top fed and mafia boss would've probably let you lay your dick on his wisdom tooth for this information. Not that that was a particularly attractive offer.

If you thought about it, it got so spooky it almost didn't seem real. So I tried not to think about it as the four of us entered the loft. I casually flipped the pizza box onto the desk and walked over to the kitchen cabinet and got out a bottle of Bushmills for the group. Had to entertain the guests and down deep, I suppose, I could use a drink myself.

'Just give me an espresso,' said Rambam. 'I've got a stake-out in Quogue, Long Island.'

443

'You can't have a stake-out in Quogue, Long Island,' said Ratso. 'It's a contradiction in terms. There's nothing there to stake out.'

I started the espresso machine and lit a cigar. Brennan poured drinks for Ratso and myself and an extremely hefty shot for himself.

'Well, it's kind of funny,' said Rambam. 'This old woman in Quogue, Long Island lost her cat and I did a door-to-door to try and find it. I found another old lady who had a lot of cats and reported that every morning around 6 a.m. a cat matching the description comes into her yard and tries to fuck one of her cats.'

'Are you giving her statement verbatim?' asked Brennan.

'Close,' said Rambam. 'Anyway, so I'm going out tonight to try to catch the cat in the act and bring him back to his owner.'

'Well,' I said, 'I can see why you'd want to go out to Quogue, Long Island and try to get that cat back for that lady. All we got here's a couple of murders and a little don that's popped up after five years.'

'The difference is,' said Rambam, pausing rather dramatically to blow on his espresso, 'that woman's paying me and you're not.'

'I'll drink to that,' said Brennan, 'we ought to get hazard pay.'

I killed my shot and took a few disbelieving puffs on the cigar.

'What's happened to you guys?' I said. 'What's happened to the fabled Village Irregulars?'

Ratso replied in a high-pitched Sly Stone inflection. 'Who *you*?' he said. 'What you *do*?'

After a tense moment or two, everyone laughed and Rambam put his large hand on my shoulder.

'Don't worry,' he said. 'Tomorrow we'll get on the track of the bad guys again. I think I know where that restaurant is in Sheepshead Bay. You and I can go out there tomorrow afternoon and talk to some people. Or we could just send Ratso.'

'Sure,' said Ratso. 'You can look for me on the third star to the left.'

'No,' I said, 'I've got something else in mind for Ratso.'

'I can hardly fucking wait,' he said.

'I can't wait either,' said Rambam. 'Got to get to the stake-out. By the way, I've checked with the DMV – that's Department of

Motor Vehicles to you – and we could have a photo of Uptown Judy soon.'

'What's soon?' I asked. Brennan's interest perked up now.

'About three weeks,' said Rambam as he headed for the door.

'Three weeks!' said Ratso. 'I still remember the shadow of Sepulveda's smile. He finds out we're onto him, we could all get rubbed out.'

'There's another reason for going out to Quogue, Long Island,' said Rambam, as he walked out the door.

After Rambam had taken his leave, the three of us had another round of Bushmills in silence. It was hard for me to believe that the closest to an establishment type that we had among us was Rambam. Maybe we were in deeper shit than I thought.

'Here's something you may need,' said Ratso. He threw my brown bandanna in the direction of the desk. It happened to land directly on top of the pizza carton.

'Cosmic,' I said.

'Now that our friendly neighborhood P.I. has left the premises,' said Brennan, 'I think I may come up with a photo a lot faster than three weeks. But things could get a little weird.'

'What do you mean "get"?' said Ratso.

'Snuff films,' said Brennan. 'I'm on the track of a guy rumoured – only rumoured – to've made a few. I've heard he might've done some sessions with Uptown Judy.'

I felt a little chill in the room. I looked over at the cat who was sleeping in kind of a half-moon position. They say you can tell by how tight a ball a cat rolls itself up in just how cold it is. Of course, this doesn't allow for the perversity of cats, who might roll themselves up into a very tight ball just to make you think it's cold. It also doesn't allow for the perversity of the weather. Otherwise, it's a pretty good indicator.

'Who is the guy?' I said.

'I don't have a name or face yet,' said Brennan, 'but I'm working on it. I've talked to burned-out hippie models from the seventies, escort service girls, porno stars. It's coming together. Newspaper morgues have been pretty helpful.'

'Couldn't McGovern help you with that?' asked Ratso.

'Reporters are just chimpanzees at typewriters,' said Brennan. 'They just never quite understand the inner workings of the photographic mind.'

The photographer's bias against reporters aside, Brennan sounded like he was clearly onto something. All I needed, I thought, was yet another possible scenario for Judy's disappearance. Was her death connected directly to Tom Baker's film? Was it a mob hit? Could a snuff film-maker have used Uptown Judy as his leading lady? Maybe she did click her red boots together three times and go back to Kansas.

Without thinking I let my hand gently graze over the red cowboy boots on the counter. Ratso observed this, apparently, and his penchant for dead person's shoes must've kicked in.

He said: 'Those were hers? Can I try 'em on?'

'Well,' I said, 'it's not a request we get every day from gentlemen callers but why not?'

'They are moderately uni-sexual,' said Brennan, no doubt trying to ease the embarrassment both of us felt.

Ratso set down his drink and picked the boots up off the counter. He had a lot of dead people's shoes and clothing and, no doubt, he was already visualizing the boots standing in a place of honor in the clutter of his closet floor. He walked over to the chair by the desk to try them on. I turned away from the rather obscene spectacle and poured myself another shot of Bushmills. I killed the shot and tried not to listen to the gruntings and rantings of Ratso as he forced his feet into the boots. I poured out another shot for both myself and Mick Brennan and we made a little cocktail chatter to compete with a noise that sounded like the Stoney Mountain Cloggers live from the Grand Ole Opry.

When I turned around again Ratso was already back in the chair trying, rather unsuccessfully, to get the boots off. I could see that they were several sizes too small and it was not going to be easy. He was clearly in some pain.

'Motherfucker!' he shouted.

'As a fellow American,' I said, 'let me help you take them off.'

Eventually, the feat was accomplished, and the feet which

446

remained on the floor of my loft, clad in green socks with little red hockey players, seemed quite relieved.

Ratso leaned back in the chair like a dead man. After a long interval, he spoke in a wistful mock-tragic tone.

He said: 'Sometimes I wonder if I'll *ever* find my Prince Charming.'

'Mate,' said Brennan. 'Have you tried Fort Dicks?'

28

The morning broke cold and lonely over the city, almost as if it knew I was going to call Tom Baker's father. Possibly the problem for me was that finding the film had become almost a spiritual task. Now that I'd found it I had to admit that Tom Baker was really dead. If it can be said that crazy Irishmen ever die. Personally, I doubt it. I think they come back like the green buds of springtime, leprechauns bringing courage and irrational cheer to the loneliest moments of all our lonely lives.

'Mr Baker,' I said. 'It's Kinky in New York.'

'I know,' said Tom Baker's father. 'It's kinky out here in San Francisco, too.'

The apple never fell far from the tree, I thought. Of course, as Allen Ginsberg once reminded me, 'Sometimes the tree falls down.'

'We've found Tom's movie,' I said.

'That's great news, Kinky. I got a call a few days ago from a woman who's Joe Franklin's secretary. She said the film had been stolen and wondered if I had a copy. Of course I didn't.'

'Like I said, we've got the film. I'll have a copy made and send you the original as soon as I check out a few things.'

'That's wonderful. Tom was very proud of his work.'

'I'm proud of Tom's work, too,' I said.

'We've put Tom's ashes on the Embarcadero. You know he grew up there. Played there as a kid.'

We talked a while longer, promised to keep in close touch, then we hung up and I walked over to the kitchen window. The cat jumped up on the sill and stood next to me. I stroked her gently until her purring seemed to rise above the noise of the street and fill the loft with something akin to peace of mind. I wasn't sure whose mind. It almost didn't matter.

I didn't know what the Embarcadero looked like but I hoped to hell it wasn't as drab as Vandam Street that morning. I knew it was somewhere by the ocean. Probably a beautiful view. Pick up a sea breeze every now and then. A little sunshine. A little rain.

'Must go familiar place,' I said to the cat.

The cat said nothing. But her eyes were green.

29

Most people who live in Manhattan are about as likely to visit Khazakstan as they are to ever go to Brooklyn. This does not necessarily reflect negatively upon Brooklyn. It just shows how small-town big-city people are. Rambam, of course, lived in Brooklyn, and was probably one of the reasons people in Manhattan didn't like to go there. Nonetheless, later that morning, I found myself arguing with him on the blower, in favour of making the trip.

'Let's go on out there to that restaurant,' I said. 'Soak up some ambience. After all, if we can find where the Don Sepulveda sighting took place, something may start to happen.'

'We can find it all right,' said Rambam. 'And something no doubt will start to happen. But it'd be safer if we use the old hardboiled computer method.'

'What is the old hardboiled computer method?'

'We access wire transfers from the bank. Say a hundred credit cards used that night the Elvis impersonator was there. Find a guy in his fifties with a credit history of only a couple years. Could be our man.'

'What if he paid cash?'

'We're fucked.'

'Look, let's use the old Sam Spade approach. Let's go to the fair and see the bear. No computer ever devised knows how to follow a hunch.'

'And I was so looking forward to cross-referencing databases.'

448

And so it was that I found myself looking out over the fishing boats on Sheepshead Bay and wondering what our own catch would be by the end of the afternoon. Off to the right were the bay and the fishing fleet, and on the left were lobster restaurants, clam joints, and old men who looked like Don Sepulveda impersonators drinking espresso at outdoor tables.

'Those guys must have iron balls,' I said.

'They go inside when it snows,' said Rambam. He slowed the car a bit and seemed to be looking for the place by Italian radar.

'Why do they call this Sheepshead Bay?' I asked. 'Some guy wake up one morning with a sheep's head in bed next to him?'

'Nothing that exciting. Several hundred years ago there used to be a sheep *shed* here and over the years the name became perverted.'

'So did everybody in New York,' I said.

It didn't take Rambam long to park the car and point across the way to a certain restaurant.

'How do you know that's the place?' I said. 'They all look the same.'

'Not to an Italian.'

'What do we do now?' The place suddenly did not look all that inviting.

'We go in, order an espresso, drop a name, and hope it's the right one.'

'Maybe we should first try cross-referencing some databases.'

Rambam got out of the car. 'Let's go, Sam Spade,' he said.

We went in, ordered two espressos, and struck up a rather lifeless conversation with the only thing who seemed to be moving in the place, a heavy-set, tough-looking guy named Dominick. Obviously, the name Rambam dropped has been changed to protect both of our asses, but the pertinent conversation, as I heard it, went something like this:

Rambam: 'You know, I'm a friend of Frankie Lasagna's. If you'd help us out I think he'd really appreciate it.'

Dominick: 'I don't know nuttin'.'

Rambam: 'That time you had that Elvis impersonator down here, that must've been a wild night.'

449

Dominick: 'You want a cannoli with that?'

Rambam: 'No thanks. You guys use a mailing list or anything for that Elvis impersonator show?'

Dominick: 'I don't know nuttin'.'

Rambam: 'Look, I'm just doing a favor for Frankie Lasagna. Can we have a look at the credit card stubs for that night?'

Dominick: 'I don't know nuttin'.'

At this point, Dominick glowered at us and walked away through a door in the kitchen.

'That Frankie Lasagna name really opens the doors, doesn't it,' I said. I lit a cigar and took a few puffs to settle my nerves.

'Watch that kitchen door,' said Rambam. 'When it opens he's either going to be carrying two espressos or an uzi.'

'Too bad we didn't have a meal here. It'd be a nice digestive aid.'

'I tell you, Frankie Lasagna should've worked.'

'Maybe he don't know nuttin',' I said.

Moments later, the kitchen door opened and Dominick came out with two espressos and a scowl. We drank the espressos. I smoked the cigar.

As we went over to pay the check, Rambam took out a card and wrote a number on it.

'If you decide to know something,' he said, 'give me a call.'

We left the place and walked to the car without looking back.

'I don't think he knows anything,' said Rambam.

'He made that pretty clear,' I said. 'But doesn't this make you kind of nervous?'

'Why should I be nervous?' said Rambam. 'I gave him your phone number.'

30

I didn't sleep very well that night. I dreamed that Dominick was holding me at gunpoint with some large unpleasant Wyatt Earp kind of handgun. Dominick was smoking a cigar and, to make things more painful for me, a slower death, he kept one end of the cigar in his mouth and the other, the lit end, held against the hammer mechanism of the gun. He was waiting for it to get hot enough to explode and kill me and I was becoming quite agitated waiting for a pizza to be delivered.

'I *ordered* pepperoni,' I said, 'I expect them to *bring* me pepperoni.'

'I'm sure I don't know a thing about this matter,' said Dominick in a highly cultivated British accent.

The pizza in the dream finally arrived. It was brought to me by Uptown Judy. There was a black funeral wreath on top of the pizza box. She was wearing her red cowboy boots.

'Nice boots,' I said.

'I need them,' she said. 'I'm headin' for the last round-up.'

There were some important questions I knew I wanted to ask her, but, in the irritating fashion of dreams, I could not put the right words together. All I could do was keep repeating my petulant little pepperoni monologue and watch Dominick puff away on his cigar.

'Why you lookin' at me,' he said, vaselining back to his Italian persona. 'I don't know nuttin'.'

'But I do,' said Uptown Judy, and she opened the pizza box.

Her flesh began melting.

'How're you gonna find me,' she said in a voice that was fading with the dream. 'How're you gonna find me if you don't know who I am?'

Some of her flesh, I noticed, was now falling directly onto the pizza in rather neat little circles that bore an uncanny resemblance to pepperoni. Her eyes fell somewhere into the pizza like two olives and I found, as I stared into their empty sockets, that I could no longer remember if they were green or they were blue or if they merely resembled Elton John's. As the dream ended, I heard a dull explosion somewhere in the near distance and woke up to find the circulation to my scrotum rather severely restricted by an unfortunate twist in my sarong.

I stumbled out of bed, rectified the situation, and noticed that the cat had knocked one of Judy's red cowboy boots off the counter, no doubt causing the muffled explosion at the end of the dream. There's a lot of reality in our dreams. Fortunately, we

Kinky Friedman

manage to sleep through most of it. There's also a great deal of dream material in our lives. Fortunately, we manage to live through most of it.

Just at the moment things looked black indeed for myself and the cat. In my case, I was out of espresso. In my maddening search for the cabinets and drawers in the kitchen, some of them having not been opened in many years, all I found was a small jar of decaffeinated instant, left there long ago, no doubt, by some forgotten lover. I always have believed that if you drink enough instant decaff you will cease to exist.

The cat's situation was equally precarious. She was obviously very hungry and all she had left was one can of cat food. Southern Gourmet Dinner.

To add to our problems the phones began ringing rather ominously. I walked over to the desk and picked up the blower on the left.

'Dis is Dominick,' said the voice.

'Yeah,' I said. This couldn't be happening so soon after my dream.

'Me and da boys're comin' over – '

'That's very cute, Rambam.'

'There's as much chance of him calling as there is of Jesus coming back in a Studebaker.'

'How about a Christler?' I quipped, quite elated to have escaped mob vengeance for another day.

'Look, I'm working on the hardboiled computer approach, but if this guy faked his own death successfully he's too smart to fall into some credit history trap. He's probably got a string of false identities that'd reach from Vandam Street to Sheepshead Bay.'

'There's a route I won't be taking again.'

'You won't have to,' said Rambam. 'I think the solution to your little problem lies much closer to home. You don't know much about Uptown Judy. You don't know what she was really all about. You didn't even know her dad was a big-time mobster. You want to find what happened to her you've got to fill in her background more fully. I can't believe you were hosing somebody and you don't really know a fucking thing about her.'

452

'Okay, so I was slightly amphibious,' I protested. 'I didn't even know who I was. How the hell am I supposed to remember who she was.'

'Well, that's what you've got to find out. You got the Elvis documentary back for Baker's dad. You correctly connected Uptown Judy with the film. But now you're in deeper waters. Not just doing a favor for a dead friend's family. You're investigating two murders. Because you don't know shit about the victims – the first thing every good investigator tries to learn – you're all over the road. You can't get a focus on things. You really got no case at all until you find out more about who was this person you call Uptown Judy.'

Having the attention span of a cocker spaniel, it was one of the longest incoming wounded monologues I'd listened to in years without interrupting. Of course, I was fairly brain-dead at the time because of the espresso situation. But I was very glad I'd listened.

'Thanks,' I said. 'You've really put the thing in perspective for me.' Even if he'd spent the previous morning on a cat stake-out, I knew Rambam was making sense.

'Forget it,' he said. 'You're handling a tricky case here. My gut feeling – my Jewish-Italian intuition – tells me that these two murders could well have been connected but they probably weren't done by the mob.'

'I'll be sure and tell that to Dominick when he calls,' I said.

'He's not gonna call,' said Rambam. 'Whether or not this case gets solved is going to depend on only one thing.'

'And what would that be?' I asked. I lit a cigar and waited but I still wasn't ready for Rambam's reply when it came.

'How many brain cells you haven't fried,' he said.

After I cradled the blower I sat at the desk for a long while in the manner of your everyday catatonic. My mind was humming along on about one cylinder. I knew Rambam was right. In the final analysis it would devolve to me to solve this case. The Village Irregulars, invaluable as they often were, could only clearly see the parts of the puzzle that had been delegated to each of them. If anybody could see the whole picture, it ought to be me. Good luck, I thought. At the moment I had my hands full coordinating the motor control to relight my cigar.

Finally, I gave up the task, put the cigar in the ashtray, picked up the cat, and, still in my brain-dead state, walked over to the couch for a little power nap. I'd only been awake for about half an hour but it'd been very taxing. Already there appeared to be some leakage between the pizza dream and the Rambam phone call. They were starting to run together like my old tie-dyed pair of socks.

I laid down on the couch with the cat on my chest and tried to imagine Uptown Judy's face. It was a blank like Inspector Maigret's. For a moment, I thought I had something. Something familiar in a smile, in the eyes. Then I lost it – thanks largely to the nightmare whirlwind of drugs, booze and fast-lane insanity that at one time I called my life.

I kept mixing Uptown Judy in with all the others and losing her in dark, disembodied images percolating up from someplace in my not-so-distant past. It was the kind of thing that, providing you were sane at the moment, could drive you crazy.

At least I knew Maigret's habits and mannerisms and style – could see him smoking his pipe, could see his raincoat hanging up by the radiator, could see him familiarizing himself with the victim of the case, patiently, passionately, ruthlessly, almost as one would with a lover.

' "How do I love thee," ' I said to the cat. ' "Let me count the ways." '

31

'Hell no,' I said to Downtown Judy, 'we don't need your help locating Don Sepulveda. We're already on his trail, it's too dangerous for womenfolk, and, besides, you've interrupted my power nap.'

'But I want to help,' she said plaintively. I held the blower in one hand and lit a post-power-nap cigar with the other.

'To quote my friend Chinga: "A woman's place is on my face," '

I said stolidly. 'The mob already has my number, Judy. I don't want them to get yours.'

'Wait a minute,' she said. 'I'm supposed to be told as much about the case as the other guys. I thought this was the Village Irregulars. All for one and one for all!'

'Fuck the Village Irregulars,' I said, 'and feed 'em Froot Loops.'

'Fuck you!' said Judy, her voice breaking with emotion.

'All right, look,' I said. 'You could help Brennan track down his crazy story about the guy with the illustrious past in the snuff film industry. Supposedly, according to lowly-placed sources, he may also have some photos of Uptown Judy which we badly need to circulate and which I badly need to jump-start my memory bank. Right now, the times I was with her seem almost like a dream. Maybe she wanted it that way.'

There was silence on the line and I wondered briefly if jealousy was again rearing its ugly green head.

Then Judy said: 'What's a snuff film?'

Oh Christ, I thought, we're sending a lamb to the slaughter. Nonetheless, it seemed at the time to be safer for Judy to be helping Brennan run down a rumour about a snuff film-maker than to be stumbling around the trail of a desperate mafia don with Pelligrino in his veins.

'A snuff film,' I said, 'is an illegal, amoral actual cinematic documentation of a person getting croaked. An actor has to really be desperate to take the job. There are of course, no sequels.'

'Jesus,' said Judy. 'Have you ever seen one?'

'No, but I've seen a lot of performances that have made me wish the movie was a snuff film.'

'And this guy may have photos of Uptown Judy?'

'Yes. And he may be very dangerous to children and green plants. If you locate him or his studio don't mess with him. Call me.'

I gave Judy Brennan's phone number, told her to work closely with Mick, and warned her again that if they should miraculously find the monster, not to approach it. She was almost in a state of sexual excitement when I hung up the phone. I was not in a state of sexual excitement when I picked up the blower again and called Ratso.

'Can you meet me at the Garden in a few hours?' I said.

'The Garden?'

'You know, the place you go about 79 times a week to watch hockey. I want you to take me through that rat maze, pardon the expression, so we can talk to a few of Uptown Judy's employers or co-workers.'

'Okay,' said Ratso, 'but the meter's running. This'll cost you at least one more big hairy steak.'

'Done,' I said.

'Medium-rare,' said Ratso. 'By the way, I've found out some interesting shit about Elvis. Did you know they now believe Elvis was Jewish?'

'That's funny,' I said. 'He didn't look Jewish.'

I cradled the blower, picked up a few cigars, and told the cat she was in charge of the boots, the pizza box, and the loft while I was gone. I put on my cowboy hat and hunting vest and stepped into a half-frozen, steel-gray afternoon. Nobody had their picnic basket out. A guy living in a cardboard box down the street was cutting little windows out of the sides like you used to do when you were a kid. If anybody was ever a kid.

I walked to Seventh Avenue to a little deli-grocery store run by some kind of born-again Koreans. More and more I was beginning to believe that I had the soul of a Korean businessman. I did not waste time on the window dressing of life. I survived only on the bare essentials. And these I stockpiled fairly heavily. If things got much worse in the city I might not want to go out again.

I bought enough cat food for all nine lives, enough cat litter to accommodate a snow leopard if any still existed, and enough espresso to keep Little Italy awake past its bedtime which is never. I also made a fairly sizable investment in toilet paper.

As I lugged my purchases up Vandam Street, my thoughts were not on meeting Ratso at the Garden. Or on Judy and Mick and the snuff film character. Or on Rambam cross-referencing databases. Or on the whereabouts of Don Sepulveda. Or on Elvis impersonators. Not even on my own horror at how the Swiss cheese effect had hamstrung my mind to where I could barely recall a woman I'd been to bed with.

My thoughts instead were of a bright vivid long-ago summer day on our ranch in Texas. I'd gone into the storeroom and come out with three rolls of toilet paper. My friend Slim sitting on a wooden Coke crate, leaning against the dining hall and drinking a can of warm Jax, his old black sun-blinded face under a paper Rainbow Bread cap watching the world go by. As I emerged from the storeroom carrying the three rolls of toilet paper, Slim had made a comment that I have never forgotten and one that has been a guiding spiritual force through many of my life's darkest hours.

'How many assholes you got?' he'd said.

32

Several hours later, Ratso and I met at the Will Call window of Madison Square Garden. We'd met there many times before but this particular afternoon it was not to get tickets to a Ranger game. This was not a game. We weren't going into the Garden. Instead, we walked to a nearby building called 4 Penn Plaza which housed the Garden's executive offices. We signed in, rode elevators, talked to receptionists, all the things that little people usually do in big skyscrapers.

After two-and-a-half hours of listening to Ratso wheedle, worm, charm, and cajole his way into practically every office remotely related to the activities of the Garden, an interesting pattern emerged. No one had ever heard of Judy Sepulveda. At the public relations office where I was under the impression Judy had worked, a three-thousand-year-old woman trotted out her computer to show that no one named Judy had ever held a full-time position there. Much less Sepulveda. But it did seem to ring a distant bell to her. Maybe she'd heard it somewhere else.

As we left the building and decided to walk a few blocks down Seventh Avenue, Ratso commented that he was surprised I was in such an upbeat mood.

'Finally,' I said, 'after two-and-a-half hours of hell I'm able to light a cigar without some hemorrhoid-ridden nerd in a monkey suit telling me to put it out.'

'You got an extra cigar?' said Ratso.

'They don't make 'em extra,' I said, but I fished one out of my coat pocket and handed it to Ratso who then borrowed my butt-cutter, my matches, and my last nerve.

'C'mon,' said Ratso. 'You're in a good mood. You're not disappointed. It's like you expected this. What's up?'

'I'm just filled with admiration for you. I knew you were good but I didn't know you had a PhD in name-dropping.'

Ratso looked slightly hurt. 'I wasn't name-dropping,' he said. 'I just know a lot of people who know a lot of people.'

I smiled at Ratso as we walked up Seventh, puffing on our cigars, vaguely enjoying the ever-changing human scenery.

'And none of whom,' I said, 'seem to know Uptown Judy.'

Ratso claimed he still had some work to do at the *Lampoon*, so after another block or two, he grabbed a cab and I continued walking toward the Village. For a while now something had been tickling at the back of my mind and, finding that Uptown Judy had apparently fabricated her job at the Garden, turned the tickle into a shower massage of my medulla oblongata. It was a veritable symphony of wrong notes. I couldn't name the work or the composer yet, but it was most assuredly a virtuoso performance.

I walked all the way back to the Village to clear my head and then, when that didn't work, I stopped at a little Irish bar to mess it up again. When I got to the loft it was ten o'clock and I didn't know where my children were. I wasn't even sure what had happened to my imaginary childhood friends.

I made a little small talk with the cat and a little before bedtime cocktail for myself. I put *South Pacific* on the victrola, my feet up on the desk, and all thoughts of Uptown Judy in abeyance. I considered briefly Ratso's offer for me to write an article for *High Times* magazine, a popular drug and paraphernalia publication of which Ratso was a former editor. *High Times* often featured a pull-out centerfold section devoted to high-fashion photographs of high-quality cocaine. It was never clear how widely read the mag was but a lot of people liked to try to snort the centerfold.

Ratso had made two suggestions for the subject matter of the proposed article. One was a piece about my Peace Corps experiences in the jungles of Borneo. The other was a piece about my almost total repression of my experiences with Uptown Judy. In either case, Ratso had suggested that the title of the article should be: 'My Scrotum Flew Tourist – A Personal Odyssey.'

I had my doubts.

I patted the pizza box a few times affectionately, killed the lights, and headed off to bed at an obscenely early hour. The week ahead promised to be a very busy and productive one. A still, small voice within was beginning to whisper to me. This had occurred before, and it was always a harbinger of the solution of a case being just within my grasp. The possibility existed, of course, that it could just be gas. But something about the voice caused me to do what my mother always believed I could: Listen with my heart. Something about the voice told me that when I solved the case, and I had no doubt now that I would, it would always remain, in some very significant ways, spiritually insoluble.

Because of these inner circumstances, I very briefly considered a bedtime prayer. Then I said to hell with it. Let the good Christians around the world pray for my eternal soul. Let the little old man with a beanie traverse the slums of South America and tell the hopeless, starving, uneducated families of twelve not to use rubbers. It cost forty million dollars for him to make the trip. Why couldn't the Catholic church spend it on feeding all the cats left behind by all the witches of the world that it had burned?

The cat and I were about halfway to Sandland when the phones began ringing violently. We both leaped sideways and I collared the little slightly effeminate princess bedside blower that remained from a former occupant. Probably the guy in the floral kimono at Uptown Judy's place. Judy herself, of course, seemed now almost certainly to be on perpetual call forward.

'Let's have it,' I said into the ridiculous little pink speaker.

'Kinky!' screamed Downtown Judy. 'Kinky!' She was clearly hysterical.

'Hold the weddin',' I said. 'Tell me what's happened.'

'It's Mick,' she said. 'Mick Brennan's been burned to death!'

33

It wasn't far from Sandland to hell, but the ride over in the hack seemed interminable. The driver, a gaunt woman, who vaguely resembled a witch to the superstitious mind, managed to catch every pothole and every red light. The potholes didn't bother me but each red light seemed to be taking the gestation period of an elephant off my life. For a brief fantastic moment I wished I were Dumbo the Elephant. With my big, floppy-disc ears I would fly like the Kayan witches of Borneo, collect Jiminy Cricket or that tedious circus mouse somewhere along the way, and arrive in time to save Mick Brennan with the coffee-colored water from the Baram River in my trunk. I blew my nose in a black bandanna. I didn't know what it meant in the homosexual color code but it hardly seemed to matter at the moment.

'C'mon,' I shouted to the driver, after waiting several years at a red light. 'It's an emergency.'

'Okay, it's an emergency,' she said. 'Where's the fire?'

As we pulled over to the address on Canal Street we saw it. It was a five-story warehouse type building and fire was engulfing the top floor. The flames were painfully visible in the top floor windows like hellish heretical tongues licking lasciviously at the New York night.

With the sounds of sirens far in the distance I threw some money at the driver and ran to a small landing on the side of the building. The bottom floor looked cool and collected. No one around. There was an intercom and a row of rusty buttons that seemed like they belonged on the uniform of a soldier on the Russian Front. The names meant nothing to me. The door felt cold. I tried it for the hell of it. It opened big and slowly like a children's storybook.

I looked up and saw black smoke beginning to wreath the top of the building. The pope was dead, I thought. But I was not ready to give up on Mick Brennan.

'Mick!' I shouted. 'Judy!'

Nothing but the sirens getting closer, always, seemingly, infuriatingly, taking their time at times like this. I looked around for any sign of life on the planet. It was a dark corner of Canal and Nowhere and, of course, there was nothing. I entered slowly, carefully, as if the fiery building were a virgin. As I came to the first stairwell, it began vaguely dawning on me what the place probably was. The studio of the reputed snuff film photographer. That would make sense. Judy had called Brennan and they'd agreed to rendezvous here.

I ran up to the second floor, still seeing no signs of the fire. In fact, there was no activity at all. Possibly, the bottom floors were warehouses or offices of some kind. At the third floor I began to hear crackling noises and things exploding above me. I still couldn't smell the smoke but my beezer was not the best after years of cigar-smoking, cat fur, and recreational drug use. I shouted for Mick and Judy again. Nothing.

On the fourth level I smelled the smoke and began hearing noises both above and below me. Downstairs, the rescue units were entering the building. Upstairs, I could only imagine. On the way up to the top floor I could see the smoke and feel the heat. On the landing at the top of the stairs a form was moving. Crouching to stay under a layer of smoke, I made my way carefully toward it. It was Downtown Judy.

Her face was smudged and she looked disoriented, and she wandered dazedly along the stairwell. 'Oh, God,' she said. 'Mick told me the guy's studio was up here and the guy definitely had the photos of Uptown Judy. He told me to wait outside and watch in case the guy came back. Then Mick went up and – I saw the fire – I heard him screaming – I tried to get through – '

'Stay right here,' I said.

I crawled under the smoke to the door of the guy's studio. I kicked at the door but it didn't budge. Behind it I could hear what hell must be like – rushing, hissing, cracking, swooshing sounds – the kind of noises most people usually only hear in their dreams. I banged on the door and burned my hand. I yelled repeatedly for Mick. I was still yelling his name when a hand grabbed me hard from the back. It was a guy from the fire department rescue unit.

'Let's rock 'n' roll,' he said.

461

Outside in the cold, Judy and I huddled in a blanket as the rescue teams went to work. Her eyes had a glazed look and she was shivering.

'Where'd you call me from?' I said.

She didn't seem to hear my question. I asked her again.

'When I heard the screaming I ran up there. I couldn't get in the door and the wall was hot. I ran back down to the payphone around the corner and called 911. Then I called you. Then I – must've run back up to try to help Mick.'

'You did your best,' I said.

We waited for a long time while the crews brought men and equipment into the building. Somebody gave us some coffee.

'Is there any hope for someone up there?' I asked a fireman standing by a truck.

'There's always hope,' he said. 'I've seen 'em bring 'em out of places lots worse than this.'

Something collapsed upstairs. Sparks went shimmering up into the skyline. My guts seemed to turn inside me. There was hope all right. It was the 'thing with feathers that perches in the soul.' There was also death. It was the thing that disappears like little fireflies into the cold gray canopy of heaven.

Moments later, two rescue guys carried a large black canvas bag with a zipper all down the side of it. I'd seen those bags before. Most recently when they'd taken a guitar player named Tequila out of my rain room and left his face and half his brains behind in the rub. I didn't have to ask anybody if there was any hope now.

'Can I see the body?' I asked one of the guys carrying the bag. 'Maybe I can identify it.'

'Forget it,' he said. 'If you'd known this guy since he was a kid, you wouldn't know him now. Gonna take dental records, my man.'

I decided to take Judy and go over to McGovern's. I left his number with a guy from the rescue unit in case anything further transpired. Not that anyone expected anything. Once they've shown you the body bag it's pretty hard for them to Part II you.

After a cab ride that I hardly remember, we rang McGovern's buzzer about seven times and he finally let us in. He took one look at the two of us and knew it was bad. He didn't know how bad. He and Brennan had been close for.a lot of years. Not enough to i.d. the contents of a body bag, but just about enough to break your heart.

I'll spare you the tragic details but a lot of Irish Whiskey got drunk in the next hour or two. I did a lot of pacing in front of McGovern's fireplace, McGovern sat in his old overstuffed chair staring at the fire, and Judy remembered a few more pieces of information, including the name of the snuff film photog that owned the studio. It was Dennis Malowitz. Not that this knowledge meant a damn to any of us anymore. I felt as drunk and numb as I'd ever been in my life and that was going a ways.

McGovern was still in the same position, Judy was sitting like a ragdoll in a chair by the little table, and I'd halfway passed out on the couch which had been to England and back on the QE2. Mick Brennan had made that trip across the ol' herring pond many times in his life, but he'd never make it again.

I was deciding whether to hang myself from McGovern's shower rod or wait a while and do it when I got to my place. Mick's death was as much my fault, I felt, as if I'd killed him with my own hands. I could let Stephanie DuPont take the cat. Of course, Clemmie and Daisy might not go for that. Maybe Winnie Katz'd take her again. I didn't have to tell her that this time it'd be forever. Maybe –.

The buzzer rang.

I started to get up but McGovern was already there pushing the voice button. For a large, drunken Irishman, he could move pretty fast.

'Mate,' we heard a voice say. 'Mate. It's Brennan. Let me in the fuckin' door.'

The three of us ran down the hallway and McGovern picked Brennan up about four feet off the floor in a giant bear hug. When we got Brennan into McGovern's apartment he didn't look any the worse for wear except for the sizable knot on his head. Apparently, he'd never gotten into the building at all. He'd left Judy at the rendezvous point nearby and somebody'd waylaid him on the side street off Canal. When he came to, the rescue unit gave him McGovern's number.

'Now where's the Bushmills?' said Brennan.

We hollered and celebrated and hugged Mick and jumped around for a while until the old lady downstairs began jabbing her ceiling rather violently with the broom.

'Fuck her,' said McGovern. 'Mick! I never thought I'd be this happy to see you.'

'You probably never will be again, mate,' said Brennan.

McGovern's loud Irish laughter filled the little apartment and shook the piles of old newspapers like a small earthquake. We had another round or two, and then, as dawn began surreptitiously slithering through the dusty Venetian blinds, Brennan turned to me quite seriously.

'Bit odd, isn't it, mate,' he said. 'They clear Uptown Judy's photos out of her flat. Now they knock me on the head and torch this bloke's studio.'

I toasted Brennan's health with a final shot of Black Bush for the road. I lit a cigar.

'Some people,' I said, 'don't like to have their pictures taken.'

34

'So this is sort of a secular Last Supper,' I said, 'for the Village Irregulars.'

'Oh,' said Chinga, 'can I be Judas?'

I ignored the comment. It was several days since the snuff film fire and I'd invited the whole group to Luna's Restaurant in Little Italy. Unlike Jesus, whose last words at the end of the meal reportedly were 'Separate checks', I was rather grudgingly happy to reward everybody for their hard work.

'We're here,' I said, 'to celebrate Mick Brennan's presence among us – '

'Cheers, mates,' said Brennan, holding up a glass of wine. 'I'd like to propose a toast to myself – '

'Who he?' said Ratso in his Sly Stone falsetto.

' – to celebrate Mick Brennan's presence among us,' I continued, 'which is already starting to get up my sleeve, and to inform you all that, while the search for Uptown Judy and for the mysterious person on the Elvis film (whom we will not mention because of our present locus) continues, we are asking the Village Irregulars to oblige us by taking a little sabbatical.'

'Who's we?' said Rambam. 'You got a mouse in your pocket?'

'Just the little ol' royal "we",' I said. 'I appreciate everything all of you have done.'

'He's solved the case,' said Ratso. 'I know you, Sherlock.'

'My dear Ratso,' I said, 'it is true that we've cleverly recovered the Elvis film for Tom Baker's father, but the case itself is far from solved. Some patterns, however, are beginning to emerge.'

'Some patterns,' said Ratso, 'are beginning to emerge in my *zuppa da pesce*.'

'Hey,' said Chinga, 'I just got aboard this ship and you're already puttin' it in mothballs.'

'Yeah,' I said, 'but it's a mighty big moth.'

Reactions among the group varied from relief to irritation to ennui. I tried to assure them that I was not permanently disbanding the Village Irregulars, just asking them to give it a rest.

'You want us to cut you some slack,' said Chinga, 'while you and Rambam solve the case.'

'Lighten up on the Kinkster,' said Downtown Judy. 'Whatever his methods are, they've worked in the past. He must have good reasons for doing what he's doing.'

'Right,' said Ratso. 'Let's celebrate. Let's order some champagne.'

'How about some Dom Perignon?' said Judy.

'That's *very* coochi-poochi-boomalini,' I said. 'I'll just have some more wine.'

'Yeah,' said McGovern, 'let's have some dago red.'

'Let's just watch our mouth,' said Rambam, as the large Italian waiter hovered near by.

Downtown Judy prevailed and ordered several bottles of Dom Perignon, which rapidly were poured down the throats of the Village Irregulars, some of whom were becoming not a little inebriated.

465

Kinky Friedman

'What if we're just sittin' here,' said Brennan, 'and a guy comes in wearing strange old-country garb. You know an old felt hat and a coat that's several decades out of fashion.'

'Yeah?' said Rambam. 'What's your point?'

'The guy's kinda familiar-lookin', wearing this old funny hat and suddenly the room gets real quiet.'

'I don't like where this is going,' I said to McGovern.

'Nobody can control the little fucker,' said McGovern, as Brennan filled his champagne glass with a maniacal expression on his face. 'That's why they call him the "Poison Dwarf".'

'I heard that,' said Brennan. 'But we'll let it pass, mate.'

'Christ,' said McGovern, 'that's a relief.'

'I wanta hear the story,' said Chinga.

'Don't worry,' said McGovern. 'You will.'

Somehow another bottle of Dom Perignon had gotten itself ordered and Brennan was already working on it. I hadn't brought my abacus with me but it was a good thing that the only currency I valued, in the words of the great Mahatma, was the 'coin of the spirit'. That was about all I was going to have left when we closed the place.

'There he is!' shouted Brennan. 'There's the bloke right there!'

The restaurant *had* gotten rather quiet. Standing in the doorway was just such a strange character as Brennan had earlier described.

'It's Don Sepulveda!' he shouted. 'Don! C'mon, mate! Join us! Have a drink!'

McGovern and Rambam had both made moves towards Brennan but it was too late. The man at the door looked at all of us as if he were marking our faces for an extremely unpleasant method of extinction. If ever a guy looked like a godfather, he was it. Of course, in Little Italy, any old fart dressed in odd, old-world garb can assume a demeanor, make a dramatic entrance into a place, and come off like a godfather. Nevertheless, the place, with the exception of Brennan, had gotten pretty damn quiet. Either the other patrons were stunned just like I was, or the guy *was* some kind of mob big shot.

'Nice hat,' said Brennan, in an only slightly more modulated voice.

466

McGovern was struggling with Brennan as the guy in the doorway shrugged almost imperceptibly, walked through Luna's, and disappeared into a back room. I remembered Michael Bloomfield making fun of a guy's hat in Luna's once. Now he was dead.

'I tell you, mate,' Brennan was saying, 'he's a godfather impersonator.'

'You see what I mean,' said Rambam. 'You're an amateur and these are all just your assistant amateurs. This kind of shit is goddamn dangerous. How could you let them get involved in this?'

'I don't know,' I said. 'I must've had a nail in my head.'

35

'This has been unlike any case I've ever handled,' I said to the cat. 'We've turned up the missing Elvis film. We've learned that Don Sepulveda, contrary to popular opinion, is still alive. Maybe we should let it go at that.'

The cat said nothing. She stared at me with the gaze usually reserved for anyone insane enough to serve her anything other than tuna. The cat didn't give a damn about the personal or professional peccadillos of people. I didn't either.

It was later in the week and the cat and I were alone in the loft. I was smoking my JFK pipe, which now had a mildly aromatic flavour, no doubt as a result of residual cat vomit. In weeks to come people would quite possibly comment on the distinctive, somewhat exotic, aroma of the tobacco. No doubt, I would have to field many questions about what kind of tobacco it was and where I'd gotten it. I would, in that event, offer my guests a little port, tamp the tobacco a trifle, sit back in my chair and puff away rather complacently. Then I would tell them that a cat had vomited in my pipe. They would laugh. I would laugh. We'd laugh and laugh and garbage trucks would ponderously roll by, birds would sing in perfect quadraphonic stereo, little toy trains would derail, and people who really loved each other would go their separate ways in this cantilevered remedial world.

I had never particularly minded being alone and I minded it

even less now that everybody was gone. I had the cat and JFK. Who else did I need? I thought of what Amelia Earhart once had told people who'd asked her how she felt flying so long alone in the cockpit, alone in the sky. 'I felt as if I were among friends,' Amelia had said.

Among friends, I thought? With friends like mine I didn't need a brown bandanna in my left hip pocket. My mind drifted back to the Last Supper scene several days ago at Luna's. I had almost forgotten it. Almost. Now I saw again clearly the strange old man in the strange old-world garb. He wasn't Don Sepulveda, of course. But he was somebody with a mystical, ancient, evil aura about him. Somebody you shouldn't say 'Nice hat' to.

Rambam may have been right. The case was far too dangerous to unnecessarily involve amateurs. Maybe that included me. Now that I thought about it, Uptown Judy had been one of the most mysterious women I'd ever known. Perhaps she'd always be. Maybe the very fact that I was having so much trouble getting her photo was significant in itself. Clap your hands if you believe in vampires.

I got up, made some hot chocolate, and paced around the loft a bit, sipping from a chipped, happy-face mug and puffing fitfully on JFK. The cat was sitting on her rocker busying herself scratching what, apparently, was an exceedingly troublesome flea. Every now and then she looked up at me with pity in her eyes.

'Something tells me,' I said, 'that one of the reasons this case hasn't been solved is that I don't really want to know.'

The cat said nothing.

That was fine with me.

36

The following afternoon, Downtown Judy, JFK, and I were sitting by my kitchen window. Two of us were smoking contentedly.

'That's nice-smelling tobacco,' she said. 'Has kind of a sweet, tangy smell to it. Where'd you get it?'

'Don't ask,' I said.

'Okay,' she said. 'Then let me ask you something else. How're you coming along on the Don Sepulveda case now that you've fired all the Village Irregulars?'

'I didn't fire the Village Irregulars. I just asked them to get a life while they were still breathing. There's already been so much death surrounding this case – Uptown Judy, Legs, Malowitz the snuff film king. About the only source of hope for our souls is the apparent resurrection of Don Sepulveda.'

'So you think you'll find him?'

'Secrets like this, my dear, don't remain secrets very long. Too many people know already. There've been too many deaths for me not to follow it through. Don Sepulveda has very little chance now. If I don't find him, the killer or killers of Uptown Judy will. Other mob factions will. Possibly, even the police will. The net's already closing in around Sepulveda as it is around those who murdered Uptown Judy.'

Here, I paused dramatically to re-light my pipe. I paced a bit with the pipe and found, as opposed to the cigar, it seemed to lend an additional credence to my words. Smelled good, too.

'Very soon now Rambam will be getting Uptown Judy's photograph from DMV – that's Department of Motor Vehicles to you – and McGovern will be running the pic on the society page of the *Daily News*. That'll stir the hunter's stew a little. I may even decide to call the Village Irregulars out of retirement. But, in the meantime, let's just sit tight and watch what happens.'

What happened next caused both of us to experience a leap sideways situation. We heard a not-of-this-earth type of keening coming at us from a point which appeared to be about four inches outside the kitchen window. I looked down into the few feeble rays of afternoon sunlight that somehow had sandwiched their ways between the skyscrapers, warehouses, hammered metal, billboards, and other crap that blotted out the sky and would've made it hard even for Amelia to be alone. A giant of a man was standing in the shadows of the sidewalk and gesticulating violently toward us. It was McGovern, and, from his demeanor, one would judge that he'd been there quite a while. I opened the window and looked blandly outside.

'Whatever does he want?' I said.

'Throw down the fucking puppet head!' shouted McGovern. It was a little colder out there than I'd realized.

I went over to the top of the refrigerator where the little Negro puppet head was forever smiling down on me like a small, friendly Aztec god. I took the puppet head with the key in its mouth and the parachute attached, and hurled it out the window. I shut the window, turned, and without looking back, continued my pacing.

'It won't be long now,' I said.

'Till you catch Don Sepulveda?' said Judy teasingly. She did not relish the idea of having finally been included in the Village Irregulars just to have them go on sabbatical when things were getting interesting.

'No,' I said. 'Till McGovern finishes off my Jameson's.'

Indeed, it wasn't long before McGovern entered the loft holding the puppet head. For some reason the two spheres, the puppet's head and McGovern's head, appeared like a child's display of the solar system. True to form, McGovern went right to my liquor cabinet and poured himself a stiff shot.

'What kind of bar you runnin' here?' said McGovern. 'At least you could have the consideration to purchase the makings of a Vodka McGovern.'

'We're short of help,' I said.

McGovern looked around at the loft with the cat asleep on the rocker, Downtown Judy sulking by the window, the dishes growing science experiments in the sink, and the evening shadows stretching all across the dusty floor like a German forest of death. Added to this was my own fairly obvious expression of irritation at having my solitude disturbed, and the truly tedious, almost unconscionable pounding coming down upon us at two second intervals like drumbeats of destruction from the Isle of Lesbos.

'When's happy hour?' said McGovern.

'Happy hour,' said Downtown Judy, 'is when the rest of us get a chance to get back on this case and all the action isn't confined to the Lone Ranger here. Or should I say, Don Quixote?'

'One don's as good as another,' I said.

'Well,' said McGovern, 'I think the Village Irregulars do add an element.'

'Unfortunately, it's plutonium,' I said. 'Look, you've all been very helpful in the past. But these are extremely sensitive and potentially dangerous waters. There may soon be a time when everyone can share and care and help solve the goddamn thing together. Right now it's time for visions and revisions, thinking and re-thinking. This case is very strange and it's not responding very well to therapy. Particularly group therapy.'

'But two heads are better than one,' said McGovern, humorously holding the little smiling black puppet head next to his own, and smiling in an uncannily similar fashion. This provoked some laughter in Judy. It is possible that I might've even smiled.

'You're all my dear friends,' I said, 'but this case is also a personal thing for me. If I've made some false assumptions somewhere in the beginning, then we're all sailing off course, and we may encounter nightmare situations that would make the horrors of the Argonauts look like rubber ducks in a bathtub.'

'It's all Greek to me,' said McGovern.

'My word of honor as a furrier,' I said, 'as soon as I get a few things straightened out in my own mind, I'll let all of you in on it. It's just that things aren't adding up the way they should. I have to know what's going on in my own mind before I commit my troops to the field again.'

'You should commit Brennan to wig city,' said McGovern.

'There's nothing wrong with Brennan,' I said. 'There's nothing wrong with you, Judy, or with you, McGovern. It's just something I have to work out for myself. And I think I'll be able to do it. Fortunately, I carry my inventory between my ears.'

McGovern poured us all a shot at this point and we raised our glasses in a brief toast. 'To quote Tom Baker,' he said. ' "Use your head for something besides a hat rack." '

37

As the afternoon ratcheted down into evening, Rambam came over and, possibly sensing a boy's club ambience, Judy began making preparatory movements toward leaving. She made a phone call or two, looked around for her purse, then, as she was actually departing, walked past the red cowboy boots on the counter and stopped to admire them. In an almost enchanting way, the woman in her suddenly came to the surface and she forgot she was in a loft on Vandam Street and imagined for a moment she was looking into a fashionable window somewhere along Fifth Avenue. McGovern, Rambam, and I were suddenly passers-by on the sidewalk.

'Are these evidence or something?' she asked finally. 'I mean, can I try them on?'

'Why not?' I said. 'Everybody else has. Including Ratso.'

'Why does that not surprise me?' said Rambam.

As Judy took the boots over to the sofa to try them on, I left Rambam and McGovern to entertain themselves momentarily, walked over to the desk, and set JFK down to rest in an ashtray that had been cast in the shape of the state of Texas. Fitting resting place. JFK was only an airport now, but there'd been a time when he'd been an inspiration to many Americans and one of them had been me. I wouldn't have joined the Peace Corps if it hadn't been for JFK. I wouldn't have lived for two years in the jungles of Borneo. Ratso wouldn't be encouraging me to write 'My Scrotum Flew Tourist – A Personal Odyssey.'

I lit a cigar.

I was just about wrapping up my revery when Judy came Texas two-stepping across the room. I took a few patient puffs on the cigar and watched the spectacle.

'Try one floor up,' I said.

'They fit!' she shouted, as she danced by the desk. 'They fit me perfectly!'

She danced around the counter and wound up the little

impromptu number with a curtsy to Rambam. He looked at her with no sign of humanity in his eyes.

' "A drive-in Cinderella," ' I said, ' "in a Chevy named desire." Take the boots.'

'I couldn't,' said Judy hopefully.

'Take 'em,' I said. 'Somebody ought to get some use out of 'em. Just remember what Sergeant Cooperman always tells me: "Don't leave the city." '

'You mean there's someplace else to go besides New York?' said Rambam.

'There's a whole world out there, Rambam,' I said. 'It's not as perverse, jaded, crowded, dirty, sordid, or evil as New York, but, believe me, it's there.'

'Come on,' said Rambam, 'there's nothing out there and you know it.'

'There used to be a place once called Chicago,' said McGovern, as he fiddled with the Magnavox and landed on some old ball-room music. When McGovern listened to old-time ballroom music you could almost hear the silk gowns rustling across the floor of his brain.

As I walked Downtown Judy to the elevator, McGovern was lost in the land of was and Rambam was locked in a rather intense communication with his answering machine.

'The past and the present,' I remarked to Judy out in the hall-way. 'Both may be tense. But the future looks bright. Like the great Sherlock, I can't tell you everything I know or suspect, but I can say that I will have unraveled the parallel tales of the Sepulveda Family, father and daughter, very shortly now.'

'I wish I could help,' said Judy wistfully.

'You already have,' I said.

Just as Judy was entering the elevator I remembered to double-check the name and address of the custom boot manufacturer inside the cowboy boots. I got in with her and asked her to take one of them off. She tried and couldn't. When the cowboy boots fit really well they're hell to take off. Especially in a freight elevator.

After some pushing and pulling and twisting I got the bastard off, jotted down the pertinent information, and told Judy it could be an important lead and that I'd follow it up in the next day or two. I'd started to help her on with the boot just as the doors of the elevator opened to the lobby. With the red cowboy boot in one hand and Judy's foot in the other, my eyes locked with the Sapphic orbs of Winnie Katz, who'd evidently taken a brief break from her upstairs activities.

'Pretty kinky,' she said, as she entered and Judy hopped out of the elevator.

I handed her the boot through the open door. She shot me a quizzical look at Winnie.

'That's just Winnie,' I said, gesturing to the impatient feminine form on the far side of the otis box. 'She runs the wonderful alternative-lifestyle dance class in the loft above me. You may not've heard of it but you've certainly heard it.'

'It's not a dance class,' said Winnie evenly. 'It's a place where uninhibited women are not afraid to be who they are.'

'Don't forget that,' I said to Judy, and I winked just before the doors closed.

'Four, please,' I said to Winnie, who was obviously not in a position to reach the buttons which were only about two inches away from my right iris.

Winnie laughed a strange and knowing laugh, which, for some reason, made me feel uncomfortable. Then she said in a world-weary voice: 'Just push the buttons you know how to push.'

Einstein and Davy Crockett did not understand women, and there was no particular reason why I should either. No man really knew what went on between the earrings. You pushed the buttons you knew how to push. Winnie and I rode up in silence.

There was a time when Winnie'd been interested in me as her great heterosexual hope. I'd been interested in her, I suppose, if I were honest with myself, for the reason most men are fascinated with lesbians. To see if we have the social, spiritual, and sexual ability to wean them from their warped, wicked, womanizing ways. It fell a little short of being a noble aim. But love so often is driven by baser emotions, like a sleek, fast vehicle built with precision by remorseless Teutonic hands. Love would always be an expensive import in this world.

But all love aside, Winnie'd said something fairly cogent to the current state of affairs. She'd referred to her dance class as a 'place where uninhibited women are not afraid to be who they are.' Who were they anyway? And what the hell did they want? Not only was I fresh out of answers but it seemed that in the recent past a smattering of knowledge in this department might've been crucial to my understanding of a number of things. One of them was what happened to Uptown Judy. The elevator doors opened at my floor.

'Nice ride, elevator boy,' said Winnie.

I walked out and turned to look at her before the doors closed. There was something almost poignant in her mockery. There were aspects of life that would always elude the woman in her that wanted to be a man.

'You've come a long way, baby,' I said. 'But you still can't write your name in the snow.'

I entered the loft to find a rather surrealistic situation in progress. Before I'd even said a word, Rambam was holding his finger to his lips apparently imploring me to put a sock on my vocal mike. With his other hand he was scribbling furiously on a piece of paper. The Magnavox speaker was not pouring forth old-time ballroom music from the FM station on the far right of the dial. Instead, McGovern's own rich Irish baritone was emanating from the speaker. Either McGovern was a very highly accomplished ventriloquist or I was riding a hell of a cat vomit high. McGovern himself looked like he was about ready to fall down and suck the carpet.

'Jesus, Joseph, and Mary!' McGovern and the Magnavox said simultaneously. 'What in the fuck is going on?'

It was a fair question.

As McGovern and the Magnavox rambled on in tandem, Rambam shoved the note he'd written under my beezer. It read: DON'T SAY A FUCKIN' WORD! THE PLACE IS *BUGGED!* IF YOU SPEAK, MAKE IT DIS-INFORMATION. REPEAT. DIS-INFORMATION!

I wondered briefly if Rambam perhaps had been watching a few too many foreign intrigue movies lately, but something very out of the ordinary was definitely going on so I followed the written

475

directive. Not only did I not say a word, but, in addition, I put my finger to my own lips so the cat could see. While I was conducting this secret operation, Rambam was showing the note to McGovern, who appeared to be quite relieved.

A flood of thoughts went through my head now and none of them were very pleasant. It's hard to think of situations and conversations retroactively and God only knew how long the bug had been there. And who in hell could've planted it? The mob? The feds? It all seemed like a crazy charade but the longer we stood there and listened to our hair grow, the less light-hearted the bizarre tableau appeared.

Rambam came over and whispered in my ear something to the effect that if a bug were an amateur operation, it could sometimes be detected through the FM frequency of a radio. This made about as much sense as anything else that had happened lately. I sat down at my desk, lit a cigar, and watched Rambam begin to case the room, checking the obvious places, under tables, the counter, the window sills. Occasionally, he'd whistle a bit in different directions. McGovern was watching Rambam, too. Then I saw him pour himself a stout shot and read the contents of the note again.

The silence was deafening. I got up and had another round with McGovern. When I got back to my chair I saw him re-reading the note as if it were a vital cipher that required enormous de-coding capabilities to understand. I sat in my chair for a while puffing the cigar in silence. Even the place where uninhibited women were not afraid to be who they were was silent. Then I heard the Magnavox and McGovern speak in loud clear tones together.

They said: 'The invasion will *not* take place at Normandy.'

38

The following morning I was slurping some *wonton mein* soup at Big Wong's and listening to Ratso try to put another bug in my ear about Elvis's background and extremely personal affairs. While Ratso was running down a *megillah* bigger than Texas he was also hard at work masticating a large order of roast pork over scrambled eggs and rice. Not only was it a rather unpleasant visual experience, but Ratso's detailed, arcane information on Elvis seemed to be interminable. I felt like Howard Hughes when he reportedly watched the movie *Ice Station Zebra* 250 times in the months just before his death.

'Of course, you know Elvis's favorite meal,' said Ratso. Once he got started on something it was almost a clinical recall.

'The case has taken a dark and unexpected turn, Ratso,' I said. 'The life of Elvis is now quite a peripheral matter. As are the lives of Jesus, Hitler, and Bob Dylan.'

'Well,' said Ratso, 'his favorite meal was peanut butter and banana sandwiches fried in Crisco.'

' – As are our own lives,' I said despondently.

'On white bread,' said Ratso.

'There's a shocker.'

'Oh yeah,' said Ratso, 'and with every meal he only drank ice water.'

'Ever the health nut.'

'You also know the bedside library he had when he died?'

'Let me guess,' I said. 'Was it *Polish War Heroes, Jewish Business Ethics, Two Hundred Years of German Humor*, and *Black Yachtsmen I Have Known?*'

'Close,' said Ratso. 'He had a book on the Kennedy Assassination, a book on reincarnation, and the Physician's Desk Reference guide which tells the name and properties of every pill in the world.'

Except you, I thought to myself, possibly a little unkindly. To preserve my sanity, my mind went wandering back to the evening before as Ratso continued to ramble on obliviously. Rambam, mostly through his whistling technique, had finally located the bug and squashed it. He'd found it inside the porcelain Sherlock Holmes head on my desk.

'An inside job,' I'd remarked, somewhat humorously, at the time.

'Anybody could've gotten in here and done it,' said Rambam. 'People who plant illegal bugs almost always have to break and enter to do their job. There's no security here to speak of.'

'There's the cat,' I'd said.

'Fuck the cat,' Rambam had replied.

' – The fuckin' cat really had some weird hobbies,' Ratso was saying. 'He used to like to watch teenage girls wrestle in their white panties with their little tufts of pubic hair curling out. He had 'em do it right on his bed while he watched. He probably did more than watch, according to my sources. Anyway, he used to send his wife Priscilla out at four o'clock in the morning for polaroid film.'

'Pretty kinky,' I said, absently quoting Winnie Katz. I thought of what Ronnie Hawkins once told me: 'When it gets too kinky for the rest of the world it's gettin' just right for me.'

If the bug had been an amateur job as Rambam had implied, then that, one would think, ruled out the feds as culprits. The only remotely logical explanation I could think of was that somehow some faction of the mob had placed the bug in the loft to learn what I knew about Don Sepulveda. If they thought they were going to learn much, they were mistaken. The more intriguing question was: How did they even know he was alive? A possible corollary to that question was how long would I be alive with mobsters sneaking into my loft and planting bugs inside my Sherlock Holmes head? At least they hadn't taken any cigars.

' – very strong speculation that Elvis was Jewish,' Ratso was saying. 'When his grandmother on his mother's side was dying, she called the whole family to her bedside. Said she had a very important announcement to make. Something she'd never told a soul. So with all these god-fearing, southern Baptist crackers – including little Elvis – around her bedside, she says with her last words: "Ah'm a Jeeeeeeeewww!" '

I looked around the little restaurant but none of our fellow diners seemed to be paying any attention to Ratso's story. Of course, almost none of them spoke English. But they did know Elvis. They probably had always suspected he was part Chinese.

'There also have been recurring rumours,' continued Ratso, relentless as a Gatling gun, 'about an Elvis bar mitzvah in some town in Mississippi. I haven't as yet been able to substantiate this.'

'Come now, my dear Ratso,' I said, 'this could be very important. But you must be more precise about the matter. There are three questions that absolutely must be answered before we can get to the bottom of this: Where exactly did the bar mitzvah take place? Who was the rabbi? And who was the caterer?'

'Joke about it if you want,' said Ratso, 'but you asked me to research Elvis's background and I did. Besides, I've always been fascinated with how an ancient religion like Judaism still has an effect and an influence on our modern world.'

'I appreciate your help,' I said. 'But there is one further thing I'd like you to do.'

'What's that?' said Ratso.

'Pass the roast pork,' I said.

39

That very night the hatchet fell and it wasn't just the waiter bringing me the check. Rambam and I were leaving Asti's on Twelfth Street, an Italian restaurant where the bottles behind the bar and the cash register become musical instruments, and everybody from the bartenders to the busboys sing opera. We had said goodbye to Augie, the owner of the place, and, as we stepped out into the unusually mild night air, I was still singing 'Stout-Hearted Men' with some fervor.

'Gives you sort of a warm feeling down your leg, doesn't it?' said Rambam to a well-dressed woman walking a chihuahua.

I continued singing the old Sigmund Romberg song that Augie and about 49 waiters had performed an ace-boon-coon version of several hours ago. It was now a question of which would stay with me longer, the song or the spicy garlic calamari. There was only a homeless man going through a large plastic garbage bag, the woman and the chihuahua, who had also stopped to inspect the garbage bag, and two blow-dried, polo-shirted types talking on a stairwell. I'd performed for worse crowds than this.

I sang:

> Give me some men who are
> stout-hearted men

Who will fight for the rights they
adore.
Start me with ten who are
stout-hearted men
And I'll soon give you ten
thousand more!

The audience was not really into it. Only the chihuahua, whose name, upon inquiry from Rambam, was Coco Joe, appeared to be a Romberg appreciator. Nevertheless, I persevered. If I could reach one person out there, I considered myself a success.

Shoulder to shoulder and bolder
and bolder
We go as we march to the fore
When – stout-hearted men
Get together man to man.

I had paused to light a cigar and to think of the next verse, when suddenly, out of the corner of my right eye, I saw something flash by like a dragon-fly wing. Almost instantaneously, I heard a sick crack and a bellow of pain from Rambam. He fell back hard against the homeless man and the garbage bag, clutching his right arm.

'You dickheads took Frankie Lasagna's name in vain,' said a voice. It sounded cool, collected, business as usual, totally void of any old-time mobster accent. It sounded intelligent, almost what we like to call college-educated. For some reason I found this a bit unnerving.

Then I saw the guy. He was advancing toward me, fighting back a little smile. In his hands he held a Louisville Slugger baseball bat, obviously the same one he'd just taken Rambam downtown with. I found this a bit unnerving, too.

As old-fashioned and out of style as the human mind is when compared to the computer, it is still, nonetheless, very wiggy to consider just how many images, impressions, and ideas can be rapidly processed through that ancient archaic mortal circuitry when someone in dress slacks with little tassels on his shoes approaches you in a menacing fashion holding a Louisville Slugger. Rambam had told me some time ago about the 'new mafia'. Young guys who never said 'dese' or 'dose' and had no roots whatsoever to old country customs or values. The new guys looked like they'd be at home on anybody's lacrosse team. The only things they shared with the old-time mob characters were an unredeemably criminal mind, and the ability to enjoy with equal relish killing someone or eating a nice healthy non-fat frozen yoghurt. Viewed in this light, the little polo player on the guy's shirt looked positively evil.

One of the guys stood slightly up the street to run interference, and the guy with the baseball bat moved in on me and Rambam. As he came closer, the well-dressed woman stood in frozen horror and dropped the leash on the chihuahua. Coco Joe, like many small dogs with great hearts, knew no fear, and went right for the guy's tassels. The guy took a murderous golf swing at the little fellow and missed by less than an inch, putting him on the final green. This bought a little time. From the guy's methodical approach and his partner's almost bored attitude, it seemed as if time was not a problem to them. They'd stay until they got the job done. But it gave me a chance to scuttle backwards like a crab in black bean sauce. It also gave me a chance to yell for help at the blinking neon Asti's sign. Unfortunately, inside the place, a large roomful of people were singing:

> Give me some men who are
> stout-hearted men
> Who will fight for the rights they adore
> Start me with ten –

I could've used a few myself. I tried reasoning with the guy as he moved in but he wasn't buying any. His eyes looked like Little Orphan Annie's. With Coco Joe still snapping at his tassels, he took two vicious swipes at me and backed me into a narrow corner between a brick wall and an iron railing. He was young and athletic and taking pretty good cuts. I didn't know if he could hit a curve but there wasn't much doubt he'd take me out of the game if he got another swing.

The well-dressed woman was now screaming and I was the one

frozen in horror. There was no place for me to go except right into the bat. I dimly recall Coco Joe biting at the guy's ankles, and the guy's sidekick shouting at him to 'finish it.' The homeless man, who was wearing the last Mondale-Ferraro T-shirt in the world, was watching the whole thing as if it were street theater. In a sense, it was.

The attacker drew the bat way back over his right shoulder. Then the homeless man and I watched it arc toward my head.

At the last moment, the little polo player pitched sideways onto the sidewalk along with the guy who was wearing it. The bat clattered into the gutter. Rambam, using only his left hand, had windmilled the guy with the garbage bag.

'Grab some bench, motherfucker!' yelled Rambam in a rage. I remember thinking how fortunate it was that there was always garbage on the streets of New York. Any place else, I'd be looking for my head.

The other guy was coming over to help his fallen partner but Rambam had by this time awkwardly extracted a gun from a chest holder with his left hand. He showed the gun and the guy bolted for Fifth Avenue. The other guy wasn't moving.

I picked up Coco Joe and brought him over to the lady, who took him from me quickly and got the hell out of there. She didn't want to get involved. Maybe she was onto something.

'Coco Joe's a hero dog,' I called after her. She never looked back.

'First time I've ever liked a fuckin' chihuahua,' said Rambam, wincing with pain as he tried to move his arm.

'He spoke highly of you,' I said.

With me holding the baseball bat and Rambam holding his arm, we walked back into Asti's. Augie, correctly sensing something was amiss, rushed up to us. At that moment, an Ezio Pinhead impersonator got up onto the little stage and began singing:

> Some enchanted evening
> You may meet a stranger –

'What happened?' asked Augie, wringing his hands.
'We just met one,' I said.

40

Didn't see Steve Rambam for a while after that. Didn't even get to sign his cast. With him at least temporarily out of commission, and with most of the old gang either coming out of or going into a sort of cosmic perpetual snit, I had time to daydream again. And daydreaming, as most government analysts today agree, can be hazardous to your health. Of course, as most government analysts today also agree, so can everything else.

The only bit of business I had to do all day was check out the store where Uptown Judy had bought her red cowboy boots. On the face of it, it didn't seem like a very strong lead, but a little Joan of Arc sort of voice kept telling me this was going to be my lucky day. Not that you should ever actually *listen* to those kind of voices.

I was reading Mark Twain's *Pudd'nhead Wilson* to the cat when I came across a particularly appropriate passage.

' "If you pick up a starving dog," ' I read, ' "he will not bite you." '

The cat, sitting alertly on the desk, looked mildly interested. Thusly encouraged, I continued.

' "This is the principal difference," ' I quoted, ' "between a dog and a man." '

The cat kept waiting and looking at me as if there should be more.

' "This is the principal *difference*," ' I repeated, ' "between a *dog* and a *man*." '

The cat, unwilling, or unable to draw the distinction between the two, walked over to the side of the desk and began sniffing the bowl of the JFK pipe. In resignation, I took a cigar out of Sherlock Holmes's head and chewed on it thoughtfully in the manner of Lt Columbo. I closed *Pudd'nhead Wilson* and was placing it in a desk drawer when I heard the Joan of Arc voices again. As if guided by them, I reached a little further into the drawer and came up only with an old arabic shawl or *kaffiyeh* that had once belonged to a friend of mine. She'd sent it to me before she died. Under the *kaffiyeh* were some old photographs I hadn't even realized were there.

I put the *kaffiyeh* and the photographs on the desk, walked over to the kitchen, caressed the espresso machine until it purred. The loft, I reflected, was turning into a halfway house for relics of dead friends. The red cowboy boots had finally walked out with Downtown Judy, but the *kaffiyeh* was still loitering around, and I had yet to remove Baker's Elvis film from the pizza box to have it copied for his dad. There were a number of other items in the loft that spoke of death as well. Too bad garbage sales were against my religion.

Sometime later I was sitting at the desk, sipping an espresso, flipping through the old photographs, sifting the cold ashes of my youth. I picked up an old photo Kacey had once given me. She was a child of about seven or eight, holding her father's hand at some beautiful, forgotten, faraway airport. The father, affectionately known as Jake the Snake, was wearing a dapper hat and trench coat and you could see he loved his daughter and she loved him. He had been a good-looking gambling man when the picture was taken, but by the time I finally met him life had put him in a wheelchair and me in a bad mood.

Kacey's eyes were shimmering roulette wheels of childhood, spinning stars into my soul, making me imagine that the child knew she was destined to die young and to frolic forever in the airport waiting lounge I was pleased to call my mind. And in her eyes I saw every woman I'd ever loved.

I no longer had to wait for Brennan or Rambam to track down Uptown Judy's photo or anything else. In a very real sense, I already held the answer in my hands. It was incredible, but it was the only one that fit.

Nice ride, elevator boy.

41

I took a long walk to Amado's Shoe Shop on Eighth Avenue in the thirties. Well before I got there I felt like an Adlai Stevenson impersonator in the wheel department. I figured I might as well have my own wheels fixed while I checked on the purchase of Uptown Judy's boots. As I walked, the sad, undecaffeinated truth kept stepping up and slapping me in the face. I'd been had very bad. Been looking at things through the wrong end of a telescope and they seemed very far away when, in truth, they were close enough for slow dancing in the make-believe ballroom of McGovern's brain. Things had been right under my nose, so to speak. Unfortunately, I'd already snorted most of the flowers before I'd had a chance to stop and smell them.

The cat was unable or unwilling to draw any real distinctions between a dog and a man. Both were large, potentially dangerous, not too bright. I had been unable or unwilling to draw distinctions, thanks largely to a cocaine snowstorm at the base of my brain, between a woman and women. Of course, I couldn't remember Uptown Judy very clearly. When things die they fade in reality and in memory. Besides, Uptown Judy hadn't wanted me to remember her too clearly.

But the chain of evidence was so strong that it almost physically dragged against me as I walked. I felt like Hercule Poirot, who, when he finally solves a difficult mystery, invariably condemns himself in rather brutal fashion for not solving it sooner. 'What a stupid oxen have I been!' 'I am like the blind man tapping with the cane!' 'I am the fool!' 'How could I not have seen?' 'I am the idiot!' Easy pal, I thought. Move it on over, Inspector Poirot. There's an old dog movin' in.

By the time I got to the shoe store, the chain of evidence seemed to be irrefutable. I walked slowly like an over-zealous Christian wearing a giant cross heavy enough to drown a Budweiser Clydesdale. It was no longer that crucial what I'd find or rather, not find, at Amado's. But nonetheless, I had to follow out the lead. I had to be absolutely certain. Even when you're wrong, it's good to be certain.

The place was pretty much of a one-man operation, which was good, because I was becoming pretty much of a one-man operation myself. When I asked Amado about sales records for the past year or two he didn't look very happy. I wasn't very happy either. I could get along with this man.

'The record was stolen,' he said. 'By a customer. When my back was turned.'

'Same here,' I said.

'Happened yesterday. Don't know which customer.'

'I didn't know my customer either,' I said.

There wasn't a hell of a lot to do while I waited for Amado to repair my boots. There never is. I could've made the next move myself in this chance-ridden chess game of life, but something was holding me back. I took out a cigar, lopped the butt off, and fired it up with my phlegm-colored Bic. I puffed on the cigar and wondered what was holding me back. It might've been weakness. It might've been compassion. It depended on who was throwing the stone.

Sometime later I corraled a hack and rode it down to Canal Street. I got out at a corner where a familiar-looking building stood. The top floor appeared to be burned out, not unlike many people that I knew. I went to the corner and found the payphone, took a quarter out of my pocket, and realized the receiver'd been ripped off. There was rust on the metal at the point where it'd been severed. It didn't surprise me. Most payphones in the city were in the same condition. People here were animals. They'd steal Jesus if he wasn't nailed down.

It was dark when I got back to the loft. I knew what I had to do. I turned on the lights, fed the cat, and called the cops.

Cooperman was in.

I didn't really want to tell him what I had to tell him but I had to tell him. Or so I thought. But just as I'd resolved my moral dilemma in favor of handing Cooperman the solution, he wouldn't take it. He wouldn't even hear of it. The fickle finger of fate for once had pointed the way for me out of the labyrinth.

Cooperman, according to Cooperman, had successfully closed the case of Uptown Judy. Not only did he not want to hear my crazy theories, he insisted upon telling me his own. I threw on some spiritual bacon and let him rouse the whole barnyard.

'So we're supposed to be officially off the case,' said Cooperman, 'but really we're still kind of keepin' an eye on it. Follow me, Tex?'

'Like a detour sign,' I said.

'Don't get smart. Anyways, while you and your friends are out sharin' your feelings with Elvis impersonators, we put out a few feelers to a few wop operatives we know. They lead us to a guy used to work for Don Sepulveda before he got whacked. Ever hear of Frankie Lasagna?'

'Yeah,' I said. 'My grandmother used to cook him for dinner.'

'So anyways, about five years ago *babañia* started comin' in big time. You know what is *babañia*, Tex?'

'Is it a Hebrew word?'

'Heroin, Tex, heroin. Anyways, some of Sepulveda's people wanted to handle it and as best we can figure, Sepulveda himself didn't approve of it. So he got spliced and it wasn't nice. Never did find the body. So what do you think happens next?'

'Lasagna gets big in *babañia*?'

'You're a funny little Negro, Tex. That's why I like you so much. But that *is* what happened. And Lasagna starts to get well known and he don't need us but he'd like us to stay away from his action. So every once in a while he throws a little tip our way. So we put the word out through these wop operatives I believe I mentioned that we could use some help on this Uptown Judy thing. Word comes back he wants to talk and after exhaustive efforts on our part he tells us the word on the street is she was polished by the same soldier who is believed to have done her father.'

'Who was that soldier?'

'Nice young fella. Hit man. Worked for another family. Name of Sally Lorello.'

I couldn't believe what I was hearing. I fished a fresh Cuban cigar out of Sherlock's head.

'Sounds just like Inspector Lestrade,' I said to the head.

'What'd you say?'

'Sorry, I was talking to somebody else. I must've said "God!" '

God rhymed with Lestrade just about as well as Lasagna rhymed with *babañia*. Otherwise, there was nothing in Cooperman's whole case that made any sense at all when brought up against what I knew to be the truth. But if I had forever, I couldn't have proved it. Sometimes it takes longer than a life.

'You really believe Lorello killed Uptown Judy?' I said.

'I don't believe it,' said Cooperman. 'I *know* it. He's already confessed. He's implicated others in the Sepulveda rub-out. He's cooperating with the D.A. He's killed so many people he can't even remember all of'em. He'll be going into a witness protection program.'

I sat there in sort of a shell-shocked silence, taking it all in. Even though he was wrong, Cooperman was obviously joined at the hip to his solution of the case and so were the official powers that be. It was convenient for them. It served a purpose. And besides, I thought, there was really very little innocence in this world left to protect. I looked across the desk at Sherlock. He looked back at me. 'It's just showbusiness,' said the head.

'You still there, Tex?' said Cooperman.

'More or less,' I said. 'What about Legs?'

'Separate deal. Like I told you. Probably drug-related.'

'Probably.'

'You still don't fuckin' get it, do you, Tex? This was an internal mob thing. We got the guy. The books are closed. Everybody's happy.'

I looked at Sherlock's face. He did not look happy.

'One more thing,' said Cooperman, making a displeasing sound that I came to realize was chuckling. 'What made you think *Elvis* had anything to do with this?'

I took a puff on a cigar and sent a cool trail of blue smoke upward toward the now-silent Isle of Lesbos. It moved gracefully in the air in slow motion smoke somersaults like the faraway fog rolling in on the Embarcadero.

'I don't know,' I said. 'I must've had a nail in my head.'

42

I went to bed feeling like the kind of middle-aged person young nerds always tell to get a life. I had a life. Unfortunately, it had been a fairly tedious life for some time now. Maybe I could recycle the goddamn thing, I thought, as I languidly counted Elvis impersonators to no avail. Perhaps next time around I'd be the cat in the court of the King. Let somebody else play the chess game to a stalemate. Let some other player find it too painful to make the next move. And what if the next move is wrong? What if Cooperman's right and the game is over and I just don't know it yet? I'd almost gotten to the point where I'd have preferred Cooperman's solution to my own. It was wrong, but in the sad, empty eyes of the world, it would look cleaner.

Suddenly, Tom Baker in all his glory descended a celestial staircase and gave me a jaunty little left-handed salute and a smile that carried lightly across the lonely years of man. With that gesture and that smile, he banished all resignation, all despair, all sense of loss. I knew I was dreaming but I wasn't going to let it stop me now. I was on a roll.

Baker walked across to a small bar in a glittering ballroom, empty except for a skinny long-haired guy sitting on a barstool. The guy got up and hugged Baker like they were long-lost friends. They were. It was Jim Morrison. Lead singer of the Doors. He'd gone missing in action in Paris in 1971. It'd taken Baker over a decade to find him again but he finally had.

The two of them lifted their glasses in a toast. 'May the best of the past be the worst of the future,' said Baker. They drank. It was one of the two things they did the best together. The other was raise hell.

They sat there drinking, talking, laughing, catching up, for a long time and I could only seem to hear bits of the conversation. But I could tell they were very happy and at peace with themselves. It was more than we the living, even we the dreaming, could say.

I heard Morrison call Baker the 'greatest method drinker of all time', and I heard Baker tell Morrison it was incredible but he still looked 'like a hippie janitor'. Then they discussed for some length of time a particularly crazy notion. Baker had performed nude in a Warhol film, causing Hollywood to blacklist him from its pristine milieu. Jim had taken his johnson out for some fresh air during a concert in Florida, causing anybody that wasn't already upset with Baker to be upset with Morrison. I listened closer to be sure I heard them correctly.

I had.

They were talking about getting agents for their penises.

They closed the place together, stumbling out onto some star-lit, tree-lined California avenue, walking hand in hand like the last scene of *Breaker Morant*, into a grainy, black-and-white sunset. Tom Baker was home and I knew it. Even in the dream, or possibly, especially in the dream, I knew I was far from it. Maybe the cursed place didn't exist on this spinning ghost of a planet.

Jim Morrison had died before I'd even met Tom Baker. They'd been heroic friends locked in a fast-lane death dance in a rock-'n'-roll time beyond anybody's control. A piece of Tom had died when Jim Morrison died. But a piece of Tom still lived with me. Come tomorrow, I vowed, I would play that piece.

As Baker and Morrison disappeared through the doors of my perception, I traded a haunting dream for a ringing telephone. Not much of a deal but these days you take what you can get. I put a choke-hold on the blower by the bedside.

'Mit – Mit – Mit,' said a familiar voice.

'McGovern,' I said. 'What time is it?'

'Five-thirty in the morning. Are you sitting down?'

'I'm *lying* down, for Christsake.'

'Well, I thought you'd want to hear this. It just came over the wire. Don Sepulveda's been killed again. Happened earlier tonight in Bay Ridge.'

'You're sure?'

'They found fifteen bulletholes in him. This time, even *he* knows he's dead.'

43

When I stumbled out of the loft that morning they were waiting for me in the hallway. If you wanted to be uncharitable you could say I was taken by surprise. If you wanted to give me the benefit of the doubt, you could say I'd known for some time it would happen. I just hadn't realized it would quite be *now*. Now is always a bit sudden, as General Custer remarked to the captain of the *Titanic*, when he passed by in the night on cloud eight and a half.

The mind of a murderer, even when the deed may almost be justified, moves at a killer pace. It is driven always by that fateful, pilled-to-the-gills trio of teamsters: desperation, paranoia, and necessity. The criminal mind makes the normal mind, if indeed, such an animal exists, appear rather slow out of the chute. And any mind can become a criminal mind. All you have to do is taste somebody else's blood.

'I was expecting you two to walk up here sooner or later,' I said.

There was no one in the hallway, of course. Just a pair of slightly scuffed red cowboy boots. Though they stood there mute, I knew they were speaking to me from their souls. I took them back inside and, for some reason, put them by my bed.

Maybe there was still time, I thought. There'd be lots of it around later to sit and wonder where it all had gone. I slipped into my hunting vest, put on my hat, and grabbed a few cigars out of Sherlock's head. If I'd taken a few other things from Sherlock's head, the story might not be ending this way.

I didn't own a gun but if I did, I probably wouldn't have taken it. Unlike many god-fearing, wonderful Americans, I'd never had a love affair with guns. If somebody was determined to blow me away they damn sure better remember to bring their own. I headed out the door in a hurry.

I left the cat in charge.

Riding in the back of a hack in a hurry was beginning to seem commonplace to me. At least I didn't say 'follow that car'. The spiritual hallmark of this case, of course, had been that there was no car to follow. I was afraid there was no passenger either now. Just a shadow in a dream. Just a girl I used to know.

It was getting on to be a bright sunny morning when I stepped out of the hack at the address I'd given the driver. A downtown address. The building was Downtown Judy's.

I pushed the buzzer by her name until my finger got tired. Then I tried the others on the same floor. I got a few cranky replies, explained briefly what I wanted, and somebody let me in. Somebody always does.

It was a fifth-floor walk-up and I legged it all the way. Past a child crying, a young couple arguing, somebody cooking some kind of zingy Pakistani breakfast. I walked ever upward past the routine archaeological layers of life, toward what I expected would be the last known address of a murderer. That didn't bother me. There was very little left to forward anyway.

A girl was standing at the end of the hallway on the fifth floor. She was kind-looking, carried a frail sensuality about her, and also, she carried a cat, gently stroking its head. She repeated what she'd told me through the speaker downstairs.

'She left in a hurry late last night. Said she was going to the airport.'

'Say where she was going?'

'No.'

'Say when she's coming back?'

'No,' said the girl, as she stroked the furry little head soothingly. 'But she gave me her cat.'

There was a certain finality to that remark that made further questioning unnecessary. I tried the door to Judy's apartment and knocked a few times kind of like you'd kick the tires of a car you knew you weren't going to buy. The girl continued to watch me and look kind. Both of us knew Judy wasn't coming back.

I patted the cat a few times myself, told him – his name was Atticus – that I had a cat of my own, and said goodbye to the girl. Never did get her name. There are millions of girls and millions of cats in this world and sometimes I wonder if we ever really get to know any of them.

The phones were ringing when I walked back into the loft. It was Ratso, burning with determination to give me some newly discovered 'background material' on Elvis.

'It's a favorite recipe of the King's,' he said. 'It's called "Coca-Cola Salad".'

'Ratso,' I said bluntly, 'this strikes me as totally extraneous information having no bearing whatsoever on the case.'

'But Kinkstah! The recipe is killer bee. I made a batch myself. You really oughta try it. Now write this down in your big chief tablet.'

'Ratso,' I said, 'I already know more than I wish to know about Elvis. But, in the interest of spiritual trivia, such as the fact that Richard Nixon met his wife at a tap dancing class, I'll take down this recipe. Now spit it.'

I got out an imaginary pen and a piece of paper and feigned an effort at jotting down the recipe. It was the least I could do. Ratso had worked hard on the case. He just didn't realize that it was over.

'Okay,' he said. 'First, take a large package of black cherry-flavored jello.'

'I hate it already.'

'Now add one 15-ounce can of crushed pineapple. Got it?'

'Roger.'

'One cup seedless golden raisins.'

'Unpleasant.'

'One cup apple chopped.'

'Ratso, I'm begging you to stop talking.'

'One half cup pecans chopped.'

'Why don't you chop your own nuts off and throw 'em in there?'

'One half cup white grapes. Am I going too fast?'

'Do chickens have lips?'

'One 8-ounce package of cream cheese.'

'Maybe he *was* Jewish.'

'One king-size coke. *King*-size, get it? Now this is important. You put the coke in *last*. Then you stir.'

'Ratso, I'm begging you to hang up the phone.'

'Now you pour into an oiled mold and refrigerate for six hours.' I took out a cigar and began my pre-nuptial arrangements. For some reason my brain was beginning to feel like an oiled mold.

'Let me check my notes,' I said, as I gazed blandly down at the blank sheet of paper. It was still blank, of course. I found that to be mildly comforting. I lit the cigar. It doesn't cost anything to be kind to a sick friend, I thought.

493

'Serves six to eight,' said Ratso.

'Does that refer to the number of guests or to their ages?' I still had a number of things to do today besides laying on the phone with Ratso like middle-aged housewives sharing recipes. I was definitely red-lining in the humoring-an-old-friend department.

'Okay,' said Ratso. 'That's it. Let's hear it back now.'

I looked again at the blank sheet of paper.

'Can't,' I said.

'Why not?' asked Ratso. I took a rather paternalistic puff on the cigar.

'Because you left out the most important ingredient.'

'What'd I leave out?'

'One half cup of the case is solved,' I said.

44

It didn't take Ratso long to find his way over to Vandam Street. From the kitchen window I could hear him shouting and see him pointing to a newspaper he was holding. He looked like an extremely well-fed adult David Copperfield. I went and fetched the puppet head from the top of the refrigerator, opened the window, and tossed it to the figure standing on the sunny sidewalk. The shouting ceased. I closed the window, walked over to my desk, and waited. In his own way, Ratso had worked hard on the case, and he deserved to hear the truth. I planned to give it to him whether he wanted to hear it or not. That was the trouble with truth, unfortunately. The supply always exceeded the demand.

Yet even in the rare circumstance where the truth was sought, the truth-teller invariably found himself or herself subjected to ridicule, scorn, crucifixion, burning at the stake, or having to give Ratso a rather long, laborious explanation. I thought of the old Turkish proverb: 'When you tell the truth, have one foot in the stirrup.'

Moments later, the puppet head was back on top of the refrigerator, the cat had quite ungraciously retired to the bedroom, and

Ratso, also somewhat ungraciously, was pacing the room, parading the paper in front of me, and demanding an explanation.

'What's goin' on, Sherlock?' he shouted. ' "Police Catch Killer of Mobster's Daughter"? "Sergeant Mort Cooperman says Sally Lorello is the man we've been looking for?" '

'Don't believe everything you read in the papers,' I said.

I finally persuaded Ratso to let me have the newspaper. It was the *Daily News*. Not McGovern's by-line, I was gratified to note. But it was a front-page story and Cooperman, in typically modest, self-effacing fashion, was taking full credit for cracking the case. It bothered me less than I'd thought it would.

I looked to Sherlock Holmes for courage. I took a fresh cigar out of his head, fired it up, and searched his gray ceramic eyes for a clue. He'd uncovered the truth on any number of occasions, and the police, the press, and the public of his day had chosen to ignore it. Now he just smoked his old pipe and looked at me. I smoked my cigar and looked at him.

'What're you and that porcelain head gonna do?' said Ratso. 'Sit there and smoke all day?'

'Ah, my dear Ratso,' I said, 'but smoke is all Cooperman's case is. It's a good solution. A convenient solution. But it's not what happened.' Ratso sat down heavily on the chair by the desk.

'So why don't you tell me, Sherlock,' he said. 'And I'm talkin' to *you*. Not the head on the desk that's never held anything but a bug and a bunch of cigars.'

'All right,' I said. 'You want to know what really happened to Uptown Judy? I'll tell you. She wasn't killed by some mob hitman named Sally Lorello. What happened to her was a lot weirder than that.'

I got up and went to the counter. I poured a stout shot of Jameson's into the bull horn. I offered Ratso a shot but he shook his head, kept looking at me for answers. I killed the shot. Then I gave him what he was looking for.

'There's a string of clues in this case,' I said, 'that stand out like a gaudy neon necklace of winking motel signs along an interstate that all of us seem to have traveled by too quickly. Nobody saw them for what they were, and nobody, especially me, put them

495

together until it was too late. I'll bumper-sticker them for you quickly because if I stopped and thought about all the clues and signs and suggestive occurrences too long it would make me viscerally ill.'

Ratso took a sandwich out of a bag he'd brought with him and began setting it out on the desk like a little one-man picnic.

'Got any salt?' he said.

I brought him the salt in an antique Aunt Jemima shaker just as the cat came out of the bedroom and took a ring-side seat on her rocker. I waited for Ratso to almost ritually salt the sandwich and for the cat to scratch a flea. Then, with all eyes upon me, I began what, even to myself, seemed an incredible narrative.

'First of all,' I said, 'let's remember that her background is very significant.'

'Uptown Judy's,' said Ratso.

'No. Downtown Judy's. And the fact that she was having her period was very suggestive.'

'Downtown Judy?'

'No. Uptown Judy.'

I lit a cigar and started slowly pacing. The cat and Ratso followed my progress across the floor with their eyes, Ratso moving the sandwich as necessary.

'She seemed a bit too strivey. Always popping up into my life at unexpected moments.'

'That's Downtown Judy.'

'No. Uptown Judy. And then, of course, although it's rather obvious, the boots did fit her perfectly.'

'That's Uptown Judy.'

'No. Downtown Judy.'

Ratso looked confused. The cat looked bored. I looked out the kitchen window at a line of dark storm clouds advancing on the city like Greek ships closing in on Troy.

'I can understand your confusion,' I said to Ratso. 'I thought I knew both of them but I was wrong. Now, to paraphrase Henny Youngman, take Uptown Judy. The times I was with her I was always cookin' on another planet. Why was that? It was almost like she knew. Then her father, Don Sepulveda, fakes his own death five years ago. That's an important precedent. Then there's the blood that Cooperman found on the floor of her apartment the same night Downtown Judy only wanted to cuddle because she was having her period.

'Then there was the phone call to Tom Baker's father from a woman who claimed to be with the Joe Franklin Show. She said the film had been stolen. Wanted to know if he had another copy. But the Joe Franklin Show received the film from Legs. How would they know to call Tom Baker's father?

'Then there was Downtown Judy's stunned reaction to the man doing the *lambada* on stage at Fort Dicks.'

'Don't remind me,' said Ratso.

'Yes, my dear Ratso, but I now believe it was not the man dancing in his codpiece that shocked her. It was the picture on the screen of Don Sepulveda.

'Now I have no doubt that it was some mob stunt to put the bug in the loft. Probably they thought we knew more about Don Sepulveda than we did. But, by sheer chance, I happened to tell Downtown Judy about my plan to check the boot shop while the two of us were out in the hallway. Nobody but me and Downtown Judy knew I planned to run down that lead. Sure enough, somebody robbed the store of its sales receipts.

'No, my dear Ratso, we've been dealing with this case from the wrong mind set. If the boots fit, wear them. Downtown Judy was a very desperate person, a former actress, and the blood found on Uptown Judy's floor that fateful night was not Uptown Judy's. It was Downtown Judy's. And because she didn't want her body scarred so I would notice, I'm now quite sure it was menstrual blood. Deliberately planted menstrual blood.'

Ratso jumped up like a member of the House of Lords. 'Wait a minute! Wait a minute!' he cried.

I waited.

'You're telling me that Downtown Judy killed Uptown Judy?' he shouted.

'No, my dear Ratso,' I said. 'I'm telling you that Downtown Judy *was* Uptown Judy.'

45

A rare moment of silence was observed at 199B Vandam. For all the world Winnie Katz's lesbian dance class might've morphosed into a mime troupe. Ratso stood mute by the window looking very much like a statue.

'You stand like that much longer,' I said, 'a pigeon's going to shit on your hat.'

'But Sherlock,' he said finally, 'what was Judy's motive in all this?'

'Uptown Judy created Downtown Judy as sort of an escape hatch for her own life. She left my name at the scene of her supposed abduction to help draw me into the case in the hope that I might help lead her to her father. I theorize that the same mob forces that caused Don Sepulveda to do a bunk were also pressuring his daughter. Maybe they suspected he was alive but couldn't find him. Neither could she without a little help from her friends.

'After the don was whacked, for real, I mean, she could no longer afford to remain here in grave danger of being lamped by the feds, the mob, and, of course, yours truly. As I said, she invented Downtown Judy years ago. As a frustrated former actress, as well as a normal perverse human being, it became almost a game with her to flirt with me and to flaunt her theatrical talents. In fact, it was probably her best role. She certainly fooled me.'

'In the condition you were in, it wouldn't have required an Oscar-winning performance.'

'Sad but true. In my defense, though, with make-up, wigs, and various other nefarious techniques and disguises, creative women today can invent new identities almost at will. They are far more cunning than we are. As Ambrose Bierce said: "Here's to woman! Would that we could fall into her arms without falling into her hands." '

'But she's still a killer,' said Ratso. 'She killed Legs. She's probably the one who torched that snuff film character, too. And you're acting like her defense attorney.'

'Ah, my dear Ratso, but Legs was almost certainly blackmailing her with the threat of exposure of her dad, and she was protecting him at all costs. She was being a good daughter. She most likely did burn Malowitz's studio to keep us from obtaining damaging photographic evidence of her identity. She knew even I could figure it out if I could study her photos in a rational frame of mind. She lied when she told me she'd called from the outside payphone. It has no receiver. She probably called from Malowitz's phone before she torched the place. Anyway, he was a bad guy. No loss to the world. Maybe he was working in the darkroom and she didn't even know he was there.'

Ratso shook his head in dismay. 'Jesus Christ,' he said, 'I can't believe I'm hearing this.' He looked around dramatically for support but saw only the cat sitting on the rocker. She refused to meet his gaze.

'Listen, Ratso,' I said. 'Judy's gone now. She may be living in Quogue, Long Island for all we know under a totally new identity. New York is the world capital of anonymity. You want to lose yourself, you've come to the right place. And besides, I can't go to Cooperman or the press with this. Who'd ever believe me? I can't prove a damn bit of it.'

'But you could try.'

'I could. But there's something else.'

'You're soft on her.'

I took a puff or two on the cigar and glanced out the window. The dark clouds were over the city now, obliterating the sun.

'I admire her,' I said. 'Judy had nothing to do with Baker's death. And she had nothing to do with what kind of family she was born into. But she did what she felt she had to. In a strange way, I have a new-found respect for her.'

'You *let* her get away, Sherlock. You let your heart overrule your head.'

'Hold the weddin',' I said. 'Did it occur to you that what I've just told you is only a theory of mine. It does explain the facts, but it is only a theory. Downtown Judy may pop up nonchalantly in a few days. Tell us she's just been to visit her aunt in Hoboken.'

'Not Hoboken. Make it somewhere else.'

Kinky Friedman

'St Penisberg, Florida. Lufkin, Texas. Who cares? The point is, Cooperman could conceivably be correct.'

'It'd be a first.'

All the theorizing had made Ratso and myself hungry, so we set forth to Chinatown in the rain. Cabs were scarce. By the time we got there we were wetter than wonton noodles. But there is something very soulful and uplifting about being in Chinatown in the rain. The sights and smells and sounds and neon signs all seem to run together.

As we walked up Canal Street toward Mott, discussing Nicaraguan politics and why I hated the Mets and Ratso loved them, both of us soaked to the skin, he returned to a familiar theme.

'Two things bother me,' he said.

'Me, too. The Mets and Nicaragua.'

'Seriously, Sherlock. How could you not realize, even in the pathetic shape you were in at the time, that the two women you were hosing were one and the same?'

'I don't know,' I said. 'I must've had a nail – '

'And don't give me that "I must've had a nail in my head" shit.'

'Ratso, to quote a few lines from an old song: "We come to see what we want to see" in this world. "We come to see, but we never come to know." '

Ratso thought it over for a block or two. Finally, he said: 'All right, I'll buy that. But why, if you think Cooperman is so dead wrong, are you letting the case go?'

'My dear Ratso, it's time for us to move on just like Downtown Judy may possibly have done. Leave behind old friends and relationships. Cut ourselves adrift from the excess luggage of life. We must go forward and poison new relationships.'

'You've had a lot of practice.'

'Ratso, there's a wise old Texas saying that applies to this case – '

'A wise old Texas saying is an oxymoron,' said Ratso.

Between the raindrops Ratso must've seen some transient expression briefly cross my face, for he suddenly softened his attitude.

'Sherlock, you look sad. Go ahead. Tell me the wise old Texas saying.'

I took a cigar out of the pocket of my overcoat but it was raining too hard to light it. I looked forward into the wet, shiny, neon-reflecting streets.

'Elvis lives,' I said.

46

One bright morning about two weeks later, a messenger arrived from Chinga's advertising agency, Chavin-Lambert, on lower Fifth Avenue. He brought with him a new copy of Tom Baker's Elvis impersonator documentary, Chinga having sent the original to Baker's father. Along with the copy was a nice new film container to keep it in. I looked over at the old, empty pizza carton still sitting on the edge of my desk like an empty funeral urn. I knew the comfort of closure would not be realized until I got rid of it. Yet I didn't want to just throw the empty carton into the trash.

Finally, I decided to burn the box right on the kitchen counter. Cremate it along with the Bakerman and Joan of Arc, and a sizable percentage of the population of Hiroshima, who at least had been spared from watching Jerry Lewis do incessant Japanese impersonations in the years to follow.

I moved the pizza box from the desk to the counter and, mumbling a belated farewell to Tom, fired it up with my phlegm-colored Bic. Soon, two little bonfires glowed in the eyes of the cat. I poured two shots of Jameson's out on the counter. I drank one. Left the other for Elijah or the Bakerman, whoever came back first.

As I watched the pizza box burn down to primeval ash, I vaguely remembered something I'd read in the *National Enquirer*. They were interviewing someone from the Domino's Pizza delivery staff and he was discussing the trials and tribulations of the job. I poured and killed another shot of Jameson's to see if it might goose my retrieval system. It did.

' "The longer the driveway," ' I said to the cat, ' "the lower the tip." '

The cat looked at me as if I'd suggested we both grab violins and dance around the funeral pyre. But that was exactly what the pizza delivery guy had said, and, as mundane remarks often do, it applied to more than delivering the pizza. It was germane to the spiritual obstacle course I'd been through recently, and to the hell we've all been through and continue to go through in life itself.

The cat said nothing.
There was nothing left to say.

Later that morning I rang up Stephanie DuPont. It was agreed that if I refrained from licking her door frame until the weekend she would accompany me to dinner on Saturday night. This time, I suggested, we would both leave our animal companions at home.

As I walked over to the window I saw a small group of things with feathers perching on the outer sill. Some people called them pigeons. It was within the realm of possibility, I thought, if I could stop smoking cigars and Stephanie could stop referring to me as 'Fuckball', that one of them might soon take up a perch again in my soul. God knows there was room at the inn.

It was nudging Gary Cooper time when I heard a strange keening noise crescendoing upward from the sidewalk below. I looked down and observed Ratso, my second favorite housepest. My first was everybody else.

The postman was arriving at almost the same time, so, instead of tossing down the puppet head, I shouted at Ratso to come in with the mailman and bring up the mail. Kill two birds and get stoned, I figured. Also save wear and tear on the puppet head.

Ratso was up to the task. Mere moments later, he entered the loft with an envelope and a question.

'What's a Vittoria Sepulveda?' he asked.

'That's Don Sepulveda,' I said. 'Judy's father. Recently deceased. Why?'

'Where's Valhalla Gardens? Sounds familiar.'

'It is. It's a bone orchard. Babe Ruth's buried there. You want to give me my letter?'

'It's not addressed to you.'

After a brief struggle I was able to procure the envelope from Ratso. It was indeed addressed to Vittorio Sepulveda, Valhalla

Gardens, Valhalla, New York. My own name and address were in the upper left hand corner of the envelope.

'There's a pattern we've seen before in this case,' I said. 'My name appearing in places it shouldn't. But I was expecting something like this. You'll notice there's no postmark.'

Ratso grabbed the envelope and studied it carefully. I took a cigar out of Sherlock's head and meticulously went through pre-ignition.

'It's an old Abbie Hoffman trick,' I said. 'No stamp. No postmark. Probably sent from JFK or somewhere. After a few weeks the post office eventually sends it back to the return address.'

'And you save the price of a stamp.'

'There's that. But also it doesn't reveal where you are when you sent it and it buys time before it reaches its destination. And, more importantly for us, the contents of this letter will most assuredly determine who was correct – Sgt Cooperman or myself. Ratso, the envelope please.'

As he forked it over to me, I struggled to keep my hands from trembling. Amazing, I thought, that it all came down to this. If nothing else, if I never went public with it or told another soul, it promised a kind of personal vindication that I now very much desired.

I opened the envelope.

I read the letter.

I smiled a crooked little moral victory smile. The way Hank Williams used to do. It was far from a perfect resolution of the story. And all compromise brings a certain sadness. The longer the driveway. If I'd been slightly off the mark in my judgment, at least I'd been correct in my basic assessment of human nature.

Ratso, observing my demeanor with interest, clutched the page from my hand. I let it go like a leaf in autumn.

'What the hell does this mean?' said Ratso. 'Some kind of code?'

'Yeah,' I said, 'but it's not the moral code some people are so fond of. It just tells me she's safe. She made it.'

I couldn't explain it to Ratso. The message consisted of only three little words, but sometimes that makes it easier to read between the lines. It told me that she was far away and almost certainly never coming back. That she was sorry for what she'd done but there'd been no other way. That it was useless to try to look for her. Useless to blame myself. That, this time, she was really starting a new life.

'We have another wise old saying in Texas, my dear Ratso.'

'And what would that be, Sherlock?'

'When the horse dies,' I said, 'get off.'

Later that night, long after Ratso had left, I read Judy's letter to the cat like a man in a mental hospital. Then I opened the desk drawer and took out Kacey's picture. Kacey would understand, I thought. Another little girl running away from herself.

I glanced around the corner at the red cowboy boots still standing beside the bed. They'd ridden their last rodeo. Sometimes it takes longer than a life.

In a sense, Judy got away with murder.

In a sense, Elvis lived.

In a sense, innocence.

I put Judy's letter and the picture back in the drawer together so Kacey could read it, too.

It wouldn't be hard.

All it said was: 'Elvis . . . Jesus . . . Coca-Cola.'

Epilogue

On January 4, 1993, the cat in this book, and the books that preceded it, was put to sleep in Kerrville, Texas by Dr W. H. Hoegemeyer and myself. Cuddles was fourteen years old, a respectable age. She was as close to me as any human being I have ever known.

Cuddles and I spent many years together, both in New York, where I first found her as a little kitten on the streets of Chinatown, and later on the ranch in Texas. She was always with me, on the table, on the bed, by the fireplace, beside the typewriter, on top of my suitcase when I returned from a trip.

I dug Cuddles' grave with a silver spade, in the little garden by the stream behind the old green trailer where both of us lived in summertime. Her burial shroud was my old New York sweatshirt and in the grave with her is a can of tuna and a cigar.

A few days ago I received a sympathy note from Bill Hoegemeyer, the veterinarian. It opened with a verse by Irving Townsend: 'We who choose to surround ourselves with lives even more temporary than our own live within a fragile circle . . .'

Now, as I write this, on a gray winter day by the fireside, I can almost feel her light tread, moving from my head and my heart down through my fingertips to the keys of the typewriter. People may surprise you with unexpected kindness. Dogs have a depth of loyalty that often we seem unworthy of. But the love of a cat is a blessing, a privilege in this world.

They say when you die and go to heaven all the dogs and cats you've ever had in your life come running to meet you.

Until that day, rest in peace Cuddles.

Kinky Friedman
Medina, Texas
February 5, 1993

505